THE COMPLETE
SHORT STORIES OF
THOMAS WOLFE

THOMAS WOLFE was born in Asheville, North Carolina, in 1900, the precocious eighth child of a Pennsylvania Dutch stonecutter and a woman from the Appalachian highlands. After completing his studies at the University of North Carolina, which he had entered at the age of fifteen, Wolfe was determined to pursue a career in playwriting and enrolled in George P. Baker's famous 47 Workshop at Harvard. But his apprenticeship in theater was not successful and he turned to teaching English at New York University, soon falling in love with a designer, completing a first novel, and finally, in 1930, receiving a Guggenheim Fellowship. Thereafter he devoted his time to writing fiction and, with the encouragement of noted editor Maxwell Perkins, would eventually establish himself among the finest fiction writers of his day. The author of *Look Homeward Angel, Of Time and the River*, other novels, and numerous short stories died of a brain infection in 1938.

FRANCIS E. SKIPP is professor of English at the University of Miami, where he has taught American literature for the past twenty-five years. His scholarly articles have appeared in many academic journals, and he is currently at work on a book about the literary group, including such writers as Jack London and Ambrose Bierce, who lived in and around Carmel, California, in 1910.

JAMES DICKEY, poet, novelist, screenwriter, and critic, is the author of the novels *Deliverance* and *Alnilam*, and of numerous poetry collections, including *Puella* (1982) and *Buckdancer's Choice*, which received the National Book Award for poetry in 1966. He lives in Columbia, South Carolina.

Books by Thomas Wolfe

LOOK HOMEWARD, ANGEL

OF TIME AND THE RIVER

FROM DEATH TO MORNING

THE STORY OF A NOVEL

THE FACE OF A NATION

THE WEB AND THE ROCK

YOU CAN'T GO HOME AGAIN

THE HILLS BEYOND

LETTERS TO HIS MOTHER

A STONE, A LEAF, A DOOR

THE LETTERS OF THOMAS WOLFE

THE COMPLETE SHORT STORIES OF THOMAS WOLFE

Edited by Francis E. Skipp

FOREWORD BY JAMES DICKEY

COLLIER BOOKS

Macmillan Publishing Company   New York

Collier Macmillan Publishers   London

Collier Books
Macmillan Publishing Company
866 Third Avenue, New York, NY 10022
Collier Macmillan Canada, Inc.

"The Bums at Sunset," "Circus at Dawn," "Dark in the Forest, Strange as Time," "Death the Proud Brother," "The Face of the War," "The Far and the Near," "The Four Lost Men," "Gulliver, the Story of a Tall Man," "In the Park," "No Door," "Old Catawba," "One of the Girls in Our Party," "Only the Dead Know Brooklyn," and "Polyphemus," from *From Death to Morning,* by Thomas Wolfe, copyright 1935 Charles Scribner's Sons, renewal copyright © 1963 Paul Gitlin, C.T.A., Administrator of the Estate of Thomas Wolfe; copyright 1932, 1933, 1934 Charles Scribner's Sons, renewal copyright © 1960, 1961, 1962 Pincus Berner; copyright 1934, 1935 Charles Scribner's Sons, renewal copyright © 1962, 1963 Paul Gitlin, C.T.A., Administrator of the Estate of Thomas Wolfe; copyright 1935 F-R Publishing Corporation, Condé Nast Publications, Inc., International Magazine Company, Inc., Harper's Bazaar, Inc., Virginia Quarterly Review, North American Review Corporation, renewal copyright © 1963 Paul Gitlin, C.T.A., Administrator of the Estate of Thomas Wolfe.

"An Angel on the Porch," from *Look Homeward, Angel,* by Thomas Wolfe, copyright 1929 Charles Scribner's Sons, renewal copyright © 1957 Edward C. Aswell as Administrator, C.T.A., of the Estate of Thomas Wolfe and/or Fred W. Wolfe.

"For Professional Appearance," "The Names of the Nation," "The Sun and the Rain," and "The Train and the City," from *Of Time and the River,* by Thomas Wolfe, copyright 1935 Charles Scribner's Sons, renewal copyright © 1963 Paul Gitlin, C.T.A., Administrator of the Estate of Thomas Wolfe.

"The House of the Far and Lost," from *Scribner's Magazine,* 1934, copyright 1934 Charles Scribner's Sons, renewal copyright © 1962 Paul Gitlin, C.T.A., Administrator of the Estate of Thomas Wolfe.

Permission is granted by Paul Gitlin, C.T.A., Administrator of the Estate of Thomas Wolfe, to reprint the following stories: "Fame and the Poet," "A Note on Experts: Dexter Vespasian Joyner," "Old Man Rivers," "A Prologue to America," and "The Return," copyright 1936, 1938, 1939, 1947 by Thomas Wolfe; "Justice Is Blind," first published in *The Enigma of Thomas Wolfe,* by Richard Walser (Cambridge, Mass.: Harvard University Press, 1953); "No More Rivers," first published in *Beyond Love and Loyalty,* by Richard S. Kennedy (Chapel Hill, N.C.: The University of North Carolina Press, 1983); and to include "The Spanish Letter," here published for the first time.

Permission is granted by Harper & Row, Publishers, Inc., to reprint the following stories: "The Anatomy of Loneliness," "Arnold Pentland," "The Bell Remembered," "Chickamauga," "The Lion at Morning," "The Lost Boy," "The Newspaper" (originally published as "Gentlemen of the Press"), "No Cure for It," "On Leprechauns," "The Plumed Knight," "Portrait of a Literary Critic," and "Return of the Prodigal," from *The Hills Beyond,* by Thomas Wolfe, copyright 1935, 1936, 1937, 1939, 1941 by Maxwell Perkins as Executor, renewed 1969 by Paul Gitlin, C.T.A., Administrator of the Estate of Thomas Wolfe; "April, Late April," "The Birthday," "The Child by Tiger," "His Father's Earth," "Mr. Malone," "Oktoberfest," "Three O'Clock," and "The Winter of Our Discontent," from *The Web and the Rock,* by Thomas Wolfe, copyright 1937, 1938, 1939 by Maxwell Perkins as Executor, renewed 1967 by Paul Gitlin, C.T.A., Administrator of the Estate of Thomas Wolfe; "Boom Town," "The Company," "The Dark Messiah," "E, a Recollection," "The Hollow Men," "The Hollyhock Sowers," "Katamoto," "Nebraska Crane," "The Promise of America," and "So This Is Man," from *You Can't Go Home Again,* by Thomas Wolfe, copyright 1934, 1937, 1938, 1939, 1940 by Maxwell Perkins as Executor, renewed 1968 by Paul Gitlin, C.T.A., Administrator of the Estate of Thomas Wolfe.

Library of Congress Cataloging-in-Publication Data
Wolfe, Thomas, 1900–1938.
[Short stories]
The complete short stories of Thomas Wolfe/edited by Francis E. Skipp; foreword by James Dickey.—1st Collier Books ed.
p. cm.
Includes index.
ISBN 0-02-040891-9
I. Skipp, Francis E. II. Title.
PS3545.O337A15 1989
813'.52—dc19 88-38324 CIP

First Collier Books Edition 1989

10 9 8 7 6 5 4 3 2 1

Printed in the United States of America

Contents

The Complete Short Stories
of Thomas Wolfe
[Titles in Order of First Publication]

Contents / vii

Foreword

BY JAMES DICKEY

One cannot stir out of doors, one cannot loose the letter *W* on the American literary air these days, without provoking a backtracking, apologetic "explanation" of Thomas Wolfe, but more often a condescending dismissal, such as that of Stanley Edgar Hyman, who tells us that writing a book on Wolfe is like trying to "sculpt in Jell-O." Writers who have felt the thrust, compulsion, and intensity of Wolfe early in life and cannot shake them off are likely, now that they know better and feel less, to hedge and dodge this way and that, finding, out of guilt and loss, some point of positive merit that they grudgingly bestow with faint praise, less believable than their condescension, and often with a touch of hypocrisy that diminishes them.

During the past forty years the New Critics have come down hard on Wolfe, and the doctrines of Henry James, in the fictional realm the equivalent of those of T. S. Eliot, I. A. Richards, and R. P. Blackmur in poetry, have assigned inferior status to Wolfe's obsessive rhetoric and his haunting on-surging power in favor of concision, event-selection, word-selection, proportion, "form." Out of this attitude have come many ingenious rationalizations leading to a downplay of Wolfe's unique gift. One of the easiest to agree with, one of the most pat and most misleading, is Wright Morris's assertion that Wolfe, with his insatiable appetite for experience, actually died of impoverishment, of a kind of spiritual starvation.

> He bolted both life and literature in such a manner he failed to get real nourishment from either. Nothing that he devoured, since it was not digested, satisfied his insatiable appetite. He was aware of that himself, and his now legendary hunger haunted him like the hound of heaven, and it became, in time, synonymous with life itself. *Appetite.* Slabs of raw life were reduced to crates of raw manuscript. The figure of Wolfe, a piece of manuscript in hand, standing beside a bulging crate of typewritten paper, convincingly symbolizes our raw-material myth and attests to our belief in it. Both the size of the man and the size of the crate are in *scale.*
>
> No greater paradox could be imagined than this raw young giant, a glutton for life, whose experience, in substance, was essentially vicarious. He got it

from books. He gives it back to us in books. His lyrical rhetoric and his sober narration—the full range, that is, of his style—derives from his reading, and his reading, like his living, was something he bolted.

It would be hard to find a statement, or an assumption, further from the truth of Wolfe's personality, his fate, or his writing. Of *course* Wolfe had read a good many other writers, including Whitman, and it is also true that he probably read them too quickly—or "bolted" them, as Morris says—but this is in keeping with his reaction to all the things of experience, from the railroad engines, the small night-bound towns, the bridges and tugs of Brooklyn, to the dithyrambs of Whitman and the "massy gold, the choked-in richness, the haunting fall and faery, of John Keats." If one is aware of literary influence in reading Wolfe, it is so secondary as to seem—and be—incidental. For readers who have no interest in the similarities between, say, Whitman's description of New York harbor and Wolfe's, or the influence of James Joyce on certain scenes of *Look Homeward, Angel* (and there is some), the effect of Wolfe's prose is that of a man who has never read anything at all, of some kind of chthonic force that just happens to be American, of a voice speaking both from the heights and from the depths, of a spirit going all out to suggest what in the final analysis cannot be said but can be felt.

The formalists would call—do call—this assumption a cop-out. Nonsense: What can be felt can also be said; nothing is beyond the powers of articulation of the real artist. In this light, Wolfe seems bumbling indeed, with his insistent repetition of "nameless," "unspoken," "tongueless," "untold," "wordless," "speechless," and "secret." Authorities like Allen Tate, one of the most intelligent, cite the Ancients, like Longinus—also intelligent—in an effort to put Thomas Wolfe and the "contemporary lyrical novel" in their place.

> Theodorus calls it the mock-inspired. It is emotion out of place and empty where there is no need of it, or lack of proportion where proportion is needed. Some writers fall into a maudlin mood and digress from their subject into their own tedious emotion. Thus they show bad form and leave their audience unimpressed: necessarily, for they are in a state of rapture, and the audience is not.

But *is* the audience not? one asks, back through the ages. Is not the result of Wolfe's rhetoric, as lengthy and repetitious as it sometimes is, to bring the reader into the state undergone by the author? As Seymour Krim says:

> The majority of professional literary critics are primarily concerned with an author's accomplishment; the more responsible the critic the more painstaking he will be in trying to assess the final value of the books that pass his desk. But the average intelligent reader is not concerned with this at all. He reads for the most personal of reasons, and the books he likes best are those that mean the most to *him*: inspire him, exalt him and increase his capacity for feeling.

Probably of all the writers of his generation in America, Wolfe had this effect on the largest number of readers. They did not, and apparently still do not, care that his books are not "well-made" or that the author under another name is the hero of each. What they do care urgently about is what these books make *them* feel; how the intensity of Wolfe's quest carries past the page into their own lives and stirs them as no American novelist of the same period can do. For the non-professional reader a novel is an extension of his private life; and when a writer like Wolfe can make him participate completely in the literary experience—make him feel that he himself, bound to his job, wife, family, bills, is King for a Day—it is natural and inevitable that he will esteem that writer. (There is nothing we will not give to the person who can show us the undiscovered world within ourselves, for most of us are unaware of the possibilities we hold.)

That could hardly be better said. What Krim indicates is certainly true of my own first encounter with Wolfe when I was in the Air Force in early 1943. Like many another young person I was shocked and released; I felt that I was reading about myself, or, really the self that I contained but had never freed. Wolfe had made me understand that I was settling for too little of life, and far too little of myself. No other writer has ever had such an *actual* effect on me; the essential quality that Wolfe's example gave me was daring: that first, and then a sense of possibility, of psychic adventure within the situations that life brought me, and most particularly those given by chance. There was no longer any need for inhibition or hang-back; there had never been any need. I would go with what was there, all around me wherever I happened to find myself; I would go with it, and I would go all the way.

In a famous letter to Scott Fitzgerald, Wolfe characterizes himself, in contrast to the Flaubertian "taker-outer," as a "great putter-inner," of the company of Balzac and Sterne. He wants to include anything at all that is relevant to his presentation; selectivity is secondary to inclusion.

Suppose we were to take a situation wherein two writers treat the same subject, the first with the classical purity of understatement, the incisiveness and technical balance of the skilled poet, and the other with the length and copiousness of Wolfe; thus doing, we might gain insight into two good and opposite ways of doing things. Quietly, and with telling understatement and balance, Edwin Arlington Robinson, for example, speaks of prostitutes, those "Veteran Sirens," in this way:

> *But they, though others fade and are still fair,*
> *Defy their fairness and are unsubdued;*
> *Although they suffer, they may not forswear*
> *The patient ardor of the unpursued.*

This observation, as incisive and powerful as that of Baudelaire's poem on the same theme, "Le Jeu," has the compression and quotability of the best poetry; it brings to bear, it uses the dynamics of the language, including the predictably rhythmical; it leaves out a great deal, but the details it touches on, the quiet, resigned quality of the rendering imagination, the use of the devices of traditional poetic form combine to make the passage one of the most memorable evocations of the subject that we have. Yet to insist upon the qualities that Robinson displays as those essential to *any* literary effort is to omit much that should be kept. Here are some prostitutes from Wolfe's "The Face of the War":

> And this timid, yet inherent desire for some warmer and more tender relation even in the practice of their profession was sometimes almost ludicrously apparent as they moved warily about among the tables soliciting patronage from the men they served. Thus, if a man addressed them harshly, brutally, savagely, with an oath—which was a customary form of greeting—they would answer him in kind. But if he spoke to them more quietly, or regarded them with a more kindly smiling look, they might respond to him with a pathetic and ridiculous attempt at coquetry, subduing their rasping voices to a kind of husky, tinny whisper, pressing against him intimately, bending their bedaubed and painted faces close to his, and cajoling him with a pitiable pretense at seductiveness, somewhat in this manner:
>
> "Hello there, big boy! . . . Yuh look lonesome sittin' there all by yourself. . . .Whatcha doin' all alone? . . . Yuh want some company? Huh?"—whispered hoarsely, with a ghastly leer of the smeared lips, and pressing closer—"Wanta have some fun, darling? . . . Come on!"—coaxing, imperatively, taking the patron by the hand—"I'll show yuh a big time."

This passage has a fullness of effect that concentration, brevity, restraint cannot, of necessity, give. The concision of Robinson may suggest the essence of the whores' meaning, their sadness and seriocomic condition, but it does not and cannot, to the extent that Wolfe's treatment does, give the physical actuality of their situation, what it feels like to be among them, to listen to them, to look at them in detail, to experience being near them and with them. This kind of fullness demands amplitude, specificity, or what I choose to call "reach." Only by a process wherein nothing was omitted could Wolfe give what he had to give, trusting that each subject, each event, would have its truthful say through him, if he did not stand in its way with cautiousness and paraphernalia.

It has been leveled against Wolfe that there is no sense of proportion in his writing: that the sight of a rusty iron railing evokes as much emotion in him as the death of his father, an absurd and even monstrous lack of discrimination. But *is* it? Is it truly? If such is the reaction, why not acknowledge it? And from the standpoint of an artist, use it? The whole sense of "proportionate response" needs to be gone into. A good many respected critics, Yvor Winters among them, seem to believe that there exists a kind of limiting factor that says that one event, one subject, one involvement must be superior in importance to another, that certain emotions are *legiti-*

mately the result of certain events and that there is some kind of inflexible criterion that determines this, some standard that we can discover and use. In his preliminary problems from *The Anatomy of Nonsense*, for example, Winters offers these conjectures:

> Is it possible to say that Poem A (one of Donne's "Holy Sonnets," or one of the poems of Jonson or of Shakespeare) is better than Poem B (Collins' "Ode to Evening") or vice versa?
>
> If not, is it possible to say that either of these is better than Poem C ("The Cremation of Sam Magee," or something comparable)?
>
> If the answer is no in both cases, then any poem is as good as any other. If this is true, then all poetry is worthless; but this obviously is not true, for it is contrary to all our experience.

All *whose* experience? Presuming literacy the only classification possible for "our," either the pronoun refers to the general reading public or to the vested interests, to the critics, professors, and others in the professional or semiprofessional evaluation game. If democratic principles were involved, "Sam Magee" would win with almost no opposition! What troubles me is that there is in Winters's statement the assumption that there is—or should be—a definite proportion between what is observed and experienced and the emotional reaction it evokes; a kind of law, a totalitarian censor. It should be obvious that even if this were a possible condition—which it is not—it would clamp a very mechanical hand, a dead hand, on all true individual reaction, all real emotion, all response as it exists rather than as it is supposed to exist; in the end, all creativity depends precisely on authenticity of reaction and cannot but be traduced by criteria outside itself. The notion that there is some kind of inflexible standard that sets emotional proportions is a mistake, and a denial of the actual spontaneous—even biological—reflex out of which creation comes. Thomas Wolfe insisted on having this kind of artistic freedom, which involved energy and excess, and on an overall application of Blake's maxim "Exuberance is beauty."

It is true also, however, that in Wolfe's work another law is working, and working against rather than for: a kind of principle of diminishing returns. With so *much* rhetoric this is bound to happen, especially since the rhetoric involves repetition to the extent that it does in Wolfe's. One tires of the evocation of the same things, over and over—the trains, the ships leaving harbors, the dazzle of water on city rivers—and tires even more quickly of the same words used in connection with them, many of these conventionally grandiose: terrific, great, tremendous, huge.

Yet again . . . again; something much more important overrides these objections, and that is the vision, projected in everything Wolfe wrote, of the world as a place for total encounters: a place in which one may *connect* with the objects of life, its people, its events, and mysteries in an absolutely maximum way, to the limit of human capacity. Whatever doubts Wolfe's example may raise, this talent is his beyond any other writer's. Everything he sees, touches, or remembers, every object or person in his memory is someone or something to deliver himself to with absolute abandon regardless of the consequences, to go for broke every second of his writing life and of his actual life, to give the world in its multifariousness his best shot, in a kind of Olympic Games of the emotions and the reactions, not with a gold medal on the line but with life-meaning itself. Nothing can be missed. Wolfe not only serves as his own best example of this attitude, but he encourages it, brings it forth in others. The process is, in its way, a kind of morality.

Here are fifty-eight of Thomas Wolfe's stories, a good many of them episodes extracted from the novels. If one wishes to employ conventional fictional standards, it is likely that one would end up by citing "The Child by Tiger," a stark and terrible account of a lynching, as being the best selection in this book. It is very good, but the paradox that one must also note is that it is not the best Wolfe. As Scott Fitzgerald wrote, "The more valuable parts of Tom were the more lyrical parts or, rather, those moments when his lyricism was best combined with his powers of observation." This quality is more readily found—more directly felt—in the stories where lyricism and observation do fuse, such as the reverie on four presidents of Wolfe's father's time, all of them veterans of the Civil War.

Then Garfield, Arthur, Harrison, and Hayes had paused by the bridge-head for a moment and were still, seeing the bright blood at noon upon the trampled wheat, feeling the brooding hush of six o'clock across the fields where all the storming feet had passed at dawn, seeing the way the rough field hedge leaned out across the dusty road, the casual intrusions of the coarse field grasses and the hot dry daisies to the edges of the road, seeing the rock-bright shallows of the creek, the sweet cool shade and lean of river trees across the water.

They paused then by the bridge-head looking at the water. They saw the stark blank flatness of the old red mill that somehow was like sunset, coolness, sorrow, and delight, and looking at the faces of dead boys among the wheat, the most-oh-most familiar plain, the death-strange faces of the dead Americans, they stood there for a moment, thinking, feeling, thinking, with strong wordless wonder in their hearts:

"As we leaned on the sills of evening, as we stood in the frames of the marvelous doors, as we were received into silence, the flanks of the slope and the slanted light, as we saw the strange hushed shapes upon the land, the muted distances, knowing all things then—what could we say except that all our comrades were spread quietly around us and that noon was far?"

This is what you read Thomas Wolfe for: complete immersion in a scene, imaginative surrender to whatever a situation or a memory evokes; quite simply, the sense of life submitted to and entered. In everything he wrote, Wolfe tells us that we have settled—are settling—for too little. We have not lived enough; we are capable of more. Wolfe places us where we all, critics included, secretly wish to be; beyond criticism and at the center of our lives, called there by words beyond the narrowness of academic judgment. Our lives and all their million particulars and possibilities are around us at every second. All we need to do is to feel what we actually feel, and go with it where it takes us, to the lowest depths of despair and hopelessness or to the heights of whatever heights there are. The risk is great, but as another writer, D. H. Lawrence, said, "I will show you how not to be a dead man in life." Wolfe stands us in good stead here, in these stories as elsewhere, which tell us in bewildering and heartening plenty to open up entirely to our own experience, to possess it, to go the whole way into it and with it, to keep nothing back, to be cast on the flood.

Preface

This book gives the reader all fifty-eight of Thomas Wolfe's short stories, presented in the order in which they first appeared. Everything of his originally published as a short story, other than his apprentice work and his short novels, is included. Thirty-five of these fifty-eight stories have never before been collected. One of them, "The Spanish Letter," is published here for the first time.

The texts of the stories correspond as closely as the surviving documents allow us to infer to the texts Thomas Wolfe intended to publish. Since Wolfe's intention was often modified to meet the requirements of commercial publishing, a number of the stories most familiar to his readers will be found to show here a somewhat unaccustomed face and figure. In this connection, it should be borne in mind that Thomas Wolfe died in September 1938, in his thirty-eighth year, leaving behind with his second editor, Edward Aswell of Harper and Brothers, a manuscript of well over two million words. From this enormous deposit Aswell drew the materials for two novels, *The Web and the Rock* (1939) and *You Can't Go Home Again* (1940), and all of the stories in this volume following "The Portrait of a Literary Critic." Eleven of these twenty-one stories Aswell published in *The Hills Beyond* (1941), and of the twenty-one Wolfe probably thought only two of them—"No More Rivers" and "Old Man Rivers"—as suitable for independent publication.

The method I adopted to present these stories as Wolfe intended them to be read is simple in outline. First, I collected them in all of their published versions. Next, I scrutinized all of the surviving manuscripts in Wolfe's own hand, all of the surviving typescripts derived from the manuscripts, and all of the surviving typescripts Wolfe dictated directly to a stenographer.

I followed the changes, from the earliest version discoverable to the latest: typically, a Wolfe manuscript, bearing corrections in his hand, became a typescript corresponding to the edited manuscript. That typescript then underwent further changes either assignable to Wolfe or to some second or third hand, or perhaps to all three. If there was evidence in the typescript or elsewhere establishing the changes Wolfe introduced as the last made, it was assumed that he acquiesced in or even directed the others. When

Wolfe's place in this order could not be logically inferred, the changes introduced by other hands were ignored. Usually at the end of a series of typescript versions, one could be found bearing only a few corrections and these unmistakably in Wolfe's hand. Such a typescript became the copy-text. Any later typescript in that series disclosing changes but not bearing Wolfe's autograph was excluded.

In the many instances when no typescript of a story bearing autograph corrections had survived, a copy-text could not be established with such confidence. Since, however, the authorship of the typescript was rarely in question, a reasonably satisfactory solution to the problem was at hand, derived from a knowledge of the way Thomas Wolfe was ordinarily edited.

Wolfe's creative bent was toward the copious. Consequently, editors with limited space and conventional ideas about what the length of a story should be usually called for cuts in the typescript Wolfe submitted. Reluctantly, he came to accept the idea that his work to be published had to be cut, but he winced with every word torn, as he felt it to have been, from its body. We can take it as axiomatic that the initiative to cut never lay with Thomas Wolfe but with his editors. Cutting was therefore at its best a collaborative endeavor with the editor proposing and Wolfe resisting and under necessity acquiescing only so far as his conscience would allow. At its worst it was unilateral and arbitrary.

It follows, therefore, that when an unedited typescript unquestionably of Wolfe's authorship, collated with its published forms, discloses cuts, the unedited typescript is almost certainly the better expression of authorial intention and should be adopted as the copy-text. When no typescript can confidently be chosen as copy-text by virtue of its bearing Wolfe's autograph, the fullest typescript version of a story unquestionably of Thomas Wolfe's authorship is the best alternative. In the few instances where no complete and coherent manuscript or typescript exists, I have used as the copy-text for a story its first independently published form.

The difficulty in establishing a reliable copy-text for the short stories of Thomas Wolfe comes about partly because Wolfe almost never sat down to the task of writing a short story. While *Look Homeward, Angel* was going through the press in the summer of 1929, Wolfe undertook at Scribners suggestion to write some short stories, but he never produced them. As he himself said of his story "Boom Town" in April 1934, the month before it was published by the *American Mercury,* "Like practically everything else I have written in the last four years, [it] is a chapter out of this enormous book."

By "this enormous book" Wolfe meant the manuscript that became *Of Time and the River* (1935), his second novel, and a major part of the great creative work to which he gave his energies almost exclusively: the transforming into fiction of the whole story of his life. It was from the ever-growing manuscript produced by this creative scheme that all his novels were drawn, and virtually every story, as well. What became Wolfe's short fiction was not intended to be short fiction when it was written. Its publication was the product either of his editor's blue pencil, the desire of his publishers to keep his name before the reading public between novels, or the consequence of a need for money that sent his literary agents prospecting into the mountain of his manuscript. And because Wolfe's stories were thus almost always drawn from large manuscripts he intended to shape into novels, even those stories which appear to belong more properly to the essay form were first part of a larger fiction and may, with a little license, be called stories.

The process can be seen at its beginning in a long letter Wolfe wrote from Switzerland in the summer of 1930, describing to Maxwell Perkins, his editor at Charles Scribner's Sons, the plan for a novel he was then calling "The October Fair" and whose protagonist he had named David Hawke:

> We understand that David is a member of an American family two or three hundred of whose members are buried in different parts of the American earth, and we get the stories and wanderings of some of these people. In the letter of the tourist from Prague, he is referred to by name; in the chapter "On the Rails," we know that he is on the train, although the story is that of the engineer; in the chapter "The Bums at Sunset," we know that he has seen them waiting at the water-tower; in the chapter called "The Congo," the wandering negro who goes crazy and kills people and is finally killed as he crosses a creek, is known to David, the boy—etc.

The "tourist from Prague" was to become Miss Blake in "One of the Girls in Our Party," a story first published in *Scribner's Magazine* in January 1935, and later that year included among the thirteen stories (and one short novel) in Wolfe's first collection, *From Death to Morning* (1935). The story of the engineer was to appear in the July 1935 *Cosmopolitan* as "Cottage by the Tracks," and with small changes as "The Far and the Near" (Wolfe's title, and the one used in this volume) in *From Death to Morning*. The chapter Wolfe called "The Congo" furnished something in the nature of a scenario which Wolfe later fleshed out and then revised into a story (from the evidence of the typescripts with heavy editorial assistance) that was to be his only appearance in the *Saturday Evening Post* when it was published there on September 11, 1937, under the fine title he gave it, "The Child by Tiger." After Wolfe's death in 1938, this story became, with changes and omissions, chapter eight of his third novel, *The Web and the Rock* (1939). All four of these stories had been cut from the manuscript of *Of Time and the River* and set aside, not because as episodes they were inferior but because in the course of editorial trimming and shaping they had become irrelevant to the larger story the novel was to tell.

Most of Wolfe's published stories resulted from such setting aside of material during the editing of his novels, but his short fiction emerged from the long manuscript in other ways, too. Wolfe's heroic scheme for *Of Time and the River* had gotten out of control and the manuscript grew ever longer without coming much closer to a conclusion. To impose some rational form upon it, Wolfe and Perkins devised a simple chronology of events selected from among the many the manuscript held. Some of the sections contained episodes connected to one another and to the larger narrative by theme, but widely separated in narrative sequence. To match the manuscript to the outline, Perkins disassembled such sections and slipped each component episode into its proper place in the chronology. Before being disassembled, however, its unity of theme made the section suitable for independent publication. This process is illustrated by the editorial history of "No Door," published in *Scribner's Magazine* in July 1933.

"No Door" was a long section from the manuscript of *Of Time and the River* the magazine had bought from Wolfe earlier that year. To fit it to the space set aside for it in the magazine, the editor, Alfred Dashiell, cut "No Door" about in half. There was no question about the merit of the material Dashiell cut: Scribners for a time had planned to publish the entire section in its original length. Furthermore, the bulk of the material cut from "No Door" was to appear in *Scribner's Magazine* in August 1934 as "The House of the Far and Lost," one of Wolfe's best. It gives the "no door" theme of the incommunicability of experience a poignant and particular illustration. That Dashiell published it a year later lets us suppose that he, too, recognized its quality; indeed, as Wolfe wrote to a North Carolina friend, Maxwell Perkins had found in it "the same haunting strangeness as 'La Belle Dame Sans Merci.'" And yet, as Wolfe added in the same letter, it was cut from the magazine version of "No Door" "as being something which could go." Wolfe, feeling that the conventions of publishing confined his talent cruelly, suffered "anguish and groans" because "some of the things which were left out are now painful to think about."

What Alfred Dashiell had done to cause Wolfe anguish over "No Door" was slight by comparison to what Maxwell Perkins was to do to fit the material of the story into the chronological outline for the novel. Perkins set aside the entire first part of the story, the part that tells of the narrator's life in "the huge and rusty jungle of the earth that is known as Brooklyn" and of "Mad Maude Whitaker" and her eccentric family. Next, he took the Harvard passages, the passages telling of the narrator's return to his North Carolina home, and the Oxford passages of the magazine version and inserted each into its chronological position in the story the novel was to tell. He then did the same for "The House of the Far and Lost." Finally, the chronological outline dictated that he cut all of the narrator's reminiscences of his jealousy for the woman Esther, together with his recollections of his life in lower Manhattan.

The first part of the "No Door" material which Perkins had set aside in preparing the typescript for *Of Time and the River* he used in *From Death to Morning* where under the "No Door" title it stands as if it were the story entire. It is not, of course; but the entire story is given in this volume by reprinting the *Scribner's Magazine* version, augmented by about three thousand words, the "things left out" which had caused Wolfe "anguish and groans."

After "No Door," the story on which the most extensive restoration has been performed for this volume is "Death the Proud Brother." The bulk of the restoration of over twenty-two hundred words returns to the story a long passage from the narrator's account of a death witnessed in the New York subway. One could explain the deletion by conceding that the elderly Irish waiter is shown reacting to the crowd of onlookers rather than to the dead man himself, but such an explanation is thin. The rich portrait of the waiter is tightly composed and unforgettable and should be back in the story. If the quality of the writing had been the criterion, the vignette of the callous young couple who abuse the dignity in death of a hobo, dead at a Greenwich Village construction site, might better have been deleted. But Wolfe's editor no doubt saw the portrait of the waiter simply as a long passage not absolutely essential to the narrative. Once again, it was "something that could go."

It is easier to account for other deletions here restored to "Death the Proud Brother." Wolfe originally had included in his story a passage of about nine hundred words in which the city, personified, speaks to a member of the "man-swarm." "Little man," Wolfe writes,

> You sweat, you toil, you hope, you suffer, I kill you in an instant with a stroke, or let you grub and curse your way along to your own death, but I do not care a jot whether you live or die, survive or are beaten, swim in my great tides, or smother there. I am neither kind, cruel, loving, or revengeful—I am only indifferent to you all, for I know that others will come when you have vanished, more will be born when you are dead, millions arise when you have fallen— and that the City, the everlasting City, will surge forever like a great tide upon the earth.

Here and in the remainder of the long passage, and elsewhere in the story where the city emerges briefly to speak contemptuously to the "little man," the style is mannered and at odds with the surrounding narrative. One can understand how an editor, shortening a long typescript, could see it as a growth easily enucleated without damage to the surrounding tissue. Mannered or not, the passage stands as an example of explicit naturalism in a writer whose protagonist lived an inner-directed life in the romantic tradition of *Sturm und Drang*.

"The Four Lost Men," a third example out of *From Death to Morning*, was first published by *Scribner's Magazine* in July 1933. Wolfe's intention in that story seems to have been to discover in the hungry visions of young Americans of the late nineteenth century the origins of some of our national myths and to recreate the sharp actuality out of which those myths and visions grew.

Wolfe's method is original and his success impressive. His narrator, the unnamed but inferrable Eugene Gant, recollects his father, vivid on the boardinghouse veranda, spitting tobacco juice and entrancing the boarders with a rodomontade of political reminiscence. With this device, Wolfe introduces the four lost men: Garfield, Arthur, Harrison, and Hayes. Through the father's voice remembered, the four presidents come to represent for Eugene his own vagueness about a significant era of the American past. The four, he tells us, were "the lost Americans: their gravely vacant bewhiskered faces mixed, melted, swam together in the sea-depths of a past intangible, immeasurable, and unknown as the buried city of Persepolis." He asks, "Which had the whiskers, which the burnsides, which was which?"

To give them an actuality, tangible, measurable, and known, he creates a fiction about their young lives that almost from the beginning and increasingly takes on a symbolic quality. They become all antebellum American youth. They become the soldiers of the Civil War. They become the war's survivors who hunger to taste the promise of America.

The story in the February 1934 *Scribner's Magazine* is nearly a fifth longer than it is in *From Death to Morning*. For publication in the book, "The Four Lost Men" was cut mainly in the section where the four men, wholly symbols now and speaking in chorus, express their hunger for America in terms of the mythical attributes of the women of the South, the West, the North, and the East. Gone entirely from the story as we read it in *From Death to Morning* are the passages on the women of the South, West, and North. Without them the story is damaged, its statement muted. Only the women of the East remain, silken, sensual, desirable, and pampered, amidst the walnut-paneled opulence of commercial Manhattan.

Like "No Door," "Death the Proud Brother," and "The Four Lost Men," "The Bums at Sunset" is among the stories in *From Death to Morning*. It had appeared in the October 1935 *Vanity Fair* and was altered for book publication only to the extent of changing the words "indeterminate" to "indeterminable" and "fragrant" to "pungent." The typescript, however, contains the ending Wolfe intended his story to have, an ending that extends both the magazine and book versions by about six hundred words. The reader of this edition can find the passage on pages 277–78. It follows the sentence "The boy sat there quietly, listening, and said nothing." Whether or not one sees in this concluding passage more of Wolfe's vision of America than in the narrative that precedes it, this at least is inarguable: the story as it stands here is the story as Thomas Wolfe intended it to be read.

One of the best things Thomas Wolfe ever wrote, "The Lost Boy," was first published in the November 1937 *Redbook Magazine*. In the years since, most readers have known it only as it was republished in Wolfe's second collection of stories, *The Hills Beyond* (1941). In that collected version, part one of "The Lost Boy" tells, in a third-person narrative, the story of the twelve-year-old Grover Gant, whose encounter with a stingy and dishonest confectioner is lodged between two mystical moments in which the gentle boy experiences "the union of Forever and Now." There follow in part two and part three, the monologues of the mother, Eliza, and of the older sister, Helen, as they remembered Grover, long since dead of typhoid fever. Part four returns the narrative to the third person to tell through the consciousness of the adult Eugene the story of his pilgrimage to St. Louis and to the house and room of Grover's death and of Eugene's memories, retained from infancy, of the older brother who wore upon his neck a birthmark, "a berry of warm brown."

A comparison would show that for this version in *The Hills Beyond,* the *Redbook* story had been polished a bit and a few minor changes and additions made. Of greater significance by far would be the discovery that the four divisions of the *Redbook* story had been numbered and titled for *The Hills Beyond* to identify the voices of "The Mother," "The Sister," and "The Brother"; that the names given the characters in the *Redbook* version had been changed for *The Hills Beyond* to identify them as members of the Gant family; and that part four had been changed from a narrative by an unidentified first person to a narrative in the third person and its voice designated "Eugene."

As they stand, the numbering of the parts of the story and the labeling of their voices serve to assist the dull who would not otherwise recognize that the shift to a new diction and a new speech rhythm at the end of the mother's section signals a new narrative voice, that of the sister. But the intelligent reader finds the changes unnecessary, and in terms of what appears to be Wolfe's intention, undesirable. All of this numbering and labeling was, I think, a mistake, and the labeling of the brother's section a grave mistake made worse by the shifting of the narrative voice from the first person to the third.

The consequence of this editorial tinkering was to give us, in *The Hills Beyond,* Grover, "the lost boy," in four pieces, four pieces set apart typographically, numbered, and in three of its numbered parts, titled. The *Redbook* text, on the other hand, collects in the consciousness of the first-person narrator of part four all of the events that precede his entrance into the story. Although addressed by the reminiscing mother and sister, he remains unnamed because he is not hearing for the first time the stories the mother and the sister tell but through his memory is retelling and reshaping them. It dawns on the reader that he has been present at this creative process when he discovers that the consciousness narrating part four is the creative mind that has given form to the whole story.

The significant omission of the narrator's name makes us understand that after his return from St. Louis, where he sought some elusive revelation, it was he who fashioned the narrative of part one, of the quiet boy who saw the light come and go upon the square and heard "the booming strokes of three o'clock beat out across the town in thronging bronze."

In the *Redbook* version, the version here reprinted, the story of the lost boy thus circles back upon itself to make of its parts a beautiful roundness, in which the first told comes to be seen as the last wrought. Three sources of the story are explicit: mother, sister, and artist-brother. The fourth source, the father, is implicit and logically and aesthetically necessary. All are fused in the imagination of the pilgrim-artist who gave it the form in which is caught the light that came and went and came again into the square to show us all we need to know of that gentle boy who had experienced the union of Forever and Now.

Not a part of either early collection, "April, Late April" appeared in the *American Mercury* of September 1937. In it, the unnamed male character expresses his sexual appetite for his mistress in images of food and eating declaimed in scenes of romping hilarity where a cannibal desire seems to stop just short of satisfaction only because the aroma of more sanctioned food surrounds the bedded and playful pair.

The story has power to seize our attention even in this liberated day principally, I suppose, because we see all this kinkiness as belonging unmistakably to Wolfe himself. "He would look at her," he writes, ". . . with a lustful hunger, and then seize her once again in his fierce grip. 'Why, you delicate and delectable little wench!' he cried. 'I will eat you, devour you, entomb you in me: I will make you a part of me and carry you with me wherever I go.'"

"April, Late April" stands, with interlardings and cuts, between pages 441 and 452 in Wolfe's 1939 novel *The Web and the Rock,* but bowdlerized sufficiently to make the violence approach the bathetic. Until now, to read the story as Wolfe wrote it, one would have had to find it on the foxed pages of a periodical long defunct.

"Boom Town," which stands in its original form in the *American Mercury* of May 1934, and "The Company," whose full version crumbles on the acidic pages of the *New Masses* of January 11, 1938, are similar cases. Their stories were intertwined and reshaped, shuffled together by Edward Aswell at Harper and Brothers to create a part of Wolfe's second posthumous novel, *You Can't Go Home Again.* The central triad of the *Mercury*'s "Boom Town" story, John Hawke, his brother, Lee, and their mother, Delia Elizabeth Hawke, are not to be found in the novel. John Hawke, of course, has become Monk Webber, the protagonist of Wolfe's last two novels, but the mother and the brother, Lee, have been transformed into sister and brother, Margaret Shepperton and Randy. A real estate broker, a Mrs. Delia Flood, has been invented to supplant the mother, and the funeral of Aunt Maw contrived to bring Monk, Margaret, and Mrs. Flood to the cemetery overlooking Libya Hill for that important scene.

In the novel, between the events in the city and the scene on cemetery hill with which "Boom Town" ends, the story of "The Company" has been inserted. The insertion is truer to the *New Masses* original than is the novelized version of "Boom Town," but Wolfe's castigation of American business in his account of the unrelenting pressure beneath which the sales force of

"The Federal Weight, Scales, and Computing Company" at all levels of rank and responsibility worked and lived is decidedly lightened. One cannot imagine Thomas Wolfe, in his newfound commitment to political principles "whereon the pillars of this world are founded, toward which the conscience of the world is tending," acquiescing in an editor's moderating so clear a political statement.

For the copy-text of "Boom Town" I have used a typescript of the story bearing Wolfe's autograph revisions and his autograph designation, "final draft of SS." In this connection it is interesting to note that the editor of the *Mercury,* Charles Angoff, claimed to have made large cuts in the "Boom Town" typescript. However, this final draft bearing Wolfe's autograph revisions is virtually the same as what Angoff published.

There is no surviving manuscript or typescript for part one and part three of "The Company." The typescript for part two bears Wolfe's autograph corrections and corresponds exactly to part two as published in the *New Masses*. I have therefore used the story as it stands in the *New Masses* as the copy-text.

The editing of the chest-high stack of unarticulated typescript Thomas Wolfe left behind at his premature death in September 1938 produced from "Boom Town" and "The Company" the synthetic chapter discussed above for his fourth novel, *You Can't Go Home Again* (1940). Similarly, chapter 38, "The Dark Messiah," as Richard S. Kennedy tells us in his critical biography of Thomas Wolfe, *The Window of Memory,* was created by Wolfe's posthumous editor, Edward Aswell. In 1937, Donald Ogden Stewart of the American Writers League had asked Wolfe, as he had asked other prominent American writers, for his views on the Spanish Civil War. In responding, Wolfe produced a twenty-page typescript. Finding what he wrote too good to squander as a statement of opinion on a contemporary issue, he revised and fictionalized its opening pages and set it aside, to be chinked somewhere into his enormous manuscript.

Coming upon this typescript as he shaped *You Can't Go Home Again,* Aswell excerpted pages 6–7, 15–20, and 9–14. To these, Kennedy continues, Aswell added some material "from Wolfe's writings on fame and the poet, then supplied an introduction and some transitional paragraphs." In August 1940, two months before the novel appeared, Aswell published "The Dark Messiah" as a story in *Current History and Forum.* As chapter 38 in the novel, the story appears with some additions and changes on pages 621–22, 625–31, and 633.

"The Dark Messiah," consequently, is synthetic Wolfe. It is included in this volume in the interest of completeness; but to offer a corrective of sorts, "The Spanish Letter," as Wolfe himself called it, is included and here published for the first time. It stands as new testimony to the clarity with which he came to see that the evil of fascism in Spain was but a reflection of the evil of the Third Reich and to the passion with which he detested it. "The

Spanish Letter" should take its place among other late writings of Thomas Wolfe to help lift from his neck the albatross of racial prejudice he carried so long, hung there by the circumstances of his upbringing.

Some of the stories Thomas Wolfe published in periodicals were never thereafter adapted to the requirements of one of his novels or collected in *From Death to Morning* or *The Hills Beyond*. Such, indeed, was the fate of "A Prologue to America," where Wolfe is at the top of his lyrical form. Its publication came about because the editors of *Vogue* had invited Wolfe to contribute to its first "Americana" issue. As Aldo Magi tells us in the foreword to an edition of the story he published in 1978, Wolfe "submitted a four thousand word chant-like paean of a ride in a train, its whistle wailing across America. The editors of *Vogue* were highly pleased with it; yet like most magazine editors faced with a Wolfe manuscript, felt it was entirely too long. They wanted only about two thousand words." Magi goes on to add that Wolfe held out, and, indeed, added another fifteen hundred words. *Vogue* eventually printed all of Wolfe's nearly fifty-five hundred words.

The material Wolfe first sent to *Vogue* was from the manuscript of his never-completed "book of the night," and in the end, the only thing the *Vogue* editors insisted on was their own title. Wolfe had wanted to call it by a title he had cherished for years, "The Hound of Darkness." *Vogue,* with the Americana theme before them, published it as "A Prologue to America" but gave it pride of place as the lead contribution.

It is a pity, of course, that Wolfe's fine title was lost, but suit the Americana theme his paean to a nation did. This is the way it ends:

> For everywhere, through the immortal dark, across the land, there has been something moving in the night, and something stirring in the hearts of men, and something crying in their wild unuttered blood, the wild unuttered tongues' huge prophecies. Where shall we go now? And what shall we do? Smoke-blue by morning in the chasmed slant, on-quickening the tempo of the rapid steps, up to the pinnacles of noon; by day and ceaseless, the furious traffics of the thronging streets; forever now, upbuilding through the mounting flood-crest of these days, sky-hung against the crystal of the frail blue weather, the slamming racketing of the girdered steel, the stunning riveting of the machines.
>
> And blazing moonlight on the buttes to-night, a screen door slammed, the clicking of a latch and silence in ten thousand little towns, and people lying in the darkness, waiting, wondering, listening as we—"Where shall we go now and what shall we do?"
>
> For something is marching in the night; so soon the morning, soon the morning—oh, America.

The reader will hear elsewhere in Wolfe's "Prologue" something of Walt Whitman, his ties and ballasts dropped, floating above the land he loved, and hear echoes of Nathanael West and *The Day of the Locust*. In the final passage given above we hear hints of "The Waste Land" and "The Bridge."

But the little Wolfe has borrowed here—he was never much of a borrower—he has made his own, and all the rest is his unmistakably.

The foregoing discussion presents a number of notable examples of the ways in which the editorial method described at the beginning of this preface has worked out in practice. All of Thomas Wolfe's short stories, apart from his apprentice work, are here between one set of covers, for better or for worse pretty much as he intended them to be read. This large corpus of work is at last readily accessible to the many thousands who already know Thomas Wolfe and stands as a trustworthy introduction to him for those others who meet him here for the first time.

FRANCIS E. SKIPP

Acknowledgments

I am indebted to Mr. Paul Gitlin, Administrator of the Estate of Thomas Wolfe, not only for allowing me to undertake this book, but for his good offices in advancing agreement among all those whose interests were concerned in bringing it into being. I owe him my thanks, as well, for permission to consult the William B. Wisdom Collection of Thomas Wolfe at Harvard. In this connection I am grateful to Harvard University and to Mr. Rodney Dennis, Curator of Manuscripts at Harvard's Houghton Library, for letting me work there, and to the Houghton staff for their efficient and indefatigable help. Finally, I wish to thank Professor Richard S. Kennedy for pointing out in my preface errors I otherwise would have allowed to stand and for giving me the benefit of his knowledge of all that relates to Thomas Wolfe while I was performing the research upon which the text of this book rests. For whatever shortcomings remain, I alone am responsible.

THE COMPLETE
SHORT STORIES OF
THOMAS WOLFE

An Angel on the Porch

Late on an afternoon in young summer Queen Elizabeth came quickly up into the square past Gant's marble-shop. Surrounded by the stones, the slabs, the cold carved lambs of death, the stonecutter leaned on the rail and talked with Jannadeau, the faithful burly Swiss who, fenced in a little rented place among Gant's marbles, was probing with delicate monocled intentness into the entrails of a watch.

"There goes the Queen," said Gant, stopping for a moment their debate. "A smart woman. A pippin as sure as you're born," he added with relish.

He bowed gallantly with a sweeping flourish of his great-boned frame of six feet five. "Good evening, madame."

She replied with a bright smile which might have had in it the flicker of an old memory, including Jannadeau with a cheerful impersonal nod. For just a moment she paused, turning her candid stare upon smooth granite slabs of death, carved lambs and cherubim within the shop, and finally on an angel poised on cold phthisic feet, with a smile of soft stone idiocy, stationed beside the door upon Gant's little porch. Then, with her brisk firm tread, she passed the shop, untroubled by the jeweler's heavy stare of wounded virtue, as he glowered up from his dirty littered desk, following her vanishing form with a guttural mutter of distaste.

They resumed their debate:

"And mark my words," proceeded Gant, wetting his big thumb, as if he had never been interrupted, and continuing his attack upon the Democratic party, and all the bad weather, fire, famine, and pestilence that attended its administration, "if they get in again we'll have soup-kitchens, the banks will go to the wall, and your guts will grease your backbone before another winter's over."

The Swiss thrust out a dirty hand toward the library he consulted in all disputed areas—a greasy edition of *The World Almanac*, three years old— saying triumphantly, after a moment of dirty thumbing, in a strange wrenched accent: "Ah—just as I thought: the muni-*cip*-al taxation of Milwaukee under De-*moc*-ratic administration in 1905 was two dollars and twenty-five cents the hundred, the lowest it had been in years. I cannot ima-*gine* why the total revenue is not given."

Judiciously reasonable, statistically argumentative, the Swiss argued with animation against his Titan, picking his nose with blunt black fingers, his broad yellow face breaking into flaccid creases, as he laughed gutturally at Gant's unreason, and at the rolling periods of his rhetoric.

Thus they talked in the shadow of the big angel that stood just beyond the door upon Gant's porch, leering down upon their debate with a smile of idiot benevolence. Thus they talked, while Elizabeth passed by, in the cool damp of Gant's fantastical brick shack, surrounded by the stones, the slabs, the cold carved lambs of death. And as they talked, the gray and furtive eyes of the stonecutter, which darkened so seldom now with the shade of the old hunger—for stone and the cold wrought face of an angel—looked out into the square at all the pullulation of the town, touched, as that woman passed his door with gallant tread, by a memory he thought had died forever. The lost words. The forgotten faces. Where? When?

He was getting on to sixty-five, his long, erect body had settled, he stooped a little. He spoke of old age often, and he wept in his tirades now because of his great right hand, stiffened by rheumatism, which once had carved so cunningly the dove, the lamb, the cold joined hands of death (but never the soft stone face of an angel). Soaked in pity, he referred to himself as "the poor old cripple who has to provide for the whole family."

That proud and sensual flesh was on its way to dust.

The indolence of age and disintegration was creeping over him. He rose now a full hour later, he came to his shop punctually, but he spent long hours of the day extended on the worn leather couch of his office, or in gossip with Jannadeau, bawdy old Liddell, Cardiac, his doctor, and Fagg Sluder, who had salted away his fortune in two big buildings on the square, and was at the present moment tilted comfortably in a chair before the fire department, gossiping eagerly with members of the ball club, whose chief support he was. It was after five o'clock; the game was over.

Negro laborers, grisly with a white coating of cement, sloped down past the shop on their way home. The draymen dispersed slowly, a slouchy policeman loafed along the steps of the city hall picking his teeth, and on the market side, from high grilled windows, there came the occasional howls of a drunken Negress. Life buzzed slowly like a fly.

The sun had reddened slightly; there was a cool flowing breath from the hills, a freshening relaxation over the tired earth, the hope, the ecstasy, of evening in the air. In slow pulses the thick plume of fountain rose, fell upon itself, and slapped the pool in lazy rhythms. A wagon rattled leanly over the big cobbles; beyond the firemen, the grocer Bradly wound up his awning with slow creaking revolutions.

Across the square at its other edge the young virgins of the eastern part of town walked lightly home in chattering groups. They came to town at four o'clock in the afternoon, walked up and down the little avenue several times, entered a shop to purchase small justifications, and finally went into the chief drug-store, where the bucks of the town loafed and drawled in lazy, alert groups. It was their club, their brasserie, the forum of the sexes. With confident smiles the young men detached themselves from their group and strolled back to booth and table.

"Hey theah! Wheahd you come from?"

"Move ovah theah, lady. I want to tawk to you."

Gant looked and saw. His thin mouth was tickled by a faint sly smile. He wet his big thumb quickly.

While his furtive eyes roved over the east end of the square, Gant talked with Jannadeau. Before the shop the comely matrons of the town came up from the market. From time to time they smiled, seeing him, and he bowed sweepingly. Such lovely manners!

"The King of England," he observed, "is only a figurehead. He doesn't begin to have the power of the President of the United States."

"His power is severely li*mit*ed," said Jannadeau gutturally, "by custom but not by statute. In actua*lity* he is still one of the most powerful monarchs in the world." His black fingers probed carefully into the viscera of a watch.

"The late King Edward, for all his faults," said Gant, wetting his thumb, "was a smart man. This fellow they've got now is a nonentity and a nincompoop." He grinned faintly, with pleasure, at the ghost of his old rhetoric, glancing furtively at the Swiss to see if the big words told.

His uneasy eyes followed carefully the stylish carriage of Queen Elizabeth's well-clad figure as she came down by the shop again. She smiled pleasantly, bound homeward for her latticed terrace. He bowed elaborately.

"Good evening, madame," he said.

She disappeared. In a moment she came back decisively and mounted the broad steps. He watched her approach with quickened pulses. Twelve years.

"How's the madam?" he said gallantly as she crossed the porch. "Elizabeth, I was just telling Jannadeau you were the most stylish woman in town."

"Well, that's mighty sweet of you, Mr. Gant," she said in her cool, poised voice. "You've always got a good word for everyone."

She gave a bright pleasant nod to Jannadeau, who swung his huge scowling head ponderously around and muttered at her.

"Why, Elizabeth," said Gant, "you haven't changed an inch in fifteen years. I don't believe you're a day older."

She was thirty-eight and cheerfully aware of it.

"Oh, yes," she said, laughing. "You're only saying that to make me feel good. I'm no chicken any more."

She had pale, clear skin, pleasantly freckled, carrot-colored hair, and a thin mouth live with humor. Her figure was trim and strong—no longer young. She had a great deal of energy, distinction and elegance in her manner.

"How are all the girls, Elizabeth?" he asked kindly.

Her face grew sad. She began to pull her gloves off.

"That's what I came to see you about," she said. "I lost one of them last week."

"Yes," said Gant gravely, "I was sorry to hear of that."

"She was the best girl I had," said Elizabeth. "I'd have done anything in the world for her. We did everything we could," she added. "I've no regrets on that score. I had a doctor and two trained nurses by her all the time."

She opened her black leather handbag, thrust her gloves into it, and pulling out a small blue-bordered handkerchief, began to weep quietly.

"Huh-huh-huh-huh-huh," said Gant, shaking his head. "Too bad, too bad, too bad. Come back to my office," he said. They went back to the dusty little room and sat down. Elizabeth dried her eyes.

"What was her name," he asked.

"We called her Lily—her full name was Lilian Reed."

"Why, I knew that girl," he exclaimed. "I spoke to her not over two weeks ago." He convinced himself permanently that this was true.

"Yes," said Elizabeth, "she went like that—one hemorrhage after another. Nobody knew she was sick until last Wednesday. Friday she was gone." She wept again.

"T-t-t-t-t," he clucked regretfully. "Too bad, too bad. She was pretty as a picture."

"I couldn't have loved her more, Mr. Gant," said Elizabeth, "if she had been my own daughter."

"How old was she?" he asked.

"Twenty-two," said Elizabeth, beginning to weep again.

"What a pity! What a pity!" he agreed. "Did she have any people?"

"No one who would do anything for her," Elizabeth said. "Her mother died when she was thirteen—she was born out here on the Beetree Fork—and her father," she added indignantly, "is a mean old devil who's never done anything for her or anyone else. He didn't even come to her funeral."

"He will be punished," said Gant darkly.

"As sure as there's a God in heaven," Elizabeth agreed, "he'll get what is coming to him in hell. The dirty old crook!" she continued virtuously, "I hope he rots!"

"You can depend upon it," he said grimly. "He will. Ah, Lord." He was silent for a moment while he shook his head with slow regret.

"A pity, a pity," he muttered. "So young." He had the moment of triumph all men have when they hear some one has died. A moment, too, of grisly fear—sixty-four.

"I couldn't have loved her more," said Elizabeth, "if she had been one of my own. A young girl like that with all her life before her."

"It's pretty sad when you come to think of it," he said. "By God, it is!"

"And she was such a fine girl, Mr. Gant," said Elizabeth, weeping softly. "She had such a bright future before her. She had more opportunities than

I ever had, and I suppose you know"—she spoke modestly—"what I've done."

"Why," he exclaimed, startled, "you're a rich woman, Elizabeth—damned if I don't believe you are. You own property all over town."

"I wouldn't say that," she answered, "but I've enough to live on without ever doing another lick of work. I've had to work hard all my life. From now on I don't intend to turn my hand over."

She looked at him with a shy, pleased smile, and touched a coil of her fine hair with a small competent hand. He looked at her attentively, noting with pleasure her firm uncorseted hips, moulded compactly into her tailored suit, and her cocked comely legs tapering into graceful feet, shod in neat little slippers of tan. She was firm, strong, washed, and elegant—a faint scent of lilac hovered over her. He looked at her candid eyes, lucently gray, and saw that she was quite a great lady.

"By God, Elizabeth," he said, "you're a fine-looking woman!"

"I've had a good life," she said. "I've taken care of myself."

They had always known each other—since first they met. They had no excuses, no questions, no replies. The world fell away from them. In the silence they heard the pulsing slap of the fountain, the high laughter of bawdry in the square. He took a book of models from the desk and began to turn its slick pages. They showed modest blocks of Georgia marble and Vermont granite.

"I don't want any of those," she said impatiently. "I've already made up my mind. I know what I want."

He looked up surprised. "What is it?"

"I want the angel out front."

His face was startled and unwilling. He gnawed the corner of his thin lip. No one knew how fond he was of the angel. Publicly he called it his white elephant. He cursed it and said he had been a fool to order it. For six years it had stood on the porch, weathering in all the wind and rain. Now it was brown and fly-specked. But it had come from Carrara in Italy, and it held a stone lily delicately in one hand. The other hand was lifted in benediction, it was poised clumsily on the ball of one phthisic foot, and its stupid white face wore a smile of soft stone idiocy.

In his rages Gant sometimes directed vast climaxes of abuse at the angel. "Fiend out of hell," he roared, "you have impoverished me, you have ruined me, you have cursed my declining years, and now you will crush me to death—fearful, awful, and unnatural monster that you are."

But sometimes when he was drunk he fell weeping on his knees before it, called it Cynthia, the name of his first wife, and entreated its love, forgiveness, and blessing for its sinful but repentant boy. There was from the square laughter.

"What's the matter?" said Elizabeth. "Don't you want to sell it?"

"It will cost you a good deal of money, Elizabeth," he said evasively.

"I don't care," she answered positively. "I've got the money. How much do you want?"

He was silent, thinking for a moment of the place where the angel stood. He knew he had nothing to cover or obliterate that place—it left a barren crater in his heart.

"All right," he said finally. "You can have it for what I paid for it—four hundred and twenty dollars."

She took a thick sheaf of bank notes from her purse and counted the money out for him. He pushed it back.

"No. Pay me when the job's finished and it has been set up. You want some sort of inscription, don't you?"

"Yes. There's her full name, age, place of birth, and so on," she said, giving him a scrawled envelope. "I want some poetry, too—something that suits a young girl taken off like this."

He pulled his tattered little book of inscriptions from a pigeonhole and thumbed its pages, reading her a quatrain here and there. To each she shook her head. Finally he said:

"How's this one Elizabeth?" He read:

> *"She went away in beauty's flower,*
> *Before her youth was spent,*
> *Ere life and love had lived its hour*
> *God called her and she went.*
>
> *Yet whispers Faith upon the wind:*
> *No grief to her was given.*
> *She left your love and went to find*
> *A greater one in heaven."*

"Oh, that's lovely—lovely!" she said. "I want that one."

"Yes," he agreed, "I think that's the best one."

In the musty, cool smell of his little office they got up. Her gallant figure reached his shoulder. She buttoned her kid gloves over the small pink haunch of her palms and glanced about her. His battered sofa filled one wall, the line of his long body was printed in the leather. She looked up at him. Her face was sad and grave. They remembered.

"It's been a long time, Elizabeth," he said.

They walked slowly to the front through aisled marbles. Sentineled just beyond the wooden doors, the angel leered vacantly down. Jannadeau drew his great head turtlewise a little farther into the protective hunch of his burly shoulders. They went out onto the porch.

The moon stood already like its own phantom in the clear-washed skies of evening. A little boy with an empty paper delivery-bag swung lithely by, his freckled nostrils dilating pleasantly with hunger and the fancied smell of supper. He passed, and for a moment, as they stood at the porch edge, all life seemed frozen in a picture: the firemen and Fagg Sluder had seen Gant, whispered, and were now looking toward him; a policeman, at the high side-porch of the police court, leaned on the rail and stared; at the edge of the central plot below the fountain a farmer bent for water at a bubbling jet, rose dripping, and stared; from the tax collector's office, city hall, up-stairs, Yancy, huge, meaty, shirt-sleeved, stared.

And at that second the slow pulse of the fountain was suspended, life was held, like an arrested gesture, in photographic abeyance, and Gant felt him-self alone move deathward in a world of seemings as, in 1910, a man might find himself again in a picture taken on the grounds of the Chicago Fair, when he was thirty, and his mustache black; and noting the bustled ladies and the derbied men fixed in the second's pullulation, remember the dead instant, seek beyond the borders for what (he knew) was there. Or as a veteran who finds himself upon his elbow near Ulysses Grant before the march, in pictures of the Civil War, and sees a dead man on a horse. Or, I should say, like some completed Don, who finds himself again before a tent in Scotland in his youth, and notes a cricket-bat, long lost and long forgot-ten; the face of a poet who had died, and young men and the tutor as they looked that Long Vacation when they read nine hours a day for greats.

Where now? Where after? Where then?

The Train and the City

Spring came that year like magic and like music and like song. One day its breath was in the air, a haunting premonition of its spirit filled the hearts of men with its transforming loveliness, wreaking its sudden and incredible sorcery upon gray streets, gray pavements, and on gray faceless tides of manswarm ciphers. It came like music faint and far, it came with triumph and a sound of singing in the air, with lutings of sweet bird-cries at the break of day and the high swift passing of a wing, and one day it was there upon the city streets with a strange and sudden cry of green, its sharp knife of wordless joy and pain.

"Sweet is the breath of morn, her rising sweet, the charm of earliest birds"—and that is the way the springtime came that year, and instantly this weary earth cast off the hag's pelt of the harsh and barren winter: the earth burst into life with a thousand singing unities of joy, of magical and delicate hues and lights, shifting as strangely and as poignantly as all the thousand strange and subtle weathers of man's heart and spirit, wreaking upon his soul the invisible mystery of its presence, its music of unrest and longing, its arrows of pain and joy, its thousand evanescent and impalpable griefs and glories, so strangely mixed of triumph and of singing, of passion, pride, and sorrow, love, and death.

A flame, a light, a glory, and a moth of light, a far lost cry, a triumph and a memory, a song, a paean and a prophecy, a moment lost forever and a word that would never die, a spurt of fire, a moment's twist of passion and of ecstasy, a brevity of poignant days and a haunting wild sorrow and regret, a thorn, a cry, a triumph, and a wordless and intolerable grief for beauty that must die, for buried dust that trembled to the passing of a wheel, for rooted lip and bone and for the cages of the heart where welled the vine, a goading of hunger and desire that maddened the brain, twisted the flesh, and tore the heart asunder with its savage and incommunicable passion of ecstasy and grief—that was the way that springtime came that year, and nowhere on the earth did it come with greater glory than on the streets and pavements of the city.

Not the whole glory of the great plantation of the earth could have outdone the glory of the city streets that spring. Neither the cry of great green fields, nor the song of the hills, nor the glory of young birch trees bursting into life again along the banks of rivers, nor the oceans of bloom in the flowering orchards, the peach trees, the apple trees, the plum and cherry trees, all of the singing and the gold of spring, with April bursting from the earth in a million shouts of triumph, and the visible stride, the flowered feet of the springtime as it came on across the earth, could have surpassed the wordless and poignant glory of a single tree in a city street, that spring, the waking to life of the bird song in the morning.

Over the immense and furious encampment of the city there trembled the mighty pulsations of a unity of hope and joy, a music of triumph and enchantment that suddenly wove all life into the fabric of its exultant harmonies. It quelled the blind and brutal stupefaction of the streets, it pierced into a million cells, and fell upon ten thousand acts and moments of man's life and business, it hovered above him in the air, it gleamed and sparkled in the flashing tides that girdled round the city, and with a wizard's hand it drew forth from the tombs of winter the gray flesh of the living dead.

Suddenly the streets were bursting into life again, they foamed and glittered with a million points of life and color, and women more beautiful than flowers, more full of juice and succulence than fruit, appeared upon them in a living tide of love and beauty. Their glorious eyes were shining with a single tenderness; they were a rhyme of teeth, a red rose of loveliness of lip, a milk and honey purity, a single music of breast, buttock, thigh and lip and flashing hair, a chorus of beauty in the exultant and triumphant harmony of spring.

In the backyard of the old brick house in which I lived that year, one of those old fenced backyards of a New York house, a minute part in the checkered pattern of a block, there was out of the old and worn earth a patch of tender grass, and a single tree of a slender and piercing green was growing there.

That spring, day by day, I watched the swift coming of that tree into its moment's glory of young leaf again, until one day I looked into its heart of sudden and magical green, and saw the trembling lights that came and went into it, the hues that deepened, shifted, changed before one's eye to every subtle change of light, each delicate and impalpable breeze, so real, so vivid, so intense that it made a magic and a mystery evoking the whole poignant dream of time and of our life upon the earth, and instantly the tree became coherent with my destiny, and my life was one with all its brevity from birth to death.

And always when this happened, when I had worked with hope, with triumph, and with power, and looked again into the heart of that green tree, I could not hold the joy and hunger that I felt in me: it would burst out of its tenement of blood and bone like the flood tide bursting through a dam, and everything on earth would come to life again.

I would start up from a furious burst of work, tired but with a huge joy pulsing in me, and suddenly I would see again that tree of magic green. I would see the evening sunlight painted without violence or heat, and with a fading and unearthly glow upon the old red brick of rusty buildings, and instantly the whole earth would begin to live with an incomparable intensity, in all its panoply of color, odor, warmth, and movement. It was living instantly in one single and exultant harmony of life and joy.

I would look out the backyard window and see the tree and shout over to the waitresses in the hospital annex, who would be ironing out as usual their two pairs of drawers and their flimsy little dresses in their shabby rooms; and I would watch a cat that crept along the ridges of the fence; and see some handsome women or some girls taking the air and reading, as they lolled back at ease in big garden chairs; and hear all the shouts and sounds of children in the streets, the voices of the people in the houses; and watch the cool steep shadows, and how the evening light was moving in the little squares of yards, each of which had in it something intimate, familiar, and revealing—a flower-plot in which a woman would work earnestly for hours, wearing a big straw hat and canvas gloves; a little patch of grass watered solemnly every evening by a man with a square red face and a bald head; a little shed or playhouse or workshop for some business-man's spare time hobby; or a gay-painted table, some easy lounging chairs, and a huge bright-striped garden parasol to cover it, and a good-looking girl who sat there reading with a tall drink at her side.

Everything would come to life at once. The old house I lived in, its red brick walls, its rooms of noble height and spaciousness, its old dark woods and floors that creaked, seemed to be living with the life of all its ninety years, and to be enriched and given a great and living silence, a profound, calm, and lonely dignity, by all the livers it had sheltered. The house was like a living presence all about me, and my sense of all these vanished lives would grow so strong that I seemed to live among them as their son and brother, and through them to reach back into a living and unbroken past, as real as all the life that passed about me.

My books leaned right and left upon the shelves as if some powerful inner energy was thrusting them that way, others had fallen off onto the floor, were stacked in tottering heaps upon the table, were flung and hauled in a dynamic circle round my cot, and were strewn everywhere about the room, until they seemed literally to move and breathe, to walk off their shelves and move around the place, even when I put them straight the hour before.

House, brick, walls, rooms, the old and worn woods, chairs, tables, even the way a half-wet bath towel hung from the shower ring above the bath tub, the way a coat was thrown down upon a chair, and finally the wild and yet organic movement and confusion of my papers, manuscripts, and books—all seemed to have an animate vitality of their own, and to leap instantly into a furious and living design.

But now everything seemed fine and wonderful to me! I loved the old house I lived in and the two disordered rooms; and suddenly it would seem to me that I knew all about the lives of the people all around me. Then, through the delicate, fragrant, and living air, I would get the smell of the sea, the fresh half-rotten river smell, which would come to me with an instant and intolerable evocation of the harbor, the traffic of its mighty ships.

And this odor, with its exultant and unutterable promise of the voyage, would be mixed with the odors of the earth and of the city. It was mixed with the smell of the ground, the fragrance of leaf and flower, and with all the warm, tarry exhalations of the street. It was mixed with the great and glorious taint of the city air, with the thousand smells of life and business that made everything palpable, warm, and sensuous with life, not only the immense and tidal flow of life that passed forever in the street, but gray pavement, old red brick, and rusty metal, old houses and great towers blazing in the air.

And instantly, an intolerable desire would awaken in me to go out in the streets. I would feel, with a feeling of wild longing, pain, and joy, that I was missing something rare and glorious, that I was allowing some superb happiness and good fortune to escape from me by staying in my room. It seemed to me that some enormous joy, some glorious and fortunate event— some fulfillment of glory, wealth, or love—was waiting for me everywhere through the city. I did not know where I must go to find it, on which of the city's thousand corners it would come to me, and yet I knew that it was there, and had no doubt at all that I would find and capture it—that I was going to achieve the greatest power and happiness that any man had ever known. Every young man on the earth has felt this.

And every child has felt it, too, for when I was a child on the great plantation of the earth there had been no waste or barren places; there was only the rich tapestry of an immense and limitlessly fertile domain forever lyrical as April, and forever ready for the harvest touched with the sorcery of a magic green, bathed forever in a full-hued golden light. And at the end, forever at the end of all the fabled earth, there hung the golden vision of the city, itself more fertile, richer, and more full of joy and bounty than the earth it rested on. Far-off and shining, it rose upward in my vision from an opalescent mist, upborn and sustained as lightly as a cloud, yet firm and soaring with full golden light. It was a vision simple, golden, unperplexed, carved from deep substances of light and shade, and exultant with its prophecy of glory, love, and triumph.

I heard, far-off, the deep and bee-like murmur of its million-footed life, and all the mystery of the earth and time was in that sound. I saw its thousand streets peopled with a flashing, beautiful, infinitely varied life. The city flashed before me like a glorious jewel, blazing with the thousand rich and brilliant facets of a life so good, so bountiful, so strangely and constantly beautiful and interesting that it seemed intolerable that I should miss a moment of it. I saw the streets swarming with the figures of great men and glorious women, and I walked among them like a conqueror, winning fiercely and exultantly by my talent, courage, and merit, the greatest tributes that the city had to offer, the highest prize of power, wealth, and fame, and the great emolument of love. There would be knavery as black and sinister as hell, but I would smash them with a blow, and drive them cringing to their hole; there would be heroic men and lovely women, and I would win and take a place among the highest and most fortunate people on earth.

Thus, in a vision hued with all the strange and magic colors of that time—a time which later somehow seemed to find its deepest meaning and fulfillment in the figures "1908"—I walked the streets of my great legendary city. Sometimes I sat among the masters of the earth in rooms of man-like opulence: dark wood, heavy leathers, solid lavish brown were all around me. Again I walked in great chambers of the night rich with the warmth of marble and the majesty of great stairs, and that were sustained on great columns of onyx, soft and deep with crimson carpets in which the foot sank down in noiseless tread. And through this room, filled with a warm and undulant music, the deep and mellow thrum of violins, there walked a hundred beautiful women, and all were mine, if I would have them, and the loveliest of them all was mine. Long of limb, and slender, yet lavish and deep of figure, they walked with an undulant movement and a proud straight look on their fragile and empty faces, holding their gleaming shoulders superbly, and their clear depthless eyes alive with love and tenderness. A firm golden light fell over them and over all my love, but I walked also in steep canyoned streets, blue and cool with a frontal steepness of money and great business, brown and rich somehow with the sultry and exultant smell of coffee, the good green smell of money, and the fresh half-rotten odor of the harbor and its tide of ships.

Such was my vision of the city—childish, fleshly, and erotic, but drunk with innocence and joy, and made strange and wonderful by the magic lights of gold and green and lavish brown in which I saw it, given a strange and trembling quality and tone, which was indefinable but unmistakable, so that I never could forget it later, and yet so strange, impalpable, and enchanted that later it would seem to me to have come from another life, a different world.

And more than anything, it was the light—oh, above all else, it was the light, the light, the tone, the texture of the magic light in which I saw that city and the earth, that made it wonderful. The light was golden, deep, and full with all rich golden lights of harvest; the light was golden like the flesh of women, lavish in their limbs, true, depthless, tender as their glorious eyes, time spun and maddening as their hair, as unutterable with desire as their fragrant nests of spicery, their melon-heavy breasts. The light was golden like a morning golden light that shines through ancient glass into a room of old dark brown. The light was brown, dark lavish brown, hued with rich lights of gold like the sultry and exultant fragrance of ground coffee; the light was lavish brown like old stone houses gulched in morning on a city street, brown like exultant breakfast smells that come from basement areas in the brownstone houses where the rich men lived; the light was blue, steep frontal blue, like morning underneath the frontal cliffs of buildings, the light was vertical cool blue, hazed with a thin morning mist, the light was blue, cold flowing harbor blue of clean cool waters, rimed brightly with the blue-black of the morning gulch and canyon of the city, blue-black with cool morning shadow as the ferry, packed with its thousand small white staring faces turned one way, drove bluntly toward the rusty weathered slips.

The light was amber brown in vast dark chambers shuttered from young light where in great walnut beds the glorious women stirred in sensual warmth their lavish limbs. The light was brown-gold like ground coffee, merchants, and the walnut houses where they lived, brown-gold like old brick buildings grimed with money and the smell of trade, brown-gold like morning in great gleaming bars of swart mahogany, the fresh beer-wash, lemon-rind, and the smell of angostura bitters. Then full-golden in the evening in the theaters, shining with full-golden warmth and body on full-golden figures of the women, on gilt sheaves and cupids and the cornucopias, on the fleshly, potent, softly-golden smell of the people; and in great restaurants the light was brighter gold, but full and round like warm onyx columns, smooth warmly tinted marble, old wine in dark round age-encrusted bottles, and the great blonde figures of naked women on rose-clouded ceilings. Then the light was full and rich, brown-golden like the great fields in autumn; it was full-swelling-golden like mown fields, bronze-red, picketed with fat rusty sheaves of corn and governed by huge barns of red and the mellow winey fragrance of the apples.

Such was the tone and texture of the lights that qualified my vision of the city and the earth.

But that childhood vision of the city was gathered from a thousand isolated sources, from the pages of books, the words of a traveler, a picture of the Bridge with its great wing-like sweep, the song and music of its cables, even the little figures of the men with derby hats as they advanced across it— these and a thousand other things all built the picture of the city in my mind, until now it possessed me and had got somehow, powerfully, exultantly, ineradicably, into everything I did or thought or felt.

That vision of the city blazed outward not only from those images and objects which would evoke it literally—as the picture of the Bridge had done; it was now mixed obscurely and powerfully into my whole vision of the earth, into the chemistry and rhythm of my blood, into a million things with which it had no visible relation. It came in a woman's laughter in the street at night, in sounds of music and the faint thrumming of a waltz in the guttural rise and fall of the bass violin; and it was the odor of new grass in April, in cries half heard and broken by the wind, and in the hot doze and torpid drone of Sunday afternoon. It came in all the smells and noises of a carnival, in the smell of confetti, gasoline, in the high excited clamors of the people, the wheeling music of the carousel, the sharp cries and strident voices of the barkers: and it was in the circus smells and sounds, as well—in the ramp and reek of lions, tigers, elephants, and in the tawny camel smell. It came somehow in frosty autumn nights, and it was in all clear sharp frosty sounds of Halloween; and it came to me intolerably at night in the receding whistle-wail of a distant and departing train, the faint and mournful tolling of its bell, and the pounding of great wheels upon the rail. It came also from the sight of great strings of rusty freight cars on the tracks and in the sight of a rail, powerful, shining, and exultant with a music of space and flight, as it swept away into the distance and was lost from sight.

In things like these and countless others like them the vision of the city somehow came alive and stabbed me like a knife; and most of it came from the sight of one of those old motor cars with their rich warmth and redolence, their strong, sultry smell of rubber, oil, and gasoline, of old warm wood and deep luxurious leather.

And somehow the dilapidated old ruin of an ancient bakery delivery truck which gasped and panted by my mother's house each day a little before three o'clock could evoke these powerful emotions of wandering, and the vision of the city as I thought it must be, as nothing else could do. The sharp and sultry odor of the old machine, the strong congruent smells of warm worn rubber, gasoline, and leather, touched my sense with a powerful and nameless excitement, the meaning of which I could not define, but which had in it, somehow, the exultancy of flight, the voyage, and deserving, and in addition to these odors of the machine there was the warm and maddening fragrance of new baked bread, of fresh buns and pies, and crisp new rolls.

Such had been my vision of the city when I was a child and before I ever had seen the city, and now, that spring, the vision was the same again.

I would rush out on the streets at evening like a lover going to a meeting with his mistress. I would hurl myself into the terrific crowds of people that swarmed incredibly, unaccountably, from work—five million bees that hummed with furious sound and movement from a thousand soaring hives. And instead of the old confusion, weariness and despair and desolation of the spirit, instead of the old and horrible sensation of drowning, smothering, in the numberless manswarm of the earth, I knew nothing but triumphant joy and power.

The city seemed carved out of a single rock, shaped to a single pattern, moving forever to a single harmony, a central all-inclusive energy—so that not only pavements, buildings, tunnels, streets, machines, and bridges, the whole terrific structure that was built upon its stony breast, seemed made from one essential substance, but the tidal swarms of people on its pavements were filled and made out of its single energy, moving to its one rhythm or repose. I moved among the people like a swimmer riding on the tide; I felt their weight upon my shoulders as if I carried them, the immense and palpable warmth and movement of their lives upon the pavements as if I were the rock they walked upon.

I seemed to find the source, the well-spring from which the city's movement came, from which all things proceeded—and having found it, my heart rose with a cry of triumph, and it seemed to me that I possessed it all.

And what did I do? How did I live? What did I enjoy, possess, and make my own in April, late April, of that year? I had all and nothing! I owned the earth; I ate and drank the city to its roots; and I left not even a heel print on its stony pavements.

And just as this tremendous fugue of hunger and fulfillment, of wild longing and superb content, of having everything and owning nothing, of finding the whole glory, warmth, and movement of the city in one small moment of my seeing, and of being maddened with desire, because I could not be everywhere at once and see everything—just as these great antagonists of wandering forever and the earth again worked furiously in me all the time, in a conflict of wild forces which strove constantly with each other and yet were all coherent to a central unity, a single force—so now did the city seem to join the earth it rested on, and everything on earth to feed the city.

Therefore, at any moment on the city streets, I would feel an intolerable desire to rush away and leave the city, if only for the joy I felt in being there. And at every moment when I was away from it, I would feel the same longing to return, to see if the city was still there, and still incredible, to find it once more blazing in my vision, in all its fabulous reality, its eternal unity of fixity and variousness, its strange and magic light of time.

Sometimes that spring, I would leave the city, going away just for the sheer joy I felt in coming back to it. I would go out in the country and come back at the end of day; or at the week-end, when I had no class to teach at the university where I was employed as an instructor, I would go away to other places where I had known people, or where I had once lived. I would go to Baltimore, to Washington, into Virginia, to New England, or among my father's people in a country town near Gettysburg, in Pennsylvania.

One Saturday, on one of those instant and overwhelming impulses, I went to the station, and got on a train that was going south into the State where I was born. This journey was never completed: I left the train that night at a station in Virginia, caught another train bound north, and was back in the city again the next afternoon. But on the trip into the South an incident occurred which I could not forget, and which became as much a part of my whole memory of the city as everything I saw that year.

It was this: that afternoon about three o'clock, as the train was pounding south across New Jersey, another train upon the inside track began to race with us, and for a distance of ten miles the two trains thundered down the tracks in an even, thrilling, and tremendous contest of steel and smoke and pistoned wheel that blotted out everything, the vision of the earth, the thought of the journey, the memory of the city, for every one who saw it.

The other train, which was bound for Philadelphia, appeared so calmly and naturally that at first no one suspected that a race was on. It came banging up slowly, its big black snout swaying and bucking with a clumsy movement, as it came on, its shining pistons swinging free and loose, and with short intermittent blasts of smoke from its squat funnel. It came up so slowly and naturally, past our windows, that at first it was hard to understand at what terrific speed the train was running, until one looked out of the windows on the other side and saw the flat, formless and uncharactered earth of New Jersey whipping by like pickets on a fence.

The other train came slowly on with that huge banging movement of the terrific locomotive, eating its way up past our windows, until the engine cab was level with me and I could see across two or three scant feet of space and see the engineer. He was a young man cleanly jacketed in striped blue and wearing goggles. He had a ruddy color, and his strong, pleasant face, which bore on it the character of courage, dignity, and an immense and expert knowledge these men have, was set in a good-natured and determined grin, as with one gloved hand held steady on the throttle, he leaned upon his sill, with every energy and perception in him fixed with a focal concentration on the rails. Behind him his fireman, balanced on the swaying floor, his face black and grinning, his eyes goggled like a demon and lit by the savage flare of his terrific furnace, was shoveling coal with all his might. Meanwhile, the train came on, came on, eating its way past foot by foot until the engine cab disappeared from sight, and the first coaches of the train came by.

And now a wonderful thing occurred. As the heavy rust-red coaches of the other train came up and began to pass us, the passengers of both trains suddenly became aware that a race between the trains was taking place. A tremendous excitement surged up in them, working its instant magic on all these travelers, with their gray hats, their worn gray city faces, and their dull tired eyes, which just the moment before had been fastened dully and wearily on the pages of a newspaper, as if, having been hurled along this way beneath the lonely skies so many times, the desolate face of the earth had long since grown too familiar to them, and they never looked out the windows any more.

But now the faces that had been so gray and dead were flushed with color, the dull and lusterless eyes had begun to burn with joy and interest. The passengers of both trains crowded to the windows, grinning like children for delight and jubilation.

Meanwhile, our own train, which for a space had been holding its rival even, now began to fall behind. The other train began to slide past our windows with increasing speed, and when this happened the joy and triumph of its passengers were almost unbelievable. Meanwhile, our faces had turned black and bitter with defeat. We cursed, we muttered, we scowled malevolently at them, and turned away with an appearance of indifference, as if we had no further interest in the thing, only to come back again with a fascinated and bitter look as their accursed windows slid by us with the inevitability of death and destiny.

Meanwhile, the crews of the two trains had shown as keen and passionate an interest, as intense a rivalry, as had the passengers. The conductors and porters were clustered at the windows or against the door in the car-ends, and they grinned and jeered just as the rest of us had done; but their interest was more professional, their knowledge more intimate and exact. The conductor would say to the porter—"Whose train is that? Did you see John McIntyre aboard?" And the Negro would answer positively, "No, sah! Dat ain't Cap'n McIntyre. Old man Rigsby's got her. Dere he is now!" he cried, as another coach moved past, and the grizzled and grinning face of an old conductor came in sight.

Then the conductor would go away, shaking his head, and the Negro would mutter and chuckle to himself by turns. He was a fat and enormous darkey, with an ink-black skin, a huge broad bottom, teeth of solid grinning white, and with a big fatty growth on the back of his thick neck. He shook like jelly when he laughed. I had known him for years because he came from my native town, and the Pullman car in which I rode, which was known as K 19, was the car that always made the journey of seven hundred miles between my home town and the city. Now the Negro sprawled upon the green upholstery of the end seat in the Pullman and grinned and muttered at his fellows in the other train.

"All right, boy. All right, you ole slew-footed niggah!" he would growl at a grinning darkey in the other train. "Uh! Uh!" he would grunt ironically. "Don't you think you's somp'n dough! You's pullin' dat train by yo'self, you is!" he would laugh sarcastically, and then suddenly and impatiently conclude, "Go on, boy! Go on! I sees you! I don't care how soon I loses you! Go on, niggah! Go on! Git dat ugly ole livah-lipped face of yo'n out o' my way!"

And the grinning and derisive face would also vanish and be gone, until the whole train had passed us, and vanished from our sight. And our porter sat there staring out the window, chuckling and shaking his head from time to time, as he said to himself, with a tone of reproof and disbelief:

"Dey ain't got no right to do dat! Dey ain't got no right to run right by us like we wasn't here!" he chuckled. "Dey ain't nothin' but a little ole Philadelphia local! Dey're not supposed to make the time we is! We's de limited! We got de outside rail!" he bragged, but immediately shaking his head, he said: "But Lawd, Lawd! Dat didn't help us none today. Dey've gone right on by us! We'll never ketch dem now!" he said mournfully, and it seemed that he was right.

Our train was running in free light and open country now, and the passengers, resigned finally to defeat, had settled back into their former dozing apathy. But suddenly our train seemed to start and leap below us with a living energy, its speed increasing visibly, the earth began to rush by with an ever-faster stroke, the passengers looked up and at one another with a question in their eyes, and an awakened interest.

And now our fortune was reversed, our train was running through the country at terrific speed, and in a moment more we began to come up on the rival train again. And now, just as the other train had slid by us, we began to walk by its windows with the calm imperious stride of our awakened and irresistible power. But where, before, the passengers of both trains had mocked and jeered at one another, they now smiled quietly and good-naturedly, with a friendly, almost affectionate, interest. For it seemed that they—the people in the other train—now felt that their train had done its best and made a manful showing against its mighty and distinguished competitor, and that they were now cheerfully resigned to let the limited have its way.

And now we walked up past the windows of the dining-car: we could see the smiling white-jacketed waiters, the tables covered with their snowy white and heavy gleaming silver, and the people eating, smiling and looking toward us in a friendly manner as they ate. And then we were abreast the heavy parlor cars: a lovely girl, blonde haired, with a red silk dress, and slender shapely legs crossed carelessly, holding an opened magazine face downward in one hand, and with the slender tapering fingers of the other hand curved inward toward her belly where they fumbled with a charm or locket hanging from a chain, was looking at us for a moment with a tender and good-natured smile. And opposite her, with his chair turned toward her, an old man, dressed elegantly in a thin, finely woven, and expensive-looking suit of gray, and with a meager, weary, and distinguished face, that had brown spots upon it, was sitting with his thin phthisic shanks crossed, and for a moment I could see his lean hands, palsied, stiff, and folded on his lap, with brown spots on them; and I could see a stiff, corded, brittle-looking vein upon the back of one old hand.

And outside there was raw and desolate-looking country, bursting suddenly into flares of April—a tree in bloom, a patch of grass, a light of flowers—incredible, unutterable, savage, immense, and delicate. And outside there were the great steel coaches, the terrific locomotives, the shining rails, the sweep of the tracks, the vast indifferent dinginess and rust of colors, the powerful mechanical expertness, and the huge indifference to suave finish. And inside there were the opulent green and luxury of the Pullman cars, the soft glow of the lights, and the people fixed there for an instant in incomparably rich and vivid little pictures of their life and destiny, as we were all hurled onward, a thousand atoms, to our journey's end somewhere upon the mighty continent, across the immense and lonely visage of the everlasting earth.

And we looked at one another for a moment, we passed and vanished and were gone forever, yet it seemed to me that I had known these people, that I knew them better than the people in my own train, and that, having met them for an instant under immense and timeless skies as we were hurled across the continent to a thousand destinations, we had met, passed, vanished, yet would remember this forever. And I think the people in the two trains felt this, also: slowly we rode past them now, and our mouths smiled and our eyes were friendly, but I think there was some sorrow and regret in what we felt. For, having lived together as strangers in the immense and swarming city, we now had met upon the everlasting earth, hurled past each other for a moment between two points in time upon the shining rails, never to meet, to speak, to know each other any more, and the briefness of our days, the destiny of man, was in that instant greeting and farewell.

Therefore, in this way, we passed and vanished, the coaches slipped away from us until again we came up level with the high cab of the locomotive. And now the young engineer no longer sat in his high window with a determined grin and with his hard blue eyes fixed on the rail. Rather, he stood now in the door, his engine banging away deliberately, slowed down, bucking and rocking loosely as we passed. His attitude was that of a man who has just given up a race. He had just turned to shout something to his fireman, who stood there balanced, arms akimbo, black and grinning, as we moved up by them. The engineer had one gloved hand thrust out against the cab to support him, he held the other on his hip, and he was grinning broadly at us with solid teeth edged with one molar of bright gold—a fine, free, generous, and good-humored smile, which said more plain than any words could do: "Well, it's over now! You fellows win! But you'll have to admit we gave you a run for your money while it lasted!"

Then we drew away and lost the train forever. And presently our own train came in to Trenton, where it stopped. And suddenly, as I was looking at some Negroes working there with picks and shovels on the track beside the train, one looked up and spoke quietly to our fat porter, without surprise or any greeting, as casually and naturally as a man could speak to some one who has been in the same room with him for hours.

"When you comin' back dis way, boy?" he said.

"I'll be comin' back again on Tuesday," said our porter.

"Did you see dat ole long gal yet? Did you tell huh what I said?"

"Not yet," the porter said, "but I'll be seein' huh fo' long! I'll tell yo what she says."

"I'll be lookin' fo' you," said the other Negro.

"Don't fo'git now," said our fat black porter, chuckling; and the train started, the man calmly returned to his work again; and this was all. What that astounding meeting of two black atoms underneath the skies, that casual, incredible conversation meant, I never knew; but I did not forget it.

And the whole memory of this journey, of this race between the trains, of the Negroes, of the passengers who came to life like magic, crowding and laughing at the windows, and particularly of the girl and the vein upon the old man's hand, was fixed in my brain forever. And like everything I did or saw that year, like every journey that I made, it became part of my whole memory of the city.

And the city would always be the same when I came back. I would rush through the immense and glorious stations, murmurous with their million destinies and the everlasting sound of time, that was caught up forever in their roof—I would rush out into the street, and instantly it would be the same as it had always been, and yet forever strange and new.

I felt as if by being gone from it an instant I had missed something priceless and irrecoverable. I felt instantly that nothing had changed a bit, and yet it was changing furiously, every second before my eyes. It seemed stranger than a dream, and more familiar than my mother's face. I could not believe in it—and I could not believe in anything else on earth. I hated it, I loved it, I was instantly engulfed and overwhelmed by it, and yet I thought at once that I could eat and drink it all, devour it, have it in me. It filled me with an intolerable joy and pain, an unutterable feeling of triumph and sorrow, a belief that all of it was mine, and a knowledge that I could never own or keep even a handful of its dust.

I brought back to it the whole packed glory of the earth, the splendor, power, and beauty of the nation. I brought back to it a tremendous memory of space, and power, and of exultant distances; a vision of trains that smashed and pounded at the rails, a memory of people hurled past the window of my vision in another train, of people eating sumptuously from gleaming silver in the dining cars, of cities waking in the first light of morning, and of a thousand little sleeping towns built across the land, lonely and small and silent in the night, huddled below the desolation of immense and cruel skies.

I brought to it the memory of the loaded box-cars slatting past at fifty miles an hour, of swift breaks like openings in a wall when coal cars came between, and the sudden feeling of release and freedom when the last caboose whipped past. I remembered the dull rusty red, like dried blood, of the freight cars, the lettering on them, and their huge gaping emptiness and joy as they curved in among raw piney land upon a rusty track, waiting for great destinies in the old red light of evening upon the lonely, savage, and indifferent earth; and I remembered the cindery look of road-beds, and the raw and barren spaces in the land that ended nowhere; the red clay of railway cuts, and the small hard lights of semaphores—green red and yellow— as in the heart of the enormous dark they shone for great trains smashing at their rails their small and passionate assurances.

And somehow all these things would awaken intolerably the blazing images of all the other things which I had seen and known in my childhood in a little town, when the great vision of the shining city was living already in my mind, and was somehow legible, exultant, full of joy and menace in ten thousand fleeting things, in the tremendous pageantry of childhood. And in all I saw, felt, tasted, smelled, or heard then—in the odor of tar in

April, and the smell of smoke in late October; in cloud shadows passing on the massed green of a hill and in the tugging of a leaf upon a bough; in the face of an actor from the city as he walked cockily down the main street of the town; and in the smell of sawdust and of circuses; and of elephants coming from the cars in morning darkness, and the smells of coffee, steaks, and ham in the circus breakfast-tent; of old worn planking in a small-town baseball bleachers, and the strident voices of a barker in a carnival; in the smell of powder, confetti, gasoline, and hot dogs, and in the sad wheeling music of a carousel; and in the flame-flares of great trains pounding at the river's edge; in the smell of rivers, fresh, half-rotten; and in the cool rustling of bladed corn at night; in walnut pulp, and rotting leaves, and in the mellow winey smell of binned and cellared apples; in the voice of a traveler who had come back from the city; and in the face of a woman who had lived there; in the drowsy warmth and smell and apathy of a little country station in mid-afternoon, sparking through brooding air the electric thrill of ticking telegraphs, and the oncoming menace of the train; in pictures of the Brooklyn Bridge with its soaring web of cables, and of men with derby hats who walked across it; and in the memory of the songs we sang—in haunting memories—of "Alexander's Rag Time Band," "Has anybody here seen Kelly?" and "Yip-I-Addy-I-Ay"; and of wintry streets where the bare boughs swung in corner light; and of closed houses, drawn shades, warmly golden with the lights and fires, and thumped pianos and the sound of voices singing; and in church bells tolling through a countryside at night; and in the departing whistle-wail of trains; the scamper of leaves upon a street in autumn; and of a woman's burst of laughter in the summer dark; in the great slow yellow rivers, and the broad and lonely light of winter across the land, and in a thousand images of the embrowned, desolate, and wintry earth—in these and in ten thousand other things I had seen and dreamed as a child; and now they all came back to me.

And finally I brought back to it the heart, the eye, the vision, of the everlasting stranger, who had walked its stones, and breathed its air, and looked into its million dark and riven faces as a stranger, and who could never make the city's life his own.

I brought back to it the million memories of my fathers, who were great men and knew the wilderness, but who had never lived in cities: three hundred of my blood and bone who sowed their blood and sperm across the continent, walked beneath its broad and lonely lights, were frozen by its bitter cold, burned by the heat of its fierce suns, withered, gnarled, and broken by its savage weathers, and who fought like lions with its gigantic strength, its wildness, its limitless savagery and beauty until with one stroke of its paw it broke their backs and killed them.

I brought back to it the memory and inheritance of all these men and women who had worked, fought, drunk, loved, whored, striven, and lived and died, letting their blood soak down like silence in the earth again, letting their flesh rot quietly away into the stern and beautiful, the limitless substance of the everlasting earth from which they came, from which they were compacted, on which they worked and wrought and moved, and in whose immense and lonely breast their bones were buried and now lay, pointing eighty ways across the continent.

Above the pounding of the mighty wheels their voices seemed to well out of the everlasting earth, giving to me, the son whom they had never seen, the dark inheritance of the earth and centuries, which was mine, even as my blood and bone were mine, but which I could not fathom:

"Whoever builds a bridge across this earth," they cried, "whoever lays a rail across this mouth, whoever stirs the dust where these bones lie, go dig them up, and say your Hamlet to the engineers. Son, son," their voices said, "is the earth richer where our own earth lay? Must you untwist the vine-root from the buried heart? Have you unrooted mandrake from our brains? Or the rich flowers, the big rich flowers, the strange unknown flowers?

"You must admit the grass is thicker here. Hair grew like April on our buried flesh. These men were full of juice; you'll grow good corn here, golden wheat. The men are dead, you say? They may be dead, but you'll grow trees here; you'll grow an oak, but we were richer than an oak: you'll grow a plum tree here that's bigger than an oak, it will be filled with plums as big as little apples.

"We were great men, and mean men hated us," they said. "We were all men who cried out when we were hurt, wept when we were sad, drank, ate, were strong, weak, full of fear, were loud and full of clamor, yet grew quiet when dark came. Fools laughed at us and witlings sneered at us: how could they know our brains were subtler than a snake's? Because they were more small, were they more delicate? Did their pale sapless flesh sense things too fine for our imagining? How can you think it, child? Our hearts were wrought more strangely than a cat's, full of deep twistings, woven sinews, flushing with dull and brilliant fires; and our marvelous nerves, flame-tipped, crossed wires too intricate for their fathoming.

"What could they see," the voices rose above the sound of the wheels with their triumphant boast, "what could they know of men like us, whose fathers hewed the stone above their graves, and now lie under mountains, plains, and forests, hills of granite, drowned by a flooding river, killed by the stroke of the everlasting earth? Now only look where these men have been buried: they've heaved their graves up in great laughing lights of flowers—do you see other flowers so rich on other graves?

"Who sows the barren earth?" their voices cried. "We sowed the wilderness with blood and sperm. Three hundred of your blood and bone are recompacted with the native earth: We gave a tongue to solitude, a pulse to the desert; the barren earth received us and gave back our agony: We made the earth cry out. One lies in Oregon, and one by a broken wheel and horse's skull still grips a gunstock on the western trail. Another one has helped to make Virgina richer. One died at Chancellorsville in Union blue, and one at Shiloh walled with Yankee dead. Another was ripped open in a bar-room brawl and walked three blocks to find a doctor, holding his entrails thoughtfully in his hands.

"One died in Pennsylvania reaching for a fork: her reach was greater than her grasp; she fell, breaking her hip, cut off from rare beef and roasting-ears at ninety-six. Another whored and preached his way from Hatteras to the Golden Gate: he preached milk and honey for the kidneys, sassafras for jaundice, sulphur for uric acid, slippery elm for decaying gums, spinach for the goiter, rhubarb for gnarled joints and all the twistings of rheumatism, and pure spring water mixed with vinegar for that great ailment dear to Venus, that makes the world and Frenchmen kin. He preached the brotherhood and love of man, the coming of Christ and Armageddon by the end of 1886, and he founded the Sons of Abel, the Daughter of Ruth, the Children of the Pentateuch, as well as twenty other sects; and finally he died at eighty-four, a son of the Lord, a prophet, and a saint.

"Two hundred more are buried in the hills of home: these men got land, fenced it, owned it, tilled it; they traded in wood, stone, cotton, corn, tobacco; they built houses, roads, grew trees and orchards. Where these men went, they got land and worked it, built upon it, farmed it, sold it, added to it. These men were hill-born and hill-haunted: all knew the mountains, but few knew the sea.

"So there we are, child, lacking our thousand years and ruined walls, perhaps, but with a glory of our own, laid out across three thousand miles of earth. There have been bird-calls for our flesh within the wilderness. So call, please call! Call for the robin red-breast and the wren who in dark woods discover the friendless bodies of unburied men!

"Immortal land, cruel and immense as God," they cried, "we shall go wandering on your breast forever! Wherever great wheels carry us is home—home for our hunger, home for all things except the heart's small fence and place of dwelling—place of love.

"Who sows the barren earth?" they said. "Who needs the land? You'll make great engines yet, and taller towers. And what's a trough of bone against a tower? You need the earth? Whoever needs the earth may have the earth. Our dust wrought in this land, stirred by its million sounds, will stir and tremble to the passing wheel. Whoever needs the earth may use the earth. Go dig us up and there begin your bridge. But whoever builds a bridge across this earth, whoever lays a rail across this mouth, whoever needs the trench where these bones lie, go dig them up and say your Hamlet to the engineers.

"The dry bones, the bitter dust?" they said. "The living wilderness, the silent waste? The barren land?

"Have no lips trembled in the wilderness? No eyes sought seaward from the rock's sharp edge for men returning home? Has no pulse beat more hot with love or hate upon the river's edge? Or where the old wheel and rusted stock lie stogged in desert sand: by the horsehead a woman's skull. No love?

"No lonely footfalls in a million streets, no heart that beat its best and bloodiest cry out against the steel and stone, no aching brain, caught in its iron ring, groping among the labyrinthine canyons? Naught in that immense and lonely land but incessant growth and ripeness and pollution, the emptiness of forests and deserts, the unhearted, harsh, and metal jangle of a million tongues, crying the belly-cry for bread, or the great cat's snarl for meat and honey? All, then, all? Birth and the twenty thousand days of snarl and jangle—and no love, no love? Was no love crying in the wilderness?

"It is not true. The lovers lie beneath the lilac bush; the laurel leaves are trembling in the wood."

So did their hundred voices well up from the earth and call to me, their son and brother, above the pounding of the mighty wheel that roared above them. And the memory of their words, their triumphant tongue of deathless silence, and the full weight of the inheritance they had given me, I brought back out of the earth into the swarming canyons and the million tongues of the unceasing, the fabulous, the million-footed city.

And finally I brought back to it a memory of the immortal and unchanging stillness of that earth itself, and of quiet words still spoken on a road. I had seen once more the huge and everlasting earth, the American earth, wild, rude, and limitless, scarred with harshness, filled with emptiness, unfinished and immemorable, but bursting into life and April at ten thousand places and somehow lyric, wild, and unforgettable, lonely, savage, and unspeakable in its beauty, as no other land on earth.

And all that I had seen, all that I remembered of this earth, I brought back to the city, and it seemed to be the city's complement—to feed it, to sustain it, to belong to it. And the image of the city, written in my heart, was so unbelievable that it seemed to be a fiction, a fable, some huge dream of my own dreaming, so unbelievable that I did not think that I should find it when I returned; yet it was just the same as I remembered it. I found in it, the instant I came out of the station, the tidal swarm of faces, the brutal stupefaction of the street, the immense and arrogant blaze and sweep of the great buildings.

It was fabulous and incredible, but there it was. I saw again the million faces—the faces dark, dingy, driven, harried, and corrupt, the faces stamped with all the familiar markings of suspicion and mistrust, cunning, contriving, and a hard and stupid cynicism. There were the faces, thin and febrile, of the taxi-drivers, the faces cunning, sly, and furtive, and the hard twisted mouths and rasping voices, the eyes glittering and toxic with unnatural fires. And there were the faces, cruel, arrogant, and knowing, of the beak-nosed Jews, the brutal heavy figures of the Irish cops, and their red beefy faces, filled with the stupid, swift, and choleric menaces of privilege and power, shining forth terribly with an almost perverse and sanguinary vitality and strength among the swarming tides of the gray-faced people. They were all there as I remembered them—a race mongrel, dark, and feverish, swarming along forever on the pavements, moving in tune to that vast central energy, filled with the city's life, as with a general and dynamic fluid.

And incredibly, incredibly! these common, weary, driven, brutal faces, these faces I had seen a million times, even the sterile scrabble of harsh words they uttered, now seemed to be touched with the magic of now and forever, this strange and legendary quality that the city had, and to belong themselves to something fabulous and enchanted. The people, common, dull, cruel, and familiar-looking as they were, seemed to be a part, to comprise, to be fixed in something classic and eternal, in the everlasting variousness and fixity of time, in all the fabulous reality of the city's life: they formed it, they were part of it, and they could have belonged to nothing else on earth

And as I saw them, as I heard them, as I listened to their words again, as they streamed past, their stony gravel of harsh oaths and rasping cries, the huge single anathema of their bitter and strident tongues dedicated so completely, so constantly, to the baseness, folly, or treachery of their fellows that it seemed that speech had been given to them by some demon of everlasting hatred only in order that they might express the infamy and vileness of men, or the falseness of women—as I listened to this huge and single tongue of hatred, evil, and of folly, it seemed incredible that they could breathe the shining air without weariness, agony, and labor—that they could live, breathe, move at all among the huge encrusted taint, the poisonous congestion of their lives.

And yet live, breathe, and move they did with savage and indubitable violence, an unfathomed energy. Hard-mouthed, hard-eyed, and strident-tongued, with their million hard gray faces, they streamed past upon the streets forever, like a single animal, with the sinuous and baleful convolutions of an enormous reptile. And the magical and shining air—the strange, subtle, and enchanted weather—of April was above them, and the buried men were strewed through the earth on which they trod, and a bracelet of great tides was flashing round them, and the enfabled rock on which they swarmed swung eastward in the marches of the sun into eternity, and was masted like a ship with its terrific towers, and was flung with a lion's port between its tides into the very maw of the infinite, all-taking ocean. And exultancy and joy rose with a cry of triumph in my throat, because I found it wonderful.

Their voices seemed to form one general City-Voice, one strident snarl, one twisted mouth of outrage and of slander bared forever to the imperturbable and immortal skies of time, one jeering tongue and rumor of man's baseness, fixed on the visage of the earth, and turned incredibly, and with an evil fortitude, toward depthless and indifferent space against the calm and silence of eternity.

Filled with pugnacious recollection, that Voice said, "'Dis guy,' I says. 'Dis friend of yoehs,'" it said, "'dis cheap chiselin' bastad who owes me fawty bucks—dat you intruduced me to—when's he goin' t' givit to me?' I says." And derisive, scornful, knowing, it would snarl: "Nah! Nah! Nah! Yuh don't get duh idea at *all!* Watcha talkin' about? Yuh got it *all* wrong! Not him! Nah! Not dat guy! Dat's not the guy at all—duh *otheh* guy!" it said. And it would ask for information sharply, saying, "*Wich* guy? *Wich* guy do you mean? Duh guy dat used to come in Louie's place?" And bullying and harsh it would reply: "*Yuh* don't know? Watcha mean yuh don't know?" . . . Defiant, "*Who* don't know? . . . *Who* says so . . . *Who* told yuh so?" And jeering, "Oh, *dat* guy! . . . Is *dat* duh guy yuh mean? An' wat t' hell do *I* care wat he t'inks, f'r Chris' sake! . . . To hell wit him!" it said.

Recounting past triumphs with an epic brag, it said: "'You're comin' out of dere!' I said. 'Wat do yuh t'ink of dat?' . . . 'Oh, yeah,' he says, 'who's goin' t' make me?' So I says, 'You hoid me—yeah! . . . You're goin' to take dat little tin crate of yoeh's right out of deh! You'll take yoeh chance right on duh line wit' all the rest of us!' . . . 'Oh, yeah,' he says. . . . 'You hoid me, misteh'—an' he went!" In tones of lady-like refinement, it recounted romance into ravished ears as follows: "'Lissen,' I says, 'as far as my boss is concoined it's bizness only. . . . An' as far as Mr. Ball is concoined it's my own business (hah! hah! hah! Y' know that's wat I tol' him. . . . Jeez: it handed him a laugh, y' know!)—An' afteh five o'clock (I says) I'm my own boss. . . . At duh same time,' I says, 'deh's duh psychological side to be considehed.'"

And with the sweet accent of maternal tribulation, it admitted, "Sure! I hit her! I did! Oh, I hit her very hahd! Jeez! It was an awful crack I gave her, honestleh! My hand was boinin' f'r a half-oueh aftehwads! . . . I just blow up, y' know! . . . Dat's my on'y reason f'r dat! I jus' blow up! Dis fellah's in duh bathroom callin' f'r his eggs, duh baby's yellin' f'r his bottle, an' I jus' blow up! . . . Dat's my on'y reason f'r *dat!* Dat's duh on'y reason dat I hit her, see? I'm afraid she'll hoit duh baby, see? She bends its fingehs back. So I says, 'F'r God's sake, please, don't do dat! . . . I gotta headache' . . . an' then I jus' blow up! Sure! I hit her hahd! . . . Duh trouble is I can't stop wit' one slap, see! . . . Jeez! I hit her! My hand was boinin' f'r a half-oueh aftehwads!"

Hot with its sense of outraged decency, it said, "I went upstairs an' pounded on dat doeh! . . . 'Come out of dere,' you s of a b,' I says—Sure, I'm tellin' yuh! Dat's what I said to her, y' know! . . . 'Come out of dere, before I t'row you out,'" and regretfully it added, "Sure! I hate to do dese t'ings—it makes me feel bad lateh—but I won't have dem in my place. Dat's duh one t'ing I refuse t' do," it said. And with passionate emotion it asserted, "Sure! . . . Dat's what I'm tellin' yuh! . . . Yuh know how dat was, don't cha? Duh foist guy—her husban'—was passin' out duh sugah an' duh otheh guy—duh boy-friend—was layin' her. Can yuh ima-a-gine it?" it said.

Amazed, in tones of stupefaction, it would say, "No kiddin'! No!" And with solemn reprehension it would add, "Oh, yuh know I think that's te-e-ri-bul! I think that's aw-w-ful!"—the voice of unbelieving horror would reply.

Finally, friendly, and familiar, the great voice of the city said, "Well, so long, Eddy. I'm goin' t' ketch some sleep," it said, and answered, "Well, so long, Joe, I'll be seein' yuh." "So long, Grace," it added with an accent of soft tenderness and love, and the huge voice of the city murmured, "O.K. kid! Eight o'clock—no kiddin'—I'll be deh!"

Such were some of the tongues of that huge single Voice, as I heard them speak a thousand times, and as now instantly, incredibly, as soon as I came back to them, they spoke again.

And as I listened, as I heard them, their speech could not have been more strange to me had they been people from the planet Mars. I stared gape-mouthed, I listened, I saw the whole thing blazing in my face again to the tone and movement of its own central, unique, and incomparable energy. It was so real that it was magical, so real that all that men had always known was discovered to them instantly, so real I felt as if I had known it forever, yet must be dreaming as I looked at it; therefore I looked at it and my spirit cried:

"Incredible! Oh, incredible! It moves, it pulses like a single living thing! It lives, with all its million faces—and this is the way I always knew it was."

Death the Proud Brother

Three times already I had looked upon the visage of death in the city, and now that spring I was to see it once again. One night—on one of those kaleidoscopic nights of madness, drunkenness, and fury that I knew that year, when I prowled the great street of the dark from light to light, from midnight until morning, and when the whole world reeled about me its gigantic and demented dance—I saw a man die in the city subway.

He died so quietly that most of us would not admit that he was dead, so quietly that his death was only an instant and tranquil cessation of life's movement, so peaceable and natural in its action, that we all stared at it with eyes of fascination and unbelief, recognizing the face of death at once with a terrible sense of recognition which told us that we had always known him, and yet, frightened and bewildered as we were, unwilling to admit that he had come.

For although each of the three city deaths that I had seen before this one had come terribly and by violence, there would remain finally in my memory of this one a quality of terror, majesty, and grandeur which the others did not have.

The first of these deaths had occurred four years before in the month of April of my first year in the city. It had happened upon the corner of one of those dingy, swarming streets of the upper East Side, and in the way it had happened there had been a merciless, accidental, and indifferent quality which was far more terrible than any deliberate cruelty could have been, which spoke terribly and at once through the shining air, the joy and magic of the season, obliterating all the hope and exultancy in the hearts of men who saw it, as it spoke to them instantly its savage and inexorable judgment.

"Oh, little man," it said, "I am the city, the million-footed, million-visaged city—my life is made up of the lives of ten million men, who come and go, pass, die, are born, and die again, while I endure forever. Little man, little man," it said, "you think me cruel and merciless because I have just killed one of you, just as only a moment since you thought that I was beautiful and good because the breath of April filled your lungs with its intoxication, the smell of the tides was coming to you from the harbor with an excellent promise of Spring—warm seas, the thought of mighty ships, of voyages, and the vision of the fabled and golden countries you have never known. Yes, little man—oh! dingy meager little atom that crawls and sweats along my strong pavements, is hauled blindly, darkly, grayly, and helplessly through my savage tunnels, who swarms up from my earth in places like vermin swarming from their ratholes in the ground, and who is poured in here and doled out there, driven and hurried along here like a dead leaf on the breast of my great tides—you little man, who live, sweat, suffer, die, only as an infinitesimal particle of my everlasting sweep, my tidal energies, to whom I give brief housings in my ten million little cells, but who can leave not even the mark of your puny foot upon my savage streets to tell that you have lived here—Oh! little man, little man, thou grimy, faceless little atom in my unnumbered swarms, who sweat, curse, hate, lie, cheat, plead, love, and toil forever until your flesh grows dry and hard and juiceless as the stone it walks upon, your eyes as dark and dead as burnt-out coals, your words as harsh, sterile, and strident as the clangors of my rusty iron, a moment since you thought me kind because the sun shone warmly on you and the air was sweet with April, and now you think me cruel because I have just killed one of your number—but what do you think I care for you? Do you think that I am kind because the sun shines warmly on you in the month of April and you see a tree in leaf again? Do you think that I am beautiful because your blood begins to pulse more hot and wild with April, because your lungs draw magic from the smells of spring, and your eyes read lies of beauty, magic, and adventure into the green of a tree, the light of the sun, the flesh and fragrance of your women? Little man, little man— in gray November you have found me dull and dismal, in the glazed and gelid heat of August you have cursed me bitterly and found my walls intolerable, in October you have returned to me with wild joy and sorrow, with exulting and regret, in the grim and savage month of February you have found me cruel, merciless, and barren, in the wild and ragged month of March your life itself was like a torn cloud, filled with mad promises of spring, and with despair and dreariness, with soaring hopes and with the broad harsh lights of desolation, with the red and torn sunsets, and the howling of demented winds; and in April, late April, you have found me fair and beautiful again. But, little man, these are the lights and weathers of your own heart, the folly of your soul, the falseness of your eye. Ten thousand lights and weathers have passed over me, shone upon me, stormed and beaten at my iron front—yet I have been the same forever. You sweat, you toil, you hope, you suffer, I kill you in an instant with a stroke, or let you grub and curse your way along to your own death, but I do not care a jot whether you live or die, survive or are beaten, swim in my great tides, or smother there. I am neither kind, cruel, loving, or revengeful—I am only indifferent to you all, for I know that others will come when you have vanished, more will be born when you are dead, millions arise when you have fallen—and that the City, the everlasting City, will surge forever like a great tide upon the earth."

So did the city speak to me that first time that I saw it kill a man, and the way it killed a man was this:

I was coming along one of the dingy cross-streets in the upper east-side district—a street filled with the harsh and angular fronts of old brown-stone houses, which once no doubt had been the homes of prosperous people but were now black with the rust and grime of many years. These streets were swarming with their violent and disorderly life of dark-faced, dark-eyed, strange-tongued people, who surged back and forth, unaccountably, innumerably, namelessly, with a tidal, liquid, and swarming fluency that all dark bloods and races have, so that the lean precision, their isolation, and the severe design that the lives of northern peoples have—like something lonely, small, pitifully yet grandly itself beneath an infinite and cruel sky—are fractured instantly by this tidal darkness. The numberless and ageless manswarm of the earth is instantly revealed in all its fathomless horror and will haunt one later in dreams of madness, terror, and drowning, even if one sees only a half-dozen of these dark faces in a street. For this reason, Thomas De Quincey remarked that if he were forced to live in China for the remainder of his days, he would go mad.

Upon the corner of this swarming street, where it joined one of the great grimy streets that go up and down the city and that are darkened forever by the savage violence and noise of the elevated structure, so that not only the light which swarms through the rusty iron webbing, but all the life and movement underneath it seems harsh, broken, driven, beaten, groping, violent, bewildered, and confused—on such a corner the man was killed. He was a little middle-aged Italian who had a kind of flimsy cart or wagon which was stationed at the curb and in which he had a shabby and miscellaneous stock of cigarettes, cheap candies, bottled drinks, a big greasy-looking bottle of orange juice turned neck downward into a battered cylinder of white-enameled tin, and a small oil stove on which several pots of food—sausages and spaghetti—were always cooking.

The accident occurred just as I reached the corner opposite the man's stand. The traffic was roaring north and south beneath the elevated structure. At this moment an enormous covered van—of the kind so large, powerful, and cumbersome that it seems to be as big as a locomotive and to engulf the smaller machines around it, to fill up the street so completely that one wonders at the skill and precision of the driver who can manipulate it—came roaring through beneath the elevated structure. It curved over and around, in an attempt to get ahead of a much smaller truck in front of it, and as it did so, swiped the little truck a glancing blow that wrecked it instantly and sent it crashing across the curb into the vendor's wagon with such terrific force that the cart was smashed to splinters, and the truck turned over it completely and lay beyond it in a stove-in wreckage of shattered glass and twisted steel.

The driver of the truck, by the miracle of chance, was uninjured, but the little Italian vendor was mangled beyond recognition. As the truck smashed over him, the bright blood burst out of his head in an instant and exploding fountain so that it was incredible so small a man could have such fountains of bright blood in him. A great crowd of swarming, shouting, excited dark-faced people gathered around the dying man at once, police appeared instantly in astonishing numbers, and began to thrust and drive in brutally among the excited people, cursing and mauling them, menacing them with clubs, and shouting savagely:

"Break it up, deh! Break it up! On your way, now!" . . . "Where yuh goin'?" one snarled, grabbing a man by the slack of his coat, lifting him and hurling him back into the crowd as if he were a piece of excrement. "Break it up, deh! Break it up! G'wan, youse guys—yuh gotta move!"

Meanwhile, the police had carried the dying man across the curb, laid him down on the sidewalk, and made a circle around him from the thrusting mob. Then the ambulance arrived with its furious and dreadful clangor of bells, but by this time the man was dead. The body was taken away, the police drove and lashed the crowds before them, whipping and mauling them along, as if they were surly and stupid animals, until at length the whole space around the wreck was clear of people.

Then two policemen, clearing the street again for its unceasing traffic, half pushed, half-carried the twisted wreckage of the vendor's cart to the curb, and began to pick up his strewn stock, boxes, broken cups and saucers, fragments of broken glass, cheap knives and forks, and finally his spaghetti pots, and to throw them into the heap of wreckage. The spaghetti, pieces of brain, and fragments of the skull were mixed together on the pavement in a horrible bloody welter. One of the policemen looked at it for a moment, pushed the thick toe of his boot tentatively into it, and then turned away with a grimace on his brutal red face as he said, "Jesus!"

At this moment, a little gray-faced Jew, with a big nose, screwy and greasy-looking hair that roached backward from his painful and reptilian brow, rushed from the door of a dismal little tailor's shop across the sidewalk, breathing stertorously with excitement, and carrying a bucketful of water in his hand. The Jew ran swiftly out into the street, with a funny bandy-legged movement, dashed the water down upon the bloody welter, and then ran back into the shop as fast as he had come. Then a man came out of another shop with a bucketful of sawdust in his hand which he began to strew upon the bloody street until the stain was covered over. Finally, nothing was left except the wreckage of the truck and the vendor's cart, two policemen who conferred quietly together with notebooks in their hands, some people staring with dull fascinated eyes upon the blood-stain on the pavement, and little groups of people upon the corners talking to one another in low, excited tones, saying:

"Sure! I seen it! I seen it! Dat's what I'm tellin' yuh! I was talkin' to 'm myself not two minutes before it happened! I saw duh whole t'ing happen!

I was standin' not ten feet away from 'im when it hit him!"—as they revived the bloody moment, going over it again and again with an insatiate and feeding hunger.

Such was the first death that I saw in the city. Later, the thing I would remember most vividly, after the horror of the blood and brains, and the hideous mutilation of the man's flesh was almost forgotten, was the memory of the bloody and battered tins and pots in which the vendor had cooked his spaghetti, as they lay strewn upon the pavement, and as the policemen picked them up to fling them back into the pile of wreckage. For later it seemed these dingy and lifeless objects were able to evoke, with a huge pathos, the whole story of the man's life, his kindly warmth and smiling friendliness—for I had seen him many times—and his pitiful small enterprise, to eke out shabbily, but with constant hope and as best he could, beneath an alien sky, in the heart of the huge indifferent city, some little reward for his bitter toil and patient steadfastness—some modest but shining goal of security, freedom, escape, and repose, for which all men on this earth have worked and suffered.

And the huge indifference with which the immense and terrible city had in an instant blotted out this little life, soaking the shining air and all the glory of the day with blood, the huge and casual irony of its stroke—for the great van, which had wrecked the truck and killed the man, had thundered ahead and vanished, perhaps without its driver even knowing what had happened—was evoked unforgettably, with all its pity, pathos, and immense indifference, by the memory of a few battered pots and pans. This, then, was the first time I saw death in the city.

The second time I saw death in the city, it had come by night, in winter, in a different way.

About mid-night of a night of still bitter cold in February, when the moon stood cold and blazing in the white-blue radiance of the frozen skies, a group of people were huddled together upon the sidewalk of one of those confusing and angular streets which join Seventh Avenue near Sheridan Square. The people were standing before a new building which was being put up there, whose front stood raw and empty in the harsh brown-livid light. A few feet away, upon the curb, the watchman of the building had made a fire in a rusty ash-can, and this fire now whipped and blazed in the frozen air with a crackling flame to which some of the people of the group would go from time to time to warm their hands.

Upon the icy pavement before the building, a man was stretched upon his back and a hospital interne, with the tubes of a stethoscope fastened to his ears, was kneeling beside him, moving the instrument from place to place on the man's powerful chest, which was exposed. An ambulance, its motor throbbing with a quiet and reduced power that was somehow ominous, was drawn up at the curb.

The man on the pavement was about forty years old and had the heavy shambling figure, the brutal and powerful visage, of the professional bum. On the scarred and battered surface of that face it seemed that every savage violence of weather, poverty, and physical degradation had left its mark of iron, during the years the vagabond had wandered back and forth across the nation, until now the man's features had a kind of epic brutality in which the legend of immense and lonely skies and terrible distances, of pounding wheel and shining rail, of rust and steel and bloody brawl, and of the wild, savage, cruel, and lonely earth was plainly written.

The man lay on his back, as still and solid as a rock, eyes closed, his powerful, brutal features upthrust in the rigid and stolid attitude of death. He was still living, but one side of his head, at the temple, had been bashed in—a terrible and gaping wound which had been got when he had wandered, drunk and almost blind with the cheap alcohol or "smoke" which he had been drinking, into the building, and had fallen forward across a pile of iron beams, against one of which he had smashed his head. The great black stain of the wound had run down across one side of his face and on the ground, but it had almost ceased to bleed, and in the freezing air the blood was clotting rapidly.

The man's rag of dirty shirt had been torn open, and his powerful breast also seemed to swell forward with the same rigid and stolid immobility. No movement of breath was visible: he lay there as if carved out of rock, but a dull, flushed, unwholesome-looking red was still burning on his broad and heavy face, and his hands were clenched beside him. His old hat had fallen off, and his bald head was exposed. This bald head, with its thin fringe of hair upon each side, gave a final touch of dignity and power to the man's strong and brutal face that was somehow terrible. It was like the look of strength and stern decorum one sees on the faces of those powerful men who do the heavy work in the trapeze act at the circus, and who are usually bald-headed men.

None of the people who had gathered there about the man showed any emotion whatever. Instead, they just stood looking at him quietly with an intent yet indifferent curiosity, as if there were in the death of this vagabond something casual and predictable which seemed so natural to them that they felt neither surprise, pity, nor regret. One man turned to the man next to him, and said quietly, but with assurance, and a faint grin:

"Well, dat's duh way it happens to dem in duh end. Dey all go like dat sooner or later. I've never known it to fail."

Meanwhile, the young interne quietly and carefully, yet indifferently, moved his stethoscope from place to place, and listened. A policeman with a dark, heavy face, pitted, seamed, and brutal looking, stood over him, surveying the scene calmly as he gently swung his club, and ruminating slowly on a wad of gum. Several men, including the night watchman and a newsdealer on the corner, stood quietly, staring. Finally, a young man and a girl, both well dressed, and with something insolent, naked, and ugly in their speech and manner that distinguished them as being a cut above the others in education, wealth, and position—as young college people, young city people, young Village, painting, writing, art-theater people, young modern "post-war generation" people—were looking down at the man, observing him with the curiosity with which, and with less pity than, one would regard a dying animal and laughing, talking, jesting with each other with a contemptible and nasty callousness that was horrible, and which made me want to smash them in the face.

They had been drinking, but they were not drunk: something hard and ugly was burning nakedly in them—yet, it was not anything forced or deliberate; it was just hard-eyed, schooled in arrogance, dry and false, and fictional, and carried like a style. They had an astonishing literary reality, as if they might have stepped out of the pages of a book, as if there really were a new and desolate race of youth upon the earth that men had never known before—a race hard, fruitless, and unwholesome, from which man's ancient bowels of mercy, grief, and wild, exultant joy had been eviscerated as out of date and falsely sentimental to bright arid creatures who breathed from sullen preference an air of bitterness and hate, and hugged desolation to the bone with a hard fatality of arrogance and pride.

Their conversation had in it something secret, sweet, and precious. It was full of swift allusions, little twists and quirks and subtleties of things about which they themselves were in the know, and interspersed with all the trademarks of the rough-simple speech that at that time was in such favor with this kind of people: the "swell," the "grand," the "fine," the "simply marvelous."

"Where can we go?" the girl was asking him. "Will Louie's still be open? I thought that he closed up at ten o'clock."

The girl was pretty and had a good figure, but both face and body had no curve or fullness; body and heart and soul, there was no ripeness in her, she was something meager of breast, hard, sterile, and prognathous.

"If he's not," the young man said, "we'll go next door to Steve's. He's open all night long." His face was dark and insolent, the eyes liquid, the mouth soft, weak, pampered, arrogant, and corrupt. When he laughed, his voice had a soft welling burble in it, loose, jeering, evilly assured.

He had the look of something prized, held precious by aesthetic women; I had also seen his kind among the art-theater crowd who sometimes went to Esther's house.

"Oh, swell!" the girl was saying in her naked tone. "I'd love to go there! Let's have another party! Who can we get to go? Do you think Bob and Mary would be in?"

"Bob might be, but I don't think that you'll find Mary," said the young man, adroitly innocent.

"*No!*" the girl exclaimed incredulously. "You don't mean that she's"—and here their voices became low, eager, sly, filled with laughter, and the young man could be heard saying with the burble of soft laughter in his voice:

"Oh, I don't know! It's just another of those things! It happens in the best of families, you know."

"No!" the girl cried with a little scream of incredulous laughter. "You *know* she hasn't! After all she said about him, too! . . . I think—that's—simply—priceless!" She then said slowly: "Oh—I—think—that's—simply—*swell!*" She cried: "I'd give anything to see Bob's face when he finds out about it!"—and for a moment they laughed and whispered knowingly together, after which the girl cried once more, with her little shout of incredulous laughter:

"Oh, this is too good to be true! Oh—I think that's *marvelous,* you know!"—then added quickly and impatiently:

"Well, who can we get to go, then? Who *else* can we get?"

"I don't know," the young man said. "It's getting late now. I don't know who we can get unless"—and his soft dark mouth began to smile, and the burble of laughter appeared in his throat as he nodded toward the man on the ground "—unless you ask our friend here if he'd like to go along."

"Oh, that would be *grand!*" she cried with a gleeful little laugh. Then for a moment she stared down seriously at the silent figure on the pavement. "I'd love it!" the girl said. "Wouldn't it be swell if we could get someone like that to go with us!"

"Well—" the young man said indefinitely. Then, as he looked down at the man, his soft wet flaw of laughter welled up, and he said softly and slyly to the girl, "I hate to disappoint you, but I don't think we'll get our friend here to go. He looks as if he's going to have a bad head in the morning," and again his soft dark mouth began to smile, and the burble of soft laughter welled up in his throat.

"Stop!" the girl cried with a little shriek. "Aren't you mean?" She said reproachfully, "I think he's sweet. I think it would be simply marvelous to take some one like that on a party! He looks like a swell person," she continued, looking down at the man curiously. "He really does, you know."

"Well, you know how it is," the young man said softly. "He was a great guy when he had it!" The burble welled up richly in his soft throat. "Come on," he said. "We'd better go. I think you're trying to make him!"—and laughing and talking together in their naked and arrogant young voices, they went away.

Presently the interne got up, took the ends of the stethoscope from his ears, and spoke a few quiet and matter-of-fact words to the policeman, who scrawled something down in a small book. The interne walked over to the curb, climbed up into the back of the ambulance, and sat down on one seat with his feet stretched out upon the other one, meanwhile saying to the driver: "All right, Mike, let's go!" The ambulance moved off smoothly, slid swiftly around the corner with a slow clangor of bells, and was gone.

Then the policeman folded his book, thrust it into his pocket, and turning on us suddenly, with a weary expression on his heavy, dark, night-time face, stretched out his arms and began to push us all back gently, meanwhile saying in a patient and weary tone of voice: "All right, you guys! On your way, now. Yuh gotta move. It's all oveh."

And obedient to his weary and tolerant command, we moved on and departed. Meanwhile, the dead man lay, as solid as a rock, upon his back, with that great brutal face of power and fortitude, upthrust and rigid, bared with a terrible stillness, an awful dignity, into the face of the cold and blazing moon.

This was the second time that I saw death in the city.

The third time that I saw death in the city, it had come like this:

One morning in May the year before, I had been on my way uptown, along Fifth Avenue. The day was glorious, bright and sparkling, the immense and delicate light of the vast blue-fragile sky was firm and almost palpable. It seemed to breathe, to change, to come and go in a swarming web of iridescent and crystalline magic, and to play and flash upon the spires of the great shining towers, the frontal blaze and sweep of the tremendous buildings, and on the great crowd which swarmed and wove unceasingly on the street, with vivid and multifarious points of light and color, as if the light were shining on a lake of sapphires.

Up and down the great street as far as the eye could reach, the crowd was surging in the slow yet sinuous convolutions of an enormous brilliantly colored reptile. It seemed to slide, to move, to pause, to surge, to writhe here and to be motionless there in a gigantic and undulant rhythm that was infinitely complex and bewildering but yet seemed to move to some central and inexorable design and energy. So did the great surge of the man-swarm look from afar, but when one passed it by at close range, it all broke up into a million rich, brilliant, and vivid little pictures and histories of life, all of which now seemed so natural and intimate to me that I thought I knew all the people, to have the warm and palpable substance of their lives in my hands, and to know and own the street as if I had created it.

At one place, a powerful motor with a liveried chauffeur would snake swiftly in toward the curb, a uniformed doorman of some expensive shop would scramble with obsequious haste across the sidewalk and open the door for some rich beauty of the upper crust. The woman would get out swiftly with a brisk, sharp movement of her well-shod little feet and slender ankles, speak a few cold, incisive words of command to her attentive driver, and then walk swiftly across the sidewalk toward the shop with a driving movement of her shapely but rather tailored-looking hips and a cold impatient look on her lovely but hard little face. To her, this great affair of seduction, attraction, and adornment for which she lived—this constant affair of clothing her lovely legs to the best advantage, setting off her solid shapely little buttocks in the most persuasive fashion, getting varnished, plucked, curled, perfumed, and manicured until she smelled like an exotic flower and glittered like a rare and costly jewel—was really as stern a business as her husband's job of getting money, and not to be trifled with or smiled at for a moment.

Again, some lovely and more tender, simple, and good-natured girl would come by on the pavements, jaunty and rich with some glowing spot of color—a scarf of red or blue, or a gray hat—her hair fine spun and blown by light airs, her clear eyes fathomless and luminous with a cat-like potency and health, her delicate loins undulant with a long stride, and her firm breasts rhythmical with each step she took, her mouth touched by a vague and tender smile as she came by.

Elsewhere, dark-eyed, dark-faced, gray-faced, driven, meager, harassed, and feverish-looking men and women would be swarming along, but the shining light and magic of the day seemed to have touched them all with its sorcery, so that they, too, all seemed filled with hope, gaiety, and good nature, and to drink in as from some source of central and exultant energy the glorious intoxication of the day.

Meanwhile, in the street the glittering projectiles of machinery were drilling past incredibly in their beetle-bullet flight, the powerful red-faced police stood like towers in the middle of the street stopping, starting, driving them on or halting them with an imperious movement of their mast-like hands.

Finally, even the warm odors of the hot machinery, the smells of oils, gasoline, and worn rubber which rose from the bluish surface of the furious street, seemed wonderful, mixed as they were with the warm, earthy, and delicious fragrance of the trees, grass, and flowers in the Park, which was near by. The whole street burst into life for me immediately as it would on such a day for every young man in the world. Instead of being crushed down and smothering beneath its cruel and arrogant blaze of power, wealth, and number, until I seemed to drown in it, like a helpless, hopeless, penniless, and nameless atom, it now seemed to me to be a glorious pageantry and carnival of palpable life, the great and glamorous Fair of all the earth, in which I was moving with certitude, exultancy, and power as one of the most honored and triumphant figures.

At this moment, with the Park in view, with the sight of the trees, with their young magic green, and all the flash and play of movement, color, and machinery, in the square before the Park, I halted and began to look with particular interest at the people working on a building which was being erected there across the street. The building was not large, and neither very tall nor wide: it rose ten flights with its steel girders set against the crystal air with a graceful and almost fragile delicacy, as if already, in this raw skeleton, the future elegance and style of the building were legible.

For I knew that this building was to house the great business which was known as Stein and Rosen, and like the man who had once shaken the hand of John L. Sullivan, I had a feeling of joy, pride, and familiarity when I looked at it. For Esther's sister was vice-president of this mighty shop, second-in-command, its first in talent and in knowledge, and from Esther's merry lips I had often heard the fabulous stories of what took place daily there. She told of the glittering processions of rich women who came there for their finery; of actresses, dancers, millionaires' wives, moving-picture women, and of all the famous courtesans, who would pay as they bought and would plank down the ransom of a king in thousand-dollar bills for a coat of chinchilla fur; and of the stupendous things these legendary figures said.

Through the portals of this temple in the daytime would move the richest women and the greatest harlots in the country. And an exiled princess would be there to sell them underwear, an impoverished duchess would be there to sell them perfumery, and Mr. Rosen himself would be there to greet them. He would bend before them from the waist, he would give his large firm hand to them, he would smile and smile with his large pearly teeth, as his eyes went back and forth about his place continually. He would wear striped trousers, and he would walk up and down upon rich carpets, he would be splendid and full of power like a well-fed bull, and somehow he would be like that magnificent horse in Job who paweth in the valley and saith among the trumpets, "Ha! Ha!"

And all day long they would be calling all over the place for Esther's sister, who rarely spoke and rarely smiled. They could not get along without her, they would be asking for her everywhere, the rich women would demand her, and the famous courtesan would say she had to speak to her. And when she came to them, they would say: "I wanted to speak to you, because the rest of them know nothing. You are the only one who understands me. You are the only one I can talk to," and yet they could not talk to her, because she never spoke. But they would want to be near her, to confess to her, to pour their words into her silence: her large eyes would look at them and make them want to speak. Meanwhile, the Rosens smiled.

Thus, while the countless man-swarm of the earth thronged all around me, I stood there thinking of these things and people. I thought of Mr. Rosen, and of Esther and her sister, and of a thousand strange and secret moments in our lives. I thought how great Caesar's dust would patch a wall, and how our lives touch every other life that ever lived, how every obscure moment, every obscure life, every lost voice and forgotten step upon these pavements, had somewhere trembled in the air about us. "'Twere to consider too curiously, to consider so." "No! faith, not a jot!—" the step that passed there in the street rang echoes from the dust of Italy, and still the Rosens smiled.

And it seemed to me that all the crowded and various life of this great earth was like a Fair. Here were the buildings of the Fair, the shops, the booths, the taverns, and the pleasure-places. Here were the places where men bought and sold and traded, ate, drank, hated, loved, and died. Here were the million fashions that they thought eternal, here was the ancient, everlasting Fair, tonight bereft of people, empty and deserted, tomorrow swarming with new crowds and faces in all its million lanes and passages, the people who are born, grow old and weary, and who die here.

They never hear the great dark wings that beat in the air above them, they think their moment lasts forever, they are so intent that they scarcely ever see themselves falter and grow old. They never lift their eyes up to the deathless stars above the deathless Fair, they never hear the immutable voice of time that lives in the upper air, that never ceases, no matter what men live or die. The voice of time is distant and remote, and yet it has all of the voice of million-noted life within its murmur, it feeds on life and yet it lives above it and apart from it, it broods forever like the flowing of a river round the Fair. Here was the Fair: here were fixed flow and changeless change, immutable movement, the eternity of the earth haunted by the phantasmal briefness of our days.

Therefore when I looked at the spare webbing of this building on that shining day and knew that those ingots of lean steel, those flat blocks of fashionable limestone which already sheeted the building's basal front, and which in their slender elegance were somehow like the hips of the women that the building would adorn, had been spun marvelously from the gossamer substance of the Parisian frocks, distilled out of the dearest perfumes in the world, shaped from the cunning in man's brain, and from the magic in a woman's hands—it all seemed good and wonderful to me.

For above, beyond, and through that web of steel, and over the great surge and pulse of life in the great street, over all the sparkling surge and shift of the great Fair, I saw suddenly the blazing image of my mistress's jolly, delicate, and rosy face of noble beauty. And the image of that single face seemed to give a tongue to joy, a certitude to all the power and happiness I felt, to resume into its small circle, as into the petals of a flower, all of the glory, radiance, and variousness of life and of the street, until a feeling of such triumph and belief surged up in me that I thought I could eat and drink the city and possess the earth.

Then, quite suddenly, as I stood there looking at the little figures of the men who were working on the building, walking along high up against the crystal air with a corky and scuttling movement as they swarmed back and forth across the girders, the thing happened with the murderous nonchalance of horror in a dream. Nine floors above the earth, a little figure was deftly catching in a bucket the nails or rivets of red-hot steel which the man with tongs was tossing to him from the forge. For a moment, the feeder had paused in his work, had turned, tongs in hand, for a breather, and had spoken to a man upon another girder. The catcher, meanwhile, grateful for this respite, had put his bucket down and stood erect, a cigarette between his lips, the small flame of a match held in the cave of his brown cupped hands. Then the feeder, his throat still loud with some scrap of bawdry irrelevant to steel, turned to his forge, gripped with his tongs a glowing rivet, and his throat still trembling with its laughter, tossed deftly, absently, casually in its accustomed arc, that nail of fire. His scream broke in upon the echoes of his laughter, carrying to the glut of faultless and accurate machinery in the street below him its terrible message of human error.

His scream was "Christ!" and at that word so seldom used for love and mercy the startled eyes of the other man leaped from his match upon the death that whizzed toward him. Even in the six feet of life that still remained to him, his body had its time for several motions. It half turned, the knees bent as if for a spring out into space, the shoulder stooped, the big brown hands groping in a futile, incompleted gesture for the bucket. Then, half crouched and rigid, with palms curved out in a kind of grotesque and terrible entreaty and one foot groping horribly into thin air, he met his death squarely, fronting it. For a moment after the rivet struck him, his body paused, crouched, rigid, like a grotesque image, groping futilely and horribly into space with one clumsy foot, and with a wire of acrid smoke uncoiling at his waist. Then his shabby garments burst into flame, the man pawed out in sickening vacancy and fell, a blazing torch lit by a single scream.

So that rich cry fell blazing through the radiant and living air. It seemed to me that the cry had filled up life—for the moment I had the sense that all life was absolutely motionless and silent save for that one cry. Perhaps this was true. It is certain that all life in that building had ceased—where but a moment before there had been the slamming racket of the riveting machines, the rattling of the winches, and the hammering of the carpenters, there was now the silence of a cataleptic trance.

Above the street, delicate and spare in the blue weather, two girders swung gently in the clasp of the chain, but all machinery had stopped. The signal-man leaned over bent, staring, his hands still stretched in warning for his mate. The feeder sat astride a girder, gripping it in his curved hands, his face bent forward sightlessly in an oblivion of sick horror. The body had fallen like a mass of blazing oil waste, upon the wooden structure that covered the sidewalk, then bounced off into the street.

Then the illusion of frozen silence, which seemed to have touched all the world, was broken. That crowd, which in the city seems to be created on the spot, to spring up from the earth like Gorgon-seed for every calamity, had already grown dense at the spot where the man had fallen. Several policemen were there, mauling, cursing, thrusting back the thickening ring that terribly suggested flesh-flies that work on something dead or sweet. And all the gleaming machinery in the street—which had been halted by the traffic lights—was again in motion.

There had been threat of longer halt, a disruption of that inevitable flow, because several of the human units in the foremost squadrons of motors who had witnessed the accident refused now, under the strong drug of horror, to "click" as good machinery ought. But they were whipped into action after a moment's pause by a ponderous traffic cop, who stood in the center of the street, swinging his mighty arm back and forth like a flail, sowing the air with rich curses, his accents thickened in the long ape-like upper lip. So, the lights burned green again, the clamors in the street awoke, the hot squadrons of machinery crawled up and down: an army of great beetles driven by an ape. Then the racket of the riveters began again, high up above the street in the blue air the long arm of the derrick moved, a chain with its balanced weight of steel swung in and down.

Already the body had been carried inside the building, the police were charging like bulls into the persistent crowd, dispersing them. In a closed car, a young woman, bright with the hard enamel of city elegance, stared through the window, her little gloved hand clenched upon the glass, her face full of manicured distress. And as she looked, she kept murmuring sharply and monotonously: "Quick! quick! be quick!" Before her, her driver bent stolidly to his work. He was upset, but he could not show it. Perhaps he was thinking: "Jesus! I've got to get her out of this quick. What'll he say if she tells him about it? He can't blame me. I can't help what the *other* guy does! That's *his* lookout. You never know what is going to happen. A guy's got to think of everything at once."

He took a chance. Smoothly, swiftly, he skirted three cars and slid into the first rank between cursing drivers, just as the lights changed. The lady settled back in her seat with a look of relief. Thank Heaven, that was over! George was so smart. He got in ahead of every one: you never knew how he did it! He had done *that* beautifully!

Then I leaned against the building. I felt empty and dizzy. It seemed to me suddenly that I had only two dimensions—that everything was like something cut out of stiff paper, with no thickness.

"Brightness falls from the air." Yes, brightness had fallen suddenly from the air, and with it all the marrowy substance of life. The vitality of life and air and people was gone. What remained to me was only a painting of warmth and color that my sick eyes viewed with weariness and disbelief. Everything in that street went up and down. It seemed to me suddenly that everything was thin, two-dimensioned, without body and fullness. The street, the people, the tall thin buildings: these were all plane lines and angles. There were no curves in the street—the only thing that curved had been that one rich cry.

And just as the light of noon had gone out of the day, so had the image of that woman's face, struck by the casual horror of this death with all its evocations of a life she knew, now suffered a transforming and sorrowful change.

For where that radiant, good, and lovely face had just the moment before wrought for me its magic certitude and unity of exultant joy, now all this magic world of health and life was shattered by this nameless death, was drowned out in the torrent of this man's nameless blood, and I could see her face no longer as it had looked at noon.

Rather that man's blood and death had awakened the whole black ruin in my heart, the hideous world of death-in-life had instantly returned with all its thousand phantom shapes of madness and despair and, intolerably, un-answerably, like the unsearchable mystery of love and death, the bitter enigma of that face of radiant life was now fixed among these shapes of death to drive me mad with its unsearchable mystery.

For in the image of that face was held all the pity and the wild regret of love that had to die and was undying, of beauty that must molder into age and wither to a handful of dry dust and yet was high as a star, as timeless as a river, undwarfed beneath the whole blind horror of the universe, and taller than man's tallest towers, and more enduring than steel and stone.

And then the shapes of death would wake and move around her, and I could only see her now fixed and secure in an infamous and arrogant power, which could not be opposed or beaten by any man, and against which, like a maddened animal, I could do nothing but batter my life and brains out on the pavements, as this man had done, or madden horribly into furious death among the other nameless, faceless, man-swarm atoms of the earth.

I saw her, impregnably secure in an immense, complex, and corrupt city-life—a life poisonous, perverse, and sterile that moved smoothly in great chambers of the night ablaze with baleful suavities of vanity and hate, where the word was always fair and courteous, and the eye forever old and evil with the jubilation of a filthy consent. It was a world of the infamous dead so powerful in the entrenchments of its obscene wealth, its corruption that was amorous of death and faithlessness, its insolence of a jaded satiety, and its appalling weight of number and amount that it crushed man's little life beneath its ramified assault and killed and mutilated every living thing it fed upon—not only the heart and spirit of youth, with all the hope and pride and anguish in him, but also the life and body of some obscure worker whose name it did not know, whose death, in its remote impregnability, it would never hear or care about.

I tried to get the fingers of my hate upon that immense and shifting world of shapes and phantoms, but I could not. I could track nothing to its tangible source, trace nothing to some fatal certitude. Words, whispers, laughter, even an ounce of traitorous flesh, all the immense and moving tapestry of that cruel and phantasmal world, were all impalpable and hovered above me, the deathless and invincible legend of scorn and defeat.

Then, even as I stood there in the street, the blind horror left me with the magic instancy in which it always came and went; all around me people seemed to live and move, and it was noon, and I could see her face the way it was again, and thought that it was the best face in the world, and knew that there was no one like her.

Two men came rapidly back across the street from the dispersing crowd and one of them was talking in a low earnest tone to the other:

"Jeez!" he said. "Dat gul! Did yuh see her? Sure, sure, he almost fell on top of her! . . . She fainted! . .. Dey had to carry her into a stoeh! . . . Jeez!" he said. In a moment and in a quietly confidential tone he added: "Say—dat makes duh fourth one on dat building—did yuh know dat?"

Then I saw a man beside me with a proud, shrinking, and sensitive face, set in a blind sightless stare that kept looking through people, feeding on something that could not be seen. As I looked, he moved, turned his head slowly, and presently, in the dull voice of some one who has had an opiate, he said, "What? The fourth? The fourth?"—although no one had spoken to him. Then he moved his thin hand slowly, and with an almost meditative gesture over his forehead and eyes, sighed wearily and slowly like some one waking from a trance or some strong drug, and then began to walk ahead uncertainly.

This was the third time I saw death in the city.

Later, the thing I was to remember vividly about these three deaths, in contrast to the fourth one, which I will now describe to you, was this: That where the first three deaths had come by violence, where almost every circumstance of horror, sudden shock, disgust, and terror was present to convulse the hearts and sicken and wither up the flesh of those who saw death come, the city people, when their first surprise was over, had responded instantly to death, accepting its violence, bloody mutilation, and horror calmly, as one of the consequences of daily life. But the fourth time I saw death come, the city people were stunned, awed, bewildered, and frightened, as they had not been before; and yet the fourth death had come so quietly, easily, and naturally that it seemed as if even a child could have looked at it without terror or surprise.

This is the way it happened:

At the heart and core of the most furious center of the city's life—below Broadway at Times Square—a little after one o'clock in the morning, bewildered, aimless, having no goal or place to which I wished to go, with the old chaos and unrest inside me, I had thrust down the stairs out of the great thronging street, the tidal swarm of atoms who were pressing and hurrying forward in as fierce a haste to be hurled back into their cells again as they had shown when they had rushed out into the streets that evening.

Thus, we streamed down from free night into the tunnel's stale and fetid air again, we swarmed and hurried across the floors of gray cement, we rushed and pushed our way along as furiously as if we ran a race with time, as if some great reward were to be won if only we could save two minutes, or as if we were hastening onward, as fast as we could go, toward some glorious meeting, some happy and fortunate event, some goal of beauty, wealth, or love on whose shining mark our eyes were fastened.

Then, as I put my coin into the slot and thrust on through the wooden turnstile, I saw the man who was about to die. The place was a space of floor, a width of cement which was yet one flight above the level of the trains, and the man was sitting on a wooden bench which had been placed there to the left, as one went down the incline to the tunnel.

The man just sat there quietly at one end of the bench, leaned over slightly to his right with his elbow resting on the arm of the bench, his hat pulled down a little, and his face half lowered. At this moment, there was a slow, tranquil, hardly perceptible movement of his breath—a flutter, a faint sigh—and the man was dead. In a moment, a policeman who had watched him casually from a distance walked over to the bench, bent down, spoke to him, and then shook him by the shoulder. As he did so, the dead man's body slipped a little, his arm slid over the end of the bench and stayed so, one hand hanging over, his shabby hat jammed down, a little to one side, upon his head, his overcoat open, and his short right leg drawn stiffly back. Even as the policeman shook him by the shoulder, the man's face was turning gray, and yet no one would say so. By this time a few people out of the crowds that swarmed constantly across the floor had stopped to look, stared curiously and uneasily, started to go on, and then had come back. Now a few of them were standing there, just looking, saying nothing, casting uneasy and troubled looks at one another from time to time.

And yet I think that we all knew that the man was dead. By this time another policeman had arrived, was talking quietly to the other one, and now he, too, began to look curiously at the dead man, went over and shook him by the shoulder as the other one had done, and then after a few quiet words with his comrade, had walked off rapidly. In a minute or two he came back again, and another policeman was with him. They talked together quietly for a moment. One of them bent over and searched his pockets, finding a dirty envelope, a wallet, and a grimy-looking card. After prying into the purse and taking notes upon their findings, they just stood beside the dead man, waiting.

The dead man was a shabby-looking fellow of an age hard to determine, but he was scarcely under fifty, and hardly more than fifty-five. And had one sought long and far for the true portrait of the pavement cipher, the composite photograph of the man-swarm atom, he could have found no better specimen than this man. His only distinction was that there was nothing to distinguish him from a million other men. He had the kind of face one sees ten thousand times a day upon the city streets but cannot remember later.

This face, which even when alive, it is true, was of a sallow, sagging, somewhat paunchy and unwholesome hue and texture, was dryly and unmistakably Irish—city Irish—with the mouth thin, sunken, slightly bowed, and yet touched with something loose and sly, a furtive and corrupt humor. And the face was so surly, hang-dog, petulant, and servile—the face of one of those little men—a door-man at a theater, a janitor in a shabby warehouse, office building, or cheap apartment house, the father-in-law of a policeman, the fifth cousin of a desk-sergeant, the uncle of a ward-heeler's wife, a pensioned door-opener, office-guarder, messenger, or question-evader for some Irish politician, schooled to vote dutifully for "the boys" on election day, and flung his little scrap of patronage for service rendered and silence kept, apt at servility, fawning, cringing to those sealed with the mark of privilege and favor, and apt at snarling, snapping, gratuitous, and impudent discourtesy to those who had no power, no privilege, no special

mark of favor or advancement to enlarge them in his sight. Such was indubitably the man who now sat dead upon the subway bench.

And that man was legion, his number myriad. On his gray face, his dead
sunken mouth, the ghost of his recent life and speech sat incredibly, until it
seemed we heard him speak, listened to the familiar tones of his voice again,
knew every act and quality of his life, as certainly as if he were alive, as he
snarled at one man: "I can't help dat, I don't know nuttin' about dat, misteh. All I know is dat I got my ordehs, an' my ordehs is to keep every one
out unless dey can prove dey've gotta a date wit' Misteh Grogan. How do
I know who you are? How can *I* tell what yoeh business is? What's dat got
to do wit' me? No, seh! Unless you can prove you gotta date wit' Misteh
Grogan, I can't let yuh in. . . . Dat may be true . . . and den again it may
not be. . . . Wat t'hell am *I* supposed t'be? A mind-readeh, or somp'n? . . .
No, misteh! Yuh can't come in! . . . I got my ordehs an' dat's all I know."

And yet, the next moment, this same voice could whine with a protesting
servility its aggrieved apology to the same man, or to another one: "W'y
didn't yuh say yuh was a friend of Misteh Grogan's? . . . W'y didn't yuh tell
me befoeh you was his brudder-in-law? . . . If yuh'd told me dat, I'd a-let
yuh by in a minute. Yuh know how it is," here the voice would drop to
cringing confidence, "so many guys come in here every day an' try to bust
dere way right in to Misteh Grogan's office when dey got no bizness
dere. . . . Dat's duh reason dat I gotta be kehful . . . But now dat I know
dat you're O.K. wit' Misteh Grogan," it would say fawningly, "you can go
in any time yuh like. Any one dat's O.K. wit' Misteh Grogan is *all right*,"
that voice would say with crawling courtesy. "Yuh know how it is," it whispered, rubbing sly, unwholesome fingers on one's sleeve, "I didn't mean
nuttin'—but a guy in my position has gotta be kehful."

Yes, that was the voice, that was the man, as certainly as if that dead
mouth had moved, that dead tongue stirred and spoken to us its language.
There he was, still with the sallow hue of all his life upon his face, as it faded
visibly, terribly before us to the gray of death. Poor, shabby, servile, fawning, snarling, and corrupt cipher, poor, meager, cringing, contriving,
cunning, drearily hopeful, and dutifully subservient little atom of the
million-footed city. Poor, dismal, ugly, sterile, shabby little man—with your
little scrabble of harsh oaths, and cries and stale constricted words, your
pitiful little designs and feeble purposes, with your ounce of brain,
your thimbleful of courage, the huge cargo of your dull and ugly supersti-
tions. Oh, you wretched little thing of dough and tallow, you eater of poor
foods and drinker of vile liquors. Joy, glory, and magnificence were here for
you upon this earth, but you scrabbled along the pavements rattling a few
stale words like gravel in your throat, and would have none of them, because the smell of the boss, the word of the priest, the little spare approvals
of Mike, Mary, Molly, Kate, and Pat were not upon them—and tonight stars
shine, great ships are blowing from the harbor's mouth, and a million more

of your own proper kind and quality go stamping on above your head, while you sit here *dead* in your gray tunnel!

Yes—Stamp! Stamp! Stamp your feet, little man, little man, proud City, as you pass over us. We look at you tonight, and we shall not forget you. We look at your dead face with awe, with pity, and with terror, because we know that you are shaped from our own clay and quality. Something of us all, the high, the low, the base, and the heroic, the rare, the common, and the glorious, lies dead here in the heart of the unceasing city, and the destiny of all men living, yes, of the kings of the earth, the princes of the mind, the mightiest lords of language, and the deathless imaginers of verse, all the hope, hunger, and earth-consuming thirst that can incredibly be held in the small prison of a skull, and that can rack and rend the little tenement of bright blood and agony in which it is confined, is written here upon this shabby image of corrupted clay.

The dead man was wearing nondescript clothing, and here again, in these dingy garments, the whole quality, the whole station, of his life was evident, as if the clothes he wore had a tongue, a character, and a language of their own. They said that the man had known poverty and a shabby security all his life, that his life had been many degrees above the vagabond and pauper, and many degrees below any real security, substance, or repose. His garments said that he had lived from month to month rather than from day to day, always menaced by the fear of some catastrophe—sickness, the loss of his job, the coming on of age—that would have dealt a ruinous blow to the slender resource which he built between him and the world, never free from the fear of these calamities, but always just escaping them.

He wore an unpressed baggy gray suit which he filled out pretty well, and which had taken on the whole sagging, paunchy, and unshapely character of his own body. He had a small pot belly, a middling fleshiness and fullness which showed that he had known some abundance in his life, and had not suffered much from hunger. He was wearing a dingy old brown felt hat, a shabby gray overcoat, and a ragged red scarf—and in all these garments there was a quality of use and wear and shabbiness that was inimitable and that the greatest costume artist in the world could never have duplicated by intent.

The lives of millions of people were written in these garments. In their sagging hang and worn dingy textures, the shabby lives of millions of pavement ciphers were legible, and this character was so strong and legible that as the dead man sat there and his face took on the corpsen gray of death, his body seemed to shrink, to dwindle, to withdraw visibly before our eyes out of its last relationship with life, and the clothes themselves took on a quality and a character that were far more living than the shape they covered.

Meanwhile, the dead man's face had grown ghastly with the strange real-unreality of death that has such a terrible irony in it, for as one looks, the face and figure of the dead man seem to have no more substance of mortal flesh than a waxen figure in a museum, and to smile, to mock, to stare, to mimic life in the same ghastly and unreal manner that a waxen figure would. So it was with this man: above his sunken mouth, about which a thin corrupted smile still seemed to hover, he had a close-cropped moustache of iron gray; his chin, which was somewhat long, full, and Irish, had a petulant, hang-dog, old man's look, and was covered by a short furze or stubble of gray beard. His eyes were half-lidded: the dead eyeballs glittered bluishly with a dull dead fisheye stare.

Meanwhile, the turnstiles kept clicking with their dull wooden note, the hurrying people kept swarming past over the gray cement floor, the trains kept roaring in and out of the station below with a savage grinding vibrance, and from time to time, out of these swarming throngs, some one would pause, stare curiously for a moment, and stay. By this time, a considerable number of people had gathered in a wide circle about the bench on which the dead man sat, and curiously, although they would not go away, they did not press in, or try to thrust their way up close, as people do when some violent, bloody, or fatal accident has occurred.

Instead, they just stood there in that wide semi-circle, never intruding farther, looking at one another in an uneasy and bewildered manner, asking each other questions in a low voice from time to time which, for the most part, went unanswered since the person asked would squirm, look at his questioner uneasily and with wavering eyes, and then, muttering, "I don't know," with a slight gesture of his arms and shoulders, would sidle or shuffle away. And from time to time, the policemen, whose number by this time had grown to four, and who just stood around the man's body with a waiting and passive vacancy, would suddenly start, curiously and almost comically, into violent activity, and would come thrusting and shoving at the ring of people, pushing them back and saying in angry and impatient voices: "All right, now! Break it up! Break it up! Break it up! Go on! Go on! Go on! Yuh're blockin' up duh passageway! Go on! Go on! Break it up, now! Break it up!"

And the crowd obediently would give ground, withdraw, shuffle around, and then, with the invincible resiliency of a rope of rubber or a ball of mercury, would return, coming back once more into their staring, troubled, uneasily whispering circle.

Meanwhile, the wooden stiles kept clicking with their dull, dead, somewhat thunderous note, the people kept thronging past to get their trains, and in their glances, attitudes, and gestures when they saw the ring of staring people and the man upon the bench, there was evident all of the responses which it is possible for men to have when they see death.

Some people would come by, pause, stare at the man, and then begin to whisper to one another in low uneasy tones: "What's wrong with him? Is he sick? Did he faint? Is he drunk—or something?" to which a man might answer, looking intently for a moment at the dead man's face, and then crying out heartily, with a hard, derisive movement of his hand, and yet with something troubled and uncertain in his voice: "Nah! He's not sick. Duh guy is drunk! Dat's all it is. Sure! He's just passed out. . . . Look at dem all standin' dere, lookin' at duh guy!" he jeered. "Yuh'd t'ink dey neveh saw a drunk befoeh. Come on!" he cried. "Let's go!" And they would hurry on, while the man mocked at the crowd with hard derisive laughter.

And indeed, the dead man's posture and appearance as he sat there on the bench with his shabby old hat pushed forward over his head, one leg drawn stiffly back, his right hand hanging over the edge of the bench, and his thin, sunken Irish mouth touched by a faint, loose, rather drunken smile, were so much like the appearance of a man in a drunken stupor that many people, as soon as they saw his gray ghastly face, would cry out with a kind of desperate relief in their voices: "Oh! He's only drunk. Come on! Come on! Let's go!"—and would hurry on, knowing in their hearts the man was dead.

Others would come by, see the dead man, start angrily, and then look at the crowd furiously, frowning, shaking their head in a movement of strong deprecation and disgust, and muttering under their breath before they went on, as if the crowd were guilty of some indecent or disorderly act which their own decent and orderly souls abhorred. Thus an old man—unmistakably, somehow, a waiter—came by, paused, stared, and went on shaking his head and muttering angrily in this way. The waiter was a man past sixty, Irish, but tall, lean, and dignified in appearance. He had silvery gray hair, really very white and fine spun, a long thin face, with handsome and dignified features, which were marked with long seamed lines of care, disappointment, and quiet bitterness and disgust, and a skin that could flame and flush up hotly in a moment and that was always a tender, choleric, rose-pink color.

Everything about this man spoke out its message of decorum, respectability, and ordered restraint. His manner, dress, and bearing said as plain as words: "I have always gone about my business in this world in a quiet and dignified and decent manner, held my tongue and kept my counsel, not mixed up with what did not concern me, went home to my wife and children every night when my work was over, and kept myself free from this low riff-raff and rabble all around me. If you want to keep out of trouble, take my advice and do likewise."

The waiter was wearing upon his silvery hair a neat black derby hat; he had on a neat black suit, which was a little threadbare, but neatly brushed and pressed, and a dignified black overcoat, with a collar of black velvet, which was buttoned and set well on his long, thin, rather distinguished-looking figure. Finally, he was carrying a neat package wrapped up in a newspaper underneath one arm, and he wore long black patent-leather shoes, which looked very elegant, but which he had notched with vent-holes at the toes. He walked a trifle painfully, with a careful, somewhat flat-footed and gouty shuffle, which had all the old waiters in the world in it, and it was evident that, another day's work being over, with all its disappointment, acrimony, and fatigue, he was going quietly and decently home to his quiet and decent family.

When the waiter saw the dead man and the ring of staring people, he paused, started angrily, and then his rose-pink face began to flame and burn with a choleric and almost apoplectic fury. For a moment he started, and even took a step forward toward the ring of people as if he was going to cuff their ears, then muttering angrily, he looked at them, shaking his head with a glance full of distaste, disgust, and affronted decency, as if they had done some shameful, deliberate, and ruffianly act against public order and propriety. Then, still shaking his head and muttering angrily under his breath, and without another glance in the direction of the dead man, the old waiter had shuffled rapidly away, his neck, his features, and his forehead rose-pink with fury to the roots of his silvery hair.

Meanwhile, three little Jewesses and a young Jewish boy had come in together, and pressed up in a group into the circle of the crowd. For a moment the girls stood there, staring, frightened, huddled in a group, while the boy had looked in a rather stupid and bewildered manner at the dead man, finally saying nervously in a high stunned tone of voice: "What's wrong wit' him? Have dey called duh ambulance yet?"

No one in the ring of silent people answered him, but in a moment a taxi-driver, a man with a brutal heavy night-time face, a swarthy, sallow, and pitted skin, and black hair and eyes, who wore a cap, a leather jacket, and a shirt of thick black wool—this man turned and, jerking his head contemptuously toward the boy without looking at him, began to address the people around him in a jeering and derisive tone:

"Duh *ambulance!*" he cried. "Duh *ambulance!* Wat t'hell's duh use of duh *ambulance!* Jesus! Duh guy's dead an' he wants t'know if any one has called duh ambulance!" he cried, jerking his head contemptuously toward the boy again, and evidently getting some kind of security and assurance from his own jeering and derisive words. "Jesus!" he snorted. "Duh guy's dead an' he wants to know w'y some one doesn't call duh ambulance!" And he went off snorting and sneering by himself, saying, "Jesus!" and shaking his head, as if the stupidity and folly of people was past his power of understanding and belief.

Meanwhile, the boy kept staring at the dead man on the bench with a dull, fascinated eye of horror and disbelief. Presently he moistened his dry lips with his tongue, and spoke nervously and dully in a bewildered tone:

"I don't see him breathe or nuttin'," he said. "He don't move or nuttin'."

Then the girl beside him, who had been holding his arm all this time, and who was a little Jewess with red hair, thin meager features, and an enormous nose that seemed to overshadow her whole face, now plucked nervously and almost frantically at the boy's sleeve, as she whispered:

"Oh! Let's go! Let's get away from heah! . . . Gee! I'm shakin' all oveh!

Gee! I'm tremblin'—look!" she whispered, holding up her hand, which was trembling visibly. "Let's go!"

"I don't see him breathin' or nuttin'," the boy muttered dully, staring.

"Gee! Let's go!" the girl whispered, pleading again. "Gee! I'm so noivous I'm tremblin' like a leaf—I'm shakin' all oveh! Come on!" she whispered. "Come on! Let's go!" And all four of them, the three frightened girls and the stunned bewildered-looking boy, hurried away in a huddled group, and went down the incline into the tunnel.

And now the other people, who up to this time had only stood, looked uneasily at one another, and asked perplexed and troubled questions which no one answered, began to talk quietly and whisper among themselves, and one caught the sound of the word "dead" several times. Having spoken and heard this word, all the people grew very quiet and still, and turned their heads slowly toward the figure of the dead man on the bench, and began to stare at him with a glance full of curiosity, fascination, and a terrible feeding hunger.

At this moment a man's voice was heard speaking quietly, and with an assurance and certainty which seemed to say for every one what they had been unable to say for themselves.

"Sure, he's dead. The man's dead." The quiet and certain voice continued, "I knew all the time he was dead."

And at the same time a big soldier, who had the seamed and weathered face of a man who has spent years of service in the army, turned and spoke with a quiet and familiar assurance to a little dish-faced Irishman who was standing at his side.

"No matter where they kick off," he said, "they always leave that little black mark behind them, don't they?" His voice was quiet, hard, and casual as he spoke these words, and at the same time he nodded toward a small wet stain upon the cement near the dead man's foot where it had been drawn stiffly back—a stain which we had noticed and which, from his remark, was probably urine.

The little dish-faced Irishman nodded as soon as the soldier had spoken, and with an air of conviction and agreement, said vigorously:

"You said it!"

At this moment, there was a shuffling commotion, a disturbance in the crowd near the gate beside the turnstiles, the people pressed back respectfully on two sides, and the ambulance doctor entered, followed by two attendants, one of whom was bearing a rolled stretcher.

The ambulance surgeon was a young Jew with full lips, a somewhat receding chin, a little silky moustache, and a rather bored, arrogant, and indifferent look upon his face. He had on a blue jacket, a flat blue cap with a visor which was pushed back on his head, and even as he entered and came walking slowly and indifferently across the cement floor, he had the tubes of the stethoscope fastened in his ears and was holding the end part in his hand. The two attendants followed him.

About every move that the ambulance doctor made there was an air of habit, boredom, even weariness, as if he had been summoned too many times on errands such as this to feel any emotion of surprise, interest, or excitement any longer. As he approached the policemen, they separated and opened up a path for him. Without speaking to them, he walked over to the dead man, unbuttoned his shirt and pulled it open, bent, and then began to use the stethoscope, listening carefully and intently for some seconds, then moving it to another place upon the dead man's tallowy, hairless, and ghastly-looking breast and listening carefully again.

During all this time his face showed no emotion whatever of surprise, regret, or discovery. Undoubtedly, the doctor had known the man was dead the moment that he looked at him, and his duties were only a part of that formality which law and custom demanded. But the people during all this time surged forward a little, with their gaze riveted on the doctor's face with awe, respect, and fascinated interest as if they hoped to read upon the doctor's face the confirmation of what they already knew themselves or as if they expected to see there a look of developing horror, pity, or regret which would put the final stamp of conviction on their own knowledge. But they saw nothing in the doctor's face but deliberation, dutiful intentness, and a look almost of weariness and boredom.

When he had finished with the stethoscope, he got up, took it out of his ears, and then casually opened the half-shut eyelids of the dead man for a moment. The dead eyes stared with a ghastly bluish glitter. The doctor turned and spoke a few words quietly to the police who were standing around him with their note-books open, with the same air of patience, custom, and indifference, and for a moment they wrote dutifully in their little books. One of them asked him a question and wrote down what he said, and then the doctor was on his way out again, walking slowly and indifferently away, followed by his two attendants, neither of whom showed any curiosity or surprise. The dead man, in fact, seemed to be under the control of a regime which worked with a merciless precision, which could not be escaped or altered by a jot, and whose operations all of its servants—doctors, stretcher-bearers, policemen, and even the priests of the church—knew with a weary and unarguable finality.

The police, having written in their books and put the books away, turned and came striding toward the crowd again, thrusting and pushing them back, and shouting as they had before: "Go on! Go on! Break it up, now! Break it up!"—but even in the way they did this, there was this same movement of regime and custom, a sense of weariness and indifference, and when the people surged back into their former positions with the maddening mercurial resiliency, the police said nothing and showed no anger or impatience. They took up their station around the dead man again, and waited stolidly, until the next move in their unalterable program should occur.

And now the people, as if the barriers of silence, restraint, and timidity had been broken and the confusion and doubt in their own spirits dispersed by a final acknowledgment, and the plain sound of the word "death," which had at last been spoken openly, began to talk to one another easily and naturally, as if they had been friends or familiar associates for many years.

A little to one side, and behind the outer ring of the crowd, three sleek creatures of the night and of the great street which roared above our heads—a young smooth Broadwayite wearing a jaunty gray hat and a light spring overcoat of gray, cut inward toward the waist, an assertive and knowing-looking Jew, with a large nose, an aggressive voice, and a vultur-esque smile, and an Italian, smaller, with a vulpine face, ghastly yellow night-time skin, glittering black eyes and hair, all three smartly dressed and overcoated in the flashy Broadway manner—now gathered together as if they recognized in one another men of substance, worldliness, and knowl-edge. They began to philosophize in a superbly knowing manner, bestow-ing on life, death, the brevity of man's days, and the futility of man's hopes and aspirations the ripe fruit of their experience. The Jew was dominantly the center of this little group, and did most of the talking. In fact, the other two served mainly as a chorus to his harangue, punctuating it whenever he paused to draw breath with vigorous nods of agreement and such remarks as "You said it!" "And I don't mean maybe!" or "Like I was sayin' to a guy duh otheh day—" an observation which was never completed, as the phi-losopher would be wound up and on his way again:

"And they ask us, f'r Christ's sake, to save for the future!" he cried, at the same time laughing with jeering and derisive contempt. "For the future!" Here he paused to laugh scornfully again. "When you see a guy like that, you ask what for? Am I right?"

"You said it!" said the Italian, nodding his head with energetic assent.

"Like I was sayin' to a guy duh otheh day"—the other younger man began.

"Christ!" cried the Jew. "Save for the *future!* W'y the hell should *I* save for the future?" he demanded in a dominant and aggressive tone, tapping himself on the breast belligerently, glancing around as if some one had just tried to ram this vile proposal down his throat. "What's it goin' to getcha? You may be dead tomorrow! What the hell's the use in saving, f'r Christ's sake! We're only here for a little while. Let's make the most of it, f'r Christ's sake!—Am I right?" he demanded pugnaciously, looking around, and the others dutifully agreed that he was.

"Like I was sayin' to a guy duh otheh day," the young man said, "it only goes to show dat yuh—"

"Insurance!" the Jew cried at this point, with a loud scornful laugh. "The insurance companies, f'r Christ's sake! W'y the hell should any one spend their dough on insurance?" he demanded.

"Nah, nah, nah," the Italian agreed gutturally, with a smile of vulpine scorn, "dat's all a lotta crap."

"A lotta baloney," the young man said, "like I was sayin' to a guy duh otheh—"

"Insurance!" said the Jew. "W'y, to listen to *those* bastuds talk you'd think a guy was gonna live forever! Save for the future, f'r Christ's sake," he snarled. "Put something by f'r your old age—your *old* age, f'r Christ's sake," he jeered, "when you may get what this guy got at any minute! Am I right?"

"You said it!"

"Put something by for a rainy day! Leave something for your children when you kick off!" he sneered. "W'y should *I* leave anything for *my* children, f'r Christ's sake?" he snarled, as if the whole pressure of organized society and the demands of fifteen of his progeny had been brought to bear on him at this point. "No, sir!" he said. "Let my children look out for themselves the way *I* done!" he said. "Nobody ever did anything f'r me!" he said. "W'y the hell should *I* spend *my* life puttin' away jack for a lot of bastuds to spend who wouldn't appreciate it, noway! Am I right?"

"You said it," said the Italian, nodding. "It's all a lotta crap!"

"Like I was sayin' to dis guy—" the young man said.

"No, sir!" said the Jew in a hard positive tone, and with a smile of bitter cynicism. "No, sir, misteh! Not for me! When I kick off and they all gatheh around the big cawfin," he continued with a descriptive gesture, "I want them *all* to take a good long look," he said. "I want them all to take a good long look at me and say: 'Well, he didn't bring nothing with him when he came, and he's not taking anything with him when he goes—but there was a guy,'" the Jew said loudly, and in an impressive tone, "'there was a guy who spent it when he had it—and *who didn't miss a thing!*'" Here he paused a moment, grasped the lapels of his smart overcoat with both hands, and rocked gently back and forth from heel to toe, as he smiled a bitter and knowing smile.

"Yes, sir!" he said presently in a tone of hard assurance.

"Yes, sir! When I'm out there in that graveyahd pushin' daisies, I don't want no bokays! I want to get what's comin' to me here and now! Am I right?"

"You said it!" the Italian answered.

"Like I was sayin' to a guy duh otheh day," the young man now concluded with an air of triumph, "yuh neveh can tell. No, sir! Yuh neveh can tell what's goin' t'happen. You're here one day an' gone duh next—so wat t'hell!" he said. "Let's make duh most of it."

And they all agreed that he was right, and began to search the dead man's face again with their dark, rapt, fascinated stare.

Elsewhere now, people were gathering into little groups, beginning to talk, philosophize, even to smile and laugh, in an earnest and animated way. One man was describing his experience to a little group that pressed around him eagerly, telling again and again, with unwearied repetition, the story of what he had seen, felt, thought, and done when he first saw the dead man.

"Sure! Sure!" he cried. "Dat's what I'm tellin' yuh. I seen him when he passed out. I was standin' not ten feet away from 'im! Sure! I watched 'im when he stahted gaspin' t' get his bret'. I was standin' dere. Dat's what I'm sayin'. I tu'ns to duh cop an' says, 'Yuh'd betteh look afteh dat guy,' I says. 'Deh's somet'ing wrong wit' 'im,' I says. Sure! Dat's when it happened. Dat's what I'm tellin' yuh. I was standin' dere," he cried.

Meanwhile, two men and two women had come in and stopped. They all had the thick, clumsy figures, the dull-red smouldering complexions, the thick taffy-colored hair, bleared eyes, and broad, blunted, smeared features of the Slavic races—of Lithuanians or Czechs—and for a while they stared stupidly and brutally at the figure of the dead man, and then began to talk rapidly among themselves in coarse thick tones, and a strange tongue.

And now, some of the people began to drift away, the throng of people swarming homeward across the cement floor had dwindled noticeably, and the circle of people around the dead man had thinned out, leaving only those who would stay like flesh-flies feeding on a carrion, until the body was removed.

A young Negro prostitute came through the gate and walked across the floor, glancing about her quickly with every step she took and smiling a hideous empty smile with her thin encarmined lips. When she saw the circle of men, she walked over to it and after one vacant look toward the bench where the dead man sat, she began to glance swiftly about her from right to left, displaying white, shining, fragile-looking teeth.

The thin face of the young Negress, which was originally of a light coppery color, had been so smeared over with rouge and powder that it was now a horrible, dusky yellow-and-purplish hue, her black eyelashes were coated with some greasy substance which made them stick out around her large dark eyes in stiff greasy spines, and her black hair had been waved and was also coated with this grease.

She was dressed in a purple dress, wore extremely high-heels which were colored red, and had the wide hips and long, thin, ugly legs of the Negress. There was something at once horrible and seductive in her figure, in her thin stringy lower legs, her wide hips, her mongrel color, her meager empty little whore's face, her thin encarmined lips, and her thin shining frontal teeth, as if the last atom of intelligence in her bird-twitter of brain had been fed into the ravenous maw of a diseased and insatiable sensuality, leaving her with nothing but this varnished shell of face, and the idiot and sensual horror of her smile, which went brightly and impudently back and forth around the ring of waiting men.

Meanwhile, the Italian with the vulpine face, whose former companions, the Jew and the sleek young Broadwayite, had now departed, sidled stealthily over toward the Negress until he stood behind her. Then he eased up on her gently, his glittering eye and livid face feeding on her all the time in a reptilian stare, until his body was pressed closely against her buttocks, and his breath was hot upon her neck. The Negress said nothing but looked swiftly around at him with her bright smile of idiot and sensual vacancy, and in a moment started off rapidly, stepping along on her high red heels and long, stringy legs, and looking back swiftly toward the Italian, flashing her painted lips and shining teeth at him in a series of seductive invitations to pursuit. The man craned his neck stealthily at the edges of his collar, looked furtively around with his glittering eyes and vulpine face, and then started off rapidly after the girl. He caught up with the girl in the corridor beyond the stiles, and they went on together.

Meanwhile, the stiles still turned with their blunt, dull wooden note, belated travelers came by with a lean shuffle of steps upon the cement floors, in the news-stand the dealer sold his wares, giving only an occasional and wearily indifferent glance at the dead man and the people, and in the cleared space around the bench the police were standing, waiting, with a stolid, weary, and impassive calm. A man had come in, walked across the space, and was now talking to one of the police. The policeman was a young man with a solid strong-necked face that was full of dark color. He talked quietly out of the side of his mouth to the man who questioned him, and who was taking notes in a small black book. The man had a flabby yellowish face, weary eyes, and a flabby roll of flesh below his chin.

Meanwhile, the people who remained, having greedily sucked the last drop of nourishment from conversation, now stood silent, staring insatiably at the dead man with a quality of vision that had a dark, feeding, glutinous, and almost physical property, and that seemed to be stuck upon the thing they watched.

By this time an astonishing thing had happened. Just as the dead man's figure had appeared to shrink and contract visibly within its garments, as if before our eyes the body were withdrawing out of a life with which it had no further relationships, so now did all the other properties of space and light, the dimensions of width, length, and distance that surrounded him, undergo an incredible change.

And it seemed to me that this change in the dimensions of space was occurring visibly and momently under my eyes, and just as the man's body seemed to dwindle and recede, so did the gray cement space around him. The space that separated him from the place where the police stood, and the gray space which separated us from the police, together with the distance of the tiled subway wall behind, all grew taller, wider, longer, enlarged themselves terrifically while I looked. It was as if we were all looking at the man across an immense and lonely distance. The dead man looked like a lonely little figure upon an enormous stage, and by his very littleness and loneliness in that immense gray space, he seemed to gain an awful dignity and grandeur.

And now, as it seemed to me, just as the living livid gray-faced dead men of the night were feeding on him with their dark insatiate stare, so did he return their glance with a deathless and impassive irony, with a terrible mockery and scorn, which was as living as their own dark look, and would endure forever.

Then, as suddenly as it had come, that distorted vision was gone, all shapes and things and distances swam back once more into their proper focus. I could see the dead man sitting there in the gray space and the people as they looked and were. And the police were driving forward again and thrusting at the people all about me.

But they could not bear to leave that little lonely image of proud death, that sat there stiffly with its grotesque, drunken dignity, its thin smile, as men are loyal to a lifeless shape, and guard and watch and will not leave it till the blind earth takes and covers it again. And they would not leave it now because proud death, dark death, sat grandly there upon man's shabby image, and because they saw nothing common, mean, or shabby on earth, nor all the fury, size, and number of the million-footed city could alter for an instant the immortal dignities of death, proud death, even when it rested on the poorest cipher in the streets.

Therefore they could not leave it from a kind of love and loyalty they bore it now; and because proud death was sitting grandly there and had spoken to them, and had stripped them down into their nakedness; and because they had built great towers against proud death, and had hidden from him in gray tunnels, and had tried to still his voice with all the brutal stupefactions of the street, but proud death, dark death, proud brother death, was striding in their city now, and he was taller than their tallest towers, and triumphant even when he touched a shabby atom of base clay, and all their streets were silent when he spoke.

Therefore they looked at him with awe, with terror and humility, and with love, for death, proud death, had come into their common and familiar places, and his face had shone terribly in gray tainted air, and he had matched his tongue, his stride, his dignities against the weary and brutal custom of ten million men, and he had stripped them down at length, and stopped their strident and derisive tongues, and in the image of their poorest fellow had shown them all the way that they must go, the awe and terror that would clothe them—and because of this they stood before him lonely, silent, and afraid.

Then the last rituals of the law and church were followed, and the dead man was taken from their sight. The dead-wagon of the police had come. Two men in uniform came swiftly down the stairs and entered carrying a rolled stretcher. The stretcher was rolled out upon the cement floor, swiftly the dead man was lifted from the bench and laid down on the stretcher, and at the same moment, a priest stepped from the crowd, and knelt there on the floor beside the body.

He was a young man, plump, well-kept, and very white, save for his garments, pork-faced, worldly, and unpriestly, and on his full white jaws was the black shaved smudge of a heavy beard. He wore a fine black over-coat with a velvet collar, and had on a scarf of fine white silk, and a derby hat, which he removed carefully and put aside when he knelt down. His hair was very black, fine-spun as silk, and getting thin on top. He knelt swiftly beside the dead man on the stretcher, raised his white, hairy hand, and as he did so, the five policemen straightened suddenly, whipped off their visored hats with a military movement, and stood rigidly for a moment, with their hats upon their hearts as the priest spoke a few swift words above the body which no one could hear. In a moment a few of the people in the crowd also took off their hats awkwardly, and presently the priest got up, put on his derby hat carefully, adjusted his coat and scarf, and stepped back into the crowd again. It was all over in a minute, done with the same inhuman and almost weary formality that the ambulance doctor had shown. The two uniformed stretcher-men bent down, took the handles of the stretcher, and speaking in low voices to each other, lifted it. Then they started off at a careful step, but as they did so, the dead man's gray-tallow hands flapped out across the edges of the stretcher and began to jog and jiggle in a grotesque manner with every step the stretcher-bearers took.

One of the men spoke sharply to another, saying, "Wait a minute! Put it down! Some one get his hands!"

The stretcher was laid down upon the floor again, a policeman knelt beside the body and quickly stripped the dead man's tie from his collar, which had been opened by the doctor and now gaped wide, showing a brass collar-button in the neck band of the shirt and the round greenish discoloration of the brass collar-button in the dead yellowed tissues of the neck. The policeman took the dead man's necktie, which was a soiled, striped, and stringy thing of red and white, and quickly tied it in a knot around the dead man's wrists in order to keep his hands from jerking.

Then the stretcher-bearers lifted him again, and started off, the police striding before them toward the gate-way, thrusting the people back, and crying: "Get back, there! Get back! Make way! Make way! Make way!"

The dead man's hands were silent now, tied together across his stomach, but his shabby old garments trembled, and his gray-yellow cheek-flanks quivered gently with every step the stretcher-bearers took. The gaping collar ends flapped stiffly as they walked, and his soiled white shirt was partially unbuttoned, revealing a dead, bony, tallowy-yellow patch of breast below, and his battered old brown hat was now pushed down so far over his face that it rested on his nose, and, together with the thin sunken smile of his mouth, intensified the grotesque and horrible appearance of drunkenness.

As for the rest of him—the decaying substance that had been his body—this seemed to have shrunk and dwindled away to almost nothing. One was no longer conscious of its existence. It seemed lost, subsided to nothing and indistinguishable in a pile of shabby old garments—an old gray overcoat, baggy old trousers, an old hat, a pair of scuffed and battered shoes. This in fact was all he now seemed to be: a hat, a thin, grotesquely drunken smile, two trembling cheek-flanks, two flapping collar-ends, two gray-grimy claws tied with a stringy necktie, and a shabby heap of worn, dingy, and nondescript garments that moved and oscillated gently with every step the stretcher-bearers took.

The stretcher men moved carefully yet swiftly through the gate and up the stairs of an obscure side opening which was marked "Exit." As they started up the grimy iron steps, the body sloped back a little heavily, and the old brown hat fell off, revealing the dead man's thin, disordered, and gray-grimy hair. One of the policemen picked up the hat, saying to one of the stretcher-bearers, "O.K., John, I've got it!" then followed him up-stairs.

It was now early morning, about half-past three o'clock, with a sky full of blazing and delicate stars, an immense and lilac darkness, a night still cool, and full of chill, but with all the lonely and jubilant exultancy of spring in it. Far-off, half-heard, immensely mournful, wild with joy and sorrow, there was a ship lowing in the gulf of night, a great boat blowing at the harbor's mouth.

The street looked dark, tranquil, almost deserted—as quiet as it could ever be, and at that brief hour when all its furious noise and movement of the day seemed stilled for a moment's breathing space, and yet preparing for another day, the taxis drilled past emptily, sparely, and at intervals, like projectiles, the feet of people made a lean and picketing noise upon the pavements, the lights burned green and red and yellow with a small, hard, lovely radiance that somehow filled the heart with strong joy and victory and belonged to the wild exultancy of the night, the ships, the springtime, and of April. A few blocks farther up the street where the great shine and glitter of the night had burned immensely like a huge censer steaming always with a dusty, pollinated, immensely brilliant light, that obscene wink had now gone dull, and shone brownly, still livid but subdued.

When the stretcher-men emerged from the subway exit, the green deadwagon of the police was waiting at the curb, and a few taxi-drivers with dark dingy faces had gathered on the sidewalk near the door. As the stretcher-men moved across the pavement with their burden, one of the taxi-drivers stepped after them, lifted his cap obsequiously to the dead man, saying eagerly:

"Taxi, sir! Taxi!"

One of the policemen, who was carrying the dead man's hat, stopped suddenly, turned around laughing, and lifted his club with jocular menace, saying to the taxi-man:

"You son-of-a-bitch! Go on!"

Then the policeman, still laughing, saying "Jesus!" tossed the dead man's hat into the green wagon, into which the stretcher-men had already shoved the body. Then one of the stretcher-men closed the doors, went around to the driver's seat where the other was already sitting, took out a cigarette and lit it between a hard cupped palm and a twisted mouth, climbed up beside the driver, saying, "O.K. John," and the wagon drove off swiftly. The police looked after it as it drove off. Then they all talked together for a moment more, laughed a little, spoke quietly of plans, pleasures, and duties of the future, said good-night all around, and walked off, two up the street toward the dull brown-livid smoulder of the lights, and three down the street, where it was darker, quieter, more deserted, and where the lights would shift and burn green, yellow, red.

Meanwhile, the jesting taxi-man who had offered his services to the dead man on the stretcher turned briskly to his fellows with an air of something ended, saying sharply and jocosely:

"Well, wattya say, boy! Wattya say!"—at the same time sparring sharply and swiftly at one of the other drivers with his open hands. Then the taxi drivers walked away toward their lines of shining, silent machines, jesting, debating, denying, laughing in their strident and derisive voices.

And again, I looked and saw the deathless sky, the huge starred visage of the night, and heard the boats then on the river, a great ship baying at the harbor's mouth. And instantly an enormous sanity and hope of strong exultant joy surged up in me again; and like a man who knows he is mad with thirst, yet sees real rivers at the desert's edge, I knew I should not die and strangle like a mad dog in the tunnel's dark, I knew I should see light once more and know new coasts and come into strange harbors, and see again, as I had once, new lands and morning.

The face of the night, the heart of the dark, the tongue of the flame—I had known all things that lived or stirred or worked below her destiny. I was the child of night, a son among her mighty family, and I knew all that moved within the hearts of men who loved the night. I had seen them in a thousand places, and nothing that they ever said or did was strange to me. As a child, when I had been a route boy on a morning paper, I had seen them on the streets of a little town—that strange and lonely company of men who prowl the night. Sometimes they were alone, and sometimes they went together in a group of two or three, forever in mid-watches of the night in little towns prowling up and down the empty pavements of bleak streets, passing before the ghastly waxen models in the windows of the clothing stores, passing below hard bulbous clusters of white light, prowling before the facades of a hundred darkened stores, pausing at length in some little lunch-room to drawl and gossip quietly, to thrust snout, lip, and sallow jowl into the stained depths of a coffee mug, or dully to wear the slow gray ash of time away without a word.

The memory of their faces, and their restless prowling of the night, familiar and unquestioned at the time, returned now with the strangeness of a dream. What did they want? What had they hoped to find as they prowled past a thousand doors in those little, bleak, and wintry towns?

Their hope, their wild belief, the dark song that the night awoke in them, this thing that lived in darkness while men slept and knew a secret and exultant triumph, and that was everywhere across the land, were written in my heart. Not in the purity and sweetness of dawn with all the brave and poignant glory of its revelation, nor in the practical and homely lights of morning, nor in the silent stature of the corn at noon, the drowsy hum and stitch of three o'clock across the fields, nor in the strange magic gold and green of its wild lyric wooded earth, nor even the land that breathed quietly the last heat and violence of day away into the fathomless depth and brooding stillness of the dusk—as brave and glorious as these times and lights have been—had I felt and found the mystery, the grandeur, and the immortal beauty of America.

I had found the dark land at the heart of night, of dark, proud, and secret night: the immense and lonely land lived for me in the brain of night. I saw its plains, its rivers, and its mountains spread out before me in all their dark immortal beauty, in all the space and joy of their huge sweep, in all their loneliness, savagery, and terror, and in all their immense and delicate fecundity. And my heart was with the hearts of all men who had heard the exultant and terrible music of wild earth, triumph, and discovery, singing a strange and bitter prophecy of love and death.

For there was something living on the land at night. There was a dark tide moving in the hearts of men. Wild, strange, and jubilant, sweeping on across the immense and sleeping earth, it had spoken to me in a thousand watches of the night, and the language of all its dark and secret tongues was written in my heart. It had passed above me with the rhythmic sustentions of its mighty wing, it had shot away with bullet cries of a demonic ecstasy on the swift howlings of the winter wind, it had come softly, numbly, with a dark impending prescience of wild joy in the dull, soft skies of coming snow, and it had brooded, dark and wild and secret, in the night, across the land, and over the tremendous and dynamic silence of the city, stilled in its million cells of sleep, trembling forever in the night with the murmurous, remote, and mighty sound of time.

And always, when it came to me, it had filled my heart with a wild exultant power that burst the limits of a little room, and that knew no stop of time or place or lonely distances. Joined to that dark illimitable energy of night, like a page to the wind, and westward, my spirit rushed across the earth with the wild post of the exultant furies of the dark, until I seemed to inhabit and hold within my compass the whole pattern of the earth, the huge wink of the enormous seas that feathered its illimitable shores, and the vast structure of the delicate and engulfing night.

And I was joined in knowledge and in life with an indubitable certitude to the great company of men who lived by night and knew and loved its mystery. I knew all joys and labors and designs that such men know. I knew the life of the engineer, lit by the intermittent flares of savage furnace fires as he sat behind his throttle, in the swaying cab of his terrific locomotive, as his eyes peered out into the darkness at the spaced and lonely beacons of the semaphores, winking into the enormous dark, green, red, and white, their small and passionate assurances, and seeing the level wall of the golden wheat, lit for a moment by his furnace flare, the huge and secret earth that leaped instantly with all its mystery into the glare of the great headlight, and that was swallowed and engulfed again beneath the terrific drive of pistoned wheels.

And I knew the passionate heart of the boy who from the darkness of his berth watched, with a wild exultancy of joy and hope and sorrow, the great stroke and fanlike sweep of the immense and imperturbable earth. Field and fold and sleeping wood, it swept past him with its strange enigma of storm-swift flight and immortal stillness, of something found and lost forever in an instant, and with a dark tongue that spoke of morning, and the sea, and the triumph of a shining city.

I knew the secret glory that the brakeman knew, as through the night he moved along his runway on the tops of reeling freights, and saw light break before him in the east and the cool blind fragrance of the night emerge into the still pure sculpture of first light. I saw the fields and woods awake then in young sunlight, peach bloom, and the singing of the birds. And I saw the outposts of the town appear in the vast spread and flare of forty rails, as the engine swept into its final destination. I knew the fear, the ecstasy, the trembling, growing resolution of a boy who prowled outside the brothels of a sleeping town. I had seen and known the dark heart of a boy's desire a thousand times and in a hundred little places, and it had given a tongue to darkness, an animate stillness to silent streets and bolted doors, a heart of fire and passion and wild longing to all the waste and lone immensity of night.

I had known as well all other joys and labors of the night: the quiet voices of a country station, and the huge and brooding song of the dark Southern earth; the clean and quiet tremble of great dynamos in power stations and the perilous flares of bluish light that came from cutting torches, the showers of golden fire that exploded from them, and the intent and goggled faces of the men who used them.

Finally, I knew the joys and labors and designs that such men know. I had known all things living on the earth by night, and finally, I had known by night the immortal fellowship of those three with whom the best part of my life was passed—proud Death, and his stern brother, Loneliness, and their great sister, Sleep. I had watched my brother and my father die in the dark mid-watches of the night, and I had known and loved the figure of proud Death when he had come. I had lived and worked and wrought alone with Loneliness, my friend, and in the darkness, in the night, in all the sleeping silence of the earth, I had looked a thousand times into the visages of Sleep, and had heard the sound of her dark horses when they came.

Therefore, immortal fellowship, proud Death, stern Loneliness, and Sleep, dear friends, in whose communion I shall live forever, out of the passion and substance of my life, I have made this praise for you:

To you, proud Death, who sits so grandly on the brows of little men— first to you! Proud Death, proud Death, whom I have seen by darkness, at so many times, and always when you came to nameless men, what have you ever touched that you have not touched with love and pity, Death? Proud Death, wherever we have seen your face, you came with mercy, love, and pity, Death, and brought to all of us your compassionate sentences of pardon and release. For have you not retrieved from exile the desperate lives of men who never found their home? Have you not opened your dark door for us who never yet found doors to enter and given us a room who, roomless, doorless, unassuaged, were driven on forever through the streets of life? Have you not offered us your stern provender, Death, with which to stay the hunger that grew to madness from the food it fed upon, and given all of us the goal for which we sought but never found, the certitude, the peace, for which our overladen hearts contended, and made for us, in your dark house, an end of all the tortured wandering and unrest that lashed us on forever? Proud Death, proud Death, not for the glory that you added to the glory of the king, proud Death, nor for the honor that you imposed upon the dignities of famous men, proud Death, nor for the final magic that you have given to the lips of genius, Death, but because you come so gloriously to us who never yet knew glory, so proudly and sublimely to us whose lives were nameless and obscure, because you give to all of us—the nameless, faceless, voiceless atoms of the earth—the awful chrism of your grandeur, Death, because I have seen and known you so well, and have lived alone so long with Loneliness, your brother, I do not fear you any longer, friend, and have made this praise for you.

Now, Loneliness forever and the earth again! Dark brother and stern friend, immortal face of darkness and of night, with whom the half part of my life was spent, and with whom I shall abide now till my death forever, what is there for me to fear as long as you are with me? Heroic friend, blood-brother of proud Death, dark face, have we not gone together down a million streets, have we not coursed together the great and furious avenues of night, have we not crossed the stormy seas alone, and known strange lands, and come again to walk the continent of night, and listen to the silence of the earth? Have we not been brave and glorious when we were together, friend, have we not known triumph, joy, and glory on this earth—and will it not be again with me as it was then, if you come back to me? Come to me, brother, in the watches of the night, come to me in the secret and most silent heart of darkness, come to me as you always came, bringing to me again the old invincible strength, the deathless hope, the triumphant joy and confidence that will storm the ramparts of the earth again.

Come to me through the fields of night, dear friend, come to me with the horses of your sister, Sleep, and we shall listen to the silence of the earth and darkness once again, we shall listen to the heartbeats of the sleeping men as with soft and rushing thunder of their hooves the strange dark horses of great Sleep come on again.

They come! Ships call! The hooves of night, the horses of great Sleep, are coming on below their manes of darkness. And forever the rivers run. Deep as the tides of Sleep the rivers run. We call!

As from dark winds and waters of our sleep on which a few stars sparely look, we grope our feelers in the sea's dark bed. Whether to polyped spore, blind sucks or crawls or seavalves of the brain, we call through slopes and glades of night's dark waters on great fish. Call to the strange dark fish, or to the dart and hoary flaking of electric fins, or to the sea-worms of the brain that lash great fish to bloody froth upon the seafloor's coral stipes. Or, in vast thickets of our sleep to call to blue gulphs and deep immensities of night, call to the cat's bright blazing glare and ceaseless prowl; call to all things that swim or crawl or fly, all subtlest unseen stirs, all half-heard, half-articulated whisperings, O forested and far!—call to the hooves of sleep through all the waste and lone immensity of night: "Return! Return!"

They come: My great dark horses come! With soft and rushing thunder of their hooves they come, and the horses of Sleep are galloping, galloping over the land.

Oh, softly, softly the great dark horses of Sleep are galloping over the land. The great black bats are flying over us. The tides of Sleep are moving through the nation; beneath the tides of Sleep and time strange fish are moving.

For Sleep has crossed the worn visages of day, and in the night time, in the dark, in all the sleeping silence of the towns, the faces of ten million men are strange and dark as time. In Sleep we lie all naked and alone, in Sleep we are united at the heart of night and darkness, and we are strange and beautiful asleep; for we are dying in the darkness, and we know no death, there is no death, there is no life, no joy, no sorrow, and no glory on the earth but Sleep.

Come, mild and magnificent Sleep, and let your tides flow through the nation. Oh, daughter of unmemoried desire, sister of Death, and my stern comrade, Loneliness, bringer of peace and dark forgetfulness, healer and redeemer, dear enchantress, hear us: come to us through the fields of night, over the plains and rivers of the everlasting earth, bringing to the huge vexed substance of this world and to all the fury, pain, and madness of our lives the merciful anodyne of your redemption. Seal up the porches of our memory, tenderly, gently, steal our lives away from us, blot out the vision of lost love, lost days, and all our ancient hungers, great Transformer, heal us!

Oh, softly, softly, the great dark horses of Sleep are galloping over the land. The tides of Sleep are moving in the hearts of men, they flow like rivers in the night, they flow with lapse and reluctation of their breath, with glut and fullness of their dark unfathomed strength into a million pockets of the land and over the shores of the whole earth. They flow with the full might of their advancing and inexorable flood across the continent of night, across the breadth and sweep of the immortal earth, until the hearts of all men living are relieved of their harsh weight, the souls of all men who have ever drawn in the breath of anguish and of labor are healed, assuaged, and conquered by the vast enchantments of dark, silent, all-engulfing sleep.

Sleep falls like silence on the earth, it fills the hearts of ninety million men, it moves like magic in the mountains, and walks like night and darkness across the plains and rivers of the earth, until low upon the lowlands, and high upon the hills, flows gently sleep, smooth-sliding sleep—oh, sleep—sleep—sleep!

No Door

A STORY OF TIME AND
THE WANDERER

. . . *of wandering forever and the earth again . . . of seed-time, bloom, and the mellow-dropping harvest. And of the big flowers, the rich flowers, the strange unknown flowers.*

Where shall the weary rest? When shall the lonely of heart come home? What doors are open for the wanderer, and in what place, and in what land, and in what time?

Where? Where the weary of heart can abide forever, where the weary of wandering can find peace, where the tumult, the fever, and the fret shall be forever stilled.

Who owns the earth? Did we want the earth that we should wander on it? Did we need the earth that we were never still upon it? Whoever needs the earth shall have the earth: he shall be still upon it, he shall rest within a little space, he shall dwell in one small room forever.

Did he feel the need of a thousand tongues that he sought thus through the moil and horror of ten thousand furious streets? He shall need a tongue no longer, he shall need no tongue for silence and the earth: he shall speak no word through the rooted lips, the snake's cold eye will peer for him through the sockets of the brain, there will be no cry out of the heart where wells the vine.

The tarantula is crawling through the rotted oak, the adder lisps against the breast, cups fall: but the earth will endure forever. The flower of love is living in the wilderness, and the elmroot threads the bones of buried lovers.

The dead tongue withers and the dead heart rots, blind mouths crawl tunnels through the buried flesh, but the earth will endure forever; hair grows like April on the buried breast, and from the sockets of the brain the death-flowers will grow and will not perish.

O flower of love whose strong lips drink us downward into death, in all things far and fleeting, enchantress of our twenty thousand days, the brain will madden and the heart be twisted, broken by her kiss, but glory, glory, glory, she remains:

Immortal love, alone and aching in the wilderness, we cried to you: You were not absent from our loneliness.

I

October: 1931

It is wonderful with what warm enthusiasm well-kept people who have never been alone in all their life can congratulate you on the joys of solitude. I know whereof I speak. I have been alone a great deal of my life—more than anyone I know, and I also knew, for one short period of my life, a few of these well-kept people. And their passionate longing for the life of loneliness is astonishing. In the evening they are driven out to their fine house in the country where their wives and children eagerly await them; or to their magnificent apartments in the city where their lovely wife or charming mistress is waiting for them with a tender smile, a perfumed, anointed, and seductive body, and the embrace of love. And all this is as a handful of cold dust and ashes, and a little dross.

Sometimes one of them invites you out to dinner: your host is a plump and pleasant gentleman of forty-six, a little bald, healthily plump, well-nourished-looking, and yet with nothing gross and sensual about him. Indeed, he is a most aesthetic-looking millionaire, his features, although large and generous, are full of sensitive intelligence, his manners are gentle, quietly subdued, his smile a little sad, touched faintly with a whimsy of ironic humor, as of one who has passed through all the anguish, hope, and tortured fury youth can know, and now knows what to expect from life and whose "eye-lids are a bit weary," patiently resigned, and not too bitter about it.

Yet life has not dealt over-harshly with our host: the evidences of his interest in un-monied, precious things is quietly, expensively, all around him. He lives in a penthouse apartment near the East River: the place is furnished with all the discrimination of a quiet but distinguished taste, he has several of Jacob Epstein's heads and figures, including one of himself which the sculptor made "two years ago when I was over there," and he also has a choice collection of rare books and first editions, and after admiring these treasures appreciatively, you all step out upon the roof for a moment to admire the view you get there of the river.

Evening is coming fast, and the tall frosted glasses in your hands make a thin but pleasant tinkling, and the great city is blazing there in your vision in its terrific frontal sweep and curtain of star-flung towers, now sown with the diamond pollen of a million lights, and the sun has set behind them, and the old red light of fading day is painted without heat or violence upon the river—and you see the boats, the tugs, the barges passing, and the wing-like swoop of bridges with exultant joy—and night has come, and there are ships there—there are ships—and a wild intolerable longing in you that you cannot utter.

When you go back into the room again, you feel very far away from Brooklyn, where you live, and everything you felt about the city as a child, before you ever knew about it, now seems not only possible, but about to happen.

The great vision of the city is living in your heart in all its enchanted colors just as it did when you were twelve years old and thought about it. You think that same glorious happiness of fortune, fame, and triumph will be yours at any minute, that you are about to take your place among great men and lovely women in a life more fortunate and happy than any you have ever known—that it is all here, somehow, waiting for you and only an inch away if you will touch it, only a word away if you will speak it, only a wall, a door, a stride from you if you only knew the place where you may enter.

And somehow the old wild wordless hope awakes again that you will find it—the door that you can enter—that this man is going to tell you. The very air you breathe now is filled with the thrilling menace of some impossible good fortune. Again you want to ask him what the magic secret is that has given his life such power, authority, and ease, and made all the brutal struggle, pain, and ugliness of life, the fury, hunger, and the wandering, seem so far away, and you think he is going to tell you—to give this magic secret to you—but he tells you nothing. And finally, you are certain of nothing—except that your drink is very good and that dinner is ahead of you. And all the old bewilderment and confusion of the soul you always felt when you thought of the mystery of time and the city returns to you. You remember how the city blazed before you like a fable the first time when you came through the portals of the mighty station and saw it—how it was like something you had always known and yet could not believe was possible, and how unbelievably it was true and was set there in its legend of enchanted time so that even the million dark and driven faces on its swarming pavements had this same legend of enchanted time upon them—a thing that was City-Time, and not your time, and that you always had lived in as a stranger, and that was more real than morning, and more phantasmal than a dream to you.

And for a moment this old unsearchable mystery of time and the city returns to overwhelm your spirit with the horrible sensations of defeat and drowning. You see this man, his mistress, and all the other city people you have known in shapes of deathless brightness, and yet their life and time are stranger to you than a dream, and you think that you are doomed to walk among them always as a phantom who can never grasp their life or make their time your own. It seems to you now that you are living in a world of creatures who have learned to live without weariness or agony of the soul, in a life which you can never touch, approach, or apprehend; a strange city-race who have never lived in a dimension of time that is like your own, and that can be measured in minutes, hours, days, and years, but in dimensions of fathomless and immemorable sensation; who can be remembered only at some moment in their lives nine thousand enthusiasms back, twenty thousand nights of drunkenness ago, eight hundred parties, four million cruelties, nine thousand treacheries or infidelities, two hundred love affairs gone by—and whose lives therefore take on a fabulous and horrible age of sensation, that has never known youth or remembered innocence and that induces in you the sensation of drowning in a sea of horror, a sea of blind, dateless, and immemorable time. There is no door.

But now your host, with his faintly bitter and ironic smile, has poured himself out another good stiff drink of honest rye into a tall thin glass that has some ice in it, and smacked his lips around it with an air of rumination, and after two or three reflective swallows, begins to get a trifle sorrowful about the life harsh destiny has picked out for him.

While his mistress sits prettily upon the fat edge of an upholstered chair, stroking her cool and delicate fingers gently over his knit brows, and while his good man Ponsonby or Kato is quietly "laying out his things" for dinner, he stares gloomily ahead, and with a bitter smile congratulates you on the blessed luck that has permitted you to live alone in the Armenian section of South Brooklyn.

Well, you say, living alone in South Brooklyn has its drawbacks. The place you live in is shaped just like a pullman car, except that it is not so long and has only one window at each end. There are bars over the front window that your landlady has put there to keep the thugs in that sweet neighborhood from breaking in; in winter the place is cold and dark, and sweats with clammy water; in summer you do all the sweating yourself, but you do get plenty of it, quite enough for any one; the place gets hot as hell.

Moreover—and here you really begin to warm up to your work—when you get up in the morning the sweet aroma of the old Gowanus Canal gets into your nostrils, into your mouth, into your lungs, into everything you do, or think, or say! It is, you say, one gigantic Stink, a symphonic Smell, a vast organ-note of stupefying odor, cunningly contrived, compacted, and composted of eighty-seven separate several putrefactions; and with a rich and mounting enthusiasm, you name them all for him. There is in it, you say, the smell of melted glue and of burned rubber. It has in it the fragrance of deceased, decaying cats, the odor of rotten cabbage, prehistoric eggs, and old tomatoes; the smell of burning rags and putrefying offal; mixed with the fragrance of a boneyard horse, now dead, the hide of a skunk, and the noisome stenches of a stagnant sewer: it has as well the—

But at this moment your host throws his head back and, with a look of rapture on his face, draws in upon the air the long full respiration of ecstatic satisfaction, as if, in this great panoply of smells, he really had found the breath of life itself, and then cries:

"Wonderful! Wonderful! Oh, simply *swell! Marvelous!*" he cries and throws back his head again, with a shout of exultant laughter.

"Oh, John!" his lady says at this point with a troubled look upon her lovely face, "I don't think you'd like a place like that at *all*. It sounds simply *dreadful!* I don't like to hear about it," she says, with a pretty little shudder of distaste. "I think it's simply terrible that they let people live in places like that!"

"Oh!" he says, "it's wonderful! The power, the richness, and the beauty of it all!" he cries.

Well, you agree, it's wonderful enough. And it's got power and richness—sure enough! As to the beauty—that's a different matter. You are not so sure of that—but even as you say this you remember many things. You remember a powerful big horse, slow-footed, shaggy in the hoof, with big dappled spots of iron gray upon it, that stood one brutal day in August by the curb. Its driver had unhitched it from the wagon, and it stood there with its great patient head bent down in an infinite and quiet sorrow, and a little boy with black eyes and a dark face was standing by it, holding some sugar in his hand, and its driver, a man who had the tough seamed face of the city, stepped in on the horse with a bucket full of water which he threw against the horse's side. For a second, the great flanks shuddered gratefully and began to smoke, the man stepped back on to the curb and began to look the animal over with a keen deliberate glance, and the boy stood there, rubbing his hand quietly into the horse's muzzle, and talking softly to it all the time.

Then you remember how a tree that leaned over into the narrow little alley where you live had come to life that year, and how you watched it day by day as it came into its moment of glory of young magic green. And you remember a raw, rusty street along the waterfront, with its naked and brutal life, its agglomeration of shacks, tenements, and slums and huge grimy piers, its unspeakable ugliness and beauty, and you remember how you came along this street one day at sunset, and saw all the colors of the sun and harbor, flashing, blazing, and shifting in swarming motes, in an iridescent web of light and color for an instant on the blazing side of a proud white ship.

And you start to tell your host what it was like and how the evening looked and felt—of the thrilling smell and savor of the huge deserted pier, of the fading light upon old brick of shambling houses, and of the blazing beauty of that swarming web of light and color on the ship's great prow, but when you start to tell about it, you cannot, nor ever recapture the feeling of mystery, exultancy, and wild sorrow that you felt then.

Yes, there has been beauty enough—enough to burst the heart, madden the brain, and tear the sinews of your life asunder—but what is there to say? You remember all these things, and then ten thousand others, but when you start to tell the man about them, you cannot.

Instead, you just tell him about the place you live in: of how dark and hot it is in summer, how clammy and cold in winter, and of how hard it is to get anything good to eat. You tell him about your landlady who is a hard-bitten ex-reporter. You tell him what a good and liberal-hearted woman she is; how rough and ready, full of life and energy, how she likes drinking and the fellowship of drinking men, and knows all the rough and seamy side of life which a newspaper reporter gets to know.

You tell how she has been with murderers before their execution, got the story from them or their mothers, climbed over sides of ships to get a story, forced herself in at funerals, followed burials to the graveyard, trampled upon every painful, decent, and sorrowful emotion of mankind—all to get that story; and still remains a decent woman, an immensely good, generous, and lusty-living person, and yet an old maid, and a puritan, somehow, to the roots of her soul.

You tell how she went mad several years before and spent two years in an asylum: you tell how moments of this madness still come back to her, and of how you went home one night several months before, to find her stretched out on your bed, only to rise and greet you as the great lover of her dreams—Doctor Eustace McNamee, a name, a person, and a love she had invented for herself. Then you tell of her fantastic family, her three sisters and her father, all touched with the same madness, but without her energy, power, and high ability; and of how she has kept the whole crowd going since her eighteenth year.

You tell about the old man who is an inventor who does not invent; of how he invented a corkscrew with a cork attached that would not cork; an unlockable lock; and unbreakable looking-glass that wouldn't look. And you tell how the year before he inherited $120,000—the first money he had ever had—and promptly took it down to Wall Street where he was promptly shorn of it, meanwhile sending his wife and daughters to Europe in the nuptial suite of a palatial liner and cabling them when they wanted to come back: "Push on to Rome, my children! Push on, push on! Your father's making millions!"

Yes, all this, and a hundred other things about this incredible, mad, fantastic, and yet high-hearted family which I had found in a dingy alleyway in Brooklyn I could tell my host. And I could tell him a thousand other things about the people all about me—of the Armenians, Spaniards, Irishmen in the alley who came home on week days and turned on the radio, until the whole place was yelling with a hundred dissonances, and who came home on Saturday to get drunk and beat their wives—the whole intimate course and progress of their lives published nakedly from a hundred open windows with laugh, shout, scream, and curse.

I could tell him how they fought, got drunk, and murdered; how they robbed, held up, and blackjacked, how they whored and stole and killed—all of which was part of the orderly and decent course of life for them—and yet, how they could howl with outraged modesty, complain to the police, and send a delegation to us when the young nephew of my landlady lay for an hour upon our patch of backyard grass clad only in his bathing trunks.

"Yuh gotta nekkid man out deh!" they said, in tones of hushed accusatory horror.

Yes, we—good sir, who are so fond of irony—we, old Whittaker, the inventor, and Mad Maude, his oldest daughter, who would grumble at a broken saucer, and then stuff lavish breakfasts down your throat, who would patiently water twenty little feet of backyard earth from April until August, and until the grass grew beautifully, and then would turn twenty skinny, swarthy, and half-naked urchins loose into it to stamp it into muddy ruin in twenty minutes while she played the hose upon their grimy little bodies; we, this old man, his daughters, and his grandson, three bank clerks, a cartoonist, two young fellows who worked for Hearst, and myself; we, good sir, who sometimes brought a girl into our rooms, got drunk, wept, confessed sinful and unworthy lives, read Shakespeare, Milton, Whitman, Donne, the Bible—and the sporting columns—we, young, foolish, old, mad, and bewildered as we were, but who had never murdered, robbed, or knocked the teeth out of a woman; we, who were fairly decent, kind, and liberal-hearted people as the world goes, were the pariahs of Balcony Square—called so because there was neither square nor balconies, but just a little narrow alleyway, a long brick wall, and a row of dingy little houses, made over from the stables and coach houses of an earlier and more wealthy day.

Yes, we were suspect, enemies to order and public morals, shameless partakers in an open and indecent infamy, and our neighbors looked at us with all the shuddering reprehension of their mistrustful eyes as they beat their wives like loving husbands, cut each other's throats with civic pride, and went about their honest toil of murder, robbery, and assault like the self-respecting citizens they were.

Meanwhile, a man was murdered, with his head bashed in, upon the step of a house three doors below me; and a drunken woman got out of an automobile one night at two o'clock, screaming indictments of her escort to the whole neighborhood.

"Yuh gotta pay me, ya big bum!" she yelled. "Yuh gotta pay me now! Give me my three dollehs, or I'll go home and make my husband beat it out of yah! No son-of-a-bitch alive is goin' to —— me an' get away wit' it f'r nothin'!!! Come on an' pay me now!" she yelled.

"Staht actin' like a lady!" said the man in lower tones. "I wont pay yuh till yuh staht actin' like a lady! Yuh gotta staht actin' like a lady!" he insisted, with a touching devotion to the rules of gallantry.

And this had continued until he started the engine of his car and drove off at furious speed, leaving her to wander up and down the alleyway for hours, screaming and sobbing, cursing foully and calling down the vengeance of her husband on this suitor who had thus misused her—an indictment that had continued unmolested until three young ambitious thugs had seized the opportunity to go out and rob her; they passed my window, running, in the middle of the night, one fearful and withdrawing, saying, "Jeez! I'm sick! I don't feel good! Wait a minute! Youse guys go on an' do it by yourself! I want a cup of coffee!"—And the others snarling savagely:

"Come on! Come on, yuh yellah bastad! If yah don't come on, I'll moi-duh yuh!" And they had gone, their quick feet scampering nimbly in the dark, while the woman's drunken and demented howls came faintly from the other end, and then ceased.

Your host has been enchanted by that savage chronicle. He smites himself upon the brow with rapture, crying, "Oh, grand! *Grand!* What a lucky fellow you are! If I were in your place, I'd be the happiest man alive!"

You take a look about you and say nothing.

"To be free! To go about and see these things!" he cries. "To live among real people! To see life as it is, in the raw—the *real* stuff, not like this!" he says with a weary look at all the suave furnishings of illusion that surround him. "And above all else, to be *alone!*"

You ask him if he has ever been alone, if he knows what loneliness is like. You try to tell him, but he knows about this, too. He smiles faintly, ironically, and dismisses it, and you, with a wise man's weary tolerance of youth: "I know! I know!" he sighs. "But all of us are lonely, and after all, my boy, the real loneliness for most of us is *here!*"—and he taps himself a trifle to the left of the third shirt stud, in the presumptive region of his heart. "But you! Free, young, and footloose, with the whole world to explore—You have a fine life! What more, in God's name, could a man desire?"

Well, what is there to say? For a moment, the blood is pounding at your temples, a hot retort springs sharp and bitter to your lips, and you feel that you could tell him many things. You could tell him, and not be very nice or dainty with it, that there's a hell of a lot more that a man desires: good food and wonderful companions, comfort, ease, security, a lovely woman like the one who sits beside him now, and an end to the loneliness—but what is there to say?

For you are what you are, you know what you know, and there are no words for loneliness, black, bitter, and aching loneliness, that gnaws the roots of silence in the night. It lies beside us in the darkness while the river flows, it fills us with wild secret song and the unmeasured desolations of gray time, and it abides with us forever, and is still, until we cannot root it from our blood or pluck it from our soul or unweave it from our brain. Its taste is acrid, sharp, and bitter at the edges of our mouth, and it is with us, in us, around us all the time, our jail, our captive, and our master, all in one, whose dark visage we cannot decipher from our own, whom we have fought, loved, hated, finally accepted, and with whom we must abide now to our death forever.

So what is there to say? There has been life enough, and power, grandeur, joy enough, and there has been also beauty enough, and God knows there has been squalor and filth and misery and madness and despair enough; murder and cruelty and hate enough, and loneliness enough to fill your bowels with the substance of gray horror, and to crust your lips with its hard and acrid taste of desolation.

And oh, there has been time enough, even in Brooklyn there is time enough, strange time, dark secret time enough, dark million-visaged time enough, forever flowing by you like a river, in the daytime, in the dark, flowing round you like a river, making your life its own as it makes all lives and cities of the earth its own, mining into its tides the earth as it mines the million dark and secret moments of your life into its tides, mining against the sides of ships, moving across the edges of your soul, foaming about the piled crustings of old wharves in darkness, sliding like time and silence by the vast cliffs of the city, girdling the stony isle of life with moving waters— thick with the wastes of earth, dark with our stains, and heavied with our dumpings, rich, rank, beautiful, and unending as all life, all living as it flows by us, by us, by us, to the sea.

Oh! there has been time enough, dark-visaged time enough—even in cellar-depths in Brooklyn there is time enough, but when you try to tell the man about it, you cannot, for what is there to say?

For suddenly you remember how the tragic light of evening falls even on the huge and rusty jungle of the earth known as Brooklyn and on the faces of all the men with dead eyes and with flesh of tallow gray, and of how even in Brooklyn they lean upon the sills of evening in that sad hushed light. And you remember how you lay one evening on your couch in your cool cellar depth in Brooklyn, and listened to the sounds of evening and to the dying birdsong in your tree; and you remember how two windows were thrown up, and you heard two voices—a woman's and a man's—begin to speak in that soft tragic light. And the memory of their words came back to you, like the haunting refrain of some old song—as it was heard and lost in Brooklyn.

"Yuh musta been away," said one, in that sad light.

"Yeah, I been away. I just got back," the other said.

"Yeah? Dat's just what I was t'inkin'," said the other. "I been t'inkin' dat yuh musta been away."

"Yeah, I been away on my vacation. I just got back."

"Oh, yeah? Dat's what I t'ought meself. I was t'inkin' just duh otheh day dat I hadn't seen yuh f'r some time, 'I guess she's gone away,' I says."

And then for seconds there was silence—save for the dying birdsong, voices in the street, faint sounds and shouts and broken calls, and something hushed in evening, far, immense, and murmurous in the air.

"Well, wat's t' noos since I been gone?" the voice went on in quietness in soft tragic light. "Has anyt'ing happened sinct I was away?"

"Nah! Nuttin's happened," the other made reply. "About duh same as *usual—you* know?" it said with difficult constraint, inviting intuitions for the spare painfulness of barren tongues.

"Yeah, I know," the other answered with a tranquil resignation—and there was silence then in Brooklyn.

"I guess Fatheh Grogan died sinct you was gone," a voice began.

"Oh, yeah?" the other voice replied with tranquil interest.

"Yeah."

And for a waiting moment there was silence.

"Say, dat's too bad, isn't it?" the quiet voice said with comfortless regret.

"Yeah. He died on Sattidy. When he went home on Friday night he was O.K."

"Oh, yeah?"

"Yeah."

And for a moment they were balanced in strong silence.

"Gee, dat was tough, wasn't it?"

"Yeah. Dey didn't find him till duh next day at ten o'clock. When dey went to look for him, he was lyin' stretched out on duh bat' room floeh."

"Oh, yeah?"

"Yeah. Dey found him lyin' deh," it said.

And for a moment more the voices hung in balanced silence.

"Gee, dat's too bad. . . . I guess I was away when all dat happened."

"Yeah. Yuh musta been away."

"Yeah, dat was it, I guess. I musta been away. Oddehwise I woulda hoid. I was away."

"Well, so long, kid. . . . I'll be seein' yuh."

"Well, so long!"

A window closed, and there was silence; evening and far sounds and broken cries in Brooklyn, Brooklyn, in the formless, rusty, and unnumbered wilderness of life.

And now the old red light fades swiftly from the old red brick of rusty houses, and there are voices in the air, and somewhere music, and we are lying there, blind atoms in our cellar-depths, gray voiceless atoms on the manswarm desolation of the earth, and our fame is lost, our names forgotten, our powers are wasting from us like mined earth, while we lie here at evening and the river flows . . . and dark time is feeding like a vulture on our entrails, and we know that we are lost, and cannot stir . . . and there are ships there! there are ships! . . . and Christ! we are all dying in the darkness! . . . and yuh musta been away . . . yuh musta been away. . . .

And that is a moment of dark time, that is one of strange, million-visaged time's dark faces. Here is another:

II

October: 1923

My life, more than the life of any one I know, has been spent in solitude and wandering. Why this is true, or how it happened, I have never known; yet it is so. From my fifteenth year—save for a single interval—I have lived about as solitary a life as modern man can have. I mean by this that the number of hours, days, months, and years—the actual time that I have spent alone—has been immense and extraordinary.

And this fact is all the more astonishing because I never seemed to seek out solitude, nor did I shrink from life or seek to build myself into a wall away from all the fury and turmoil of the earth. I loved life so dearly that I was driven mad by the thirst and hunger that I felt for it, a hunger so literal, cruel, and physical that it wanted to devour the earth and all the people in it.

At college, I would prowl the stacks of the great library at night pulling books out of a thousand shelves and reading them like a mad man. The thought of these vast stacks of books would drive me mad; the more I read, the less I seemed to know; the greater the number of books I read, the greater the immense uncountable number of those which I could never read would seem to be. Within a period of ten years I read at least twenty thousand volumes—deliberately I have set the figure low—and opened the pages and looked through many times that number. If this seems unbelievable, I am sorry for it, but it happened. Yet all this terrific orgy of the books brought me no comfort, peace, or wisdom of the mind and heart. Instead, my fury and despair increased from what it fed upon, my hunger mounted with the food it ate.

And it was the same with everything I did.

For this fury which drove me on to read so many books had nothing to do with scholarship, nothing to do with academic honors, nothing to do with formal learning. I was not in any way a scholar and did not want to be one. I simply wanted to know about everything on earth, and it drove me mad when I saw that I could not do this. In the midst of a furious burst of reading in the enormous library, the thought of the streets outside and the great city all around me would drive through my body like a sword. It would now seem to me that every second that I passed among the books was being wasted—that at this moment something priceless, irrecoverable, was happening in the streets, and that if I could only get to it in time and see it, I would somehow get the knowledge of the whole thing in me—the source, the well, the spring from which all men and words and actions and every design upon this earth proceed.

And I would rush out in the streets to find it, be hurled through the tunnel into Boston and then spend hours in driving myself savagely through a hundred streets, looking into the faces of a million people, trying to get an instant and conclusive picture of all they did and said and were, of all their million destinies. And I would search the furious streets until bone and brain and blood could stand no more—until every sinew of my life and spirit was wrung, trembling and exhausted, and my heart sank down beneath its weight of despair and desolation.

Yet a furious hope, a wild extravagant belief was burning in me all the time. I would write down enormous charts and plans and projects of all that I proposed to do in life—a program of work and living which would have exhausted the energies of ten thousand men. I would get up in the middle of the night to scrawl down insane catalogs of all that I had seen and done:

the number of books I had read, the number of miles I had traveled, the number of people I had known, the number of women I had slept with, the number of meals I had eaten, the number of towns I had visited, the number of states I had been in.

And at one moment I would gloat and chuckle over these stupendous lists like a miser gloating over his hoard, only to groan bitterly with despair the next moment, and to beat my head against the wall, as I remembered the overwhelming amount of all I had not seen or done, or known. Then I would begin another list filled with enormous catalogs of all the books I had not read, all the food I had not eaten, all the women I had not slept with, all the states I had not been in, all the towns I had not visited. Then I would write down plans and programs whereby all these things must be accomplished, how many years it would take to do it all, and how old I would be when I had finished. An enormous wave of hope and joy would surge up in me, because it now looked easy, and I had no doubts at all that I could do it.

I never asked myself how I was going to live while this was going on, where I was going to get the money for this gigantic adventure, and what I was going to do to make it possible. Although I had a good mind in some respects, I was no better than a child when it came to things like this; the fact that to explore and devour the world, as I was going to do, would require the fortune of a millionaire had no meaning to me at all. If I thought about it, it seemed to have no importance or reality whatever—I just dismissed it impatiently, or with a conviction that some old man would die and leave me a fortune; that I was going to pick up a purse containing hundreds of thousands of dollars while walking in the Fenway, and that the reward would be enough to keep me going; or that a beautiful and rich young widow, true-hearted, tender, loving and voluptuous, who had carrot-colored hair, little freckles on her face, a snub nose and luminous gray-green eyes with something wicked, yet loving and faithful, in them, and one gold filling in her solid little teeth, was going to fall in love with me, marry me, and be forever true and faithful to me while I went reading, eating, drinking, whoring, and devouring my way around the world; or finally that I would write a book or play every year or so, which would be a great success, and yield me fifteen or twenty thousand dollars at a crack.

Thus I went storming away at the whole earth about me, sometimes mad with despair, weariness, and bewilderment; and sometimes wild with jubilant and exultant joy and certitude as the conviction came to me that everything would happen as I wished. Then at night I would hear the vast sounds and silence of the earth and of the continent of night, until it seemed to me it was all spread before me like a map—rivers, plains, and mountains and ten thousand sleeping towns; it seemed to me that I saw everything at once.

Then I would think about the State of Kansas, of Wyoming, Colorado, or some other place where I had never been, and I could sleep no more, and I would twist about in bed, and tear the sheets, get up and smoke, and walk around the room. I would feel an intolerable desire to go and see these places, to hear the voices of the people, to step out of the train upon the earth, and it seemed to me if I could do this only for five minutes I would be satisfied. I would become obsessed with the notion that the earth of these places would look and feel different from anything I had ever known, that it had a quality and texture of its own, a kind of elastic quality so that the foot would spring upon it, and also a feeling of depth and solidity which the earth in the East did not have. And I felt that I could never rest in peace again until I had stepped upon this earth, and tested it.

Meanwhile, the great antagonists of fixity and everlasting change, of wandering forever and return, of weariness intolerable and insatiate thirst, of certitude and peace and no desire and everlasting torment of the soul, had begun to wage perpetual warfare in me. And now I hardly ever thought of home. Rather, like a man held captive in some green land of sorcery who does not know the years are passing while he dreams his life away, the enormous plant of time, desire, and memory flowered and fed forever with a cancerous growth through all the tissues of my life until the earth I came from, and the life that I had known seemed remote and buried as the sunken cities of Atlantis.

Then, one day I awoke at morning and thought of home. A lock-bolt was shot back in my memory, and a door was opened. Suddenly, as if a curtain of dark sorcery had been lifted from my vision, I saw the earth I came from, and all the people I had known in shapes of deathless brightness. And instantly an intolerable desire to see them all again began to burn in me. I said: "I must go home again!" And this, too, all men who ever wandered on the earth have said.

Three years had passed by like a dream. During this time my father had died. That year I went home for the last time in October.

October had come again, and that year it was sharp and soon: frost was early, burning the thick green on the mountain sides to the massed brilliant hues of blazing colors, painting the air with sharpness, sorrow, and delight. Sometimes, and often, there was warmth by day, and ancient drowsy light, a golden warmth and pollinated haze in afternoon, but over all the earth there was the premonitory breath of frost, an exultancy for all men who were returning and for all those who were gone and would not come again.

My father was dead, and now it seemed to me that I had never found him. He was dead, and yet I sought him everywhere, and could not believe that he was dead, and was sure that I would find him. It was October and that year, after years of absence and of wandering, I had come home again.

I could not think that he had died, but I had come home in October, and all the life that I had known there was strange and sorrowful as dreams. And yet I saw it all in shapes of deathless brightness—the town, the streets, the magic hills, and the plain prognathous faces of the people I had known as if I had revisited the shores of this great earth with a heart of fire, a cry of pain and ecstasy, a memory of intolerable longing and regret for all that glorious and exultant life which I must visit now forever as a fleshless ghost, never to touch, to hold, to have its palpable warmth and substance for my own again. I had come home again, and yet I could not believe that he was dead, and I thought I heard his great voice ringing in the street again and that I would see him striding toward me across the Square with his gaunt earth-devouring stride, or find him waiting every time I turned the corner, or lunging toward the house bearing the tremendous provender of his food and meat, bringing to us all the deathless security of his strength and power and passion, bringing to us all again the roaring message of his fires that shook the firefull chimney throat with their terrific blast, giving to us all again the exultant knowledge that the good days, the magic days, the golden weather of our lives, would come again, and that this dream-like and phantasmal world in which I found myself would waken instantly, as it had once, to all the palpable warmth and glory of the earth, if only my father would come back to make it live, to give us life, again.

Therefore, I could not think that he was dead. And at night, in my mother's house, I would lie in my bed in the dark, hearing the wind that rattled dry leaves along the empty pavement, hearing far-off across the wind, the barking of a dog, feeling dark time, strange time, dark secret time, as it flowed on around me, remembering my life, this house, and all the million strange and secret visages of time, thinking, feeling, thinking:

"October has come again, has come again. . . . I have come home again and found my father dead . . . and that was time . . . time . . . time. . . . Where shall I go now? What shall I do? For October has come again, but there has gone some richness from the life we knew, and we are lost."

Storm shook the house at night—the old house, my mother's house—where I had seen my brother die. The old doors swung and creaked in the darkness, darkness pressed against the house, the darkness filled us, filled the house at night, it moved about us soft and secret, palpable, filled with a thousand secret presences of sorrowful time and memory, moving about me as I lay below my brother's room in darkness, while storm shook the house and something creaked and rattled in the wind's strong blast.

Wind beat at us with burly shoulders in the night. The darkness moved there in the house like something silent, palpable—a spirit breathing in my mother's house, a demon and a friend—speaking to me its silent and intolerable prophecy of flight, of secrecy and of storm, moving about me constantly, prowling about the edges of my life, ever beside me, in me, whispering:

"Child, child—come with me—come with me to your brother's grave tonight. Come with me to the places where the young men lie whose bodies have long since been buried in the earth. Come with me where they walk and move again tonight, and you shall see your brother's face again, and hear his voice, and see again, as they march toward you from their graves, the company of the young men who died, as he did, in October, speaking to you their messages of flight, of triumph, and the all-exultant darkness, telling you that it all will be again as it was once."

And I would lie there thinking:

"October has come again—has come again"—feeling the dark around me, not believing that my father could be dead, thinking: "The strange and lonely years have come again. . . . I have come home again . . . come home again . . . and will it not be with us as it has been again?"—feeling darkness as it moved about me, thinking, "Is it not the same darkness that I knew in Childhood, and have not I lain here in bed before, and felt this darkness moving all about me? . . . Did we not hear dogs that barked in darkness, in October," I then thought. "Were not their howls far-broken by the wind? . . . And hear dry leaves that scampered on the streets at night . . . and the huge and burly rushes of the wind . . . and hear limbs that stiffly creak in the remote demented howlings of the wind . . . and something creaking in the wind at night . . . and think, then, as we think now, of all the men who have ever gone and never will come back again, and of our friends and brothers who lie buried in the earth? . . . Oh, has not October now come back again," I cried, "as always—as it always was?"—and hearing the great darkness softly prowling in my mother's house at night, and thinking, feeling, thinking, as I lay there in the dark:

"And now October has come again, which in our land is different from October in other lands. The ripe, the golden month has come again, and in Virginia the chinquapins are falling. Frost sharps the middle music of the seasons, and all things living on the earth turn home again. The country is so big you cannot say the country has the same October. In Maine, the frost comes sharp and quick as driven nails; just for a week or so the woods, all of the bright and bitter leaves, flare up: the maples turn a blazing bitter red, and other leaves turn yellow like a living light, falling about you as you walk the woods, falling about you like small pieces of the sun, so that you cannot say where sunlight shakes and flutters on the ground, and where the leaves.

"Meanwhile the Palisades are melting in massed molten colors, the season swings along the nation, and a little later in the South dense woodings on the hill begin to glow and soften, and when they smell the burning wood-smoke in Ohio, the children say, 'I'll bet that there's a forest fire in Michigan.' As the mountaineer goes hunting down in North Carolina, he stays out late with mournful flop-eared hounds; a rind of moon comes up across the rude lift of the hills: what do his friends say to him when he stays out late? Full of hoarse innocence and laughter, they will say: 'Mister, yore ole woman's goin' to whup ye if ye don't go home.'"

Oh, return, return!

"October is the richest of the seasons: the fields are cut, the granaries are full, the bins are loaded to the brim with fatness, and from the cider-press the rich brown oozings of the York Imperials run. The bee bores to the belly of the yellowed grape, the fly gets old and fat and blue, he buzzes loud, crawls slow, creeps heavily to death on sill and ceiling, the sun goes down in blood and pollen across the bronzed and mown fields of old October.

"The corn is shocked: it sticks out in hard yellow rows upon dried ears, fit now for great red barns in Pennsylvania, and the big stained teeth of crunching horses. The indolent hoof kicks swiftly at the boards, the barn is sweet with hay and leather, wood and apples. This, and the clean dry crunchings of the teeth, is all: the sweat, the labor, and the plow are over. The late pears mellow on a sunny shelf; smoked hams hang to the warped barn rafters; the pantry shelves are loaded with three hundred jars of fruit. Meanwhile, the leaves are turning up in Maine, the chestnut burrs plop thickly to the earth in gusts of wind, and in Virginia the chinquapins are falling.

"There is a smell of burning in small towns in afternoons, and men with buckles on their arms are raking the leaves in yards as boys come by with straps slung back across their shoulders. The oak leaves, big and brown, are bedded deep in yard and gutter: they make deep wadings to the knee for children in the streets. The fire will snap and crackle like a whip, sharp, acrid smoke will sting the eyes, in mown fields the little vipers of the flame eat past the coarse black edges of burnt stubble like a line of locusts. Fire drives a thorn of memory in the heart.

"The bladed grass, a forest of small spears of ice, is thawed by noon: summer is over, but the sun is warm again, and there are days throughout the land of gold and russet. The summer is dead and gone, the earth is waiting, suspense and ecstasy are gnawing at the hearts of men, the brooding prescience of frost is there. The sun flames red and bloody as it sets, there are old red glintings on the battered pails, the great barn gets the ancient light as the boy slops homeward with warm foaming milk. Great shadows lengthen on the fields, the old red light dies swiftly, and the sunset barking of the hounds is faint and far and full of frost: there are shrewd whistles to the dogs of frost and silence—this is all. Wind scuffs and rattles at the old brown leaves, and through the night the great oak leaves keep falling.

"Trains cross the continent in a swirl of dust and thunder, the leaves fly down the track behind them: the great trains cleave through gulch and gulley, they rumble with spoked thunder on the bridges over the powerful brown wash of mighty rivers, they toil through hills, they skirt the rough brown stubble of shorn fields, they whip past empty stations in the little towns, and their great stride pounds its even pulse across America. Field and hill and lift and gulch and hollow, mountain and plain and river, a wilderness with fallen trees across it, a thicket of bedded brown and twisted undergrowth, a plain, a desert, and a plantation, a mighty landscape with no fenced niceness, an immensity of fold and convolution that can never be remembered, that can never be forgotten, that has never been described—weary with harvest, potent with every fruit and ore, the immeasurable richness embrowned with autumn, rank, crude, unharnessed, careless of scars or beauty, everlasting and magnificent, a cry, a space, an ecstasy!—American earth in old October.

"And the great winds howl and swoop across the land: they make a distant roaring in great trees, and boys in bed will stir in ecstasy, thinking of demons and vast swoopings through the earth. All through the night there is the clean, the bitter, rain of acorns, and the chestnut burrs are plopping to the ground.

"And often in the night there is only the living silence, the distant frosty barking of a dog, the small clumsy stir and feathery stumble of the chickens on the limed roosts, and the moon, the low and heavy moon of autumn, now barred behind the leafless poles of pines, now at the pinewood's brooding edge and summit, now falling with ghost's dawn of milky light upon rimed clods of fields and on the frosty scurf of pumpkins, now whiter, smaller, brighter, hanging against the church spire's slope, hanging the same way in a million streets, steeping all the earth in frost and silence.

"Then a chime of frost-cold bells may peal out on the brooding air, and people lying in their beds will listen. They will not speak or stir, silence will gnaw the darkness like a rat, but they will whisper in their hearts:

"'Summer has come and gone, has come and gone. And now—?' but they will say no more, they will have no more to say: they will wait listening, silent and brooding as the frost, to time, strange ticking time, dark time that haunts us with the briefness of our days. They will think of men long dead, of men now buried in the earth, of frost and silence long ago, of a forgotten face and moment of lost time, and they will think of things they have no words to utter.

"And in the night, in the dark, in the living sleeping silence of the towns, the million streets, they will hear the thunder of the fast express, the whistles of the great ships upon the river.

"What will they say then? What will they say?"

Only the darkness moved about me as I lay there thinking; feeling in the darkness: a door creaked softly in the house.

"October is the season for returning: the bowels of youth are yearning with lost love. Their mouths are dry and bitter with desire: their hearts are torn with the thorns of Spring. For lovely April, cruel and flowerful, will tear them with sharp joy and wordless lust. Spring has no language but a cry; but crueler than April is the asp of time.

"October is the season for returning: Even the town is born anew," I thought. "The tide of life is at the full again, the rich return to business or to fashion, and the bodies of the poor are rescued out of heat and weariness. The ruin and the horror of the summer is forgotten—a memory of hot cells and humid walls, a hell of ugly sweat and labor and distress and hopelessness, a limbo of pale greasy faces. Now joy and hope have revived again in the hearts of millions of people, they breathe the air again with hunger, their movements are full of life and energy. The mark of their summer's suffering is still legible upon their flesh, there is something starved and patient in their eyes, and a look that has a child's hope and expectation in it.

"All things on earth point home in old October: Sailors to sea, travelers to walls and fences, hunters to field and hollow and the long voice of the hounds, the lover to the love he has forsaken—all things that live upon this earth return, return: Father, will you not, too, come back again?

"Where are you now, when all things on earth come back again? For have not all these things been here before, have we not seen them, heard them, known them, and will they not live again for us as they did once, if only you come back again?

"Father, in the night time, in the dark, I have heard the thunder of the fast express. In the night, in the dark, I have heard the howling of the winds among great trees, and the sharp and windy raining of the acorns. In the night, in the dark, I have heard the feet of rain upon the roofs, the glut and gurgle of the gutter spouts, and the soaking, gulping throat of all the mighty earth, drinking its thirst out in the month of May—and heard the sorrowful silence of the river in October. The hill-streams foam and welter in a steady plunge, the mined clay drops and melts and eddies in the night, the snake coils cool and glistening under dripping ferns, the water roars down past the mill in one sheer sheet-like plunge, making a steady noise like the wind, and in the night, in the dark, the river flows by us to the sea.

"The great maw slowly drinks the land as we lie sleeping: the mined banks cave and crumble in the dark, the dark earth melts and drops into its tide, great horns are baying in the gulf of night, great boats are baying at the river's mouth. Thus, thick with the wastes of earth, dark with our stains, and heavied with our dumpings, rich, rank, beautiful, and unending as all life, all living, the river, the dark immortal river, full of strange tragic time, is flowing by us—by us—by us—to the sea.

"All this has been upon the earth, and will abide forever. But you are gone, our lives are ruined and broken in the night, our lives are mined below us by the river, are whirled away into the sea and darkness, and we are lost unless you come to give us life again.

"Come to us, father, in the watches of the night, come to us as you always came, bringing to us the invincible sustenance of your strength, the limitless treasure of your bounty, the tremendous structure of your life that will shape all lost and broken things on earth again into a golden pattern of exultancy and joy. Come to us, father, while the winds howl in the darkness, for October has come again, bringing with it huge prophecies of death and life and the great cargo of the men who will return. For we are ruined, lost, and broken if you do not come, and our lives, like rotten chips, are whirled about us onward in the darkness to the sea."

So, thinking, feeling, speaking, I lay there in my mother's house, but there was nothing in the house but silence and the moving darkness: storm shook the house and huge winds rushed upon us, and I knew then that my father would not come again, and that all the life that I had known was now lost and broken as a dream.

Suddenly I knew that every man who ever lived has looked, is looking, for his father, and that even when his father dies, his son will search furiously the streets of life to find him, and that he never loses hope but always feels that some day he will see his father's face again. I had come home again in October, and there were no doors, there were no doors for me to enter, and I knew now that I could never make this life my own again. Yet, in all the huge unrest that was goading me to flight, I had no place or door or dwelling-place on earth to go, and yet must make for myself a life different from the one my father made for me or die myself.

Storm shook the house at night, and there was something calling in the wind. It spoke to me and filled my heart with the exultant prophecies of flight, darkness, and discovery, saying with a demon's whisper of unbodied joy:

"Away! Away! Away! There are new lands, morning, and a shining city! Child, child, go find the earth again!"

That was another moment of dark time. That was another of time's million faces.

Here is another:

III
October: 1926

Smoke-gold by day, the numb, exultant secrecies of fog, a fog-numb air filled with the solemn joy of nameless and impending prophecy, an ancient yellow light, the old smoke-ochre of the morning, never coming to an open brightness—such was October in England that year. Sometimes by night in stormy skies there was the wild, the driven moon, sometimes the naked time-far loneliness, the most—oh, most—familiar blazing of the stars that shine on men forever, their nameless, passionate dilemma of strong joy and empty desolation, hope and terror, home and hunger, the huge twin tyranny of their bitter governance—wandering forever and the earth again.

They are still-burning, homely particles of night that light the huge tent of the dark with their remembered fire, recalling the familiar hill, the native earth from which we came, from which we could have laid our finger on them, and making the great earth and home seem near, most near, to wanderers; and filling them with naked desolations of doorless, houseless, timeless, and unmeasured vacancy.

And everywhere that year there was something secret, lonely, and immense that waited, that impended, that was still. Something that promised numbly, hugely, in the fog-numb air, and that never broke into any open sharpness, and that was almost keen and frosty October in remembered hills—oh, there was something there incredibly near and most familiar, only a word, a stride, a room, a door away—only a door away and never opened, only a door away and never found. Such was October in that land that year, and all of it was strange and as familiar as a dream.

At night, in the lounging rooms of the old inn, crackling fires were blazing cheerfully, and people sat together drinking small cups of black bitter liquid mud that they called coffee.

The people were mostly family groups who had come to visit their son or brother in the university. They were the most extraordinary, ugly, and distinguished-looking people I had ever seen. There was the father, often the best looking of the lot: a man with a ruddy weathered face, a cropped white mustache, iron gray hair—an open, driving, bull-dog look of the country carried with tremendous style. The mother was very ugly with a long horse face and grimly weathered cheek-flanks that seemed to have the tough consistency of well-tanned leather. Her grim bared smile shone in her weathered face and was nailed forever round the gauntness of her grinning teeth. She had a neighing voice, a shapeless figure, distinguished by the bony and angular width of the hip structure, clothed with fantastic dowdiness—fantastic because the men were dressed so well, and because everything they wore, no matter how old and used it might be, seemed beautiful and right.

The daughter had the mother's look: a tall, gawky girl with a bony, weathered face and a toothy mouth, she wore an ill-fitting evening or party dress of a light, unpleasant blue, with a big meaningless rosette of ruffles at the waist. She had big feet, bony legs and arms, and she was wearing pumps of dreary gray and gray silk stockings.

The son was a little fellow with ruddy apple-cheeks, crisp, fair, curly hair, and baggy gray trousers; and there was another youth, one of his college friends, of the same cut and quality, who paid a dutiful but cold attention to the daughter, which she repaid in kind and with which everyone was completely satisfied.

They had to be seen to be believed, but even then, one could only say, like the man who saw the giraffe: "I don't believe it." The young men sat stiffly on the edges of their chairs, holding their little cups of coffee in their hands, bent forward in an attitude of cold but respectful attentiveness, and the conversation that went among them was incredible. For their manner was impregnable, they were cold, remote, and formal almost to the point of military curtness, and yet one felt among them constantly an utter familiarity of affection, a strange secret warmth, past words or spoken vows, that burned in them like glacial fire.

You had to get almost on top of them to understand what they were saying, and even then you listened in a state of fascinated disbelief, following the sound and meanings of the words like a man who has a very competent understanding of a foreign language, but who is conscious at every moment of the effort of translation, and never once forgets that the language is not his own.

But when you got ten or fifteen feet away from them, their language could not have been more indecipherable if they had spoken in Chinese; but it was fascinating just to listen to the sounds. For there would be long mounting horse-like neighs, and then there would be reedy flute-like notes, and incisive cold finalities and clipped ejaculations and sometimes a lovely and most musical speech. But the horse-like neighs and the clipped ejaculations would predominate; and suddenly I understood how strange these people seemed to other races, and why the Frenchmen, Germans, and Italians would sometimes stare at them with gape-mouthed stupefaction when they heard them talking.

Once when I passed by them, they had the family vicar or some clergyman of their acquaintance with them. He was a mountain of a man, and he, too, was hardly credible: the huge creature was at least six and a half feet tall, and he must have weighed three hundred pounds. He had a flaming moon of face and jowl, at once most animal and delicate, and he peered out keenly with luminous smoke-gray eyes beneath a bushy hedge-growth of gray brows. He was dressed in the clerical garb, and his bulging grossly sensual calves were encased in buttoned gaiters. As I went by, he was leaning forward with his little cup of muddy coffee held delicately in the huge mutton of his hand, peering keenly out beneath his beetling bush of brow at the young man who was the brother's friend. And what he said was this:

"Did you ever read—that is in recent yöhs—the concluding chaptahs in 'The Vicah of Wakefield'?" Carefully he set the little cup down in its saucer. "I was reading it again the other day. It's an extraordinary thing!" he said.

It was impossible to reproduce the sound of these simple words, or the effect they wrought upon my senses. For in them was packed such a mingled measure of the horse-like neigh, the reedy, flute-like note, the solemn portentousness of revealed authority, and the long-breathing whisper of unctuous reverence, that it seemed incredible such simple words could hold the weight of all the meaning that was treasured in them.

For first, the words "Did you ever" were delivered in a delicate rising-and-falling neigh, the word "read" really came out with a long reedy sound, the words "that is in recent yöhs," in a parenthesis of sweetly gentle benevolence, the phrase "the concluding chaptahs in 'The Vicah of Wakefield,'" in full, deliberate, satisfied tones of titular respect, the phrase "I was reading it again the other day," thoughtfully, reedily, with a subdued, gentle, and mellow reminiscence, and the final decisive phrase "It's an extraordinary thing," with passionate conviction and sincerity that passed at the end into such an unction of worshipful admiration that the words "extraordinary thing" were not spoken, but breathed out passionately, and had the sound "*'strawd'n'ry* thing!"

"Ow!" the young man answered distantly, and in a rather surprised tone, with an air of coldly startled interest, "Now! I can't say that I have—not since my nursery days, at any rate!" He laughed metallically.

"You should read it again," the mountainous creature breathed unctuously. "A *'strawd'n'ry* thing! A *'strawd'n'ry* thing." Delicately he lifted the little cup of muddy black in his huge hand again and put it to his lips.

"But *frightfully* sentimental, down't you think?" the girl neighed sharply at this point. "I mean all the lovely-woman-stoops-to-folly sawt of thing, you now. After all, it is a bit thick to expect people to swallow *that* nowadays," she neighed, "particularly after all that's happened in the last twenty yöhs. I suppose it mattuhed in the eighteenth centureh, but after all," she neighed with an impatient scorn, "who cares today? Who cares," she went on recklessly, "*what* lovely woman stoops to? I can't see that it makes the *slightest* difference. It's not as if it mattuhed any longah! No one cares! It doesn't mattuh what she does!"

"Ow!" the young man said with his air of coldly startled interest. "Yes, I think I follow you, but I don't entirely agree. How can we be certain what is sentimental and what's not?" he cried. "It may be we're the sentimental ones ourselves—and the time may come when we turn again to the kind of life and manners Goldsmith wrote about."

"That *would* be jolly, wouldn't it?" the girl said quietly and ironically.

"It *would* be, yes," the youth replied. "But stranger things than *that* have happened, haven't they?"

"But it seems to me that he misses the whole point!" the girl exclaimed with one full mouth-like rush. "After all," she went on scornfully, "no one is interested in woman's folly any longah—the ruined-maiden, broken-vows sawt of thing. If that was what she got, she should jolly well have known what she wanted to begin with! *I'll* not waste any pity on her," she said grimly. "The greatest folly is in not knowing what you want to do! The whole point today is to live as cleveleh as possible! That's the only thing that mattahs! If you know what you want and go about it cleveleh, the rest will take care of itself."

"Um," the mother now remarked, her gaunt smile set grimly, formidably, on her weathered face. "That takes a bit of doin', *doesn't* it?" And as she spoke these quiet words, her grim smile never faltered for an instant, and there was a hard, an obdurate, an almost savage irony in her intonation, which left them all completely unperturbed.

"Oh, a *'strawd'd'ry* thing! A *'strawd'nr'y* thing!" the huge clerical creature whispered dreamily at this point, as if he had not heard them. And delicately he set his little cup back on the saucer.

One's first impulse when he saw and heard them was to shout with an astounded laughter—and yet, somehow, one never laughed. They had a formidable and impregnable quality that silenced laughter: a quality that was so assured in its own sense of its inevitable rightness that it saw no other way except its own, and was so invincibly sure of its own way that it was indifferent to all others. It could be taken among strange lands and alien faces, and to the farthest and most savage colonies on earth, and would never change or alter by a jot, and would be invincibly immune to the invasions of any life except its own.

Yes, they had found a way, a door, a room to enter, and there were walls about them now, and the way was theirs. The mark of dark time and the architecture of unnumbered centuries of years were on them, and had made them what they were, and what they were, they were, and would not change.

I did not know if their way was a good way, but I knew it was not mine. Their door was one I could not enter. And suddenly the naked empty desolation filled my life again, and I was walking on beneath the timeless sky, and had no wall at which to hurl my strength, no door to enter by, and no purpose for the furious unemployment of my soul. And now the worm was eating at my heart again. I felt the slow, interminable waste and wear of gray time all about me, and my life was passing in the darkness, and all the time a voice kept saying: "Why? Why am I here now? And where shall I go?"

When I got out into High Street after dinner, the dark air would be thronging with the music of great bells, and there would be a smell of fog and smoke and old October in the air, the premonitory thrill and menace of some intolerable and nameless joy. Often at night, the visage of the sky would by some magic be released from the thick grayness that had covered it by day, and would shine forth barely, blazing with flashing and magnificent stars. And sometimes the sky would be wild and stormy, and one could see the wild moon driving on above the stormy tatters of the scudding clouds.

And, as the old bells thronged through the smoky air, the students would be passing along the street, singly or in groups of two or three, briskly, and with the eager haste that told of meetings to come, appointments to be kept, or the expectation of some good fortune, happiness, or pleasure toward which they hurried on.

The soft glow of lights would shine from the ancient windows of the colleges, and one could hear the faint sounds of voices, laughter, sometimes music in the colleges.

Then I would go to different pubs and drink until closing time. Sometimes the proctors would come into a pub where I was drinking, speak amicably to every one, and in a moment more go out again.

Somehow I always hoped that they would take me for a student. I could see them stepping up to me, as I stood there at the bar, saying courteously, yet gravely and sternly:

"Your name and college, sir?"

Then I could see the look of astonished disbelief on their grim red faces when I told them I was not a student, and at last, when I had convinced them, I could hear their crestfallen muttered-out apologies, and would graciously excuse them.

But the proctors never spoke to me, and the bar-man, seeing me look at them as they went out one night, misunderstood the look, and laughed with cheerful reassurance:

"You've nothing at all to worry about, sir. They won't bother you. It's only the gentlemen at the University they're after."

"How do they know I'm not there?"

"That I couldn't tell you, sir," he answered cheerfully, "but they 'ave a way of knowin'! Ah, yes!" he said with satisfaction, slapping a wet cloth down on the bar. "They 'ave a way of knowin', right enough! They're a clever lot, those chaps. A very clever lot, sir, and they always 'ave a way of knowin' when you're not." And smiling cheerfully, he made a vigorous parting swipe across the wood, and put the cloth away below the counter.

My glass was almost empty, and I looked at it and wondered if I ought to have another. I thought they made them very small, and kept thinking of the Governors of North Carolina and South Carolina. It was a fine, warm, open sort of pub, and there was a big fire-place just behind me, crackling smartly with a fire of blazing coals: I could feel the warmth upon my back. Outside, in the fog-numb air, people came by with lonely, rapid footsteps and were lost in fog-numb air again.

At this moment the bar-maid, who had bronze-red hair and the shrewd, witty visage of a parrot, turned and called out in a cheerful, crisply peremptory tone: "Time, please, gentlemen. Closing time."

I put the glass down empty. I wondered what the way of knowing was.

It was October, about the middle of the month, at the opening of the Michaelmas term. Everywhere there was the exultant thrill and bustle of returning, of new life, beginning in an ancient and beautiful place that was itself enriched by the countless lives and adventures of hundreds of years. In the morning there was the numb excitement of the foggy air, a smell of good tobacco, beer, grilled kidneys, ham and sausages, and grilled tomatoes, a faint nostalgic smell of tea, and incredibly, somehow, in that foggy old-gold light, a smell of coffee—a maddening, false, delusive smell, for when one went to find the coffee, it would not be there: it was black liquid mud, bitter, lifeless, and undrinkable.

Everything was very expensive, and yet it made you feel rich yourself just to look at it. The little shops, the wine shops with their bay windows of small leaded glass, and the crusty opulence of the bottles of old port and sherry and the burgundies, the mellow homely warmth of the interior, the tailor shops, the tobacco shops with their selected grades of fine tobacco stored in ancient crocks, the little bell that tinkled thinly as you went in from the street, the decorous, courteous, yet suavely good-natured proprietor behind the counter, who had the ruddy cheeks, the flowing brown mustache, and the wing-collar of the shopkeeper of solid substance, and who would hold the crock below your nose to let you smell the moist fragrance of a rare tobacco before you bought, and would offer you one of his best cigarettes before you left—all of this gave to the simplest acts of life and business a ritualistic warmth and sanctity, and made you feel wealthy and secure.

And everywhere around me in the morning there was the feeling of an immanent recovery, a recapture of a life that had always been my own. This familiar look kept shining at me through the faces of the people. It was in the faces of tradesmen—people in butcher shops, wine shops, clothing stores—and sometimes it was in the faces of women, at once common, fine, familiar, curiously delicate and serene, going to the markets, in the foggy old-bronze light of morning, and of men who passed by wearing derby hats and wing-collars. It was in the faces of a man and his son, good-humored little red-faced bullocks, packed with life, who ran a pub in Cowley Road near the house where, later, I went to live.

It was a look round, full, ruddy, and serene in its open good-nature and had more openness and mellow humor in it than I had found in the faces of the people of New England. It was more like the look of country people and small-town people in the South. Sometimes it had the open tranquil ruddiness, the bovine and self-satisfied good humor of my uncle, Crockett Pentland, and sometimes it was like Mr. Bailey, the policeman, whom the Negro killed one winter's night, when snow was on the ground and all the bells began to ring. And then it was full and hearty like the face of Mr. Ernest Pegram, who was the City Plumber and lived next door to my father, or it was plump, common, kindly, invincibly provincial, ignorant, and domestic like the face of Mrs. Higginson, who lived across the street, and had herself been born in England and whose common kindly face had the same animal, gentle, smoke-like delicacy of expression round the mouth that some of these men and women had.

It was a life that seemed so near to me that I could lay my hand on it and make it mine at any moment. I seemed to have returned to a room that I had always known, and to have paused for a moment without any doubt or perturbation of the soul outside the door, since at any time I chose I had only to turn the knob, open the door, and step into a life that was mine as naturally and thoughtlessly as a man throws himself into his own familiar chair when he returns from a long journey.

But I never found the door, or turned the knob, or stepped into the room. When I got there, I couldn't find it. It was as near as my hand if I could only touch it, only a hand's breadth off if I could span it, a word away if I would speak it. Only a stride, a move, a step away was all the peace, the certitude, the joy—and home forever—for which my life was panting, and I was drowning in the darkness.

I never found it. The old-smoke-gold of morning would be full of hope and joy and immanent discovery, but afternoon would come, and the soft gray humid skies would press down on me with their huge numb waste and weight and weariness of intolerable time, and the empty naked desolation filled my guts.

I would walk that legendary street past all those visible and enchanted substances of time, and see the students passing through the college gates, the unbelievable velvet green of college quads, and see the huge dark room of peace and joy that time had made, and I had no way of getting into it.

Each day I walked about the town and breathed the accursed languid softness of gray foreign air, that had no bite or sparkle in it, and went by all their fabulous age-encrusted walls of Gothic time, and wondered what in the name of God I had to do with all their walls or towers, or how I could feed my hunger on the portraits of the Spanish king, and why I was there, why I had come!

Around me was the whole structure of an enchanted life—a life hauntingly familiar—and now that I was there, I had no way of getting into it. The inn itself was ancient, legendary, beautiful, elfin, like all the inns I had ever read about, and yet all of the cheer, the warmth, the joy and comfort I had dreamed of finding in an inn was lacking.

Upstairs the halls went crazily up and down at different levels, one mounted steps, went down again, got lost and turned around in the bewildering design of the ancient added-on-to structure—and this was the way I had always known it would be. But the rooms were small, cold, dark, and dreary, the lights were dim and dismal, you stayed out of your room as much as possible, and when you went to bed at night, you crawled in trembling between clammy sheets. When you got up in the morning, there was a small jug of warm water at your door with which to shave, but the jug was too small. You got out of the room and went downstairs as quickly as you could.

Downstairs it would be fine. There would be a brisk fire crackling in the hearth, the old smoke-gold of morning and the smell of fog, the crisp cheerful voices of the people and their ruddy competent morning look, and the cheerful smells of breakfast, always liberal and good, the best meal they had: kidneys and ham and eggs and sausages, toast and marmalade and tea.

But at night would come the huge boiled-flannel splendor of the dinner, the magnificent and prayerful service of the waiter, who served you with such reverent grace from heavy silver platters that you felt the food must be as good as everything looked. But it never was.

I ate at a large table in the center of the dining-room provided by a thoughtful staff for such isolated waifs and strays as myself. The food looked very good, and was, according to the genius of the nation, tasteless. How they ever did it I could never tell: everything was of the highest quality, and you chewed upon it mournfully, wearily, swallowing it with the dreary patience of a man who has been condemned forever to an exclusive diet of boiled unseasoned spinach. There was a kind of evil sorcery, a desolate mystery in the way they could take the choicest meats and vegetables and extract all their succulence and native flavor from them, and serve them up to you magnificently with every atom of their former life reduced to the general character of stewed hay or well-boiled flannel.

There would be a thick, heavy soup of dark mahogany, a piece of boiled fish covered with a nameless, tasteless sauce of glutinous white, roast beef that had been done to death in dish-water, and solid, perfect, lovely brussels sprouts for whose taste there was no name whatever. It might have been the taste of boiled wet ashes, or the taste of stewed green leaves, with all the bitterness left out, pressed almost dry of moisture, or simply the taste of boiled clouds and rain and fog. For dessert there would be a pudding of some quivery yellow substance, beautifully moulded, which was surrounded by a thin sweetish fluid of sickly pink. And at the end there would be a cup of black bitter liquid mud.

I felt as if these dreary ghosts of food would also come to life at any moment, if I could only do some single simple thing—make the gesture of an incantation, or say a prayer, or speak a magic word, a word I almost had, but couldn't quite remember.

It was the food that plagued my soul with misery, bitter disappointment, and bewilderment. For I liked to eat, and they had written about food better than anyone on earth. Since my childhood there had burned in my mind a memory of the food they wrote about. It was a memory drawn from a thousand books (of which *Quentin Durward,* curiously, was one), but most of all it came from that tremendous scene in *Tom Brown's School-Days* which described the boy's ride through the frosty darkness on an English stagecoach, the pause for breakfast at an inn, blazing fire, cheerful room, snowy table groaning with spiced meats, waiter reeling in with steaks, grilled kidneys, eggs and bacon, piping hot.

I could remember with a gluttonous delight the breakfast which that hungry boy had devoured. It was a memory so touched with the magic relish of frost and darkness, and smoking horses, the thrill, the ecstasy of the journey and a great adventure, the cheer, the warmth, the bustle of the inn, and the delicious abundance of the food they gave the boy, that the whole thing was evoked with blazing vividness, and now it would almost drive me mad with hunger when I thought of it.

Now it seemed to me that these people had written so magnificently about food not because they always had it, but because they had it rarely and therefore made great dreams and fantasies about it, and that this same quality—the quality of *lack* rather than of *possession,* of desire rather than fulfillment—had got into everything they did, and made them dream great dreams, and do heroic acts, and had enriched their lives unmeasurably.

They had been the greatest poets in the world because the love and substance of great poetry were so rare among them. Their poems were so full of the essential quality of sunlight because their lives had known sunlight briefly, and so shot through with the massy substance of essential gold (a matchless triumph of light and color and material in which they had beaten the whole world by every standard of comparison) because they had known so much fog and rain, so little gold. And they had spoken best of April because April was so brief with them.

Thus, from the grim gray of their skies they had alchemied gold, and from their hunger, glorious food, and from the raw bleakness of their lives and weathers they had drawn magic. And what was good among them had been won sternly, sparely, bitterly, from all that was ugly, dull, and painful in their lives, and when it came, was more rare and beautiful than anything on earth.

But that, I knew, was also theirs: it was another door I could not enter.

The day before I went away, the Rhodes scholars invited me to lunch. That was a fine meal: we ate together in their rooms in college, they opened their purses to the college chef and told him not to spare himself and go the limit. Before the meal we drank together a bottle of good sherry wine, and as we ate, we drank the college ale, strong, brown, and mellow, and when we came to coffee, we all finished off on a bottle of port apiece.

There was a fine thick seasonable soup, of the color of mahogany, and then a huge platter piled high with delicate brown-golden portions of filet of sole, and a roast of mutton, tender, fragrant, and delicious as no other mutton that I ever ate, with red currant jelly, well-seasoned sprouts, and boiled potatoes to go with it, and at the end a fine apple tart, thick cream, sharp cheese and crackers.

It was a fine meal, and when we finished with it, we were all happy and exultant. We were beautifully drunk and happy, with that golden, warm, full-bodied, and most lovely drunkenness that can come only from good rich wine and mellow ale and glorious and abundant food—a state that we recognize instantly when it comes to us as one of the rare, the priceless, the unarguable joys of living, something stronger than philosophy, a treasure on which no price can be set, a sufficient reward for all the anguish, weariness, and disappointment of living, and a far, far better teacher than Aquinas ever was.

We were all young men, and when we had finished, we were drunk, glorious, and triumphant as only young men can be. It seemed to us now that we could do no wrong, or make no error, and that the whole earth was a pageantry of delight which had been shaped for our happiness, possession, and success. The Rhodes scholars no longer felt the old fear, confusion, loneliness, and bitter inferiority and desolation of the soul which they had felt since coming there.

The beauty, age, and grandeur of the life about them were revealed as they had never been before, their own fortune in living in such a place seemed impossibly good and happy, nothing seemed strange or alien in this life around them now, and they all felt that they were going to win and make their own a life among the highest and most fortunate people on earth.

As for me, I now thought of my departure exultantly, and with intolerable desire, not from some joy of release, but because everything around me now seemed happy, glorious, and beautiful, and a token of unspeakable joys that were to come. A thousand images of trains, of the small rich-colored joy and comfort and precision of their trains, of England, lost in fog, and swarming with its forty million lives, but suddenly not dreary, but impossibly small, and beautiful and near, to be taken at a stride, to be compassed at a bound, to enrich me, to fill me, be mine forever in all its joy and mystery and magic smallness.

And I thought of the huge smoky web of London with this same joy; of the suave potent ale I could get in one place there, of its squares and ancient courts, and age-grimed mysteries, and of the fog-numb strangeness of ten million passing men and women. I thought of the swift rich projectile of the channel train, the quays, the channel boats, and darkness, night, the sudden onslaught of the savage choppy seas outside the harbor walls, and England fading, and the flashing beacon lights of France, the quays again, the little swarming figures, the excited tongues, the strange dark faces of the Frenchmen, the always-alien, magic, time-enchanted strangeness of the land, the people, and the faces; and then Paris, the nostalgic, subtle, and incomparably exciting fabric of its life, its flavor, its smell, the strange opiate of its time, the rediscovery of its food, its drink, the white, carnal, and luxurious bodies of the whores.

We were all exultant, wild, full of joy and hope and invincible belief as we thought of all these things and all the glory and mystery that the world held treasured in the depths of its illimitable resources for our taking; and we shouted, sang, shook hands, and roared with laughter, and had no doubts, or fears, or dark confusions, as we had done in other, younger, and more certain times.

Then we started out across the fields behind the colleges, and the fields were wet and green, the trees smoky-gray and blurred in magic veils of bluish mist, and the worn path felt, looked, and seemed incredibly familiar, like a field we had crossed, a path we had trod, a million times. And at length we came to their little creek-wise river, their full, flowing little river of dark time and treasured history, their quiet, narrow, deeply flowing little river, uncanny in the small perfection of its size, as it went past soundlessly among the wet fresh green of fields that hemmed it with a sweet, kept neatness of perfection.

Then, having crossed, we went up along the river path until we came to where the crews were waiting—the Merton crew before, another college behind, and the students of both colleges clustered eagerly on the path beside their boats, exhorting their comrades in the shell, waiting for the signal that would start the race.

Then, even as the Rhodes scholars pounded on my back and roared at me with an exuberant affection that "You've got to run with us! You belong to Merton now!" the starting gun cracked out, the crews bent furiously to their work, the long blades bit frantically the cold gray water, and the race was on, and we were racing lightly, nimbly now, two packs of young men running on the path, each yelping cries of sharp encouragement to his crew as he ran on beside it.

At first it seemed so wild, so sharp, so strong and lithe and eager, as I ran. I felt an aerial buoyancy: my step was light, my stride was long and easy, my breath came softly, without labor, and the swift feet of the running boys thudded before, behind, around me on the hard path pleasantly, and I was secure in my strength and certitude again, and thought I was one of them, and could run with them to the end of the world and back, and never feel it.

I thought that I had recovered all the lean sinew and endurance of a boy, that the storm-swift flight, the speed, the hard condition and resilient effort of the boy were mine again, that I had never lost them, that they had never changed. Then a leaden heaviness began to steal along my limbs. I felt the weariness of effort for the first time, a thickening slowness in the muscles of my legs, a numb weight-like heaviness tingling at my finger tips, and now I no longer looked so sharply and so smartly at the swinging crew below me, the nimbly running boys around me.

I began to pound ahead with dogged and deliberate effort, my heart pounding like a hammer at my ribs; my breathing was laboring hoarsely in my throat, and my tongue felt numb and thick and swollen in my mouth, and blind motes were swimming drunkenly before my eyes. I could hear my voice, unfamiliar and detached, weirdly unreal, as if someone else was speaking in me, as it panted hoarsely:

"Come on, Merton! . . . Come on, Merton! . . . Come on, Merton!"

And now the nimbler running footsteps all around me had passed, had gone ahead of me, had vanished. I could no longer see the crews nor know if they were there. I ran on blindly, desperately, hearing, seeing, saying nothing any longer, an anguished leaden creature, weighted down with a million leaden hours and weary efforts, pounding heavily, blindly, mindlessly along beneath gray timeless skies of an immortal weariness, across the gray barren earth of some huge planetary vacancy—where there was neither shade nor stay nor shelter, where there would never be a resting place, a room, nor any door which I could enter, and where I must pound blindly, wearily along, alone, through the huge vacancy forever.

Then voices swarmed around me once again, and I could feel strong hands upon me. They seized me, stopped me, and familiar faces swarmed forward at me through those swimming motes of blind gray vacancy. I could hear again the hoarse ghost-unreality of my own voice panting, "Come on, Merton!" and see my friends again, now grinning, laughing, shouting as they shook me, "Stop! The race is over! Merton won!"

IV

Late April: 1928

Before me, all that Spring, in the broad window of the dingy storage house across the street, a man sat, in a posture that had never changed, looking out the window. It was an old building with a bleak and ugly front of a rusty, indurated brown, a harsh webbing of fire escapes, and a battered old wooden sign which stretched across the whole width of the facade, and on which in faded letters was inscribed this legend: The Security Distributing Corporation. I did not know what a Distributing Corporation was, nor the purport of its business, but every day since I had come into this street to live, enormous motor vans and powerful horse-drawn trucks had driven up before this dingy building, had backed cleanly and snugly against the floor of old, worn planking that ended with a sharp, sheared emptiness three feet above the sidewalk pavement. And instantly the quiet musty depths of the old building would burst into a furious energy of work: the drivers and their helpers would leap from their seats to the pavements, and the air would be filled with the harsh, constricted cries and shouts of the city:

"Back it up, deh! Back it up! Cuh-*mahn!* Cuh-*mahn!* Givvus a hand, youse guys! Hey-y! *You! Lightnin'!*" They looked at one another with hard smiling faces of derision, quietly saying, "Jesus!" They stood surlily upon their rights, defending truculently the narrow frontier of their duty: "Wadda *I* care where it goes? Dat's *yoeh* look-out! Wat t'hell 'sit got to do wit me!" And they worked furiously, unamiably, with high exacerbated voices, spurred and goaded by their harsh unrest. They worked with speed and power and splendid aptness, shouting: "Hey-y! Youse guys! D'yuhth t'ink all we got to do is run aroun' wit youse all night? . . . Back it up, deh! Back it up!"

They had the tough, seamed face, the thick, dry skin without hue of freshness or of color, the constricted speech, the hard assurance of men born and nurtured from the city's iron breast, and yet there was a bitter savor to them, too. Born to a world of brick and stone and savage conflict, torn from their mother's womb into a world of crowded tenements and swarming streets, stunned into sleep at childhood beneath the sudden, slamming racket of the elevated trains, taught to fight, to menace, and to struggle in a world of savage violence and incessant din, the qualities of that world had been stamped into their flesh and movements, written into their tongue and brain and vision, distilled through all the tissues of their flesh until their lives, schooled in the city's life, had taken on its special tones and qualities. Its harsh metallic clangors sounded from their strident tongues, the savage speed and violence of its movement were communicated to their acts and gestures, the rhythm of its furious dissonance, its vertical heights and canyoned narrowness, and the vast illusion of its swarming repetitions, had yielded them the few words and oaths and gestures, the perfect, constant, cat-like balance that they needed, and stunned their senses to a competent and undaunted tonelessness, cutting the pattern of their lives sparely into its furious and special groove.

The city was their stony-hearted mother, and they had drawn a harsh nurture from its breast. Surly of act and ready in an instant with a curse, their pulse beat with the furious rhythm of the city's stroke, their tongues were bitter with its strident and abusive languages, and their hearts were filled with an immense and secret pride, a dark, unspoken tenderness when they thought of it.

Their souls were like the implacable asphalt visage of a city street: each day the movement of a furious life, a thousand new and alien pageantries, the violent colors of a thousand new sensations, swept across the visage of that soul, and each day all sound and sight and fury were erased from its unyielding surfaces. Ten thousand furious days had passed about them, and they had no memory: they lived like creatures born full-grown into present time, shedding the whole accumulation of the past with every step they took, with every breath they drew, and their lives were written in the passing of each moment of dark time.

And they were sure and certain, forever wrong, but always confident; and they had no hesitations, they confessed no ignorance, nor error, and they knew no doubt. They began each morning with a jibe, a shout, an oath of harsh impatience; eager for the tumult of the day, they sat strongly in their seats at furious noon, and through fumes of oil and hot machinery addressed their curses to the public at the tricks and strategies of cunning rivals, the tyranny of the police, the stupidity of the pedestrian, and the errors of less skillful men than they. Each day they faced the million perils and confusions of the streets with as calm a heart as if they were alone upon a country road. Each day, with an undaunted and untroubled mind, they embarked upon an adventure at which the hearts of men bred only to the wilderness would have recoiled in horror and desolation. They were the city's true-born children, and they possessed it utterly. They possessed it to the last, remotest arm of its unnumbered ganglia, to the remotest spot in all its mighty web, and each day, they hurled their great machines across its length and breadth as if it was just the hand's breadth of a native and familiar earth, meeting each instant crisis, shock, or peril with a skill, a masterful certainty, a bold authority that was incomparable.

The power and precision with which they worked stirred in me a strong and deep emotion of respect, and it also touched in me a sense of regret and humility. For whenever I saw it, my own life, with its tormented desires, its fury of love and madness, its wild and uncertain projects and designs, its labors begun in hope and confidence and ended in despair and incompletion, its obscure purposes and bewilderments, by a cruel comparison with the lives of these men, who had learned to use their strength and talents perfectly in a life demanding manual skill, and mastery of sensuous materials, seemed blind, faltering, baffled, still lost in clouds and chaos and confusion. And I had seen them as I saw them now, three hundred times, in their brief and violent intrusions in the street. In the winter they wore shirts of thick black wool and leather jackets, in the spring they worked with naked tattooed arms, brown and lean with the shift and play of whip-cord muscles. And the end and purposes of their work had always been a mystery to me.

Five times a week at night, the mighty vans were lined up at the curb in an immense and waiting caravan. Their huge bulk was covered now with huge bolts of canvas, on each side a small green lamp was burning, and the drivers, their faces faintly lit with small, respiring points of red tobacco ash, were talking quietly in the shadow of their great machines. Once I had asked one of the drivers the destination of these nightly journeys, and the man had told me that they went to Philadelphia, and would return again by morning.

That spring the picture of these great vans at night, immense, somber, and yet alive with a powerful and silent expectancy, the small green glow of the lamps and the quiet voices of the drivers waiting for the word to start, had given me a sense of mystery and joy. I could not have said what emotion the scene evoked in me, but in it was something of the cruel loveliness of April, the immense space and loneliness of the land at night, the lilac dark, sown with its glittering panoply of stars, and the drivers moving in their great dark vans through sleeping towns, and out into the fragrant country-side again, and into first light, cities, April, and the birdsong of morning.

Their lives seemed splendid to me in the darkness of the night and April. They were a part of that great company of men throughout the earth who love the night, and I felt a sense of union with them. For I had loved the night more dearly than the day. The energies of my life had risen to their greatest strength at night, and at the center of my life had always been the secret and exultant heart of darkness. Night had brought to me madness, drunkenness, a thousand cruel images of hatred, lust, and murder, and of woman's falseness, but it had never brought to me, as day had done, the weariness, the confusion, the sense of smothering and drowning on the eyeless, mindless, crawling seafloors of the earth.

I knew the joys and labors of such men as these, who drove their huge vans through the country in the night. I could see and feel with the literal concreteness of an experience in which I had shared all hours and move-ments of their journey. I could see the dark processional of vans lumbering through the sleeping towns, and feel the darkness, the cool fragrance of the country, on my face again. I could see the quiet, seamed faces of the drivers dimly lit by lantern flares, and I knew the places where they stopped to eat, the little all-night lunch rooms or the lunch wagon warm with greasy light, now empty, save for the dozing authority of the night-time Greek, and now filled with the heavy shuffle of the drivers' feet, the hard and casual intru-sions of their voices.

I could smell the pungent solace of strong, fragrant, fresh tobacco, the plain, priceless, and uncostly joy of the first cigarette lit between the cupped flame of a hard hand and a strong-seamed mouth, in slow fumes of deep-drawn luxury from the nostrils of a tired man. Then I could smell the sultry, excellent excitement of black boiling coffee, the clean, hungry spur and savor of the frying eggs and onions, and the male and meaty relish of strong frying hamburgers. I could see and smell and taste the strong coarse pats of forcemeat red, smacked by a greasy hand upon the blackened sheet of frying plate, turning, in a coil of pungent smoke, from ground, spicy, sanguinary beef into a browned and blackened succulence, crisp on its surface, juicy at the core with the good raw grain of meat.

They ate coarsely, thrusting at plate and cup with strong, hoarse gulpings, goatily, with jungle lust, with the full sharp relish of male hunger and the pleasant weariness of a strong fatigue. They ate with bestial concentration, grained to the teeth with coarse, spicy meat, coating their sandwiched hamburgers with the liberal unction of the thick tomato ketchup, and rending with hard blackened fingers soft yielding slabs of fragrant baker's bread.

Oh, I was with them, of them, for them, blood brother of their joy and hunger to the last hard gulping of the craw, the last deep ease and glow of strong, hungry bellies, the last slow coil of pungent blue expiring from the bellows of their grateful lungs.

Their lives seemed glorious to me in the magic of the dark and April. They swept strongly, invincibly, into the heart of desolation, through all the fury, pain, and madness of my soul, speaking to me again their exultant prophecies of new lands, triumph, and discovery, the morning of new joy upon the earth again, the resurrection of man's ancient, deathless, and triumphant labor of creation, saying again to me with an invincible contention that we who were dead should live again, we who were lost be found, and that the secret, wild, and lonely heart of man was young and living in the darkness, and could never die.

All that Spring in the window of the warehouse, the man sat at a desk, staring out into the street. I had seen this man three hundred times, and yet I had never seen him do anything but look out the window with a fixed abstracted stare. At first, the man seemed so natural and unobtrusive a part of his surroundings that his personality had faded quietly into them, as much a part of the old warehouse building as its dusty brick and dingy planking, and he had gone unnoticed.

Then Esther, with her merry, quick, and sharp observance, had caught and fixed him in her memory, had looked quietly at him day by day and then, one day, with laughter, had pointed to him, saying, "There's our friend in the Distributing Corp. again! What do you suppose he distributes? I've never seen him do anything but look out the window! Have you noticed him? Hah?" she said eagerly and merrily, clapping her small hand to her ear. "God! It's the strangest thing I ever saw! He sits there day by day, and he does nothing!" she cried with a rich laugh of astonishment. "Have you seen him? He spends all his time in looking out the window." She paused, making a slight movement of bewildered protest. "Isn't it queer?" she said, after a moment, with serious wonder. "What do you suppose a man like that can do? What do you suppose he's thinking of?"

"Oh, I don't know," I said indifferently. "Of nothing, I suppose."

And yet from that moment the man's face had been fixed in my memory.

For several weeks thereafter when she came in every day, she would look across the street and cry out in a jolly voice that had in it the affectionate satisfaction and assurance that people have when they see some familiar and comforting object in their memory.

"Well, I see our old friend, the Distributing Corp., is still looking out his window! I wonder what he's thinking of today?" And she would turn away, laughing, her faced flushed with merriment and good humor. Then, for a moment, with child-like fascination which words and rhythms had for her, she meditated their strange beat with an abstracted gravity, silently framing and pronouncing with her lips a series of meaningless sounds such as "Corp—Borp—Forp—Dorp—Torp—," and at length singing out in an earnest and gleeful chant, and with an air of triumphant discovery: "The Distributing Corp, the Distributing Corp, He sits all day and he does no Worp!" And in spite of my protest that her rhyme had neither sense nor reason in it, she cast back her encrimsoned face, and roared with laughter, a rich full woman's yell of delight and triumph.

Then we had laughed no more about the man. For incredible, comical as his indolence had been when we first noticed it, as obscure and mysterious as his employment seemed, there came to be something formidable, immense, and impressive in the quality of that fixed stare. Day by day a thronging traffic of life and business passed before him in the street. Day by day the great vans and wagons came, the drivers, handlers, packers, swarmed before his eyes, filling the air with their harsh cries, irritably intent with driving labor, but the man in the window never wavered in his fixed abstracted stare.

That man's face remained forever in my memory. It was fixed there like one of those unforgettable images that a man remembers from his whole city life, and became for me a timeless image of fixity and judgment, the impartial, immutable censor of all the blind confusion and oblivion of a thousand city days, and of the tortured madness and unrest of my own life.

For night would come, and I would see the night's dark face again, and live again the crowded century of darkness that stretched from light to light, from midnight until morning.

From the meditation of a half-heard phrase, the hard mockery of a scornful eye, a young thug's burst of jeering laughter as he passed below my window with his comrades, or from some incident remembered, the inflection of a tone, the protraction of a smile, the hideous distortion of any casual act or word or circumstance, or from no visible cause whatever, the tidal flood of madness, hatred, and despair would awake with evil magic, poisoning me, bone, brain, and blood, swarming through every tissue of my life the foul corruption of its malignant taint, becoming the instant and conclusive proof of the faithlessness and treachery of my mistress.

Then would I call the woman on the phone, and if she answered me, I would curse and taunt her foully, ask her where her lover was, and if she had him with her at that moment, and believe I heard him whispering and snickering behind her even when she swore no one was there. Feeling even as I cursed at her a rending anguish of inexpiable regret, I would tell her never to come back, rip the phone out of its moorings in the wall, hurl it on the floor, and smash and trample it to fragments underneath my feet, as if the instrument itself had been the evil agent of my ruin.

I would drain the bottle to its last raw drop, feel for a moment its fatal, brief, and spurious illusions of deliberation and control, and then rush out into the streets of night to curse and fight with people, with the city, with all life. Into the tremendous fugue of all-receiving night was packed a century of living, the death, despair, and ruin of a hundred lives. Night would reel about me lividly the huge steps of its demented dance, and day would come incredible like birth, like hope, like joy again, and I would be rescued out of madness to find myself upon the Bridge again, walking home across the Bridge, and with morning, bright, shining morning, blazing incredible upon the terrific frontal cliff and wall of the great city.

I would come home into my street at morning, and find the living stillness of my rooms that had been waiting to receive me, and see again, after all the madness, death, and million blind confusions of the night, the stolid, fixed, unchanging judgment of that face set in the warehouse window, staring out into the street forever with its look of sorrow, stern repose, and tranquil prophecy, its immutable judgment of dark time.

The man's thick white face, fixed there like the symbol of some permanence among the blind rush and sweep of all the million things that pass, the furious and immeasurable erosions of time, was connected somehow with another image which came to me that Spring among all the blazing stream of visions that passed constantly, a train of fire across my brain and this one, unlike the others, was wordless and inexplicable, and neither dream nor fantasy.

And that image, which was to haunt me sorrowfully, was this:

In an old house at the end of day, a man was sitting by the window. Without violence or heat the last rays of the sun fell on the warm brick of the house, and painted it with a sad unearthly light. In the window the man sat always looking out. He never spoke, he never wavered in his gaze, and his face was neither the face of the man in the warehouse window, nor any other face that I had ever seen, but it looked at me quietly, and the immutable exile of an imprisoned spirit was legible upon it, and it was the calmest and the most sorrowful face that I had ever seen.

I saw that image plainly; I knew it utterly, like something I had lived and made my own. And that man's face became for me the face of darkness and of time. It was fixed above the memory of that Spring like some dark judge or destiny, some sorrowful and yet impassive witness of all the fury and anguish in the lives of men.

It never spoke a word to me that I could hear, its mouth was closed, its language was unspeakable—and yet what it said to me was more plain and inevitable than any spoken word could ever be. It was a voice that seemed to have the whole earth in it, and to resume into itself that murmurous and everlasting sound of time, that, day and night, hovers forever above the earth, and all the furious streets of life, unchanging and eternal in its sustenance, no matter what men live or die.

It was the voice of evening and of night, and in it were all the million tongues of all those men who have passed through the heat and fury of the day, and who now lean quietly upon the sills at evening. In it was the whole vast hush and weariness that seemed to come upon the city at the hour of dusk, when the blind and savage chaos of another day is ended—and when everything, streets, buildings, and ten million men and women seem to breathe slowly with a sorrowful and weary joy, and when all sound, all violence and movement in the city's life, seems stilled in this same light of sorrow, peace, and resignation.

The knowledge of their million tongues was in that single tongueless voice, the wisdom of man's life of labor, fury, and despair, spoke to me from it in the hour of evening, and remained with me in all the madness and despair that I would know at night. And what this tongueless image said to me, was this:

"Child, child," it said. "Have patience and belief, for life is many days, and all this present grief and madness of your life will pass away. Son, son, you have been mad and drunken, furious and wild, filled with hatred and despair, and all the dark confusions of the soul—but so have we. Your thirst and hunger were so great you thought that you could eat and drink the earth, but it has been this way with all men dead or living in their youth. You found the earth too great for your one life, you found your brain and sinew smaller than the hunger and desire that fed on them—but child, this is the chronicle of the earth and of all life. And now because you have known madness and despair, because you will grow mad and desperate again before this night is over, we, made of your earth and quality, men who have known all of the madness, anguish, and despair that youth can know, we who have stormed the ramparts of the furious earth and been hurled back, we who have been maddened by the unknowable and bitter mystery of love, the passion of hatred and desire, of faith and jealousy, grief and longing, we who can now lean quietly on the sills of evening, watching the tumult, pain, and frenzy of this life, now call upon you to take heart and hope again, for we can swear to you that these things pass, and we can tell you there are things that never change and are the same forever.

"Because we shall not go into the dark again, nor suffer madness, nor admit despair; because we have found doors—Because we shall build walls about us now, and find a place, and see a few things clearly, letting millions pass. . . .

"Because we have known so many things, we have seen so many things, we have lived so long and lived alone so much and thought so many things; and because there is a little wisdom in us now; because, belly and back and bone and blood, we have made our own a few things now, and we know what we know, we have what we have, we are what we are . . .

"We shall not strike against the wall at night and cry, 'No more!'; we shall not hear the clocks of time strike out on foreign air, we shall not wake at morning in some foreign land to think of home, nor hear the hoof and wheel come down the streets of memory again; because we shall not go again, we shall not go again, because our wandering is over and our hunger fed—O brother, son and comrade, famished youth, over the dust and fury of ten thousand days, over all the madness of our hunger and unrest, we had a vision of things that never change, we had a vision of things that last forever, and we made this song for you:

"Some things will never change. Some things will always be the same. Lean down your ear upon the earth, and remember there are things that last forever. Behold: because we have been set here in the shift and glitter of so many fashions, because we have seen so many things that come and go, so many words forgotten, so many fames that flared and were destroyed; because our brains were bent and sick and driven by the rush, the jar, the million shocks of multitude and number, because we were a grain of dust, a cellulate and dying atom, a dwarfed wanderer among the horror of immense architectures, a stranger whose footfalls had not worn away the millionth part of an inch from the million streets of life; a sinew of bright blood and agony staggering under the weight of its desire, exploded by its everlasting hunger; and because our proudest songs were lost in all the snarl of voices, our vision broken and bewildered by the buildings, because we thought men so much less than mortar, our hearts grew mad and desperate, and we had no hope.

"But we know that the vanished step is better than the stone it walked upon, that one lost word will live when all the towers have fallen down, we know that the vanished men, the dead that they motored to swift burials and at once forgot, the cry that was wasted, the gesture that was half remembered, the forgotten moments of a million obscure lives, will live here when these pavements are forgotten, and the dust of the buried lovers will outlast the city's dust. Lift up your heart, then, as you look at those proud towers: for we tell you they are less than blade and leaf, for the blade and leaf will last forever.

"Some things will never change. Some things will always be the same. The tarantula, the adder, and the asp will always be the same. The sound of the hoof in the street will never change, the glitter of the sunlight on the roughened water will always be the same, and the leaf that strains there in the wind upon the boughs will always be the same. April again! Patches of sudden green, the feathery blur and smoky buddings of young boughs, and something there that comes and goes and never can be captured, the thorn of Spring, the sharp, the tongueless cry! These things will always be the same.

"The voice of forest water in the night, the silence of the earth that lives forever, the glory of the proud and deathless stars, a woman's laughter in the dark—and a cry! a cry!—these things will always be the same.

"Hunger and pain and death will never change, the lids of dark, the innocence of morning, the clean, hard rattle of raked gravel, the cricketing stitch of mid-day in hot meadows, the stir and feathery stumble of hens upon the roost, the smell of sea in harbors, and the delicate web of children's voices in bright air, these things will always be the same.

"All things belonging to the earth will never change—the leaf, the blade, the flower, the wind that cries and sleeps, and wakes again, the trees whose stiff arms clash and tremble in the dark, and the dust of lovers long since buried in the earth—all things proceeding from the earth to seasons, all things that lapse and change and come again upon the earth—these things will always be the same, for they come up from the earth that never changes, they go back into the earth that lasts forever; only the earth endures, but it endures forever.

"Under the pavements trembling like a pulse, under the buildings trembling like a cry, under the waste of time, the hoof of the beast again above the broken bones of cities, there will be something growing like a flower, forever bursting from the earth, forever deathless, faithful, coming into life again like April."

The Four Lost Men

Suddenly, at the green heart of June, I heard my father's voice again. That year I was sixteen; the week before I had come home from my first year at college, and the huge thrill and menace of war, which we had entered just two months before, had filled our hearts. And war gives life to men as well as death. It fills the hearts of young men with wild song and jubilation. It wells up in their throats in great-starred night the savage goat-cry of their pain and joy. And it fills them with a wild and wordless prophecy not of death, but life, for it speaks to them of new lands, triumph, and discovery, of heroic deeds, the fame and fellowship of heroes, and the love of glorious unknown women—of shining triumph and a grand success in a heroic world, and of a life more fortunate and happy than they have ever known.

So it was with us all that year. Over the immense and waiting earth, the single pulse and promise of the war impended. One felt it in the little towns at dawn, with all their quiet, casual, utterly familiar acts of life beginning. One felt it in the route-boy deftly flinging the folded block of paper on a porch, a man in shirt-sleeves coming out upon the porch and bending for the paper, the slow-clopping hoofs of the milk horse in a quiet street, the bottle-clinking wagon, and the sudden pause, the rapid footsteps of the milkman and the clinking bottles, then clopping hoof and wheel, and morning, stillness, the purity of light, and the dew-sweet bird-song rising in the street again.

In all these ancient, ever-new, unchanging, always magic acts of life and light and morning one felt the huge impending presence of the war. And one felt it in the brooding hush of noon, in the warm, dusty stir and flutter of the feathery clucking of the sun-warm hens at noon. One felt it in the ring of the ice-tongs in the street, the cool whine of the ice-saws droning through the smoking block. One felt it poignantly somehow, in the solid lonely liquid leather shuffle of men in shirt-sleeves coming home to lunch in one direction in the brooding hush and time-enchanted spell of noon, and in the screens that slammed and sudden silence. And one felt it in the humid warmth and hungry fragrance of the cooking turnip greens, in leaf and blade and flower, in smell of tar, and the sudden haunting green-gold summer absence of street-car after it had gone.

In all these ancient, most familiar things and acts and colors of our lives, one felt, with numbing ecstasy, the impending presence of the war. The war had got in everything: it was in things that moved, and in things that were still, in the animate red silence of an old brick wall as well as in the thronging life and traffic of the streets. It was in the faces of the people passing and in the thousand familiar moments of man's daily life and business.

And lonely, wild, and haunting, calling us on forever with the winding of its far lost horn, it had got into the time-enchanted loneliness of the magic hills around us, in all the sudden, wild, and lonely lights that came and passed and vanished on the massed green of the wilderness.

The war was in far cries and broken sounds and cow bells tinkling in the gusty wind, and in the far, wild, wailing joy and sorrow of a departing train, as it rushed eastward, seaward, war-ward through a valley of the South in the green spell and golden magic of full June. The war was in the ancient red-gold light of fading day that fell without violence or heat upon the streets of life, the houses where men lived, the brief flame and fire of sheeted window panes.

And it was in field and gulch and hollow, in the sweet green mountain valleys, fading into dusk, and in the hill-flanks reddened with the ancient light and slanting fast into steep cool shade and lilac silence. It was in the whole earth breathing the last heat and weariness of day out in the huge hush and joy and sorrow of oncoming night.

Finally, the war had gotten into all sounds and secrecies, the sorrow, longing, and delight, the mystery, hunger, and wild joy that came from the deep-breasted heart of fragrant, all-engulfing night. It was in the sweet and secret rustling of the leaves in summer streets, in footsteps coming quiet, slow, and lonely along the darkness of a leafy street, in screen doors slammed, and silence, the distant barking of a dog, far voices, laughter, faint pulsing music at a dance, and in all the casual voices of the night, far, strangely near, most intimate and familiar, remote as time, as haunting as the briefness of our days.

And suddenly, as I sat there under the proud and secret mystery of huge-starred, velvet-breasted night, hearing my father's great voice sounding from the porch again, the war, with a wild and intolerable loneliness of ecstasy and desire, came to me in the sudden throbbing of a racing motor, far-away silence, an image of the cool sweet darkness of the mountainside, the white flesh and yielding tenderness of women. And even as I thought of this, I heard the low, rich, sensual welling of a woman's voice, voluptuous, low, and tender, from the darkness of a summer porch across the street.

What had the war changed? What had it done to us? What miracle of transformation had it wrought upon our lives? It had changed nothing; it had heightened, intensified, and made glorious all the ancient and familiar things of life. It had added hope to hope, joy to joy, and life to life; and from that vital wizardry it had rescued all our lives from hopelessness and despair, and made us live again who thought that we were lost.

The war seemed to have collected in a single image of joy, and power, and proud compacted might all of the thousand images of joy and power and all-exulting life which we had always had, and for which we had never had a word before. Over the fields of silent and mysterious night it seemed that we could hear the nation marching, that we could hear, soft and thunderous in the night, the million-footed unison of marching men. And that single, glorious image of all-collected joy and unity and might had given new life and hope to all of us.

My father was old, he was sick with a cancer that flowered and fed forever at his entrails, eating from day to day the gaunt sinew of his life away beyond a hope or remedy, and we knew that he was dying. Yet under the magic life and hope the war had brought to us, his life seemed to have revived again out of its grief and pain, its death of joy, its sorrow of irrevocable memory.

For a moment he seemed to live again in his full prime. And instantly we were all released from the black horror of death and time that had menaced us for years. Instantly we were freed from the evil spell of sorrowful time and memory that had made his living death more horrible than his real one could ever be.

And instantly the good life, the golden and jubilant life of childhood, in whose full magic we had been sustained by the power of his life, and which had seemed so lost and irrevocable that it had a dreamlike strangeness when we thought of it, had under this sudden flare of life and joy and war returned in all its various and triumphant colors. And for a moment we believed that all would be again for us as it had been, that he never could grow old and die, but that he must live forever, and that the summertime, the orchard and bright morning, would be ours again, could never die.

I could hear him talking now about old wars and ancient troubles, hurling against the present and its leaders the full indictment of his soaring rhetoric that howled, rose, fell, swept out into the night, piercing all quarters of the darkness with the naked penetration which his voice had in the old days when he sat talking on the porch in summer darkness, and the neighborhood attended and was still.

Now as my father talked, I could hear the boarders on the porch attending in the same way, the stealthy creak of a rocker now and then, a low word spoke, a question, protest, or agreement, and then their hungry, feeding, and attentive silence as my father talked. He spoke of all the wars and troubles he had known, told how he had stood, "a bare-foot country boy," beside a dusty road twelve miles from Gettysburg and had watched the ragged rebels march past upon the road that led to death and battle and the shipwreck of their hopes.

He spoke of the faint and ominous trembling of the guns across the hot brooding silence of the countryside, and how silence, wonder, and unspoken questions filled the hearts of all the people, and how they had gone about their work on the farm as usual. He spoke of the years that had followed on the war when he was a stone-cutter's apprentice in Baltimore, and he spoke of ancient joys and labors, forgotten acts and histories, and he spoke then with familiar memory of the lost Americans—the strange, lost, time-far, dead Americans, the remote, voiceless, and bewhiskered faces of the great Americans, who were more lost to me than Egypt, more far from me than the Tartarian coasts, more haunting strange than Cipango or the lost faces of the first dynastic kings that built the Pyramids—and whom he had seen, heard, known, found familiar in the full pulse, and passion, and proud glory of his youth: the lost, time-far, voiceless faces of Buchanan, Johnson, Douglas, Blaine—the proud, vacant, time-strange and bewhiskered faces of Garfield, Arthur, Harrison, and Hayes.

"Ah, Lord!" he said—his voice rang out in darkness like a gong, "Ah, Lord!—I've known all of 'em since James Buchanan's time—for I was a boy of six when he took office!" Here he paused a moment, lunged forward violently in his rocking chair, and spat cleanly out a spurt of strong tobacco juice across the porch-rail into the loamy earth, the night-sweet fragrance of the geranium beds. "Yes, sir," he said gravely, lunging back again, while the attentive, hungry boarders waited in the living darkness and were still, "I remember all of them since James Buchanan's time, and I've seen most of them that came since Lincoln!—Ah, Lord!" he paused briefly for another waiting moment, shaking his grave head sadly in the dark. "Well do I remember the day when I stood on a street in Baltimore—poor friendless orphan that I was!" my father went on sorrowfully, but somewhat illogically, since at this time his mother was alive and in good health, upon her little farm in Pennsylvania, and would continue so for almost fifty years— "A poor friendless country boy of sixteen years, alone in the great city where I had come to learn my trade as an apprentice—and heard Andrew Johnson, then the President of this *great* nation," said my father, "speak from the platform of a horse-car—and he was so drunk—so *drunk*—" he howled, "the President of this country was so *drunk* that they had to stand on each side of him and hold him as he spoke—or he'd a-gone head over heels into the gutter!" Here he paused, wet his great thumb briefly, cleared his throat with considerable satisfaction, lunged forward violently again in his rocking chair, and spat strongly a wad of bright tobacco juice into the loamy fragrance of the dark geranium bed.

"The first vote I ever cast for President," my father continued presently, as he lunged back again, "I cast in 1872, in Baltimore, for that *great* man— that brave and noble soldier—U.S. Grant! And I have voted for every Republican nominee for President ever since. I voted for Rutherford Hayes of Ohio in 1876—that was the year, as you well know, of the great Hayes-Tilden controversy, in 1880 for James Abram Garfield—that *great* good man," he said passionately, "who was so foully and brutally done to death by the cowardly assault of a murderous assassin." He paused, wet his thumb, breathing heavily, lunged forward in his rocking chair, and spat again. "In 1884, I cast my vote for James G. Blaine in the year that Grover Cleveland defeated him," he said shortly, "for Benjamin Harrison in 1888, and for Harrison again in 1892, the time that Cleveland got in for his second term—a time that we will all remember to our dying days," my father said grimly, "for the Democrats were in and we had soup kitchens. And, you can mark my words," he howled, "you'll have them again, before these next four years are over—your guts will grease your backbone as sure as there's a God in heaven before that fearful, that awful, that cruel, inhuman, and blood-thirsty Monster who kept us out of war," my father jeered derisively, "is done with you—for hell, ruin, misery, and damnation commence every time the Democrats get in. You can rest assured of that!" he said shortly, cleared his throat, wet his thumb, lunged forward violently, and spat again. And for a moment there was silence, and the boarders waited.

"Ah, Lord!" my father said at length sadly, gravely, in a low, almost in-audible tone. And suddenly, all the old life and howling fury of his rhetoric had gone from him: he was an old man again, sick, indifferent, dying, and his voice had grown old, worn, weary, sad.

"Ah, Lord!" he muttered, shaking his head sadly, thinly, wearily in the dark. "I've seen them all. . . . I've seen them come and go . . . Garfield, Arthur, Harrison, and Hayes . . . and all . . . all . . . all of them are dead. . . . I'm the only one that's left," he said illogically, "and soon I'll be gone, too." And for a moment he was silent. "It's pretty strange when you come to think of it," he muttered. "By God it is!" And he was silent, and darkness, and mystery, and night were all about us.

Garfield, Arthur, Harrison, and Hayes—time of my father's time, blood of his blood, life of his life, had been living, real, and actual people in all the passion, power, and feeling of my father's youth. And for me they were the lost Americans: their gravely vacant and bewhiskered faces mixed, melted, swam together in the sea-depths of a past intangible, immeasurable, and unknowable as the buried city of Persepolis.

And they were lost.

For who was Garfield, martyred man, and who had seen him in the streets of life? Who could believe his footfalls ever sounded on a lonely pavement? Who had heard the casual and familiar tones of Chester Arthur? And where was Harrison? Where was Hayes? Which had the whiskers, which the burn-sides: which was which?

Were they not lost?

Into their ears, as ours, the tumults of forgotten crowds, upon their brains the million printings of lost time, and suddenly upon their dying sight the brief, bitter pain and joy of a few death-bright, fixed, and fading memories: the twisting of a leaf upon a bough, the grinding felloe-rim against the curb, the long, and distant retreating thunder of a train upon the rails.

Garfield, Hayes, and Harrison were Ohio men; but only the name of

Garfield has been brightened by his blood. But at night had they not heard the howlings of demented wind, the sharp, clean, windy raining to the earth of acorns? Had all of them not walked down lonely roads at night in winter and seen a light and known it was theirs?

Had they not known the smell of old bound calf and well-worn leathers, the Yankee lawyer's smell of strong tobacco spit and court-house urinals, the smell of horses, harness, hay, and sweating country men, of jury rooms and court rooms—the strong male smell of justice at the county seat, and heard a tap along dark corridors where a drop fell in darkness with a punctual crescent monotone of time, dark time?

Had not Garfield, Hayes, and Harrison studied law in offices with a dark brown smell? Had not the horses trotted past below their windows in wreaths of dust along a straggling street of shacks and buildings with false fronts? Had they not heard below them the voices of men talking, loitering up in drawling heat? Had they not heard the casual, rich-fibered, faintly howling country voices, and heard the rustling of a woman's skirt, and waiting silence, slyly lowered tones of bawdry and then huge guffaws, slapped meaty thighs, and high, fat, choking laughter? And in the dusty dozing heat, while time buzzed slowly, like a fly, had not Garfield, Arthur, Harrison, and Hayes then smelled the river, the humid, subtly fresh, half-rotten river, and thought of the white flesh of the women then beside the river, and felt a slow, impending passion in their entrails, a heavy rending power in their hands?

Then Garfield, Arthur, Harrison, and Hayes had gone to war, and each became a brigadier or major general. All were bearded men: they saw a spattering of bright blood upon the leaves, and they heard the soldiers talking in the dark of food and women. They held the bridge-head in bright dust at places with such names as Wilson's Mill and Spangler's Run, and their men smashed cautiously through dense undergrowth. And they heard the surgeons cursing after battle and the little rasp of saws. They had seen boys standing awkwardly holding their entrails in their hands, and pleading pitifully with fear-bright eyes: "Is it bad, General? Do you think it's bad?"

When the canister came through, it made a ragged hole. It smashed through tangled leaves and boughs; sometimes it plunked solidly into the fiber of a tree. Sometimes when it struck a man, it tore away the roof of his brain, the wall of his skull, raggedly, so that his brains seethed out upon a foot of wilderness, and the blood blackened and congealed, and he lay there in his thick clumsy uniform, with a smell of urine in the wool, in the casual, awkward, and incompleted attitude of sudden death. And when Garfield, Arthur, Harrison, and Hayes saw these things, they saw that it was not like the picture they had had as children; it was not like the works of Walter Scott and William Gilmore Simms. They saw that the hole was not clean and small and in the central front, and the field was not green nor fenced, nor mown. Over the vast and immemorable earth the quivering heated light of afternoon was shining, a field swept rudely upward to a lift of rugged wood, and field by field, gulley by gulch by fold, the earth advanced in rude, sweet, limitless convolutions.

Then Garfield, Arthur, Harrison, and Hayes had paused by the bridge-head for a moment and were still, seeing the bright blood at noon upon the trampled wheat, feeling the brooding hush of six o'clock across the fields where all the storming feet had passed at dawn, seeing the way the rough field hedge leaned out across the dusty road, the casual intrusions of the coarse field grasses and the hot, dry daisies to the edges of the road, seeing the rock-bright shallows of the creek, the sweet cool shade and lean of river trees across the water.

They paused then by the bridge-head, looking at the water. They saw the stark blank flatness of the old red mill that somehow was like sunset, cool-ness, sorrow, and delight, and looking at the faces of the dead boys among the wheat, the most-oh-most familiar plain, the death-strange faces of the dead Americans, they stood there for a moment, thinking, feeling, thinking, with strong wordless wonder in their hearts:

"As we leaned on the sills of evening, as we stood in the frames of the marvelous doors, as we were received into silence, the flanks of the slope and the slanted light, as we saw the strange hushed shapes upon the land, the muted distances, knowing all things then—what could we say except that our comrades were spread quietly around us and that noon was far?

"What can we say now of the lonely land—what can we say now of the deathless shapes and substances—what can we say who have lived here with our lives, bone, blood, and brain, and all our tongueless languages, hearing on many a casual road the plain familiar voices of Americans, and tomorrow will be buried in the earth, knowing the fields will steep to silence after us, the slant light deepen on the slopes, and peace and evening will come back again, at one now with the million shapes and single substance of our land, at one with evening, peace, the huge stride of the undulant oncoming night, at one, also, with morning?

"Silence receive us and the field of peace, hush of the measureless land, the unabated distances, shape of the one and single substance and the mil-lion forms, replenish us, restore us, and unite us with your vast images of quietness and joy. Stride of the undulant night, come swiftly now, engulf us, silence, in your great-starred secrecy; speak to our hearts of stillness, for we have, save this, no speech.

"There is the bridge we crossed, the mill we slept in, and the creek. There is a field of wheat, a hedge, a dusty road, an apple orchard, and the sweet wild tangle of a wood upon that hill. And there is six o'clock across the fields again, now and always as it was and will be to the world's end forever. And some of us have died this morning coming through the field—and that was time—time—time. We shall not come again, we never shall come back again as we did once at morning—so, brothers, let us look again before we go. . . . There is the mill, and there the hedge, and there the shallows of the rock-bright waters of the creek, and there the sweet and most familiar cool-ness of the trees—and surely we have been this way before!" they cried.

"Oh, surely, brothers, we have sat upon the bridge, before the mill, and sung together by the rock-bright waters of the creek at evening, and come across the wheat field in the morning and heard the dew-sweet bird-song rising from the hedge before! You plain, oh-most-familiar and most homely earth, proud earth of this huge land unutterable, proud nobly swelling earth, in all your delicacy, wildness, savagery, and terror—grand earth in all your loneliness, beauty and wild joy, terrific earth in all your limitless fe-cundities, swelling with infinite fold and convolution into the reaches of the west forever—American earth!—bridge, hedge, and creek and dusty road— you plain tremendous poetry of Wilson's Mill where boys died in the wheat this morning—you unutterable far-near, strange-familiar, homely earth of magic, for which a word would do if we could find it, for which a word would do if we could call it by its name, for which a word would do which never can be spoken, that can never be forgotten, and that will never be revealed—oh, proud, familiar, nobly swelling earth, it seems we must have known you before! It seems that we must have known you forever, but all we know for certain is that we came along this road one time at morning, and now our blood is painted on the wheat, and you are ours now, we are yours forever—and there is something here we never shall remember— there is something here we never shall forget!"

Had Garfield, Arthur, Harrison, and Hayes been young? Or had they been born with flowing whiskers, sideburns, and wing-collars, speaking gravely from the cradle of their mother's arms the noble vacant sonorities of far-seeing statesmanship? It could not be. Had they not been young men in the Thirties, the Forties, and the Fifties? Did they not, as we, cry out at night along deserted roads into demented winds? Did they not, as we, cry out the fierce goat-cry of ecstasy and exultancy, as the full measure of their hunger, their potent and inchoate hope, went out into that single wordless cry?

Did they not, as we, when young, prowl softly up and down past brothels in the dark hours of the night, seeing the gas lamps flare and flutter on the corner, falling with livid light upon the corners of old cobbled streets of brownstone houses? Had they not heard the lonely clopping of a horse, the jounting wheels of a hansom cab, upon those barren cobbles? And had they not waited, trembling in the darkness till the horse and cab had passed, had vanished with the lonely recession of shod hoofs, and then were heard no more?

And then had Garfield, Arthur, Harrison, and Hayes not waited, waited in the silence of the night, prowling up and down the lonely cobbled street, with trembling lips, numb entrails, pounding hearts? Had they not set their jaws, made sudden indecisive movements, felt terror, joy, a numb impend-ing ecstasy, and waited, waited then—for what? Had they not waited, hear-ing sounds of shifting engines in the yards at night, hearing the hoarse, gaseous breath of little engines through the grimy fan-flare of their funnels, the racketing clack of wheels upon the light, ill-laid, ill-joined rails? Had they not waited in that dark street with the fierce lone hunger of a boy, feeling around them the immense and moving quietness of sleep, the heart-beats of ten thousand sleeping men, as they waited, waited, waited in the night?

Had they not, as we, then turned their eyes up and seen the huge starred visage of the night, the immense and lilac darkness of America in April? Had they not heard the sudden, shrill, and piping whistle of a departing engine? Had they not waited, thinking, feeling, seeing then the immense mysterious content of night, the wild and lyric earth, so casual, sweet and strange-familiar, in all its space and savagery and terror, its mystery and joy, its limitless sweep and rudeness, its delicate and savage fecundity? Had they not had a vision of the plains, the mountains, and the rivers flowing in the darkness, the huge patter of the everlasting earth and the all-engulfing wilderness of America?

Had they not felt, as we have felt, as they waited in the night, the huge lonely earth of night time and America, on which ten thousand lonely sleeping little towns were strewn? Had they not seen the fragile network of the light, racketing, ill-joined little rails across the land, over which the lonely little trains rushed on in darkness, flinging a handful of lost echoes at the river's edge, leaving an echo in the cut's resounding cliff, and being engulfed then in huge lonely night, in all-brooding, all-engulfing night? Had they not known, as we have known, the wild secret joy and mystery of the everlasting earth, the lilac dark, the savage, silent, all-possessing wilderness that gather in around ten thousand lonely little towns, ten million lost and lonely sleepers, and waited and abode forever, and was still?

Had not Garfield, Arthur, Harrison, and Hayes then waited, feeling the goat-cry swelling in their throats, feeling wild joy and sorrow in their hearts, and a savage hunger and desire—a flame, a fire, a fury—burning fierce and lean and lonely in the night, burning forever while the sleepers slept? Were they not burning, burning, burning, even as the rest of us have burned? Were Garfield, Arthur, Harrison, and Hayes not burning in the night? Were they not burning forever in the silence of the little towns with all the fierce hunger, savage passion, limitless desire that young men in this land have known in the darkness?

Were they not burning with the wild and wordless hope, the incredible belief that all young men have known before the promise of that huge mirage, the deathless dupe and invincible illusion of this savage, all-exultant land where all things are impending and where young men starve? Were they not burning in the enfabled magic, mystery, and joy of the lilac dark, the lonely, savage, secret, everlasting earth on which we lived, and wrought, and perished, mad with hunger, unfed, famished, furious, unassuaged? Were they not burning, burning where a million doors of glory, love, unutterable fulfillment, impended, waited in the dark for us, were here, were here around us in the dark forever, were ready to our touch forever, and that duped us, mocked forever at our hunger, maddened our hearts and brains with searching, took our youth, our strength, our love, our life, and killed us, and were never found?

Had Garfield, Arthur, Harrison, and Hayes not waited then, as we have waited, with numb lips and pounding hearts and fear, delight, strong joy, and terror stirring in their entrails as they waited in the silent street before a house, proud, evil, lavish, lighted, certain, secret, and alone? And as they heard the hoof, the wheel, the sudden whistle, and the immense and sleeping silence of the town, the lonely, wild, and secret earth, the lilac dark, the huge starred visage of the night—did they not wait there in the dark, thinking:

"Oh, there are new lands, morning, and a shining city. Soon, soon, soon!"

And then as Garfield, Arthur, Harrison, and Hayes prowled softly up and down in the dark cobbled streets, hearing the sudden shrill departure of the whistle in the night, the great wheels pounding at the river's edge, feeling the lilac dark, the heart-beats of the sleeping men, and the attentive silence, the terror, savagery, and joy, the huge mystery and promise of the immense and silent earth, thinking, feeling, thinking, with wild silent joy, intolerable desire, did they not say:

"Oh, there are women in the West, and we shall find them. They will be waiting for us, calm, tranquil, corn-haired, unsurprised, looking across the wall of level grain with level eyes, looking into the flaming domains of the red, the setting sun, at the great wall and the soaring vistas of the western ranges. Oh, there are lavish corn-haired women in the West with tranquil eyes," cried Garfield, Arthur, Harrison, and Hayes, "and we shall find them waiting in their doors for us at evening!

"And there are women in the South," they said, "with dark eyes and the white magnolia faces. They are moving beneath the droop of tree-barred levels of the South. Now they are moving on the sweep of ancient lawns, beside the great slow-flowing rivers in the night! Their step is light and soundless as the dark, they drift the white ghost-glimmer of their beauty under ancient trees, their words are soft and slow and hushed, and sweeter far than honey, and suddenly their low and tender laugh, slow, rich, and sensual, comes welling from the great vat of the dark. The perfume of their slow white flesh is flower-sweet, magnolia strange, and filled with all the sweet languors of desire! Oh, there are secret women in the South," they cried, "who move by darkness under drooping trees the white ghost-glimmer of magnolia loveliness, and we shall find them!

"And there are women in the North," cried Garfield, Arthur, Harrison, and Hayes, "who wait for us with Viking eyes, the deep breasts and the great limbs of the Amazons. There are powerful and lovely women in the North," they said, "whose eyes are blue and depthless as a mountain lake. Their glorious hair is braided into ropes of ripened grain, and their names are Lundquist, Nielsen, Svenson, Jorgenson, and Brandt. They are waiting for us in the wheat fields of the North, they are waiting for us at the edges of the plains, they are waiting for us in the forests of great trees. Their eyes are true and level, and their great hearts are the purest and most faithful on the earth, and they will wait for us until we come to them.

"There are ten thousand lonely little towns at night," cried Garfield, Arthur, Harrison, and Hayes, "ten thousand lonely little towns of sleeping men, and we shall come to them forever in the night. We shall come to them like storm and fury, with a demonic impulse of wild joy, dark chance, dropping suddenly upon them from the fast express at night—leaving the train in darkness, in the dark mid-watches of the night, and being left then to the sudden silence, mystery, and promise of an unknown little town. Oh, we shall come to them forever in the night," they cried, "in winter among howling winds and swirling snow. Then we shall make our tracks along the sheeted fleecy whiteness of an empty silent little street, and find our door at length, and know the instant that we come to it that it is ours.

"Coming by storm and darkness to the lonely, chance, and secret towns," they said, "we shall find the well-loved face, the longed-for step, the well-known voice, there in the darkness while storm beats about the house and the white mounting drifts of swirling snow engulf us. Then we shall know the flower-whiteness of a face below us, the night-time darkness of a cloud of hair across our arm, and know all the mystery, tenderness, and surrender, of a white-dark beauty, the fragrant whiteness, the slow bounty of a velvet undulance, the earth-deep fruitfulness of love. And we shall stay there while storm howls about the house," they said, "and huge drifts rise about us. We shall leave forever in the whitened silence of the morning, and always know the chance, the secret, and the well-beloved will be there waiting for us when storms howl at night, and we come again through swirling snow, leaving our footprints on the whitened, empty, silent streets of unknown little towns, lost at the heart of storm and darkness upon the lonely, wild, all-secret mystery of the earth."

And finally did not Garfield, Arthur, Harrison, and Hayes, those fierce and jubilant young men, who waited there, as we have waited, in the silent barren street with trembling lips, numb hands, with terror, savage joy, fierce rapture alive and stirring in their entrails—did they not feel, as we have felt, when they heard the shrill departing warning of the whistle in the dark, the sound of great wheels pounding at the river's edge? Did they not feel, as we have felt, as they awaited there in the intolerable sweetness, wildness, mystery, and terror of the great earth in the month of April, and knew themselves alone, alive and young and mad and secret with desire and hunger in the great sleep-silence of the night, the impending, cruel, all-promise of this land? Were they not torn, as we have been, by sharp pain and wordless lust, the asp of time, the thorn of spring, the sharp, the tongueless cry? Did they not say:

"Oh, there are women in the East—and new lands, morning, and a shining city! There are forgotten fume-flaws of bright smoke above Manhattan, the forest of masts about the crowded isle, the proud cleavages of departing ships, the soaring web, the wing-like swoop and joy of the great bridge, and men with derby hats who come across the bridge to greet us—come, brothers, let us go to find them all! For the huge murmur of the city's million-footed life, far, bee-like, drowsy, strange as time, has come to haunt our ears with all its golden prophecy of joy and triumph, fortune, happiness, and love such as no men before have ever known. Oh, brothers, in the city, in the far-shining, glorious, time-enchanted spell of that enfabled city we shall find great men and lovely women, and unceasingly ten thousand new delights, a thousand magical adventures! We shall wake at morning in our rooms of lavish brown to hear the hoof and wheel upon the city street again, and smell the harbor, fresh, half-rotten, with its bracelet of bright tides, its traffic of proud sea-borne ships, its purity and joy of dancing morning gold—and feel, with an unspeakable sorrow and delight, that there are ships there, there are ships—and something in our hearts we cannot utter.

"And we shall smell the excellent sultry fragrance of boiling coffee and think of silken luxury of great walnut chambers in whose shuttered amber morning-light proud beauties slowly stir in sensual warmth their lavish limbs. Then we shall smell, with the sharp relish of young hunger, the grand breakfast smells: the pungent bacon, crisping to a turn, the grilled kidneys, eggs, and sausages, and the fragrant stacks of gold-brown wheat cakes smoking hot. And we shall move, alive and strong and full of hope, through all the swarming lanes of morning and know the good green smell of money, the heavy leathers and the walnut of great merchants, the power, the joy, the certitude and ease of proud success.

"We shall come at furious noon to slake our thirst with drinks of rare and subtle potency in sumptuous bars of swart mahogany in the good fellowship of men, the spicy fragrance of the lemon rind and angostura bitters. Then, hunger whetted, pulse aglow, and leaping with the sharp spur of our awakened appetite, we shall eat from the snowy linen of the greatest restaurants in the world. We shall be suavely served and tenderly cared for by the pious unction of devoted waiters. We shall be quenched with old wine and fed with rare and priceless honesty, the maddening succulence of grand familiar food and noble cooking, fit to match the peerless relish of our hunger!

"Street of the day, with the unceasing promise of your million-footed life, we come to you!" they cried. "Streets of the thunderous wheels at noon, streets of the great parades of marching men, the band's bright oncoming blare, the brave stick-candy whippings of a flag, street of the cries and shouts, the swarming feet, the man-swarm ever passing in its million-footed weft—street of the jounting cabs, the ringing hooves, the horse-cars and the jingling bells, the in-horse ever bending its sad nodding head toward its lean and patient comrade on the right—great street of furious life and movement, noon, and joyful labors, your image blazes in our hearts forever, and we come!

"Street of the morning, street of hope!" they cried. "Street of coolness, slanted light, the frontal cliff and gulch of steep blue shade, street of the dancing morning-gold of waters on the flashing tides, street of the rusty weathered slips, the blunt-nosed ferry foaming in with its packed wall of small white staring faces, all silent and intent, all turned toward *you*—proud street! Street of the pungent sultry smells of new-ground coffee, the good green smell of money, the fresh half-rotten harbor smells with all its evocation of your mast-bound harbor and its tide of ships, great street!—Street of the old buildings grimed richly with the warm and mellow dinginess of trade—street of the million morning feet forever hurrying onward in the same direction—proud street of hope and joy and morning, in your steep canyon we shall win the wealth, the fame, the power, and the esteem which our lives and talent merit!

"Street of the night!" they cried. "Great street of mystery and suspense, terror and delight, eagerness and hope, street edged forever with the dark menace of impending joy, and unknown happiness and fulfilment, street of gaiety, warmth, and evil, street of the great hotels, the lavish bars and restaurants, and the softly golden glow, the fading lights and empetaled whiteness of a thousand hushed white thirsty faces in the crowded theaters, street of the tidal flood of faces, lighted with your million lights and all thronging, tireless, and unquenched in their insatiate searching after pleasure, street of the lovers coming along with slow steps, their faces turned toward each other, lost in the oblivion of love among the everlasting web and weaving of the crowd, street of the white face, the painted mouth, the shining and inviting eye—oh, street of night, with your mystery, joy, and terror—we have thought of you, proud street.

"And we shall move at evening in the noiseless depths of sumptuous carpets through all the gaiety, warmth, and brilliant happiness of great lighted chambers of the night, filled with the mellow thrum and languor of the violins, and where the loveliest and most desirable women in the world—the beloved daughters of great merchants, bankers, millionaires, or rich young widows, beautiful, loving, and alone—are moving with a slow proud undulance, a look of depthless tenderness in their fragile lovely faces. And the loveliest of them all," they cried, "is ours, is ours forever, if we want her! For brothers, in the city, in the far-shining, magic, golden city we shall move among great men and glorious women and know nothing but strong joy and happiness forever, winning by our courage, talent, and deserving the highest and most honored place in the most fortunate and happy life that men have known, if only we will make it ours!"

So thinking, feeling, waiting, as we have waited, in the sleeping silence of the night in silent streets, hearing, as we have heard, the sharp blast of the warning whistle, the thunder of great wheels upon the river's edge, feeling, as we have felt, the mystery of night time and of April, the huge impending presence, the wild and secret promise, of the savage, lonely, everlasting earth, finding, as we have found, no doors to enter, and being torn, as we were torn, by the thorn of spring, the sharp, the wordless cry, did they not carry—these young men of the past, Garfield, Arthur, Harrison, and Hayes—even as we have carried, within their little tenements of bone, blood, sinew, sweat, and agony, the intolerable burden of all the pain, joy, hope, and savage hunger that a man can suffer, that the world can know?

Were they not lost? Were they not lost, as all of us have been, who have known youth and hunger in this land, and who have waited lean and mad and lonely in the night, and who have found no goal, no wall, no dwelling, and no door?

The years flow by like water, and one day it is spring again. Shall we ever ride out of the gates of the East again, as we did once at morning, and seek again, as we did then, new lands, the promise of the war, and glory, joy, and triumph, and a shining city?

O youth, still wounded, living, feeling with a woe unutterable, still grieving with a grief intolerable, still thirsting with a thirst unquenchable—where are we to seek? For the wild tempest breaks above us, the wild fury beats about us, the wild hunger feeds upon us—and we are houseless, doorless, unassuaged, and driven on forever; and our brains are mad, our hearts are wild and wordless, and we cannot speak.

Boom Town

I

Through the windows of the train he could see the flat, formless earth of New Jersey, loaded with its swarming weight of men and cities, with slum, swamp, and filthy tenement, with suburb and the ugliness of industry—cinder and yard and rust and waste, stubble and field and wood, steel and smoke-glazed glass and factory chimney, stroking forever past the moving windows into the infinite progressions of the stifled land. All through the early afternoon this flat uncharactered earth faded away into the powerful and weary hazes of the heat: the earth was parched and dusty looking, hot with coarse yellowed grasses and the withered stalks of flowerless weeds. Then, under a glazed and burning sky the train pounded down across the States of Pennsylvania, Delaware, and Maryland, paused for forty minutes in the fading glow of a weary day at Washington, and toward dark slowly rumbled over the Potomac and entered the broad heat-stricken Commonwealth of Virginia. It was the end of June: already the weather had grown very hot, and there had been no rain for weeks.

A gigantic panorama of a continent gasping for its breath unfolded as the train rushed on: everywhere within the hot green airless depth of the train and outside, at stations on the pauses of the journey, the talk was all of drought and heat: in great engines steaming slowly on the tracks, or passive as great cats, the engineers were wiping wads of blackened waste across their grimy faces, the wilted passengers in other trains fanned feebly at their faces a sheaf of languid paper, or sat in a soaked and sweltering dejection.

All through the night he lay in his dark berth and watched, as he had watched so many times before, the old earth of Virginia as it stroked past him in the dream-haunted silence of the moon. Field and hill and gulch and stream and bridge and dreaming wood, then field and hill and gulch and stream and wood again, the old earth, the everlasting earth of America, kept stroking past him in the steep silence of the moon.

All through the ghostly stillness of the land the train made on forever its tremendous noise fused of a thousand sounds and haunted by the spell of time. And that sound evoked for him a million images: old songs, old faces

120

and forgotten memories, and all strange, wordless, and unspoken things men know and live and feel, and never find a language for, the legend of dark time, the sad brevity of their days, the strange and bitter miracle of life itself. And through the thousand rhythms of this one design he heard again, as he had heard ten thousand times in childhood, the pounding wheel, the tolling bell, the whistle wail. Far, faint, and lonely as a dream, it came to him again through that huge spell of time and silence and the earth, evoking for him, as it had always done, its tongueless prophecy of life, its wild and secret cry of joy and pain, and its intolerable promises of the new lands, morning and a shining city.

But now the strange and lonely cry of the great train, which had haunted his whole life and which, far and faint from some green mountain of the South, had come to him so often as a child at night, bringing to him huge promises of flight and darkness, was speaking to him with an equal strangeness of return. For he was going home again. And sudden, blind, and furious as all his wandering had been, was his return. He was going home again, and he did not know the reason for his going.

What was he looking for? What did he hope to find at home? He did not know. A restless wanderer, twenty-five years old, an obscure instructor at one of the universities in the city, a nameless atom in the terrific manswarm of the city's life, he was not by any standard which his native town could know—"successful," "a success." And more than anything, he feared the sharp, the appraising eye, the worldly judgments of that little town. Yet now he was returning to it. Why?

Suddenly, a memory of his years away from home, the years of wandering in many lands and cities, returned to him. He remembered how many times he had thought of home with such an intensity of passion that he could close his eyes and see the scheme of every street in town, and every house upon each street, and the faces of ten thousand people, as well as the memory of all their words, the densely woven fabric of all their histories.

Why had he felt so, thought so, remembered with such blazing accuracy, if it had not mattered, and if, in the vast homeless unrest of his spirit, this little town, and the immortal hills around it, was not the only home he had on earth? He did not know. All that he knew was that the years flow by like water and that one day men come home again.

The train rushed onward through the moonlit land.

II

When he looked from the windows of the train the next morning, the hills were there again: they towered immense and magical into the blue weather, and suddenly coolness was there, the winey sparkle of the air and the shining brightness, and it seemed to him that he had never left them and that all which had passed in the years between was like a dream.

Above him was the huge bulk of the hills, the looming shapes around him, the dense massed green of the wilderness, the cloven cuts and gulches of the mountain passes, the dizzy steepness, and the sudden drops below. He could see the little huts stuck to the edge of bank and gulch and hollow, set far below him in the gorges, toy-small, yet closer, nearer than a dream. All this, so far, so near, so strange, and so familiar, refound like something we have always known and remembered, lost the instant that we find it, the everlasting stillness of the earth now meeting the intimate toiling slowness of the train as it climbed upward round the sinuous curves, was near and instant as a vision, more lost yet more familiar than his mother's face.

At last the train came sweeping down the long sloping bend into the suburban junction two miles from town, where his family always met him when he came home. But even before the train had come to a full halt at the little station, he had looked out the windows and seen with this same sense of instant recognition the figures of his mother and his brother, waiting for him on the platform as he knew he would find them.

He could see his brother, Lee, teetering restlessly from one flat foot to another as his glance went back and forth along the windows of the train in search of him. He could see his mother's strong short figure, planted solidly, her hands clasped across her waist in their loose and powerful grip, her white face with its delicate pursed mouth turned toward the windows of the train, her glance darting back and forth with the curious, startled, animal-like swiftness and intensity all her family had.

And even as he swung down from the car-steps of the Pullman and, valise in hand, strode toward the platform across the rock ballast of the roadbed and the powerful gleaming rails, he knew instantly, with this intuitive feeling of strangeness and recognition, just what they would say to him at the moment of their meeting.

Now his mother and his brother had seen him. He could see his mother speak excitedly to his brother, and motion toward him. And now his brother was coming toward him on the run, his broad clumsy hand extended in a gesture of welcome, his rich tenor shouting greetings at him as he came:

"How are you, boy?" he shouted. "Put it there!" he cried heartily as he came up and vigorously wrung him by the hand. "Glad to see you, John."

And still shouting greetings, he reached over and attempted to take the valise. The inevitable argument, vehement and protesting, began immediately, and in another moment, as always, the older brother was in triumphant possession, and the two were walking together toward the platform, Lee shouting scornfully all the time in answer to the other's protests: "Oh, for God's sake! Forget about it! I'll let you do as much for me when I come up to the Big Town to visit you! . . . Here's mama!" he said abruptly, as they came up on the platform. "I know she'll be glad to see you!"

She was waiting for him with the bridling and rather confused movement that was characteristic of her in moments of strong excitement. Her powerful and delicate mouth was smiling tremulously, her worn faded brown eyes were wet with the tears which the sight of a train arriving and departing always seemed to cause.

"Hello, mama," he said, somewhat thickly and excitedly. "How are you, mama?"

He hugged her hard, planting a clumsy kiss on her white face. In a moment they released each other, and his mother, holding his hand in her strong warm clasp, stepped back a pace and regarded him with the old tremulous, half-bantering expression she had used so often when he was a child.

"Well, well, well!" she said. "Hm-m!" she said, making a little humming noise as she spoke. "My ba-aby!"

John reddened in the face, making an awkward and indefinite gesture, and could find nothing adequate to say. Then he looked quickly at his brother; for a moment they regarded each other with a tormented glance, then both began to grin at the same time, he sullenly, his brother with a wide, swiftly developing grin of wild exuberance, which suddenly split his handsome face with an idiotic and exultant glee. That grin was followed immediately by the tremendous chortling of mad laughter, the huge "Whah—whah-h!—Haw-w" his brother cried, smiting his forehead with the back of one clumsy hand. "'My baby'—haw-w!" he cried again, and smote himself. "God-damn!"

"Well, now, sonny boy," his mother now said briskly, "come on, now! I've got a good breakfast waiting for you when you get home!"

"How's Helen, mama," John broke in, somehow disturbed by the failure of his sister to meet him.

"Hah? What say? Helen?" she said quickly, in a sharp, surprised kind of tone. "Oh, she's all right. And yes, now! She called up before we left this morning and said to give you her love and tell you she'd be over later. Said she wanted to come along to meet you but had to stay at home because Roy McIntyre had 'phoned her he had a prospect for that place of theirs on Weaver Street and wanted to bring him over right away to look at it. Of course, she and Hugh are anxious to sell, want to move out there and build on one of those lots they own on Grovewood Terrace. Say they'll take eight thousand for the house—two thousand down, but I told her to take cash. I told her not to listen to Roy McIntyre if he tries to trade in on the deal any of those lots he's got up there on the hill in Ridgewood."

Here she gestured toward the hill that swept back in a slope of massed leafy green behind the railroad tracks, and with a short and almost compulsive tremor of her strong, pursed face, she shook her head in a movement of emphatic negation.

"Mama!" Lee, who during the course of these remarks had been teetering restlessly back and forth on his large feet, thrusting his fingers through his flashing hair in a distracted manner, and finally consulting his watch uneasily, now spoke in a tone of patient but somewhat strained courtesy:

"I think if we get started—"

"Why, yes!" she cried instantly in a tone of briskly cheerful but rather startled agreement. "That's the very thing. This very minute, sir! I'm ready any time you are! Come on!" and she started to move off with a confused and bridling movement of her strong frame.

"But as I say, now," she continued quickly, turning to John again, "I told her not to listen to him if he wants to swap. No, sir!" Here she shook her head emphatically. "I told her if that's what he's trying to do I'd pay no attention to him for a minute! Hm!"—she shook her head with a little scornful smile—"That's what he was trying to do. Why, here, now! Yes! You see what he was up to, don't you? Why, didn't he try the same trick on me? Didn't he come to me? Didn't he try to trade with me? Oh, here, along you know the first part of last April," she said impatiently with a dismissing gesture of her broad hand, as if all this splintered and explosive information must be perfectly clear to everyone—"with Dr. Gibbs, Rufe Mears, Erwin Featherstone, and all the rest of that crowd that's in with him. Says: 'I'll tell you what I'll do. We know you're a good trader, we respect your judgment, and we want you in,' he says, 'and just to have you with us, why, I'll trade you three fine lots I own up there on Pinecrest Road in Ridgewood for that house and lot you own on Preston Avenue.'

"Says: 'You won't have to put up a cent of your own money. Just to get you in with us I'll make an even swap with you!' 'Well,' I says—"

III

"Mama," John broke in desperately, stunned and bewildered by this mad obsession which had so completely filled and conquered her that everything else on earth—home, friends, children, absence and return, the whole chronicle of her life—had been submerged and for the time forgotten:

"Mama," he began desperately again, but bewildered, not knowing what to say, "don't you think it would be better if . . . "

"Hah? What say?" Startled from that flood-tide of her obsession, she looked suddenly at him with the quick, instant attentiveness of a bird. "Well, as I say, you see now," she went on, seeing that he did not answer. "Said to him when they first came to me—Roy McIntyre, old Gibbs, and then, of course, that's so—" she went on reflectively, "Rufe Mears was there as . . . "

"Couldn't we?" John blurted out with the blind confusion of a man who has suddenly come upon an undiscovered continent. "Why couldn't we go home now, and eat our breakfast and then call up Helen—couldn't we—"

"Why, yes! The very thing! I'm ready, sir!"

"I think, mama," Lee now said gently with the tortured pleading, almost comic patience of exasperation, "I think that if we could—" and at this moment his tormented eyes suddenly met, stopped, rested for a moment on the astounded, bewildered look his brother gave him. For a minute they looked at each other with earnest, asking looks—then suddenly the bursting of wild glee upon his brother's face.

"Haw-w," Lee yelled, "haw-w," prodding his brother in the ribs, "*haw-w!*" he cried. "You'll see—oh, you'll see, all right!" he gloated. "Frankly I have to laugh when I think about it. Frankly I do!" he said earnestly. Then, looking at the astonished face before him, he burst into the devastating roar again: "Haw-w! Whah-whah-h! You'll see," he said mysteriously and mockingly. "Oh, you'll get it now," he cried. "Nineteen hours a day, from daybreak to three o'clock in the morning—no holts barred!" he chortled. "They'll be waiting for us when we get there," he said. "They're all lined up there on the front porch in a reception committee to greet you and to cut your throat, every damn mountain grill of a real estate man in town. Old Horse Face Hines, the undertaker; Skin-em-alive Roy McIntyre; Skunk-eye Rufe Mears the demon promoter; and old squeeze-your-heart's-blood Gibbs, the widder and orphan man from Arkansas;—they're all there!" he said gloatingly. "She told 'em you're a prospect, and they're waiting for you—every cut-throat swindler of a real estate man in town! It's your turn now!" he yelled. "She's told 'em that you're on the way, and they're drawin' lots right now to see which one gets your shirt and which one takes the pants and B.V.D.s. Haw-w! Whah-whah-h!" he poked his younger brother in the ribs.

"They'll get nothing from me," John said angrily, "for I haven't got it to begin with."

"Haw-w! *Whah-whah-h!*" Lee yelled. "That doesn't matter. If you've got an extra collar button, they'll take that as the first installment, and then and then—haw-w!—they'll collect your goddam cufflinks, socks, and your pants suspenders in easy installments," he said gloatingly, "as the years roll on. Haw-w! *Whah-h!*" he yelled, prodding his brother with clumsy fingers as he saw the sullen and astounded look upon his face. Then, seeing his mother's white, pursed, and reproving face, he suddenly prodded *her* in the ribs, at which she shrieked in a vexed manner and slapped his rough hand.

"I'll vow, boy!" she cried fretfully. "What on earth's the matter with you? Why, you act like a regular idiot. I'll vow you do!"

"Haw! Whah-h!" he yelled again. Then, still grinning, he picked up the valise and started rapidly across the station platform toward his battered little car, which was parked at the curb not more than twenty yards away.

And in this manner, accompanied every foot of the way by his mother's torrential discourse, which gave him with encyclopedic fullness the speculative history of every piece of real estate they passed, punctuated from time to time by his brother's prodding fingers in his ribs, the limitless and exultant madness of his great "whah-whah-h," the youthful native, after years of wandering, returned to his own town again—and found there a strange mad life, a glittering city, a wild and drunken fury he had never seen before.

IV

The streets were foaming with a mad exuberant life, crowded with strange expensive traffic, with a thousand points of glittering machinery, winking and blazing imperially in the hot bright air, filled with new faces he had never seen. And the faces of the people he had known shone forth from time to time like a remembered door, like a street he had gone to once, or like lights in the enormous darkness of a lonely coast. And yet on the faces of everyone, natives and strangers alike, there was burning the drunken glow of an unholy glee. Their feet swarmed and scampered on the pavements, their bodies darted, dodged, thrust, and twisted as if the leaping energy of some powerful drug was driving them on. For the first time he witnessed the incredible spectacle of an entire population which was drunk—drunk on the same powerful liquors, drunk with an intoxication which never wore off and which never made them weary, dead, or sodden, but which drove them on constantly to new heights of leaping and scampering exuberance.

The people he had known all his life cried out to him along the streets, they seized his hand and shook it, saying, "Hi there, boy! . . . Glad to see you home again! . . . Going to be with us for a while now? Good! I'll be seeing you, I've got to go on now, I've got to meet a fellow down the street to sign some papers! Glad to see you, boy!"—and they would vanish, having uttered this tempestuous greeting without a pause and without the loss of a stride, pulling and dragging him along with them as they wrung his hand.

The conversation was terrific and incessant—a tumult of voices united in variations of a single chorus: speculation and real estate. They were gathered in groups before the drug stores, before the post-office, along the curbs, before the court house and the city hall. They hurried along the pavements talking together with a passionate absorption of earnestness, bestowing a half-abstracted nod of greeting from time to time on some acquaintance who was passing. The real estate men were everywhere. Their motors and buses roared through all the streets of the town and out into the country, bearing crowds of prospective clients. One could see them on the porches of houses unfolding blue prints and prospectuses as they shouted enticements and promises of sudden wealth into the ears of deaf old women. Everyone was game for them—the lame, the halt, and the blind, Civil War veterans or their decrepit pensioned widows, as well as high school boys and girls, Negro truck drivers, soda-jerkers, elevator-boys, boot-blacks.

Everyone bought real estate; and everyone was a "real estate man" either in name or in practice. The barbers, the lawyers, the grocers and butchers and builders and clothiers were all engaged now in a single interest, a common obsession. And there seemed to be only one rule, a dominant and infallible law—to buy, always to buy, to pay whatever price was asked and to sell again within two days at whatever price one chose to fix. It was fantastic: within the town, along any of its streets, the property was being sold by the inch, the foot—thousands of dollars were being paid for each front foot of earth along these streets, and when the supply of streets was exhausted, new streets were created feverishly, and even before these streets were paved or a house had been built upon them, the land was being sold by the inch, the foot, for hundreds and thousands of dollars.

A spirit of drunken waste and wild destructiveness was everywhere apparent: the fairest places in town were mutilated at a cost of millions of dollars. In the center of town, for instance, there was a beautiful green hill, opulent with rich lawn and lordly trees, with beds of flowers and banks of honeysuckle, and surmounted with an immense rambling old wooden hotel. It was a glorious old place which was a labyrinth of wings and corridors, of great parlors, porches, halls, and courts, which had for forty years been the most delightful place in town, and from which as lovely and magical a landscape as the earth can offer—the vast panorama of the ranges of the "Smokies"—could be seen. Now they advanced upon this enchanted hill.

John could remember the immense and rambling old hotel with its wide porches and comfortable rockers, its countless eaves and gables, elfin, Gothic, capricious, and fantastic, the thick red carpets of the wide corridors, and the old lobby, a place of old red leather hollowed and shaped by the backs of men, of the smells of tobacco and the iced tinkle of tall drinks. It had a splendid mellow dining-room filled with laughter and quiet voices, and unctuous expert niggers, bending and scraping and chuckling with glee over the jokes of the rich men from the North as with prayerful grace they served them delicious foods out of old silver dishes.

He could remember all these things as well as the tender or smiling looks and glances of the glorious women, the rich men's wives and daughters. And he would be touched with the unutterable mystery of all these things— of beauty and wealth and fame, and of these splendid travelers who had come great distances, who brought with them somehow a marvelous evocation of the whole golden and unvisited world, with its thousand fabulous cities and with all its proud, passionate song of glory, fame, and love.

Now this was gone: an army of men and shovels had advanced upon this great green hill and leveled it down to an ugly mound of clay, and they had paved that clay with a desolate horror of hard white concrete, they had built stores and garages and office buildings and parking spaces—raw and new— and they had built a new hotel where the old one was. It was a structure of sixteen stories of pressed brick and concrete, harsh and sharp and raw, which seemed to have been stamped out of the same mold as a thousand others throughout the country by some gigantic biscuit-cutter of hotels, and which was called, sumptuously, the Ritz-Altamont.

V

Suddenly, one day, in the midst of this glittering tumult, he met Robert Weaver, a classmate at college, and a boyhood friend. He came down the thronging street swiftly at his anxious lunging stride, and immediately, without a word of greeting, broke hoarsely into the abrupt and fragmentary speech that had always been characteristic of him, but that now, in the pulsing stimulation of this atmosphere, seemed feverish and emphasized.

"When did you get here? . . . How long are you going to stay? . . . What do you think of the way things look here?" Then, without waiting for an answer, he demanded with a brusque, challenging, and almost impatient scornfulness: "Well, what do you intend to do—be a two-thousand-dollar-a-year school-teacher all your life?"

The contemptuous tone with its implication of superiority—an implication which among this swarm of excited people big with their importance of imagined achievement and great wealth he had felt keenly since his return—now stung John to retort sharply:

"There are worse things than teaching school! Being a paper millionaire is one of them! As for the two thousand dollars a year, you really get it, Robert. It's not real estate money, it's money you can spend. You can buy a ham sandwich with it."

He laughed sharply. "You're right!" he said. "I don't blame you. It's the truth!" He began to shake his head slowly. "Lord, Lord!" he said. "They've all gone clean out of their heads here . . . Never saw anything like it in my life . . . Why, they're all crazy as a loon," he swore. "You can't talk to them . . . You can't reason with them . . . They won't listen to you . . . They're getting prices for property here you couldn't get in New York."

"Are they *getting* it?"

"Well," he said, with a falsetto laugh, "they get the first five hundred dollars . . . You pay the next five hundred thousand on time."

"How much time?"

"God!" he said, "I don't know . . . All you want, I reckon . . . Forever . . . It doesn't matter . . . You sell the next day for a million."

"On time?"

"That's it!" he cried, laughing. "You make a half million just like that."

"On time?"

"You've got it!" said Robert. "On time . . . God! Crazy, crazy, crazy." He kept laughing and shaking his head. "That's the way they make it," he said.

"Are you making it, too?"

His manner at once became feverish, earnest, and excited: "Why, it's the damnedest thing you ever heard of!" he said. "I'm raking it in hand over fist . . . Made three hundred thousand dollars in the last two months . . . Why, it's the truth! . . . Made a trade yesterday and turned around and sold the lot again not two hours later. . . . Fifty thousand dollars just like that!" he snapped his fingers. "Does your mother want to sell that house on Spring Street? . . . Have you talked to her about it? . . . Would she consider an offer?"

"Yes, if she gets enough."

"How much does she want?" he demanded impatiently. "Would she talk two hundred and fifty thousand?"

"Could you get it for her?"

"I could get it within twenty-four hours," he said. "I know a man who'd snap it up in five minutes . . . I'll tell you what I'll do, John. If you persuade her to sell, I'll split the commission with you . . . I'll give you five thousand dollars."

"All right, Robert, it's a go. Could you let me have fifty cents on account?"

"Do you think she'll sell?" he said feverishly.

"I don't think so. I think she's going to hold on."

"Hold on! What's she going to hold on for? Now's the time when things are at the peak. She'll never get a better offer!"

"I know, but we're expecting to strike oil out in the backyard at any time now."

At this moment there was a brilliant disturbance among the tides of traffic in the street. A magnificent motor car detached itself from the stream of humbler vehicles and crawled in swiftly to the curb where it came to a smooth stop—a panther of opulent machinery, a glitter of nickel, glass, and burnished steel. From it, a gaudily attired creature stepped down to the pavement with an air of princely indolence, tucked a light malacca cane carelessly under its right arm-pit, and slowly and fastidiously withdrew from its nicotined fingers a pair of lemon gloves, at the same time saying to the liveried driver: "You may go, James. Call for me again in hal-luf and houah!"

The creature's face was thin, sunken, and as swarthy as a Mexican's; its coal-black eyes glittered with the unnatural fires of the drug addict; its toothless jaws had been so bountifully furnished forth with a set of glittering false teeth that they now grinned and clattered at the world with the prognathous bleakness of a skeleton. The whole figure, although heavy and shambling, had a caved-in and tottering appearance that suggested a stupendous debauchery. It moved forward with its false bleak grin, leaning heavily upon the stick, and suddenly John recognized that native ruin which had been known to him since childhood as Rufus—or Rufe—Mears.

VI

J. Rufus Mears—the "J" was a recent and completely arbitrary addition of his own, fitting in, no doubt, with his ideas of financial and personal grandeur and matching the dizzy pinnacle at the summit of the town's affairs on which he was now perched—was the black sheep of a worthy and industrious family in the community.

From the beginning, Rufe's career had been lurid, capricious, and disgraceful. A dark and corrupt energy was boiling ceaselessly within him to wrest a living and quick wealth from life in some shady and precarious fashion. He was haunted constantly by the apparition of "easy money." On one occasion he had been sentenced to a term in jail for operating gambling machines; on another he had been sent to the chain gang for running a "blind tiger"; on yet another, he had got into serious difficulties when he began to tour the small towns in the district with a burlesque musical show, the chorus of which had been recruited from ignorant girls in the neighborhood who had had no experience in the theater whatever and were lured into the unsavory enterprise by Rufe's plausible dark tongue.

In recent years, his physical and mental disintegration had been marked; he had become an addict of cocaine, and his swarthy eyes usually burned with a feverish drugged glitter. It was well known that he was no longer mentally responsible for his acts. He had spent other terms in prison, and once, after having telegraphed to the morning newspaper a thrilling and moving account of his death by violence in another city, he had been sent for a period to the State asylum for the insane.

This was Rufe Mears as John remembered him, and as all of them had seen and known him, and who now stood before them in the fantastic trappings of a clown of royalty, the visible and supreme embodiment of their unbelievable and extravagant madness. For, like gamblers who will stake a fortune on some moment's whimsy of belief or superstition, thrusting their money in a stranger's hand and bidding him to play with it because the color of his eye is lucky, or as race-track men will rub the hump upon a cripple's back to bring them luck, the people of the town now listened prayerfully to every word that Rufe Mears might utter. They greedily sought his opinion in all their staggering speculations, and they acted instantly on his suggestion or command. He had become—in what way, for what reason, upon what proof of competence no one knew—the high priest and prophet of this insanity of waste.

They knew that he was witless, that he was criminal, that he was drugged, diseased, and broken, but they used him as men once used divining rods, they deferred to him as people in Russia were said to have deferred to idiots in the village—with an absolute and incredible faith that some divine power of intuition in him made all his judgments infallible. It was this creature who now stood before them, on whom already the respectful gaze of the passerby was directed, and to whom Robert now turned with a movement of feverish eagerness, saying to John abruptly and peremptorily as he left him: "Wait a minute . . . I've got to speak to Rufe Mears about something . . . Wait till I come back."

John watched the astounding scene—Rufe Mears still drawing the gloves off his stained and yellowed fingers with that movement of bored casualness, walked over toward the entrance to the drug store, while Robert, in an attitude of obsequious entreaty, kept at his elbow, bent his tall stiff form toward him, and hoarsely and abruptly poured a torrent of frenzied interrogation of which John could hear glittering fragments. ". . . Property in West Altamont . . . Seventy-five thousand dollars . . . Option expires tomorrow at noon . . . John Ingram has the piece above mine . . . Won't sell. . . . Holding for hundred fifty . . . Mine's the best location . . . But Fred Bynum says too far from the main road. . . . What do you think, Rufe? . . . Is it worth it?"

During the course of this torrential appeal Rufe Mears did not even once turn to look at his petitioner. In fact, he gave no evidence whatever that he was paying the slightest attention to what Robert was saying. Instead, he finished taking off his gloves, thrust them in his pocket, cast his glittering eye feverishly around in a series of disordered glances, and suddenly grew rigid, shuddering convulsively, and began to root into himself violently with a clutching, thrusting hand. This operation completed, he shuddered once again and, like a man who is just coming out of a trance, seemed for the first time to become aware that Robert was waiting in an attitude of prayerful entreaty.

"What's that? What did you say, Robert?" he said rapidly in his dark drugged tone. "How much did they offer you for it? . . . Don't sell . . . Don't sell!" he said suddenly and with violent emphasis. "Now is the time to buy, not to sell . . . The trend is upwards . . . Don't sell . . . . That's my advice!"

"I'm not selling, Rufe," Robert cried excitedly. "I'm thinking of buying."

"Oh yes, yes, yes!" Rufe muttered rapidly. "I see, I see . . . " He turned abruptly for the first time and fixed his glittering eye upon his questioner. "Where did you say it was?" he demanded sharply. "Rosemont. . . . Good. . . . Good! . . . Can't go wrong! Buy! Buy!"

Suddenly he started to walk away into the drug-store; the lounging idlers split obsequiously. Robert rushed after him frantically, and caught him by the arm, shouting, "No, no, Rufe! It's not Rosemont! It's the other way . . . I've been telling you . . . It's West Altamont!"

"What's that?" Rufe cried sharply. "West Altamont . . . Why didn't you say so? . . . That's different! Buy! Buy! . . . Can't go wrong! . . . Whole town's moving in that direction . . . Values double out there in six months . . . How much do they want?"

"Seventy-five thousand," Robert panted. "Option expires tomorrow . . . Five years to pay it up . . . The old Buckner place, only fifteen minutes away!"

"Buy! Buy!" Rufe barked, and began to walk away into the store at a lunging and disjointed step, as if his legs would fly away below him at any moment.

Robert turned and strode back toward John, his eyes blazing with excitement, his every stride and gesture a fierce interrogation.

"Did you hear him? Did you hear what he said?" he demanded hoarsely. "You heard him, didn't you? . . . Best damned judge of real estate that ever lived . . . Never known to make a mistake! . . . Buy! Buy! . . . Will double in value in six months . . . You were standing right here?" he said hoarsely and accusingly, glaring at him. "You heard what he said, didn't you?"

"Yes. I heard him."

Robert glanced wildly and confusedly about him, passed his hand feverishly through his hair several times, and then said, sighing heavily and shaking his head in a movement of astonished wonderment: "Seventy-five thousand dollars' profit in one deal! . . . Never heard anything like it in my life! . . . Lord, Lord!" he cried. "What are we coming to?"

VII

On Sunday afternoon, the mother and her two sons drove out to the only plot of land in town which had been preserved from the furious invasion of the real estate men. This was the cemetery, where all the members of their family who had died were buried.

On the way out, as they drove through the streets of the town, the mother, who was sitting in the back seat of the car, kept up a constant, panoramic, and exhaustive commentary on the speculative history of every piece of property they passed. She talked incessantly about real estate, pausing from time to time to nod deliberately to herself in a movement of strong affirmation, gesturing briefly and casually with her strong wide hand, and meditating her speech frequently with the strong lips of deliberative silence.

"You see, don't you," she said, nodding slowly to herself with a movement of conviction and tranquilly indifferent whether they listened or not so long as the puppets of an audience were before her. "You see what they're goin' to do here, don't you? Why, Fred Arthur, Roy McIntyre, and Dr. Gibbs—all that crowd—why, yes—here! Say!" she cried, frowning meditatively. "Wasn't I reading it? Didn't it all come out in the paper—why, here, you know, a week or two ago—how they proposed to tear down that whole block of buildings there and were going to put up the finest garage in this part of the country. Oh! say, it will take up the whole block, you know, with a fine eight-story building over it, with storage space upstairs for more cars, and doctors' offices—why, yes! they're even thinking of puttin' in a roof garden and a big restaurant on top. Say, the whole thing will cost 'em over half a million dollars before they're done with it—oh, paid two thousand dollars a foot for every inch of it!" she cried. "But pshaw! Why, those are

Main Street prices—you can get business property up in town for *that!*—I could have told him—but hm!"—again the scornful little tremor of the head—"He'll never do it—no, sir! He'll be lucky if he gets out with his skin!"

Near the cemetery they passed a place beside the road where an unpaved road of clay went upward among fields toward some lonely pines. The place beside the road was flanked by two portaled shapes of hewn granite blocks set there like markers of a splendid city yet unbuilt which would rise grandly from the hills that swept back into the green wilderness from the river—this and a large sign planted in the field was all.

But even as they passed by this loneliness of field and pine and waning light, they read some words upon the sign. The large word on the top was RIVERCREST—and down below they saw in small letters the word "Dedicated."

"Hah? What say?" she cried out in a sharply startled tone. "What does it say below? Dedicated?"

"Wait a minute!" Lee cried abruptly, jamming his large flat foot onto the brake so violently that they were flung forward with a stunning jolt. They halted with a jarring skid and peered out at the letters of the sign:

RIVERCREST
Dedicated to All the People of This
Section and to the Glory of the Greater
City They Will Build.

They read the words in silence for a moment, and then she repeated them slowly and with obvious satisfaction. "Ah-hah!" she said, nodding her head slowly with deliberate agreement, "that's just exactly it!" Then they started to move on again.

"Dedicated!" Lee muttered to himself. "Dedicated to all the people of this section," he muttered distractedly, pushing his clumsy fingers through his hair. "To the glory of the Greater City they will build. . . . Uh-huh! Ah-hah!" he sang out madly. "Dedicated! . . . Now ain't that nice," he said slowly, and in a tone of mincing and delicate refinement. "Dedicated to the service of all the people of this section." The crazy grin split wide and sudden on his handsome face. *"Haw-w!"* he yelled suddenly and smote himself upon the temple with the heel of his large and clumsy hand. "Dedicated to cutting your goddamn throat and bleeding you white of every nickel that you've got. Dedicated! Haw-w! Whah *whah!*"

When they got to the cemetery, they drove slowly in around a circling road and at length came to a halt on the rounded crest of the hill where the family burial lot was situated. It was a good lot—perhaps the best one on the hill—and it looked out across the deep dense green of the wooded slopes and hollows toward the central business part of town. The ramparts, spires, and buildings of the town, the old ones as well as the splendid new ones—the hotels, office buildings, garages, and arcades and concrete squares of boom development which exploded from the old design with glittering violence—were plainly visible. It was a fine view.

For a moment, after getting out of the car, the mother stood looking at the burial lot, her strong hands loosely clasped across her waist. Then shaking her head rapidly with a pursed mouth of depreciation and regret, she said: "Hm! Hm! Hm! Too bad, too bad, too bad!"

"What's that, mama?" Lee said. "What's too bad?"

"Why, that they should have ever chosen such a place as this for the cemetery," she said regretfully. "Why, as I told Frank Candler just the other day, they've gone and deliberately given away the two best building sites in town to the niggers and the dead people! That's just exactly what they've done! I've always said as much—that the two finest building sites in town for natural beauty are Niggertown and Riverview Cemetery. I could have told them that long years ago—they should have known as much themselves if any of them could have seen an inch beyond his nose—that someday the town would grow up and this would be valuable property! Why, why on earth! When they were looking for a cemetery site—why on earth didn't they think of findin' one across the river, up there on Patton Hill, say, where you get a beautiful view—out of town somewhere, where property is not so valuable? But *this!*" she cried. "This by rights is *building* property! And as for the niggers, I've always said that they'd have been better off if they were put down there on those old flats in the depot section! Now it's too late, of course,—nothin' can be done—but it was certainly a grave mistake," she said, and shook her head. "I've always known it."

"Well, I guess you're right," Lee muttered absently. "I never thought of it before, but I guess you're right."

"And to think," the mother went on in a moment, with that curious fragmentary semblance of irrelevance which was not irrelevant at all, "—and to think that he would go and move her—to think that any man could be so hard-hearted as to—o-oh!" She shuddered with a brief convulsive pucker of revulsion. "It makes my blood run cold to think of it—and I told him so!— to think he would have no more mercy in him than to go and move her from the place where she lay buried."

"Why, who was that, mama?" Lee said absently. "Move who?"

"Why, Lydia, of course, child!" she said impatiently, gesturing briefly to the old and weather-rusted stone beneath which her husband's first wife lay buried. "That's the thing that started all this moving! We'd never have thought of coming here if it hadn't been for Lydia!—And here," she cried fretfully, "the woman had been dead and in her grave more than a year when he gets this notion in his head he's got to move her—and you couldn't reason wuth him! You couldn't argue wuth him!" she cried with vehement surprise. "I tried to talk to him about it, but it was like talking to a stone wall—no, sir!" Here, with a movement of strong decision, she shook her head. "He'd made up his mind, he was determined—and he wouldn't budge from it an inch! . . . 'But see here, man,' I said. 'The thing's not right!—The woman ought to stay where she's buried!' I didn't like the look of it! 'Even the dead have got their rights,' I said"—again the powerful short tremor of the face—"'Where the tree falls there let it lie!'—but no! he wouldn't listen, you couldn't talk to him. He says, 'I'll move her if it's the last thing I ever live to do! I'll move her if I have to dig her up myself and carry the coffin on my back to Riverview—but that's where she's going, and you needn't argue any more!' Well, I saw then that he had his mind made up and that it wouldn't do any good to talk to him about it. But oh! an *awful* mistake, an awful mistake!" she muttered with the powerful short movement of the head—"All that moving and expense for nothing—if he'd felt that way he should have gone to Riverview in the beginning when she died—but that's when he bought this lot, all right," she now said tranquilly—"And that's the reason that the rest of them are buried here. That's how it was all right," she said, "but I've always regretted it! I was against it from the start."

And for a moment she was silent, looking with the contemplation of a grave-eyed memory at the weather-rusted stone.

"Well, as I say, then," she went on calmly, "when I saw he had his mind made up and that there was no use to try to change him—Well, I went out to the old cemetery the day they moved her—oh! one of those raw windy days you get in March! The very kind of day she died on. And old Mrs. Wrenn and Amy Williamson—of course, they had both been good friends of Lydia's—they went along, too. And, of course, when we got out there, they were curious, they wanted to have a look, you know," she went on calmly, describing this grisly desire with no surprise whatever, "and they tried to get me to take a look at it, too. 'No,' I said. 'You go on and satisfy your curiosity if that's what you want to do, but I won't look at it!' I said, 'I'd rather remember her the way she was.' Well, they went ahead and did it, then. They got old Prov—you know, he was the old nigger man that worked for us—to open up the coffin, and I turned my back and walked away a little piece until they got through lookin'," she said tranquilly, "and pretty soon, I heard them comin'. Well, I turned around and looked at them, and let me tell you something," she said gravely, "their faces were a study. Oh, they turned pale and they trembled. 'Well, are you satisfied?' I said. 'Did you find what you were lookin' for?' 'Oh-h,' says old Mrs. Wrenn, pale as a ghost, shakin' and wringin' her hands, you know, 'Oh, Delia,' she says, 'it was awful. I'm sorry that I looked,' she said.

"'Ah-hah!' I says. 'What did I tell you! You see, don't you?' Says, 'Oh-h, it was all gone—all gone—all rotted away to nothing so you couldn't recognize her. The face was all gone until you could see the teeth, and the nails had all grown out long—but Delia!' she says, 'the hair!—the hair!—oh! I tell you what,' she says, 'the hair was beautiful! It had grown out until it covered everything—the finest head of hair I ever saw on anyone. But the rest of it—oh! I'm sorry that I looked!' she says. 'Well, I thought so! I thought so!' I said. 'I knew you'd be sorry, so I wouldn't look!'—But that's the way it was all right," she concluded with the tranquil satisfaction of omniscience.

VIII

At one corner of the burial lot a tall locust tree was growing: its pleasant shade was divided between the family lot and the adjacent one where members of the mother's family, the Pentlands, had been buried. The gravestones in the family lot (which was set on a gentle slope) were arranged in two parallel rows. In the first row were buried John's brothers, Arthur McFarlane Hawke and Edward Madison Hawke, who were twins: also his mother's first child, Margaret Ann.

Facing these was the family monument. It was a square massive chunk of gray metallic granite, brilliantly burnished, one of the finest and most imposing monuments in the cemetery. It bore the family name in raised letters upon its shining surface, and on each end were inscriptions for his father and his mother. His father was buried at the end of the monument which faced the town. His inscription read: "William Oliver Hawke—Born near Gettysburg, Pennsylvania, April 16, 1851—Died, Altamont, Old Catawba, June 21, 1922." The mother's inscription was at the other end of the monument, facing her own people, and read: "Delia Elizabeth Hawke—née Pentland—Born at the Forks of Ivy, Old Catawba, February 16, 1860— Died—"

All of the monuments, save his father's and mother's, had, in addition to the name and birth and death inscription, a little elegiac poem, carved in a fine italicized script, and reading somewhat as follows:

> *Still is the voice we knew so well*
> *Vanished the face we love*
> *Flown his spirit pure to dwell*
> *With Angels up above.*
> *Ours is the sorrow, ours the pain*
> *And ours the joy alone*
> *To clasp him in our arms again*
> *In Heaven by God's throne.*

In the drowsy waning light of the late afternoon, John could see people moving across the great hill of the dead, among the graves and monuments of other burial lots. The place had the brooding hush a cemetery has on a summer day, and in the fading light even the figures of the people had a dream-like and almost phantasmal quality as they moved about.

The mother stood surveying the scene reflectively, her hands held at the waist in their loose strong clasp. She looked at the gravestones in the family lot, reading the little elegiac verses, and although she had read these banal phrases a thousand times, she did so again with immense satisfaction, framing the words with her lips and then nodding her head slowly and deliberately in a movement of emphatic affirmation, as if to say: "Ah-hah! That's it exactly!"

For a moment longer, she stood looking at the stones. Then she went over to Ed's grave, picked up a wreath of laurel leaves which someone had left there a few weeks before, and which had already grown withered and faded looking, and set it at the head of the grave against the base of the stone. Then she moved about among the graves, bending with a blunt, strong movement and weeding out tufts of the coarse grass which had grown weedily about the bases of some of the monuments.

When she had finished, she stood looking down at Margaret's stone, which was weathered, stained, and rusty looking. She read the inscription of the old faded letters, and then turning to her youngest son, spoke quietly:

"This morning at eight o'clock, thirty-nine years ago, I lost the first child that I ever had. Your sister Margaret died today—July the fourteenth—four days less than nine months old. She was the most perfect baby I ever saw— the brightest and most sensible child for her age." And again she nodded her head slowly and deliberately, in a movement of powerful affirmation.

"Time went on, I had other children, kept my hands full, and to a certain degree," she said reflectively, "kept my mind off sorrow. No time for sorrow!" cried the mother, with the strong convulsive tremor of the head. "Too much to do for sorrow! . . . Then, when years had passed, the hardest blow of all fell. Arthur was taken. It seemed I had given up all. Could have borne as well if all the others had been taken! I can't understand why!" And for a moment her brown worn eyes were wet. "But it had grown a part of me—felt somehow that he was to lead the others, and when I realized that he was gone, it seemed that everything was lost.

"I never got to know Ed," she said quietly. "I always wanted to talk to him, but could not. I felt a part of him was gone—maybe he felt so, too. It was hard to give Ed up, but I had suffered the first great loss in giving up his twin, the other part."

She paused, looking down at the two tombstones for a moment, and then said gravely and proudly: "I believe that they have joined each other, and if they are happy, I'll be reconciled. I believe I'll meet them in a Higher Sphere, along with all the members of our family—all happy and all leading a new life."

She was silent for another moment, and then, with a movement of strong decision, she turned away and looked out toward the town where already the evening lights were going on, were burning hard and bright and steady in the dusk.

"Come now, my sonny boys!" she cried briskly and cheerfully. "It's getting dark, and there are people waiting for us.

"Son," she said, laying her broad hand on John's shoulder in a warm, strong, and easy gesture, and speaking in the old half-bantering manner that she had used so often when he was a child, "I've been a long time livin' on this earth, and as the fellow says, the world do move. You've got your life ahead of you, and lots to learn and many things to do, but let me tell you something, boy!" and for a moment she looked at him in a sudden, straight, and deadly fashion, with a faint smile around the edges of her mouth. "Go out and see the world, and get your fill of wanderin', and then," she cried, "come back and tell me if you've found a better place than home! I've seen great changes in my time, and I'll see many more before I die, and there are great things yet in store for us—great progress, great inventions, it will all come true. Perhaps I'll not live to see it, but you *will!* We've got a fine town here, and we've got fine people here to make it go, and we're not done yet. I've seen it all grow up out of a country village—and some day we will have a great city here."

IX

A great city? These words, he knew, had come straight from his mother's heart, from all the invincible faith of her brave spirit which had endured the anguish, grief, and suffering of a hundred lives and which would never change. That unshaken spirit would, he knew, face toward the future to the last hour of her life with this same unyielding confidence, and would be triumphant over all the ruinous error and mischance of life. And for her, he knew, this "great city" that she spoke of now was the city of her heart, her faith, her spirit—the city of the everlasting future, and her quenchless hope, the fortunate, good, and happy life that some day she was sure would be found here on the earth for all men living.

But that other city, this glittering and explosive shape of man's destructive fury which now stood sharply in their vision in the evening light—what did the future hold for that place and its people? In this strange and savage hunger for what she had spoken of as a better life, a greater city, in this delirium of intoxication which drove them on, there was really a fatal and desperate quality, as if what they hungered for was ruin and death. It seemed to him that they were ruined: it seemed that even when they laughed and shouted and smote one another on the back, the knowledge of their ruin was in them—and they did not care, they were drunk and mad and amorous of death.

But under all their flash and play of life, the paucity of their designs—the starved meagerness of their lives—was already apparent to them. The better life resolved itself into a few sterile and baffled gestures—they built an ugly and expensive house and bought a car and joined a country club; they built a larger, uglier, and more expensive house, bought a more expensive car, and joined a larger and more expensive country club—they pursued this routine through all the repetitions of an idiot monotony, building new houses, new streets, new country clubs with a frenzied haste, a wild extravagance, but nowhere was there food to feed their hunger, drink to assuage their thirst. They were stricken and lost, starved squirrels chasing furiously the treadmill of a revolving cage, and they saw it, and they knew it.

A wave of ruinous and destructive energy had welled up in them—they had squandered fabulous sums in meaningless streets and bridges, they had torn down the ancient public buildings, court house, and city hall, and erected new ones, fifteen stories tall and large enough to fill the needs of a city of a million people; they had leveled hills and bored through mountains, building magnificent tunnels paved with double roadways and glittering with shining tiles—tunnels which leaped out on the other side into Arcadian wilderness. It was mad, infuriate, ruinous; they had flung away the earnings of a lifetime and mortgaged those of a generation to come; they had ruined themselves, their children and their city, and nothing could be done to stop them.

Already the town had passed from their possession, they no longer owned it, it was mortgaged under a debt of fifty million dollars, owned by bonding companies in the North. The very streets they walked on had been sold beneath their feet—and still they bought, bought, bought, signing their names to papers calling for the payment of a king's ransom for forty feet of earth, reselling the next day to other mad men who signed away their lives with the same careless magnificence. On paper, their profits were fabulous, but their "boom" was already over, and they could not see it. They were staggering below obligations to pay that none of them could meet—and still they bought.

And then, when it seemed that they had exhausted all the possibilities of ruin and extravagance in town, they had rushed out into the wilderness, into the calm eternity of the hills, into the lyrical immensities of wild earth where there was land enough for all men living, where any man could take as much earth as he needed, and they had madly staked off little plots and wedges of the wilderness, as one might try to stake a picket fence out in the middle of the ocean. They had given fancy names to all their plots and stakings—"Wild Boulders"—"Shady Acres"—"Eagle's Crest." They set prices to an acre of the wilderness that might have bought a mountain, and made charts and drawings, showing populous and glittering communities of shops, houses, streets, roads, and clubs in regions where there was no road, no street, no house, and which could not be reached in any way save by a group of resolute and desperate pioneers armed with axes, or by airplane.

These places were to be transformed into idyllic colonies for artists and critics and writers—all the artists and critics and writers in the nation—and there were colonies as well for preachers, doctors, actors, dancers, golfplayers, and retired locomotive engineers. There were colonies for everyone, and what is more, they sold them!

It was the month of July 1929—that fatal year which brought ruin to millions of people all over the country. They were now drunk with an imagined victory, pressing and shouting in the dusty tumult of the battle, most beaten where they thought their triumph the greatest, so that the desolate and barren panorama of their ruin would not be clearly known to them for several years to come.

X

And now, as John stood there looking at this new strange town, this incredible explosion of a town which had gone mad and frenzied over night, he suddenly remembered the barren night-time streets of the town he had known so well in his childhood. The gaunt pattern of their dreary and unpeopled desolation had burned its acid print upon his memory. Bare, wintry, and deserted—by ten o'clock at night those streets had been an aching monotony and weariness of hard light and empty pavements, a frozen torpor broken only occasionally by the footfalls of some prowler of the night, by desperate famished lonely men who hoped past hope and past belief for some haven of comfort, warmth, and love there in the wilderness, for the sudden opening of a magic door into some secret, rich, and more exultant life. They never found it. They were dying in the darkness, and they knew it—without a goal, a wall, a certain purpose, or a door.

For that was the way the thing had come. That was the way the thing had happened. Yes, it was there—on many a night long past and wearily accomplished in ten thousand little towns and in ten million barren streets where all the passion, hope, and hunger of the famished men beat like a great pulse through the fields of night—it was there and nowhere else that all this madness had been brewed.

And yet, what really had changed in life? Below their feet, the earth was still and everlasting as it had always been. And around them in the cemetery the air brooded with a lazy drowsy warmth. There was the cry of the sweet-singing birds again, the sudden thrumming of bullet noises in undergrowth and leaf, and the sharp cricketing stitch of afternoon, the broken lazy sounds from far away, a voice in the wind, a boy's shout, a cry, the sound of a bell, as well as all the drowsy fragrance of a thousand warm intoxicating odors—the resinous smell of pine, and the smells of grass and warm sweet clover. It was all as it had always been, but the town where he had spent his childhood and which lay stretched out before him in the evening light had changed past recognition: the town, with its quiet streets and the old frame houses, which were almost obscured beneath the massed leafy spread of trees, was now scarred with hard raw patches of concrete on which the sun fell wearily, or with raw clumps and growths of new construction—skyscrapers, garages, hotels, glittering residential atrocities of stucco and raw brick—or it was scored and scarred harshly by new streets and roads.

The place looked like a battle field; it was cratered and shelltorn with savage explosions of brick and concrete all over town. And in the interspaces the embowered remnants of the old and pleasant town remained, timid, retreating, overwhelmed, to remind one, in all this harsh new din, of foot-falls in a quiet street as men went home at noon, of laughter and quiet voices and the leafy rustle of the night. For this was lost!

This image of his loss, and theirs, had passed through his mind with the speed of light, the instancy of thought, and now he heard his mother's voice again:

"And you'll come back!" he heard her saying. "There's no better or more beautiful place on earth than in these mountains, boy—and some day you'll come back again," she cried with all the invincible faith and hopefulness of her strong heart.

An old and tragic light was shining like the light of dreams on the rocky little river which he had seen somewhere, somehow, from the windows of a train long, long ago, in his childhood, somewhere before memory began, and which wound its deathless magic in his heart forever. And that old and tragic light of fading day shone faintly on their faces, and suddenly they were fixed there like a prophecy with the hills and river all around them— and there was something lost, intolerable, foretold, and come to pass, and like old time and destiny—some magic that he could not say.

Down by the river's edge in darkness he heard the bell, the whistle, and the pounding wheel. It brought to him, as it had done ten thousand times in childhood, its great promise of morning, new lands, and a shining city.

And now, receding, far and faint, he heard again the whistle of the great train pounding on the rails across the river. It swept away from them, leaving the lost and lonely thunder of its echoes in the hills, the flame-flare of its terrific furnace for a moment, and then just heavy wheels and rumbling loaded cars—and, finally, nothing but the silence it had left behind it.

Now, even farther off and almost lost, he heard for the last time its wailing and receding cry, bringing to him again all its wild and secret prophecy, its pain of going, and its triumphant promise of new lands. He saw them fixed forever in his vision, and the lonely light was shining on their faces, and he felt an intolerable pain, an unutterable joy and triumph, as he knew that he would leave them. And something in his heart was saying like a demon's whisper of unbodied joy that spoke of flight and darkness, new earth he could touch and make his own again: Soon! Soon! Soon!

Then they all got into the car again and drove rapidly away from the green hill of the dead, the woman toward the certitude of lights, the people, and the town; the young man toward the train, the city, and the voyages— all of the gold-bright waters of the morning, the seas, the harbors, and the magic of the ships.

The Sun and the Rain

When he awoke, he was filled with a numb excitement. It was a gray wintry day with snow in the air, and he expected something to happen. He had this feeling often in the country in France: it was a strange mixed feeling of desolation and homelessness, of wondering with a ghostly emptiness why he was there—and a momentary feeling of joy, and hope, and expectancy, without knowing what it was he was going to find.

In the afternoon he went down to the station and a took a train that was going to Orléans. He did not know where Orléans was. The train was a mixed train, made up of goods cars and passenger compartments. He bought a third-class ticket and got into one of the compartments. Then the shrill little whistle blew, and the train rattled out of Chartres into the countryside, in the abrupt and casual way a little French train has, and that was disquieting to him.

There was a light mask of snow on the fields, and the air was smoky: the whole earth seemed to smoke and steam and from the windows of the train one could see the wet earth and the striped cultivated pattern of the fields, and now and then some farm buildings. It did not look like America: the land looked fat and well kept, and even the smoky wintry woods had this well-kept appearance. Far off sometimes one could see the tall lines of poplars and knew there was water there.

In the compartment he found three people—an old peasant and his wife and daughter. The old peasant had sprouting mustaches, a seamed and weather-beaten face, and small rheumy-looking eyes. His hands had a rock-like heaviness and solidity, and he kept them clasped upon his knees. His wife's face was smooth and brown, there were fine webs of wrinkles around her eyes, and her face was like an old brown bowl. The daughter had a dark sullen face and sat away from them next to the window as if she were ashamed of them. From time to time when they spoke to her she would answer them in an infuriated kind of voice without looking at them.

The peasant began to speak amiably to him when he entered the compartment. He smiled and grinned back at the man, although he did not understand a word the man was saying, and the peasant kept on talking then, thinking he understood.

The peasant took from his coat a package of the cheap powerful to-bacco—the *'bleu*—which the French Government provides for a few cents for the poor, and prepared to stuff his pipe. The young man pulled a pack-age of American cigarettes from his pocket and offered them to the peasant.

"Will you have one?"

"My faith, yes!" said the peasant.

He took a cigarette clumsily from the package and held it between his great stiff fingers, then held it up to the flame the young man offered, puff-ing at it in an unaccustomed way. Then he fell to examining it curiously, revolving it in his hands to read the label. He turned to his wife, who had followed every movement of this simple transaction with the glittering in-tent eyes of an animal, and began a rapid and excited discussion with her.

"It's American, this."

"Is it good?"

"My faith, yes—it's of good quality."

"Here, let me see! What does it call itself?"

They stared dumbly at the label.

"What do you call this?" said the peasant to the young man.

"Licky Streek," said the youth, dutifully phonetical.

"L-L-Leek-ee?" they stared doubtfully. "What does that wish to say in French?"

"*Je ne sais pas,*" he answered.

"Where are you going?" the peasant said, staring at the youth with rheumy little eyes of fascinated curiosity.

"Orléans."

"How?" the peasant asked with a puzzled look on his face.

"Orléans."

"I do not understand," the peasant said.

"Orléans! Orléans!" the girl shouted in a furious tone. "The gentleman says he is going to Orléans."

"Ah!" the peasant cried with an air of sudden illumination. "*Orléans!*"

It seemed to the youth that he had said the word just the same way the peasant said it, but he repeated again:

"Yes, Orléans."

"He is going to Orléans," the peasant said, turning to his wife.

"Ah-h!" she cried knowingly, with a great air of illumination; then both fell silent, and began to stare at the youth with curious eyes again.

"What region are you from?" the peasant asked presently, still intent and puzzled, staring at him with his small eyes.

"How's that? I don't understand."

"I say—what region are you from?"

"The gentleman is not French!" the girl shouted, as if exasperated by their stupidity. "He is a foreigner. Can't you see that?"

"Ah-h!" the peasant cried, after a moment, with an air of astounded enlightenment. Then, turning to his wife, he said briefly, "He is not French. He is a stranger."

"Ah-h!"

And they both turned their small round eyes on him and regarded him with a fixed, animal-like attentiveness.

"From what country are you?" the peasant asked presently. "What are you?"

"I am an American."

"Ah-h! An American. . . . He is an American," he said, turning to his wife.

"Ah-h!"

The girl made an impatient movement and continued to stare sullenly out the window.

Then the peasant, with the intent curiosity of an animal, began to examine his companion carefully from head to foot. He looked at his shoes, his clothes, his overcoat, and finally lifted his eyes to the young man's valise on the rack above his head. He nudged his wife and pointed to the valise.

"That's good stuff, eh?" he said in a low voice. "It's real leather."

"Yes, it's good, that."

And both of them looked at the valise for some time and then turned their curious gaze upon the youth again. He offered the peasant another cigarette, and the old man took one, thanking him.

"It's very fine, this," he said, indicating the cigarette. "That costs dear, eh?"

"Six francs."

"Ah-h! . . . that's very dear," and he began to look at the cigarette with increased respect.

"Why are you going to Orléans?" he asked presently. "Do you know someone there?"

"No, I am just going to see the town."

"How?" The peasant blinked at him uncomprehendingly. "You have business there?"

"No. I am going just to visit—to see the place."

"How?" the peasant said stupidly in a moment, looking at him. "I do not understand."

"The gentleman says he is going to see the town," the girl broke in furiously. "Can't you understand anything?"

"I do not understand what he is saying," the old man said to her. "He does not speak French."

"He speaks very well," the girl said angrily. "I understand him very well. It is you who are stupid—that's all."

The peasant was silent for some time now, puffing at his cigarette and looking at the young man with friendly eyes.

"America is very large—eh?" he said at length—making a wide gesture with his hands.

"Yes, it is very large. Much larger than France."

"How?" the peasant said again with a puzzled, patient look. "I do not understand."

"He says America is much larger than France," the girl cried in an exasperated tone. "I understand all he says."

Then, for several minutes, there was an awkward silence: nothing was said. The peasant smoked his cigarette, seemed on the point of speaking several times, looked bewildered and said nothing. Outside, rain had begun to fall in long slanting lines across the fields, and beyond, in the gray blown sky, there was a milky radiance where the sun should be, as if it were trying to break through. When the peasant saw this, he brightened, and leaning forward to the young man in a friendly manner, he tapped him on the knee with one of his great stiff fingers, and then pointing toward the sun, he said very slowly and distinctly, as one might instruct a child:

"*Le so-leil.*"

And the young man obediently repeated the word as the peasant had said it:

"*Le so-leil.*"

The old man and his wife beamed delightedly and nodded their approval, saying, "Yes. Yes. Good. Very good." Turning to his wife for confirmation, the old man said:

"He said it very well, didn't he?"

"But, yes! It was perfect!"

Then, pointing to the rain and making a down-slanting movement with his great hands, he said again, very slowly and patiently:

"*La pluie.*"

"*La pluie,*" the young man repeated dutifully, and the peasant nodded vigorously, saying:

"Good, good. You are speaking very well. In a little time you will speak good French." Then, pointing to the fields outside the train, he said gently:

"*La terre.*"

"*La terre,*" the young man answered.

"I tell you," the girl cried angrily from her seat by the window, "he knows all these words. He speaks French very well. You are too stupid to understand him—that is all."

The old man made no reply to her, but sat looking at the young man with a kind, approving face. Then more rapidly than before, and in succession, he pointed to the sun, the rain, the earth, saying:

"*Le soleil . . . la pluie . . . la terre.*"

The young man repeated the words after him, and the peasant nodded with satisfaction. Then for a long time no one spoke, there was no sound except for the uneven rackety-clack of the little train, and the girl continued to look sullenly out the window. Outside, the rain fell across the fertile fields in long slanting lines.

Late in the afternoon, the train stopped at a little station, and every one rose to get out. This was as far as the train went: to reach Orléans it was necessary to change to another train.

The peasant, his wife, and his daughter collected their bundles, and got out of the train. On another track, another little train was waiting, and the peasant pointed to this with his great stiff finger, and said to the young man:

"Orléans. That's your train there."

The young man thanked him, and gave the old man the remainder of the package of cigarettes. The peasant thanked him effusively, and before they parted, he pointed again rapidly toward the sun, the rain, and the earth, saying with a kind and friendly smile:

"*Le soleil . . . la pluie . . . la terre.*"

And the young man nodded to show that he understood, repeating what the old man had said. And the peasant shook his head in vigorous approval, saying:

"Yes, yes. It's very good. You will learn fast."

At these words, the girl, who with the same sullen, aloof, and ashamed look had walked on ahead of her parents, now turned, and cried out in a furious and exasperated tone:

"I tell you, the gentleman knows all that! . . . Will you leave him alone now! . . . You are only making a fool of yourself!"

But the old man and old woman paid no attention to her, but stood looking at the young man with a friendly smile, and shook hands warmly and cordially with him as he said good-bye.

Then he walked on across the tracks and got up into a compartment on the other train. When he looked out the window again, the peasant and his wife were standing on the platform, looking toward him with kind and eager looks on their old faces. When the peasant caught his eye, he pointed his great finger toward the sun again, and called out:

"*Le soleil.*"

"*Le soleil,*" the young man answered.

"Yes, yes!" the old man shouted with a laugh. "It's very good."

Then the daughter looked toward the young man sullenly, gave a short and impatient laugh of exasperation, and turned angrily away. The train began to move then, but the old man and woman stood looking after him as long as they could. He waved to them, and the old man waved his great hand in answer, and laughing, pointed toward the sun. And the young man nodded his head and shouted, to show that he had understood. Meanwhile, the girl had turned her back with an angry shrug and was walking away around the station.

Then they were lost from sight, the train swiftly left the little town behind, and now there was nothing but the fields, the earth, the smoky and mysterious distances. The rain fell steadily.

$$\mathcal{C}\mathcal{X}\mathcal{X}\mathcal{S}$$

The House of the Far and Lost

In the fall of that year I lived out about a mile from town in a house set back from the Ventnor Road. The house was called a "farm"—Hill-top Farm, or Far-end Farm, or some such name as that—but it was really no farm at all. It was a magnificent house of the weathered gray stone they have in that country, as if in the very quality of the wet heavy air there is the soft thick gray of time itself, sternly yet beautifully soaking down forever on you—and enriching everything it touches—grass, foliage, brick, ivy, the fresh moist color of people's faces, and old gray stone with the incomparable weathering of time.

The house was set back off the road at a distance of several hundred yards, possibly a quarter of a mile, and one reached it by means of a road bordered by rows of tall trees which arched above the road and which made me think of home at night when the stormy wind howled in their tossed branches. On each side of the road were the rugby fields of two of the colleges, and in the afternoon I could look out and down and see the fresh moist green of the playing fields and watch young fellows, dressed in their shorts and jerseys and with their bare knees scurfed with grass and turf, as they twisted, struggled, swayed, and scrambled for a moment in the scrimmage-circle, and then broke free, running, dodging, passing the ball as they were tackled, filling the moist air with their sharp cries of sport. They did not have the desperate, the grimly determined, the almost professional earnestness that the college teams at home have; their scurfed and muddy knees, their swaying scrambling scrimmages, the swift breaking away and running, their panting breath and crisp clear voices gave them the appearance of grown-up boys.

Once when I had come up the road in afternoon while they were playing, the ball got away from them and came bounding out into the road before me, and I ran after it to retrieve it as we used to do when passing a field where boys were playing baseball. One of the players came over to the edge of the field and stood there waiting with his hands upon his hips while I got the ball: he was panting hard, his face was flushed, and his blond hair tousled, but when I threw the ball to him, he said, "Thanks very much!" crisply and courteously—getting the same sound into the word "*very*" that

147

they got in "*American*," a sound that always repelled me a little because it seemed to have some scornful aloofness and patronage in it.

For a moment I watched him as he trotted briskly away on to the field again: the players stood there waiting, panting, casual, their hands upon their hips; he passed the ball into the scrimmage, the pattern swayed, rocked, scrambled, and broke sharply out into open play again, and everything looked incredibly strange, near, and familiar.

I felt that I had always known it, that it had always been mine, and that it was as familiar to me as everything I had seen or known in my childhood. Even the texture of the earth looked familiar, and felt moist and firm and springy when I stepped on it, and the stormy howling of the wind in that avenue of great trees at night was wild and desolate and demented, as it had been when I was eight years old and could lie in my bed at night and hear the great oaks howling on the hill above my father's house.

The name of the people in the house was Coulson: I made arrangements with the woman at once to come and live there: she was a tall, weathered-looking woman of middle age, we talked together in the hall. The hall was made of marble flags and went directly out onto a graveled walk.

The woman was crisp, cheerful, and worldly-looking. She was still quite handsome. She wore a well-cut skirt of woolen plaid and a silk blouse: when she talked, she kept her arms folded because the air in the hall was chilly, and she held a cigarette in the fingers of one hand. A shaggy brown dog came out and nosed upward toward her hand as she was talking, and she put her hand upon its head and scratched it gently. When I told her I wanted to move in the next day, she said briskly and cheerfully:

"Right you are! You'll find everything ready when you get here!" She then asked if I was at the university. I said no, and added, with a feeling of difficulty and naked desolation, that I was a "writer" and was coming there to work. I was twenty-four years old.

"Then I am sure that what you do will be *very, very* good!" she said cheerfully and decisively. "We have had several Americans in the house before, and all of them were very clever! All the Americans we have had here were very clever people," said the woman. "I'm sure that you will like it." Then she walked to the door with me to say good-bye. As we stood there, there was the sound of a small motor car coming to a halt, and in a moment a girl came swiftly across the gravel space outside and entered the hall. She was tall, slender, very lovely, but she had the same bright hard look in her eye that the woman had, the same faint, hard smile around the edges of her mouth.

"Edith," the woman said in her crisp, curiously incisive tone, "this young man is an American—he is coming here tomorrow." The girl looked at me for a moment, with her hard bright glance, thrust out a small gloved hand, and shook hands briefly, a swift firm greeting.

"Oh! How d'ye do!" she said. "I hope you will like it here." Then she went on down the hall, entered a room on the left, and closed the door behind her.

Her voice had been crisp and certain like her mother's, but it was also cool, young, and sweet, with music in it, and later, as I went down the road, I could still hear it.

That was a wonderful house, and the people there were wonderful people. Later, I could not forget them. I seemed to have known them all my life, and to know all about their lives. They seemed as familiar to me as my own blood, and I knew them with a knowledge that went deep below the roots of thought or memory. We did not talk together often, or tell of our lives to one another. It will be very hard to tell about it—the way we felt and lived together in that house—because it was one of those simple and profound experiences of life which people seem always to have known when it happens to them, but for which there is no language.

And yet, like a child's half-captured vision of some magic country he has known, and which haunts his days with strangeness and the sense of immanent, glorious re-discovery, the word that would unlock it all seems constantly to be almost on our lips, waiting just outside the gateway of our memory, just a shape, a phrase, a sound away the moment that we choose to utter it—but when we try to say the thing, something fades within our mind like fading light, and something melts within our grasp like painted smoke, and something goes forever when we try to touch it. It is the greatest perceiver of moonlight and magic that this earth has known—"For if a man should dream that he had gone to heaven and waking found within his hand a flower as token that he had really been there—ay, and what then?" What then!

The nearest I could come to it was this: In that house I sometimes felt the greatest peace and solitude that I had ever known. But I always knew the other people in the house were there. I could sit in my sitting room at night and hear nothing but the stormy moaning of the wind outside in the great trees, the small gaseous flare and jet from time to time of the coal fire burning in the grate—and silence, strong living lonely silence that moved and waited in the house at night—and I would always know that they were there.

I did not have to hear them enter or go past my door, nor did I have to hear doors close or open in the house, or listen to their voices: if I had never seen them, heard them, spoken to them, it would have been the same—I should have known they were there.

It was something I had always known, and had known it would happen to me, and now it was there with all the strangeness and dark mystery of an awaited thing. I knew them, felt them, lived among them with a familiarity that had no need of sight or word or speech. And the memory of that house and of my silent fellowship with all the people there was somehow mixed with an image of dark time. It was one of those sorrowful and unchanging images which, among all the blazing stream of images that passed constantly their stream of fire across my mind, was somehow fixed, detached, and everlasting, full of sorrow, certitude, and mystery that I could not fathom, but that wore forever on it the old sad light of waning day—a light from which all the heat, the violence, and the substance of furious dusty day had vanished, and was itself like time, unearthly-of-the-earth, remote, detached, and everlasting. For though that image was remote from life, it was essential to it, yet subject to no change and connected to no source of living or event that I could trace.

And that fixed and changeless image of dark time was this: In an old house of time I lived alone, and yet had other people all around me, and they never spoke to me, or I to them. They came and went like silence in the house, but I always knew that they were there. I would be sitting by a window in a room, and I would know then that they were moving in the house, and darkness, sorrow, and strong silence dwelt within us, and our eyes were quiet, full of sorrow, peace, and knowledge, and our faces dark, our tongues silent, and we never spoke. I could not remember how their faces looked, but they were all familiar to me as my father's face, and we had known one another forever, and we lived together in the ancient house of time, dark time, and silence, sorrow, certitude, and peace were in us. Such was the image of dark time that was to haunt my life thereafter, and into which, somehow, my life among the people of that house had passed.

In the house that year there lived, besides myself and Morison, the Coulsons, the father and mother and their daughter, and three men who had taken rooms together, and who were employed in a factory where motor cars were made, two miles from town.

I think the reason that I could never forget these people later and seemed to know them all so well was that there was in all of them something ruined, lost, or broken—some precious and irretrievable quality which had gone out of them and which they could never get back again. Perhaps that was the reason that I liked them all so much, because with ruined people it is either love or hate: there is no middle way. The ruined people that we like are those who desperately have died, and lost their lives because they loved life dearly, and had that grandeur that makes such people spend prodigally the thing they love the best, and risk and lose their lives because it is so precious to them, and die at length because the seeds of life were in them. It is only the people who love life in this way who die—and these are the ruined people that we like.

The ruined people that we hate are those who died because they hated life and always had the seeds of death within them, and who, when dead, talk fatally and with an evil desperation of the vast land of the earth, but never go into the rain without their rubbers, or paint their corpse up with the hues of life, and try to put their leper's touch upon the living flesh of man. These are the people who are old and evil, full of cunning and cold caution, who ensnare the heart of youth in death and desperation with false faces of gallantry and who finally risk nothing. These are the ruined people that we hate, for they are dead, yet will not die, and try to spread corruption at the heart of life.

But the people in the house were people who had lost their lives because they loved the earth too well, and somehow had been slain by their hunger. And for this reason I liked them all, and could not forget them later: there seemed to have been some magic that had drawn them all together to the house, as if the house itself was a magnetic center for lost people.

Certainly, the three men who worked at the motor car factory had been drawn together for this reason. Two were still young men in their early twenties. The third man was much older. He was a man past forty, his name was Nicholl, he had served in the army during the war and had attained the rank of captain.

He had the spare, alert, and jaunty figure that one often finds in army men, an almost professional military quality that somehow seemed to set his figure upon a horse as if he had grown there, or had spent a lifetime in the cavalry. His face also had the same lean, bitten, professional military quality: his speech, although good-natured and very friendly, was clipped, incisive, jerky, and sporadic, his lean weather-beaten face was deeply, sharply scarred and sunken in the flanks, and he wore a small cropped mustache, and displayed long frontal teeth when he smiled—a spare, gaunt, toothy, yet attractive smile.

His left arm was withered, shrunken, almost useless, part of his hand and two of the fingers had been torn away by the blast or explosion which had destroyed his arm, but it was not this mutilation of the flesh that gave one the sense of a life that had been ruined, lost, and broken irretrievably. In fact, one quickly forgot his physical injury: his figure looked so spare, lean, jaunty, well-conditioned in its energetic fitness that one never thought of him as a cripple, nor pitied him for any disability. No: the ruin that one felt in him was never of the flesh, but of the spirit. Something seemed to have been exploded from his life—it was not the nerve-centers of his arm, but of his soul, that had been destroyed. There was in the man somewhere a terrible dead vacancy and emptiness, and that spare, lean figure that he carried so well seemed only to surround this vacancy like a kind of shell.

He was always smartly dressed in well-cut clothes that set well on his trim spruce figure. He was always in good spirits, immensely friendly in his clipped spare way, and he laughed frequently—a rather metallic cackle which came suddenly and ended as swiftly as it had begun. He seemed, somehow, to have locked the door upon dark care and worry, and to have flung the key away—to have lost, at the same time that he lost more precious things, all the fretful doubts and perturbations of the conscience most men know.

Now, in fact, he seemed to have only one serious project in his life. This was to keep himself amused, to keep himself constantly amused, to get from his life somehow the last atom of entertainment it could possibly yield, and in this project the two young men who lived with him joined in with an energy and earnestness which suggested that their employment in the motor car factory was just a necessary evil which must be borne patiently because it yielded them the means with which to carry on a more important business, the only one in which their lives were interested—the pursuit of pleasure.

And in the way in which they conducted this pursuit, there was an element of deliberate calculation, concentrated earnestness, and focal intensity of purpose that was astounding, grotesque, and unbelievable, and that left in the mind of one who saw it a formidable and disquieting memory because there was in it almost the madness of desperation, the deliberate intent of men to cover up or seek oblivion at any cost of effort from some hideous emptiness of soul.

Captain Nicholl and his two young companions had a little motor car so small that it scuttled up the road, shot around and stopped in the gravel by the door with the abruptness of a wound-up toy. It was astonishing that three men could wedge themselves into this midget of a car, but wedge themselves they did, and used it to the end of its capacity, scuttling away to work in it in the morning, and scuttling back again when work was done, and scuttling away to London every Saturday, as if they were determined to wrest from this small motor, too, the last ounce of pleasure to be got from it.

Finally, Captain Nicholl and his two companions had made up an orchestra among them, and this they played in every night when they got home. One of the young men, who was a tall fellow with blond hair which went back in even corrugated waves across his head as if it had been marcelled, played the piano, the other, who was slight and dark, and had black hair, performed upon a saxophone, and Captain Nicholl himself took turns at thrumming furiously on a banjo, or rattling a tattoo upon the complex arrangement of trap drums, bass drums, and clashing cymbals that surrounded him.

They played nothing but American jazz music or sobbing crooners' rhapsodies or nigger blues. Their performance was astonishing. Although it was contrived solely for their own amusement, they hurled themselves into it with all the industrious earnestness of professional musicians employed by a night-club or a dance hall to furnish dance music for the patrons. The little dark fellow who played the saxophone would bend and weave prayerfully with his grotesque instrument, as the fat gloating notes came from its unctuous throat, and from time to time he would sway in a half circle, or get up and prance forward and back in rhythm to the music as the saxophone players in dance orchestras sometimes do.

Meanwhile, the tall blond fellow at the piano would sway and bend above the keys, glancing around from time to time with little nods and smiles as if he were encouraging an orchestra of forty pieces or beaming happily in an encouraging fashion at a dance floor crowded with paying customers.

While this was going on, Captain Nicholl would be thrumming madly on the strings of a banjo. He kept his instrument gripped somehow below his withered arm, fingering the end strings with his two good fingers, knocking the tune out with his good right hand, and keeping time with a beating foot. Then, with a sudden violent movement, he would put the banjo down, snatch up the sticks of the trap drum, and begin to rattle out a furious accompaniment, beating the bass drum with his foot meanwhile, and reaching over to smash cymbals, chimes, and metal rings from time to time. He played with a kind of desperate fury, his mouth fixed in a strange set grin, his bright eyes burning with a sharp wild glint of madness.

They sang as they played, bursting suddenly into the refrain of some popular song with the same calculated spontaneity and spurious enthusiasm of the professional orchestra, mouthing the words of Negro blues and jazz with obvious satisfaction, with an accent which was remarkably good, and yet which had something foreign and inept in it, which made the familiar phrases of American music sound almost as strange in their mouths as if an orchestra of skillful patient Japanese were singing them.

They sang:

> *Yes, sir! That's my baby*
> *Yes, sir! Don't mean maybe*
> *Yes, sir! That's my baby now!*

or:

> *Oh, it ain't gonna rain no more, no more*
> *It ain't gonna rain no more*

or:

> *I got dose blu-u-ues————*

the young fellow at the piano rolling his eyes around in a ridiculous fashion, and mouthing out the word "blues" extravagantly as he sang it, the little dark fellow bending forward in an unctuous sweep as the note came gloating fatly from the horn, and Captain Nicholl swaying sideways in his chair as he strummed upon the banjo strings, and improvising a mournful accompaniment of his own somewhat as follows: "I got dose blu-u-ues! Yes, suh! Oh! I got dose blues! Yes, suh! I sure have got 'em—dose blu-u-ues—blu-u-ues—blu-u-ues!"—his mouth never relaxing from its strange fixed grin, nor his eyes from their bright stare of madness as he swayed and strummed and sang the words that came so strangely from his lips.

It was a weird scene, an incredible performance, and somehow it pierced the heart with a wild nameless pity, an infinite sorrow and regret.

They were all lost and ruined and hopeless. Something precious, irrecoverable had gone out of them, and they knew it. They fought the emptiness in them with this deliberate, formidable, and mad intensity of a calculated gaiety, a terrifying mimicry of mirth, and the storm howled around us in the dark trees, and I felt that I had known them forever, and had no words to say to them—and no door.

There were four in the Coulson family: the father, a man of fifty years, the mother, somewhere in the middle forties, a son, and a daughter, Edith, a girl of twenty-two who lived in the house with her parents. I never met the son: he had completed his course at Oxford a year or two before, and had gone down to London where he was now employed. During the time I lived there, the son did not come home.

They were a ruined family. How the ruin had fallen on them, what it was, I never knew, for no one ever spoke to me about them. But the sense of their disgrace, of a shameful inexpiable dishonor, for which there was no pardon, from which there could never be redemption, was overwhelming. In the most astonishing way I found out about it right away, and yet I did not know what they had done, and no one ever spoke a word against them.

Rather, the mention of their name brought silence, and in that silence there was something merciless and final, something that belonged to the temper of the country, and that was far more terrible than any open word of scorn, contempt, or bitter judgment could have been, more savage than a million strident, whispering, or abusive tongues could be, because the silence was unarguable, irrevocable, complete, as if a great door had been shut against their lives forever.

Everywhere I went in town, the people knew about them, and said nothing—saying everything—when I spoke their names. I found this final, closed, relentless silence everywhere—in tobacco, wine, and tailor shops, in book stores, food stores, haberdashery stores—wherever I bought anything and gave the clerk the address to which it was to be delivered, they responded instantly with this shut finality of silence, writing the name down gravely, sometimes saying briefly, "Oh! Coulson's!" when I gave them the address, but more often saying nothing.

But whether they spoke or simply wrote the name down without a word, there was always this quality of instant recognition, this obdurate, contemptuous finality of silence, as if a door had been shut—a door that could never again be opened. Somehow I disliked them even more for this silence than if they had spoken evilly: there was in it something ugly, sly, knowing, and triumphant that was far more evil than any slyly whispering confidence of slander, or any open vituperation of abuse, could be. It seemed somehow to come from all the evil and uncountable small maggotry of the earth, the cautious little hatred of a million nameless ciphers, each puny, pallid, trivial in himself, but formidable because he added his tiny beetle's ball of dung to the mountainous accumulation of ten million others of his breed.

It was uncanny how these clerk-like faces, grave and quiet, that never spoke a word, or gave a sign, or altered their expression by a jot, when I gave them the address, could suddenly be alive with something secret, foul, and sly, could be more closed and secret than a door, and yet instantly reveal the naked, shameful, and iniquitous filth that welled up from some depthless source. I could not phrase it, give a name to it, or even see a certain sign that it was there, no more than I could put my hand upon a wisp of fading smoke, but I always knew when it was there, and somehow when I saw it my heart went hard and cold against the people who revealed it, and turned with warmth and strong affection toward the Coulson family.

There was, finally, among these grave clerk-like faces one face that I could never forget thereafter, a face that seemed to resume into its sly suave surfaces all of the nameless abomination of evil in the world for which I had no name, for which there was no handle that I could grasp, no familiar places or edges I could get my hands upon, which slid phantasmally, oilily, smokily away whenever I tried to get my hands upon it. But it was to haunt my life for years in dreams of hatred, madness, and despair that found no frontal wall for their attack, no word for their vituperation, no door for the shoulder of my hate—an evil world of phantoms, shapes, and whispers that was yet as real as death, as ever-present as man's treachery, but that slid away from me like smoke whenever I tried to meet, or curse, or strangle it.

This face was the face of a man in a tailor shop, a fitter there, and I could have battered that foul face into a bloody pulp, distilled the filthy refuse of his ugly life out of his fat swelling neck and through the murderous grip of my fingers if I could only have found a cause, a logic, and an act for doing it. And yet I never saw the man but twice, and briefly, and there had been nothing in his suave, sly careful speech to give offense.

Edith Coulson had sent me to the tailor's shop: I needed a suit, and when I asked where to go to have it made, she had sent me to this place because her brother had his suits made there and liked it. The fitter was a heavy shambling man in his late thirties: he had receding hair, which he brushed back flat in a thick pompadour, yellowish, somewhat bulging eyes, a coarse heavy face, loose-featured, red, and sensual, a sloping meaty jaw, and large discolored buck teeth which showed unpleasantly in a mouth that was always half open. It was, in fact, the mouth that gave his face its sensual, sly, and ugly look, for a loose and vulgar smile seemed constantly to hover about its thick coarse edges, to be deliberately, slyly restrained, but about to burst at any moment in an open, evil, foully sensual laugh. There was always this ugly suggestion of a loose, corrupt, and evilly jubilant mirth about his mouth, and yet he never laughed or smiled.

This man's speech had this same quality. It was suave and courteous, but even in its most urbane assurances, there was something non-committal, sly, and jeering, something that slid away from you, and was never to be grasped, a quality that was faithless, tricky, and unwholesome. When I came for the final fitting, it was obvious that he had done as cheap and shoddy a job as he could do; the suit was vilely botched and skimped, sufficient cloth had not been put into it, and now it was too late to remedy the defect.

Yet, the fitter gravely pulled the vest down till it met the trousers, tugged at the coat, and pulled the thing together where it stayed until I took a breath or moved a muscle, when it would all come apart again, the collar bulging outward from the shoulder, the skimpy coat and vest crawling backward from the trousers, leaving a hiatus of shirt and belly that could not be remedied now by any means.

Then, gravely, he would pull the thing together again, and in his suave, yet oily, sly, and non-committal phrases, say:

"Um! Seems to fit you very well."

I was choking with exasperation, and knew that I had been done, because I had foolishly paid them half the bill already, and now knew no way out of it except to lose what I had paid, and get nothing for it, or take the thing, and pay the balance. I was caught in a trap, but even as I jerked at the coat and vest speechlessly, seized my shirt, and thrust the gaping collar in his face, the man said smoothly:

"Um! Yes! The collar. Should think all that will be all right. Still needs a little alteration." He made some chalk marks on me. "Should think you'll find it fits you very well when the tailor makes the alterations."

"When will the suit be ready?"

"Um. Should think you ought to have it by next Tuesday. Yes. I think you'll find it ready by Tuesday."

The sly words slid away from me like oil: there was nothing to pin him to or grasp him by, the yellowed eyes looked casually away and would not look at me, the sensual face was suavely grave, the discolored buck teeth shone obscenely through the coarse loose mouth, and the suggestion of the foul loose smile was so pronounced now that it seemed that at any moment he would have to turn away with heavy trembling shoulders, and stifle the evil jeering laugh that was welling up in him. But he remained suavely grave and non-committal to the end, and when I asked him if I should come again to try it on, he said, in the same oily tone, never looking at me:

"Um. Shouldn't think that would be necessary. Could have it delivered to you when it's ready. What is your address?"

"The Far-end Farm—it's on the Ventnor Road."

"Oh! Coulson's!" He never altered his expression, but the suggestion of the obscene smile was so pronounced that now it seemed he had to out with it. Instead, he only said:

"Um. Yes. Should think it could be delivered to you there on Tuesday. If you'll just wait a moment, I'll ask the tailor."

Gravely, suavely, he took the coat from me and walked back toward the tailor's room with the coat across his arm. In a moment, I heard sly voices whispering, laughing slyly, then the tailor saying:

"Where does he live?"

"Coulson's!" said the fitter chokingly, and now the foul awaited laugh did come—high, wet, slimy, it came out of that loose mouth, and choked and whispered wordlessly, and choked again, and mingled then with the tailor's voice in sly, choking, whispering intimacy, and then gasped faintly, and was silent. When he came out again, his coarse face was red and swollen with foul secret merriment, his heavy shoulders trembled slightly, he took out his handkerchief and wiped it once across his loose half-opened mouth, and with that gesture wiped the slime of laughter from his lips. Then he came toward me, suave, grave, and courteous, evilly composed, as he said smoothly:

"Should think we'll have that for you by next Tuesday, sir."

"Can the tailor fix it so it's going to fit?"

"Um. Should think you'll find that everything's all right. You ought to have it Tuesday afternoon."

He was not looking at me: the yellowish bulging eyes were staring casually indefinitely, away, and his words again had slid away from me like oil. He could not be touched, approached, or handled: there was nothing to hold him by, he had the impregnability of smoke or a ball of mercury.

As I went out the door, he began to speak to another man in the shop, I heard low words and whispered voices, then, gasping, the word "Coulson's!" and the slimy, choking smothered laughter as the street door closed behind me. I never saw him again. I never forgot his face.

That was a fine house: the people in it were exiled, lost, and ruined people, and I liked them all. Later, I never knew why I felt so close to them, or remembered them with such warmth and strong affection.

I did not see the Coulsons often and rarely talked to them. Yet I felt as familiar and friendly with them all as if I had known them all my life. The house was wonderful as no other house I had ever known because we all seemed to be living in it together with this strange speechless knowledge, warmth, and familiarity, and yet each was as private, secret, and secure in his own room as if he occupied the house alone.

Coulson himself I saw least of all: we sometimes passed each other going in or out the door, or in the hall: he would grunt "Morning," or "Good day," in a curt blunt manner, and go on, and yet he always left me with a curious sense of warmth and friendliness. He was a stocky well-set man with iron-gray hair, bushy eyebrows, and the red weathered face which wore the open color of the country on it, but also had the hard dull flush of the steady heavy drinker.

I never saw him drunk, and yet I think that he was never sober: he was one of those men who have drunk themselves past any hope of drunkenness, who are soaked through to the bone with alcohol, saturated, tanned, weathered in it so completely that it could never be distilled out of their blood again. Yet even in this terrible excess one felt a kind of grim control—

the control of a man who is enslaved by the very thing that he controls, the control of the opium eater who cannot leave his drug but measures out his dose with a cold calculation, and finds the limit of his capacity, and stops there, day by day.

But somehow this very sense of control, this blunt ruddy style of the country gentleman which distinguished his speech, his manner, and his dress, made the ruin of his life, the desperate intemperance of drink that smouldered in him like a slow fire, steadily, nakedly apparent. It was as if, having lost everything, he still held grimly to the outer forms of a lost standard, a ruined state, when the inner substance was destroyed.

And it was this way with all of them—with Mrs. Coulson and the girl, as well: their crisp, clipped friendly speech never deviated into intimacy, and never hinted at any melting into confidence and admission. Upon the woman's weathered face there hovered, when she talked, the same faint set grin that Captain Nicholl had, and her eyes were bright and hard, a little mad, impenetrable, as were his. And the girl, although young and very lovely, sometimes had this same look when she greeted anyone or paused to talk. In that look there was nothing truculent, bitter, or defiant: it was just the look of three people who had gone down together, and who felt for one another neither bitterness nor hate, but that strange companionship of a common disgrace, from which love has vanished, but which is more secret, silent, and impassively resigned to its fatal unity than love itself could be.

And that hard bright look also said this plainly to the world: "We ask for nothing from you now, we want nothing that you offer us. What is ours is ours, what we are we are, you'll not intrude nor come closer than we let you see!"

Coulson might have been a man who had been dishonored and destroyed by his women, and who took it stolidly, saying nothing, and drank steadily from morning until night, and had nothing for it now but drink and silence and acceptance. Yet I never knew for certain that this was so, it just seemed inescapable, and seemed somehow legible not only in the slow smouldering fire that burned out through his rugged weathered face, but also in the hard bright armor of the women's eyes, the fixed set grin around their lips when they were talking—a grin that was like armor, too. And Morison, who had referred to Coulson, chuckling, as a real "bottle-a-day-man," had added quietly, casually, in his brief, indefinite, but blurted-out suggestiveness of speech:

"I think the old girl's been a bit of a bitch in her day. . . . Don't know, of course, but has the look, hasn't she?" In a moment he said quietly, "Have you talked to the daughter yet?"

"Once or twice. Not for long."

"Ran into a chap at Magdalen other day who knows her," he said casually. "He used to come out here to see her." He glanced swiftly, slyly, at me, his face reddening a little with laughter. "Pretty hot, I gather," he said quietly, smiling, and looked away. It was night: the fire burned cheerfully in the grate, the hot coals spurting in small gaseous flares from time to time. The house was very quiet all around us. Outside we could hear the stormy wind in the trees along the road. Morison flicked his cigarette into the fire, poured out a drink of whiskey into a glass, saying as he did so: "I say, old chap, you don't mind if I take a spot of this before I go to bed, do you?" Then he shot some seltzer into the glass and drank. And I sat there, without a word, staring sullenly into the fire, dumbly conscious of the flood of sick pain and horror which the casual foulness of the man's suggestion had aroused, stubbornly trying to deny now that I was thinking of the girl all the time.

One night, as I was coming home along the dark road that went up past the playing field to the house, and that was bordered on each side by grand trees whose branches seemed to hold at night all the mysterious and de- mented cadences of storm, I came upon her standing in the shadow of a tree. It was one of the grand wild nights that seemed to come so often in the autumn of that year: the air was full of a fine stinging moisture, not quite rain, and above the stormy branches of the trees I could see the sky, wild, broken, full of scudding clouds through which at times the moon drove in and out with a kind of haggard loneliness. By that faint, wild, and broken light, I could see the small white oval of the girl's face—somehow even more lovely now just because I could not see it plainly. And I could see as well the rough gleaming bark of the tree against which she leaned.

As I approached, I saw her thrust her hand into the pocket of her over- coat, a match flared, and for a moment I saw Edith plainly, the small flower of her face framed in the wavering light as she lowered her head to light her cigarette.

The light went out, I saw the small respiring glow of her cigarette before the white blur of her face, I passed her swiftly, head bent, without speaking, my heart filled with the sense of strangeness and wonder which the family had aroused in me.

Then I walked on up the road, muttering to myself. The house was dark when I got there, but when I entered my sitting room the place was still warmly and softly luminous with the glow of hot coals in the grate. I turned the lights on, shut the door behind me, and hurled several lumps of coal upon the bedded coals. In a moment the fire was blazing and crackling cheerfully, and getting a kind of comfort and satisfaction from its activity, I flung off my coat, went over to the sideboard, poured out a stiff drink of scotch from a bottle there, and coming back to the fire, flung myself into a chair, and began to stare sullenly into the dancing flames.

How long I sat there in this stupor of sullen and nameless fury, I did not know, but I was sharply roused at length by footsteps light and rapid on the gravel, shocked into a start of surprise by a figure that appeared suddenly at one of the French windows that opened directly from my sitting room to the level sward of velvet lawn before the house.

I peered through the glass for a moment with an astonished stare before

I recognized the face of Edith Coulson. I opened the doors at once, she came in quickly, smiling at my surprise, and at the glass which I was holding foolishly, half-raised in my hand.

I continued to look at her with an expression of gape-mouthed astonishment and in a moment became conscious of her smiling glance, the cool sweet assurance of her young voice.

"I say!" she was saying cheerfully. "What a lucky thing to find you up! I came away without any key—I should have had to wake the whole house up—so when I saw your light—" she concluded briskly, "—what luck! I hope you don't mind."

"Why no-o, no," I stammered foolishly, still staring dumbly at her. "No—no-o—not at all," I blundered on. Then, suddenly coming to myself with a burst of galvanic energy, I shut the windows, pushed another chair before the fire, and said:

"Won't you sit down and have a drink before you go?"

"Thanks," she said crisply. "I will—yes. What a jolly fire you have." As she talked, she took off her coat and hat swiftly and put them on a chair. Her face was flushed and rosy, beaded with small particles of rain, and for a moment she stood before the mirror arranging her hair, which had been tousled by the wind.

The girl was slender, tall, and very lovely with the kind of beauty they have when they are beautiful—a beauty so fresh, fair, and delicate that it seems to be given to just a few of them to compensate for all the grimly weathered ugliness of the rest. Her voice was also lovely, sweet, and musical, and when she talked, all the notes of tenderness and love were in it. But she had the same hard bright look in her eye that her mother had, the faint set smile around her mouth: as we stood there talking, she was standing very close to me, and I could smell the fragrance of her hair, and felt an intolerable desire to put my hand upon hers and was almost certain she would not draw away. But the hard bright look was in her eye, the faint set smile around her mouth, and I did nothing.

"What'll you have?" I said. "Whiskey?"

"Yes, thank you," she said with the same sweet crisp assurance with which she always spoke, "and a splash of soda." I struck a match and held it for her while she lit the cigarette she was holding in her hand, and in a moment returned to her with the drink. Then she sat down, crossed her legs, and for a moment puffed thoughtfully at her cigarette, as she stared into the fire. The storm moaned in the great trees along the road, and near the house, and suddenly a swirl of rain struck the windows with a rattling blast. The girl stirred a little in her chair, restlessly, shivered:

"Listen!" she said. "What a night! Horrible weather we have here, isn't it?"

"I don't know. I don't like the fog and rain so well. But this—the way it is tonight—" I nodded toward the window—"I like it."

She looked at me for a moment.

"Oh," she said non-committally. "You do." Then, as she sipped her drink, she looked curiously about the room, her reflective glance finally resting on my table where there was a great stack of ledgers in which I wrote.

"I say," she cried again. "What are you doing with all those big books there?"

"I write in them."

"Really?" she said, in a surprised tone. "I should think it'd be an awful bother carrying them around when you travel."

"It is. But it's the best way I've found of keeping what I do together."

"Oh," she said, as before, and continued to stare curiously at me with her fair, lovely young face, the curiously hard, bright, and unrevealing glance of her eye. "I see. . . . But why do you come to such a place as this to write?" she said presently. "Do you like it here?"

"I do. As well as any place I've ever known."

"Oh! . . . I should think a writer would want a different kind of place."

"What kind?"

"Oh—I don't know—Paris—London—some place like that where there is lots of life—people—fun—I should think you'd work better in a place like that."

"I work better here."

"But don't you get awfully fed up sitting in here all day long and writing in those enormous books?"

"I do, yes."

"I should think you would . . . I should think you'd want to get away from it sometime."

"Yes. I do want to—every day—almost all the time."

"Then why don't you?" she said crisply. "Why don't you go off some week-end for a little spree. I should think it would buck you up no end."

"It would—yes. Where should I go?"

"Oh, Paris, I suppose. . . . Or London! London!" she cried. "London is quite jolly if you know it."

"I'm afraid I don't know it."

"But you've *been* to London," she said in a surprised tone.

"Oh, yes. I lived there for several months."

"Then you know London," she said impatiently. "Of course you do."

"I'm afraid I don't know it very well. I don't know many people there—and after all, that's the thing that counts, isn't it?"

She looked at me curiously for a moment with the faint hard smile around the edges of her lovely mouth. "—Should think that might be arranged," she said with a quiet, an enigmatic humor. Then, more directly, she added: "That shouldn't be difficult at all. Perhaps I can introduce you to some people."

"That would be fine. Do you know many people there?"

"A good many," she said. "I go there often—whenever I can." She got up with a swift decisive movement, put her glass down on the mantel and cast her cigarette into the fire. Then she faced me, looking at me with a curiously bold, an almost defiant directness of her hard bright eyes, and she fixed me with this glance for a full moment before she spoke.

"In fact," she said slowly in a moment, as she looked at me, "in fact—I am going there this week—to meet a friend."

"Oh," I said, looking at her stupidly. "When?"

Her gaze did not waver.

"Saturday," she said. "I am going to meet someone there Saturday— Good night," she said crisply. "Thanks awfully for letting me in—and for the drink."

"Good night," I said, and she was gone before I could say more, and I had closed the door behind her, and I could hear her light swift footsteps going down the hall and up the steps. And then there was nothing in the house but sleep and silence, and storm and darkness in the world around me, and for a long time—until the fire had crumbled to a fading glow of coals—I sat there staring at the flame.

Mrs. Coulson came into my room just once or twice while I was there. One morning she came in, spoke crisply and cheerfully, and walked over to the window looking out upon the velvet lawn and at the dreary impenetrable gray of foggy air. Although the room was warm, and there was a good fire burning in the grate, she clasped her arms together as she looked and shivered a little:

"Wretched weather, isn't it?" she said in her crisp tones, her gaunt weathered face and toothy mouth touched by the faint fixed grin as she looked out with her bright hard stare. "Don't you find it frightfully depressing? Most Americans do," she said, getting the sharp disquieting sound into the word.

"Yes. I do, a little. We don't have this kind of weather very often. But this is the time of year you get it here, isn't it? I suppose you're used to it by now."

"Used to it," she said crisply, turning her hard bright gaze upon me. "Not at all. I've known it all my life, but I'll never get used to it. It is a wretched climate."

"Still, you wouldn't feel at home anywhere else, would you? You wouldn't want to live outside of England."

"No?" she said, staring at me with the faint set grin around her toothy mouth. "Why do you think so?"

"Because your home is here."

"My home? My home is where they have fine days, and where the sun is always shining."

"I wouldn't like that. I'd get tired of sunlight all the time. I'd want some gray days and some fog and snow."

"Yes, I suppose you would. But then, you've been used to having fine days all your life, haven't you? With us, it's different. I'm so fed up with fog and rain that I could do without it nicely, thank you, if I never saw it again. . . . I don't think you could understand how much the sunlight means to us," she said slowly. She turned, and for a moment looked out the window with her hard bright stare, the faint set grin about her mouth. "Sunlight— warmth—fine days forever! Warmth everywhere—in the earth, the sky, in the lives of people all around you—nothing but warmth and sunlight and fine days!"

"And where would you go to find all that? Does it exist?"

"Oh, of course!" she said crisply and good-naturedly, turning to me again. "There's only one place to live—only one country where I want to live."

"Where is that?"

"Italy," she said. "That's my real home. . . . I'd live the rest of my life there if I could." For a moment longer she looked out the window, then turned briskly, saying:

"Why don't you run over to Paris some week-end? After all, it's only seven hours from London: if you left here in the morning you'd be there in time for dinner. It would be a good change for you. I should think a little trip like that would buck you up tremendously."

Her words gave me a wonderful feeling of confidence and hope: I think she had traveled a great deal, and she had the casual, assured way of speaking of a voyage that made it seem very easy, and filled one with a sense of joy and adventure when she spoke about it. When I tried to think of Paris by myself, it had seemed very far away and hard to reach: London stood between it and me, and when I thought of the huge smoky web of London, the soft gray skies above me, and the enormous weight of lives that were hidden somewhere in that impenetrable fog, gray desolation and weariness of the spirit filled me. It seemed to me that I must draw each breath of that soft gray air with heavy weary effort, and that every mile of my journey would be a ghastly struggle through some viscous and material substance of soft heavy gray that weighted down my steps and filled my heart with desolation.

But when Mrs. Coulson spoke to me about it, suddenly it all seemed wonderfully easy and good. England was magically small, the Channel to be taken at a stride, and all the thrill, the joy, the mystery of Paris mine again—the moment that I chose to make it mine.

I looked at her gaunt weathered face, her toothy mouth with the faint fixed grin, the hard bright armor of her eyes, and wondered how anything so clear, so sharp, so crisp, and so incisive could have been shaped and grown beneath these soft and humid skies that numbed me, mind and heart and body, with their thick numb substance of gray weariness and desolation.

A day or two before I left, Edith came into my room one afternoon bearing a tray with tea and jam and buttered bread. I was sitting in my chair before the fire, and had my coat off: when she came in I scrambled to my feet, reached for my coat and started to put it on. In her young crisp voice she told me not to, and put the tray down on the table, saying that the maid was having her afternoon away.

Then for a moment she stood looking at me with her faint and enigmatic smile.

"So you're leaving us?" she said presently.

"Yes. Tomorrow."

"And where will you go from here?" she said.

"To Germany, I think. Just for a short time—two or three weeks."

"And after that?"

"I'm going home."

"Home?"

"Back to America."

"Oh," she said slowly. "I see." In a moment she added, "We shall miss you."

I wanted to talk to her more than I had ever wanted to talk to anyone in my life, but when I spoke, all that I could say, lamely, muttering, was:

"I'll miss you, too."

"Will you?" She spoke so quietly that I could scarcely hear her. "I wonder for how long?" she said.

"Forever," I said, flushing miserably at the sound of the word, and yet not knowing any other word to say.

The faint hard smile about her mouth was a little deeper when she spoke again.

"Forever? That's a long time when one is as young as you," she said.

"I mean it. I'll never forget you as long as I live."

"We shall remember you," she said quietly. "And I hope you think of us sometime—back here buried, lost, in all the fog and rain and ruin of England. How good it must be to know that none of the failure of the past can pull you down—that there will always be another day for you—a new beginning. I wonder if you Americans will ever know how fortunate you are," the girl said.

"And yet you could not leave all this," I said with a kind of desperate hope. "This old country you've lived in, known all your life. A girl like you could never leave a place like this to live the kind of life we have in America."

"*Couldn't* I?" she said with a quiet but unmistakable passion of conviction. "There's nothing I'd like better."

I stared at her blindly, dumbly, for a moment; suddenly all that I wanted to say and had not been able to say found release in a movement of my hands. I gripped her by the shoulders and pulled her to me and began to plead with her:

"Then why don't you? I'll take you there!—Look here—" my words were crazy, and I knew it, but as I spoke them, I believed all I said—"Look here!

I haven't much money—but in America you can make it if you want to! I'm going back there. You come, too—I'll take you when I go!"

She had not tried to free herself; she just stood there passive, unresisting, as I poured that frenzied proposal in her ears. Now, with the same passive and unyielding movement, the bright armor of her young eyes, she stepped away, and stood looking at me silently for a moment, the faint hard smile at the edges of her mouth. Then, slowly, with an almost imperceptible movement, she shook her head. "Oh, you'll forget about us all," she said quietly. "You'll forget about our lives here—buried in fog—and rain—and failure—and defeat."

"Failure and defeat won't last forever."

"Sometimes they do," she said with a quiet finality that froze my heart.

"Not for you—they won't!" I said, and took her by the hand again with desperate entreaty. "Listen to me—" I blundered on incoherently, with the old feeling of nameless shame and horror. "You don't need to tell me what it is—I don't want to know—but whatever it is for you—it doesn't matter—you can get the best of it."

She said nothing, but just looked at me through that hard bright armor of her eyes, the obdurate finality of her smile.

"Good-bye," she said, "I'll not forget you either." She looked at me for a moment curiously before she spoke again. "I wonder," she said slowly, "if you'll ever understand just what it was you did for me by coming here."

"What was it?"

"You opened a door that I thought had been closed forever," she said, "a door that let me look in on a world I thought I should never see again—a new bright world, a new life and a new beginning—for us all. And I thought that was something which would never happen to anyone in this house again."

"It will to you," I said, and took her hand again with desperate eagerness. "It can happen to you whenever you want it to. It's yours, I'll swear it to you, if you'll only speak."

She looked at me with her direct hard glance, an almost imperceptible movement of her head.

"I tell you I know what I'm talking about."

Again she shook her head.

"You don't know," she said. "You're young. You're an American. There are some things you'll never be old enough to know. For some of us there's no return. Go back," she said, "go back to the life you know—the life you understand—where there can always be a new beginning—a new life."

"And you—" I said dumbly, miserably.

"Good-bye, my dear," she said so low and gently I could scarcely hear her. "Think of me sometime, won't you—I'll not forget you." And before I could speak, she kissed me once and was gone, so light and swift that I did not know it, until the door had closed behind her. And for some time, like a man in a stupor, I stood there looking out the window at the gray wet light of England.

The next day I went away, and never saw any of them again, but I could not forget them. Although I had never passed beyond the armor of their hard bright eyes, or breached the wall of their crisp, friendly, and impersonal speech, or found out anything about them, I always thought of them with warmth, with a deep and tender affection, as if I had always known them—as if, somehow, I could have lived with them or made their lives my own if only I had said a word, or turned the handle of a door—a word I never knew, a door I never found.

Dark in the Forest,
Strange as Time

Some years ago, among the people standing on one of the platforms of the Munich railway station, beside the Swiss express, which was almost ready to depart, there were a woman and a man—a woman so lovely that the memory of her would forever haunt the mind of him who saw her, and a man on whose dark face the legend of a strange and fatal meeting was already visible.

The woman, who was about thirty-five years old, was at the flawless summit of a mature and radiant beauty. She was a glorious creature, packed to the last red ripeness of her lip with life and health, a miracle of loveliness in whom all the elements of beauty had combined with such exquisite proportion and so rhythmical a balance that even as one looked at her he could scarcely believe the evidence of his eyes, so magically did it change and yet remain itself.

Thus, although not over tall, she seemed at times to command a superb and queenly height, then to be almost demurely small and cozy as she pressed close to her companion. Again, her lovely figure seemed never to have lost the lithe slenderness of girlhood, yet it was full, lavish, undulant with all the voluptuous maturity of womanhood, and every movement she made was full of seductive grace.

The woman was fashionably, smartly, and expensively dressed; her little toque-like hat fitted snugly down over a crown of coppery reddish hair and shaded her eyes, which had a smoke-blue and depthless quality that could darken almost into black, and change with every swiftest change of feeling that passed across her face. She was talking to the man in low and tender tones, smiling a vague and voluptuous smile as she looked at him. She spoke eagerly, earnestly, gleefully to him, and from time to time burst into a little laugh that came welling low, rich, sensual, and tender from her throat.

As they walked up and down the platform talking, the woman thrust her small gloved hand through the arm of his heavy overcoat and snuggled close to him, sometimes nestling her lovely head, which was as proud and graceful as a flower, against his arm. Again they would pause, and look steadfastly at each other for a moment. Now she spoke to him with playful reproof, chided him, shook him tenderly by the arms, pulled the heavy furred lapels of his expensive overcoat together, and wagged a small gloved finger at him warningly.

And all the time the man looked at her, saying little, but devouring her with large dark eyes that were burning steadily with the fires of death, and that seemed to feed on her physically, with an insatiate and voracious tenderness of love. He was a Jew, his figure immensely tall, cadaverous, and so wasted by disease that it was lost, engulfed, forgotten, in the heavy and expensive garments that he wore.

His thin white face, which was wasted almost to a fleshless integument of bone and skin, converged to an immense hooked nose, so that his face was not so much a face as a great beak of death, lit by two blazing and voracious eyes and colored on the flanks with two burning flags of red. Yet, with all its ugliness of disease and emaciation, it was a curiously memorable and moving face, a visage somehow nobly tragic with the badge of death.

But now the time had come for parting. The guards were shouting warnings to the passengers; all up and down the platform there were swift and serried movements, hurried eddyings among the groups of friends. One saw people embracing, kissing, clasping hands, crying, laughing, shouting, going back for one more hard swift kiss, and then mounting hastily into their compartments. And one heard in a strange tongue the vows, oaths, promises, the jests and swift allusions, that were secret and precious to each group and that sent them off at once in roars of laughter, the words of farewell that are the same the world over:

"Otto! Otto! . . . Have you got what I gave you? . . . Feel! Is it still there?" He felt; it was still there; fits of laughter.

"Will you see Else?"

"How's that? Can't hear"—shouting, cupping hand to ear, and turning head sideways with a puzzled look.

"I—say—will—you—see—Else?" fairly roared out between cupped palms above the tumult of the crowd.

"Yes. I think so. We expect to meet them at St. Moritz."

"Tell her she's got to write."

"Hey? I can't hear you." Same pantomime as before.

"I—say—tell—her—she's—got—to write" another roar.

"Oh, yes! yes!" nodding quickly, smiling, "I'll tell her."

"—or I'll be mad at her!"

"What? Can't hear you for all this noise"—same business as before.

"I—say—I'll—be—mad—if—she—doesn't—write" roared again at the top of his lungs.

Here a man who had been whispering slyly to a woman, who was trembling with smothered laughter, now turned with a grinning face to shout something at the departing friend, but was checked by the woman, who seized him by the arm and with a face reddened by laughter, gasped hysterically:

"No! No!"

But the man, still grinning, cupped his hands around his mouth and roared:

"Tell Uncle Walter he has got to wear his ——"

"How's that? Can't hear!"—cupping ear and turning head to one side as before.

"I—say," the man began to roar deliberately.

"No! No! No! Sh-h!" the woman gasped frantically, tugging at his arm.

"—to—tell—Uncle Walter—he—must—wear—his—woolen ——"

"No! No! No!—Heinrich! . . . Sh-h!" the woman shrieked.

"The—heavy—ones—Aunt—Bertha—embroidered—with—his—initials!" the man went on relentlessly.

Here the whole crowd roared, and the woman screamed with laughter, shrieking protests, and saying:

"Sh-h! Sh-h!" loudly.

"*Ja*—I'll tell him!" the grinning passenger yelled back at him as soon as they had grown somewhat quieter. "Maybe—he—hasn't—got—'em—any—more," he shouted as a happy afterthought. "Maybe—one—of—the—Frauleins—down—there—" he gasped and choked with laughter.

"Otto!" the woman shrieked. "Sh-h!"

"Maybe—one—of—the—Frauleins—got—them—away—from—" He began to gasp with laughter.

"O-o-o-t-to! . . . Shame on you—Sh-h!" the woman screamed.

"Souvenir—from—old—Munchen," roared back his fellow wit, and the whole group was convulsed again. When they had recovered somewhat, one of the men began in a wheezing and faltering tone, as he wiped his streaming eyes:

"Tell—Else—" Here his voice broke off in a feeble squeak, and he had to pause to wipe his eyes again.

"What?" the grinning passenger yelled back at him.

"Tell—Else," he began more strongly, "that Aunt—Bertha—Oh, my God!" he groaned weakly again, faltered, wiped at his streaming eyes, and was reduced to palsied silence.

"What?—What?" shouted the grinning passenger sharply, clapping his hand to his attentive ear. "Tell Else what?"

"Tell—Else—Aunt—Bertha—is—sending—her—recipe—for—layer—cake," the man fairly screamed now, as if he would get it out at any cost before his impending total collapse. The effect of that apparently meaningless reference to Aunt Bertha's layer cake was astonishing: nothing that had gone before could approach the spasmodic effect it had upon this little group of friends. They were instantly reduced to a shuddering paralysis of laughter, they staggered drunkenly about, clasped one another feebly for support, tears streamed in torrents from their swollen eyes, and from their wide-open mouths there came occasionally feeble wisps of sound, strangled gasps, faint screams from the women, a panting, palsied fit of mirth from which they finally emerged into a kind of hiccoughing recovery.

What it was—the total implication of that apparently banal reference which had thrown them all into such a convulsive fit of merriment—no stranger could ever know, but its effect upon the other people was infectious; they looked toward the group of friends, and grinned, laughed, shook their heads at one another. And so it went all up and down the line. Here were people grave, gay, sad, serious, young, old, calm, casual, and excited; here were people bent on business and people bent on pleasure; here were people sharing by every act, word, and gesture the excitement, joy, and hope which the voyage awakened in them, and people who looked wearily and indifferently about them, settled themselves in their seats, and took no further interest in the events of the departure—but everywhere it was the same.

People were speaking the universal language of departure that varies not the whole world over—that language which is often banal, trivial, and even useless, but on this account curiously moving, since it serves to hide a deeper emotion in the hearts of men, to fill the vacancy that is in their hearts at the thought of parting, to act as a shield, a concealing mask to their true feeling.

And because of this there was for the youth, the stranger and the alien who saw and heard these things, a thrilling and poignant quality in the ceremony of the train's departure. As he saw and heard these familiar words and actions—words and actions that beneath the barrier of an alien tongue were identical to those he had seen and known all his life, among his own people—he felt suddenly, as he had never felt before, the overwhelming loneliness of familiarity, the sense of the human identity that so strangely unites all the people in the world, and that is rooted in the structure of man's life, far below the tongue he speaks, the race of which he is a member.

But now that the time had come for parting, the woman and the dying man said nothing. Clasped arm to arm they looked at each other with a stare of burning and voracious tenderness. They embraced, her arms clasped him, her living and voluptuous body drew toward him, her red lips clung to his mouth as if she could never let him go. Finally, she fairly tore herself away from him, gave him a desperate little push with her hands, and said, "Go, go! It's time!"

Then the scarecrow turned and swiftly climbed into the train, the guard came by and brutally slammed the door behind him, the train began to move slowly out of the station. And all the time the man was leaning from a window in the corridor looking at her, and the woman was walking along beside the train, trying to keep him in sight as long as she could. Now the train gathered motion, the woman's pace slowed, she stopped, her eyes wet, her lips murmuring words no one could hear, and as he vanished from her sight, she cried, *"Auf Wiedersehen!"* and put her hand up to her lips and kissed it to him.

For a moment longer the young man, who was to be this specter's brief companion of the journey, stood looking out the corridor window down the platform toward the great arched station sheds, seeming to look after the group of people departing up the platform, but really seeing nothing but the tall lovely figure of the woman as she walked slowly away, head bent, with a long, deliberate stride of incomparable grace, voluptuous undulance. Once she paused to look back again, then turned and walked slowly as before.

Suddenly she stopped. Someone out of the throng of people on the platform had approached her. It was a young man. The woman paused in a startled manner, lifted one gloved hand in protest, started to go on, and in the next moment they were locked in a savage embrace, devouring each other with passionate kisses.

When the traveler returned to his seat, the dying man, who had already come into the compartment from the corridor and had fallen back into the cushions of his seat, breathing hoarsely, was growing calmer, less exhausted. For a moment the young man looked intently at the beak-like face, the closed weary eyes, wondering if this dying man had seen that meeting on the station platform, and what knowledge such as this could now mean to him. But the mask of death was enigmatic, unrevealing; the youth found there nothing that he could read. A faint and luminous smile was playing at the edges of the man's thin mouth, and his burning eyes were now open, but far and sunken, and seemed to be looking from an unspeakable depth at something that was far away. In a moment, in a profound and tender tone, he said:

"That was my wife. Now in the winter I must go alone, for that is best. But in the spring, when I am better, she will come to me."

All through the wintry afternoon the great train rushed across Bavaria. Swiftly and powerfully it gathered motion, it left the last scattered outposts of the city behind it, and swift as dreams, the train was rushing out across the level plain surrounding Munich.

The day was gray, the sky impenetrable and somewhat heavy, and yet filled with a strong, clean, Alpine vigor, with that odorless and yet exultant energy of cold mountain air. Within an hour the train had entered Alpine country; now there were hills, valleys, the immediate sense of soaring ranges, and the dark enchantment of the forests of Germany, those forests which are something more than trees—which are a spell, a magic, and a sorcery, filling the hearts of men, and particularly those of strangers who have some racial kinship with that land, with a dark music, a haunting memory, never wholly to be captured.

It is an overwhelming feeling of immediate and impending discovery, such as men have who come for the first time to their father's country. It is like coming to that unknown land for which our spirits long so passionately in youth, which is the dark side of our soul, the strange brother and the complement of the land we have known in our childhood. And it is revealed to us instantly the moment that we see it with a powerful emotion of perfect recognition and disbelief, with that dream-like reality of strangeness and familiarity which dreams and all enchantments have.

What is it? What is this wild fierce joy and sorrow swelling in our hearts? What is this memory that we cannot phrase, this incessant recognition for which we have no words? We cannot say. We have no way to give it utterance, no ordered evidence to give it proof, and scornful pride can mock us for a superstitious folly. Yet we will know the dark land at the very moment we come to it, and though we have no tongue, no proof, no utterance for what we feel, we have what we have, we know what we know, we are what we are.

And what are we? We are the lonely naked men, the lost Americans. Immense and lonely skies bend over us, and ten thousand men are marching in our blood. Where does it come from, the constant hunger and the rending lust, and the music, dark and solemn, elfin, magic, sounding through the wood? How is it that this boy, who is American, has known this strange land from the moment that he saw it?

How is it that from his first night in a German town he has understood the tongue he never heard before, has spoken instantly, saying all he wished to say, in a strange language which he could not speak, speaking a weird argot which was neither his nor theirs, of which he was not even conscious, so much did it seem to be the spirit of a language, not the words, he spoke, and instantly, in this fashion, understood by everyone with whom he talked?

No. He could not prove it, yet he knew that it was there, buried deep in the old swarm-haunted brain and blood of man, the utter knowledge of this land and of his father's people. He had felt it all, the tragic and insoluble admixture of the race. He knew the terrible fusion of the brute and of the spirit. He knew the nameless fear of the old barbaric forest, the circle of brutal and barbaric figures gathered round him in their somber and unearthly ring, the sense of drowning in the blind forest horrors of barbaric time. He carried all within himself, the slow gluttony and lust of the unsated swine, as well as all the haunting, strange, and powerful music of the soul.

He knew the hatred and revulsion from the never-sated beast—the beast with the swine-face and the quenchless thirst, the never-ending hunger, the thick, slow, rending hand that fumbled with a brutal, smouldering, and unsated lust. And he hated that great beast with the hate of hell and murder because he felt and knew it in himself and was himself the prey of its rending, quenchless, and obscene desires. Rivers of wine to drink, whole roast oxen turning on the spit, and through the forest murk, the roaring wall of huge beast-bodies and barbaric sound around him, the lavish flesh of the great blonde women, in brutal orgy of the all-devouring, never-sated maw of the great belly, without end or surfeit—all was mixed into his blood, his life, his spirit.

It had been given to him somehow from the dark time-horror of the ancient forest together with all that was soaring, glorious, haunting, strange, and beautiful: the husky horn-notes sounding faint and elfin through the forests, the infinite strange weavings, dense mutations of the old swarm-haunted and Germanic soul of man. How cruel, baffling, strange, and sorrowful was the enigma of the race: the power and strength of the incorruptible and soaring spirit rising from the huge corrupted beast with such a radiant purity, and the powerful enchantments of grand music, noble poetry, so sorrowfully and unalterably woven and inwrought with all the blind brute hunger of the belly and the beast.

It was all his, and all contained in his one life. And it could, he knew, never be distilled out of him, no more than one can secrete from his flesh his father's blood, the ancient and immutable weavings of dark time. And for this reason, as he now looked out the window of the train at the haunting and lonely Alpine land of snow and dark enchanted forest, he felt the sense of familiar recognition instantly, the feeling that he had always known this place, that it was home. And something dark, wild, jubilant, and strange was exulting, swelling in his spirit like a grand and haunting music heard in dreams.

And now, a friendly acquaintance having been established, the specter, with the insatiate, possessive curiosity of his race, began to ply his companion with innumerable questions concerning his life, his home, his profession, the journey he was making, the reason for that journey. The young man answered readily, and without annoyance. He knew that he was being pumped unmercifully, but the dying man's whispering voice was so persuasive, friendly, gentle, his manner so courteous, kind, and insinuating, his smile so luminous and winning, touched with a faint and yet agreeable expression of weariness, that the questions almost seemed to answer themselves.

The young man was an American, was he not? . . . Yes. And how long had he been abroad—two months? Three months? No? Almost a year! So long as that! Then he liked Europe, yes? It was his first trip? No? His fourth?—The specter lifted his eyebrows in expressive astonishment, and yet his sensitive thin mouth was touched all the time by his faint, wearily cynical smile.

Finally, the boy was pumped dry: the specter knew all about him. Then for a moment he sat staring at the youth with his faint, luminous, subtly mocking, and yet kindly smile. At last, wearily, patiently, and with the calm finality of experience and death, he said:

"You are very young. Yes. Now you vant to see it and to haf it all—but you haf nothing. Zat is right—yes?" he said with his persuasive smile. "Zat vill all change. Some day you vill vant only a little—maybe, then, you haf a little—" and he flashed his luminous winning smile again. "And dat iss better—Yes?" He smiled again, and then he said wearily, "I know. I know. Myself, I had gone everyvere like you. I haf tried to see everyt'ing—and I haf had nothing. Now I go no more. Everyvere it iss de same," he said wearily, looking out the window, with a dismissing gesture of his thin white hand. "Fields, hills, mountains, rifers, cities, peoples—You vish to know about zem all. One field, one hill, one rifer," the man whispered, "zat iss enough!"

He closed his eyes for a moment: when he spoke again, his whisper was almost inaudible—"One life, one place, one time."

Darkness came, and the lights in the compartments were turned on. Again that whisper of waning life made its insistent, gentle, and implacable demand upon the youth. This time it asked that the light in the compartment be extinguished, while the specter stretched himself out upon the seat to rest. The younger man consented willingly and even gladly: his own journey was near its end, and outside, the moon, which had risen early, was shining down upon the Alpine forests and snows with a strange, brilliant, and haunting magic which gave to the darkness in the compartment some of its own ghostly and mysterious light.

The specter lay quietly stretched out upon the cushions of the seat, his eyes closed, his wasted face, on which the two bright flags of burning red now shone with a vermilion hue, strange and ghastly in the magic light as the beak of some great bird. The man scarcely seemed to breathe: no sound or movement of life was perceptible in the compartment except the pounding of the wheels, the leathery stretching and creaking sound of the car, and all the strange-familiar and evocative symphony of sounds a train makes— that huge symphonic monotone which is itself the sound of silence and forever.

For some time held in that spell of magic light and time, the youth sat staring out the window at the enchanted world of white and black that swept grandly and strangely past in the haunting and phantasmal radiance of the moon. Finally he got up, went out into the corridor, closing the door carefully behind, and walked back down the narrow passageway through car after car of the rocketing train until he came to the dining car.

Here all was brilliance, movement, luxury, sensual warmth and gaiety. All the life of the train now seemed to be concentered in this place. The waiters, surefooted and deft, were moving swiftly down the aisle of the rocketing car, pausing at each table to serve people from the great platters of well-cooked food which they carried on trays. Behind them the *sommelier* was pulling corks from tall frosty bottles of Rhine wine: he would hold the bottle between his knees as he pulled, the cork would come out with an exhilarating pop, and he would drop the cork into a little basket.

At one table a seductive and beautiful woman was eating with a jaded-looking old man. At another a huge and powerful-looking German, with a wing-collar, a shaven skull, a great swine face, and a forehead of noble and lonely thought, was staring with a concentrated look of bestial gluttony at the tray of meat from which the waiter served him. He was speaking in a guttural and lustful tone, saying, *"Ja! . . . Gut! . . . und etwas von diesem hier auch . . ."*

The scene was one of richness, power, and luxury, evoking as it did the feeling of travel in a crack European express which is different from the feeling one has when he rides on an American train. In America, the train gives one a feeling of wild and lonely joy, a sense of the savage, unfenced, and illimitable wilderness of the country through which the train is rushing, a wordless and unutterable hope, as one thinks of the enchanted city toward which he is speeding; the unknown and fabulous promise of the life he is to find there.

In Europe, the feeling of joy and pleasure is more actual, ever-present. The luxurious trains, the rich furnishings, the deep maroons, dark blues, the fresh, well-groomed vivid colors of the cars, the good food and the cosmopolitan look of the travelers—all of this fills one with a powerful sensual joy, a sense of expectancy about to be realized. In a few hours' time one goes from country to country, through centuries of history, a world of crowded culture, and whole nations swarming with people, from one famous pleasure-city to another.

And instead of the wild joy and nameless hope one feels as he looks out the window of an American train and sees the lonely, savage, and illimitable earth that strokes past calmly and imperturbably like the visage of time and eternity, one feels here (in Europe) an incredible joy of realization, an immediate sensual gratification, a feeling that there is nothing on earth but wealth, power, luxury, and love, and that one can live and enjoy this life, in all the infinite varieties of pleasure, forever.

When the young man had finished eating and paid his bill, he began to walk back again through corridor after corridor along the length of the rocketing train. When he got back to his compartment, he saw the specter lying there as he had left him, stretched out upon the seat, with the brilliant moonlight still blazing on the great beak of his face.

The man had not changed his position by an atom, and yet at once the boy was conscious of some subtle, fatal change he could not define. What was it? He took his seat again and for some time stared fixedly at the silent ghostly figure opposite him. Did he not breathe? He thought, he was almost sure, he saw the motion of his breathing, the rise and fall of the emaciated breast, and yet he was not sure. But what he saw plainly now was that a line, vermilion in its moon-dark hue, had run out of the corner of the firm-set mouth, and that there was a large vermilion stain upon the floor.

What should he do? What could be done? The haunted light of the fatal moon seemed to have steeped his soul in its dark sorcery, in the enchantment of measureless and inert calmness. Already, too, the train was slackening its speed, the first lights of the town appeared, it was his journey's end.

Was it not well to leave all things as he had found them in silence at the end? Might it not be that in this great dream of time in which we live and are the moving figures, there is no greater certitude than this, that having met, spoken, known each other for a moment, as somewhere on this earth we were hurled onward through the darkness between two points of time, it is well to be content with this, to leave each other as we met, letting each one go alone to his appointed destination, sure of this only, needing only this—that there will be silence for us all and silence only, nothing but silence in the end?

And now the train was slowing to a halt. There were the flare of rails, the switch-lights of the yard, small, bright, and hard, green, red, and yellow, poignant in the dark, and on other tracks he could see the little goods cars and the strings of darkened trains, all empty, dark, and waiting with their strange attentiveness of recent life. Then the long station quays began to slide slowly past the windows of the train, and the sturdy goat-like porters were coming on the run, eagerly saluting, speaking, calling to the people in the train who had already begun to pass their baggage through the windows.

Softly the boy took his overcoat and suit-case from the rack above his head and stepped out into the narrow corridor. Quietly he slid the door of the compartment shut behind him. In the semi-darkness of the compartment the spectral figure of the cadaver lay upon the cushions, did not move. Already the train had come to a full stop. The boy went down the corridor to the end, and in a moment, feeling the bracing shock of the cold air upon his lungs, he was going down the quay with a hundred other people, all moving in the same direction, some toward certitude and home, some toward a new land, hope, and hunger, the swelling prescience of joy, the promise of a shining city. He knew that one day he was going home again.

For Professional Appearance

(A SATIRE)

The purposes of Professor Hatcher's celebrated school for dramatists seemed, as stated, to be plain and reasonable enough. Professor Hatcher himself prudently forbore from making extravagant claims concerning the benefits to be derived from his course. He did not say that he could make a dramatist out of any man who came to take his course. He did not predict a successful career in the professional theater for every student who had been a member of his class. He did not even say he could teach a student how to write plays. No. He made, in fact, no claims at all. Whatever he said about his course was very reasonably, prudently, and temperately put: it was impossible to quarrel with it.

All Professor Hatcher said about his course was that if a man had a genuine dramatic and theatrical talent to begin with, he might be able to derive from Professor Hatcher's course a technical and critical guidance which it would be hard to get elsewhere, and which he might find for himself only after years of painful and even wasteful experiment.

Certainly this seemed reasonable enough. Moreover, Professor Hatcher felt that the artist would benefit by what was known as the "round table discussion"—that is, by the comment and criticism of the various members of the class, after Professor Hatcher had read them a play by one of their group. He felt that the spirit of working together, of seeing one's play produced and assisting in the production, of being familiar with all the "arts" of the theater—lighting, designing, directing, acting, and so on—was an experience which should be of immense value to the young dramatist of promise and talent. In short, although he made no assertion that he could create a talent where none was, or give life by technical expertness to the substance of a work that had no real life of its own, Professor Hatcher did feel that he might trim the true lamp to make it burn more brightly by the beneficent tutelage of this influence.

And although it was possible to take issue with him on some of his beliefs—that, for example, the comment and criticism of "the group" and a community of creative spirits were good for the artist—it was impossible to deny that his argument was reasonable, temperate, and conservative in the statement of his purposes.

And he made this plain to every member of his class. Each one was made to understand that the course made no claims of magic alchemy—that he could not be turned into an interesting dramatist if the talent was not there.

But although each member of the class affirmed his understanding of the fundamental truth, and readily said that he accepted it, most of these people, at the bottom of their hearts, believed—pitiably and past belief— that a miracle would be wrought upon their sterile, unproductive spirits, that for them, for *them,* at least, a magic transformation would be brought about upon their miserable small lives and feeble purposes—and all because they now were members of Professor Hatcher's celebrated class.

And for this reason, it was impossible to forget any of these people— poor, damned, dull, sodden, pallid, misbegotten misfits though the most part of them might be—oh, indubitably, damnably, were! For this reason it was impossible to think of them later without a swift feeling of pity and regret, a sudden sense of strangeness, loss, and wonder as one thought of the immense and cruel skies of savage time that bend above America, of all the men now buried in the everlasting earth of the great wilderness, of all the lost, the lonely, and stricken people, the frustrate groping atoms of this earth now past our vision, past our knowledge, emptied out somewhere into the all-engulfing darkness of a hundred million atoms, and a planetary vacancy.

Therefore, one could not forget the people in the class even when one forgot the plays they wrote, the designs and purposes toward which they thought they were working. For it was not the plays they wrote, the pallid aspirations of their inept unfertile spirits, or the fact that they were only the feeble adepts of a feeble cult that made them pitiable and unforgettable. It was not merely that in themselves they were evidences of that vast and tragic phenomenon of culture which had now begun to show itself all through the nation—in those millions of lost souls everywhere who felt that if they could somehow only act in a play or write a book, the vast and nameless misery, failure, vacancy, and unrest in their unprevailing lives would magically be overcome and cured. No—it was not merely this—plays, acting, artistic yearnings, and the art theater with all its portentous triviality, its feeble preciosity, and its pale designs—that made these people tragically memorable. It was not that, after one or two years in Professor Hatcher's class, most of them would accept the inevitable defeat, silently concede his irremediable lack, and then drift quietly back into his appointed corner. It was not merely that the lifeless confinements of some small safe useless place, away from the savage glare and conflict of a life too tough for his thin soul, was sanctuary where most of them must go. It was not merely that most of them could look forward only to being teachers of the drama in some little middle western college, or assistant to a fat, flatulent old woman, or a neurotic and aesthetic female in the poisonous cloisters of the art theater. It was not merely that having made art the basis of their lives without having within them the power, the energy, or the fruitfulness to serve, sustain, or reproduce the faith they followed or the religion they professed— they must have the punishment that art gives to those who thus misuse it— which is utter sterility, the eunuch's impotent hatred against life and against the artist who is able to live, produce, and use it, and finally, utter empty damnation.

No, it was not merely this special form of all their frustrate yearning that made these people memorable. It was not merely that, as cult-adepts in a lifeless cult, they were illustrative of thousands of their kind everywhere who had recoiled in terror and sought refuge and escape, at whatever price, from a life too savage, naked, brutal, and magnificent for their frail sides and tender skins.

No, it was more than this—almost, it might be said of all these people, it was in spite of their special cults rather than because of them that they were pitiable and interesting figures. For it was not merely that they were frustrate members of a cultish creed; it was that they belonged to the nameless and illimitable legion of the lost, the baffled, and the lonely everywhere across the earth, and of whatever class and quality—that made them memorable.

The members of Professor Hatcher's class belonged to the whole lost family of the earth, whose number is uncountable, and for this reason they could never be forgotten.

And, first and foremost, they belonged to that great lost tribe of people who are more numerous in America than in any other country in the world. They belonged to that unnumbered horde who think that somehow, by some magic and miraculous scheme or rule or formula, "something can be done for them." They belong to that huge colony of the damned who buy thousands of books that are printed for their kind, telling them how to run a tea shop, how to develop a pleasing personality, how to acquire "a liberal education," swiftly and easily and with no anguish of the soul, by fifteen minutes' reading every day, how to perform the act of sexual intercourse in such a way that your wife will love you for it, how to have children or keep from having children, how to write short-stories, novels, plays, and verses which are profitably salable, how to keep from having body odor, constipation, bad breath, or tartar on the teeth, how to have good manners, know the proper fork to use for every course, and always do the proper thing— how, in short, to be beautiful, "distinguished," "smart," "chic," "forceful," and "sophisticated"—finally, how to have a "brilliant personality" and to "achieve success."

Yes, for the most part, the members of Professor Hatcher's class belonged to this great colony of the lost Americans. They belonged to that huge tribe of all the damned and lost who feel that everything is going to be all right if they can only take a trip, or learn a rule, or meet a person. They belong to that futile, desolate, and forsaken horde who feel that all will be well with their lives, that all the power they lack themselves will be supplied, and all the anguish, fury, and unrest, the confusion and the dark damnation of man's soul, can magically be healed if only they eat bran for breakfast, secure an introduction to a celebrated actress, get a reading of their manuscript by a friend of Sinclair Lewis, or win admission to Professor Hatcher's celebrated class of dramatists.

And, in a curious way, the plays written by the people in Professor Hatcher's class illustrated, in one form or another, this desire. Few of the plays had any intrinsic reality, for most of these people were lacking in the first, the last, the foremost quality of the artist, without which he is lost: the ability to get out of his own life the power to live and work by, to derive from his own experience—as a fruit of all his seeing, feeling, living, joy, and bitter anguish—the palpable and living substance of his art.

Few of the people in Professor Hatcher's class possessed this power. Few of them had anything of their own to say. Their lives seemed to have grown from a stony and fruitless soil, and, as a consequence, the plays they wrote did not reflect that life, save by a curious and yet illuminating indirection.

Thus, in an extraordinary way, their plays—unreal, sterile, imitative, and derivative as most of them indubitably were—often revealed more about the lives of the people who wrote them than better and more living work could do. For, although few of the plays showed any contact with reality—with that passionate integument of blood and sweat and pain and grief and joy and laughter of which this world is made—most of them did show, in one way or another, what was perhaps the basic impulse in the lives of most of these people—the impulse that had brought them here to Professor Hatcher's class.

And this impulse was not the impulse of the living artist which is first of all the desire to know, to embrace all life, to explore it to its remotest depths, to drown in it, mix it with the currents of his blood and root it in his vitals with an insatiable hunger that consumes and drives him on forever, which knows no end or limit, and which grows forever from the food it feeds upon.

The impulse of the people in Professor Hatcher's class was not to embrace life and devour it, but rather to escape from it. And in one way or another most of the plays these people wrote were illustrative of this desire. For in these plays—unnatural, false, and imitative as they were—one could discern, in however pale and feeble a design, a picture of the world not as its author had seen and lived and known it, but rather as he wished to find it, or believe in it. Thus, these plays were really pallid figmentations of desire, neat little pictures of the world of make-believe in which their makers could find a convenient escape from all the conflict, sweat, and agony of a world too tough for them. And in all their several forms—whether gay, sad, comic, tragic, or fantastical—these plays gave evidence of the denial and fear of life.

The wealthy young dawdler from Philadelphia, for example, wrote plays that had their setting in a charming little French café. Here one was introduced to all the gay, quaint, charming Frenchmen—to Papa Duval, the jolly proprietor, and Mama Duval, his rotund and no less jolly spouse, as well as to all the quaint and curious habitués that are so prolific in theatrical establishments of this order. One met, as well, that fixture of these places: old Monsieur Vernet, the crusty, crotchety, but kindly old gentleman who is the café's oldest customer and has had the same table in the corner by the window for more than thirty years. One saw again the familiar development of the comic situation—the day when Monsieur Vernet enters at his appointed time and finds at his table a total stranger. Sacrilege! Imprecations! Tears, prayers, and entreaties on the part of Papa Duval and his wife, together with the stubborn refusal of the imperious stranger to move. Climax: old Monsieur Vernet storming out of the café, swearing that he will never return. Resolution of the conflict: the efforts of Papa and Mama Duval to bring their most prized customer back into the fold again, and their final success, the pacification and return of Monsieur Vernet amid great rejoicing, thanks to a cunning stratagem on the part of Henri, the young waiter, who wins a reward for all these efforts, the hand of Mimi, Papa and Mama Duval's charming daughter, from whom he has been separated by Papa Duval's stern decree.

Thus, custom is restored and true love reunited by one brilliant comic stroke!

And all this pretty little world, the contribution of a rich young man who came from Philadelphia! How perfectly God-damn delightful it was, to be sure!

The plays of old Seth Flint, the sour and withered ex-reporter, were, if of a different coloring, cut from the same gaudy cloth of theatrical unreality. For forty years old Seth had pounded precincts as a news-man, and had known city-rooms across the nation. Now at his life's close, he was yielding to the only self-indulgence he had ever known—a year away from the city-room of a Denver newspaper, a year away in the rare ether, among the precious and aesthetic intellects of Professor Hatcher's celebrated course, a year in which to realize the dream of a lifetime, the vision of his youth—a year in which to write the plays he had always dreamed of writing.

And what kind of plays did he write? Here was an interesting man, a creature full of courage, wisdom, understanding, humor, and the stern granite of an impregnable character. Here was a man who had seen, known, and lived as much of the horror of life as one man's life could hold. Here was a man who had known all the blood, sweat, anguish, failure, joy, hope, the savage, huge, and tortured unrest of America in all its unspeakable ugliness, in all its unutterable beauty, in all its wildness, harshness, barrenness, sweetness, desolation, and abundance—here was a man who had within his withered old mummy of a body the living stuff of life, in all its passionate integument—the living stuff from which a hundred living books or plays could be created. Here was a man who had been faithful to his young man's dream, and had now in his sixtieth year come here among these young men to fulfill his own dream of youth—to write the plays he had wanted to write as a young man. And what kind of plays did he write?

Alas! Old Seth did exactly what he set out to do, he succeeded perfectly in fulfilling his desire—and by tragic irony, his failure lay in just that fact. The plays which he produced with an astounding and prolific ease— ("Three days is enough to write a play," the old man said in his sour voice. "You guys who take a year to write a play give me a pain. If you can't write a play in a week, you can't write anything; the play's no good.")—these plays were just the plays which he had dreamed of writing as a young man, and therein was evident their irremediable fault.

For Seth's plays—so neat, brisk, glib, and smartly done—would have been good plays in a commercial way, as well, if he had only done them twenty years before. He wrote plays in which the babies got mixed up in the maternity ward of a great hospital, in which the rich man's child goes to the family of the little grocer, and the grocer's child grows up to be the heir of an enormous fortune, with all the luxuries and securities of wealth around him. And he brought about the final resolution of this tangled scheme, the meeting of these scrambled children and their bewildered parents, with a skill of complication, a design of plot, a dexterity that was astonishing. His characters—all well-known types of the theater, as of nurse tough-spoken, shop-girl slangy, reporter cynical, and so on—were well-conceived to fret their purposes, their lines well-timed and apt and deftly made. He had mastered the formula of an older type of "well-made" play with astonishing success. Only, the type was dead; the interest of the public in such plays had vanished twenty years before.

So here was a man, a live man, writing with amazing skill, dead plays for a theater that was dead, and for a public that did not exist.

"Chekov! Ibsen!" old Seth would whine sourly with a dismissive gesture of his parchmented old hand, and a scornful contortion of his bitter mouth in his old mummy of a face. "You guys make me tired the way you worship them!" he would whine out at some of the exquisite young temperaments in Professor Hatcher's class. "Those guys can't write a play! Take Chekov, now!" whined Seth. "That guy never wrote a real play in his life! He never knew how to write a play! He couldn't have written a play if he'd tried! He never learned the rules of writing a play!—That *Cherry Orchard* now," whined old Seth with a sour sneering laugh, "—that *Cherry Orchard* that you guys are always raving about! That's not a play!" he cried indignantly. "Whatever made you think it was a play? I was trying to read it just the other day," he rasped, "and there's nothing there to hold your interest! It's got no *plot!* There's no story in it! There's no suspense! Nothing happens in it. All you got is a lot of people who do nothing but talk all the time. You never get anywhere," said Seth scornfully. "And to hear you guys rave about it, you'd think it was a great play."

"Well, what do you call a great play, then, if *The Cherry Orchard* isn't one?" one of the young men said acidly. "Who wrote the great plays that you talk about?"

"Why, George M. Cohan wrote some," whined Seth instantly. "That's who. Avery Hopwood wrote some great plays. We've had plenty of guys in this country who wrote great plays. If they'd come from Russia, you'd get down and worship 'em," he said bitterly. "But just because they came out of this country they're no good!"

In the relation of the class toward old Seth Flint, it was possible to see the basic falseness of their relation toward life everywhere around them. For here was a man—whatever his defects as a playwright might have been—who had lived incomparably the richest, most varied and dangerous, and eventful life among them; he was himself far more interesting than any of the plays they wrote, and as dramatists they should have recognized and understood his quality. But they saw none of this. For their relation toward life and such people as old Seth Flint was not one of understanding. It was not even one of burning indignation—of that indignation which is one of the dynamic forces in the artist's life. It was rather one of supercilious scorn and ridicule.

They felt they were "above" old Seth, and most of the other people in the world, and for this reason they were in Professor Hatcher's class. Of Seth they said:

"He's really a misfit, terribly out of place here. I wonder why he came."

And they would listen to an account of one of Seth's latest errors in good taste with the expression of astounded disbelief, the tones of stunned incredulity which were coming into fashion about that time among elegant young men.

"No really! . . . But he never really said *that*. . . . You *can't* mean it."

"Oh, but I assure you, he did!"

". . . It's simply past belief! . . . I can't believe he's as bad as *that*."

"Oh, but he *is!* It's incredible, I know, but you've no idea what he's capable of." And so on.

And yet old Seth Flint was badly needed in that class: his bitter and unvarnished tongue caused Professor Hatcher many painful moments, but it had its use—oh, it had its use, particularly when the play was of this nature:

> IRENE (*slowly, with scorn and contempt in her voice*) So—It has come to this! This is all your love amounts to—a little petty selfish thing! I had thought you were bigger than that, John.
>
> JOHN (*desperately*) But—but, my God, Irene—what am I to think? I found you in bed with him, my best friend! (*with difficulty*) You know—that looks suspicious, to say the least!
>
> IRENE (*softly—with amused contempt in her voice*) You poor little man! And to think I thought your love was so big.
>
> JOHN (*wildly*) But I do love you, Irene. That's just the point.
>
> IRENE (*with passionate scorn*) Love! You don't know what love means! Love

is bigger than that! Love is big enough for all things, all people. *(She extends her arms in an all-embracing gesture.)* My love takes in the world—it embraces all mankind! It is glamorous, wild, free as the wind, John.

JOHN *(slowly)* Then you have had other lovers?

IRENE: Lovers come, lovers go. *(She makes an impatient gesture.)* What is that? Nothing! Only love endures—my love which is greater than all.

The youth would writhe in his seat, and clench his hands convulsively. Then he would turn almost prayerfully to the bitter, mummied face of old Seth Flint for that barbed but cleansing vulgarity that always followed such a scene:

"Well?" Professor Hatcher would say, putting down the manuscript he had been reading, taking off his eyeglasses (which were attached to a ribbon of black silk) and looking around with a quizzical smile, an impassive expression on his fine, distinguished face. "Well?" he would say again urbanely as no one answered. "Is there any comment?"

"What is she?" Seth would break the nervous silence with his rasping snarl. "Another one of these society whores? You know," he continued, "you can find plenty of her kind for three dollars a throw without any of that fancy palaver."

Some of the class smiled faintly, painfully, and glanced at each other with slight shrugs of horror; others were grateful, felt pleasure well in them and said underneath their breath exultantly:

"Good old Seth! Good old Seth!"

"Her love is big enough for all things, is it?" said Seth. "I know a truck driver out in Denver I'll match against her any day."

The youth and Ed Horton, a large and robust aspirant from the Iowa cornlands, roared with happy laughter, poking each other sharply in the ribs.

"Do you think the play will act?" someone said. "It seems to me that it comes pretty close to closet drama."

"If you ask me," said Seth, "it comes pretty close to water-closet drama. . . . No," he said sourly. "What that boy needs is a little experience. He ought to go out and get him a woman and get all that stuff off his mind. After that, he might sit down and write a play."

For a moment there was a very awkward silence, and Professor Hatcher smiled a little palely. Then, taking his eyeglasses off with a distinguished movement, he looked around and said:

"Is there any other comment?"

The Names of the Nation

Brother, I know and I know and yet it will always be the same. They said that we are base and false, our lives shabby, ugly, paltry, worthless, dull, and let them have it as they will, for I know and I know, they said that beauty, mercy, pity, peace, and love had no place in us, and I know, I know, they said there was no glory, grandeur, greatness in our lives, and I know, and I know, and I know!

But we heard a sound of marching in the night, we heard a sound of great hooves on the land by night, and in night-time, in the dark, Lee rode by us in Virginia on his great white horse.

Brother, I know and I know, and many years have passed since we rushed forward in the dark together, and the river has flowed onward in the night, and yet it will always be the same forever.

For I have heard the thousand phrases of their disbelief—the scorn of clever men, the ridicule of their bright bitter minds, the weariness and mockery of a barren people, the certain knowledge of the knowing fool, the bitter curse of exiled men, the harsh indictment of the wanderer—and all they said was true enough, but there was something yet which never has been spoken, and I knew and I knew, and it would always be the same.

"One time!" their voices cried, leaning upon a bar the bitter weight of all their discontent. "One time! I've been back one time—just once in seven years," they said, "and Jesus that was plenty! One time was enough. To hell with that damned country! What have they got now but a lot of cheap spaghetti joints and skyscrapers?" they said. "If you want a drink, you sneak down three back alleyways, get the once-over from a couple of ex-prize fighters, and then plank down a dollar for a shot of varnish that would rot the guts out of a goat! . . . And the women!"—the voices rose here with infuriated scorn. "What a nice lot of cold-blooded gold-digging bastards *they've* turned out to be! . . . I spent thirty dollars taking one of 'em to a show and to a night club afterward. When bedtime came, do you think I got anything out of it? . . . 'You may kiss my little hand,' she says . . . 'You may kiss my little ——, that's what you may do,'" the voices snarled with righteous bitterness. "When I asked her if she was going to come through, she started to yell for the cops! . . . A woman who tried to pull one like that

185

over here would get sent to Siberia! . . . A nice country I don't think! . . . Now, get this! *Me*, I'm a Frenchman, see!" the voices said with a convincing earnestness. "These guys know how to *live*, see? This is my country, where I belong. See? . . . Johnny, *luh meme chose pour mwah et m'seer!* . . . Fill 'em up again, kid."

"Carpen-*teer!*" the voices then rose jeeringly, in true accents of French pugnacity. "Sure, I'm a Frenchman—but Carpen-*teer!* Where do yuh get that stuff? Christ, Dempsey could a took that frog the best day he ever saw! . . . An accident!" the voices yelled. "Whattya mean—an accident? Didn't I see the whole thing with my own eyes? Wasn't I back there then? . . . Wasn't I talkin' t' Jack himself an hour after the fight was over? . . . An accident! Jesus! The only accident was that he let him last four rounds. 'I could have taken him in the first if I wanted to,' Jack says to me. . . . Sure, I'm a Frenchman!" the voice said with belligerent loyalty. "But Carpenteer! Jesus! Where do you get that stuff?"

And, brother, I have heard the voices you will never hear discussing the graces of a life more cultured than any you will ever know—and I know and I know, and yet it is still the same.

Bitterly, bitterly Boston one time more! the flying leaf, the broken cloud—"I think," said they, "that we will live here now I think," they said, "that we are running down to Spain next week so Francis can do a little writing. . . . And really," their gay yet cultivated tones continued, "it's wonderful what you can do here if you only have a little money. . . . *Yes*, my dear!" their refined accents continued in a tone of gay conviction. "It's really quite incredible, you know . . . I happen to know of a real honest-to-goodness château near Blois that can be had for something less than seven thousand dollars! . . . It's all rather incredible, you know," those light half-English tones went on, "when you consider what it takes to live in Brookline! . . . Francis has always felt that he would like to do a little writing, and I feel somehow the atmosphere is better here for all that sort of thing—it really is, you know. Don't you think so?" said those gay and cultivated tones of Boston which you, my brother, never yet have heard. "And after all," those cultivated tones went on in accents of a droll sincerity, "you see all the people here you care to see, I *mean*, you know! They all come to Paris at one time or other—I *mean*, the trouble really is in getting a little time alone for yourself. . . . Or do you find it so?" the voices suavely, lightly asked me. . . . "Oh, look! Look at that—there!" they cried with jubilant elation. "I mean that boy and his girl there walking along with their arms around each other! . . . Don't you just a-do-o-re it? . . . Isn't it too *ma-a-rvelous?*" those refined and silvery tones went on with patriotic tenderness. "I mean, there's something so perfectly sweet and unselfconscious about it all!" the voices said with all the cultivated earnestness of Boston. "Now *where?*—where?—would you see something like that at home?" the voices said triumphantly.

(Seldom in Brookline, lady. O rarely, seldom, almost never in the town of Brookline, lady. But on the Esplanade—did you ever go out walking on the Esplanade at night-time, in the hot and gelid month of August, lady? They are not Frenchmen, lady: they are all Jews and Irish and Italians, lady, but the noise of their kissing is like the noise the wind makes through a leafy grove—it is like the great hooves of a hundred thousand cavalry being pulled out of the marshy places of the earth, dear lady.)

"... I *mean*—these people really understand that sort of thing so much better than we do. . . . They're so much *simpler* about it . . . I mean so much more graceful with that kind of thing. . . . *Il faut un peu de sentiment, n'est-ce pas?* . . . Or do you think so?" said those light, those gay, those silvery and half-English tones of cultivated Boston which you, my brother, never yet have heard.

(I got you, lady. That was French. I know. . . . But if I felt your leg, if in a somewhat graceful Gallic way I felt your leg and said, "*Chérie! Petite chérie!*"—would you remember, lady, this is Paris?)

O bitterly, bitterly Boston one time more: their silvery voices speak an accent you will never know, and of their loins is marble made, but, brother, there are corn-haired girls named Nielsen out in Minnesota, and the blonde thighs of the Lundquist girl could break a bullock's back.

O bitterly, bitterly Boston one time more, the French have little ways about them that we do not have, but, brother, they're still selling cradles down in Georgia, and in New Orleans their eyes are dark, their white teeth bite you to the bone.

O bitterly, bitterly Boston one time more, and of their flesh is codfish made, but Big Brother's still waiting for you with his huge red fist behind the barn up in the State of Maine, and they're still having shotgun marriages at home.

Oh, brother, there are voices that you will never hear—ancestral voices prophesying war, my brother, and rare and radiant voices that you know not of, as they have read us into doom. The genteel voice of Oxenford broke once like chimes of weary unenthusiastic bells across my brain, speaking to me compassionately its judgment on our corrupted lives, gently dealing with the universe, my brother, gently and without labor—gently, brother, gently it dealt with all of us with easy condescension and amused disdain:

"I'm afraid, old boy," the genteel voice of Oxenford remarked, "you're up against it over thöh. . . . I really am . . . Thös no place thöh faw the individual any longah," the genteel voice went on, un-individual brother. "Obviously," that tolerant voice instructed me, "obviously, thöh can be no cultuah in a country so completely lackin' in tradition as is yöahs. . . . It's all so objective—if you see what I main—thös no place left faw the innah life," it said, oh outward brother! . . . "We Europeans have often obsöved (it's *very* curious, you know) that the American is incapable of any real feelin'—it seems quite impawsible faw him to distinguish between true emotion an' sentimentality—an' he *invayably* chooses the lattah! . . . *Curious,* isn't it?"—or do you think so, brother? "Of co'se, thöh is yoah beastly sex-prawblem. . . . Yoah women! . . . Oh, deah, deah! . . . Perhaps we'd bettah say no moah . . . but, thöh you *ah!*"—right in the eye, brother. "Yoah country is a matriahky, my deah fellah . . . it really is, you know" . . . if you can follow us, dear brother. "The women have the men in a state of complete subjection . . . the male is rapidly becomin' moah sexless and emasculated"—that genteel voice of doom went on—"No!—decidedly you have quite a prawblem befoah you. . . . Obviously thöh can be no cultuah while such a condition puhsists. . . . *That* is why when my friends say to me, 'You ought to see *America.* . . . You really ought, you know' . . . I say, 'No thanks. . . . If you don't mind, I'd rathah not. . . . I think I'll stay at home'" . . . "I'm sorry," the compassionate tones of Oxenford went on, "but that's the way I feel—it really is, you know. . . . Of co'se, I know you couldn't understand my feelin'—faw aftah all, you ah a Yank—but thöh you ah! Sorry!" it said regretfully, as it spoke to me its courteous and inexpiable judgments of eternal exile, brother, and removed forever the possibility of your ever knowing him. "But that's the way I feel! I hope you don't mind," the voice said gently, with compassion.

No, sir, I don't mind. We don't mind, he, she, it, or they don't mind. Nobody minds, sir, nobody minds, Because, just as you say, sir, oceans are between us, seas have sundered us, there is a magic in you that we cannot fathom—a light, a flame, a glory—an impalpable, indefinable, incomprehensible, undeniable something-or-other which I can never understand or measure because—just as you say, sir, with such compassionate regret—I am—I am—a Yank.

'Tis true, my brother, we are Yanks. Oh, 'tis true, 'tis true! I am a Yank! Yet, wherefore Yank, good brother? Hath not a Yank ears? Hath not a Yank lies, truths, bowels of mercy, fears, joys, and lusts? Is he not warmed by the same sun, washed by the same ocean, rotted by the same decay, and eaten by the same worms as a German is? If you kill him, does he not die? If you sweat him, does he not stink? If you lie with his wife or mistress, does she not whore, lie, fornicate, betray, even as a Frenchman does? If you strip him, is he not naked as a Swede? Is his hide less white than Baudelaire's? Is his breath more foul than the King of Spain's? Is his belly bigger, his neck fatter, his face more hoggish, and his eyes more shiny than a Munich brewer's? Will he not cheat, rape, thieve, whore, curse, hate, and murder like any European? Aye—Yank! But wherefore, wherefore, Yank, good brother?

My brother did not answer: the great stars blazed above us, shining faintly on his knit brows, his restless frenzied eyes, his drawn face, as the immense and mournful earth wheeled on around us, and we rushed forward forever into the limitless gulf of night.

.   .   .

Brother, I know and I know, and many years have passed since we rushed forward in the dark together, and the river has flowed onward in the night, and yet it will always be the same forever.

Wandering forever and the earth again! Yes, brother, we were living before that, and also we are living after—save that we stoop a little more, and go more slowly, and our eyes are worn a little more by hauntings of old things, and there are many things now we can't forget.

Brother, have we forgotten how the peach trees leaned across a wall, and how the blossoms drifted to the earth in Spring, in April, in the orchard of our father's house? Have we forgotten the cool and purple glade of evening marching up the hill's steep side, the dogs barking, and the soft, the sad, the come-to-meeting bells across the hush of evening countrysides? And did the broken tinkling of the fat-bellied cows as they plod home in bedded dust at night, never make echoes in an exile's brain? And then the cool, the dew-cool of the night, the after-supper sounds on the high front porches, the great rise of our father's voice, the smell of honeysuckle sagging on the old wire fence, and all of the fire-flies trembling in the dark, and over all, like time, like sleep, like blessed peace and certitude, the vast low stammer of the night?

Will they never come back to us, never again—the forgotten faces, the old lost scenes? Will we never go back to them, never feel pain for them, never return to them, never again? Have we forgotten these things and our father's face: will we rush blindly into night forever—brother and stranger and friend?

Oh, I know and I know, and it will always be the same forever. For I have lived alone ten thousand nights of solitude and darkness, and waked at morning in a foreign land, and thought of home. And the years walked proudly in my brain, my father's voice was sounding in my ear, and in the pulses of my blood the substance of my earth remained and would not die.

Oh, stored with memory our living dust, within the shadow of our eyes were held the faces of the dead who died and live forever, two hundred million men were walking in our bones, and when we heard the howling of the wind around forgotten eaves in old October, we could not sleep. And by the waters of life, by time, by time, we stood and watched the rivers of this earth flow under us, and we knew it would be the same with us forever!

Brother, have we come then from a fated stock? Augured from its birth, announced by two dark angels, named in our mother's womb? And for what? Fatherless, to grope our feelers in the sea's dark bed, among the polyped squirms, the blind sucks and crawls, the seavalves of the brain, loaded with memory that will not die? To cry our love out in the wilderness, to wake always in the night, smiting the pillow in some foreign land, thinking forever of the myriad sights and sounds of home?

"While Paris Sleeps!"—By God, while Paris sleeps, to wake and walk and not to sleep; to wake and walk and sleep and wake, and sleep again, seeing dawn come before the window square that cast its wedge before our glazed, half-sleeping eyes, seeing soft hated foreign light, and breathing soft dull languid air that could not bite and tingle up the blood. Seeing legend and lie and fable wither in our sight, as we saw what we saw, we knew what we knew.

Sons of the lost and lonely father, sons of the wanderers, children of the hardy loins, the savage earth, the pioneers, what had we to do with all their bells and churches? Could we feed our hunger on portraits of the Spanish king? Brother, for what? For what? To kill the giant of loneliness and fear, to slay the hunger that would not give us rest.

Of wandering forever and the earth again. Brother, for what? For what? For the wilderness, the immense and lonely land. For the unendurable hunger, the unendurable ache, the incurable loneliness. For the exultancy whose only answer is the wild goat-cry. For a million memories, ten thousand sights and sounds and shapes and smells and names of things that only we can know.

For what? For what? Not for a nation. Not for a people, not for an empire, not for a thing we love or hate.

For what? For a cry, a space, an ecstasy. For a savage and nameless hunger. For a living and intolerable memory that may not for a second be forgotten, since it includes all the moments of our lives, it includes all we do and are. For a living memory; for ten thousand memories; for a million sights and sounds and moments; for something like nothing else on earth; for something which possesses us.

For something under our feet, and around us and over us; something that is in us and part of us, and proceeds from us, that beats in the pulses of our blood.

Brother, for what?

First, for the thunder of the imperial names, the names of men and battles, the names of places and great rivers, the mighty names of the States. The name of the Wilderness; the names of Antietam, Chancellorsville, Shiloh, Bull Run, Fredricksburg, Cold Harbor, the Wheat Fields, Ball's Bluff, and the Devil's Den; the name of Cowpens, Brandywine, and Saratoga; of Death Valley, Chickamauga, and the Cumberland Gap. The names of the Nantahalas, the Bad Lands, the Painted Desert, the Yosemite, and the Little Big Horn; the names of Yancey and Cabarras counties; and the terrible name of Hatteras.

Then for the continental thunder of the States: the names of Montana, Texas, Arizona, Colorado, Michigan, Maryland, Virginia, and the two Dakotas, the names of Oregon and Indiana, of Kansas and the rich Ohio; the powerful name of Pennsylvania, and the name of Old Kentucky; the undulance of Alabama; the names of Florida and North Carolina.

.   .   .

In the red-oak thickets at the break of day long hunters lay for bear: the rattle of arrows in laurel leaves, the war-cries round the painted buttes, and the majestical names of the Indian nations: the Pawnees, the Algonquins, the Cherokees, the Sioux, the Hurons, the Mohawks, the Navahos, the Utes, the Omahas, the Onandagas, the Chippewas, the Creeks, the Chickasaws, the Arapahos, the Catawbas, the Dakotas, the Apaches, the Croatans, and the Tuscaroras. The names of Powhatan and Sitting Bull, and the name of Great Chief Rain-In-The-Face.

Of wandering forever and the earth again: in red-oak thickets at the break of day long hunters lay for bear. The arrows rattle in the laurel leaves, and the elmroots thread the bones of buried lovers. There have been war-cries on the western trails, and on the plains the gunstock rusts into a handful of bleached bones. The barren earth? Was no love living in the wilderness?

The rails go westward in the dark. Brother, have you seen the starlight on the rails? Have you heard the thunder of the fast express?

Of wandering forever and the earth again: the names of the mighty rails that bind the nation, the wheeled thunder of the names that net the continent: the Pennsylvania, the Union Pacific, the Santa Fe, the Baltimore and Ohio, the Chicago and Northwestern, the Southern, the Louisiana and Northern, the Seaboard Air Line, the Chicago, Milwaukee, and St. Paul; the Lackawanna; the New York, New Haven, and Hartford; the Florida East Coast; the Rock Island; and the Denver and Rio Grande.

Brother, the names of the engines, the engineers, and the sleeping cars: the great engines of the Pacific type, the articulated mallets with three sets of eight-yoked driving wheels, the four hundred ton thunderbolts with J. T. Cline, T. J. McRae, and the demon hawkeyes of H. D. Campbell on the rails.

The names of the great tramps who range the nation on the fastest trains: the names of the great tramps Oklahoma, Red Fargo Pete, Dixie Joe, Iron Mike, the Frisco Kid, Nigger Dick, Ike the Kike, and the Jersey Dutchman.

By the waters of life, by time, by time, Lord Tennyson stood among the rocks, and stared. He had long hair, his eyes were deep and somber, and he wore a cape; he was a poet, and there was magic and mystery in his touch, for he had heard the horns of Elfland faintly blowing. And by the waters of life, by time, by time, Lord Tennyson stood among the cold gray rocks and commanded the sea to break—break —break! And the sea broke, by the waters of life, by time, by time, as Lord Tennyson commanded it to do, and his heart was sad and lonely as he watched the stately ships (of the Hamburg-American Packet Company, fares forty-five dollars and up, first class) go on to their haven under the hill, and Lord Tennyson would that his heart could utter the thoughts that arose in him.

By the waters of life, by time, by time: the names of the mighty rivers, the alluvial gluts, the drains of the continent, the throats that drink America (Sweet Thames, flow gently till I end my song). The names of the men who pass and the myriad names of the earth that abides forever: the names of the men who are doomed to wander and the name of that immense and lonely land on which they wander, to which they return, in which they will be buried—America! The immortal earth that waits forever, the trains that thunder on the continent, the men who wander, and the women who cry out, "Return."

Finally, the names of the great rivers that are flowing in the darkness (Sweet Thames, flow gently till I end my song).

By the waters of life, by time, by time: the names of the great mouths, the mighty maws, the vast wet coiling never glutted and unending snakes that drink the continent. Where, sons of men, and in what other land, will you find others like them, and where can you match the mighty music of their names?—the Monongahela, the Colorado, the Rio Grande, the Columbia, the Tennessee, the Hudson (Sweet Thames!); the Kennebec, the Rappahannock, the Delaware, the Penobscot, the Wabash, the Chesapeake, the Swannanoa, the Indian River, the Niagara (Sweet Afton!), the Saint Lawrence, the Susquehanna, the Tombigbee, the Nantahala, the French Broad, the Chattahoochee, the Arizona, and the Potomac (Father Tiber!)— these are a few of their great proud glittering names, fit for the immense and lonely land that they inhabit.

O Tiber! Father Tiber! You'd only be a suckling in that mighty land! And as for you, Sweet Thames, flow gently till I end my song: flow gently, gentle Thames, be well-behaved, sweet Thames, speak softly and politely, little Thames, flow gently till I end my song.

By the waters of life, by time, by time, and of the yellow cat that smites the nation, of the belly of the snake that coils across the land—of the terrible names of the rivers in flood, the rivers that foam and welter in the dark, that smash the levees, that flood the lowlands for two thousand miles, that carry the bones of the cities seaward on their tides: of the awful names of the Tennessee, the Arkansas, the Missouri, the Mississippi, and even the little mountain rivers, brother, in the season of the floods.

Delicately they dive for Greeks before the railway station: the canoe glides gently through the portals of the waiting room (for whites). Full fathom five the carcass of old man Lype is lying (of his bones is coral made) and delicately they dive for lunch-room Greeks before the railway station.

Brother, what fish are these? The floatage of sunken rooms, the sodden bridal veils of poverty, the slime of ruined parlor plush, drowned faces in the family album; and the blur of long-drowned eyes, blurred features, white, bloated flesh.

Delicately they dive for Greeks before the railway station. The stern good half-drowned faces of the brothers Trade and Mark survey the tides. Cardui! Miss Lillian Leitzel twists upon one arm above the flood, the clown, half-sunken to the waist, swims upward out of the swirling yellow, the tiger bares his teeth above the surges of a river he will never drink. The ragged tatters of circus posters are plastered on soaked boards. And delicately they dive for Greeks before the railway stations.

Have you not seen them, brother?

And finally, brother, the mighty name of the earth itself, on which we live and move, that wheels past us with immortal stroke and calm and silence, as we rush onward into the night.

For only the earth endures, but this earth is America, and America is this earth, and while this earth endures, America endures. America is immense and everlasting: it must endure forever. The wheel will rust, the tallest towers will topple down like smoke, the hundred thousand towns and cities, the new and old, the permanent and the impermanent, those built for a day and those built forever, will melt before the waters of time. They will be compacted into earth and dust as the bones of the wanderers and those weary of wandering have been compacted into earth and dust, but the great rivers of America will drink the continent, and the earth will endure forever.

For only the earth endures, the immense and everlasting earth whereon we have all lived as wanderers and strangers. Only the earth endures, the terrific earth that needed giants, and that broke the backs of mighty men. Only the earth endures, the enormous earth with its incredible beauty, its terrific desolation, the American earth that can never be remembered, that can never be forgotten, and that has never been described. Only the earth endures, that strange and lonely continent of earth that bred the race of wanderers, that secret and mysterious earth which has always been unknown.

Brother, it has possessed the bones of our father, it has possessed and knit with elmroot the bones of buried lovers, it has possessed and made its own the million secret moments of our lives. In it is our life and our destiny, and our immense and secret history.

By the waters of life, by time, by time, the slow tides and secret movings of dark time, the dust of our cities melts into earth: it will possess and drink into itself the bones of the cities, the ruins of great towers and ten million streets—yes! it will possess strong steel and the iron of great wheels and make its own great engines, as it makes our dust its own.

For what are we, brother? We are a phantom flare of grieved desire, the ghostling and phosphoric flickers of immortal time, a brevity of days haunted by the eternity of the earth. We are an unspeakable utterance, an insatiable hunger, an unquenchable thirst; a lust that bursts our sinews, explodes our brains, sickens and rots our guts, and rips our heart asunder. We are a twist of passion, a moment's flame of love and ecstasy, a sinew of bright blood and agony, a lost cry, a music of pain and joy, a haunting of brief sharp hours, an almost captured beauty, a demon's whisper of unbodied memory. We are the dupes of time.

We are the sons of our father, whose face we shall never see again, we are the sons of our father, whose voice we shall hear no more, we are the sons of our father, to whom we have cried for strength and comfort in our agony, we are the sons of our father, whose life like ours was lived in solitude and darkness, we are the sons of our father, to whom only can we wreak out the strange dark burden of our heart and spirit, we are the sons of our father who is dead, and we shall follow the print of his foot forever.

One of the Girls in Our Party

The mid-day meal was ended and "the tour"—a group of thirty women, all of them teachers from the public schools of the American Middle West— had got up from their tables and left the dining-room of the sedate little Swiss hotel where they were quartered. Now they were gathered in the hall beyond: their voices, shrill, rasping, and metallic, could be heard lifted in a united clamor of strident eagerness. In a moment one of the older women, who wore an air of authority, returned to the dining room, and looking through the door at two young women who were still seated at one of the tables hastily bolting a belated luncheon, she called imperatively:

"Miss Turner! Miss Blake! Aren't you coming? The bus is here."

"All right!" Miss Turner, the smaller of the two women, was the one who answered. "In a moment."

"Well, you hurry, then," the woman said in an admonishing tone as she turned to go. "Everyone else is ready: we're waiting on you."

"Come on," Miss Turner said quickly, in a lowered tone, as she turned to Miss Blake, "I guess we'd better go. You know how cranky they get if you keep them waiting."

"Well, you go on, then," said Miss Blake calmly. "I'm not coming." Miss Turner looked at her with surprise. "I've decided to pass this one up. I've got some letters to answer, and if I don't do it now, they just won't get answered."

"I know," said Miss Turner. "I haven't written a word to anyone in two weeks. The way they keep you on the go, there's no time to write." The two women got up from the table, moved toward the door, and there faced each other in a gesture of instinctive farewell. Then for a moment each stood in a constrained and awkward silence, as if waiting for the other one to speak. It was Miss Turner who first broke the pause:

"Well, I guess that means I won't see you again, will I?"

"Why?" Miss Blake said. "You'll come back here before you get your train, won't you?"

"No," said Miss Turner, "I don't think so. They've taken our baggage to

195

the station, and I think we're going to get out there on the way back—I mean, all the girls in *my* party."

"Well," Miss Blake said, in her curiously flat and toneless way, "I guess I won't see you, then—not until we get to Vienna, anyway. I'll see you there."

"Yes," Miss Turner agreed, "and I want to hear all about it, too. I almost wish I were going along with you—I've always wanted to see Italy—I'd almost rather go there than where we're going, but you can't take in everything at one time, can you?"

"No," Miss Blake agreed, "you certainly can't."

"But I think it's just wonderful how much you do see!" Miss Turner went on with considerable enthusiasm. "I mean, when you consider that the whole tour only lasts six weeks from the time you leave home, it's wonderful how much you do take in, isn't it?"

"Yes," Miss Blake said, "it certainly is."

"Well, good-bye. I guess I'd better go."

"Yes, you'd better," Miss Blake answered. "I wouldn't want you to miss the bus. Good-bye."

"Good-bye," Miss Turner answered. "I'll see you in Vienna. Have a good time, and take care of yourself, now."

"All right," Miss Blake said flatly. "You do the same."

Miss Blake watched the bus go, then turned and went quickly upstairs to her room and set to work on her unfinished letters. She wrote:

England was the first place we went to when we left the ship. We were in England a whole week, but it rained all the time we were in London. The coffee that they drink is awful. All the traffic goes to the left in London, and none of the girls could get used to this. Miss Cramer, who is one of the girls in our party, came within an inch of being run over one day because she was looking in the wrong direction; I know they have a lot of accidents. London was also the place where Miss Jordan slipped and fell and sprained her ankle when getting out of the bus. She is one of the girls in our party. She didn't get to see anything in London because she was in bed all the time we were there and has been walking on a cane with her ankle taped ever since. But we took two bus-tours while we were in London that covered the whole city. In the morning we saw the Bank of England and the Tower of London and the Crown Jewels and came back to an old inn where Doctor Johnson, who was a good friend of Shakespeare's, used to eat. Miss Barrett was especially interested in this, as she teaches English literature in the Senior High at Moline. She is one of the girls in our party. After lunch we saw Trafalgar Square with Nelson's Monument and the National Gallery. We didn't stay long at the National Gallery, we just stopped long enough to say we'd seen it. Then we visited the Houses of Parliament, Westminster Abbey with the Poet's Corner, and Buckingham Palace with the sentinels on duty walking up and down. We got there just as the King and Queen were driving out; we got a good look at her, but you could hardly see the King because of that big hat she was wearing. You couldn't help feeling sorry for the poor man. As Miss Webster said, he did look so small and henpecked peeking out behind the edges of that big hat. Miss Webster is one of the girls in our party.

We also spent a day at Oxford. We had good weather there; it didn't rain at all the day we were there. Then we spent a day at Stratford-on-Avon where Shakespeare was born. But as Miss Webster said, they've fixed that house up a lot since he lived in it. It didn't rain the morning of the day we went to Stratford-on-Avon, but it started in again when we were coming back. It rained most of the time we were in England. No wonder everything is so green.

The next country we visited was Holland. Of all the countries we have been to I like Holland best. Everything was so clean in Holland. We spent three days in Holland, and it didn't rain the whole time we were there. We were in Amsterdam for a day, and we went out to the Island of Marken where all the people were dressed up in their quaint costumes and even the children wore wooden shoes, just the same as they have done for hundreds of years. Miss Turner took some pictures of some children. She is making a collection to show her classes when she gets back home. It is a very interesting collection, and most of the pictures came out very well. Miss Turner is one of the girls in our party.

We spent another whole day at Haarlem and The Hague. We saw the Palace of Peace and some pictures by Rembrandt, including "The Anatomy Lesson," which of course was interesting to me and some more "grist for the mill," as I will be able to make use of all this material in drawing class when school takes up again.

In Holland we had the nicest guide we had on the whole trip. Everyone was crazy about him; we have thought so often of him, and laughed so much about him, since. He was an old man named Mr. Vogelsang, and when Miss Watson, who is one of the girls in our party, asked him what that name meant, he said the name meant Song-Bird, so after that we called him our Song-Bird. You couldn't get the best of Mr. Vogelsang, no matter what you said. He always had an answer ready for you. We have laughed so much about it since whenever we thought of Mr. Vogelsang.

Vogelsang iss my name unt dat means Sonk-birt. Sonk-birt by name, sonk-birt by nature; if you are nice to me, perhaps I sink for you. Now ve are commink to de olt shot-tower. It vas conshtructed in de year uff sixteen hundert unt t'venty-nine mit contribushions mait by all de burghers uff de town. De roof iss all uff golt unt silver conshtructed vich vas gifen by de laities from deir chewells, ornaments, unt odder brecious bossessions. De two fickures dat you see on top uff de olt glock iss subbosed to represent de burgermeister uff dot beriod, Pieter van Hondercoetter, unt his vife Matilda. Upon de shtroke uff t'ree o'glock you vill see dem come out on de platform, turn, unt shtrike mit golten mallets on de bell—so! It comes now, vatch it!—So! *Vun!* de burgermeister shtrikes upon his seit vun time—you see?—So! Now! *Two!*—de laity shtrikes upon her seit vun time—So! Now! *T'ree*—de burgermeister shtrikes upon his seit—now it iss t'ree o'glock—all iss ofer for anodder hour—unt laities, dat's de only time dat a man has efer been known to haf de last vort mit a voman.

Oh, you couldn't get the best of Mr. Vogelsang, we used to tease him but he always had an answer ready for you.

Now, laities, dis tower was erected at a cost of twelluf million guilders vich iss fife million dollars in real money. It took ofer sixteen years to built it; de golt, chewells, unt odder brecious metals in de roof alone iss vort ofer vun million two hundert unt fifty t'ousand dollars. De tower iss two hundert unt sixty-t'ree feet tall from top to bottom unt dere iss t'ree hundert sixty-fife shtone shteps in de shtair case, vun for efery day in de year engrafed mit de name uff a citizen who gave money for de tower. If you vould like to gount de shteps yourself, you gan now glimb to de top, but ass for me, I t'ink I shtay here. For aldough my name iss Sonk-birt, I am now too olt to fly.

Mr. Vogelsang always had a joke for everything. Well, we all climbed up to the top of the tower then, and when we got back down, Miss Powers said that Mr. Vogelsang was wrong, because she had counted three hundred and sixty-seven steps both ways, and Miss Turner swore that he was right, that she had made it three hundred and sixty-five both up and down. And then Mr. Vogelsang said: "Vell, laities, I tell you how it iss. You are both wronk, because I liet to you. I forgot to tell you dis iss leap year, unt ven leap year comes, dere iss alvays vun shtep more. Dis year you find dat dere iss t'ree hundert sixty-six if you gount again."

Well, we had to laugh then, because you couldn't get the best of Mr. Vogelsang. But Miss Powers was awfully mad and swore she was right, that she had counted three hundred and sixty-seven both ways. She and Miss Turner had an argument about it, and that's why they've hardly spoken to each other since. But we all liked Holland, it didn't rain there, and everyone was crazy about Mr. Vogelsang.

We were in Paris for four days, and it only rained once. We were really there only three days, we got there late at night, and we were all so tired that we went to bed as soon as we got to the hotel. But we didn't get much sleep, it was the noisiest place you ever saw, and those little taxi horns they have kept tooting all night long under your window until it almost drove you crazy. Some of the girls thought they'd lost their baggage, it failed to arrive when we did, they almost had a fit. It didn't get there until the day we left for Switzerland, and Miss Bradley said her whole stay in Paris was ruined by worrying about it. Miss Bradley is one of the girls in our party.

We took a bus tour the first day and saw Notre Dame and the Latin Quarter, the Eiffel Tower, and the Arc de Triumph, and came back and had lunch at the hotel. After lunch some of the girls went shopping, but the rest of us went to the Louvre. We didn't stay long, just long enough to see the Mona Lisa. One night we all had tickets for the Opera, where we saw Faust. The next night we went to the Folies Bergeres, and last night we went up to Montmartre in buses to see the night life there.

Today we are in Montreux: this is the place where the tour splits up, some of the party leaving us to take the trip along the Rhine, and then to Munich, Salzburg, and the Bavarian Alps, while the rest of us are seeing Switzerland and Italy. After visiting Milan, Venice, Florence, Rome, and the Austrian Tyrol, we will join up with the other group in Vienna two weeks from now.

All of us were sorry to say good-bye to most of the girls, but we know it will be for only two weeks' time, and we are looking forward eagerly to our meeting in Vienna and relating our experiences to one another. But, frankly, there are one or two girls we wouldn't miss if we never saw them again. There are always one or two on a party like this who can't adjust themselves to the group and do their best to spoil the trip for everyone. That Miss Powers was one of them. She was always losing her baggage, or forgetting something, and leaving it behind; we got so tired of having her yapping all the time that there were three hundred and sixty-seven steps in that old shot-tower, that she was right and Miss Turner wrong, until Miss Turner finally said: "All right, have it your own way—there were three hundred and sixty-seven—who cares about it? Only, for heaven's sake, forget about it and give the rest of us some peace."

Of course, that only made Miss Powers madder than ever, she was furious about it. She was certainly a pest, if I ever saw one. She was forever coming up to one of the girls and asking her to write something in her memory book. She carried that memory book with her wherever she went; I believe she slept with it under her pillow.

Now when one of the girls wants to be funny, she says, "Won't you please write something in my memory book?"—it's become a regular joke with us. But Miss Powers was certainly a nuisance, and none of the girls are sorry to say good-bye to her.

We have been spending the day in Switzerland. We all visited the League of Nations in Geneva and the famous castle of Chillon this morning. This afternoon, while I am writing this letter, everyone has gone for a bus tour through the Alps. We are leaving for Rome tonight.

Well, it has been a wonderful trip and a wonderful experience, as well as being very educational. I can hardly wait now until I get home and have time to think over the many beautiful things I have seen.

The tour has been well run and well conducted from start to finish. And on the whole the girls are enthusiastic about the way the trips have been managed. Of course when you have to cover so many countries—we will have covered nine countries—England, Holland, Belgium, France, Switzerland, Italy, Austria, Czechoslovakia, and Germany—by the time we set sail for home again, just thirty-one days after we disembarked—it is wonderful to think of all you do take in in such a short space of time.

I get a little confused sometimes when I try to remember all the places we have been to and all the wonderful things we have seen, and if I come back again, I think I will take it a little more slowly and travel in a smaller party, with just a friend or two. But I'm certainly glad I took this tour, it gives you a chance to look around and pick out the high spots, so you will know what you want to see when you come back a second time. And it has certainly been very educational. Still, I won't be sorry to see home again. I am looking forward to it already.

I'm dying to see you and have a good long talk with you as soon as I get back. I'm starved for news. What has happened? Is Ted still going with the Trumbull girl, or has he found himself a new "enamorata"? ("Ain't love grand?" Especially when you are seventeen—hah! hah!) Have you been out to the lodge this summer, and were Bill and Lola there? Couldn't we get them to take us out the first week-end after I get back? It will be good to get a cup of real coffee for a change. Summer has come and gone before I knew it, and soon autumn will be here again.

. . . and the smell of the woodsmoke in Ohio and the flaming maples, the nights of the frosty stars, the blazing moons that hang the same way in a thousand streets, slanting to silence on the steeple's slope, nights of the wheel, the rail, the bell, the wailing cry along the river's edge, and of the summer's ending, nights of the frost and silence and the barking of a dog, of people listening, and of words unspoken and the quiet heart, and nights of the old October that must come again, must come again, while we are waiting, waiting, waiting in the darkness for all of our friends and brothers who will not return.

I'll see you in September.

Circus at Dawn

There were times in early autumn—in September—when the greater circuses would come to town—the Ringling Brothers, Robinson's, and Barnum and Bailey shows, and when I was a route-boy on the morning paper——on those mornings when the circus would be coming in——I would rush madly through my route in the cool and thrilling darkness that comes just before the break of day, and then I would go back home and get my brother out of bed.

Talking in low excited voices, we would walk rapidly back toward town under the rustle of September leaves, in cool streets just grayed now with that still, that unearthly and magical first light of day which seems suddenly to rediscover the great earth out of darkness, so that the earth emerges with an awful, a glorious sculptural stillness, and one looks out with a feeling of joy and disbelief, as the first men on this earth must have done, for to see this happen is one of the things that men will remember out of life forever and think of as they die.

At the sculptural still square where at one corner, just emerging into light, my father's shabby little marble shop stood with a ghostly strangeness and familiarity, my brother and I would "catch" the first street-car of the day bound for the "depot" where the circus was—or sometimes we would meet someone we knew, who would give us a lift in his automobile.

Then, having reached the dingy, grimy, and rickety depot section, we would get out, and walk rapidly across the tracks of the station yard, where we could see great flares and steamings from the engines, and hear the crash and bump of shifting freight cars, the swift sporadic thunders of a shifting engine, the tolling of bells, the sounds of great trains on the rails.

And to these familiar sounds, filled with their exultant prophecies of flight, the voyage, morning, and the shining cities—to all the sharp, thrilling odors of the trains—the smell of cinders, acrid smoke, of musty, rusty freight cars, the clean pine-board of crated produce, and the smells of fresh stored food—oranges, coffee, tangerines and bacon, ham and flour and beef—there would be added now, with an unforgettable magic and familiarity, all the strange sounds and smells of the coming circus.

The gay yellow sumptuous-looking cars in which the star performers lived and slept, still dark and silent, heavily and powerfully still, would be drawn up in long strings upon the tracks. And all around them the sounds of the unloading circus would go on furiously in the darkness. The receding gulf of lilac and departing night would be filled with the savage roar of lions, the murderously sudden snarling of great jungle cats, the trumpetings of the elephants, the stamp of the horses, and with the musty, pungent, unfamiliar odor of the jungle animals: the tawny camel smells, and the smells of panthers, zebras, tigers, elephants, and bears.

Then, along the tracks, beside the circus trains, there would be the sharp cries and oaths of the circus men, the magical swinging dance of lanterns in the darkness, the sudden heavy rumble of the loaded vans and wagons as they were pulled along the flats and gondolas, and down the runways to the ground. And everywhere, in the thrilling mystery of darkness and awakening light, there would be the tremendous conflict of a confused, hurried, and yet orderly movement.

The great iron-gray horses, four and six to a team, would be plodding along the road of thick white dust to a rattling of chains and traces and the harsh cries of their drivers. The men would drive the animals to the river which flowed by beyond the tracks, and water them; and as first light came, one could see the elephants wallowing in the familiar river and the big horses going slowly and carefully down to drink.

Then, on the circus grounds, the tents were going up already with the magic speed of dreams. All over the place (which was near the tracks and the only space of flat land in the town that was big enough to hold a circus) there would be this fierce, savagely hurried, yet orderly confusion. Great flares of gaseous circus lights would blaze down on the seared and battered faces of the circus toughs as, with the rhythmic precision of a single animal—a human riveting machine—they swung their sledges at the stakes, driving a stake into the earth with the incredible instancy of accelerated figures in a motion picture. And everywhere, as light came and the sun appeared, there would be a scene of magic, order, and of violence. The drivers would curse, and talk their special language to their teams; there would be the loud, gasping, and uneven labor of a gasoline engine, the shouts and curses of the bosses, the wooden riveting of the driven stakes, and the rattle of heavy chains.

Already in an immense cleared space of dusty beaten earth, the stakes were being driven for the main exhibition tent. And an elephant would lurch ponderously to the field, slowly lower his great swinging head at the command of a man who sat perched upon his skull, flourish his gray wrinkled snout a time or two, and then solemnly wrap it around a tent pole as big as the mast of a racing schooner. Then the elephant would back slowly away, dragging the great pole with him as if it were a stick of matchwood.

And when this happened, my brother would break into his great "whah-

whah" of exuberant laughter, and prod me in the ribs with his clumsy fingers. And farther on, two town darkeys, who had watched the elephant's performance with bulging eyes, would turn to each other with ape-like grins, bend double as they slapped their knees, and howl with swart rich nigger-laughter, saying to each other in a kind of rhythmic chorus of question and reply:

"He don't play with it, do he?"

"No, *suh!* He don't send no boy!"

"He don't say, 'Wait a minute,' do he?"

"No, suh! He say, 'Come with me!' That's what he say!"

"He go 'Boogety-boogety!'" said one, suiting the words with a prowling movement of his black face toward the earth.

"He go rootin' faw it!" said the other, making a rooting movement with his head.

"He say, 'Ar-rumpf!'" said one.

"He say, 'Big boy, we is on ouah way!'" the other answered.

"Har! Har! Har! Har! Har!"—and they choked and screamed with their rich laughter, slapping their thighs with a solid smack as they described the elephant's prowess to each other.

Meanwhile, the circus food-tent—a huge canvas top without concealing sides—had already been put up, and now we could see the performers seated at long trestled tables underneath the tent, as they ate breakfast. And the savor of the food they ate—mixed as it was with our strong excitement, with the powerful but wholesome smells of the animals, and with all the joy, sweetness, mystery, jubilant magic, and glory of the morning and the coming of the circus—seemed to us to be the most maddening and appetizing succulence of any food that we had ever known or eaten.

We could see the circus performers eating tremendous breakfasts, with all the savage relish of their power and strength: they ate big fried steaks, pork chops, rashers of bacon, a half dozen eggs, great slabs of fried ham and great stacks of wheat-cakes which a cook kept flipping in the air with the skill of a juggler, and which a husky-looking waitress kept rushing to their tables on loaded trays held high and balanced marvelously on the fingers of a brawny hand. And above all the maddening odors of the wholesome and succulent food, there brooded forever the sultry and delicious fragrance— that somehow seemed to add zest and sharpness to all the powerful and thrilling life of morning—of strong boiling coffee, which we could see sending off clouds of steam from an enormous polished urn, and which the circus performers gulped down, cup after cup.

And the circus men and women themselves—these star performers— were such fine-looking people, strong and handsome, yet speaking and moving with an almost stern dignity and decorum, that their lives seemed to us to be as splendid and wonderful as any lives on earth could be. There was never anything loose, rowdy, or tough in their comportment, nor did the circus women look like painted whores, or behave indecently with the men.

Rather, these people in an astonishing way seemed to have created an established community which lived an ordered existence on wheels, and to observe with a stern fidelity unknown in towns and cities the decencies of family life. There would be a powerful young man, a handsome and magnificent young woman with blonde hair and the figure of an Amazon, and a powerfully-built, thick-set man of middle age, who had a stern, lined, responsible-looking face and a bald head. They were probably members of a trapeze team—the young man and woman would leap through space like projectiles, meeting the grip of the older man and hurling back again upon their narrow perches, catching the swing of their trapeze in mid-air, and whirling thrice before they caught it, in a perilous and beautiful exhibition of human balance and precision.

But when they came into the breakfast tent, they would speak gravely yet courteously to other performers, and seat themselves in a family group at one of the long tables, eating their tremendous breakfasts with an earnest concentration, seldom speaking to one another, and then gravely, seriously, briefly.

And my brother and I would look at them with fascinated eyes: my brother would watch the man with the bald head for a while and then turn toward me, whispering:

"D-d-do you see that f-f-fellow there with the bald head? W-w-well he's the heavy man," he whispered knowingly. "He's the one that c-c-catches them! That f-f-fellow's got to know his business! You know what happens if he misses, don't you?" said my brother.

"What?" I would say in a fascinated tone.

My brother snapped his fingers in the air.

"Over!" he said. "D-d-done for! W-w-why, they'd be d-d-d-dead before they knew what happened. Sure!" he said, nodding vigorously. "It's a f-f-f-fact! If he ever m-m-m-misses, it's all over! That boy has g-g-g-got to know his s-s-s-stuff!" my brother said. "W-w-w-why," he went on in a low tone of solemn conviction, "it w-w-w-wouldn't surprise me if they p-p-p-pay him seventy-five or a hundred dollars a week! It's a fact!" my brother cried vigorously.

And we would turn our fascinated stare again upon these splendid and romantic creatures, whose lives were so different from our own, and whom we seemed to know with such familiar and affectionate intimacy. And at length, reluctantly, with full light come and the sun up, we would leave the circus grounds and start for home.

And somehow the memory of all we had seen and heard that glorious morning, and the memory of the food-tent with its wonderful smells, would waken in us the pangs of such a ravenous hunger that we could not wait until we got home to eat. We would stop off in town at lunch-rooms and, seated on tall stools before the counter, we would devour ham-and-egg sandwiches, hot hamburgers red and pungent at their cores with coarse spicy sanguinary beef, coffee, glasses of foaming milk and doughnuts, and then go home home to eat up everything in sight upon the breakfast table.

His Father's Earth

As the boy stood looking at the circus with his brother, there came to him two images, which had haunted his childhood and the life of every boy who ever lived, but were now for the first time seen together with an instant and magic congruence. And these two images were the images of the circus and his father's earth.

He thought then he had joined a circus and started on the great tour of the nation with it. It was spring: the circus had started in New England and worked westward and then southward as the summer and autumn came on. His nominal duties—for, in his vision, every incident, each face and voice and circumstance were blazing real as life itself—were those of ticket seller, but in this tiny show, everyone did several things: the performers helped put up and take down the tents, load and unload the wagons, and the roustabouts and business people worked wherever they were needed.

The boy sold tickets, but he also posted bills and bartered with tradesmen and farmers in new places for fresh food. He became very shrewd and clever at this work, and loved to do it—some old, sharp, buried talent for shrewd trading, that had come to him from his mountain blood, now aided him. He could get the finest, freshest meats and vegetables at the lowest prices. The circus people were tough and hard, they always had a fierce and ravenous hunger, they would not accept bad food and cooking, they fed stupendously, and they always had the best of everything.

Usually the circus would arrive at a new town very early in the morning, before daybreak. He would go into town immediately: he would go to the markets, or with farmers who had come in for the circus. He felt and saw the purity of first light, he heard the sweet and sudden lutings of first birds, and suddenly he was filled with the earth and morning in new towns, among new men: he walked among the farmers' wagons, and he dealt with them on the spot for the prodigal plenty of their wares—the country melons bedded in sweet hay of wagons, the cool sweet prints of butter wrapped in clean wet cloths, with dew and starlight still on them, the enormous battered cans foaming with fresh milk, the new laid eggs which he bought by the gross and hundred dozens, the tender limy pullets by the score, the rude country wagons laden to the rim with heaped abundancies—with delicate bunches of green scallions, the heavy red ripeness of huge tomatoes, the sweet-leaved lettuces crisp as celery, the fresh podded peas and the succulent young beans, as well as the potatoes spotted with the loamy earth, the powerful winey odor of the apples, the peaches, and the cherries, the juicy corn stacked up in shocks of living green, and the heavy blackened rinds of home-cured hams and bacons.

As the market opened, he would begin to trade and dicker with the butchers for their finest cuts of meat: they would hold great roasts up in their gouted fingers, they would roll up tubs of fresh ground sausage, they would smack with their long palms the flanks of beeves and porks: he would drive back to the circus with a wagon full of meat and vegetables.

At the circus ground the people were already in full activity. He could hear the wonderful timed tattoo of sledges on driven stakes, the shouts of men riding animals down to water, the slow clank and pull of mighty horses, the heavy rumble of the wagons as they rolled down off the circus flat cars. By now the eating table would be erected, and as he arrived, he could see the cooks already busy at their ranges, the long tables set up underneath the canvas with their rows of benches, their tin plates and cups, their strong readiness. There would be the amber indescribable pungency of strong coffee, and the smell of buckwheat batter.

And the circus people would come in for their breakfast: hard and tough, for the most part decent and serious people, the performers, the men and women, the acrobats, the riders, the tumblers, the clowns, the jugglers, the contortionists, and the balancers would come in quietly and eat with a savage and inspired intentness.

The food they ate was as masculine and fragrant as the world they dwelt in: it belonged to the stained world of mellow sun-warmed canvas, the clean and healthful odor of the animals, and the mild sweet lyric nature of the land in which they lived as wanderers, and it was there for the asking with a fabulous and stupefying plenty, golden and embrowned: they ate stacks of buckwheat cakes, smoking hot, soaked in hunks of yellow butter which they carved at will with a wide free gesture from the piled prints on the table, and which they garnished (if they pleased) with ropes of heavy black molasses, or with the lighter, freer maple syrup.

They ate big steaks for breakfast, hot from the pan and lashed with onions, they ate whole melons, crammed with the ripeness of the deep pink meat, rashers of bacon, and great platters of fried eggs, or eggs scrambled with calves' brains, they helped themselves from pyramids of fruit piled up at intervals on the table—plums, peaches, apples, cherries, grapes, oranges, and bananas—they had great pitchers of thick cream to pour on everything, and they washed their hunger down with pint mugs of strong deep-savored coffee.

For their mid-day meal they would eat fiercely, hungrily, with wolfish gusts, mightily, with knit brows and convulsive movements of their corded throats. They would eat great roasts of beef with crackled hides, browned in their juices, rare and tender, hot chunks of delicate pork with hems of fragrant fat, delicate young boiled chickens, only a mouthful for these ravenous jaws, twelve-pound pot roasts cooked for hours in an iron pot with new carrots, onions, sprouts, and young potatoes, together with every vegetable that the season yielded: huge roasting ears of corn, smoking hot, stacked like cord wood on two-foot platters, tomatoes cut in slabs with wedges of okra and succotash, and raw onion, mashed potatoes whipped to a creamy smother, boats swimming with pure beef gravy, new carrots, turnips, fresh peas cooked in butter, and fat string beans seasoned with the flavor of big chunks of cooking-pork. In addition, they had every fruit that the place and time afforded: hot crusty apple, peach and cherry pies, encrusted with cinnamon, puddings and cakes of every sort, and blobbering cobblers inches deep.

Thus the circus moved across America, from town to town, from state to state, eating its way from Maine into the great plains of the West, eating its way along the Hudson and the Mississippi rivers, eating its way across the prairies and from the North into the South, eating its way across the flat farm lands of the Pennsylvania Dutch colony, the eastern shore of Maryland and back again across the states of Virginia, North Carolina, Tennessee, and Florida—eating all good things that this enormous, this inevitably bountiful and abundant cornucopia of a continent yielded.

They ate the cod, bass, mackerel, halibut, clams, and oysters of the New England coast, the terrapin of Maryland, the fat beeves, porks, and cereals of the Middle West, and they had, as well, the heavy juicy peaches, watermelons, cantaloupes of Georgia, the fat sweet shad of the Carolina coasts, and the rounded and exotic citrus fruits of the tropics: the oranges, tangerines, bananas, kumquats, lemons, guavas down in Florida, together with a hundred other fruits and meats—the Vermont turkeys, the mountain trout, the bunched heaviness of the Concord grapes, the red winey bulk of the Oregon apples, as well as the clawed, shelled, and crusted dainties, the crabs, the clams, the pink meated lobsters that grope their way along the sea-floors of America.

The boy awoke at morning in three hundred towns with the glimmer of starlight on his face; he was the moon's man; then he saw light quicken in the east, he saw the pale stars drown, he saw the birth of light, he heard the lark's wing, the bird tree, the first liquorous liquefied lutings, the ripe-aired trillings, the plumskinned birdnotes, and he heard the hoof and wheel come down the streets of the nation. He exulted in his work as food-producer for the circus people, and they loved him for it. They said there had never been anyone like him—they banqueted exultantly, with hoarse gulpings and with joy, and they loved him.

Slowly, day by day, the circus worked its way across America, through forty states and through a dozen weathers. It was a little world that moved across the enormous loneliness of the earth, a little world that each day began a new life in new cities, and that left nothing to betray where it had been save a litter of beaten papers, the droppings of the camel and the elephant in Illinois, a patch of trampled grass, and a magical memory.

The circus men knew no other earth but this; the earth came to them with the smell of the canvas and the lion's roar. They saw the world behind the lights of the carnival, and everything beyond these lights was phantasmal and unreal to them; it lived for them within the circle of the tent as men and women who sat on benches, as the posts they came to, and sometimes as the enemy.

Their life was filled with the strong joy of food, with the love of traveling, and with danger and hard labor. Always there was the swift violence of change and movement, of putting up and tearing down, and sometimes there was the misery of rain and sleet, and mud above the ankles, of wind that shook their flimsy residence, that ripped the tent stakes from their moorings in the earth and lifted out the great center pole as if it were a match. Now they must wrestle with the wind and hold their dwelling to the earth; now they must fight the weariness of mud and push their heavy wagons through the slime; now, cold and wet and wretched, they must sleep on piles of canvas, upon the flat cars in a driving rain, and sometimes they must fight the enemy—the drunk, the savage, the violent enemy, the bloody man, who dwelt in every place. Sometimes it was the city thug, sometimes the mill hands of the South, sometimes the miners in a Pennsylvania town—the circus people cried, "Hey, Rube!" and fought them with fist and foot, with pike and stake, and the boy saw and knew it all.

When the men in a little town barricaded the street against their parade, they charged the barricade with their animals, and once the sheriff tried to stop the elephant by saying: "Now, damn ye, if you stick your God-damned trunk another inch, I'll shoot."

The circus moved across America foot by foot, mile by mile. He came to know the land. It was rooted in his blood and his brain forever—its food, its fruit, its fields and forests, its deserts, and its mountains, its savage lawlessness. He saw the crimes and the violence of the people with pity, with mercy, and with tenderness: he thought of them as if they were children. They smashed their neighbors' brains out with an ax, they disemboweled one another with knives, they were murderous and lost upon this earth they dwelt upon as strangers.

The tongueless blood of the murdered men ran down into the earth, and the earth received it. Upon this enormous and indifferent earth the little trains rattled on over ill-joined rails that loosely bound the sprawling little towns together. Lost and lonely, brief sawings of wood and plaster and cheap brick ugliness, the little towns were scattered like encampments through the wilderness. Only the earth remained, which all these people had barely touched, which all these people dwelt upon but could not possess.

Only the earth remained, the savage and lyrical earth with its rude potency, its thousand vistas, its heights and slopes and levels, with all its violence and delicacy, the terrible fecundity, decay, and growth, its fierce colors, its vital bite and sparkle, its exultancy of space and wandering. And the memory of this earth, the memory of all this universe of sight and sense, was rooted in this boy's heart and brain forever. It fed the hungers of desire and wandering, it breached the walls of his secret and withdrawn spirit. And for every memory of place and continent, of enormous coffee-colored rivers and eight hundred miles of bending wheat, of Atlantic coast and midland prairie, of raw red Piedmont and tropic flatness, there was always the small, fecund, perfect memory of his father's land, the dark side of his soul and his heart's desire, which he had never seen, but which he knew with every atom of his life, the strange phantasmal haunting of man's memory. It was a fertile, nobly swelling land, and it was large enough to live in, walled with fulfilled desire.

Abroad in this ocean of earth and vision he thought of his father's land, of its great red barns and nobly swelling earth, its clear familiarity and its haunting strangeness, and its dark and secret heart, its magnificent, its lovely and tragic beauty. He thought of its smell of harbors and its rumors of the seas, the city, and the ships, its wine-red apples and its brown-red soil, its snug weathered houses, and its lyric unutterable ecstasy.

A wonderful thing happened. One morning he awoke suddenly to find himself staring straight up at the pulsing splendor of the stars. At first he did not know where he was, but he knew instantly, even before he looked about him, that he had visited this place before. The circus train had stopped in the heart of the country, for what reason he did not know. He could hear the languid and intermittent breathing of the engine, the strangeness of men's voices in the dark, the casual stamp of the horses in their cars, and all around him the attentive and vital silence of the earth.

Suddenly he raised himself from the pile of canvas on which he slept. It was the moment just before dawn: against the east, the sky had already begun to whiten with the first faint luminosity of day, the invading tides of light crept up the sky, drowning the stars out as they went. The train had halted by a little river which ran swift and deep next to the tracks, and now he knew that what at first had been the sound of silence was the swift and ceaseless music of the river.

There had been rain the night before, and now the river was filled with the sweet clean rain-drenched smell of earthy deposits. He could see the delicate white glimmer of young birch trees leaning from the banks, and on the other side he saw the winding whiteness of the road. Beyond the road, and bordering it, there was an orchard with a wall of lichened stone: a row of apple trees, gnarled and sweet, spread their squat twisted branches out across the road, and in the faint light he saw that they were dense with blossoms: the cool intoxication of their fragrance overpowered him.

As the wan light grew, the earth and all its contours emerged sharply, and he saw again the spare, gaunt loneliness of the earth at dawn, with all its sweet and sudden cries of spring. He saw the worn and ancient design of lichened rocks, the fertile soil of the baked fields, he saw the kept order, the frugal cleanliness, with its springtime overgrowth, the mild tang of opulent greenery. There was an earth with fences, as big as a man's heart, but not so great as his desire, and after his giant wanderings over the prodigal fecundity of the continent, this earth was like a room he once had lived in. He returned to it as a sailor to a small closed harbor, as a man, spent with the hunger of his wandering, comes home.

Instantly he recognized the scene. He knew that he had come at last into his father's land. It was a magic that he knew but could not speak; he stood upon the lip of time, and all of his life now seemed the mirage of some wizard's spell—the spell of canvas and the circus ring, the spell of the tented world which had possessed him. Here was his home, brought back to him while he slept, like a forgotten dream. Here was the dark side of his soul, his heart's desire, his father's country, the earth his spirit dwelt on as a child. He knew every inch of the landscape, and he knew, past reason, doubt, or argument, that home was not three miles away.

He got up at once and leaped down to the earth; he knew where he would go. Along the track there was the slow swing and dance of the brakemen's lamps, that moving, mournful, and beautiful cloud of light along the rails of the earth, that he had seen so many times. Already the train was in motion; its bell tolled and its heavy trucks rumbled away from him. He began to walk back along the tracks, for less than a mile away, he knew, where the stream boiled over the lip of a dam, there was a bridge. When he reached the bridge, a deeper light had come: the old red brick of the mill emerged sharply and with the tone and temper of deep joy fell sheer into bright shining waters.

He crossed the bridge and turned left along the road: here it moved away from the river, among fields and through dark woods—dark woods bordered with stark poignancy of fir and pine, with the noble spread of maples, shot with the naked whiteness of birch. Here was the woodland maze: the sweet density of the brake and growth. Sharp thrummings, woodland flitters broke the silence. His steps grew slow, he sat upon a wall, he waited.

Now rose the birdsong in first light, and suddenly he heard each sound the birdsong made. Like a flight of shot the sharp fast skaps of sound arose. With chittering bicker, fast-fluttering skirrs of sound, the palmy honeyed bird-cries came. Smooth drops and nuggets of bright gold they were. Now sang the birdtrees filled with lutings in bright air: the thrums, the lark's wing, and tongue-trilling chirrs arose now. The little nameless cries arose and fell with liquorous liquified lutings, with lirruping chirp, plumbellied smoothness, sweet lucidity.

And now there was the rapid kweet kweet kweet kweet kweet of homing birds and their pwee pwee pwee: others with sharp cricketing stitch, a mosquito buzz with thin metallic tongues, while some with rusty creakings, high shrew's caws, with eerie rasp, with harsh far calls—all birds that are awake in the sweet woodland tangles: and above, there passed the whirr of hidden wings, the strange lost cry of the unknown birds, in full flight now, in which the sweet confusion of their cries was mingled.

Then he got up and went along that road where, he knew, like the prophetic surmise of a dream, the house of his father's blood and kin lay hidden. At length, he came around a bending in the road, he left the wooded land, he passed by hedges and saw the old white house, set in the shoulder of the hill, worn like care and habit in the earth; clean and cool, it sat below the clean dark shelter of its trees: a twist of morning smoke coiled through its chimney.

Then he turned in to the rutted road that led up to the house, and at this moment the enormous figure of a powerful old man appeared around the corner prophetically bearing a smoked ham in one huge hand. And when the boy saw the old man, a cry of greeting burst from his throat, and the old man answered with a roar of welcome that shook the earth.

Then the old man dropped his ham, and waddled forward to meet the boy: they met half down the road, and the old man crushed him in his hug; they tried to speak but could not; they embraced again and in an instant all the years of wandering, the pain of loneliness and the fierce hungers of desire, were scoured away like a scum of frost from a bright glass.

He was a child again, he was a child that had stood upon the lip and leaf of time and heard the quiet tides that move us to our death, and he knew that the child could not be born again, the book of the days could never be turned back, old errors and confusions never righted. And he wept with sorrow for all that was lost and could never be regained, and with joy for all that had been recovered.

Suddenly he saw his youth as men on hilltops might look at the whole winding course of rivers to the sea, he saw the blind confusions of his wanderings across the earth, the horror of man's little stricken mote of earth against immensity, and he remembered the proud exultancy of his childhood when all the world lay like a coin between his palms, when he could have touched the horned rim of the moon, when heroes and great actions bent before him.

And he wept, not for himself, but out of love and pity for every youth that ever hoped and wandered and was alone. He had become a man, and he had in him unique glory that belongs to men alone, and that makes them great, and from which they shape their mightiest songs and legends. For out of their pain they utter first a cry for wounded self, then, as their vision deepens, widens, the universe of their marvelous sense leaps out and grips the universe; they feel contempt for gods, respect for men alone, and with the indifference of a selfless passion, enact earth out of a lyric cry.

At this moment, also, two young men burst from the house and came running down the road to greet him. They were powerful and heavy young men, already beginning to show signs of that epic and sensual grossness that distinguished their father. Like their father, they recognized the boy instantly, and in a moment he was engulfed in their mighty energies, borne up among them to the house. And they understood all he wanted to say, but could not speak, and they surrounded him with love and lavish heapings of his plate. And the boy knew the strange miracle of return to the dark land of his heart's desire, the father's land which haunts men like a dream they never knew.

Such were the twin images of the circus and his father's land which were to haunt his dreams and waking memory and which now, as he stood there with his brother looking at the circus, fused instantly to a living whole and came to him in a blaze of light.

And in this way, before he had ever set foot upon it, he came for the first time to his father's earth.

Old Catawba

On the middle-Atlantic seaboard of the North American continent and at about a day's journey from New York is situated the American state of Old Catawba. In area and population the state might almost strike a median among the states of the union: its territory, which is slightly more than fifty thousand square miles, is somewhat larger than the territories of most of the Atlantic coastal states, and, of course, much smaller than the great areas of the immense but sparsely populated states of the Far West. Upon this area, which is a little smaller than the combined areas of England and Wales, there live about three million people, of whom about the third part are black. Catawba, therefore, is about as big as England, and has about as many people as Norway.

The state possesses however a racial type and character that is probably much more strongly marked and unified than that of any European country. In fact, although America is supposed by many of her critics to be a confusion of races, tongues, and peoples, as yet unwelded, there is perhaps nowhere in the world a more homogeneous population than that of Old Catawba. Certainly, there are far greater differences in stature, temperament, speech, and habit between a North German and a South German, between a North Frenchman and a Southern Frenchman, a North of England man and a Devon man, a North Italian and a South Italian, than between a Catawban from the East and one from the West.

The name "Catawba" is, of course, an Indian name: it is the name of a tribe that is now almost extinct but which at one time flourished in considerable strength and number. The chief seat of the tribe was in South Carolina, and there is at the present time a reservation in York County of that state where the remnant is gathered together.

The way in which the State of Catawba got its name rests entirely upon misconception: the tribes that early explorers encountered were not Catawbas; they belonged to a tribe that is now probably wholly extinct. Yet, so strong is the power of usage and association that any other name would now seem unthinkable to a native of that state. People outside the state have often said that the name has a somewhat tropical laziness in its sound, particularly when prefixed with the word "old," but there is very little that is tropical or exotic in the appearance and character of Catawba itself, or of the people who inhabit it. To them, the name Catawba perfectly describes the state: it has the strong, rugged, and homely quality that the earth has.

In the state documents during the period of the royal proprietors, the territory is invariably referred to as "Catawba," or "His Majesty's Colony in the Catawbas": the name "Old Catawba" does not begin to appear in state papers until twenty or thirty years before the Revolution, and for what reason no one knows. The typical American method in naming places has been to prefix the word "new" to the name—*New* England, *New* York, *New* Mexico—to discriminate these places from their older namesakes. But if *New* York indicates the existence somewhere of an *old* York, *old* Catawba does not indicate the existence of a new one. The name undoubtedly grew out of the spirit of the people who had dwelt there over a century, and the name did not come from a sentimental affection; it grew imperatively from a conviction of the spirit. It is one of those names that all men begin to use at about the same time, a perfect and inevitable name that has flowered secretly within them, and that now must be spoken.

Anyone who has ever lived in the state for any length of time is bound to feel this: the word "old" is not a term of maudlin affection, it describes exactly the feeling that the earth of that state inspires—the land has a brooding presence that is immensely old and masculine, its spirit is rugged and rather desolate, yet it broods over its people with stern benevolence. The earth is a woman, but Old Catawba is a man. The earth is our mother and our nurse, and we can know her, but Old Catawba is our father, and although we know that he is there, we shall never find him. He is there in the wilderness, and his brows are bowed with granite: he sees our lives and deaths, and his stern compassion broods above us. Women love him, but only men can know him: only men who have cried out in their agony and their loneliness to their father, only men who have sought throughout the world to find him, can know Catawba: but this is all the men who ever lived.

The Catawba people are great people for all manner of debate and reasoned argument. Where the more fiery South Carolinian or Mississippian will fly into a rage and want to fight the man who doubts his word or questions his opinion, the eye of the Catawban begins to glow with fire of another sort—the lust for debate, a Scotch love of argument. Nothing pleases a Catawban better than this kind of dispute. He will say persuasively, "Now let's see if we can't see through this thing. Let's see if we can't git to the bottom of this." A long, earnest, and even passionate discussion will ensue in which the parties on both sides usually maintain the utmost good temper, kindliness, and tolerance, but in which they nevertheless pursue their arguments with great warmth and stubbornness. In these discussions several interesting traits of the Catawban quickly become manifest: the man is naturally a philosopher—he loves nothing better than to discuss abstract and difficult questions such as the nature of truth, goodness, and beauty, the essence of property, the problem of God. Moreover, in the development of his arguments the man loves the use of homely phrases and illustration; he is full of pungent metaphors drawn from his experience and environment; and in discussing an ethical question—say, the "moral right" of a man to his property, and to what extent he may profit by it—the Catawban may express himself somewhat in this manner:

"Well, now, Joe, take a case of this sort: suppose I buy a mule from a feller over there on the place next to mine, an' suppose I pay a hundred and fifty dollars fer that mule."

"Is this a one-eyed mule or a two-eyed mule you're buyin'?" Joe demands with a broad wink around at his listening audience.

"It's a two-eyed mule," the first man says good-humoredly, "but if you've got any objections to a two-eyed mule, we'll make it a one-eyed mule."

"Why, hell, no! Jim," the other man now says, "I ain't got no objections, but it seems to me if you're goin' to have a two-eyed mule, you ought to have something better than a one-eyed argyment."

There is a roar of immense male laughter at this retort, punctuated with hearty slappings of thigh and knee, and high whoops in the throat.

"By d-*damn!*" one of the appreciative listeners cries, when he can get his breath, "I reckon that'll hold 'im fer a while."

The story of the "two-eyed mule and the one-eyed argyment" is indeed an immense success, it is the kind of phrase and yarn these people love, and it is destined for an immediate and wide circulation all over the community, accompanied by roars and whoops of laughter. It may even be raised to the dignity of proverbial usage so that one will hear men saying, "Well, that's a two-eyed mule and a one-eyed argyment if I ever saw one," and certainly the unfortunate Jim may expect to be greeted for some time to come in this way:

"Howdy, Jim. I hear you've gone into the mule business," or, "Hey, Jim, you ain't bought no two-eyed mules lately, have you?" or, "Say, Jim: you ain't seen a feller with a one-eyed argyment lookin' fer a two-eyed mule, have you?"

Jim knows very well that he is "in" for this kind of treatment, but he joins in the laughter good-humoredly, although his clay-red face burns with a deeper hue and he awaits the resumption of the debate with a more dogged and determined air.

"Well, that's all right about that," he says, when he can make himself heard. "Whether he's a one-eyed mule or a two-eyed mule is neither here nor there."

"Maybe one eye is here, an' t'other there," someone suggests, and this sets them off again at Jim's expense. But Jim has the determination of the debater and the philosopher, and although his face is pretty red by now, he sticks to his job.

"All right," he says at length, "say I got a mule, anyway, an' he's a good mule, an' I paid one hundred and fifty dollars fer him. Now," he says, pausing, and lifting one finger impressively. "I take that mule an' work him on my farm fer *four* years. He's a *good* mule an' a *good* worker, an' durin' that time he pays fer himself *twice* over! Now!" he declares again, pausing and looking triumphantly at his opponent, Joe, before resuming his argument.

"All right! All right!" Joe says patiently with an air of resignation. "I heard you. I'm still waitin'. You ain't said nothin' yet. You ain't *proved* nothin' yet."

"Now!" Jim continues slowly and triumphantly. "I gave one hundred and fifty dollars fer him, but he's earned his keep an' paid fer himself *twice* over."

"I heard you! I heard you!" says Joe patiently.

"In other words," someone says, "you got back what you paid fer the mule with one hundred and fifty dollars to boot."

"Egs-actly!" Jim says with decision to the group that is now listening intently. "I got back what I put into him, an' I got one hundred fifty dollars to boot. Now here comes another feller," he continues, pointing indefinitely toward the western horizon, "who *needs* a good mule, an' he sees *my* mule, and he *offers to buy it!*" Here Jim pauses again, and he turns and surveys his audience with triumph written on his face.

"*I* heard you. *I'm* listenin'," says Joe in a patient and monotonous voice.

"How much does he offer you?" someone asks.

"Now, wait a minute! I'm comin' to that," says Jim with a silencing gesture. "This here feller says, 'That's a perty good mule you got there!' 'I reckon he'll do!' I say. 'I ain't got no complaint to make!' 'I'm thinkin' of buyin' a mule myse'f,' he says. 'That so?' I say. 'Yes,' he says, 'I could use another mule on my farm. You ain't thinkin' of sellin' that mule there, are you?' 'No,' I say. 'I ain't thinkin' of sellin' it.' 'Well,' he says, 'would you consider an offer fer him?' 'Well,' I say, 'I might an' I might not. It all depends.' 'How much will you take fer him?' he says. 'Well,' I say, 'I ain't never thought of sellin' him before. I'd rather you'd make an offer. How much will you give?' 'Well,' he says, 'how about three hundred dollars?'"

There is a pause of living silence now while Jim turns finally and triumphantly upon his audience.

"*Now!*" he cries again, powerfully and decisively, leaning forward with one big hand gripped upon his knee and his great index finger pointing toward them.

"I'm *listenin',*" Joe says in a calm but foreboding tone.

"I *got* my money back out of that mule," Jim says, beginning a final recapitulation.

"Yes, an' you got another hundred an' fifty to boot," someone helpfully suggests.

"That makes *one* hundred percent clear profit on my 'riginal investment," Jim says. "Now here comes a feller who's willin' to pay me three hundred dollars on top of that. That makes *three* hundred percent."

He pauses now with a conclusive air.

"Well?" Joe says heavily. "Go on. I'm still waitin'. What's the argyment?"

"Why," says Jim, "the argyment is this: I *got* my money back—"

"We all *know* that," says Joe. "You got your money back an' a hundred percent to boot."

"Well," says Jim, "the argyment is this: have I any *right* to take the three hundred dollars that feller offers me?"

"Right?" says Joe, staring at him. "Why, what are you talkin' about? Of course, you got the right. The mule's yours, ain't he?"

"Ah!" says Jim with a knowing look, "that's just the point. *Is* he?"

"You *said* you bought an' *paid* fer him, didn't you?" someone said.

"Yes," says Jim, "I did that, all right."

"Why, hell, Jim," someone else says, "you just ain't talkin' sense. A man's got the right to sell his own property."

"The *legal* right," Jim says. "The *legal* right! Yes! But I ain't talkin' about the *legal* right. I'm talkin' about the *mawral* right."

They gaze at Jim for a moment with an expression of slack-jawed stupefaction mixed with awe. Then he continues:

"A man's got a right to buy a piece of property an' to sell it an' to git a fair profit on his investment, I ain't denyin' that. But has *any* man," he continues, "a right—a mawral right—to a profit of three hundred percent?"

Now Jim has made his point; he is content to rest for a moment and await the attack that comes, and comes immediately: after a moment's silence there is a tumult of protest, derisive laughter, strong cries of denial, a confusion of many voices all shouting disagreement, above which Joe's heavy baritone finally makes itself heard.

"Why, Jim!" he roars. "That's the damnedest logic I ever did hear. I did give you credit fer havin' at least a *one*-eyed argyment, but I'm damned if this argyment you're givin' us has any eyes a-tall!"

Laughter here, and shouts of agreement.

"Why, Jim!" another one says with solemn humor, with an air of deep concern, "you want to go to see a doctor, son: you've begun to talk funny. Don't you know that?"

"*All* right. *All* right! says Jim doggedly. "You can laugh all you please, but there's two sides to this here question, no matter what you think."

"Why, Jim," another man says, with a loose grin playing around his mouth. "What you goin' to do with that two-eyed mule? You goin' to *give* him away to that feller simply because you got your money out of him?"

"I ain't sayin'," Jim says stubbornly, looking very red in the face of their laughter. "I ain't sayin' what I'd do. Mebbe I would an' mebbe I wouldn't."

There is a roar of laughter this time, and the chorus of derisive voices is more emphatic than ever. But for some moments now, while this clamor has been going on, one of the company has fallen silent, he has fallen into a deep study, into an attitude of earnest meditation. But now he rouses himself and looks around with an expression of commanding seriousness.

"Hold on a moment there, boys," he says. "I'm not so sure about all this. I don't know that Jim's such a fool as you think he is. 'Pears to me there may be somethin' in what he says."

"Now!" says Joe, with an air of finality. "What did I tell you! The woods are full of 'em. Here's another 'un that ain't all there."

But the contest is just now beginning in earnest: it goes on furiously, but very seriously, from now on, with these two Horatiuses holding their bridge valiantly and gaining in strength and conviction with each assault. It is a remarkable circumstance that at almost every gathering of Catawbans there is one or more of these minority warriors who become more thoughtful and dubious as their companions grow more vociferous in their agreement and derision, and who, finally, from the first mild expression of doubt, become hotly embattled on the weaker side, and grow in courage and conviction at every breath, every word they utter, every attack they make or repel.

And it has always been the same with the Catawba people. Their character has strong Scotch markings: they are cautious and deliberate, slow to make a radical decision. They are great talkers, and believe in prayer and argument. They want to "reason a thing out," they want to "git to the bottom of a thing" through discussion, they want to settle a thing peaceably by the use of diplomacy and compromise. They are perhaps the most immensely conservative people on earth, they reverence authority, tradition, and leadership, but when committed to any decision, they stick to it implacably, and if the decision is war, they will fight to the end with the fury of maniacs.

Until very recent years these people were touched scarcely at all by "foreign" migration, whether from any of the other states, or from Europe: even today the number of "foreign-born" citizens is almost negligible; the state has the largest percentage of native-born inhabitants in the country. This stock proceeds directly from the stock of the early settlers, who were English, German, and Scotch, particularly Scotch: the frequency with which Scotch names occur—the Grahams, the Alexanders, the McRaes, the Ramsays, the Morrisons, the Pettigrews, the Pentlands, etc.—is remarkable, as is also a marked Scottishness of physique, a lean, angular, big-boned, and loose-jointed structure, a long loping stride, an immense vitality and endurance, especially among the mountaineers in the western part of the state. In fact, during the recent war, it was found by the Army examiners that Catawba furnished easily the tallest troops in the service, and that their average height was a good inch and a half above the average for the country. From this it must not be supposed, as some philological pedagogues have supposed, with the mincing and accurate inaccuracy which is usual in this kind of people, that Old Catawba is today a magnificent anachronism populated with roistering and swashbuckling Elizabethans, "singing" (the pedagogues gloatingly remark of the mountaineers) "the *very* songs their ancestors sang in England four centuries ago, in a form that is practically intact," or with warlike and mad-eyed Celts, chanting the same ballads as when they stormed across the border behind the Bruces.

No. The Catawban today is not like this, nor would he want to be. He is not a colonist, a settler, a transplanted European; during his three centuries there in the wilderness, he has become native to the immense and lonely land that he inhabits, during those three centuries he has taken on the sinew and the color of that earth, he has acquired a character, a tradition, and a history of his own: it is an obscure history, unknown to the world and not to be found in the pages of books, but it is a magnificent history, full of heroism, endurance, and the immortal silence of the earth. It lives in his heart, it lives in his brain, it lives in his unrecorded actions; and with this knowledge he is content, nor does he feel the need of ballads or armadas to trick him into glory.

He does not need to speak, he does not need to affirm or deny, he does not need to assert his power or his achievement, for his heart is a lonely and secret heart, his spirit is immensely brave and humble, he has lived alone in the wilderness, he has heard the silence of the earth, he knows what he knows, and he has not spoken yet. We see him, silent and unheralded, in the brief glare of recorded event—he is there in the ranks of the American Revolution, and eighty years later he is there, gloriously but silently, in the ranks of the Civil War. But his real history is longer and much more extraordinary than could be indicated by these flares of war: it is a history that goes back three centuries into primitive America, a strange and unfathomable history that is touched by something dark and supernatural, and that goes back through poverty and hardship, through solitude and loneliness and unspeakable courage, into the wilderness. For it is the wilderness that is the mother of that nation, it was in the wilderness that the strange and lonely people who have not yet spoken, but who inhabit that immense and terrible land from East to West, first knew themselves, it was in the living wilderness that they faced one another at ten paces and shot one another down, and it is in the wilderness that they still live, waiting until the unspeakable thing in them shall be spoken, until they can unlock their hearts and wreak out the dark burden of their spirit—the legend of loneliness, of exile, and eternal wandering that is in them.

The real history of Old Catawba is not essentially a history of wars or rebellions; it is not a history of politics or corrupt officials; it is not a history of democracy or plutocracy or any form of government; it is not a history of business men, puritans, knaves, fools, saints, or heroes; it is not a history of culture or barbarism.

The real history of Old Catawba is a history of solitude, of the wilderness, and of the immense and eternal earth, it is the history of millions of men living and dying alone in the wilderness, it is the history of the billion unrecorded and forgotten acts and moments of their lives; it is the history of the sun and the moon and the earth, of the sea that with lapse and reluctation of its breath, feathers eternally against the desolate coasts, and of great trees that smash down in lone solitudes in the wilderness; it is a history of time, dark time, strange secret time, forever flowing like a river.

The history of Old Catawba is the history of millions of men living alone in the wilderness, it is the history of millions of men who have lived their brief lives in silence upon the everlasting earth, who have listened to the earth and known her million tongues, whose lives were given to the earth, whose bones and flesh are recompacted with the earth, the immense and terrible American earth that makes no answer.

Arnold Pentland

From time to time, during his Sunday visits to his Uncle Bascom's house, Eugene would meet his cousin, Arnold Pentland. Arnold was the only one of Bascom's children who ever visited his father's house: the rest were studiously absent, saw their father only at Christmas or Thanksgiving, and then like soldiers who will make a kind of truce upon the morning of the Lord's nativity. And certainly the only reason that poor tormented Arnold ever came to Bascom's house was not out of any love he bore for him—for their relation to each other was savage and hostile as it had been since Arnold's childhood—but rather, he came through loneliness and terror, as a child comes home, to see his mother, to try to find some comfort with her if he could.

Even in the frequency of these visits, the dissonant quality of his life was evident. After months of absence he would appear suddenly, morosely, without a word of explanation, and then he would come back every Sunday for weeks. Then he would disappear again, as suddenly as he came: for several months, sometimes for a year or more, none of them would see him. The dense and ancient web of Boston would repossess him—he would be engulfed in oblivion as completely as if the earth had swallowed him. Then, after months of silence, he would again be heard from: his family would begin to receive postal cards from him, of which the meaning was often so confused that nothing was plain save that the furious resentment that sweltered in him against them was again at work.

Thus, in the same day, Bascom, his daughters, and his other son might all receive cards bearing a few splintered words that read somewhat as follows:

"Have changed my name to Arnold Penn. *Do not try to find me. It is useless!* You have made an outcast out of me—now I only want to forget that I ever knew you, have the same blood in my veins. *You have brought this upon yourselves—I hope I shall never see your faces again!* Arthur Penn."

After this explosion they would hear nothing from him for months. Then one day he would reappear without a word of explanation, and for several weeks would put in a morose appearance every Sunday.

Eugene had met him first one Sunday afternoon in February at his uncle's house: Arnold was sprawled out on a sofa as he entered, and his mother, approaching him, spoke to him in the tender, almost pleading tone of a woman who is conscious of some past negligence in her treatment of her child and who is now, pitiably too late, trying to remedy it.

"Arnold," she said coaxingly, "Arnold, will you get up now, please, dear—this is your cousin—won't you say hello to him?"

The great fat obscenity of belly on the sofa stirred, the man got up abruptly, and blurting out something desperate and incoherent, thrust out a soft, grimy hand, and turned away.

Arnold Pentland was a man of thirty-six. He could have been rather small of limb and figure had it not been for his great soft shapeless fatness—a fatness pale and grimy that suggested animal surfeits of unwholesome food. He had lank, greasy hair of black, carelessly parted in the middle, his face, like all the rest of him, was pale and soft, the features blurred by fatness and further disfigured by a greasy smudge of beard. And from this fat, pale face his eyes, brown and weak, looked out on the world with a hysterical shyness of retreat, his mouth trembled uncertainly with a movement that seemed always on the verge of laughter and hysteria, and his voice gagged, worked, stuttered incoherently, or wrenched out desperate, shocking phrases with an effort that was almost as painful as the speech of a paralytic.

His clothing was indescribably dirty. He wore a suit of old blue serge, completely shapeless, and shiny with the use of years, and spotted with the droppings of a thousand meals. Half the buttons were burst off the vest, and between vest and trousers there was a six-inch hiatus of dirty shirt and mountainous fat belly. His shoes were so worn that his naked toes showed through, and his socks were barely more than rags, exposing his dirty heels every time he took a step. The whole creature was as grievously broken, dissonant, and exploded as it is possible for a human life to be, and all the time his soft brown eyes looked out with the startled, pleading look of a stricken animal.

It was impossible to remain with him without a painful feeling of embarrassment—a desire to turn away from the gibberings of an idiot.

Dinner that day—the Sunday of Eugene's first meeting with his cousin—was an agonizing experience for everyone except Bascom. Arnold's conduct of his food was a bestial performance; he fell upon it ravenously, tearing at it, drawing it in with a slobbering suction, panting, grunting over it like an animal until layers of perspiration stood out on his pale wide forehead. Meanwhile, his mother was making a pitiable effort to distract attention from this painful performance: with a mask of attempted gaiety she tried to talk to her nephew about a dozen things—the news of the day, the latest researches in "psychology," the base conduct of the Senate "unreconcilables," or the researches of Professor Einstein, the wonder-working miracle of the human mind. At which, Arnold, looking up and glaring defiantly at both of them, would suddenly explode into a jargon of startling noises that was even more shocking than his bestial ruminations over food.

"M-m-m-man at Harvard . . . fourteen languages . . . A guh-guh-guh-guh—" he paused and glared at his mother with a look of desperate defiance while she smiled pitiable encouragement at him—"A gorilla," he marched it out at last triumphantly, "can't speak one!" and he paused again, his mouth trembling, his throat working convulsively, and then burst out again—"Put gorilla in cage with man . . . all over! . . . done for! . . . half a minute!" He snapped his fingers. "Gorilla make mince meat of him . . . Homer . . . Dante . . . Milton . . . Newton . . . Laws of Gravity. . . . Muh-muh-muh-muh—" again he gagged, craned his fat neck desperately along the edges of his dirty collar and burst out—"Mind of man! . . . Yet when dead—nothing! . . . No good! . . . Seven ten-penny nails worth more!" He paused, glaring, his throat working desperately again, and at length barked forth with triumphant concision: "Brisbane!" and was still.

"Ah-h!" Bascom muttered at this point, and his features contorted in an expression of disgust, he pushed his chair back, and turned half away—"What is he talking about, anyway! . . . Gorillas—Harvard—Fourteen languages." Here he laughed sneeringly down his nose. "Phuh! Phuh! Phuh! Phuh! Phuh! . . . Homer—Dante—Newton—seven ten-penny nails—Brisbane! . . . Phuh! Phuh! Phuh! Phuh! Phuh! . . . Did anyone ever hear such stuff since time began!" And contorting his powerful features he laughed sneeringly down his nose again.

"Yes!" cried Arnold angrily, throwing down his napkin and glaring at his father with wild resentful eyes, shot suddenly with tears—"And you, too! . . . No match for guh-guh-guh-guh *gorilla!*" he yelled. "Think you are! . . . Egotist! . .. Muh-muh-muh"—he paused, gagging, worked his neck along his greasy collar and burst out—"megalomaniac! . . . Always were! . . . But no match gorilla . . . get you!"

"Ah-h!" Bascom muttered, confiding his eloquent features into vacancy with an expression of powerful disgust. "You don't know what you're talking about! . . . He has no conception—oh, not the slightest!—not the faintest!—none whatever!" he howled, waving his great hand through the air with a gesture of scornful dismissal.

The next Sunday, when Eugene had gone to Bascom's house, he was surprised when the old man himself came to the door and opened it. In response to the boy's quick inquiry about his aunt, Bascom, puckering his face in a gesture of disgust, and jerking his head toward the kitchen, muttered:

"Ah-h! She's in there talking to that—fool! . . . But come in, my boy!" he howled, with an instant change to cordiality. "Come in, come in, come in!" he yelled enthusiastically. "We've been expecting you."

From the kitchen came the sound of voices—a woman's and a man's at first low, urgent, blurred, then growing louder; and suddenly he could hear Arnold's voice, the wrenched-out, desperate speech now passionately excited:

"Got to! . . . I tell you, mother, I've got to! . . . She needs me . . . and I've got to go!"

"But Arnold, Arnold," his mother's voice was tenderly persuasive and entreating. "Now quiet, dear, quiet! Can't you quiet yourself a moment while we talk about it?"

"Nothing to talk about!" his voice wrenched the words out desperately. "You've seen the letters, mother. . . . You see what she says, don't you?" his voice rose to a hysterical scream.

"Yes, dear, but—"

"Then what is there to talk about?" he cried frantically. . . . "Don't you see she wants me? . . . Don't you see she's in some terrible trouble with that—that brute . . . that she's begging me to come and take her away from him?"

"Oh, Arnold, Arnold!" his mother's voice was filled with pitiable entreaty, hushed with an infinite regret. "My poor boy, can't you see that all she says is that if you ever go out there she would be glad to see you?" He made some blurted-out reply that was indecipherable, and then, speaking gently but incisively, she continued:

"Arnold:—listen to me, my dear. This woman is a married woman twenty years older than yourself, with grown children of her own. . . . Don't you understand, my dear, that those letters are just the friendly letters that a woman would write to a boy she once taught in school? Don't you see how much these letters you have written her have frightened her—how she is trying in a kind way to let you know—"

"It's a lie!" he said in a choking tone—"A dirty lie! You're against me like all the rest of them! I'll not listen to you any longer! I'll go and get her— I'll bring her back with me, no matter what you say—and to hell with you!" he yelled. "To hell with all of you!"

There was a sound of scrambling confusion, and then he came flying through the swinging door that led into the kitchen, jamming his battered hat down on his head, his eyes wild with grief and anger, his lips trembling and convulsed, murmuring soundless imprecations as he fled. And his mother followed him, a small wren-like figure of a woman, her face haggard, stamped with grief and pity, calling: "Arnold! Arnold!" desperately to that untidy figure that went past like a creature whipped with furies, never pausing to look or speak or say good-bye to anyone, as he ran across the room and left the house, slamming the door behind him.

The story, with its wretched delusion, was pitiable enough. Since his second year at high school, Arnold had cherished a deep affection for a woman who had taught him at that time. She was one of the few women who had ever shown a scrap of understanding for him, and her interest had been just the kindly interest that a warm-hearted and intelligent woman might feel for a wretched little boy. To her, as to everyone else, he had been an ugly duckling, but this had awakened her protective instinct, and actually made him dearer to her than the more attractive children. And because of this she had taught him more—done more for him—than any other person he had ever known, and he had never forgotten her.

When Arnold left school, this woman had married and moved to California with her husband. But in the twenty years that had elapsed since, her old friendship with the boy—for "boy" he still was to her—had never been broken. During all that time Arnold had written her several times a year—long rambling letters filled with his plans, despairs, ambitions, hopes, and failures; the incoherent record of an incoherent personality—and the woman had always answered him with short, brisk, friendly letters of her own.

And during all these years, while he remained to her the "boy" that she had taught, her own personality was undergoing a fantastic transformation in his memory. Although she had been a mature and rather spinsterly female when he had known her, and was now a gray-haired woman in the upper fifties, it seemed to him now that she had never been anything but young and beautiful and fair.

And as that picture developed in his mind, it seemed to him that he had always loved her—as a man would love a woman—and that the only possible meaning in these casual and friendly letters that she wrote to him lay in the love she bore him.

Nothing could be done to stop him. For months now he had come to his mother with trembling haste each time that he received one of the letters. He would read them in a trembly voice, finding in the most casual phrases the declaration of a buried love. And his own replies to these friendly notes had become steadily more ardent and intimate until at last they had become the passionate and hysterical professions of a man in love. The effect of this correspondence on the woman was evident—evident to everyone but Arnold himself. At first, her replies had been written in the same friendly tone that had always characterized her notes to him, but a growing uneasiness was apparent. It was evident that in a kindly way she was trying to check this rising tide of passion, divert his emotion into the old channel of fellowship. Then, as his letters increased in the urgent ardor of their profession, her own had grown steadily more impersonal; the last, in answer to his declaration that he "must see her and would come at once," was decidedly curt. It expressed her cool regret that such a visit as he proposed was impossible—that she and her family would be "away for the summer"—told him that the journey to California would be long, costly, and unpleasant, and advised him to seek his summer's recreation in some more agreeable and less expensive way.

Even the chilling tenor of this letter failed to quench him. Instead, he "read between the lines," he insisted on finding in these curt phrases the silent eloquence of love, and though months had passed since this last letter, and he had written many ardent times since then, he was even convinced that her protracted silence was just another sign of her love—that she was being suppressed through fear, that she was held in bitter constraint by that "brute," her husband—a man for whom he had conceived a murderous hatred.

Thus, against all the persuasions of his mother, he had decided to go. And that day, when he had fled out of his father's house with bitter imprecations on his lips, had marked the final moment of decision. Nothing could be done to stop him, and he went.

He was gone perhaps a month; no one knew exactly how long he was away, for none of his family saw him for almost a year. And what the result of that strange meeting may have been, they never heard—and yet never needed to be told.

From that moment on he was completely lost to them; the legend of that last defeat, the ruin of that final and impossible hope, was written on him, inscribed on his heart and living in his eyes in letters of unspeakable terror, madness, and despair.

One night in April when Eugene had been prowling around the dark and grimy streets of the South Boston slums, he saw a familiar figure in lower Washington Street. It was his cousin, Arnold Pentland. A fine spring rain had been falling all night long, and below the elevated structure the pavements were wet and glistening. Arnold was standing at a corner, looking around with a quick distracted glance, clutching a tattered bundle of old newspapers under one arm.

Eugene ran across the street, calling to him, "Arnold! Arnold!" The man did not seem to hear at first, then looked around him in a startled way, and at last, as Eugene approached him, calling him by name again, he shrank together and drew back, clutching his bundle of old papers before him with both hands and looking at his cousin with the terror-stricken eyes of a child who has suddenly been attacked.

"Arnold!" the other cried again, "*Arnold!* Don't you know me? . . . I'm your cousin—Eugene!" And as he made another step toward the man, his hand outstretched in greeting, Arnold scrambled back with such violent terror that he almost fell and then, still holding the bundle of old papers before him protectively, stammered:

"Duh-duh-duh-don't know you . . . some mistake!"

"Oh, there's no mistake!" the boy cried impatiently. "You must know me! . . . I've met you a dozen times at Uncle Bascom's house. . . . Look here, Arnold." He took off his own hat so that the man could better see his face. "You know me now, don't you?"

"No!—No!" Arnold gasped, moving away all the time. "Wrong man. . . . Name's not Arnold!"

The other stared at him a moment in blank astonishment and then exploded:

"Not Arnold! Of course it's Arnold! Your name's Arnold Pentland, and you're my first cousin. Look here, Arnold; what the hell is this, anyway? What are you trying to do?"

"No! . . . No! . . . Mistake, I tell you. . . . Don't know you! Name's not Arnold . . . Name's Arthur Penn."

"I don't give a damn what you call yourself!" Eugene now cried angrily. "You're Arnold Pentland just the same, and you're not going to get away from me until you admit it! Look here! What kind of trick is this, anyway? What are you trying to pull on me?"—and in his excitement he took the man by the arm and shook him.

Arnold uttered a long wailing cry of terror, and wrenching free, struggled backward, crying:

"You leave me alone now! . . . All of you leave me alone! . . . I never want to see any of you again!" And turning, he began to run blindly and heavily away, a grotesque and pitiable figure, clutching his bundle of sodden newspapers, bent over toward the rain.

Eugene watched him go with a feeling of nameless pity, loneliness, and loss—the feeling of a man who for a moment in the huge unnumbered wilderness of life, the roaring jungle of America, sees a face he knows, a kinsman of his blood, and says farewell to him forever. For that moment's vision of that fat, stumbling figure running blindly away from him down a dark wet street was the last he would ever have. He never saw the man again.

The Face of the War

. . . Heat-brutal August the year the war ended: here are four moments from the face of the war. One—at Langley Field: a Negro retreating warily out of one of the rude shed-like offices of the contracting company on the flying field, the white teeth bared in a horrible grimace of fear and hatred, the powerful figure half-crouched, ape-like, ready to crouch or run, the arms, the great black paws, held outward defensively as he retreated warily under the merciless glazed brutality of the August sun, over the barren, grassless horror of hard dry clay, the white eyeballs fixed with an expression of mute unfathomable hatred, fear, and loathing upon the slouchy, shambling figure of a Southern white—a gang boss or overseer—who advanced upon him brandishing a club in his meaty hand, and screaming the high thick throat-scream of blood-lust and murder: "I'll stomp the guts out of you, you God-damned black bastard! I'll beat his God-damn brains out!"— and smashing brutally with his club, coming down across the Negro's skull with the sickening resilient thud, heard clear across the field, of wood on living bone. Behind the paunch-gut white, an office clerk, the little meager yes-man of the earth, a rat in shirt-sleeves, quick as a rat to scamper to its hiding, quick as a rat to come in to the kill when all is safe, with rat's teeth bared—advancing in the shambling wake of his protector, fear's servile seconder, murder's cringing aide, coming in behind with rat's teeth bared, the face white as a sheet, convulsed with fear and with the coward's lust to kill without mercy or reprisal, the merciless sun blazing hot upon the armband buckles on the crisp shirt-sleeve, and with a dull metallic glint upon the barrel of the squat blue automatic that he clutches with a trembling hand, offering it to his blood-mad master, whispering frantically—"Here! . . . Here, Mister Bartlett! . . . Shoot the bastard if he tries to hit you!"

Meanwhile, the Negro retreating slowly all the time, his terrible white stare of fear and hatred no longer fixed upon his enemy, but on the evil glint of that cylinder of blue steel behind him, his arms blindly, futilely, before him as his hated foe comes on, his black face, rilled and channeled first with lacings of bright blood, then beaten to a bloody pulp as the club keeps smashing down with its sickening and resilient crack:

"You . . . God-damn . . . black . . . son-of-a-bitch!" the voice thick, high,

229

phlegmy, choked with murder. "I'll teach ye—" Smash! the cartilage of the thick black nose crunches and is ground to powder by the blow "—if a God-damn Nigger can talk back to a white man!"—Smash. A flailing, horribly clumsy blow across the mouth which instantly melts into a bloody smear through which the Negro, eyes unmoving from the blue glint of the steel, mechanically spits the shattered fragments of his solid teeth—"I'll bash in his God-damned head—the damn black bastard—I'll show him if he can—" Smash! Across the wooly center of the skull and now, the scalp ripped open to the base of the low forehead, the powerful black figure staggering drunkenly, bending at the knees, the black head sagging, going down beneath the blows, the arms still blindly thrust before him, upon one knee now on the barren clay-baked earth, the head sunk down completely on the breast, blood over all, the kneeling figure blindly rocking, swaying with the blows, the arms still out until he crashes forward on the earth, his arms outspread, face to one side and then, the final nausea of horror—the murderous kick of the shoe into the blood-pulp of the unconscious face, and then silence, nothing to see or hear now but the heavy, choked, and labored breathing of the paunch-gut man, the white rat-face behind him with the bared rat's fangs of terror, and the dull blue wink of the envenomed steel.

Again: your coward's heart of fear and hate, the coward's lust for one-way killing, murder without danger to himself, the rat's salvation from the shipwreck of his self-esteem—armed with a gun now, clothed in khaki, riding the horse of his authority—as here:—Three boys, himself among them, all employed by the contracting company, are walking after supper on the borders of the flying field in the waning light of the evening, coming dark. They are walking down near the water's edge, across the flat marshy land, they are talking about their homes, the towns and cities they have known and come from, their colleges and schools, their plans for an excursion to the beach at the week-end, when they draw their pay. Without knowing it, they have approached a hangar where one of the new war-planes with which the government has been experimenting has been housed. Suddenly, the soldier who is there on guard has seen them, advances on them now, one hand upon the revolver in his holster, his little furtive eyes narrowed into slits. Face of the city rat, dry, gray, furtive, pustulate, the tallowy lips, the rasping voice, the scrabble of a few sharp oaths, the stony gravel of a sterile, lifeless speech:

"What are ya doin' here ya f—— little bastards!—Who told ya to come f—— round duh hangah?"

One of the boys, a chubby red-cheeked youngster from the lower South, fair-haired, blue-eyed, friendly and slow of speech, attempts to answer:

"Why, mister, we just thought—"

Quick as a flash, the rat has slapped the boy across the mouth; the filthy tips have left their mottled print upon the boy's red cheek, have left their loathsome, foul, and ineradicable print upon the visage of his soul forever:

"I don't give a f—— what ya t'ought, ya little p——! Annudeh woid outa ya f—— trap an' I'll shoot the s—— outa ya!" He has the gun out of its holster now, ready in his hand; the eyes of the three boys are riveted on the dull reptilian wink of its blue barrel with a single focal intensity of numb horror, fascinated disbelief.

"Now get t' f—— hell outa here!" the hero cries, giving the boy he has just slapped a violent shove with his free hand. "Get the f—— hell away from heah, all t'ree of youse! Don't f—— around' wit' me, ya little p——," the great man snarls now, eyes a-glitter, narrow as a snake's, as he comes forward with deadly menace written on his face. "Annudeh woid outa ya f—— traps, an' I'll shoot t' s—— outa youse! On yuh way, now, ya p——. Get t' hell away from me befoeh I plug ya!"

And the three boys, stunned, bewildered, filled with shame, and sickened out of all the joy and hope with which they had been speaking of their projects just a moment before, have turned, and are walking silently away with the dull shame, the brutal and corrosive hatred which the war has caused, aching and rankling in their hearts.

Again, an image of man's naked desire, brutal and imperative, stripped down to his raw need, savage and incurious as the harsh need of a starved hunger which takes and rends whatever food it finds—as here: Over the bridge, across the railway track, down in the Negro settlement of Newport News—among the dives and stews and rusty tenements of that grimy, dreary, and abominable section, a rude shack of unpainted pine boards, thrown together with the savage haste which war engenders, to pander to a need as savage and insatiate as hunger, as old as life, the need of friendless, unhoused, lonely men the world over.

The front part of this rawly new, yet squalid place, has been partitioned off by rude pine boards to form the semblance of a lunch room and soft-drink parlor. Within are several tables furnished with a few fly-specked menu cards, on which half a dozen items are recorded, and at which none of the patrons ever look, and a wooden counter, with its dreary stage property of luke-warm soda pop, a few packages of cigarettes, and a box of cheap cigars beneath a dingy little glass case; and beneath a greasy glass humidor, a few stale ham and cheese sandwiches, which have been there since the place opened, which will be there till the war is done.

Meanwhile, all through the room, the whores, in their thin, meager mummers, act as waitresses, move patiently about among the crowded tables and ply their trade. The men, who are seated at the tables, belong for the most part to that great group of unclassed creatures who drift and float, work, drift, and starve, are now in jail, now out again, now foul, filthy, wretched, hungry, out of luck, riding the rods, the rusty box cars of a freight, snatching their food at night from the boiling slum of hoboes' jungle, now swaggering with funds and brief prosperity—the floaters, drifters, and half-bums, that huge nameless, houseless, rootless, and anomalous class that swarms across the nation.

They are the human cinders of the earth. Hard, shabby, scarred, and lined of face, common, dull, and meager of visage as they are, they have the look of having crawled that morning from the box car in the train yard of another city or of having dropped off a day coach in the morning, looking casually and indifferently about them, carrying a cardboard suitcase with a shirt, two collars, and a tie. Yet a legend of great distances is written on them—a kind of atomic desolation. Each is a human spot of moving rust naked before the desolation of the immense and lonely skies that bend above him, unsheltered on the huge and savage wilderness of the earth, across which he is hurled—a spot of grimy gray and dingy brown, clinging to the brake rods of a loaded freight.

He is a kind of human cinder hurled through space, naked, rootless, nameless, with all that was personal and unique in its one life almost emptied out into that huge vacancy of rust and iron and waste and lonely and incommunicable distances in which it lives, through which it has so often been bombarded.

And this atom finds its end at length, perhaps, at some unknown place upon the savage visage of the continent, exploded, a smear of blood on the rock ballast, a scream lost in the roar of pounding wheels, a winding of entrails around the axle rods, a brief indecipherable bobbing of blood and bone and brains upon the wooden ties, or just a shapeless bundle of old ragged brown and gray slumped down at morning in a shabby doorway, on a city street, beneath the elevated structure, a bundle of ragged bone now cold and lifeless to be carted out of sight by the police, nameless and forgotten in its death as in its life.

Such for the most part were the men who now sat at the tables in this rude house of pleasure, looking about them furtively, warily, with an air of waiting, calculation, or indecision, and sometimes glancing at one another with sly, furtive, rather sheepish smiles.

As for the women who attended them, they were prostitutes recruited, for the most part, from the great cities of the North and Middle West, brutally greedy, rapacious, weary of eye, hard of visage, over-driven, harried and exhausted in the mechanical performance of a profession from which their only hope was to grasp and clutch as much as they could in as short a time as possible. They had the harsh, rasping, and strident voices, the almost deliberately exaggerated and inept extravagance of profanity and obscenity, the calculated and over-emphasized style of toughness which one often finds among poor people in the tenement sections of great cities—which one observes even in small children—the constant oath, curse, jeer, threat, menace, and truculent abuse, which really comes from the terrible fear in which they live, as if, in that world of savage aggression and brute rapacity, from which they have somehow to wrest their bitter living, they are afraid that any betrayal of themselves into a gentler, warmer, and more tolerant kind of speech and gesture will make them suspect to their fellows, and lay them open to the assaults, threats, tyrannies, and dominations they fear.

So it was with these women now: one could hear their rasping, strident voices everywhere throughout the smoke-filled room, their harsh jeering laughter, and the extravagant exaggeration and profusion with which they constantly interlarded their rasping speech with a few oaths and cries repeated with brutal monotony, such phrases as "Christ!" "Jesus!"—"What t' God-damn hell do I care?"—"Come on! Watcha goin' t' do now! I got no time t' —— around with yuh! If ya want t' ——come on an' pay me—if ya don't, get t' God-damn hell outa here"—being among the expressions one heard most frequently.

Yet, even among these poor, brutally exhausted, and fear-ridden women, there was really left, like something pitiably living and indestructible out of life, a kind of buried tenderness, a fearful, almost timid desire to find some friendship, gentleness, even love among the rabble-rout of lost and ruined men to whom they ministered.

And this timid, yet inherent desire for some warmer and more tender relation even in the practice of their profession was sometimes almost ludicrously apparent as they moved warily about among the tables, soliciting patronage from the men they served. Thus, if a man addressed them harshly, brutally, savagely, with an oath—which was the customary form of greeting—they would answer him in kind. But if he spoke to them more quietly, or regarded them with a more kindly smiling look, they might respond to him with a pathetic and ridiculous attempt at coquetry, subduing their rasping voices to a kind of husky, tinny whisper, pressing against him intimately, bending their bedaubed and painted faces close to his, and cajoling him with a pitiable pretense at seductiveness somewhat in this manner:

"Hello there, big boy! . . . Yuh look lonesome sittin' there all by yourself. . . . Whatcha doin' all alone? . . . Yuh want some company? Huh?"— whispered hoarsely with a ghastly leer of the smeared lips, and pressing closer—"Wanta have some fun, darling? . . . Come on!"—coaxingly, imperatively, taking the patron by the hand—"I'll show yuh a big time."

It was in response to some such blandishment as this that the boy had got up from his table, left the smoke-filled room accompanied by the woman, and gone out through a door at one side into the corridor that led back to the little partitioned board compartments of the brothel.

Here it was at once evident that there was nothing to do but wait. A long line of men and women that stretched from one end of the hallway to another stood waiting for their brief occupancies of the little board compartments at the other end, all of which were now obviously and audibly occupied.

As they came out into the hall, the woman with the boy called out to another woman at the front end of the line: "Hello, May! . . . Have ya seen Grace?"

"Aah!" said the woman thus addressed, letting cigarette smoke coil from her nostrils as she spoke, and speaking with the rasping, exaggerated, and brutal toughness that has been described: "I t'ink she's in number Seven here havin' a ——."

And having conveyed the information in this delicate manner, she then turned to her companion, a brawny, grinning seaman in the uniform of the United States Navy, and with a brisk, yet rather bantering humor, demanded:

"Well, whatchya say, big boy? . . . Gettin' tired of waitin'? . . . Well, it won't be long now. . . . Dey'll be troo in dere in a minute an' we're next."

"Dey better had be!" the sailor replied with a kind of jocular savagery. "If dey ain't, I'll tear down duh —— joint! . . . Christ!" he cried in an astounded tone, after listening attentively for a moment. "Holy Jeez!" he said with a dumbfounded laugh. "What t' hell are dey doin' in deh all dis time? Who is dat guy, anyway?—A whole regiment of duh Marines, duh way it sounds t' me! Holy *Jesus!*" he cried with an astounded laugh, listening again—"Christ!"

"Ah, c'mon, Jack!" the woman said with a kind of brutal, husky tenderness, snuggling close to his brawny arm meanwhile, and lewdly proposing her heavy body against his. "Yuh ain't gonna get impatient on me now, are yuh? . . . Just hold on a minute moeh an' I'll give ya somet'ing ya neveh had befoeh!—"

"If yuh do," the gallant tar said tenderly, drawing his mighty fist back now in a gesture of savage endearment that somehow seemed to please her, "I'll come back and smack yuh right in the ——, yuh son-of-a-bitch!" he amorously whispered, and pulled her to him.

Similar conversations and actions were to be observed all up and down the line: there were lewd jests, ribald laughter, and impatient and shouted demands on the noisy occupants of the little compartments to "come on out an' give some of duh rest of us a chanct, f'r Christ's sake!" and other expressions of a similar nature.

It was a brutally hot night in the middle of August: in the hallway the air was stifling, weary, greasily humid. The place was thick with tobacco smoke, the stench of the men, the powder and cheap perfume of the women and over all, unforgettable, overpowering, pungent, resinous, rude, and raw as savage nature and man's naked lust, was the odor of the new, unpainted, white-pine lumber of which the whole shambling and haphazard place had been contructed.

Finally, after a long and weary wait in that stifling place, during which time the door of the compartments had opened many times, and many men and women had come out, and many more gone in, the boy and the woman with him had advanced to the head of the line, and were next in the succession of that unending and vociferous column.

Presently, the door of the room for which they waited opened, a man came out, shut the door behind him, and then went quickly down the hall. Then for a moment there was silence, impatient mutters in the line behind them, and at length the woman with the boy muttering:

"I wondeh what t' hell she's doin' all dis time!—Hey!" she cried harshly, and hammered on the door, "Who's in dere? . . . Come on out, f'r Christ's sake! . . . Yuh're holdin' up duh line!"

In a moment, a woman's voice answered wearily:

"All right, Fay! . . . Just a minute dear. . . . I'll be right there."

"Oh," the woman with the boy said in a suddenly quiet, strangely tender, kind of voice. "It's Margaret. . . . I guess she's worn out, poor kid." And knocking on the door again, but this time gently, almost timidly, she said in a quiet voice:

"How are yuh, kid? . . . D'ya need any help?"

"No, it's all right, Fay," the girl inside said in the same tired and utterly exhausted tone. "I'll be out in a moment. . . . Come on in, honey."

The woman opened the door softly and entered the room. The only furnishings of the hot, raw, and hideous little place, besides a chair, an untidy and rumpled looking bed, and a table, was a cheap dresser on which was a doll girdled with a soiled ribbon of pink silk, tied in a big bow, a photograph of a young sailor inscribed with the words, "To Margaret, the best pal I ever had—Ed"—and a package of cigarettes. An electric fan, revolving slowly from left to right, droned incessantly, and fanned the close stale air with a kind of sporadic and sweltering breeze.

And from moment to moment, as it swung in its half orbit, the fan would play full upon the face and head of the girl, who was lying on the bed in an attitude of utter pitiable weariness. When this happened, a single strand of her shining hair, which was straight, lank, fine-spun as silk, and of a lovely red-bronze texture, would be disturbed by the movement of the fan and would be blown gently back and forth across her temple.

The girl, who was tall, slender, and very lovely, was, save for her shoes and stockings, naked, and she lay extended at full length on the untidy bed, with one arm thrust out in a gesture of complete exhaustion, the other folded underneath her shining hair, and her face, which had a fragile, transparent, almost starved delicacy, turned to one side and resting on her arm, the eyelids closed. And the eyelids also had this delicacy of texture, were violet with weariness, and so transparent that the fine net-work of veins was plainly visible.

The other woman went softly over to the bed, sat down beside her, and began to speak to her in a low and tender tone. In a moment the girl turned her head toward the woman, opened her eyes, and smiled, in a faint and distant way, as if someone who is just emerging from the drugged spell of an opiate:

"What? . . . What did you say, darling? . . . No, I'm all right," she said faintly, and sitting up, with the other woman's help, she swiftly pulled on over her head the cheap one-piece garment she was wearing, which had been flung back over the chair beside the bed. Then smiling, she stood up, took a cigarette out of the package on the dresser, lighted it, and turning to the boy, who was standing in the door, said ironically, with something of the rasping accent which the other woman used, beneath which, however, her pleasant rather husky tone was plainly evident.

"All right, Catawba! Come on in!"

He went in slowly, still looking at her with an astounded stare. He had known her the first moment he had looked at her. She was a girl from the little town where the state university, at which he was a student, was situated, a member of a family of humble decent people, well-known in the town: she had disappeared almost two years before, there had been rumor at the time that one of the students had "got her in trouble," and since that time he had neither seen nor heard of her.

"How are all the folks down home?" she said. "How's everyone in Pulpit Hill?"

Her luminous smoke-gray eyes were hard and bright as she spoke, her mouth, in her thin young face, was hard and bitter as a blade, and her voice was almost deliberately hard and mocking. And yet, beneath this defiant scornfulness, the strange, husky tenderness of the girl's tone persisted, and as she spoke, she put her slender hand lightly on his arm, with the swift, unconscious tenderness of people in a world of strangers who suddenly meet someone they know from home.

"They're all right," he stammered in a confused and bewildered tone, his face beginning to smoulder with embarrassment as he spoke.

"Well, if you see anyone I know," she said in the same ironic tone, "say hello for me. . . . Tell 'em I sent my love."

"All right," he blurted out stupidly. "I—I—certainly will."

"And I'm mad at you, Catawba," she said with a kind of mocking reproachfulness, "I'm mad at you for not telling me you were here. . . . The next time you come here, you'd better ask for me—or I'll be mad! . . . We homefolks have got to stick together. . . . So you ask for Margaret—or I'll be mad at you—do you hear?"

"All right," he stammered confusedly again. "I certainly will."

She looked at him a moment longer with her hard bright stare, her bitter, strangely tender smile. Then thrusting her fingers swiftly through her hair, she turned to the other woman and said:

"Be nice to him, Fay. . . . He's one of the folks from down my way. . . . Good-bye, Catawba. . . . When you come back, you ask for Margaret."

"Good-bye," he said, and she was gone, out of the door and down that stifling little hall of brutal, crowding, and imperative desire, into the market-place again, where for the thousandth time she would offer the sale of her slender young body to whoever would be there to buy, to solicit, take, accept the patronage of any of the thousand nameless and unknown men that the huge cylinder of chance and of the night might bring to her.

He never saw her after that. She was engulfed into the great vortex of the war, the million-threaded web of chance and of dark time, the huge dark abyss and thronging chaos of America, the immense, the cruel, the indifferent, and the magic land, beneath whose single law of perilous, fatal, million-visaged chance we all have lived, where all of us have lived and walked as strangers, where all of us have been so small, so lonely, and forsaken, which has engulfed us all at length, and in whose dark and lonely breast so many lost and nameless men are buried and forgotten.

This, then, was the third visage of calamity, the image of desire, the face of war.

Again, the speed, haste, violence, savage humor, and the instant decisiveness of war:—A sweltering room on one of the great munitions piers at Newport News where now the boy is working as a material checker. Inside the great shed of the pier, a silent sweltering heat of one hundred ten degrees, a grimy mote-filled air, pollinated with the golden dust of oats which feed through a gigantic chute into the pier in an unending river, and which are sacked and piled in tremendous barricades all up and down the length of that enormous shed.

Elsewhere upon the pier, the towering geometries of war munitions: the white hard cleanliness of crated woods containing food and shot provender of every sort—canned goods, meat, beans, dried fruits, and small arms ammunition—the enormous victualing of life and death fed ceaselessly into the insatiate and receiving maw of distant war.

The sweltering air is impregnated with the smells of all these things— with smell of oats and coarse brown sacking, with the clean fresh pungency of crated boxes, and with the huge, drowsy, and nostalgic compact of a pier—the single blend of a thousand multiform and mixed aromas, the whole compacted fragrance of the past, sharp, musty, thrilling, unforgettable, as if the savor of the whole huge earth's abundance has slowly stained, and worn through, and soaked its mellow saturation into the massive and encrusted timbers of the pier.

But now all work has ceased: all of the usual sounds of work—the unceasing rumble of the trucks, the rattling of winches and the hard, sudden labor of the donkey engines on the decks of ships, the great nets swinging up and over with their freight of boxes, the sudden rattling fall and rise again, the shouts and cries of the black sweating stevedores, the sharp commands of the gang bosses, overseers, and loading men—all this has stopped, has for the moment given over to the measured stamp of marching men, the endless streams of men in khaki uniforms who have all morning long, since early light, been tramping through the pier and filing up a gangplank into the side of a great transport which waits there to engulf them.

Meanwhile, the Negro stevedores sprawl lazily on loaded oat sacks round the grain chute, the checkers doze upon the great walled pile of grain or, kneeling in a circle down behind some oaty barricade, they gamble feverishly with dice.

Meanwhile, the troops come through. The sweltering brown columns tramp in, pause, are given rest, wearily shift the brutal impediment of the loaded knapsacks on their shoulders, take off their caps, wipe their sleeves across their red sweating faces, curse quietly among themselves, and then wait patiently for the lines to move again.

Down by the ship-side, at the gangplank's end, a group of officers are seated at a table as the troops file by them, examining each man's papers as he comes to them, passing them on from hand to hand, scrawling signatures, filing, recording, putting the stamp of their approval finally on the documents that will release each little khaki figure to its long-awaited triumph of the ship, the voyage, the new land, to all the joy and glory it is panting for, and to the unconsidered perils of battle, war, and death, disease, or mutilation, and the unknown terror, horror, and disgust.

But now a column of black troops is coming by. They are a portion of a Negro regiment from Texas, powerful big men, naive and wondering as children, incorrigibly unsuited to the military discipline. Something, in fact, is missing, wrong, forgotten, out of place, with everyone's equipment: one has lost his cap, another is without a belt, another is shy two buttons on his jacket, still another has mislaid his canteen, one is shy a good part of his knapsack equipment, and dumbly, ignorantly bewildered—everyone has lost something, left something behind, done something wrong, now misses something which he has to have.

And now, in one of the pauses in their march along the pier, each one of them pours out the burden of his complaint, into the sweltering misery of the heated air, the babel of black voices mounts. And the target of their bewilderment, the object on whom this whole burden of mischance and error is now heaped, the overburdened and exhausted ruler to whom each now turns in his distress, and with the naive and confident faith of a child, asks for an instant solution to the tangled web of error in which he is enmeshed—is an infuriated little bullock of a white man, a first lieutenant, their commander, who, during the mountainous accumulations of that catastrophic morning, has been driven completely out of his head.

Now he stamps up and down that pier like a maddened animal, the white eyeballs and the black sweat-rilled faces follow him back and forth on his stamping and infuriated lunges with the patient, dutiful, and all-confiding trustfulness of children.

His red solid little face is swollen with choked fury and exasperation: as the unending chronicle of their woes mounts up, he laughs insanely, clutches violently at the neck-band of his coat as if he is strangling, stamps drunkenly and blindly about like a man maddened with the toothache, and finally hurls his cap down on the floor and stamps on it, cursing bitterly.

And still they petition him, with the confident hope and certitude of trusting children that one word from their infallible governor will settle everything:—one tells about his missing belt, another of his forgotten canteen, another of his lost cap, his depleted and half-furnished knapsack— affectionately, incorrigibly, they address his as "Boss!" in spite of his curses, threats, entreaties, his final maddened screams that they must address him in a military manner, and the man stamps up and down, out of his wits with choking and unutterable exasperation, cursing vilely:

"You God-damned black bone-headed gang of sausage-brained gorillas!" he yells chokingly, and clutches at his throat—"Oh you damned thick-skulled solid-ivory idiot brothers of the one-eyed mule! You sweet stinking set of ape-faced sons of bitches, you! If your brains were made of dynamite you wouldn't have enough to blow your nose, you poor dumb suffering second cousins of an owl! . . . Oh, you just wait, you ink-complected bastards, you!" he now shouted with a kind of fiendish and anticipatory pleasure. "Just wait until I get you in the front-line trenches—I'll line you up there till those German bastards shoot you full of daylight if it's the last thing I ever live to do, you . . . damned . . . ignorant . . . misbegotten . . . cross . . . between a . . . a . . . a . . . walled-eyed possum and a camel's hump—why, you low-down, ignorant bunch of . . . of—"

"Boss?"

"Don't call me Boss!" in a high, choking, almost strangled gurgle. "You dumb son-of-a-bitch, how often have I got to tell you not to call me BOSS!" he yells.

"I know, Boss—" in a plaintive tone—"but my belt-buckle's busted. Is you got a piece of string?"

"*A piece of string!*" he chokes. "Why, you damned—you—you—a piece of string!" he squeaks, and finally defeated, he takes off his cap, throws it on the floor, and sobbing, stamps upon it.

But an even greater affliction is in store for this happy man. Down at the ship-side now, where the examining officers are sitting at the table, there has come a sudden pause, a disturbing interruption in the swift and mechanical dispatch with which the troops have been filing in before them. Six of the big black soldiers in a group have been stopped, sharply questioned, and then brusquely motioned out of line.

The officer picks up his cap, yells, "What in Christ's name is the matter now?" and rushes down to where they stand, in an attitude of crushed dejection, with tears rolling down their ebony cheeks. A moment's excited interrogation of the officers seated at the table informs him of the trouble: the six Negroes, all of whom are members of his command, have been under treatment for venereal diseases, but have somehow managed to sneak away from camp without a clean bill of health. Now their delinquency and stratagem of escape has been discovered, they have been denied their embarkation papers, and weeping and begging, with the pitiable confidence which all these blacks put in their commanding officer, they are fairly groveling before him, pleading with him that they be allowed to take ship with the rest of their companions.

"We ain't done nothin', Boss!" their leader, a huge ape of a man, black as ebony, is sniffling, pawing at the officer's sleeve. "Dey ain't nothin' wrong with us!"—"We don't want to stay heah in dis Gawd-damn hole, Boss!"

another sniffles. "We want to go to France wheah you is! . . . Don't leave us behind, Boss! . . . We'll do anyt'ing you say if you'll jest take us along wid you!—"

"Why, you black clappy bastards!" he snarls—"I wish you were in hell, the lot of you! . . . How the hell do you expect me to do anything now at the last moment?" he yells, and filled with a frenzy that can find no stay or answer goes stamping back and forth like a man gone mad with the very anguish of exasperation and despair. He charges into the midst of that small group of tainted and dejected blacks like a maddened little bull. He raves at them, he reviles them and curses them most foully, for a moment it seems that he is going to assault them physically. And they gather around him weeping, entreating, crying, begging him for rescue and release, until at length, as if driven frantic by their clamor, he claps both hands onto his ears and screaming, "All right, all right, all right!—I'll try—but if they let you go, I hope they kill every clappy son-of-a-bitch in the first attack"—he rushes away to the table where the examining officers are seated at their work, engages them long and earnestly in a passionate and persuasive debate, and finally wins them over to his argument.

It is decided that the infected Negroes shall be given a physical examination here and now upon the pier, and a tall medical officer, delegated for this task, rises from the table, signs briefly to the rejected men, and accompanied by their red-faced little officer, marches them away behind the concealing barrier of the great roll of sacked oats.

They are gone perhaps ten minutes: when they return the Negroes are cavorting with glee, their black faces split by enormous ivory grins, and they are capering around their little officer like frantic children. They fairly fawn upon him, they try to kiss his hands, they pat his shoulders with their great black paws—the story of their triumphant restoration to the fold is legible in every move they make, in everything they do.

The tall medical officer marches sternly ahead, but with a faint grin playing round the corners of his mouth, and the little red-faced officer is still cursing bitterly, but in his curses now there is a gentler note, the suggestion almost of a lewd tenderness.

And at length that brown, enormous, apparently interminable column has filed into the ship's great side, and there is nothing on the pier now but the far lost sounds and silence, the breath of coolness, evening, the oncoming undulous stride of all-enfolding and deep-breasted night.

Gulliver

THE STORY OF A TALL MAN

Some day someone will write a book about a man who was too tall—who lived forever in a dimension that he did not fit, and for whom the proportions of everything—chairs, beds, doors, rooms, shoes, clothes, shirts, and socks, the berths of Pullman cars, and the bunks of transatlantic liners, together with the rations of food, drink, love, and women, which most men on this earth have found sufficient to their measure—were too small.

He should write the story of that man's journey through this world with the conviction of incontrovertible authority, and with such passion, power, and knowledge that every word will have the golden ring of truth; and he will be able to do this because that man's life has been his own, because he has lived it, breathed it, moved in it, and made it his with every sinew of his life since he was fifteen years of age, and because there is no one on earth who understands that world, in all its joy and pain and strangeness of an incommunicable loneliness, as well as such a man.

The world this man would live in is the world of six feet six, and that is the strangest and most lonely world there is. For the great distances of this world are the fractional ones, the terrific differences are those we can measure by a hand, a step, a few short inches, and that shut us completely from the world we see, the life we love, the room, the door we want to enter, as if we saw them from the star-flung planetary distances of bridgeless and unmeasured vacancy. Yes, that world we see and want is even more remote from us than Mars, for it is almost ours at every instant, intolerably near and warm and palpable and intolerably far because it is so very near—only a foot away if we could utter, find, and enter it—and we are lashed on by our fury and devoured by our own hunger, captives in the iron and impregnable walls of our own loneliness.

To be a giant, to be one of those legendary creatures two miles high in the old stories—that is another thing. For a giant lives in his own world and needs and wants no other: he takes a mountain at a stride, drinks off a river in one gulp of thirst, wanders over half a continent in a day, and then comes home at night to dine in friendship with his fellow Titans, using a shelf of mountain for a table, a foothill as a stool, and the carcasses of whole roast oxen as the dainty morsels of his feast.

And to be a giant in a world of pygmy men—to be a mile-high creature in a world of foot-high men—that also is another thing. For sometimes his huge single eye is blinded by their cunning, he will make the mountains echo with his wounded cries, tear up a forest in his pain and fury, and will lash about him with an oak tree, and hurl ten-ton boulders torn from granite hills after the little ships of terror-stricken men.

He awakes at morning in a foreign land, his ship is wrecked, his comrades drowned, and he forsaken: a regiment of tiny creatures are swarming up across his body, they shoot their tiny arrows at his face and bind him down with countless weavings of a thread-like cord, and the terrific legend of his life among the pygmies becomes the instrument by which another giant whipped the folly, baseness, and corruption in the lives of men with the scorpion lash of the most savage allegory ever written.

And to be a pygmy in a world of pygmy men, that also is another thing. For where we all are inches tall, our size is only measured by proportion. We live elf-close and midget-near the earth, and desperately explore the tropic jungle of the daisy fields while monstrous birds—huge buzzing flies and booming bees and tottering butterflies—unfurl the enormous velvet sails of their slashed wings as they soar over us. We think we are as tall, as big, as strong as any men that ever lived, if thinking, seeing, makes it so, and in our three-inch world our corn and wheat is good but is no higher than the grass. We wander through great gloomy forests no taller than scrub pine, there are no Atlantic depths and Himalayan heights, our grandest mountain ranges are just mole-hill high, and if the stars seem far, most far, to us, they are no farther than they seem to other men.

Finally, to be one of those poor giants and midgets of the time in which we live—one of these paltry eight- and nine-foot Titans, two-foot dwarfs of circuses—that also is a different thing. For now they live the life, and love the lights of carnival, and the world beyond those lights is phantom and obscure. Each day the world throngs in to sit beneath the canvas top and feed its fascinated eye on their deformities, and they display themselves before that world and are not moved by interest, touched by desire, from what they see of it. Instead they live together in the world of freaks, and this world seems to them to have been framed inevitably by nature. They love, hate, play, contrive, betray, and hope, are happy, sorrowful, and ambitious like all other men. The eight-foot giant and the two-foot dwarf are bosom friends. And three times a day they sit down and eat at table in the interesting and congenial society given charm and romance by The Fat Girl and The Bearded Lady, and piquant zest by the witty repartee of Jo-Jo-What-Is-It, The Living Skeleton, and The Tattooed Man. But that, as well, is not a tall man's world: it is another door he cannot enter.

For he is earthy, of the earth, like every man. Shaped from the same clay, breathing the same air, fearing the same fears, and hoping the same hopes as all men in the world, he walks the thronging streets of life alone—those streets that swarm forever with their tidal floods of five feet eight. He walks those streets forever a stranger, and alone, having no other earth, no other life, no other door than this, and feeding upon it with an eye of fire, a heart of intolerable hunger and desire, yet walled away from all the dimensional security of that great room of life by the length of an arm, the height of a head, the bitter small denial of a foot—seeing, feeling, knowing, and desiring the life that blazes there before his eyes, which is as near as his heart, and as far as heaven, which he could put his hand upon at every moment, and which he can never enter, fit, or make his own again, no more than if he were phantasmal substances of smoke.

It is a strange adventure—the adventure of being very tall—and in its essence it comes to have a singular and instinctive humanity. In an extraordinary way, a tall man comes to know things about the world as other people do not, cannot, know them. And the reason for this lies mainly in the purely fortuitous quality of a tall man's difference from average humanity. In no respect, save in respect to his unusual height, is a tall man different from other men. In no way is he less his brother's brother, or his father's son. In fact—astonishing as this fact may seem—the overwhelming probability is that the tall man never thinks of being tall, never realizes, indeed, that he *is* tall until other people remind him of his height.

Thus, when this tall man was alone, he never thought of his great height; it never occurred to him that his dimensions were in any way different from those of most people that he saw around him every day upon the streets. In fact, he was the victim of an extraordinary delusion: for some reason which he could not define, he had a secret and unspoken conviction—an image of himself that was certainly not the product of his conscious reasoning, but rather the unconscious painting of his desire—that he was really a person of average height and size—a man of five feet eight or nine, no more. A moment's reflection would, of course, tell him that this picture of himself was wrong, but his natural and instinctive tendency was to think—or rather *feel*—himself in this perspective. It was, therefore, only natural, that when his attention was rudely and forcibly brought to a realization of his unusual height—as it was a hundred times a day now by people on the street—he should receive the news with a sense of shocked surprise, bewilderment, and finally with quick flaring anger and resentment.

He would be going along the street at five o'clock when the city was pouring homeward from its work, and suddenly he would become conscious that people were watching him: would see them stare at him and nudge each other, would see their surprised looks traveling curiously up his frame, would hear them whisper to each other in astonished voices, and see them pass him laughing, and hear their oaths and words of astonished disbelief, hilarious surprise. When this happened, he could have strangled them. As he heard their scoffs and jokes and exclamations—those dreary husks of a stale and lifeless humor which are the same the world over, which never change, and which have worn their weary rut into a tall man's heart and brain until he knows them as no one else can ever know them—he felt almost that he could *choke* them into wisdom, seize them, knock their heads together, snarl at them:

"God-damn you, but I'll show you that I am the same as you if I have to shake you into owning it!"

Thus he was the butt, a hundred times a day, of those clumsy, tiresome but well-intentioned jocularities to which, in the course of time, a tall man becomes so patiently accustomed, so wearily resigned. And his own response to them was probably the same as that of every other tall man that ever lived and had to weather the full measure of man's abysmal foolishness. At first, he felt only the fierce and quick resentment of youth, the truculent sensitivity of youth's wounded pride, its fear of ridicule, its swift readiness to take offense, to feel that it was being flouted, mocked, insulted, its desire to fight and to avenge its wounded honor.

And then he felt a kind of terrible shame and self-abasement: a feeling of personal inferiority that made him envy the lot of the average man, that made him bitterly regret the accident of birth and nature that had imprisoned a spirit fierce and proud and swift as flight and burning as a flame in such a grotesque tenement. And this feeling of shame and self-abasement and hatred of his flesh is the worst thing that a tall man knows, the greatest iniquity that his spirit suffers. For it is during this period that he comes to hate the body that has been given him by birth and nature, and by his act of hatred, he degrades himself and dishonors man. For this loathing for his body is like the ignoble hatred that a man may have for a loyal and ugly friend whose destiny is coherent with his own, and who must endure. And endure he does—this loyal ugly friend that is man's grotesque tenement— and goes with him everywhere in all his mad and furious marchings, and serves man faithfully like no other friend on earth, and suffers the insults and injuries that man heaps upon him, the frenzy, passion, and brute exhaustion, the scars, the sickness, and the pain, the surfeits of his master's intolerable hunger, and at the end, all battered, scarred, debased, befouled, and coarsened by his master's excess, is still with him, inseparable as his shadow, loyal to the end—a friend homely, true, devoted, good as no one else can ever be, who sticks with us through every trouble, stays by us through every brawl, bears the brunt of all our drinking, eating, and our brutal battery, reels in and out of every door with us, and falls with us down every flight of stairs, and whom we one day find again before us—as a madman may discover light and sanity again and see the comrade, the protector, and the victim of his madness steady there before him, grinning at him wryly through his puffed and battered lips, and saying with a rueful but an all-forgiving humor:

"Well—here we are again."

It is a strange adventure, a hard but precious education, that a tall man knows. For finally he comes to learn, through sweat and toil and a little aging, a stern but not desolate humanity. He gets a kind of lonely wisdom that no one else on earth can get. And by the strange and passionate enigma of his destiny, he is drawn close to man by the very circumstance that shuts him out. He enters life through the very door that once he thought was shut against him, is of the earth, more earthy, by the fact of his exclusion. A tall man could not escape from life, or flee the world, even if he desired it: he is at once life's exile and life's prisoner; wherever he goes, life reaches out and pulls him to it, will not let him go. And at the end, he learns the truth of Ernest Renan's bitter observation—that the only thing that can give one a conception of the infinite is the extent of human stupidity. And in the jibes, the jests, the drolleries that are shouted at him a dozen times a day in the streets because of his great height, in the questions that are asked concerning it, and in the innumerable conversations that it provokes, he acquires a huge and damning accumulation of evidence concerning man's fatal unity, the barren paucity of his invention, the desolate consonance of his rut.

It never changed, it was always the same: it went on day by day and month by month in the narrow crowded streets all around him, and it would go on year after year in a hundred cities, a dozen countries, among the thousand scattered places in all quarters of the world, and it would always be the same—a barren formula endlessly renewed with the unwearied pertinacity of an idiot monotony—it would always be the same.

He never found the slightest deviation in that barren formula. No one ever made an interesting or amusing observation about his height—and ten thousand people talked to him about it. No one ever said a funny or a witty thing about his height, and ten thousand people had their fling about it. No one ever showed the slightest understanding of the nature of a tall man's life, or asked a single shrewd and penetrating question about it—and yet the curiosity that his tallness caused was almost incredible, the conversations that he had, the questions that he had to answer, were innumerable.

The barren formula was so endlessly repeated that at length it had worn its dull grooves into his brain, and he answered without thinking, replied without listening, giving mechanically the answers that they wished to hear, the tried and trusted formula that had served its purpose so many thousand times before, knowing in advance what every one would say.

Was it wit? Then let the diligent historian of the nation's wit give ear and pay attention to these drolleries which were shouted after one tall man's receding figure as he trod the pavements of ten thousand streets:

"Hey-y!"

"Hey-y! Youse guy!"

"Hey-y-y! . . . Holy Jeez! . . . Cheezus! . . . Look ut duh guy!"

"Hey-y, Mis-teh! . . . Is it rainin' up deh? . . . Cheezus! . . . Ho-lee Chee! . . . Will yuh look at duh guy?"

"Hey-y—Mis-teh! . . . How's duh weatheh up deh? . . . Ho-lee Chee! . . . Take a look ut duh size of 'm, will yah?"

Such, then, were the evidences of the national humor upon this subject—by a high authority it can solemnly be affirmed that these evidences were all there were.

Or was it conversation of a more polite and genteel sort—well-bred consolation, soothing affirmations, suave flatteries meant to hearten and give cheer? The formula in this kind of conversation ran as follows:

"You're ver-ree tall, aren't you?"

"Yes—hah! hah!—yes—hah! hah!—I suppose I am—hah! hah!—I suppose you noticed it!"

"Yes, I did—when you got up, it did seem ra-ther overwhelming the first time—[with hasty correction]—only, of course, one doesn't notice it at *all* later . . . I *mean* one forgets all about it . . . I *ree-lee* think you'd be *awf-lee* glad you are that way . . . I *mean,* that's the way most people would like to be . . . it does give you such an advantage, doesn't it? . . . I *mean,* after *all,* everyone would be that way if they could—no one wants to be *short,* do they? . . . Every one would much rather be *tall* . . . I *mean,* it makes every one look *up* to you, doesn't it, wherever you go. . . . *Reelee,* I shouldn't think you'd *mind* at all . . . I should think you'd be glad you *are* that way . . . I *mean,* after *all,* it does give you a great advantage, *doesn't* it? . . . Do you see what I *mean?*"

"Yes . . . ah-hah-hah! . . . I certainly do! . . . ah-hah-hah! . . . Yes, I certainly do see what you mean . . . ah-hah-hah! You're right about it . . . ah-hah-hah! . . . I certainly do!"

Or was it friendly banter now, a kindly curiosity of a rougher sort, among a simple yet good-natured kind of men? Suppose a scene, then: such a scene as one has found ten thousand times within the labyrinth of night upon the seaboard of the continent. It is an airless groove in an old wall behind blind windows set in rotting birch: within, a slab of bar, its wet shine puddled here and there with rings of glasses; a battered rail of brass, not polished recently; and a radiance of hard dead light; Leo, the bar-man, with his jowled, squatty face of night, professionally attentive; and at the end, the dead stamped visages of night, the rasping snarl of drunken voices, the elbows of the bar-flies puddled in beer slop.

The buzzer rings, good Leo peers with hard mistrust through opened slot, the door is opened, and the tall man enters, to whom at once Pat Grogan, wit by nature, Celt by birth, and now the antic of good Leo's bar—approaches, with the small red eyes of rheum and murder comically a-stare, ape-shoulders stooped, ape-knees bowed and tucked under, the jowled ape-visage comically turned upward in a stare of ape-like stupefaction—all most comical to see—while good Leo looks and chuckles heavily and all the bar-flies grin. So, now, as follows:

Grogan (still crowding): "*Je-sus* . . . *Christ!* . . . *Ho-lee* Jeez! . . . What's dat guy *standin'* on, anyway? . . . (Leo and all the grinning bar-flies chortle with appreciative delight, and thus encouraged, Jolly Grogan carries on) . . . Jee-zus! (with a slow deliberate lifting of his red-jowled face, he calculates the visitor from foot to head—a delicate stroke, not lost by any means on grinning Leo and his appreciative clientele) . . . Say-y! . . . When I foist saw dat guy, I t'ought he was standin' on a box or somep'n . . . (turning to Leo with an air of fine bewilderment). . . . Take a lookut 'im, will yuh? *Ho-lee* Chee! . . . Who *is* dis guy, anyway? . . . (turning to all the grinning others) . . . When I foist sees duh guy, I says t' myself . . . What *is* dis, anyway? . . . Is duh *coicus* in town or somep'n? (turns again, gesturing to tall visitor with air of frank bewilderment) . . . Take a look at 'm, will yuh? . . . (Satisfied with his success, he rejoins his grinning and appreciative comrades, and for some time further regales them by taking astounded glances at the tall visitor, shaking his head in a bewildered way, and saying in an unbelieving tone) . . . But *Je-sus!* . . . Take a look at 'm, will yuh?" etc.

And now Leo, shaking his head slowly to himself with appreciative admiration of his client's wit, approaches the tall visitor, and still chuckling heartily at the recollection, leans over the bar and whispers confidingly:

"Dat's Misteh Grogan. . . . (a trifle apologetically) He's been drinkin' a little, so don't pay attention to anyt'ing he says. . . . He didn't mean nuttin' by it—(with ponderous assurance) Nah-h! . . . He's one of duh nicest guys you eveh saw when he's not drinkin' . . . he's only kiddin', anyway . . . he don't mean nuttin' by it . . . but *Je-sus!* (suddenly laughs heartily at the recollection, a heavy, swarthy, and deliberate hah-hah-hah that sets all his night-time jowls a-quiver) . . . When he pulled dat one aboutcha standin' on a box or somep'n, I had t' laff . . . duh way he said it! . . . Standin' on a box or somep'n—dat's a good one! . . . Hah! Hah! Hah! Hah! Hah!" . . . (and goes heavily away, heaving with slow nocturnal laughter, shaking his head slowly to himself).

Now, as the visitor stands drinking by himself, the bar-flies cluster at the other end in excited controversy, from which disputatious murmurs may be heard from time to time—such vehement scraps of affirmation or denial as the following:

"Nah-h! . . . Guh *wan!* . . . Whatcha givin' me? . . . He's more'n dat . . . I'll betcha on it! . . . Nah-h! Guh *wan!* . . He's oveh *seven* if he's an inch! . . . Guh *wan!* . . . I'll betcha on it! . . . *All* right! All right! . . . Guh-wan and *ast* him den! . . . But he's more'n dat! I'll betcha on it!" . . .

One of the debaters now detaches himself from his disputatious group and, beer glass in hand, approaches the lone visitor. . . . A face not bad, not vicious, not unfriendly: face of a city-man in the late forties—the face of the cartoonist-drawing—lean, furrowed, large-nosed, deeply seamed, a little sunken around the mouth, almost metallically stamped and wisely knowing, cynically assured—the nerve-ends stunned, the language strident, utterly, unmistakably, the city's child.

The City's Child (grinning amiably, a trifle apologetically, lowering his voice, and speaking with a natural tensity of his lips, out of the corners of his mouth): . . . "Podden me, Mac . . . I hope yuh don't mind my astin' yuh a question . . . but my frien's and me has been havin' a little oggument aboutcha . . . an' I gotta little question dat I'd like t' ast yuh. . . . Yuh don't mind, do yuh?"

The Tall Stranger (grinning mechanically and laughing an agreeable and complaisant laugh of utter falseness): "Why, no! . . . ah-hah-hah! . . . Not at all! . . . ah-hah-hah! . . . Go right ahead, it's perfectly all right. . . . Ah-hah-hah."

The City's Child: "Because if yuh do, I wantcha t' say so . . . I guess a lotta guys ast yuh the same question, an' I t'ought mebbe yuh might get tired of hearin' it—you know what I mean? . . . A lotta guys might get tired of bein' ast duh same question so many times . . . (with an expression of difficulty on his face, shrugs his shoulders expressively and says hopefully) *You* know?

The Tall Stranger: "Why . . . ah-hah-hah! . . . Yes . . . I think I do. . . . That is to say, go right ahead . . . ah-hah-hah . . . it's quite all right."

The City's Child: "I guess so many guys have ast yuh dis same question dat yuh can guess already what it is—can't yuh?"

The Tall Stranger: "Why, yes—no—ah-hah-hah! . . . That is to say—*Yes!* . . . I think I can!"

The City's Child: Well, den, Mac . . . if yuh *don't* mind . . . if it's all right . . . I was just goin' t' ast yuh . . . (whispering persuasively) . . . just to settle a little oggument I been havin' wit' my *frien's—How tall are yuh?* (lustily) . . . Now if yuh don't want t' tell me, it's O.K. . . . Yuh know how it is, *some* guys . . ."

The Tall Stranger: "Not at all—ah-hah-hah . . . that is to say, *yes*—ah-hah-hah . . . it's quite all right . . . I don't mind at all. . . . I'm between six feet five and six feet six . . . that is, I haven't measured for some time . . . but I was between six feet five and six feet six the last time that I measured. . . . (apologetically) That's been some time ago . . . several years ago since I last measured . . . but . . . ah-hah-hah . . . it was between six feet five and six feet six and I don't think I've grown much since then . . . ah-hah-hah. . . . Between six feet five and six feet six."

The City's Child (with an astonished but somewhat disappointed air): "Is *dat* a fact? . . . I t'ought yuh was more'n dat! . . . I t'ought you was aroun' seven foot . . . but anotheh guy oveh heah said you wasn't more'n six foot seven or eight (reflectively). . . . I t'ought you was more'n dat!"

The Tall Stranger: "No . . . ah-hah-hah . . . a lot of people think so . . . but I guess that's right . . . about six feet five or six."

The City's Child (jocularly): "Say! . . . Yuh know watta a guy like *you* ought to do! . . . You know what I'd do if I was big as you—"

The Tall Stranger: "Why, no . . . ah-hah-hah—What's that?"

The City's Child: "I'd go in duh ring an' fight Dempsey . . . I'd fight *all* dose guys. . . . Dat's what I'd do . . . . A guy as big as you could hit an awful wallop . . . an' wit your reach dey couldn't touch yuh. . . . Dat's what

I'd do if I had yoeh size! I'd go in duh ring—yes, sir!—Dat's just duh t'ing I'd do if I was big as *you*."

The Tall Stranger (rising glibly and mechanically to the occasion): "Well, you'd better be glad you're not. . . . You don't know how lucky you are."

The City's Child (in a slow, interested voice): "Oh, yeah?"

The Tall Stranger (getting off his little speech rapidly and glibly): "Sure. A guy like me has nothing but trouble everywhere he turns."

The City's Child (with awakened interest): "Oh, yeah?"

The Tall Stranger: "Sure. They don't make anything big enough to fit you."

The City's Child (with an air of slow, surprised revelation): "Say! I guess dat's right, at dat!"

The Tall Stranger: "Sure it is! You can't get a bed long enough to sleep in—"

The City's Child (curiously): "I guess yuh got to sleep all doubled up, heh?"

The Tall Stranger: "Sure I have. Like this, see?" (Here he makes a zigzag movement with his hand, and the City's Child laughs hoarsely.)

The City's Child: "Wat d'yuh do about clo'es? Guess yuh gotta have everyt'ing made to ordeh, huh?"

The Tall Stranger: "Sure." (And according to the formula, now he tells his fascinated listener that the one he sleeps on is a foot too short for him, that he cannot stretch out in a berth or steamer bunk, that he cracks his head against the rafters as he descends a steep flight of stairs, that he cannot find room for his knees in theaters or buses—and all the rest of it. When he has finished, the City's Child strokes his head with a movement of slow and almost disbelieving revelation, and then saying slowly, "Well, what d'yuh t'ink of dat," he returns to impart the fascinating information he has gathered to the waiting group of his expectant and interested friends.)

So, in ten thousand streets and towns and places of the earth, ran the undeviating formula:—a formula that never changed, that was the same forever—and that showed the tall and lonely man the barren unity of life, and that finally, curiously, in a poignant and inexplicable fashion, gave him faith in man, a belief in man's fundamental goodness, kindliness, and humanity, as nothing else on earth could do.

In the Park

When the show was over, we went out into the street and turned up Broadway. We were both so happy and excited that we fairly bounded along, and that was the way it was that night. It was one of the first fine days in spring, the air was cool and delicate and yet soft, and the sky was of a velvety lilac texture, and it was glittering with great stars. The streets outside the theater were swarming with hansoms, four wheelers, private carriages, and victorias; they kept driving up in front of the theater all the time, and people kept getting into them.

All of the men looked handsome, and all of the women were beautiful: everyone seemed to be as exultant and happy as we were, it seemed as if a new world and new people had burst out of the earth with the coming of spring—everything ugly, dull, sour, and harsh had vanished—the streets were flashing with life and sparkle. I saw all of it, I felt myself a part of it all, I wanted to possess it all, and there was something I wanted to say so much it made my throat ache, and yet I could not say it because I could not find the words I wanted. I could not think of anything else to say—it sounded foolish, but suddenly I seized my father's arm and cried: "Oh, to be in April now that England's there."

"Yes!" he shouted, "Also in Paris, Naples, Rome, and Dresden! Oh, to be in Budapest!" cried Daddy, "now that April's here and the frost is on the pumpkin, and the dawn comes up like thunder out of the night that covers me."

He seemed to have grown young again; he was the way he used to be when I was a little girl and I would knock at his study door and he would call out in a wonderful actor's voice, "Enter, Daughter of Des-o-la-tion into this abode of mis-er-ee."

His eyes sparkled, and he threw back his head and laughed his wild and happy laugh.

That year I think we were living with Bella; no, we weren't, I guess we were living with Auntie Kate—well, maybe we were staying with Bella: I don't know, we moved around so much, and it's so long ago. It gets all confused in my mind now; when Daddy was acting, he was always on the go, he couldn't be still a minute; sometimes he was playing in New York, and sometimes he went off on a tour with Mr. Mansfield and was gone for months.

I think it must have been the year before he died; I was about eighteen: I was a beauty—I was like peaches and cream—

In those days when he was acting, I used to meet him after the theater, and we would go somewhere to eat. There was a fellow after your heart: the very best was *just* about good enough for him. New York was awfully nice in those days. They had such nice places to go to—I don't know, they didn't have all this noise and confusion; it seems like another world sometimes. You could go to White's or Martin's or Delmonico's—there were a lot of nice places. There was also a place called Mock's; I never went there, but one of the first things I remember as a child was hearing Daddy come home late at night and say he'd been to Mock's. When he came home, I would listen at the grating of the heater in my room, and I could hear him and the other actors talking to my mother: it was fascinating; and sometimes it was all about Mock's. "Oh, you have been to Mock's?" I thought I heard my mother say. "Oh, yes! I have been to Mock's," my father said. "And what did you have at Mock's?" my mother said. "Oh, I had some oysters and a glass of beer and some mock-turtle soup at Mock's," my father said.

We used to go to White's almost every night after the show with two priests who were friends of Daddy's: Father Dolan and Father Chris O'Rourke. Father Dolan was a big man with the bluest eyes I ever saw, and Father Chris O'Rourke was a little man with a swarthy and greasy face: it was all full of black marks, it was one of the strangest faces I ever saw; but there was something very powerful and sweet about it. Father Dolan was a very fine, high sort of man: he was very kind and jolly, but he also had a fine mind, and he was very outspoken and honest. He loved the theater, he knew a great many actors, a great many of them went to his church, and he loved my father. He was a great scholar; he knew the plays of Shakespeare almost by heart—he and Daddy used to tag each other's lines, to see who knew the most. I never knew Daddy to catch him up but once, and that was on a line from "King Lear," "The prince of darkness is a gentleman"—Father Dolan said it came from "As You Like It."

How those fellows loved to eat and drink: if one of them had to say Mass the next day we had to hurry because you can't eat or drink after midnight if you are saying Mass the next day. Because of this, both priests would take out their watches and lay them on the table before them when they sat down. Father Chris O'Rourke drank nothing but beer, and as soon as he sat down, a waiter would bring him a half-dozen glasses which he would drink at once. But if these two priests had a glass of beer on the table before them when midnight came, they left it: no matter what it was, no matter whether they'd finished eating or drinking or not, when the stroke of midnight came, these fellows quit if they were going to say Mass the morning after.

Father Chris O'Rourke would eat and drink for almost an hour as if his life depended on it: he was very near-sighted, he wore thick glasses, and from time to time he would seize his watch and bring it right under his nose while he peered and squinted at it. Because of his own hurry to get through before twelve o'clock, he thought everyone else must be the same way: he was afraid someone would not get fed, and he was always urging and belaboring people to hurry up and eat. Father Dolan loved to eat, too, but he was a great talker: sometimes he would get to talking to Daddy and forget to eat: when he did this, Father Chris O'Rourke would almost go out of his head, he would keep nudging and poking at Father Dolan and pointing at his watch with a look of agony on his face, leaning over and muttering at him in an ominous sort of way. "You're going to be *late!* It is almost *twelve!*"

"Bedad, then!" said Father Dolan, "I'll be late!" He was a big man, but he had a funny little Irish voice: it was very crisp and jolly and had a little chuckling lilt in it, and it seemed to come from a long way off. "I never saw a man like ye, Chris, to be always thinkin' of his belly! Did the great Saints of the Church spend their time guzzlin' and crammin', or did they spend it in meditation and prayin' and mortifyin' their flesh? Did ye never hear of the sin of gluttony?"

"Yis," said Father Chris O'Rourke, "that I have, and I also heard of the wicked sin of wanton waste. Shame on ye, Dan Dolan, wit your talk about the great Saints of the Church: there was niver a great Saint yit that would praise a man fer wastin' what the Lord had set before him. Do you think I'll sit here an' see good food go to waste whin there's poor people all over the world tonight that's goin' witout?"

"Well," said Father Dolan, "I've read most of the argyments of the learned reasoners of the Church as well as the damnable heresies of the infidels, all the way from St. Thomas Aquinas to Spinozey, an' in me younger days I could split a hair meself wit the best of them, but in all me life I never heard the beat of that one: it makes Aristotle look like Wordsworth's Idiot Boy. Bedad, if ye can prove that what ye're doin' wit yer gorgin' is feedin' the poor all over the earth, I won't put anything past your powers of reasonin'—Chris—ye could show the Pope that Darwin was a Jesuit, and he'd believe ye!"

Well, as I say, when we got to the restaurant, the first thing Father Chris O'Rourke would do was to lay his watch upon the table, and the first thing Daddy would do was to order two or three bottles of champagne: they used to know we were coming, and it would be waiting for us in great silver buckets full of ice. Then Daddy would pick up the menu—it was a great big card, simply covered with the most delicious things to eat, and he would frown and look serious and clear his throat and say to Father Dolan, "What does the pontifical palate crave, Dan?"

After the play that night we went to White's, and these two priests were waiting for us when we got there. A little later Mr. Gates came in—he's still alive. I saw him on the street the other day, he's getting quite old. He was married to one of the most beautiful women you ever saw, and she was burned to death in an automobile accident. He saw the thing happen right under his eyes: isn't it the most horrible thing you ever heard of? Well, you could tell by the way Mr. Gates walked that he was awfully excited about something: he was another of these great fat fellows, and you could see his old jowls quivering as he came.

"Good God!" said Daddy, "here comes Bunny with a full head of steam on!" Mr. Gates began to speak to Daddy half across the room; all of the people stopped and stared at him.

"Joe! Joe!" he said—he had a funny hoarse kind of voice, one of those foggy whiskey voices. I think he drank a good deal. "Joe, do you know what I've done? I've just bought a horseless carriage. Come on! You're going for a ride with me!"

"Now, wait! Wait! Wait!" said Daddy, holding up his hand just like an actor. "Not so fast, Bunny! Sit down and have a bite to eat first, and tell us about it. When did you do this desperate deed?"

"Today," Mr. Gates said in a sort of hoarse whisper. "Do you suppose I've done right?"

He looked around at us with his old eyes simply bulging out of his head and with a sort of scared look on his face. Oh! We laughed so much about it: Father Dolan began to laugh, and Daddy had to pound him on his back, he got to coughing so!

Mr. Gates was an awfully nice man: he was a great big fat fellow, but he was so handsome: there was something so delicate about him; his mouth kept trembling and twitching so when he was excited and wanted to say something. I think that was why they called him Bunny.

So Daddy said, "Sit down and have something to eat and then we'll see."

Mr. Gates said, "Say, Joe. I've got the mechanic outside here, and I don't know what to do with him."

"You mean you've hired him for keeps?" Daddy said.

"Yes," Mr. Gates said, "and I'm damned if I'm not embarrassed! I don't know what to do with him. I mean, what is his social standing?"

"Does he wash?" Daddy said.

"Well," said Mr. Gates, looking at Father Dolan, "I think he uses holy water."

"Oh, Mr. Gates," I said. "How awful! Right before Father Dolan, too!"

But Father Dolan laughed just as I knew he would; he was a great fat fellow, he was an awfully nice man. Father Chris O'Rourke laughed, too, but I don't think he liked it so much.

"I mean," Mr. Gates said, "I don't know how to treat the man. Is he above me, or below me, or what?"

"It looks to me," Daddy said, "as if he were on top of you. I think you've gone and got yourself saddled with a black elephant."

Daddy was so wonderful like that, everybody loved him. Mr. Gates was so worried about the driver: it all seems so funny now to think back on it—he didn't know whether the man was to eat at the table with his family and be treated like one of them or what. There was something so delicate about Mr. Gates: he was big and fat, but a very sensitive, fine person.

"It looks like a neat little problem in social etiquette, Bunny," Daddy said. "Well, let's have him in here for a bite to eat. We'll see what he looks like."

So Mr. Gates went out and got him, and pretty soon he came back with him, and he was really an awfully nice young fellow: he had a little mustache, and he wore a Norfolk jacket and a flat cap, and everybody stared so, and nudged each other, he was awfully embarrassed. But Daddy was wonderful with people, he made him feel right at home. He said, "Sit down, young fellow. If we're going to run an engine, we've got to feed the driver."

So he sat down, and we had a marvelous meal: you'd get great juicy chops cooked in butter, and steaks an inch thick, and the most marvelous oysters and sea food.

I know it was pretty late in the season, but we started off with oysters and champagne: I don't think the young fellow was used to drinking. Daddy kept filling up his glass, and he got quite drunk. He was awfully funny, he kept talking about his responsibility.

"It's a terrible responsibility to know that all these lives are dependent on you," he said; then Daddy would fill up his glass again. "A moment's hesitation in a crisis," he said, "and all is lost."

"A truer word was never spoken," said Daddy, and he filled his glass up again.

"A man must have a clear brain and a steady hand," he said.

"Right your are," said Daddy. "This will make you so steady, son, that you will get practically paralyzed."

Mr. Gates and Father Dolan laughed so much that the tears began to trickle down their cheeks. Oh, we had an awfully good time in those days; there was something so innocent about everything.

Then we all got up to go, and I was really quite nervous: the poor kid could hardly stand up, and I didn't know what was going to happen. Daddy was so happy and excited, there was something so wild about him, his eyes danced like devils, and he threw back his head and laughed, and you could hear him all over the place.

Father Chris O'Rourke had to hold Mass the next morning, and he left us, but Father Dolan came along. We all went outside, with the young man being helped along by Daddy and Mr. Gates, and everyone in the restaurant followed us outside, and Mr. Gates told me to sit up front beside the driver. God! I was proud! And Daddy and Mr. Gates and Father Dolan got in behind; how they ever did it I don't know; it must have been awfully small—I think Daddy must have sat on Father Dolan's lap. Oh, yes! I know he did.

And everybody cheered as we started off: the actors followed us out of the restaurant and stood looking after us as we drove off into the lilac and velvet darkness, and I can still remember how I looked back and saw their smiling and unnatural faces, their bright masks, their lonely and haunted eyes. They kept shouting funny things at Daddy and asking if he had any last messages, and De Wolfe Hopper was there, and he ran around pretending to be a horse and neighing, and trying to climb up a lamp-post. Oh, it was thrilling!

So Mr. Gates said, "Whither away, Joe?"

And Daddy said, "To the Golden Gate and may she never stop!"

Then Daddy said to the young fellow who was driving, "How fast can she go, son?" and the young fellow said, "She can do twenty miles an hour without any trouble."

"Downhill, you mean," said Daddy just to tease him, so we started to go, and God! I was thrilled! It seemed to me we were flying. I suppose he did go twenty miles an hour, but it seemed like a hundred would now, and we passed a policeman on a horse, and the horse got frightened and tried to run away, and God! the cop was so mad: he came galloping after us and shouted for us to stop, and Daddy laughed just like a crazy man and said, "Go on, son! Go on! There's not a horse in the world that can catch you!"

But the young fellow was scared, and he slowed down, and then the cop came up and said what did we mean, and where did we think we were, and he'd a good mind to put us all under arrest for disturbing the peace at that hour of the night with "that thing"; he kept calling it "that thing" in such a scornful way, and I got so angry at him; I thought it was beautiful, it was painted the richest kind of winey red, it looked grand enough to eat, and I was so mad to think the man should talk that way.

I don't know why it made me mad, but I think the reason must have been that the car didn't seem to me like a thing at all. It's hard to tell you how it was, but it was almost as if the car was some strange and beautiful and living creature which we had never known before but which now gave to all our lives a kind of added joy and warmth and wonder. And I believe that was the way it was with those first motor cars we ever saw. Somehow each one of them seemed different from all the others, each one seemed to have a different name, a separate life and personality; and although now I know they would look crude and funny and old-fashioned, it was all different then. We had never seen or known them in the world before, we had only dreamed or heard they could exist, and now that I was riding in one, it all seemed unbelievable and yet gloriously real and strange, as every beautiful thing is when it first happens to you. The car was as magical to me as if it had come out of some other world like Mars, and yet the very moment that I saw it, I seemed to have known about it always, and it seemed to belong to that day, that hour, that year, somehow to be a part of all that happened that night; to belong to Daddy and the priests and Mr. Gates, the young mechanic, and all the haunted faces of the actors, and to all the songs we sang that year, the things we did and said, and something strange and innocent and lost long ago.

I can remember how that old car looked so well that I could close my eyes and draw it for you. I can remember its rich wine color, its great polished lamps of brass, the door that opened in its round, fat back, and all its wonderful and exciting smells—the strong and comforting smell of its deep leather, and the smells of gasoline and oil and grease that were so strong and warm and pungent that they seemed to give a kind of thrilling life and ecstasy to everything in the whole world. They seemed to hold the unknown promise of something wonderful and strange that was about to happen and that belonged to the night, and to the mystery and joy of life, the ecstasy of the lilac dark, as all the smells of flowers and leaf and grass and earth belonged to them.

So I guess that was the reason that I got so mad when I heard the policeman call the car "that thing," although I did not know the reason then. It looked as if the cop was going to run us in, but then Daddy got up out of Father Dolan's lap, and when the cop saw Father Dolan, of course he got very nice to us: and Mr. Gates talked to him and gave him some money, and Daddy joked with him and made him laugh, and then Daddy showed him his police badge, and asked him if he knew Big Jake Dietz at police headquarters, and told him he was one of Jake's best friends, and then I was so proud to see the way the cop came round.

And the cop said for us all to go into Central Park and we could ride all we damned pleased for all he cared, but you wouldn't catch him in one of those things; they'd blow up on you at any moment and then where'd you all be? And Daddy said he hoped we'd all be in Heaven, and what's more, we'd take our own priest with us, so there'd be no hitch in any of the formalities, and we all got so tickled and began to laugh, and the cop did, too, and then he began to brag about his horse, and God! it *was* a beautiful horse, and he said give him a horse always, that they'd never make one of those things that could go faster than a horse. The poor fellow! I wonder what he'd say now!

And Daddy teased him and said the time would come when you'd have to go to the zoo to see a horse, and the policeman said by that time you'd have to go to a junk-shop to see a motor car, and Daddy said, "The trouble with us is that we're anachronisms." And the policeman said well, he didn't know about that, but he wished us luck and hoped we all got out of it alive.

So we rode off, and we drove into Central Park and started off as hard as we could go and began to climb a hill, when sure enough, we broke down just as the policeman said we would. I never knew just what did happen. I guess the young fellow may have had too much to drink, he seemed wild and excited, but anyway we saw a hansom halfway up the hill in front of us, and he cried out, "Watch me pass them," and did something to the car, and just as we got even with them and were trying to go by, the car coughed and spluttered and stood still. Well, we could hear the people in the hansom laughing, and one of them shouted something back to us about the tortoise and the hare. And I felt so mad at them and so humiliated and so sorry for our driver, and Daddy said, "Never mind, son, the race may not be always to the swift, but even the hare will sometimes have his day."

But our young fellow felt so bad he couldn't say a word. He got out of the car and walked round and round it, and finally he began to explain to us the way it happened and how it could never happen again in a hundred years. And well, you see it was this way, and well, you see it was that. And we didn't understand a word of what he was saying, but we felt so sorry for him that we told him he was right. So he began to poke around inside of it, and then he would turn something here and twist something there, and grab the crank and whirl it round and round until I was afraid he was going to wring his arm off. Then he would get down on his back and crawl in under it and bang and hammer at something underneath. And nothing happened. Then he would get up and walk round and round the car again and mutter to himself. Finally, he gave up and said he was afraid we'd have to get out of the car and take a hansom if we wanted to get home without walking. So we started to get out, and the mechanic was so mad and so embarrassed at the way his car had acted that he grabbed it and shook it as if it were a brat. And nothing happened.

He gave it one last try. He grabbed the crank like a crazy man and began to whirl it round and round until he was exhausted. And when nothing happened, he suddenly shouted out, "Oh, damn that thing," kicked it in the tire as hard as he could, and collapsed across the radiator, sobbing as if his heart would break. And I don't know what that did to it or how it happened, but suddenly the car began to chug and wheeze again, and there we were ready to go, and the young fellow with a grin that stretched from ear to ear.

So we went up that hill and coasted down the next, and now we really seemed to fly. It was like soaring through the air, or finding wings you never knew you had before. It was like something we had always known about and dreamed of finding, and now we had it like a dream come true. And I suppose we must have gone the whole way round the park from one end to another, but none of us really knew how far we went or where we were going. It was like that kind of flight you make in dreams, and sure enough, just like something you are waiting for in a dream, we came tearing round a curve in the road, and there before us we could see the same hansom we had tried to pass upon the hill. And the minute that I saw it, I knew that it was bound to happen; it seemed too good to be true, and yet I had felt sure all the time that it was going to turn out this way. And that was the way it was with all of us; we threw back our heads and roared with laughter, we yelled and waved our hands at all the people in the cab, we went tearing by them as if they were rooted to the earth, and as we passed them, Daddy turned and shouted back at them, "Cheer up, my friends, they also serve who only stand and wait."

So we passed them by and left them far behind us, and they were lost; and now there was nothing all around us but the night, the blazing stars, the lilac darkness in the park, and God! but it was beautiful. It was just the beginning of May, and all the leaves and buds were coming out; they had that tender feathery look, and there was just a little delicate shaving of moon in the sky, and it was so cool and lovely, with the smell of the leaves, and the new grass, and all the flowers bursting from the earth till you could hear them grow: it seemed to me the loveliest thing I had ever known, and when I looked at my father, his eyes were full of tears, and he cried out, "Glory! Oh, glory! Glory!" and then he began in his magnificent voice, "What a piece of work is a man! How noble in reason! How infinite in faculty! In form and moving how express and admirable! in action how like an angel! in apprehension how like a god!"

And the words were so lovely, the music was so grand, that somehow it made me want to cry, and when he had finished, he cried out, "Glory!" once again, and I saw his wild and beautiful brow there in the darkness, and I turned my eyes up toward the sky and there were the tragic and magnificent stars, and a kind of fate was on his head and in his eyes, and suddenly as I looked at him I knew that he was going to die.

And he cried "Glory! Glory!" and we rode all through the night, and round and round the park, and then dawn came, and all the birds began to sing. Now broke the birdsong in first light, and suddenly I heard each sound the birdsong made: like a flight of shot, the sharp fast skaps of sound arose. With chitterling bicker, fast-fluttering skirrs of sound, the palmy, honeyed birdcries came. Smooth drops and nuggets of bright gold they were. Now sang the birdtree filled with lutings in bright air: the thrum, the lark's wing, and tongue-trilling chirrs arose now. The little brainless cries arose and fell with liquorous liquefied lutings, with lirruping chirp, plumbellied smooth-ness, sweet lucidity. And now there were the rapid kweet kweet kweet kweet of homely birds, and then their pwee-pwee-pwee: others with thin metallic tongues, a sharp cricketing stitch, a mosquito buzz, while some with rusty creakings, high shrew's caws, with eerie rasp, with harsh far calls—all birds that are awoke in the park's woodland tangles; and above them passed the whirr of hidden wings, the strange lost cry of the unknown birds; in full light now in the park, the sweet confusion of their cries was mingled.

"Sweet is the breath of morn, her rising sweet with charm of earliest birds," and it was just like that, and the sun came up, and it was like the first day of the world, and that was the year before he died, and I think we were staying at Bella's then, but maybe we were staying at the old hotel, or perhaps we had already moved to Auntie Kate's: we moved around so much, we lived so many places, it seems so long ago that when I try to think of it now it gets confused, and I cannot remember.

Only the Dead Know Brooklyn

Now is the winter of our discontent made glorious by dis mont' of May, and all the long-drowned desolation of our souls in the green fire and radiance of the Springtime buried.

We are the dead—ah! We were drowned so long ago—and now we thrust our feelers in distressful ooze upon the sea-floors of the buried world. We are the drowned—blind crawls and eyeless gropes and mindless sucks that swirl and scuttle in the jungle depths, immense and humid skies bend desolately upon us, and our flesh is gray.

We are lost, the eyeless atoms of the jungle depth, we grope and crawl and scuttle with blind feelers, and we have no way but this.

Dere's no guy livin' dat knows Brooklyn t'roo an' t'roo (only the dead know Brooklyn t'roo and t'roo), because it'd take a lifetime just to find his way aroun' duh goddam town (—only the dead know Brooklyn t'roo and t'roo, even the dead will quarrel an' bicker over the sprawl and web of jungle desolation that is Brooklyn t'roo an' t'roo).

So like I say, I'm waitin' for my train t' come when I sees dis big guy standin' deh—dis is duh foist I eveh see of him. Well, he's lookin' wild, y'know, an' I can see dat he's had plenty, but still he's holdin' it; he talks good, an' he's walkin' straight enough. So den dis big guy steps up to a little guy dat's standin' deh, an' says, "How d'yuh get t' Eighteent' Avenoo an' Sixty-seven' Street?" he says.

"Jesus! Yuh got me, chief," duh little guy says to him. "I ain't been heah long myself. Where is duh place?" he says. "Out in duh Flatbush section somewhere?"

"Nah," duh big guy says. "It's out in Bensonhoist. But I was neveh deh befoeh. How d'yuh get deh?"

"Jesus," duh little guy says, scratchin' his head, y'know—yuh could see duh little guy didn't know his way about—"yuh got me, chief. I neveh hoid of it. Do any of youse guys know where it is?" he says to me.

"Sure," I says. "It's out in Bensonhoist. Yuh take duh Fourt' Avenoo express, get off at Fifty-nint' Street, change to a Sea Beach local deh, get off at Eighteent' Avenoo an' Sixty-toid, and den walk down foeh blocks. Dat's all yuh got to do," I says.

"G'wan!" some wise guy dat I neveh seen befoeh pipes up. "Watcha talkin' about?" he says—oh, he was wise, y'knowa "Duh guy is crazy! I'll tell yuh wht yuh do," he says to duh big guy. "Yuh change to duh West End line at Toity-sixt'," he tells him. "Get off at Noo Utrecht an' Sixteent' Avenoo," he says. "Walk two blocks oveh, foeh blocks up," he says, "an' you'll be right deh." Oh, a *wise* guy, y'know.

"Oh, yeah?" I says. "Who told *you* so much?" He got me sore because he was so wise about it. "How long you been livin' heah?" I says.

"All my life," he says. "I was bawn in Williamsboig," he says. "An' I can tell you t'ings about dis town you neveh hoid of," he says.

"Yeah?" I says.

"Yeah," he says.

"Well, den, yuh can tell me t'ings about dis town dat nobody else has eveh hoid of, either. Maybe yuh make it all up yoehself at night," I says, "befoeh yuh go to sleep—like cuttin' out papeh dolls, or somep'n."

"Oh, yeah?" he says. "You're pretty wise, ain't yuh?"

"Oh, I don't know," I says. "Duh boids ain't usin' my head for Lincoln's statue yet," I says. "But I'm wise enough to know a phony when I see one."

"Yeah?" he says. "A wise guy, huh? Well, you're so wise dat someone's goin' t'bust yuh one right on duh snoot some day," he says. "Dat's how wise *you* are."

Well, my train was comin', or I'da smacked him den an' dere, but when I seen duh train was comin' all I said was, "All right, mugg! I'm sorry I can't stay to take keh of yuh, but I'll be seein' yuh sometime, I hope, out in duh cemetery." So den I says to duh big guy, who'd been standin' deh all duh time, "You come wit me," I says. So when we gets onto duh train, I says to him, "Where yuh goin' out in Bensonhoist?" I says. "What numbeh are yuh looking for?" I says. *You* know—I t'ought if he told me duh address I might be able to help him out.

"Oh," he says, "I'm not lookin' for no one. I don't know no one out deh."

"Then watcha goin' out deh for?" I says.

"Oh," duh guy says, "I'm just goin' out to see duh place," he says. "I like duh sound of duh name"—Bensonhoist, y'know—"so I t'ought I'd go out an' have a look at it."

"Watcha tryin' t' hand me?" I says. "Watcha tryin' to do, kid me?" *You* know, I t'ought duh guy was bein' wise wit me.

"No," he says, "I'm tellin yuh duh troot. I like to go out an' take a look at places wit nice names like dat. I like to go out an' look at all kinds of places," he says.

"How'd yuh know deh was such a place," I says, "if yuh neveh been deh befoeh?"

"Oh," he says, "I got a map."

"A *map*?" I says.

"Sure," he says, "I got a map dat tells me about all dese places. I take it wit me every time I come out heah," he says.

And Jesus! Wit dat, he pulls it out of his pocket, an' so help me, but he's *got* it—he's tellin' duh troot—a big map of duh whole goddam place wit all duh different pahts. Mahked out, y'know—Canarsie an' East Noo Yawk and Flatbush, Bensonhoist, Sout' Brooklyn, duh Heights, Bay Ridge, Greenpernt—duh whole goddam layout, he's got it right deh on duh map.

"You been to any of dose places?" I says.

"Sure," he says, "I been to most of 'em. I was down in Red Hook just last night," he says.

"Jesus! Red Hook!" I says. "Whatcha do down deh?"

"Oh," he says, "nuttin' much. I just walked aroun'. I went into a coupla places an' had a drink," he says, "but most of the time I just walked aroun'."

"Just walked aroun'?" I says.

"Sure," he says, "just lookin' at t'ings, y'know."

"Where'd yuh go?" I asts him.

"Oh," he says, "I don't know duh name of duh place, but I could find it on my map," he says. "One time I was walkin' across some big fields where deh ain't no houses," he says, "but I could see ships oveh deh all lighted up. Dey was loadin'. So I walks across duh fields," he says, "to where duh ships are."

"Sure," I says, "I know where yuh was. Yuh was down to duh Erie Basin."

"Yeah," he says, "I guess dat was it. Dey had some of dose big elevators an' cranes, and dey was loadin' ships, an' I could see some ships in drydock all lighted up, so I walks across duh fields to where dey are," he says.

"Den what did yuh do?" I says.

"Oh," he says, "nuttin' much. I came on back across duh fields after a while an' went into a coupla places an' had a drink."

"Didn't nuttin' happen while yuh was in dere?" I says.

"No," he says. "Nuttin' much. A coupla guys was drunk in one of duh places an' started a fight, an' dey bounced 'em out," he says, "an' den one of duh guys stahted to come back again, but duh bartender gets his baseball bat out from under duh counteh, so duh guy goes on."

"Jesus!" I said. "Red Hook!"

"Sure," he says. "Dat's where it was, all right."

"Well, you keep outa deh," I says. "You stay away from deh."

"Why?" he says. "What's wrong wit it?"

"Oh," I says, "it's a good place to stay away from, dat's all. It's a good place to keep out of."

"Why?" he says. "Why is it?"

Jesus! Whatcha gonna do wit a guy as dumb as dat? I saw it wasn't no use to try to tell him nuttin', he wouldn't know what I was talkin' about, so I just says to him, "Oh, nuttin'. Yuh might get lost down deh, dat's all."

"Lost?" he says. "No, I wouldn't get lost. I got a map," he says.

A map! Red Hook! Jesus!

So den duh guy begins to ast me all kinds of nutty questions: how big was Brooklyn an' could I find my way aroun' in it, how long would it take a guy to know duh place.

"Listen!" I says. "You get dat idea outa youeh head right now," I says. "You ain't eveh gonna get to know Brooklyn," I says. "Not in a hunderd yeahs. I been livin' heah all my life," I says, "an' I don't even know all deh is to know about it, so how do you expect to know duh town," I says, "when yuh don't even live heah?"

"Yes," he says, "but I got a map to help me find my way about."

"Map or no map," I says, "yuh ain't gonna get to know Brooklyn wit no map," I says.

"Can yuh swim?" he says, just like dat. Jesus! By dat time, y'know, I begun to see dat duh guy was some kind of nut. He'd had plenty to drink, of course, but he had dat crazy look in his eye I didn't like. "Can yuh swim?" he says.

"Sure," I says. "Can't you?"

"No," he says. "Not more'n a stroke or two. I neveh loined good."

"Well, it's easy," I says. "All yuh need is a little confidence. Duh way I loined, me oldeh bruddeh pitched me off duh dock one day when I was eight yeahs old, cloes an' all. 'You'll swim,' he says. 'You'll swim all right— or drown.' An', believe me, I *swam!* When yuh know yuh got to, you'll do it. Duh only t'ing yuh need is confidence. An' once you've loined," I says, "you've got nuttin' else to worry about. You'll neveh ferget it. It's somep'n dat stays wit yuh as long as yuh live."

"Can yuh swim good?" he says.

"Like a fish," I tells him. "I'm a regleh fish in duh wateh," I says. "I loined to swim right off duh docks wit duh odeh kids," I says.

"What would yuh do if yuh saw a man drownin'," duh guy says.

"Do? Why, I'd jump in an' pull him out," I says. "Dat's what I'd do."

"Did yuh eveh see a man drown?" he says.

"Sure," I says. "I see two guys—bot' times at Coney Island. Dey got out too far, an' neider one could swim. Dey drowned befoeh anyone could get to 'em."

"What becomes of people after dey have drowned out heah?" he says.

"Drowned out where?" I says.

"Out heah in Brooklyn."

"I don't know whatcha mean," I says. "Neveh hoid of no one drownin' heah in Brooklyn, unless yuh mean in a swimmin' pool. Yuh can't drown in Brooklyn," I says. "Yuh gotta drown somewhere else—in duh ocean, where dere's wateh."

"Drownin'," duh guy says, lookin' at his map. "Drownin'."

Jesus! By den I could see he was some kind of nut, he had dat crazy expression in his eyes when he looked at yuh, an' I didn't know what he might do. So we was comin' to a station, an' it wasn't my stop, but I got off, anyway, an' waited for duh next train.

"Well, so long, chief," I says. "Take it easy, now."

"Drownin'," duh guys say, lookin' at his map. "Drownin'."

Jesus! I've t'ought about dat guy a t'ousand times since den an' wondered what eveh happed to 'm goin' out to look at Bensonhoist because he liked duh name! Walkin' aroun' t'roo Red Hook by himself at night an' lookin' at his map! How many people did I see drowned out heah in Brooklyn! How long would it take a guy wit a good map to know all deh was to know about Brooklyn!

Jesus! What a nut *he* was! I wondeh what eveh happened to 'm, anyway! I wondeh if someone knocked 'm on duh head, or if he's still wanderin' aroun' in duh subway in duh middle of duh night wit his little map! Duh poor guy! Say, I've got to laugh, at dat, when I t'ink about him! Maybe he's found out by now dat he'll neveh live long enough to know duh whole of Brooklyn. It'd take a guy a lifetime to know Brooklyn t'roo and t'roo. An' even den, yuh wouldn't know it all.

Only the dead know Brooklyn t'roo an' t'roo.

Polyphemus

A one-eyed Spaniard, one of the early voyagers, was beating his way up the American coasts out of the tropics, perhaps on his way back home, perhaps only to see what could be seen. He does not tell us in the record he has left of the voyage how he happened to be there, but it seems likely that he was on his way home and had been driven off his course. Subsequent events show that he was in a very dilapidated condition, and in need of overhauling: the sails were rent, the ship was leaking, the food and water stores were almost exhausted. During the night in a storm off one of the cruelest and most evilly celebrated of the Atlantic capes, the one-eyed Spaniard was driven in and almost wrecked. By some miracle of good fortune he got through one of the inlets in the dark, and when light broke, he found himself becalmed in an enormous inlet of pearl-gray water.

As the light grew, he made out seaward a long almost unbroken line of sandy shoals and islands that formed a desolate barrier between the sea and the mainland, and made this bay in which he found himself. Away to the west he descried now the line of the shore: it was also low, sandy, and desolate looking. The cool gray water of morning slapped gently at the sides of his ship: he had come from the howling immensity of the sea into the desert monotony of this coast. It was as bleak and barren a coast as the one-eyed Spaniard had ever seen. And indeed, for a man who had come up so many times under the headlands of Europe, and had seen the worn escarpments of chalk, the lush greenery of the hills, and the minute striped cultivation of the earth that greeted the sailor returning from a long and dangerous voyage—and awakened in him the unspeakable emotion of earth which has been tilled and used for so many centuries, with its almost personal bond for the men who have lived there on it, and whose dust is buried in it—there must have been something particularly desolate about this coast which stretched away with the immense indifference of nature into silence and wilderness. The Spaniard felt this, and the barren and desert quality of the place is duly recorded in his log, which, for the most part, is pretty dry reading.

But here a strange kind of exhilaration seizes the Spaniard: it gets into his writing, it begins to color and pulse through the gray stuff of his record. The light of the young rising sun reddened delicately upon the waters; immense and golden, it came up from the sea behind the line of sand-dunes, and suddenly he heard the fast drumming of the wild ducks as they crossed his ship high up, flying swift and straight as projectiles. Great heavy gulls of a size and kind he had never seen before swung over his ship in vast circles, making their eerie creaking noises. The powerful birds soared on their strong even wings, with their feet tucked neatly in below their bodies; or they dove and tumbled through the air, settling to the water with great flutterings and their haunted creaking clamor: they seemed to orchestrate this desolation, they gave a tongue to loneliness, and they filled the hearts of the men who had come there with a strange exultancy. For, as if some subtle and radical changes had been effected in the chemistry of their flesh and blood by the air they breathed, a kind of wild glee now possessed the one-eyed Spaniard's men. They began to laugh and sing, and to be, as he says, "marvelous merry."

During the morning the wind freshened a little; the Spaniard set his sails and stood in toward the land. By noon he was going up the coast quite near the shore, and by night he had put into the mouth of one of the coastal rivers. He took in his sails and anchored there. There was nearby on shore a settlement of "the race that inhabits these regions," and it was evident that his arrival had caused a great commotion among the inhabitants, for some who had fled away into the woods were now returning, and others were running up and down the shore, pointing and gesticulating and making a great deal of noise. But the one-eyed Spaniard had seen Indians before: that was an old story to him now; he was not disturbed. As for his men, the strange exuberance that had seized them in the morning does not seem to have worn off; they shouted ribald jokes at the Indians, and "did laugh and caper as if they had been madde."

Nevertheless, they did not go ashore that day. The one-eyed Spaniard was worn out, and his crew was exhausted: they ate such food as they had, some raisins, cheese, and wine, and after posting a watch, they went to sleep, unmindful of the fires that flickered in the Indian village, of sounds and chants and rumors, or of the forms that padded softly up and down the shore.

The marvelous moon moved up into the skies, and blank and full, blazed down upon the quiet waters of the sound, and upon the Indian village. It blazed upon the one-eyed Spaniard and his lonely little ship and crew, on their rich dull lamps, and on their swarthy sleeping faces; it blazed upon all the dirty richness of their ragged costumes, and on their greedy little minds, obsessed then as now by the European's greedy myth about America, to which he remains forever faithful with an unwearied and idiot pertinacity: "Where is the gold in the streets? Lead us to the emerald plantations, the diamond bushes, the platinum mountains, and the cliffs of pearl. Brother, let us gather in the shade of the ham and mutton trees, by the shores of ambrosial rivers: we will bathe in the fountains of milk, and pluck hot buttered rolls from the bread vines."

Then the moon blazed down upon the vast desolation of the American coasts, and on the glut and hiss of tides, on all the surge and foaming slide of waters on lone beaches. The moon blazed down on the eighteen thousand miles of coast, on the million sucks and hollows of the shore, and on the great wink of the sea, that ate the earth minutely and eternally. The moon blazed down upon the wilderness, it fell on sleeping woods, it dripped through moving leaves, it swarmed in weaving patterns on the earth, and it filled the cat's still eye with blazing yellow. The moon slept over mountains and lay like silence on the desert, and it carved the shadows of great rocks like time. The moon was mixed with flowing rivers, and it was buried in the heart of lakes, and it trembled on the water like bright fish. The moon steeped all the earth in its living and unearthly substance, it had a thousand visages, it painted continental space with ghostly light; and its light was proper to the nature of all things it touched: it came in with the sea, it flowed with the rivers, and it was still and living on clear spaces in the forest where no men watched.

And in the woodland darkness great birds fluttered to their sleep—in sleeping woodlands strange and secret birds, the teal, the nightjar, and the flying rail went to their sleep with flutterings dark as the hearts of sleeping men. In fronded beds and on the leaves of unfamiliar plants where the tarantula, the adder, and the asp had fed themselves asleep on their own poisons, and on lush jungle-depths where green-golden, bitter red, and glossy blue proud tufted birds cried out with brainless scream, the moonlight slept.

The moonlight slept above dark herds of bison moving with slow grazings in the night, it covered lonely little Indian villages; but most of it fell upon the unbroken undulation of the wilderness where, two centuries later, it would blaze on windows, and move across the face of sleeping men.

Sleep lay upon the wilderness, it lay across the faces of the nations, it lay like silence on the hearts of sleeping men; and low on lowlands and high upon the hills, flowed gentle sleep, smooth sliding sleep—sleep—sleep.

Early the next morning, the Spaniard went ashore with several of his men. "When we reached land," he writes, "our first act was to fall down on our knees and render thanks to God and the Blessed Virgin without whose intervention we had all been dead men." Their next act was to "take possession" of this land in the name of the King of Spain and to ground the flag. As we read today of this solemn ceremony, its pathos and puny arrogance touches us with pity. For what else can we feel for this handful of greedy adventurers "taking possession" of the immortal wilderness in the name of another puny fellow four thousand miles away, who had never seen or heard of the place and could never have understood it any better than these men. For the earth is never "taken possession of": it possesses.

At any rate, having accomplished these acts of piety and devotion, the Spaniards rose from their prayers, faced the crowd of Indians who had by this time ventured quite close to all this unctuous rigmarole, and discharged a volley from their muskets at them ("lest they become too froward and threatening"). Two or three fell sprawling on the ground, and the others ran away yelling into the woods. Thus, at one blast, Christianity and government were established.

The Spaniards now turned their attention to the Indian village—they began to pill and sack it with the deftness of long experience; but as they entered one hut after another, they found no coffers of nuggets or chests of emeralds, and found indeed that not even the jugs and pots and cooking utensils were of gold or silver, but had been crudely fashioned from baked earth; their rage grew; they felt tricked and cheated, and began to smash and destroy all that came within their reach. This sense of injury, this virtuous indignation, has crept into the Spaniard's record—indeed, we are edified with a bit of early American criticism which, save for a few archaisms of phrasing, has a strangely familiar ring, and might almost have been written yesterday: "This is a wild and barbarous kind of race, full of bloudie ways, it exists in such a base and vile sort of living that is worthier of wild beestes than men: they live in darkness and of the artes of living as we know them they are ignorant, one could think that God Himself has forgot them, they are so farre remote from any lighte."

He comments with disgust on the dried and "stinkeing fysshe" and the dried meat that hung in all the huts, and on the almost total lack of metals, but he saves his finest disdain for a "kinde of weede or plante," which they also found in considerable quantity in all the dwellings. He then goes on to describe this "weede or plante" in considerable detail: its leaves are broad and coarse, and when dried, it is yellow and has a strong odor. The barbarous natives, he says, are so fond of the plant that he has seen them put it in their mouths and chew it; when his own men tried the experience, however, they quickly had enough of it, and some were seized with retchings and a puking sickness. The final use to which this plant is put seems to him so extraordinary that he evidently fears his story will be disbelieved, for he goes on, with many assurances and oaths of his veracity, to describe how the plant may be lighted and burned and how "it giveth a fowle stinkeing smoak," and most wonderful of all, how these natives have a way of setting it afire and drawing in its fumes through long tubes so that "the smoak cometh out again by their mouth and nostryls in such wyse that you mighte thinke them devils out of helle instead of mortyl men."

Before we leave this one-eyed fellow, it is ironic to note with what contempt he passes over "the gold in the streets" for which his bowels yearn. As an example of one-eyed blindness, it is hard to beat. For here was gold, the inexhaustible vein of gold which the marvelous clay of the region could endlessly produce, and which mankind would endlessly consume and pay for; and the Spaniard, devoured by his lust for gold, ignores it with a grimace of disgust and a scornful dilation of his nostrils. That act was at once a history and a prophecy, and in it is all the story of Europe's blundering with America.

For it must be said of all these explorers and adventurers, the early ones and the late ones, who came back from their voyages to the Americas embittered because they did not find gold strewn on the earth, that they failed not because there was no gold, but because they did not know where and how to look for it, and because they did not recognize it when they had it under their noses—because, in short, they were one-eyed men. That gold, real gold, the actual ore, existed in great quantities, and often upon the very surface of the earth as these men supposed, has since been abundantly shown: it is only one of the minor and less interesting episodes of American history—a casual confirmation of one of the European fairy tales. They tried to think of the most wonderful fable in the world, these money-haters, and they evolved the story of gold on the ground.

It was a story as naive and not as beautiful as a child's vision of the lemonade spring, the ice cream mountains, the cake and candy forests, but, at any rate, America confirmed this little fable about gold in one short year of her history, and then proceeded to unpocket and unearth vast stores of wealth that made the visions of these old explorers look absurd. For she unearthed rivers of rich oil and flung them skywards, she dug mountains of coal and iron and copper out of the soil, she harvested each year two thousand miles of golden wheat, she flung great rails across the desert, she bridged the continent with the thunder of great wheels, she hewed down forests of enormous trees and floated them down rivers, she grew cotton for the world, her soil was full of sugars, citric pungencies, of a thousand homely and exotic things, but still the mystery of her earth was unrevealed, her greatest wealth and potencies unknown.

The one-eyed Spaniard, however, saw none of these things. He looted the village, murdered a few of the Indians, and advanced eighty or a hundred miles inland, squinting about for treasure. He found a desolate region, quite flat, with soil of a sandy marl, a coarse and undistinguished landscape, haunted by a lonely austerity, and thickly and ruggedly forested—for the most part with large areas of long-leaf pine. As he went inland, the soil deepened somewhat in hue and texture: it had a clayey, glutinous composition, and when rain fell, he cursed it. It grew coarse grasses and tough thick brush and undergrowth: it could also grow enough of the pungent weed whose fumes had so disgusted him to fill the nostrils of the earth with smoke forever. There was abundance of wild game and fowl, so that the one-eyed Spaniard did not go hungry; but he found no nuggets and not even a single emerald.

The one-eyed Spaniard cursed, and again turned eastward toward the sea. Swift and high and straight as bullets, the ducks passed over him, flying toward the coastal marshes. That was all. The enormous earth resumed its silence. Westward in great hills that he had never seen, cloud shadows passed above the timeless wilderness, the trees crashed down at night athwart the broken bowl of clean steep waters; there was the flash and wink of a billion little eyes, the glide and thrumming stir, the brooding ululation of the dark; there was the thunder of wings, the symphony of the wilderness, but there was never the tread of a booted foot.

The Spaniard took to his ship and set sail gladly. He was one-eyed and he had found no gold.

The Far and the Near

On the outskirts of a little town upon a rise of land that swept back from the railway there was a tidy little cottage of white boards, trimmed vividly with green blinds. To one side of the house there was a garden neatly patterned with plots of growing vegetables, and an arbor for the grapes that ripened late in August. Before the house there were three mighty oaks which sheltered it in their clean and massive shade in summer, and to the other side there was a border of gay flowers. The whole place had an air of tidiness, thrift, and modest comfort.

Every day, a few minutes after two o'clock in the afternoon, the limited express between two cities passed this spot. At that moment, the great train, having halted for a breathing space at the town near by, was beginning to lengthen evenly into its stroke, but it had not yet reached the full drive of its terrific speed. It swung into view deliberately, swept past with a powerful swaying motion of the engine, a low smooth rumble of its heavy cars upon pressed steel, and then it vanished into the cut. For a moment the progress of the engine could be marked by heavy bellowing puffs of smoke that burst at spaced intervals above the edges of the meadow grass, and finally nothing could be heard but the solid clacking tempo of the wheels receding into the drowsy stillness of the afternoon.

Every day for more than twenty years, as the train had approached this house, the engineer had blown on the whistle, and every day, as soon as she heard this signal, a woman had appeared on the back porch of the little house and waved to him. At first she had a small child clinging to her skirts, and now this child had grown to full womanhood, and every day she, too, came with her mother to the porch and waved.

The engineer had grown old and gray in the service. He had driven his great train, loaded with its weight of lives, across the land ten thousand times. His own children had grown up and married, and four times he had seen before him on the tracks the ghastly dot of tragedy converging like a cannon ball to its eclipse of horror at the boiler head—a light spring wagon filled with children, with its clustered row of small stunned faces; a cheap automobile stalled upon the tracks, set with the wooden figures of people paralyzed with fear; a battered hobo walking by the rail, too deaf and old to hear the whistle's warning; and a form flung past his window with a scream—all this the man had seen and known. He had known all the grief, the joy, the peril, and the labor such a man could know; he had grown seamed and weathered in his loyal service, and now, schooled by the qualities of faith and courage and humbleness that attended his labor, he had grown old, and had the grandeur and wisdom that these men have.

But no matter what peril or tragedy he had known, the vision of the little house and the women waving to him with a brave free motion of the arm had become fixed in the mind of the engineer as something beautiful and enduring, something beyond all change and ruin, and something that would always be the same, no matter what mishap, grief, or error might break the iron schedule of his days.

The sight of the little house and of these two women gave him the most extraordinary happiness he had ever known. He had seen them in a thousand lights, a hundred weathers. He had seen them through the harsh bare light of wintry gray across the brown and frosted stubble of the earth, and he had seen them again in the green luring sorcery of April.

He felt for them and for the little house in which they lived such tenderness as a man might feel for his own children, and at length the picture of their lives was carved so sharply in his heart that he felt that he knew their lives completely, to every hour and moment of the day, and he resolved that one day, when his years of service should be ended, he would go and find these people and speak at last with them whose lives had been so wrought into his own.

That day came. At last the engineer stepped from a train onto the station platform of the town where these two women lived. His years upon the rail had ended. He was a pensioned servant of his company, with no more work to do. The engineer walked slowly through the station and out into the streets of the town. Everything was as strange to him as if he had never seen this town before. As he walked on, his sense of bewilderment and confusion grew. Could this be the town he had passed ten thousand times? Were these the same houses he had seen so often from the high windows of his cab? It was all as unfamiliar, as disquieting as a city in a dream, and the perplexity of his spirit increased as he went on.

Presently the houses thinned into the straggling outposts of the town, and the street faded into a country road—the one on which the women lived. And the man plodded on slowly in the heat and dust. At length he stood before the house he sought. He knew at once that he had found the proper place. He saw the lordly oaks before the house, the flower beds, the garden and the arbor, and farther off, the glint of rails.

Yes, this was the house he sought, the place he had passed so many times, the destination he had longed for with such happiness. But now that he had found it, now that he was here, why did his hand falter on the gate; why had the town, the road, the earth, the very entrance to this place he loved, turned unfamiliar as the landscape of some ugly dream? Why did he feel this sense of confusion, doubt, and hopelessness?

At length he entered by the gate, walked slowly up the path, and in a moment more had mounted three short steps that led up to the porch, and was knocking on the door. Presently he heard steps in the hall, the door was opened, and a woman stood facing him.

And instantly, with a sense of bitter loss and grief, he was sorry he had come. He knew at once that the woman who stood there looking at him with a mistrustful eye was the same woman who had waved to him so many thousand times. But her face was harsh and pinched and meager; the flesh sagged wearily in sallow folds, and the small eyes peered at him with timid suspicion and uneasy doubt. All the brave freedom, the warmth and the affection that he had read into her gesture, vanished in the moment that he saw her and heard her unfriendly tongue.

And now his own voice sounded unreal and ghastly to him as he tried to explain his presence, to tell her who he was and the reason he had come. But he faltered on, fighting stubbornly against the horror of regret, confusion, disbelief that surged up in his spirit, drowning all his former joy and making his act of hope and tenderness seem shameful to him.

At length the woman invited him almost unwillingly into the house, and called her daughter in a harsh shrill voice. Then, for a brief agony of time, the man sat in an ugly little parlor, and he tried to talk while the two women stared at him with a dull, bewildered hostility, a sullen, timorous restraint.

And finally, stammering a crude farewell, he departed. He walked away down the path and then along the road toward town, and suddenly he knew that he was an old man. His heart, which had been brave and confident when it looked along the familiar vista of the rails, was now sick with doubt and horror as it saw the strange and unsuspected visage of the earth which had always been within a stone's throw of him, and which he had never seen or known. And he knew that all the magic of that bright lost way, the vista of that shining line, the imagined corner of that small good universe of hope's desire, could never be got again.

The Bums at Sunset

Slowly, singly, with the ambling gait of men who have just fed, and who are faced with no pressure of time and business, the hoboes came from the jungle, descended the few feet of clay embankment that sloped to the road bed, and in an unhurried manner walked down the tracks to the water tower. The time was the exact moment of sunset, the sun indeed had disappeared from sight, but its last shafts fell remotely, without violence or heat, upon the treetops of the already darkening woods and on the top of the water tower. That light lay there briefly with a strange unearthly detachment, like a delicate and ancient bronze, it was no part of that cool, that delicious, darkening of the earth which was already steeping the woods—it was like sorrow and like ecstasy and it faded briefly like a ghost.

Of the five men who had emerged from the "jungle" above the tracks and were now advancing in a straggling procession toward the water tower, the oldest was perhaps fifty, but such a ruin of a man, such a shapeless agglomerate of sodden rags, matted hair, and human tissues, that his age was indeterminate. He was like something that has been melted and beaten into the earth by a heavy rain. The youngest was a fresh-skinned country lad with bright wondering eyes: he was perhaps not more than sixteen years old. Of the remaining three, one was a young man not over thirty with a ferret face and very few upper teeth. He walked along gingerly on tender feet that were obviously unaccustomed to the work he was now putting them to: he was a triumph of dirty elegance—he wore a pin-striped suit heavily spattered with grease stains and very shiny on the seat: he kept his coat collar turned up and his hands deeply thrust into his trousers pocket— he walked thus with his bony shoulders thrust forward as if, in spite of the day's heat, he was cold. He had a limp cigarette thrust out of the corner of his mouth, and he talked with a bare movement of his lips, and a curious convulsion of his mouth to the side: everything about him suggested unclean secrecy.

Of the five men, only the remaining two carried on them the authority of genuine vagabondage. One was a small man with a hard seamed face, his eyes were hard and cold as agate, and his thin mouth was twisted slantwise in his face, and was like a scar.

The other man, who might have been in his mid-fifties, had the powerful shambling figure, the seamed brutal face, of the professional vagabond. It was a face and figure that had a curious nobility; the battered and pitted face was hewn like a block of granite, and on the man was the tremendous story of his wanderings—a legend of pounding wheel and thrumming rod, of bloody brawl and brutal shambles, of immense and lonely skies, the savage wildness, the wild, cruel, and lonely distance of America.

This man, somehow obviously the leader of the group, walked silently, indifferently, at a powerful shambling step, not looking at the others. Once he paused, thrust a hand into the baggy pocket of his coat, and drew out a cigarette, which he lit with a single motion of his hard cupped hand. Then his face luxuriously contorted as he drew upon the cigarette, he inhaled deeply, letting the smoke trickle out slowly through his nostrils after he had drawn it into the depths of his mighty lungs. It was a powerful and brutal gesture of sensual pleasure that suddenly gave to the act of smoking and to the quality of tobacco all of their primitive and fragrant relish. And it was evident that the man could impart this rare quality to the simplest physical acts of life—to everything he touched—because he had in him somehow the rare qualities of exultancy and joy.

All the time, the boy had been keeping step behind the man, his eyes fixed steadily upon the broad back of the vagabond. Now, as the man stopped, the boy came abreast of him, and also stopped, and for a moment continued to look at the man, a little uncertainly, but with the same expression of steadfast confidence.

The bum, letting the smoke coil slowly from luxurious nostrils, resumed his powerful swinging stride, and for a moment said nothing to the boy. Presently, however, he spoke roughly, casually, but with a kind of brutal friendliness:

"Where yuh goin' kid?" he said. "To the Big Town?"

The boy nodded dumbly, seemed about to speak, but said nothing.

"Been there before?" the man asked.

"No," said the boy.

"First time yuh ever rode the rods, huh?"

"Yes," said the boy.

"What's the matter?" the bum said, grinning. "Too many cows to milk down on the farm, huh? Is that it?"

The boy grinned uncertainly for a moment, and then said, "Yes."

"I t'ought so," the bum said, chuckling coarsely. "Jesus! I can tell one of youse fresh country kids a mile off by the way yuh walk. . . . Well," he said, with a rough blunt friendliness, in a moment, "stick wit me if you're goin' to the Big Town. I'm goin' that way, too."

"Yeah," the little man with the mouth like a scar now broke in, in a rasping voice, and with an ugly jeering laugh:

"Yeah. You stick to Bull, kid. He'll see yuh t'roo. He'll show yuh de—woild, I ain't kiddin' yuh! He'll take yuh up to Lemonade Lake an' all t'roo

Breadloaf Valley—won't yuh, Bull? He'll show yuh where de ham trees are and where de toikeys grow on bushes—won't yuh, Bull?" he said with ugly yet fawning insinuation. "You stick to Bull, kid, and you'll be wearin' poils. . . . A-a-a-ah! yuh punk kid!" he now said with a sudden turn to snarling viciousness. "Wat t' hell use do yuh t'ink we got for a punk kid like you?—Dat's duh trouble wit dis racket now! . . . We was all right until all dese kids began to come along! . . . Wy t' hell should we be boddered wit him!" he snarled viciously. "Wat t' hell am I supposed to be—a noice maid or sump'n? . . . G' wan, yuh little punk," he snarled viciously, and lifted his fist in a sudden backhand movement, as if to strike the boy. "Scram! We got no use fer yuh! . . . G' wan, now. . . . Get t' hell away from here before I smash yuh one."

The man named Bull turned for a moment and looked silently at the smaller bum.

"Listen, mug!" he said quietly in a moment. "You leave the kid alone. The kid stays, see?"

"A-a-a-ah!" the other man snarled sullenly. "What is dis, anyway?—A—noic'ry or sump'n?"

"Listen," the other man said, "yuh hoid me, didn't yuh?"

"A-a-a-ah t' hell wit it!" the little man muttered. "I'm not goin' t' rock duh cradle f'r no punk kid."

"Yuh hoid what I said, didn't yuh?" the man named Bull said in a heavy menacing tone.

"I hoid yuh. Yeah!" the other muttered.

"Well, I don't want to hear no more outa your trap. I said the kid stays—and he stays."

The little man muttered sullenly under his breath, but said no more. Bull continued to scowl heavily at him a moment longer, then turned away and went over and sat down on a handcar which had been pushed up against a tool house on the siding.

"Come over here, kid," he said roughly, as he fumbled in his pocket for another cigarette. The boy walked over to the handcar.

"Got any smokes?" the man said, still fumbling in his pocket. The boy produced a package of cigarettes and offered them to the man. Bull took a cigarette from the package, lighted it with a single movement, between his tough seamed face and his cupped hand, and then dropped the package of cigarettes in his pocket, with the same spacious and powerful gesture.

"T'anks," he said as the acrid smoke began to coil luxuriously from his nostrils. "Sit down, kid."

The boy sat down on the handcar beside the man. For a moment, as Bull smoked, two of the bums looked quietly at each other with sly smiles, and then the young one in the soiled pin-stripe suit shook his head rapidly to himself, and grinning toothlessly with his thin sunken mouth, mumbled derisively:

"Cheezus!"

Bull said nothing, but sat there smoking, bent forward a little on his knees, as solid as a rock.

It was almost dark; there was still a faint evening light, but already great stars were beginning to flash and blaze in cloudless skies. Somewhere in the woods there was a sound of water. Far off, half heard and half suspected, there was a faint dynamic throbbing on the rails. The boy sat there quietly, listening, and said nothing.

O night, now, night! And from the fields and thickets of coarse grass small night things sing, the bushes and the rank stiff underbrush are thrumming with the quick blind sudden noises: within the woods small lanterns of firefly glowworm's magic wink like ghosts, the steady water makes a noise like night and silence, and through the clay and brittle mica-shale upon the banks small springs from under the earth are seeping slowly.

O night, now, night! And all of the dark is one symphonic noise, all of the dark is one rich brooding noise, all of the dark is filled with the vast rich stammer of the night! O night, now, night! The bowels of youth are yearning with lost love! The bowels of youth are stirring with the ache of loneliness and joy! O night, now, night! And on the rails here in the wilderness, here in the ancient singing wilderness, O in the night here on the everlasting land, there is faint starlight on the gleaming rails, there is a humming in the air and on the wires, and on the rails we feel, O faint and far, the thunder of the fast express.

All of the night is singing now with one rich voice, a few bright stars are winking sparely, a sliver of the moon hangs at the pine's dark edge. And on the land, across the nightly earth, the voices of the women cry: "Return! Return. . . . Return, return, our breasts are heavy with their tenderness. . . . Return, return. . . . Our limbs are heavy with our love. . . . Return, return. . . . Turn to us in the night. . . . O come to us in the darkness. . . . Lie below our roof in falling rain. . . . Draw near us when the lightning flames and strikes. . . . O clasp us, and lie cradled in our arms. . . . Come into us and be engulfed in us—O plough deeply in the secret buried earth, plunge deeply into the furrow of our flesh, return, and feel our kiss forever on your lips."

Oh, will there not be some return for all men wandering on the earth? Will not the wound that pierced our hearts in April find some appeasement at the summer's end? October is the time for all returning, and men in exile think then of their native earth. All through the land at evening women wait, their heads are leaned against the doorways of the house, and as the vast incessant brooding of the earth swells up and fills the vast dark blue immensity of night, their flesh is drinking slowly in the million rhythms of the earth: the night-time darkens on their silent faces; their eyes burn gloriously underneath the stars. Their bodies are dark cups that drink in night and all the brooding ululation of the earth. All exhalations of the earth, all rich sweet fragrances, all growth and seed-time of the dark flows in, flows in, with secret glut, with dark deep soakings; they shall inherit the earth, and their flesh is sweet, their legs are widened with waiting, patient, everlasting lust. Their faces are great pansies heavied down for love and darkness.

Of wandering forever and the earth again. They wait there in the darkness in the earth, and all of the night-time is one singing noise. Their eyes are leveled out upon dark wheat; their eyes have pinetrees in them; their faces bloom with lilac and magnolia; their eyes have cool lakes in them, and their faces burn against the granite mountains, their faces burn across the desert and the dark.

Return! Return! All of the women from the earth and darkness are crying out, "Return, return, return!"

The engineer is pounding on the gleaming rails, and his wife has heard him in the night. And the whistle cry wails back: return, return, return!

"There's Jim now blowing for the Reidsville crossing." Return return.

And the brakeman's whore is listening in the darkness; and the fireman's girl is standing in the door.

And the bums are waiting by the rails at sunset, and all of the million voices of the earth cry out, "Return!"

The Bell Remembered

I

It sometimes seems to me my whole life has been haunted by the ringing of the courthouse bell. The courthouse bell gets into almost every memory I have of youth; it beats wildly with receding and advancing waves of sound through stormy autumn days; and in the sharp burst suddenness of spring, the blade of April, and the green of May, the courthouse bell is also there with its first stroke, giving a brazen pulse to haunting solitudes of June, getting into the rustling of a leaf, cloud shadows passing on the hills near home, speaking to morning with its wake-o-day of come-to-court; jarring the drowsy torpor of the afternoon with "court again."

It was a rapid and full-throated cry; a fast stroke beating on the heels of sound; its brazen tongue, its fast hard beat was always just the same, I knew, and yet the constant rhythm of its stroke beat through my heart and brain and soul and through the pulses of my blood with all the passionate and mad excitements of man's fate and error.

I never heard it—as a boy—without a faster beating of the pulse, a sharp dry tightening of the throat, the numb aerial buoyancy of deep excitement, even though I did not always know the cause. And yet, at morning, shining morning, in the spring, it would seem to speak to me of work-a-day, to tell me the world was up-and-doing, advancing to the rattling traffics of full noon. And then, in afternoon, it spoke with still another tongue; it broke the drowsy hush of somnolent repose with its demand for action; it spoke to bodies drowsing in the mid-day warmth, and it told us we must rudely break our languorous siesta, it spoke to stomachs drugged with heavy food, crammed full of turnip greens and corn, string beans and pork, hot biscuit and hot apple pie, and it told us it was time to gird our swollen loins for labor, that man's will and character must rise above his belly, that work was doing, and that night was not yet come.

Again, in morning it would speak of civil action; of men at law and the contention of a suit; its tone was full of writs and summonses or appearances and pleading; sometimes its hard fast tongue would now cry out, "Appear!"

"Appear, appear, appear appear appear appear appear, appear appear appear!"

Or, "Your property is mine—is mine—is mine—is mine!"

Or, again, harsh and peremptory, unyielding, unexplained:

"You must come to court—to court—to court—to court—to court—to court—to court."

Or, more brutal still and more peremptory, just:

"Court—court—court—court—court—court—court—court—court—"

In afternoon, the courthouse bell spoke of more fatal punishment: murder on trial, death through the heated air, a dull, slow-witted mountain wretch who sat there in the box, with a hundred pairs of greedy eyes upon him, and still half unaware of what he did, the killer's sudden sob, itself like blood and choking in the throat, the sun gone blood-smeared in the eyes, the feel and taste of blood throughout, upon the hot air, on the tongue and in the mouth, across the visage of the sun, with all the brightness of the day gone out—and then the sudden stroke, and the gold-bright sun of day returning, a cloud shape that passes on the massed green of a mountain flank, bird-thrumming wood-notes everywhere, swift and secret, bullet-wise within the wilderness, the drowsy stitch and drone of three o'clock through coarse wet grasses of the daisied fields, and the life-blood of a murdered man soaking quietly before him down into an unsuspected hand's breadth of familiar earth on mountain meadow—all as sudden, swift, and casual as this, all swiftly done as the swift thrummings in a wood—and all unknowing of the reason why he did it; now the prisoner's box, two hundred greedy eyes upon him, a stunned animal caught in the steel traps of law, and the courthouse bell that pounds upon the torpor of hot afternoon the brutal imperative of its inflexible command:

"To kill to kill to kill to kill to kill to kill—" and then, simply:

"Kill kill kill kill kill kill kill kill kill—"

II

I sometimes wonder if the people of a younger and more urban generation realize the way the courthouse bell, the country courthouse, shaped life and destiny through America some sixty years ago. For us in Libya Hill, at any rate, it was the center of the life of the entire community, the center of the community itself—for Libya Hill was first a country courthouse, then a town—a town that grew up round the courthouse, made a Square, and straggled out along the roads that led to the four quarters of the earth.

And for the country people round about, even more than for the people who lived in the town, the courthouse was the center of their life, and of more interest to them than it was to us. They came to town to trade and barter—they came to town to buy and sell, but when their work was over, it was always to the courthouse that they turned.

When court was being held, one could always find them here. Here were their mules, their horses, ox-teams, and their covered wagons; here their social converse, their communal life; here were their trials, suits, and punishments; here their drawling talk of rape and lust and murder—the whole shape and pattern of their life, the look of it, its feel, its taste, its smell.

Here was, in sum, it seems to me, the framework of America; the abysmal gap between our preachment and performance, our grain of righteousness and our hill of wrong. Not only in the lives and voices and persons of these country people, these rude mountaineers, who sat and spat and loitered on the courthouse steps, but in the very design and shape and structure of the courthouse building itself did the framework of this life of ours appear. Here in the pseudo-Greek facade with its front of swelling plaster columns trying to resemble stone, as well as in the high square dimensions of the trial courtroom, the judge's bench, the prisoner's box, the witness stand, the lawyer's table, the railed-off area for participants, the benches for spectators behind, the crossed flags of the State and of the nation, and the steel engraving of George Washington—in all these furnishings of office, there was some effort to maintain the pomp of high authority, the dignified impartial execution of the law.

But, alas, the impartial execution of the law was, like the design and structure of the courthouse itself, not free from error, and not always sound. The imposing Doric and Corinthian columns were often found, upon inspection, to be just lath and brick and plaster trying to be stone. And no matter what pretensions to a classic austerity the courtroom itself would try to make, the tall gloomy-looking windows were generally unwashed; no matter what effect of Attic grace the grand facade could make upon the slow mind of the country man, the wide dark corridors were full of drafts and ventilations, darkness, creaking boards, and squeaking stairways, the ominous dripping of an unseen tap.

And the courthouse smell was also like the smell of terror, crime, and justice in America—a certain essence of our life, a certain sweat out of ourselves, a certain substance that is ours alone and unmistakable—the smell of courthouse justice in this land.

It was—to get down to its basic chemistries—first of all a smell of sweat, tobacco-juice, and urine—a smell of sour flesh, feet, clogged urinals, and broken-down latrines. It was, mixed in and subtly interposed with these, a smell of tarry disinfectant, a kind of lime and alum, a strong ammoniac smell. It was a smell of old dark hallways and old used floors, a cool, dark, dank, and musty cellar-smell. It was a smell of old used chairs with creaking bottoms; a smell of sweated woods and grimy surfaces; a smell of rubbed-off arm-rests, bench-rests, chair-rests, counter-, desk-, and table-rests; a smell as if every inch of woodwork in the building had been oiled, stewed, sweated, grimed, and polished by man's flesh.

In addition to all these, it was a smell of rump-worn leathers, a smell of thumb-worn calfskin, yellowed papers and black ink; it was a smell of brogans, shirtsleeves, overalls, and sweat and hay and butter; and it was a kind of exciting smell of chalk, starched cuffs that rattled, the incessant rattling of dry papers, the crackling of dry knuckles and parched fingers, the dry rubbing of white chalky hands; a country lawyer smell of starch and broadcloth.

And oh, much more than these—and all of these—it was a smell of fascination and terror, a smell of throbbing pulse and beating heart and the tight and dry constriction of the throat; it was a smell made up of all the hate, the horror, the fear, the chicanery, and the loathing that the world could know, a smell made up of the intolerable anguish of men's nerve and heart and brain and sinew; the sweat and madness of man's perjured soul enmeshed in trickery—a whole huge smell of violence and crime and murder, of shyster trickeries and broken faith—it was one small smell of justice, fairness, truth, and hope in one high mountainous stench of error, passion, guilt, and graft, and wrong.

It was, in short, America—the wilderness America, the sprawling, huge, chaotic criminal America; it was murderous America soaked with murdered blood, tortured and purposeless America; savage, blind, and mad America, exploding, through its puny laws, its pitiful pretense; America with all its almost hopeless hopes, its almost faithless faiths; America with the huge blight on her of her own error, the broken promise of her lost dream and her unachieved desire; and it was America as well with her unspoken prophecies, her unfound language, her unuttered song; and just for all these reasons it was for us all our own America, with all her horror, beauty, tenderness, and terror, with all we know of her that never has been proved, that never yet was uttered—the only one we know, the only one there is.

III

I suppose my interest in the courthouse and the courthouse bell was a double one; the sound of that great brazen bell not only punctuated almost every experience of my youth, but it also punctuated almost every memory I have of my father. He had been made a Judge of the Circuit Court some years after the War, and the whole record of his life about this period might have been chronicled in the ringing of the bell. When the bell rang, court was in session and my father was in town; when the bell did not ring, court was not in session, and my father was holding court in some other town.

Moreover, when the bell began to ring, my father was at home; and before the bell had finished ringing, he was on his way to court. The ceremony of his going was always the same; I suppose I watched him do it a thousand times, and it never changed or varied by a fraction. He would get home at one o'clock, would eat dinner in a pre-occupied silence, speaking rarely, and probably thinking of the case that he was trying at the moment. After dinner, he would go into his study, stretch himself out on his old leather sofa, and nap for three-quarters of an hour. I often watched him while he took this brief siesta; he slept with a handkerchief spread out across his face, and with only the top of his bald head visible. Often, these naps produced snores of very formidable proportions, and the big handkerchief would blow up beneath the blast like a sail that catches a full wind.

But no matter how profound these slumbers seemed to be, he would always rouse himself at the first stroke of the courthouse bell, snatch the handkerchief from his face, and sit bolt upright with an expression of intense and almost startled surprise on his red face and in his round blue eyes:

"There's the *bell!*" he would cry, as if this was the last thing on earth he had expected. Then he would get up, limp over to his desk, thrust papers, briefs, and documents into his old brief case, jam a battered old slouch hat upon his head, and limp heavily down the hall where my mother would be busy with her sewing in the sitting room.

"I'm going now!" he would announce in a tone that seemed to convey a kind of abrupt and startled warning. To this my mother would make no answer whatever, but would continue placidly at her knitting, as if she had been expecting this surprising information all the time.

Then my father, after staring at her for a minute in a puzzled and undecided manner, would limp off down the hall, pause half-way, limp back to the open door, and fairly shout:

"I say, I'm *going!*"

"Yes, Edward," my mother would answer placidly, still busy with her needles. "I heard you."

Whereupon Father would glare at her again, in a surprised and baffled manner, and finally blurt out:

"Is there anything you want from town?"

To which my mother would say nothing for a moment, but would lift the needle to the light, and squinting, thread it.

"I say," my father would shout, as if he were yelling to someone on top of a mountain, "*is—there—anything—you—want—from town?*"

"No, Edward," Mother would presently reply, with the same maddening placidity. "I think not. We have everything we need."

At these words, Father would stare at her fixedly, breathing heavily, with a look of baffled indecision and surprise. Then he would turn abruptly, grunting, "Well, good-bye, then," and limp down the hall toward the steps, and heavily and rapidly away across the yard—and that would be the last I would see of my father until evening came: a stocky, red-faced man, with a bald head and a battered-up old brief case underneath his arm, limping away up the straggling street of a little town down South some sixty years ago, while the courthouse bell beat out its hard and rapid stroke.

I have heard my father say that, outside of a battlefield, a courtroom could be the most exciting place on earth, and that the greatest opportunity for observing life and character was in a courtroom; and I think that he was right. When an interesting case was being tried, he sometimes took me with him; I saw and heard a great many wonderful and fascinating things, a great many brutal and revolting things, as well; but by the time I was fifteen I was not only pretty familiar with courtroom procedure, but I had seen men on trial for their lives; the thrilling and terrible adventure of pursuit and capture; the cunning efforts of the hounds of law to break down evidence, to compel confession, to entrap and snare—hounds running, and the fox at bay; and I had heard trials for every other thing on earth as well—for theft, assault, and robbery; for blackmail, arson, rape, and greed, and petty larceny; for deep-dyed guilt or perjured innocence—all of the passion, guilt, and cunning, all of the humor, love, and faithfulness, all of the filth and ignorance, the triumph or defeat, the pain or the fulfillment, that the earth can know, or of which a man's life is capable.

Although my father's house on College Street was just a few blocks from the courthouse on the Square—so near, in fact, that he could be in court before the bell had finished its brazen ringing—in those days we could pass a large part of the whole town's population in the course of that short journey. It certainly seemed to me, every time I went along with him, that we *spoke* to the whole town; every step of our way was punctuated by someone greeting him with "Hello, General," or "Good morning, General," or "Good afternoon"—(outside the courtroom everybody called him General)—and my father's brief, grunted-out replies as he limped along:

"'Lo, Ed," "Morning, Jim," "'Day, Tom."

He was a good walker in spite of his limp and, when in a hurry, could cover ground fast—so fast indeed that I had to stir my stumps to keep ahead of him.

Arrived at the courthouse, we were greeted by the usual nondescript conglomeration of drawling country folk, tobacco-chewing mountaineers, and just plain loafers who made the porch, the steps, and walls of the old brick courthouse their club, their prop, their stay, their fixed abode, and almost, so it seemed to me, their final resting place—certainly some of them were, in Father's phrase, "as old as God," and had been sitting on the courthouse steps or leaning against the courthouse walls longer than most of us could remember.

Chief among these ancient sons of leisure—I think he was, by tacit consent, generally considered chief of them—was the venerable old reprobate who was generally referred to, when his back was turned, as Looky Thar. My father had given him that title, and it stuck forever after, chiefly because of its exceeding fitness. Old Looky Thar's real name was Old Man Slagle; although he called himself Major Slagle, and was generally addressed as Major by his familiars, friends, and acquaintances, the title was self-bestowed, and had no other basis in fact or actuality.

Old Looky Thar had been a soldier in the War and in addition to the loss of a leg, he had suffered a remarkable injury which had earned him the irreverent and flippant name of Looky Thar. This injury was a hole in the roof of his mouth, "big enough to stick your hull fist through," in Looky

Thar's own description of its dimensions, the result of an extraordinary shrapnel wound which had miraculously spared his life, but had unfortunately not impaired his powers of speech. I think he was about the lewdest, profanest, dirtiest-minded old man I ever saw or heard, and furthermore, his obscenities were published in a high cracked falsetto and accompanied by a high cracked cackle, publishable for blocks, and easily heard by people a hundred yards away.

He was, if anything, prouder of that great hole in his mouth than he was of his wooden leg; he was more pleased about it than he would have been over election to the Legion of Honor, the bestowal of the Victoria Cross, or the winning of a famous victory. That hole in the roof of his mouth not only became the be-all and the sufficient reason for his right to live; it became the be-all for his right to loaf. Moreover, the hole not only justified him in everything he thought or felt or did; but he also felt apparently that it gave to all his acts and utterances a kind of holy and inspired authority, a divine and undebatable correctness. And if anyone had the effrontery—was upstart enough—to question any one of Looky Thar's opinions (and his opinions were incessant and embraced the universe), whether on history, politics, religion, mathematics, hog-raising, peanut-growing, or astrology, he might look forward to being promptly, ruthlessly, and utterly subdued—discomfited—annihilated—put in his place at once by the instant and infallible authority of old Looky Thar's chief "frame of reference"—the huge hole in the roof of his mouth.

It did not matter what was the subject, what was the occasion, what the debate; old Looky Thar might argue black was white, or top was bottom, that the earth was flat instead of round—but whatever his position, no matter what he said was right, was right because he said it, because a man who had a big hole in the roof of his mouth could never *possibly* be wrong about anything.

On these occasions, whenever he was questioned or opposed in anything, his whole demeanor would change in the wink of an eye. In spite of his wooden leg, he would leap up out of his old splint-bottomed chair as quick as a monkey, and so angry that he punctuated every word by digging his wooden peg into the earth with vicious emphasis. Then, opening his horrible old mouth so wide that one wondered how he would ever get it closed again, exposing a few old yellow fangs of teeth, he would point a palsied finger at the big hole, and in a high cracked voice that shook with passion, scream:

"Looky thar!"

"I know, Major, but—"

"*You* know?" old Looky Thar would sneer. "Whut do *you* know, sir? A miserable little upstart that don't know *nothin'* tryin' to talk back to a man that fit all up an' down Virginny an' that's got a hole in the roof of his mouth big enough to stick your hull fist through. . . . *You* know!" he screamed, "*Whut* do you know? . . . Looky thar!"

"All right, I can see the hole, all right, but the argument was whether the earth was round or flat, and *I* say it's round!"

"*You* say it's round," Looky Thar would sneer. "What do *you* know about it, sir—a pore little two-by-fo' upstart that *don't know nothin'*? . . . How do *you* know whether it's round or flat? . . . When you ain't *been* nowhere yet . . . and ain't *seen* nothin' yet . . . an' never been five miles from home in your hull *life!* . . . talkin' back to a man that's fit all up an' down Virginny an' that's got a hole in the roof of his mouth you could stick your hull fist through—Looky thar!" and he would dig viciously into the earth with his wooden peg, crack his jaws wide open, and point to the all-justifying hole with a palsied and triumphant hand.

Otherwise, if not opposed in any way, old Looky Thar was amiable enough, and would talk endlessly and incessantly to anyone within hearing distance, who might have leisure or the inclination to listen to unending anecdotes about old Looky Thar's experiences in war, in peace, with horses, liquor, niggers, men and women—especially with women, his alleged relations with the female sex being lecherously recounted in a high cracked voice, punctuated by high-cracked bursts of bawdy laughter, all audible for several hundred yards.

My father loathed him; he represented everything my father hated most—shiftlessness, ignorance, filth, lechery, and professional veteranism; but hate, love, loathing, anger or contempt were not sufficient to prevail above old Looky Thar; he was a curse, a burden, and a cause of untold agony, but he was there in his splint-bottomed chair against the courthouse porch, and there to stay—a burden to be suffered and endured.

Although old Looky Thar could pop up from his chair as quick and nimble as a monkey when he was mad, and someone had opposed him, when he greeted my father he became the aged and enfeebled veteran, crippled from his wounds, but resolved to make a proper and respectful greeting to his honored chief.

At Father's approach, old Looky Thar, who would have been regaling his tobacco-chewing audience with tall tales of "how we fit 'em—we fit 'em up an' down Virginny"—he would cease talking suddenly, tilt his chair forward to the ground, place his palsied hands upon the arms of the chair, and claw frantically and futilely at the floor with his wooden stump, all the time grunting and groaning, and almost sobbing for breath, like a man at the last gasp of his strength, but resolved to do or die at any cost.

Then he would pause, and still panting heavily for breath, gasp out in a voice mealy with hypocrisy and assumed humility:

"Boys, I'm ashamed to have to ask fer help, but I'm afraid I got to! Here comes the General an' I *got* to get up on my feet; will one of you fellers lend a hand?"

Of course, a dozen lending, sympathetic hands were instantly available; they would pull and hoist old Looky Thar erect. He would stagger about drunkenly and claw frantically at the floor with his wooden peg in an effort to get his balance, catch hold of numerous shoulders in an effort to regain his balance—and then, slowly, and with a noble effort, come up to the salute—the most florid and magnificent salute you ever saw, the salute of a veteran of the Old Guard saluting the Emperor at Waterloo.

There were times when I was afraid my father was going to strangle him. Father's face would redden to the hue of a large and very ripe tomato, the veins in his thick neck and forehead would swell up like whipcording, his big fingers would work convulsively for a moment into his palms while he glared at Looky Thar; then without another word he would turn and limp away into the court.

To me, however, his comment on one occasion, while brief, was violent and descriptively explosive.

"There's another of your famous veterans," he growled. "Four years in war and forty years on your hind-end. There's a fine old veteran for you."

"Well," I protested, "the man *has* got a wooden leg."

Father stopped abruptly, faced me, his square face reddened painfully as he fixed me with the earnest, strangely youthful look of his blue eyes:

"Listen to me, boy," he said very quietly, and tapped me on the shoulder with a peculiar and extraordinarily intense quality of conviction. "Listen to me; a wooden leg is no excuse for *anything!*"

I stared at him, too astonished to say anything; and not knowing what reply to make to what seemed to me one of the most extraordinary and meaningless remarks I had ever heard.

"Just remember what I tell you," he said. "A wooden leg is no excuse for anything!"

Then, his face very red, he turned and limped heavily and rapidly into the court, leaving me still staring in gape-mouthed astonishment at his broad back.

IV

One day, about six months after this conversation with my father, I was in his study reading an account of the Battle of Spottsylvania by one of the generals in Hancock's command who had been present at the fight. I had finished reading his description of the first two movements of that bloody battle—namely, Hancock's charge upon the Confederate position and the thrilling counter-charge of our own troops—and was now reading the passages that described the final movement—the hand-to-hand fighting that was waged by forces of both armies over the earth embankment—a struggle so savage and prolonged that, in the words of this officer, "almost every foot of earth over which they fought was red with blood." Suddenly I came upon this passage:

> There have been other battles of the War in which more troops were engaged, where the losses were greater, and the operations carried on on a more exten-

sive scale, but in my own estimation, there has been no fighting in modern times that was as savage and destructive as was the hand-to-hand fighting that was waged back and forth over the earth embankment there at Spottsylvania in the final hours of the battle. The men of both armies fought hand to hand and toe to toe; the troops of both sides stood on top of the embankment firing pointblank in the faces of the enemy, getting fresh muskets constantly from their comrades down below. When one man fell, another sprang up to take his place. No one was spared—from private soldier up to captain, from captain to brigade commander; I saw general officers fighting in the thick of it shoulder to shoulder with the men of their own ranks; among others, I saw Mason among his mountaineers, firing and loading until he was himself shot down and borne away by his own men, his right leg so shattered by a Minie ball that amputation was imperative—

Something blurred and passed across my eyes, and suddenly all the gold and singing had gone out of the day. I got up and walked out of the study, and down the hallway, holding the book open in my hand.

When I got to the sitting room, I looked in and saw my mother there; she looked up placidly, and then looked at me quickly, startled, and got up, putting her sewing things down upon the table as she did.

"What is it? What's the matter with you?"

I walked over to her, very steadily, I think.

"This book," I said, and held the page up to her, pointing at the place—"Read what it says here—"

She took it quickly, and read. In a moment she handed it back to me; her fingers shook a little, but she spoke calmly:

"Well?"

"What the book says—is that Father?"

"Yes," she said.

"Then," I said, staring slowly at her and swallowing hard—"does that mean that Father—"

Then I saw that she was crying; she put her arms around my shoulders and said:

"Your father is so proud—he wouldn't tell you. He couldn't bear to have his son think he was a cripple."

Then I knew what he had meant.

A cripple! Fifty years and more have passed since then, but every time the memory returns, my vision blurs, and something tightens in my throat, and the gold and singing passes from the sun as it did on that lost day in spring, long, long ago. A cripple—he a cripple!

I see his bald head and red face, his stocky figure limping heavily away to court . . . and hear the hard fast ringing of the bell . . . and remember Looky Thar, the courthouse loafers and the people passing . . . the trials, the lawyers, and the men accused . . . the generals coming to our house the way they did all through the 'eighties . . . the things they talked of and the magic that they brought . . . and my heart boy-drunk with dreams of war and glory . . . the splendid generals and my father, who was so un-warlike as I thought . . . and the unworthiness of my romantic unbelief . . . to see that burly and prosaic figure as it *limped* away toward court . . . and tried to vision him with Gordon in the Wilderness . . . or charging through the shot-torn fields and woods at Gettysburg . . . or wounded, sinking to his knees at Sharpsburg, by Antietam Creek . . . and failing miserably to see him so; and, boy-like, failing to envisage how much of madness or of magic even brick-red faces and bald heads may be familiar with . . . down the Valley of Virginia, long years ago. . . .

But a cripple!—No! He was no cripple, but the strongest, straightest, plainest, most uncrippled man I ever knew! . . . And fifty years have gone by since then, but when I think of that lost day, it all comes back . . . the memory of each blade, each leaf, each flower . . . the rustling of each leaf and every light and shade that came and went against the sun . . . the dusty Square, the hitching posts, the mules, the ox-teams, and the horses, the hay-sweet bedding of the country wagons and the smell of bedded melons . . . the courthouse loafers . . . and old Looky Thar—and Spangler's mule teams trotting by across the Square . . . each door that opened . . . and each gate that slammed . . . and everything that passed throughout the town that day . . . the women sitting on the latticed porches of their brothels at the edge of Niggertown . . . the whores respiring in warm afternoon, and certain only of one thing—that night would come! . . . all things known or un-seen—a part of my whole consciousness . . . a little mountain town down South one afternoon in May some fifty years ago . . . and time passing like the humming of a bee, time passing like the thrumming in a wood, time passing as cloud shadows pass above the hill-flanks of the mountain mead-ows or like the hard fast pounding of the courthouse bell . . . a man long dead and long since buried who limped his way to court and who had been at Gettysburg . . . and time passing . . . passing like a leaf . . . time passing like a river flowing . . . time passing . . . and remembered suddenly as here, like the forgotten hoof and wheel of sixty years ago . . . time passing as men pass who never will come back again . . . and leaving us, Great God, with only this . . . knowing that this earth, this time, this life are stranger than a dream.

Fame and the Poet

I

Fame followed him round all day long, but he did not speak to her. He always knew that she was there, however, and that her glorious eyes were fixed adoringly on him. He deliberately avoided looking at her. He knew he had her, he knew that she was his, and he thought it was just as well to let her wait a little while. And that night, just as he expected, she got into the elevator as he was going up to his room. Still he didn't speak to her or give any indication that he was aware of her presence. But her fragrance filled the elevator cage; she smelled perfectly glorious. When he got out of the elevator, Fame got out, too, and as he went down the corridor toward his room, he could hear her light and rapid footsteps following along behind him. He opened the door and walked into his room. Fame came in, too. He closed the door. Fame stood looking at him with an expression of adoring submissiveness. It was not until that moment that he spoke to her.

"Sit down," he said, in a quiet but masterful tone of voice.

Fame took a seat, and with her hands folded in her lap, continued to look at him demurely, with an expression of adoring obedience in her glorious gray eyes.

"Now, listen, Fame," our hero said, clearing his throat nervously and fumbling in his pocket for a cigarette in order to conceal his embarrassment. "There are a few things we ought to get straight right now."

"Yes, darling," the Angel replied, and leaning forward a little in an attitude of submissive respect, she indicated by her manner that she was prepared to give her master the most earnest and obedient attention.

"In the first place," the young man said, "there is this name of yours—not that I don't like it," he said quickly, as she gazed at him with wide and dewy eyes, "only—well," he hunted for a word and flushed a little with embarrassment—"it is a little formal—a little too classical for modern use."

"Is it, dear?" said Fame in a vague and tender voice, still gazing at him with star-eyed adoration.

"Yes." He cleared his throat quickly. "Now what I was thinking is—if we could only find a name for you—something a little more simple—a—a— little more adapted to everyday use."

"Whatever you say, dear," Fame replied.

"Well, now," the young man said, "I was thinking of something plain and simple like—like—Ruth, or Mary, or—or—Fay!" he cried triumphantly. "What's wrong with Fay?" he demanded. "It's a good name—short, plain, easy to remember, doesn't attract attention—a lot of girls are called Fay nowadays. What's wrong with Fay?" he said persuasively, and looked inquiringly at her.

"Nothing, darling," Fame answered. "I think it's a very nice name. Is that what you'd like to call me?"

"Yes, I think it is. It's a good name for you. So if you don't mind, I'll call you Fay hereafter."

"All right, dear," Fame said quietly. "If you like the name, I do, too."

"Good! That's settled, then!" he said with satisfaction. "After this your name is Fay. . . . Now another thing—" here he cleared his throat again, squirmed uncomfortably, and reddened. "Another thing" was not going to be easy.

II

"Yes, dear?" Fame asked inquiringly, after a moment's pause.

"Well, now, Fay—" The youth craned at his collar, flushed a deep tomato red, and strove desperately to get it out—"It's—it's—well," he blurted, and brought his palm down sharply on his knee—"it's about those wings of yours."

Fame regarded her plumage with considerable satisfaction and said, "They *are* nice, aren't they?"

"Yes," the young man said, "but—but—well, you see, Fay, girls don't wear those things nowadays. Not—not that they're not very becoming to you and all that but—but if you went around now—always wearing things like that, you'd attract an awful lot of attention—you really would. You'd— you'd have people following you in the streets, and you wouldn't like that, Fay, you know you wouldn't."

Fame looked at him, wide-eyed with astonishment. "You don't like my wings?" she said, shaking her head a little, looking at him with a troubled question in her lovely eyes.

"I *do* like them—I *do* like them," he said desperately, "—only you see, Fay, it's not the style any more."

"Most of the boys I used to go with liked them," Fame replied. "Shelley was crazy about them—he called me Angel—he was always talking about flying away with me somewhere. He always insisted that I have my wings snowy white. Keats liked them, too, only his tastes were a little loud. He liked crimson wings with golden tips: they really used to attract a lot of attention when I went out with him. Milton liked my wings, but he had very sober tastes in everything. I had to dress in gray for him; that was the way he liked me best. Then there was Walter Raleigh. Walter always liked—"

"Look here," the young man said, and stared at Fame suspiciously. "It seems to me you've been around a good deal for a girl of your age."

"Oh, no," said Fame quickly. "I really haven't. I've been almost nowhere. I've really led a very retiring sort of life."

"Well," said her lord and master, still regarding the lady with a suspicious eye, "for a girl who has led a retiring life, you certainly seem to have known a lot of men."

"No one as nice as you, darling," Fame whispered cozily and tried to snuggle in beside him. The young man repulsed her gently but firmly, still looking at her suspiciously. As he regarded her, his uneasiness increased. He didn't like the way she said the words; there was something in the tone, the cajoling manner, that bothered him. The more he thought of it, the less he liked it. It seemed to him that he had heard these very words spoken in this very tone before, and even as he wondered where he had heard them, it came to him like a flash. It was his former mistress, Mrs. Flutterly, all over again.

"Now don't hand me any of that stuff," he said brutally. "I want the truth. Have you or have you not?"

"*But*—but," Fame looked bewildered and tried to laugh it off, just as Mrs. Flutterly used to do. "*What* stuff are you talking about, darling? I'm not handing you any stuff," she protested. "Besides, I don't even know what you are talking about."

It's the same old line, he reflected, and ground his teeth: Mrs. Flutterly to a T.

"Now you look here," he said roughly. "You know damned good and well what I'm talking about, so don't try to play innocent with me."

"But—but darling, I *don't!*" Fame protested, shrugging her shoulders slightly, lifting her hands and laughing a little troubled and uncomfortable laugh. They're all alike, the youth thought gloomily, as he regarded the lady with a sullen and distempered eye; it's Mrs. Flutterly all over, even to the way she looks innocent and bewildered and shrugs her shoulders and pretends to laugh.

"If you'd only tell me what you're talking about—" Fame began.

"Come on," he said coarsely. "Quit stalling around now—you know good and well what I'm talking about. How many men you been with, huh?" the brute barked at her, and glowered evilly.

"Been with?" Fame said slowly, her voice rising on a fine inflection of puzzled doubt. "Do you mean how many men have I been *out* with?"

"Now, listen, you," he said in a tone that was distinctly full of threat. "You answer and you tell the truth or out you go. How many lovers have you had?"

"Lovers?" Fame began, "why I don't remember if—"

"You do remember," he said. "And by God, you're going to tell me the truth if I have to choke it out of you. Answer me!" he shouted again, and smote his knee so fiercely that it made her jump. "How many of those guys did you sleep with?"

"Why—why—" she faltered in a trembling tone.

"By God, you're going to tell me now," he muttered between grating teeth, and leaning forward, he seized the slender bracelet of her arm with brutal grip. "Answer!" he snarled and shook her. "Answer, I tell you!"

She burst into tears; great choking sobs welled up and filled her throat; she tried to speak but couldn't through the tears. It was, he grimly saw, the art of Mrs. Flutterly.

"There—there—" she choked.

"Answer!" he rasped back, and shook her again. "Were there or were there not? Answer!"

"—Yis," she squeaked almost inaudibly. "There were—"

"How many?" he said through clenched teeth.

"I—I—I—*two*—" she finally squeaked in a pitiable little voice.

"*Two!*" he shook her. "*Two!*" Again he shook her. "Are you sure it's *two?*" For a third time he shook her brutally. "Answer!" he yelled.

"I—I—I—*three!*" she squeaked. "Maybe three!" she gasped.

"Ah—h—h—!" his breath expired in a sough of disgust.

He straightened back in his chair and fairly flung her from him. "And maybe four—and maybe five—and maybe six—and maybe God knows how many more! You wouldn't even know yourself! There have been so damn many you've lost count! You're all alike—the whole lot of you!"

III

Gnawing his lip, he settled back in his chair, and for a moment surveyed her in glowering silence. But at length, curiosity got the best of him.

"You and Milton," he rasped harshly. "What about you and him? Was he one of them?"

"He—he—was a good man, George," Fame wept softly. "But I was so young when I met him—just a girl—he was so good—so good," she wept. "But hard—hard! There was never any joy, any laughter—any music in the house. If I tried to sing, he made me stop. He wanted to be good to me—but he was so stern. Our life was nothing but work, work, work from dawn to dark—he called it living laborious days—and he said a woman's place was in the home. I suppppose he was right," she smiled pitifully through her tears, "—but I was so young—I wanted a little joy."

"You're not answering my question," said the youth implacably. "Was Milton one of your lovers or not?"

"He—he—" Fame began in a faltering voice.

"*Yes or no?*" he snarled. "I want an answer."

Fame's ripe lip trembled. She tried to speak, her glorious eyes suffused with tears again: "Yis—" she squeaked—"He—he—Yis!—but I was so young—so young," she sobbed. "I didn't kn—o—w!"

"I thought so," said the hero with the grim finality of disgust, and leaning far back in his chair, he surveyed her a moment in gloomy silence.

"What about Shelley?" he barked so sharply that it made her jump. "Was he one of the gang, too?"

"—Oh," Fame cried, softly smiling through her tears, "he was a *saint,* an *angel.* There was something so unearthly about Percy—he was more like a disembodied spirit than a man of flesh and blood—"

"None of that guff now!" he rasped. "Did you and Percy have relations—yes or no?"

"—It—it—it was really more like disembodied spirits—" Fame went on in a rapid and faltering tone.

"*Yes or no?*"

"—Nothing—nothing physical about it at all," Fame went on. "The desire of the moth for the star—that's what Percy called—"

"Listen, you!" He leaned forward and shook her brutally. "Answer me! Did you and Percy have relations or didn't you? *Yes or no!*"

Her tender underlip trembled, she tried to speak, finally she burst into tears again, and squeaked:

"Yis! . . . but I was so young . . . so lonely . . . I didn't really mean to—"

"I thought so!" he said with a growl of fierce disgust and pushed her brutally away from him, and then for a moment longer sat regarding her with a sneer of contempt. " . . . 'He could give not what men called love!' Ah—ah—ah! The mealy-mouthed hypocrite! . . . Giving the works to every girl he met and trying to pretend he was the Holy Ghost! . . . Well, come on, now!" he said coarsely. "Let's have all the dirt and get it over with! Was Keats one of the boys, too?"

"—Johnny—" Fame began in a trembling voice, "—Johnny—"

"Was he? Yes or no?"

"—The poor kid—" she gasped. "He was all alone, he had no money, no friends—he was dying of consumption—I—I—I felt that if there was anything I could—"

"*Yes or no?*" he shouted.

"Yis," squeaked Fame, beginning to sob hysterically. "Yis! . . . Yis! . . . I've told you now! You've dragged it out of me! . . . "

She smote herself dramatically on the bosom with a small clenched fist and tried to smile bravely, pathetically, with a martyred air. " . . . But as God is my judge," she went on in a moment, in a trembling voice that faltered through her tears, "you're the only one I ever really loved—the others didn't count," she sobbed. "I was so young at the time—just a young girl—father and mother were both dead—and, oh, God!" she sobbed, "I was so alone—so alone—" Great choking sobs engulfed her, took her speech away—

she tried to speak, but could not—finally, pathetically, heartrendingly, just as Mrs. Flutterly used to do, she squeaked: "I didn't know what to *do—o—o!*"

IV

He couldn't stand it. He saw how he was being taken in, but he was still the dupe and still the gull; torn between pity and tenderness which the sight of a woman in tears stirred in him and cursing himself for his own weakness and folly in yielding, he took her in his arms and growled: "Oh, for God's sake! Stop it! Stop it!" and shook her gently.

Her arms went around him now, her fragrant mouth was pressed against his own, he breathed the fragrance of her shining hair, the flowery smell of her seductive loveliness, her voluptuous form bent back and yielded to his embrace, and he was lost.

"Get off them clothes," he panted thickly, made ungrammatical by passion, "because we're—we're—oh, damn it—how are we going to manage these wings?"

Return

I have been seven years from home, but now I have come back again. And what is there to say?

Time passes, and puts halters to debate. There is too much to say; there is so much to say that must be spoken; there is so much to say that never can be told:—we say it in the impassioned solitudes of youth, and of ten thousand nights and days of absence and return. But in the end, the answer to it all is time and silence: this answers all; and after this, there is no more to say.

So has it been with me. For there has been a time when I would wake just at the first blue-gray of dawn to feel the shoulder strap again against my arm, the canvas bag, the blocked sheet and the final shot beneath the oak tree on the lawn before the lawyer's great white house—to know my route was ended and that work was done, and that morning had come back again—so thinking, feeling, and remembering, then, that I was far away, and that I had been long from home.

Then all old things would come again—both brick and wall, and step and hedge, the way a street sloped or a tree was standing, the way a gate hung or a house was set, the very cinders of a rutted alley way—such things as these would come again, leaf, blade, and stone, and door. So much more door than any other one could ever be—like all things that belong to men— the essence of all doors that ever were because it is his own, the door that he has passed a thousand times—all things like these would come back again, the whole atomic pattern of my native earth, my town, my child- hood, and my youth, with all the faces, all lives and histories of long ago— and all forgotten weathers of man's memory would come again, there in the darkness in some foreign land, would come so poignant, swift, and vivid in the whiteness of their blazing panoply that I could feel my foot upon the street again, my hand upon the rail, the strap upon my shoulder, the whole sensuous unit of my native earth, with an intensity that I had never known before. And I could taste it, feel it, smell it, live it through again, hard to the hilt of exile, as I was born perhaps to live all things and moments, hard to the hilt, and carrying on that furious and impassioned argument of youth and solitude, contending fiercely with a thousand disputants, would think:

"I have a thing that I must tell them; I'll go home again, I'll meet them and I'll say my piece: I will lay bare my purposes, strip down the vision of my life until its bare soul's nakedness, tell my people what it is to try to shape and spin a living out of the entrails of man's life, and what he visions, why he does it—oh, some day I will go back and reveal my plan until no man living in the world can doubt it—I will show them utterly:—"

—And I have come back now: I have come home again, and there is nothing more that I can say.—All arguments are ended: saying nothing, all is said then; all is known: I am home.

Where are the words I thought that I must say, the arguments I thought that I should make, the debates and demonstrations that so often, in those years of absence, memory, wandering, youth, and new discovery I had so hotly made to solitude and to the ghostly audience of an absent fellowship, the thousand things that I would prove and show when I returned—where are they now?

For I have come home again—and what is there to say? I think that there is nothing—save the silence of our speech. I think that there is nothing—save the knowledge of our glance. I think that there is nothing—save the silent and unspoken conscience in us now that needs no speech but silence, because we know what we know, we have what we have, we are what we are.

So what is there to say?

"You've put on weight since I last saw you."

"Yes, but you are just the same."

"Have you seen Bob yet? He's been looking for you."

"No; but he came by the house last night, but I wasn't there. I'm seeing him today."

"Sam Reed was asking about you. . . . Here's Jim now."

" . . . Come on, boys! Here he is! We've got him now! He's on the spot! Let's pin him down and make him own up! . . . Wasn't that Whit Nelson you had in mind when you told about the night he bought up all the gold fish down at Wood's? . . . What's that he wrote, Ed, about the time you slept all night in Reagan's hearse and woke up scared to death next morning when you found out where you were?"

"Why, Lord, he got the facts right, but the figures were all wrong! I slept all night in Reagan's hearse, all right, but you and Jim were with me, too— and you were worse scared when you woke up in the morning than I was! That's all I objected to; he should have put that in!"

" . . . And what was that you said, Paul, when he told of how you used to take the grass widow from Paducah down to Riverside on Thursday night and buy her popcorn? . . . Come on, now . . . you can't back out on us: you know you said it—tell him what you said."

"Why, hell, I only said she wasn't forty-four, the way HE said, but forty-eight, and that instead of two gold teeth the way HE had it, she had three.

And two of them were on the side, with a great big bright one in the middle—not one above and one below the way HE told about it. And it wasn't popcorn that I bought 'her,' but a bag of peanuts. I just wanted him to get it straight, that's all!"

"Come on, now! Own up! You had us all in mind! We've got you on the spot . . . Confess! . . . Look at his face! He don't know what to say!"

"Hell, son, there's nothing that you have to say. We all understand. There were some folks around here when that book of yours first came out who thought you'd written up the town and put them in the book; and some who were mad about it for a while. But that's all forgotten now. So much has happened since those days, that anything you said was mild. You stayed away too long. We're glad that you've come home."

And there is nothing more to say.

" . . . You'll find things changed, though. It's not the place you used to know. . . . I guess you'll find it changed a lot. . . . Your father's marble shop was on this corner. . . . Do you remember the old wooden steps? . . . The draymen sitting on the steps? . . . The tombstones and the angel on the porch? . . . Your father standing there a thousand times . . . the old fire department and the city hall . . . the city market and the calaboose . . . the fountain and the street cars coming in upon the quarter hour? We've put buses in since the time you went away. . . . Have you been through the tunnel yet? . . . It's all changed so much you wouldn't know the place."

Change? There is no change. These surfaces have altered and these shapes are new. . . . There is a wrinkle by the eye we did not have before; a furrow in the cheek; a kind of worn humor in the grin about the lip, a look plain, steady, naked, touched with care that twenty did not know—our hue is rougher and our groove more deep—time passes, WE have grown older, much water and some blood has gone beneath the bridge since then: I think we know each other better—but, oh, brothers, friends, and comrades of this mortal dust—we have not changed!

For here again, again, I turn into the street, finding again the place where corners meet, looking again to see if time is there. And all of it is as it has always been: again, again, I turn, and find again the things that I have always known: the cool sweet magic of starred mountain night, the huge attentiveness of dark, the slope, the street, the trees, the living silence of the houses waiting, and the fact that April has come back again. . . . And again, again, in the old house I feel beneath my tread the creak of the old stair, the worn rail, the whitewashed walls, the feel of darkness and the house asleep, and think, "I was a child here; here the stairs and here was darkness; this was I, and here is Time."

These things will never change. Some things will never change: the groove is deeper, but the leaf, the bud, the wheel, the blade, and April will come back again.

The wheel will turn, the immortal wheel of life will turn, but it will never change. Here from this little universe of time and place, from this small core and adyt of my being where once, hill-born and bound, a child, I lay at night, and heard the whistles wailing to the west, the thunder of great wheels along the river's edge, and wrought my vision from these hills of the great undiscovered earth and my America—here, now, forevermore, shaped here in this small world, and in the proud and flaming spirit of a boy, new children have come after us, as we: as we, the boy's face in the morning yet, and mountain night, and starlight, darkness, and the month of April, and the boy's straight eye: again, again, the thudding press, the aching shoulder, and the canvas bag; the lean arm and the rifled throw again, that whacked the blocked and folded sheet against the shacks of Niggertown.

. . . These things, or such as these, will come again; so, too, the high heart and the proud and flaming vision of a child—to do the best that may be in him, shaped from this earth, as we, and patterned by this scheme, to wreak with all his might with humbleness and pride, to strike here from his native rock, I pray, the waters of our thirst, to get here from his native earth, his vision of this earth and this America, to hear again, as we, the wheel, the whistle, and the trolley bell; so, too, as we, to go out from these hills and find and shape the great America of our discovery; so, too, as we, who write these words, to know again the everlasting legend of man's youth—flight, quest, and wandering—exile and return.

Mr. Malone

It was the first literary party in the life of Joseph Doaks. As he entered the room, he had the feeling of having stepped into a Covarrubias drawing and having all the figures come to life, looking even more like their own cartoons than life itself. There was Van Vleeck, with his buck teeth, over in the corner talking to a Negro; there was Stephen Hook, leaning against the mantel with that air of bored nonchalance that was really just the screen for his excruciating shyness; there was Mr. Lloyd McHarg, or "Knuckles," as he was more familiarly known to his friends, who had done great violence to himself and nature and yet remained splendidly himself—a man—a kind of unruinable ruin, with the pale-blue eyes that looked as if they had been slightly poached in alcohol, the corrugated redness of his puckered face, the essential and terrific redness of hair, eyebrows, ears, and everything about him, the high staccato cachinnation of his speech, which was itself like the nervous clatter of a typewriter or of a page of one of his own books. There was Cottswold, the critic, a little puff-ball of a man, a lover of dear whimsy, a polished adept of envenomed treacle; and many other famous ones of art and letters in the city's life.

They all looked so much like themselves, and as Joe knew they *must* look, that he squared his shoulders, drew a breath, and muttered to himself, "Well, here we are."

And then these forms and faces, fixed there in his memory in that blinding instant of first recognition, moved and shifted, and the rosy, smiling face of Mrs. Jack bore down on him, wreathed in friendly greeting. She welcomed him and took him with her; then he heard a Voice.

It was not that this was the only voice, for everywhere there was the sound of voices, that curious, haunting medley of three dozen voices, all together, in a kind of woven fabric of bright sound, a murmurous confluence as strange as time. But over all these voices, through them and above them, instantly distinguishable from all the others, there was a single, all-pervading, all-compelling, all-concluding, and all-dominating—well, this *was* a Voice!

It was certainly by all odds the most extraordinary voice that Joe had ever heard. In the first place, it was distinguished by a perfectly astounding rich-

300

ness and an indescribable sonority that seemed to have in it the compacted resonance in the voice of every Irishman who ever lived. But this magnificently full-bodied voice was charged through and through with hell-fire, with vituperation of an unfathomable and unutterable hate. One felt with every word a kind of imminent flood of malevolent feeling for all mankind that seemed to swell up from some bottomless well of fury inside him and make instant strangulation inevitable.

The possessor of this remarkable voice was Mr. Seamus Malone, and Mr. Malone's appearance was fully as remarkable as his voice. He was a man somewhere in his early forties, of rather fragile physical mold, but giving a spurious impression of ruggedness through the possession of an astonishing beard. This beard covered all his face; it was square-cut, not long, but luxuriant, and of an inky, blue-black color. Above this beard a pair of pale-blue eyes surveyed the world with a distempered scorn; the total effect was to give Mr. Malone something of the appearance of an embittered Jesus Christ.

Mr. Malone's full-bodied voice, of course, surged through the black luxuriance of his beard. When he talked—and he talked constantly—one became uneasily aware of the presence of two pale-red lips, thick and rubbery looking, concealed in the black foliage. These lips were characterized by an astonishing flexibility; they writhed and twisted about in the beard like a couple of venomous snakes. Sometimes they parted in a ghastly travesty of a smile, sometimes they writhed clear around his face in a convulsive snarl. But they were never silent for a moment; through them poured a tide of envenomed speech.

Mr. Malone was seated at the end of a sofa, within easy distance of his highball glass and a bottle of Scotch whisky. He was surrounded by an attractive audience of several people. Prominent among these was a young man and his beautiful young wife, both of whom—mouths slightly parted, eyes shining with hypnotized fascination—were listening with a kind of breathless attentiveness to the flood of Mr. Malone's malevolent erudition.

"Obviously," Mr. Malone was saying, "obviously . . . " Oh, how to convey the richness, the sonority, the strangling contempt that was packed into that single word! "*Obviously*, the fellow has read nothing! All that he's read, apparently, are two books that every schoolboy is familiar with; namely, the *Pons Asinorum* of Jacopus Robisonius, which was printed by Parchesi in Bologna in the spring of 1497, and the *Pontifex Maximus* of Ambrosius Glutzius, which was printed in Pisa in the following year. Beyond that," snarled Mr. Malone, "he knows nothing. Of course"—and his rubber lips did a snake dance all through the thicket of his beard—"of course, in a so-called civilization, where the standard of erudite information is governed by the lucubrations of Mr. William Randolph Hearst and the masterly creations of the *Saturday Evening Post,* the pretensions of such a fellow pass, no doubt, for encyclopedic omniscience. But he *knows* nothing!" choked Mr. Malone in a kind of strangling yell, and at the same time he threw both hands up as a final gesture of exasperated futility. "He's read nothing! In God's name, what *can* you expect?"

And gasping, exhausted by his effort, he did a kind of devil's mad jig for a moment with one foot. He looked about in a maddened way, espied the whisky bottle; his thin claw-like hand shot out and seized the bottle, he poured out a tumblerful of whisky, spilling half of it upon the table, gulped down the rest, and in a moment, a little appeased, he panted out, "The whole thing's absurd—the sensation he has made! The fellow is an ignoramus, an imbecile!"

During the concluding passages of this tirade, Mrs. Jack and Joe had approached the place where the master was sitting, and waited in respectful silence until the conclusion of his remarks. Now, when he had somewhat composed himself and a light akin to reason had begun to come back into his distempered eyes, Mrs. Jack bent over him and spoke quietly.

"Seamus."

"Eh? Hey? What is it?" he said, startled. "Oh, hello, Alice. It's you!"

"Yes. I want to introduce the young man I was speaking to you about—Mr. Doaks, the one whose manuscript you have been reading."

"Oh—eh—how are you?" said Seamus Malone. He extended a clammy hand, his pale-red lips twisted in a ghastly attempt at a friendly smile. And in this smile there was something that was likewise pitiable, something that spoke of genuine warmth, a genuine instinct for friendship down below the whole tortured snarl of his life, something really engaging that peered out for just an instant behind the uncontrollable distemper of his race. It was there beneath all his swarming hatreds, jealousies, his self-pity, his feeling that life had somehow betrayed him, which it had not done, and that his talents had not had their due, which they had and more, and that infamous charlatans, fools, ignoramuses, mountebanks of every description were being acclaimed as geniuses, surfeited with the sickening adulations of a moronic population which should have been *his! His! His!* No one's but *his!* Great God! If there was an atom of truth, of honor, of intelligence in this damnable, accursed, Judas Iscariot of a so-called world!

But now, having spoken to Joe with a painful effort at friendly greeting, an "Oh, yes! How are you? I've been reading your manuscript," the confession was too much for him, and the old note of scorn began to appear in the richly sonorous tones.

"Of course, to tell the truth, I haven't read it," boomed Mr. Malone, beginning to tap impatiently upon the edges of the sofa. "*No* one who has an atom of intelligence would *attempt* to read a manuscript, but I've looked into it. I've—I've read a few pages." This admission obviously cost him a great effort, but he wrenched it out at length. "I've—I've come across one or two things in it that—that didn't seem bad. Not bad, that is"—he was snarling in good form now—"compared to the usual nauseating drivel that gets published, and that passes in this Noble and Enlightened Land of Ours for Belles-Lettres. Not bad when compared to the backwoods bilge of Mr. Sinclair Lewis. Not bad when compared to the niggling nuances of that neurotic New Englander from Missouri, Mr. T. S. Eliot, who after baffling an all-too-willing world for years by the production of such incomprehensible nonsense as 'The Waste Land' and 'The Love Song of J. Alfred Prufrock,' and gaining for himself a reputation for perfectly *enormous* erudition among the readers of Kalamazoo, has now, my friends, turned prophet, priest, and political revolutionary, and is at the present moment engaged in stunning the entire voting population of that great agnostic republic known as the British Isles with the information that *he*—God save the mark!—Mr. Eliot from Missouri, has become a *Royalist!* A *Royalist,* if you please," choked Mr. Malone, "and an Anglo-Catholic."

"No," said Mr. Malone, after a brief pause to catch his breath, "I have not read much of this young man's book—a few words here and there, a passage now and then. But compared to Mr. Eliot's portentous bilge, the perfumed piffle of Mr. Thornton Wilder"—he began to rock back and forth with the old red glitter in his eyes—"the elephantine imbecility of Mr. Theodore Dreiser, the moon-struck idiocies of the Sherwood Andersons, the Carl Sandburgs, the Ernest Hemingway 'I am dumb' school, the various forms of quackery purveyed by the various Frosts, O'Neills, and Jeffers, the Cabells, Glasgows, Peterkins, and Cathers, the Bromfields and Fitzgeralds, the Kansas Tolstois, the Tennessee Chekhovs, the Dakota Dostoevskis, and the Idaho Ibsens"—he choked—"compared to all the seven hundred and ninety-six varieties of piffle, bilge, quack-salvery, and hocus-pocus that are palmed off upon the eager citizens of this Great Republic by the leading purveyors of artistic hogwash, what this young man has written is not bad." And after struggling stertorously for breath, he at last exploded in a final despairing effort. "It's all *swill!*" he snarled. "Everything they print is swill! If you find *four* words that are *not* swill, why then"—he gasped, and threw up his hands again—"print it! *Print* it!"

And having thus disposed of a large part of modern American writing, if not to his utter satisfaction, at least to his utter exhaustion, Mr. Malone rocked back and forth for several minutes, breathing like a porpoise and doing the devil's jig of knee and toe. Finally he slopped out a staggering slug of Scotch and gulped it down, then subsided into silence, muttering once more, "*Print* it!"

There was a rather awkward pause at the conclusion of this tirade. Few people attempted to interpose an answer to the vituperations of Mr. Seamus Malone; there was in his approach to matters a kind of tornado-like completeness that rendered argument, if not impotent, at least comparatively useless.

After a painful silence, however, more to restore the aspects of polite conversation than for any other reason, one of the audience—the young man with the beautiful wife—inquired with just the right note of respectful hesitancy, "What—what do you think of Mr. Joyce?" Mr. Joyce, indeed, amid the general wreckage seemed at the moment one of the few undemolished figures left in modern literature. "You—you know him, don't you?"

It was evident at once that the question was unfortunate. Red fire began to flame again in the Malone eye, and he was already rubbing his claw-like hands back and forth across the hinges of his bony knees.

"What," Mr. Malone began in an extremely rich foreboding tone of voice, "*what* do I think of Mr. Joyce? And do I *know* him? I presume, sir," Mr. Malone continued, very slowly, "that you are asking me if I know Mr. James Joyce, formerly a citizen of Dublin, but at present"—here his pale lips writhed around in a meaningful smile—"at the present moment, if I mistake not, a resident of the Left Bank of Paris. Yes, sir, I do. I have known Mr. James Joyce for a very long time, a very long time indeed. Too, too long a time. I had the honor—call it, rather, the Proud Privilege"—the choking note was evident—"of watching young Mr. Joyce grow up in the years after I moved to Dublin. And surely, my friends, it is a proud privilege for one so *humble* as *myself*"—here he beckoned sneeringly to his frail breast—"to be able to claim such glorious intimacy with the Great Mumbo Jumbo of Modern Literature, the holy prophet of the Intelligentsia, who in one staggering tome exhausts everything there is to write about—to say nothing of *everyone* who has read it. Do I *know* Mr. Joyce? Sir, I think I may modestly claim that happy distinction," Mr. Malone remarked, with a slight convulsion of the lips. "I have known the gentleman in question for forty years, if not exactly like a brother"—jeeringly—"at least *quite* well enough. And what do I think of Mr. Joyce, you ask? Well," Mr. Malone went on in a tone of sonorous reflectiveness, "let me see, what *do* I think of Mr. Joyce? Mr. Joyce, first of all, is a little bourgeois Irishman of provincial tastes who has spent a lifetime on the continent of Europe in a completely *fruitless* attempt to overcome the Jesuit bigotry, prejudice, and narrowness of his childhood training. Mr. Joyce began his literary career as a fifth-rate poet, from there proceeded to become a seventh-rate short-story writer, graduated from his mastery in this field into a ninth-rate dramatist, from this developed into a thirteenth-rate practitioner of literary Mumbo-Jumboism which is now held in high esteem by the Cultured Few," Mr. Malone sneered, "and I believe is now engaged in the concoction of a piece of twenty-seventh-rate incoherency, as if the possibilities in this field had not already been exhausted by the master's preceding opus."

In the pause that followed, while Mr. Malone drank and in a manner composed himself, some person of great daring was heard to murmur that he *had* thought that parts of *Ulysses* were rather good.

Mr. Malone took this mild dissension very well. He rocked back and forth a little, and then, waving his thin white hand with a gesture of pitying concessiveness, remarked, "Oh, I suppose there is some slight talent there—some minor vestiges, at any rate. Strictly speaking, of course, the fellow is a school-teacher, a kind of small pedant who should be teaching the sixth form somewhere in a Jesuit seminary. But he had *something*—not a great deal, but something. Of course"—here the gorge began to rise again, and red, baleful lightnings shot out from his eyes—"of course, the amazing thing is the reputation the fellow has gotten for himself when he had no more to start with. It's extremely amusing," cried Mr. Malone, and his lips writhed horribly in an attempt at laughter. "There were at least a dozen people in Dublin at the time who could have done the job Joyce tried to do in *Ulysses*, and done it *much* better!" he choked. "Gogarty, who is twenty times the man Joyce is, could have done it. A. E. could have done it. Ernest Boyd could have done it. Yeats could have done it. Even—even Moore or Stephens could have done it." He rocked back and forth, and suddenly snarled, "*I* could have done it! And why didn't I?" he demanded furiously, thus asking a question that was undoubtedly in everyone's mind at the moment. "Why, because I simply wasn't interested! It didn't matter enough to any of us! We were interested in—in other things—in living! Of course," he choked, "that is the history of all modern literature, isn't it? All of the people who really *could* write stay out of it. Why? Because," boomed Mr. Malone, "they're not interested in it. They're interested in other things!"

He was interested in his whisky glass at the moment; he looked around and found it, reached for it, and drank. Then, with a tortured effort at a smile, he turned to the young man with the beautiful wife and said, "But come! Let's talk of something pleasanter. I hear you're going abroad soon?"

"Yes," the young man answered, with a suggestion of relief. "We're going over for a year."

"We're *terribly* thrilled over going," the young woman remarked. "We know you've lived there such a lot, and we'd be *awfully* grateful for any advice you'd give us."

"Where are you going," said Malone. "Are you—are you just traveling around"—his lips twisted, but he controlled himself—"or are you going to settle down and live in one place?"

"Oh, we're going to live in one place," the young man said quickly. "We're going to settle down in Paris."

There was a pause, then the young wife leaned toward the great man a little anxiously and said, "Don't you think that's a good idea, Mr. Malone?"

Now, if Mr. Malone had been expressing his own opinion, five minutes or five months before, he certainly *would* have thought it was a good idea to go to Paris and live there for a year. He had said so himself on many occasions—occasions when he had denounced American provincialism, American puritanism, American crassness, and American ignorance of Continental life. Moreover, he had frequently demanded *why* Americans, instead of trying to gulp all Europe down at once, didn't settle down in Paris for a year, live quietly, and observe the people. Moreover, if the young man and his wife had announced their intention of settling down in *London* for a year, the effect on Mr. Malone would have been easily predictable. His pale, rubbery lips would have twisted around scornfully in his whiskers, and he would have ironically inquired, "Why London? Why"—here he would have begun to breathe hoarsely—"why inflict the dull provincialism of English life, the dreary monotony of English food, the horrible torpor of the English mind, when only seven hours away across the Channel you have the opportunity of living *cheaply* in the most beautiful and civilized city in the world, of living comfortably, luxuriously, in *Paris* for a fraction of what your living would cost you in London, and furthermore of associating with a gay and civilized people instead of with the provincial Babbitts of the British bourgeoisie?"

Why, then, did the old red flood of vituperative scorn rise up in Mr. Malone now that the young people had expressed their intention of doing the very thing he himself would have urged them to do?

Well, first of all, they were telling him, and Mr. Malone could not brook such impudence. Second, he rather regarded the city of Paris as his own private discovery, and too many damned Americans had begun to go there. Certainly no one could go there without his consent.

So now that these two young people had decided, all by themselves, to go to Paris for a year, he found their puppy-like insolence insupportable. For a moment after the young man and his wife had spoken there was silence; red fire began to flash from the Malone eye, he rocked gently back and forth and rubbed his knees, but for the nonce controlled himself. "Why *Paris?*" he inquired, quietly enough, but with a note of ironic sarcasm in the rich timbre of his voice. "Why *Paris?*" he repeated.

"But—don't you think that's a good place to go to, Mr. Malone?" the young woman anxiously inquired. "I don't know," she went on rapidly, "but—but Paris sounds so gay, and jolly, and sort of exciting."

"Gay? Jolly? Exciting?" said Mr. Malone, with an air of serious reflection. "Oh, I suppose some gaiety is left. That is, if Midwestern tourists, avaricious hotelkeepers, and the Messrs. Thomas Cook have not utterly destroyed what was left of it. I suppose, of course," he went on with a slight choke, "that you'll do all the things your compatriots usually do—sit twelve hours a day among the literati at Le Dôme, or on the terrace of the Café de la Paix, and come back at the end of your year having seen *nothing* of Paris, *nothing* of the French, *nothing* of the real life of the people, but utterly, thoroughly convinced that you know *all!*" He laughed furiously, and said, "Really, it's most amusing, isn't it, the way all you young Americans nowadays flock to Paris? Here you are—young people, *presumably* of some intelligence—and where do you go," sneered Mr. Malone. "Paris!" He snarled the word out as if the very stench of it disgusted him. "Pa-a-ris, one of the *dullest, dreariest,* most *expensive, noisiest,* and most *uncomfortable* cities in the world, inhabited by a race of penny-pinching shopkeepers, cheating taxidrivers and waiters, the simply *appalling* French middle class, and the excursions of the Cook's tourists."

There was a stricken silence for a moment; the beautiful young wife looked crushed, bewildered; then the young man cleared his throat and said a trifle nervously, "But—but where would *you* go, Mr. Malone?"

"My dear fellow," Mr. Malone said, "there are dozens of more interesting places than Paris. Go anywhere, but don't go there!"

"But where?" the young woman said. "Where would you suggest, Mr. Malone? What other city can you think of?"

"Why—why—why, *Copenhagen!*" Mr. Malone suddenly boomed triumphantly. "By all means, go to *Copenhagen!* Of course," he sneered, "the news has probably not yet reached the Greenwich Village Bohemians on the Left Bank, Midwestern school-teachers, or other great globe-trotters of that ilk. They've probably never *heard* of the place, since it's probably a little off their beaten route. They probably would be surprised to know that Copenhagen is the *gay-est, pleasantest,* most civilized city in Europe, populated by the most charming and intelligent people in the world. The news, no doubt," he jeered, "would come as a distinct shock to our Bohemian friends on the Left Bank, whose complete conception of the geography of Europe does not extend, apparently, beyond the Eiffel Tower. But go to Copenhagen, by all means. *Pa-a-ris,*" he snarled. "Not in a million years—Copenhagen! Copenhagen!" he yelled, threw his hands up in a gesture eloquent of exasperated futility over the spectacle of human idiocy, gasped stertorously for breath, and shot claw-like fingers clutching for the whisky glass.

Then suddenly, seeing the stricken figure, the somewhat appalled face, of young Mr. Doaks, so swiftly and so sharply caught here among imagined great ones of the earth, and finding all of it so strange, Mr. Malone, as if the face of the young Doaks brought sharply back and instantly the memory of the young Malone, and of all Doakses, all Malones that ever were, put down his whisky glass and cried out warmly, richly, "But I thought that what I read was—was—" Just for a moment the pale lips writhed tormented in his beard, and then—oh, tormented web of race and man—he got it out. He smiled at the young Doaks quite winningly and said, "I liked your book. Good luck to you."

Such a man as this was Mr. Seamus Malone.

Oktoberfest

One Sunday afternoon, at the end of September, I made my way, accompanied by Heinrich Bahr, to the Theresien Fields, on the eastern edges of Munich, where the October fair was going on. As we walked along, past the railway station and toward the carnival grounds, the street, and all the streets that led to it, began to swarm with people. Most of them were native Müncheners, but a great number were also Bavarian country people. These Bavarians were brawny men and women who stained the crowd brilliantly with the rich dyes of their costume—the men in their elaborately embroidered holiday shorts and stockings, the women in their bright dresses and lace bodices, marching briskly along with the springy step of the mountaineer. These peasants had the perfect flesh and the sound teeth of animals. Their smooth round faces bore only the markings of the sun and the wind: they were unworn by the thought and pain that waste away man's strength. I looked at them with a pang of regret and envy—their lives were so strong and confident, and having missed so much they seemed to have gained so greatly. Their lives were limited to one or two desires—most of them had never read a book, a visit to this magic city of Munich was to them a visit to the heart of the universe, and the world that existed beyond their mountains had no real existence for them at all.

As we neared the Theresien Fields, the crowd became so thick that movement was impeded and slowed down. The huge noises of the fair came to us now, and I could see the various buildings. My first feeling as I entered the Fields was one of overwhelming disappointment. What lay before me and around me seemed to be a smaller and less brilliant Coney Island. There were dozens of booths and sheds filled with cheap dolls, teddy bears, candy wrappers, clay targets, etc., with all the accompanying claptrap of two-headed monsters, crazy houses, fat ladies, dwarfs, palmists, hypnotists, as well as all the elaborate machinery for making one dizzy: whirling carriages and toy automobiles that spun about on an electrified floor, all filled with people who screamed with joy when the crazy vehicles crashed together and were released again by an attendant.

Heinrich Bahr began to laugh and stare like a child. The childlike capacity of all these people for amusement was astonishing. Like children, they never seemed to grow weary of the whole gaudy show. Great fat fellows with shaven heads and creased necks rode on the whirling and whipping machines, or rode round and round, again and again, on the heaving wooden horses of the merry-go-rounds. Heinrich was fascinated: I rode with him several times on the breathless dip-and-dive of the great wooden trestle-like railway, and then was whipped and spun dizzy in several of the machines.

Finally Heinrich was content. We moved slowly along down the thronging central passage of the fair until we came to a more open space at the edge of the Fields. Here from a little platform a man was haranguing the crowd in harsh, carnival-barker's German. Beside him on the platform stood a young man whose body and arms were imprisoned in a sleeveless canvas jacket and manacled with a chain. Presently the barker stopped talking, the young man thrust his feet through canvas loops, and he was hauled aloft, feet first, until he hung face downward above the staring mob. I watched him as he began his desperate efforts to free himself from the chain and jacket that fettered him, until I saw his face turn purple, and the great veins stand out in ropes upon his forehead. Meanwhile, a woman passed through the crowd soliciting contributions, and when she had got all the money the crowd would yield, the young man, whose swollen face was now almost black with blood, freed himself very quickly and was lowered to the earth. The crowd dispersed almost, it seemed to me, with a kind of sullenness as if the thing they had waited to see had now happened but had somehow disappointed them, and while the barker began his harangue again, the young man sat in a chair recovering himself, with his hand before his eyes. Meanwhile, the woman who had collected money stood by him anxiously, looking at him, and in a moment spoke to him. And somehow just by their nearness to each other and by no other outward sign there was communicated to me a sense of tenderness and love.

My mind was reeling from all the clamorous confusion of the fair, and this last exhibition, coming as a climax to an unceasing program of monsters and animal sensations, touched me with a sense of horror. For a moment it seemed to me that there was something evil and innate in men that blackened and tainted even their most primitive pleasures.

Late afternoon had come; the days now were shortening rapidly, and the air was already that of autumn—it was crisp and chill, meagerly warmed by a thin red sunshine. Over all the fair there rose the dense and solid fabric of a hundred thousand voices. Heinrich, whose interest in the shows of the fair had been for the time appeased, now began to think of beer. Taking me by the arm, he joined in the vast oscillation of the crowd that jammed the main avenue of the carnival in an almost solid wedge.

The Germans moved along slowly and patiently, with the tremendous massivity that seems to be an essence of their lives, accepting the movement of the crowd with enormous contentment as they lost themselves and became a part of the great beast around them. Their heavy bodies jostled and bumped against one another awkwardly and roughly, but there was no anger among them. They roared out greetings or witticisms to one another and to everyone; they moved along in groups of six or eight, men and women all together with arms linked.

Heinrich Bahr had become eager and gay; he laughed and chuckled to himself constantly; presently, slipping his hand through my arm with a friendly and persuasive movement, he said: "Come! Let us go and see the Roasted Ox." And immediately at these words an enormous hunger woke in me, a hunger for flesh such as I had never known: I wanted not only to see the Roasted Ox, I wanted to devour great pieces of it. I had already noticed one characteristic of this fair that distinguished it from any other I had ever seen. This was the great number of booths, large and small, given over to the sale of hot and cold meats. Great sausages hung in ropes and festoons from the walls of some of these places, while in others there was a constant exhalation from steaming and roasting viands of all kinds and sizes. The fragrance and the odor were maddening. And it seemed to me that above this dense mass of people that swayed along so slowly, there hovered forever in the thin cold air an odor of slaughtered flesh.

But now we found ourselves before a vast long shed, gaily colored in front, and bearing above its doors a huge drawing of an ox. This was the Oxen Roastery (*Ochsen-Braterei*), but so dense was the crowd within that a man stood before the doors with his arms out, keeping back the people who wanted to enter, and telling them they must wait another fifteen minutes. Heinrich and I joined the crowd and waited docilely with all the others: to me there was communicated some of the enormous patience of this crowd, which waited and which did not try to thrust past barriers. Presently the doors were opened, and we all went in.

I found myself in a vast long shed at the end of which, through the dense cloud of tobacco smoke which thickened the atmosphere almost to the consistency of a London fog, I could see the carcasses of two great animals revolving slowly on iron spits over troughs of red-hot coals.

The place, after the chill bite of the October air, was warm—warm with a single unmistakable warmth: the warmth of thousands of bodies crowded together in an enclosed place. And mingled with this warmth, there was an overpowering odor of food. At hundreds of tables people were sitting together devouring tons of flesh—ox flesh, great platters full of sliced cold sausages, huge slabs of veal and pork, together with great stone mugs that foamed with over a liter of the cold and strong October beer. There was a heavy and incessant rumble of voices full of food, that rose and fell in brittle waves. Down the central aisles and around the sides moved and jostled another crowd, looking restlessly over the densely packed area for a vacant place. And the brawny peasant women who acted as waitresses plunged recklessly through this crowd, bearing platters of food or a half-dozen steins of beer in one hand, and brusquely thrusting human impediments out of their way with another.

Heinrich and I moved with the crowd slowly down the central aisle. The feeders, it seemed to me, were for the most part great heavy people who already had in their faces something of the bloated contentment of swine. Their eyes were dull and bleared with food and beer, and many of them stared at the people around them in a kind of stupefaction, as if they had been drugged. And indeed the air itself, which was so thick and strong it could be cut with a knife, was sufficient to drug one's senses, and I was therefore glad when, having arrived at the end of the aisle and stared for a moment at the great carcass of the ox that was turning brown as it revolved slowly before us, Heinrich suggested that we go elsewhere.

The sharp air lifted me at once from lethargy, and I began to look about me quickly and eagerly again. The crowd was growing denser as evening approached, and I knew now that the evening was to be dedicated to food and beer.

Distributed among the innumerable smaller buildings of the fair, like lions couched among a rabble of smaller beasts, there rose about us the great beer halls erected by the famous breweries. And as thick as the crowd had been before the booths and shows, it seemed small compared to the crowd that filled these vast buildings—enormous sheds that each held several thousand people. Before us now, and from a distance, I could see the great red facade of the Löwenbräu brewery, with its proud crest of two royal lions, rampant. But when we came near the vast roaring of sound the hall enclosed, we saw that it would be impossible to find a seat there. Thousands of people were roaring over their beer at the tables, and hundreds more milled up and down incessantly, looking for an opening.

We tried several other of the great beer halls of the great breweries with no better success, but at length we found one which had a few tables set about on a small graveled space before the hall, screened from the swarming crowd outside by a hedge. A few people were sitting at some of the tables, but most of the tables were vacant: darkness was now approaching, the air was sharp and frosty, and there was an almost frantic eagerness to join the fetid human warmth, enter the howling tempest of noise and drunkenness that the great hall contained. But both of us were now tired, fatigued by the excitement, by the crowd, by the huge kaleidoscope of noise, of color and sensation, we had experienced. "Let us sit down here," I said, indicating one of the vacant tables before the hall. And Heinrich, after peering restlessly through one of the windows at the smoky chaos within, through which dark figures pushed and jostled like spirits lost in the foggy vapors of Valhalla, consented and took a seat, but with a disappointment he was unable to conceal.

"It is beautiful in there," he said. "You cannot afford to miss it." Then a peasant woman bore down upon us, swinging in each of her strong hands six foaming steins of the powerful October beer. She smiled at us with a ready friendliness and said, "The light or the dark?" We answered, "Dark." Almost before we had spoken, she had set two foaming mugs before us on the table and was on her way again.

"But beer?" I said. "Why beer? Why have they come here to drink beer? Why have all these great sheds been built here by the famous breweries when all Munich is renowned for beer and there are hundreds of beer restaurants in the city?"

"Yes," Heinrich answered. "But—" he smiled and emphasized the word, "this is October beer. It is almost twice as strong as ordinary beer."

Then we seized our great stone mugs, clinked them together with a smiling "*Prosit*," and in the frosty sharp exhilaration of that air we drank long and deep the strong cold liquor that sent tingling through our veins its potent energy. All about us people were eating and drinking—near by at another table people in gay clothes had ordered beer, and now, unwrapping several paper bundles that they were carrying with them, they set out on the table a prodigious quantity of food and began to eat and drink stolidly. The man, a brawny fellow with thick mustaches and white woolen stockings that covered his powerful calves but left his feet and knees bare, pulled from his pocket a large knife and cut the heads from several salt fish, which shone a beautiful golden color in the evening light. From another paper the woman produced several rolls, a bunch of radishes, and a big piece of liver sausage, and added them to the general board. Two children, a boy and a girl, the girl with braided hanks of long blonde hair falling before her over the shoulders, both watchful and blue-eyed with the intent and focused hunger of animals, stared silently at the food as their parents cut it and apportioned it. In a moment, with this same silent and voracious attentiveness, all of them were eating and drinking.

Everyone was eating; everyone was drinking. A ravenous hunger, a hunger that knew no appeasement, that wished to glut itself on all the roasted ox flesh, all the sausages, all the salt fish in the world, seized me and held me in its teeth. In all the world there was nothing but Food—glorious Food. And beer—October beer. The world was one enormous belly—there was no higher heaven than the paradise of Cram and Gorge. All of the agony of the mind was here forgotten. What did these people know about books? What did they know about pictures? What did they know about the million tumults of the soul, the conflict and the agony of the spirit, the hopes, fears, hatreds, failures, and ambitions, the whole fevered complex of modern life? These people lived for nothing but to eat and drink—and they were right.

The doors of the great hall kept opening and shutting constantly as the incessant stream of beer drinkers pressed patiently in. And from within I heard the shattering blare of a huge brass band and the roar of five thousand beer-drunk voices, rocking together in the rhythms of "*Trink, Trink, Brüderlein, Trink!*"

Our savage hunger was devouring us: we called loudly to the bustling waitress as she passed us and were told that if we wanted hot food we must go within. But in another moment she sent another woman to our table who was carrying an enormous basket loaded with various cold foods. I took two sandwiches, made most deliciously of onions and small salted fish, and an enormous slice of liver cheese, with a crust about its edges. Heinrich also selected two or three sandwiches, and, having ordered another liter of dark beer apiece, we began to devour our food. Darkness had come on: all of the buildings and amusement devices of the fair were now blazing with a million lights; from the vast irradiant murk of night there rose and fell in wavelike nodes the huge fused roar and mumble of the crowd.

When we had devoured our sandwiches and finished our beer, Heinrich suggested that we now make a determined effort to find seats within the hall, and I, who had heretofore felt a strong repulsion toward the thick air and roaring chaos of the hall, now found to my surprise that I was ready and eager to join the vast crowd of beer-fumed feeders. Obediently now I joined the line of patient Germans who were shuffling slowly through the doors, and in a moment more I found myself enveloped in a cyclone of drunken sound, trampling patiently with a crowd that moved slowly around the great room looking for seats. Presently, peering through the veils and planes of shifting smoke that coiled and rose in the great hall like smoke above a battlefield, Heinrich spied two seats at a table near the center of the room, where, on the square wooden platform, forty men dressed in peasant costume were producing a deafening noise upon brass instruments. We plunged directly for the seats, jostling and half-falling over unprotesting bodies that were numb with beer.

And at last, dead center of that roaring tumult, we seated ourselves triumphantly, panting victoriously, and immediately ordered two liters of dark beer and two plates of schweinwurstl and sauerkraut. The band was blaring forth the strains of "*Ein Prosit! Ein Prosit!*" and all over the room people had risen from their tables and were standing with arms linked and mugs upraised while they roared out the great drinking song and swung and rocked rhythmically back and forth.

The effect of these human rings all over that vast and murky hall had in it something that was almost supernatural and ritualistic: something that belonged to the essence of a race was enclosed in those rings, something dark and strange as Asia, something older than the old barbaric forests, something that had swayed around an altar, and had made a human sacrifice, and had devoured burnt flesh.

The hall was roaring with their powerful voices, it shook to their powerful bodies, and as they swung back and forth, it seemed to me that nothing on earth could resist them—that they must smash whatever they came against. I understood now why other nations feared them so; suddenly I was myself seized with a deadly fear of them that froze my heart. I felt as if I had dreamed and awakened in a strange barbaric forest to find a ring of savage barbaric faces bent down above me—blonde-braided, blond-mustached, they leaned upon their mighty spear staves, rested upon their shields of toughened hide, as they looked down. And I was surrounded by them; there was no escape. I thought of all that was familiar to me, and it seemed far away, not only in another world but in another time, sea-sunken in eternity ages hence from the old dark forest of barbaric time. And now I thought almost with warm friendliness of the strange dark faces of the Frenchmen, their cynicism and dishonesty, their rapid and excited voices, their small scale, their little customs; even all their light and trivial adulteries now seemed friendly and familiar, playful, charming, full of grace. Or of the dogged English, with their pipes, their pubs, their bitter beer, their fog, their drizzle, their women with neighing voices and long teeth—all these things now seemed immensely warm, friendly, and familiar to me, and I wished that I were with them.

But suddenly a hand was slipped around my arm, and through that roar and fog of sound I realized that someone was speaking to me. I looked down and there beside me saw the jolly, flushed, and smiling face of a pretty girl. She tugged at my arm good-naturedly and mischievously, spoke to me, nodded her head for me to look. I turned. Beside me was a young man, her companion; he, too, smiling, happy, held his arm for me to take. I looked across and saw Heinrich, his sallow, lonely, pitted face smiling and happy as I had never seen it before. He nodded to me. In an instant we, too, were all linked together, swinging, swaying, singing in rhythm to the roar of those tremendous voices, swinging and swaying, singing all together as the band played "*Ein Prosit.*" Ended at length the music, but now all barriers broken through, all flushed and happy, smiling at one another, we added our own cheers to the crowd's great roar of affirmation when the song was ended. Then laughing, smiling, talking, we sat down again.

And now there was no strangeness any more. There were no barriers any more. We drank and talked and ate together. I drained liter after liter of the cold and heady beer. Its fumes mounted to my brain. I was jubilant and happy. I talked fearlessly in a broken jargon of my little German. Heinrich helped me out from time to time, and yet it did not matter. I felt that I had known all these people all my life, forever. The young girl, with her jolly pretty face, eagerly tried to find out who I was and what I did. I teased her. I would not tell her. I told her a dozen things—that I was a Norwegian, an Australian, a carpenter, a sailor, anything that popped into my head, and Heinrich, smiling, aided and abetted me in my foolishness. But the girl clapped her hands and gleefully cried out, "No," that she knew what I was— I was an artist, a painter, a creative man. She and all the others turned to Heinrich, asking him if this was not true. And smilingly he half inclined his head and said I was not a painter but that I was a writer—he called me a poet. And then all of them nodded their heads in satisfied affirmation; the girl gleefully clapped her hands together again and cried out that she had known it. And now we drank and linked our arms and swayed together in a ring again. And presently, now that it was growing late and people had begun to leave the hall, we, too, got up, the six of us, the girl, another girl, their two young men, and Heinrich and myself, moved out among the singing, happy crowds again, and arm in arm, linked all together, moved singing through the crowds.

And then we left them, finally, four young people from the mass of life and from the heart of Germany, whom I should never see again—four people and the happy, flushed, and smiling face of a young girl. We left them, never having asked their names, nor they our own; we left them and lost them, with warmth, with friendship, with affection, in the hearts of all of us.

We went our way, and they went theirs. The great roar and clamor of the fair suffused and faded behind us, until it had become a vast and drowsy distant murmur. And presently, walking arm and arm together, we reached again the railway station and the ancient heart of Munich. We crossed the Karlsplatz, and at last we reached our dwelling in the Theresien and Louisen streets.

And yet we found we were not tired, we were not ready to go in. The fumes of the powerful and heady beer, and more than that the fumes of fellowship and affection, of friendship and of human warmth, had mounted to our brains and hearts. We knew it was a rare and precious thing, a moment's spell of wonder and of joy, that it must end, and we were loath to see it go.

It was a glorious night, the air sharp, frosty, and the street deserted, and far away, like time, the ceaseless and essential murmur of eternity, the distant, drowsy, wavelike hum of the great fair. The sky was cloudless, radiant, and in the sky there blazed a radiant blank of moon. We paused a moment at our dwelling, then as by mutual instinct walked away. We went along the streets, and presently we had arrived before the enormous, silent, and moon-sheeted blankness of the Old Pinakothek. We passed before it, we entered on the grounds, we strode back and forth, our feet striking cleanly on clean gravel. Arm in arm we talked, we sang, we laughed together. "A poet, yes," he cried, and looked exultantly at the blazing moon. "A poet, *ja*," he cried again. "These people did not know you, and they said you were a poet. And you are."

And in the moonlight, his lonely scarred and pitted face was transfigured by a look of happiness. And we walked the streets, we walked the streets. We felt the sense of something priceless and unutterable, a world invisible that we must see, a world intangible that we must touch, a world of warmth, of joy, of imminent and impending happiness, of impossible delight, that was almost ours. And we walked the streets, we walked the streets. The moon blazed blank and cold out of the whited brilliance of the sky. And the streets were silent. All the doors were closed. And from the distance came the last and muted murmurs of the fair. And we went home.

’E

A RECOLLECTION

All through the fall and winter of that year Mr. Joseph Doaks was living in a flat in London. For him it was a memorable year, and one of the most memorable experiences of that year was his relationship with Daisy Purvis.

Mrs. Purvis was a charwoman who lived at Hammersmith and for years had worked for "unmarried gentlemen" in the fashionable districts known as Mayfair and Belgravia. Mr. Doaks inherited her, so to speak, from a young gentleman of fashion who occupied the little flat in Ebury Street before Mr. Doaks took it over. In appearance, Mrs. Purvis might have been the prototype of a whole class. She was somewhere in the middle forties, a woman inclined to plumpness, of middling height, fair-haired, blue-eyed, and pink-complexioned, with a pleasant, modest face, and a naturally friendly nature. At first, although at all times courteous, her manner toward her new employer was a little distant. She would come in in the morning, and they would formally discuss the business of the day: what they were going to have for lunch, the supplies they were going to "git in," the amount of money it would be necessary to "lay out."

"What would you like for lunch today, sir?" Mrs. Purvis would say. " ’Ave you decided?"

"No, Mrs. Purvis. What would you suggest? Let's see. We had the chump chop yesterday, didn't we, and the sprouts?"

"Yes, sir," Mrs. Purvis would reply, "and the day before, Monday, you may recall, we ’ad rump steak with potato chips."

"Yes, and it was good, too. Well, then, suppose we have rump steak again?"

"Very good, sir," Mrs. Purvis would say, with perfect courtesy, but with a rising intonation of the voice that somehow suggested that she rather thought his choice was not the best one. Feeling this, Mr. Doaks would immediately have doubts. He would say, "Oh, wait a minute. We've been having steak quite often, haven't we?"

"You ’ave ’ad it quite a bit, sir," she would say quietly. "Still, of course—" She would pause and wait.

"Well, then, what would you suggest, Mrs. Purvis?"

"Well, sir, if I may say so, a bit of gammon and peas is rather nice sometimes," with just a trace of diffidence, mixed with an engaging tinge of warmth. "I 'ad a look in at the butcher's as I came by this morning, and the gammon was nice, sir. It *was* a prime bit, sir," she said now with genuine warmth. "Prime."

After this, of course, he could not tell her that he had not the faintest notion what gammon was. He could only look delighted and respond, "Then, by all means, Mrs. Purvis, let's have gammon and peas. I think it's just the thing today."

"Very good, sir." The words had put her back within the fortress of aloofness, had put him back on his heels.

"All right, then, Mrs. Purvis," he said. "Thank you very much."

" 'Kew," she said, most formally and distantly now, and went out, closing the door gently but very firmly after her.

Mr. Doaks had a good life that year. He had never had a servant in his life before. He had been served by many people, but never before had he owned a servant body and soul, to the degree that her life was his life, her interests his interests, her whole concern devoted to the preservation of his welfare. It was perhaps not quite as absolute a devotion as has been here described. Mrs. Purvis had, in fact, for two or three hours of the day, another master, who shared with Doaks her service. This was the little man who kept doctor's offices on the floor below. From one o'clock in the afternoon until four, or thereabout, the doorbell tinkled almost constantly, and Mrs. Purvis was kept busy padding up and down the narrow stairs, admitting or ushering out an incessant stream of patients, all of whom were women.

Doaks used to tease Mrs. Purvis about this unbroken procession of female visitors, and question her on the nature of the doctor's practice. It is probable that she knew that he was not above turning an honest guinea now and then by occasional unorthodoxy. But her loyalty to anyone she served was so unquestioning that when the young man pressed her for information her manner would instantly become beautifully vague, and she would confess that, although she was not familiar with the technical details of Doctor's practice, it was, she believed, devoted to "the treatment of nervous diseases."

"Yes, but what kind of nervous diseases, Mrs. Purvis, and why?" Mr. Doaks would innocently continue. "Why is it always women who have these nervous diseases? Don't the gentlemen ever get nervous, too?"

"Ah-h," said Mrs. Purvis, nodding her head with an ejaculation of knowing profundity. "Ah-h! *There* you 'ave it!"

"Have what, Mrs. Purvis?" Mr. Doaks demanded.

" 'Ave the answer," Mrs. Purvis said. "It's this Moddun Tempo. *That's* what Doctor says," she said, loftily. "It's the pace of Moddun Life—cocktail parties, staying up to all hours, and all of that. In America, I believe, conditions are even worse," said Mrs. Purvis. "Not, of course, that they *really* are," she added quickly, as if fearing her remark might inadvertently have wounded the patriotic sensibilities of her employer. "I mean, after all, not 'avin' been there myself, I wouldn't know, would I? I must say, though," she went on tactfully after a brief pause, "the American ladies *are* very smart, aren't they, sir? They're all so very well turned out, aren't they, sir? You can always tell one when you see one. And then they're *very* clever, aren't they? I mean, quite a number of them 'ave married into the nobility, 'aven't they, sir? You're always readin' somethin' or other about them, and quite a number of them 'ave been received at court. And of course"—her voice fell to just the subtlest shade of unction, and Mr. Doaks' prophetic soul informed him what was coming—"and of course, sir, 'E . . ." Ah, there it was: immortal " 'E," who lived and moved and loved and had his being there at the central sphere of Daisy Purvis's heaven; immortal "'E," the idol of every Purvis everywhere, who, for *their* uses, *their* devotions, had no other name and needed none but " 'E."

"Of course, sir," Mrs. Purvis said, " 'E likes them, doesn't 'E? I'm told 'E's very fond of them. The American ladies must be very clever, sir, because 'E finds them so amusing. There was a picture of 'Im in the news just recently with a party of 'Is friends and a new American lady was among them. At least I'd never seen *'er* face before, and very smart she was, too—a Mrs. Somebody-or-Other—I can't recall the name. But as I say, sir," reverting to her former theme, "it's what Doctor calls the Moddun Tempo, and I've 'eard that conditions in America are"—she hesitated just perceptibly, then with unfailing tactfulness she found the proper phrase—"much the same as they are here."

Her picture of America, derived largely from the pages of tabloid newspapers, of which she was an assiduous devotee, was so delightfully fantastic that Doaks could never find it in his heart to disillusion her. So he dutifully agreed that she was right, and managed skillfully to convey the suggestion that a large proportion of America's female population spent their time going from one cocktail party to another; in fact, practically never got out of bed.

"Ah, then," said Mrs. Purvis, nodding her head wisely with an air of satisfaction, "then *you* know what it means!" And after a just perceptible pause, "Shockin' I calls it."

She called a great many things shocking. In fact, it is doubtful that any choleric Tory in London's most exclusive club could have been more vehemently concerned with the state of the nation than was Daisy Purvis. To listen to Mrs. Purvis talk, one might have thought that she was the heir to enormous estates that had been chief treasures of her country's history since the days of the Norman conquerors, but which were now being sold out of her hands, ravaged and destroyed because she could no longer pay the ruinous taxes which the government had imposed.

They used to discuss these matters long and earnestly, with dire forebodings, windy sighs, and grave shakings of the head. Mr. Doaks would sometimes work the whole night through and finally get to bed at six or seven o'clock in the dismal pea soup of a London morning. Mrs. Purvis would arrive at seven-thirty. If he was not already asleep, he would hear her creep softly up the stairs and go into the kitchen on the top floor. A little later she would rap at his door and come in with an enormous cup, smoking with a beverage, in whose soporific qualities she had the utmost faith.

" 'Ere's a nice, 'ot cup of Ovaltine," said Mrs. Purvis, "to git you off to sleep."

He was probably nearly "off to sleep" already, but this made no difference. If he was not "off to sleep," Mrs. Purvis had the Ovaltine to "git him off" again.

The real truth of the matter was that she wanted to exchange gossip with him, in especial to go over the delectable proceedings of the day's news. She would bring him crisp, fresh copies of the *Times* and *Daily Mail,* and she would have, of course, her own copy of the tabloid paper that she read.

While he propped himself up in bed and drank his Ovaltine, Mrs. Purvis would stand in the doorway, rattle her tabloid with a peremptory gesture, and thus begin: "Shockin', I calls it!"

"Why, 'ere now, listen to this, if you please!" she would say indignantly, and read as follows: " 'It was announced yesterday, through the offices of the Messrs. Merigrew & Raspe, solicitors to 'is Grace, the Duke of Basingstoke, that 'is Grace 'as announced the sale of 'is estate at Chipping Cudlington in Gloucestershire. The estate, comprising sixteen thousand acres, of which eight thousand are in 'unting preserve, and including Basingstoke 'All, one of the finest examples of early Tudor architecture in the kingdom, 'as been in the possession of 'is Grace's family since the fifteenth century. Representatives of the Messrs. Merigrew & Raspe stated, 'owever, that because of the enormous increase in estate and income taxes since the war, 'is Grace feels that it is no longer possible for 'im to maintain the estate, and 'e is accordingly putting it up for sale. This means, of course, that the number of 'is Grace's private estates 'as now been reduced to three, Fothergill 'All in Devonshire, Wintringham in Yorkshire, and the Castle of Loch McTash, 'is 'unting preserve in Scotland. 'Is Grace, it is said, 'as stated recently to friends that if something is not done to check the present ruinous trend toward higher taxation, there will not be a single great estate in England remaining in the 'ands of its original owners within a 'undred years.' "

"Ah-h," said Mrs. Purvis, nodding with an air of knowing confirmation as she finished reading this dolorous item. "There you 'ave it! Just as 'is Grace says, we're losin' all of our great estates. And wot's the reason? Why, the owners can no longer afford to pay the taxes—ruinous, 'e calls 'em, and 'e's right. If it keeps up, you mark my words, the nobility'll 'ave no place left to live. A lot of 'em are migratin' already," she said darkly.

"Migrating where, Mrs. Purvis?"

"Why," she said, "to France, to Italy, places on the Continent. They've all let their estates go. They've gone abroad to live. And why? Because the taxes are too 'igh. Shockin', I calls it!"

By this time Mrs. Purvis's pleasant face would be pink with indignation. It was one of the most astonishing demonstrations of concern young Mr. Doaks had ever seen. Again and again he would try to get to the bottom of it. He would bang down his cup of Ovaltine and burst out, "Yes, but good Lord, Mrs. Purvis, why the hell should you worry so much about it? Those people aren't going to starve. Here you get twelve shillings a week from me and eight shillings more from the doctor. He says he's going abroad to live at the end of the year, and I'm going back to America in a few months. You don't even know where you'll be, what you'll be doing, this time next year. And yet you come in here, day after day, and read me this stuff about the Duke of Basingstoke or the Earl of Pentateuch having to give up one of their half-dozen estates, as if you were afraid the whole lot of them would have to go on the dole. You're the one who will have to go on the dole if you get out of work. Those people are not going to suffer, not really, not the way you'll have to."

"Ah-h, yes," she answered, in a tone that was soft and gentle, as if she were speaking of the welfare of a group of helpless children, "but then, we're used to it, *aren't* we? And *they,* poor things, they're not."

It was appalling. He couldn't fathom it. You could call it what you liked; you could call it servile snobbishness, blind ignorance, imbecilic stupidity, but there it was. You couldn't shatter it, you couldn't even shake it. It was one of the most formidable examples of devotion and loyalty he had ever known.

These conversations would go on morning after morning until there was scarcely an impoverished young viscount whose grandeurs and whose miseries had not undergone the reverent investigation of Mrs. Purvis's anguished and encyclopedic care. But always at the end—after the whole huge hierarchy of saints, angels, captains of the host, guardians of the inner gate, and chief lieutenants of the right hand had been reverently inspected down to the minutest multicolored feather that blazed in their heraldic wings— silence would fall. It was as if some great and unseen presence had entered the room. Then Mrs. Purvis would rattle her crisp paper, clear her throat, and with holy quietness pronounce the sainted name of "'E."

"Well," she would say, and as she spoke her face was softened by a glow of tenderness, "I see by the paper 'ere that 'E's got back from the Continent. I wonder what 'E's up to now." And suddenly she laughed, a jolly and involuntary laugh that flushed her pink cheeks almost crimson and brought a mist to her blue eyes. "Ah! I tell you wot," she said, "'E *is* a deep one. You never know wot 'E's been up to. You pick up the paper one day and read where 'E's visitin' some friends in Yawkshire. The next day, before you know it, 'E turns up in Vienna. This time they say 'E's been in Scandinavia—it wouldn't surprise me if 'E's been over there visitin' one of them young princesses. Of course"—her tone was now tinged with the somewhat pompous loftiness with which she divulged her profounder revelations to the incondite Mr. Doaks—"of course, there's been talk about that for some time past. Not that 'E would care! Not 'Im. 'E's too independent, 'E is! 'Is mother found that out long ago. She tried to manage 'Im the way she does the others. Not 'Im! That chap's got a will of 'Is own. 'E'll do wot 'E wants to do and no one will stop 'Im, that's 'ow independent 'E is."

She was silent a moment, reflecting with misty eyes upon the object of her idolatry. Then suddenly her pleasant face again suffused with ruddy color, and a short, rich, almost explosive laugh burst from her as she cried, "The dev-*ill!* You know, they do say that 'E was comin' 'ome one night not long ago, and that"—her voice lowered confidingly—"they do say 'E'd 'ad a bit too much, and"—her voice sank still lower, and in a tone in which a shade of hesitancy was mixed with laughter, she went on—"well, sir, they do say 'E was 'avin' 'Is troubles in gittin' 'ome. They say that really 'E was 'avin' to support himself, sir, by the fence around St. James's Palace. But they do say, sir, that—ooh! ha-ha-ha!"—she laughed suddenly and throatily—"You must excuse me, sir, but I 'ave to larf when I think of it!" And then, slowly, emphatically, with an ecstasy of adoration, Mrs. Purvis whispered, "They do say, sir, that the bobby on duty just outside the palace saw 'Im, and came up to 'Im and said, 'Can I 'elp you, sir?' But not *'Im!* 'E wouldn't be 'elped! 'E's too proud, 'E is! That's the way 'E's always been. I'll tell you wot, 'E is a dev-*ill!*" And still smiling, her strong hands held before her in a worn clasp, she leaned against the door and lapsed into the silences of misty contemplation.

"But Mrs. Purvis," Doaks remarked presently, "do you think he'll ever get married? I mean, do you really, now? After all, he's no chicken any longer, is he? And he must have had lots of chances, and if he was going to do anything about it—"

"Ah!" said Mrs. Purvis, in that tone of lofty recognition that she always used at such a time. "*Ah!* Wot I always says to *that* is, 'E *will!* 'E'll make up 'Is mind to it when 'E 'as to, but not before! 'E won't be driven into it, not 'Im! 'E'll do it when 'E knows it's the proppuh time."

"Yes, Mrs. Purvis," her questioner persisted, "but what is the proper time?"

"Well," said Mrs. Purvis, "after all, there *is* 'Is father, isn't there? And 'Is father is not so young as 'e used to be, *is* 'e?" She was silent for a moment, diplomatically allowing the tactful inference to sink in by itself. "Well, sir," she concluded very quietly, "I mean to say, sir, a time *will* come, sir, won't it?"

"Yes, Mrs. Purvis," the young man persisted, "but *will* it? I mean, can you be sure? You know, you hear all sorts of things—even a stranger like myself hears them. For one thing, you hear that he doesn't want it very much, and then, of course, there *is* his brother, isn't there?"

"Oh, '*im*," said Mrs. Purvis, " '*im!*" For a moment she said nothing more, but had she filled an entire dictionary with the vocabulary of bitter and unyielding hostility, she could not have said more than she managed to convey in the two letters of that tiny little pronoun " '*im*."

"Yes, but," Doaks persisted somewhat cruelly, "after all, he *wants* it, doesn't he?"

" 'E does," said Mrs. Purvis grimly.

"And he *is* married, isn't he?"

" 'E is," said Mrs. Purvis, if anything a trifle more grimly than before.

"And *he* has children, hasn't he?"

" 'E *'as,* yes," said Mrs. Purvis, somewhat more gently. In fact, for a moment her face glowed with its look of former tenderness, but it grew grim again very quickly, and in a moment she said, "But '*im!* Not '*im!*" She was more deeply stirred by this imagined threat to the ascendancy of her idol than Doaks had ever seen her. Her lips worked tremulously for a moment, then she shook her head with a quick movement of inflexible denial and said, "Not 'im." She was silent for a moment more, as if a struggle was going on between her desire to speak and the cool barrier of her natural reserve. Then she burst out, "I tell you, sir, I never liked the look of 'im! Not that one—no!" She shook her head again in a half-convulsive movement; then in a tone of dark confidingness, she almost whispered, "There's something *sly* about 'is face that I don't like! 'E's a sly one, '*e* is, but 'e don't fool *me!*" Her face was now deeply flushed, and she nodded her head with the air of a person who had uttered her grim and final judgment and would not budge from it. "That's my opinion, if you ask me, sir! That's the way I've always felt about 'im. And 'er. '*Er!* She wouldn't like it, *would* she? Not 'arf she wouldn't!" She laughed suddenly, the bitter and falsetto laugh of an angry woman. "Not '*er!* Why, it's plain as day, it's written all over 'er! But a lot of good it'll do 'em," she said grimly. "*We* know wot's wot!" She shook her head again with grim decision. "The *people* know wot's wot; they can't be fooled. So let them get along with it!"

"You don't think, then, that they—"

"*Them!*" said Mrs. Purvis strongly. "*Them!* Not in a million years, sir! Never! Never! . . . 'E"—her voice fairly soared to a cry of powerful conviction—" 'E's the one! 'E's *always* been the one! And when the time comes, sir, 'E—'E will be King!"

April, Late April

I

Autumn was kind to them, winter was long to them—but April, late April, all the gold sang. . . .

Each day he heard her step upon the stairs at noon. By noon, by high, sane noon, with all its lights of health and joy, she was the one he loved, the mistress of his big disordered room, the bringer of marvelous food, the inspired cook, the one whose brisk small footsteps on the stairs outside his door could wake a leaping jubilation in his heart. Her face was like a light and like a music in the light of noon: it was jolly, small, and tender, as delicate as a plum, and as rosy as a flower. It was young and good and full of health and delight; its sweetness, strength, and noble beauty could not be equaled anywhere on earth. He kissed it a thousand times because it was so good, so wholesome, and so radiant in its loveliness.

Everything about her sang out with hope and morning joy and the music of good life. Her little tender face was full of a thousand shifting plays of jolly humor, as swift and merry as a child's, and yet it had in it always, like shadows in the sun, all the profound and sorrowful depths of beauty. And her hands, which were so small, so certain, and so strong, could cook food so maddening that the table of an emperor would have been put to shame beside it, food such as no one else had read, heard, or dreamed about before.

Thus, when he heard her step upon his stairs at noon, her delicate knuckles briskly rapping at his door, she brought the greatest health and joy to him that he had ever known: she came in from the brutal stupefaction of the streets like a cry of triumph, like a shout of music in the blood, like the deathless birdsong in the first light of morning. She was the bringer of hope, the bearer of princely food, the teller of good news. A hundred sights and magical colors which she had seen in the streets that morning, a dozen tales of life and work and business, sprang from her merry lips with the eager insistence of a child, and as he heard her, as he looked at her, he saw and felt her freshness, youth, and loveliness anew.

She got into the conduits of his blood, she began to sing and pulse through the vast inertia of his flesh, still heavied with great clots of sleep, until he sprang up, seized, engulfed, and devoured her, and felt there was nothing on earth he could not do, nothing on earth he could not conquer. She gave a tongue to joy, a certainty to all the music of the Spring whose great pulsations trembled in the gold and sapphire singing of the air.

Everything—the stick-candy whippings of a flag, the shout of a child, the smell of old worn plankings in the sun, the heavy tarry exhalations of the Spring-warm streets, the thousand bobbing, weaving colors and points of light upon the pavements, the smell of the markets, of fruits, flowers, vegetables and loamy earth, and the heavy shattering *baugh* of a great ship as it left its wharf at noon on Saturday—was given intensity, structure, and the form of joy because of her.

She had never been as beautiful as she was that Spring, and sometimes it drove him almost mad to see her look so fresh and fair. Even before he heard her step upon the stair at noon, he always knew that she was there. Sunken in sleep at twelve o'clock, drowned fathoms deep at noon in strange wakeful sleep, his consciousness of her was so great that he knew instantly the moment when she entered the house, whether he heard a sound or not.

She seemed to be charged with all the good and joyful living of the earth, and as she stood there in the high rare light of noon, her little face was as strange and delicate as a flower, as red and tender as a cherry. And in all that was at once both rich and delicate in her little bones, her trim rich figure, slim ankles, full swelling thighs, deep breast, and straight small shoulders, rose lips and flower face, and all the winking lights of her gold hair—she seemed as rare, as rich, as high and grand a woman as any one on earth could be. The first sight of her at noon always brought hope, confidence, and belief, and sent through the huge inertia of his flesh, still drugged with the great anodyne of sleep, a tidal surge of invincible strength.

She would fling her arms around him and kiss him furiously; she would throw herself down beside him on his cot and cunningly insinuate herself into his side, presenting her jolly glowing little face insatiably to be kissed, covered, plastered with a thousand kisses: she was as fresh as morning, as crisp as celery, as delicate and tender as a plum, her rare and tender succulence was so irresistible he felt he could devour her in an instant and entomb her in his flesh forever. And then, when he had embraced her to his will, she would rise and set briskly about the preparation of a meal for him.

There is no spectacle on earth more appealing than that of a beautiful woman in the act of cooking dinner for someone she loves. Thus, the sight of his mistress as, delicately flushed, she bent with the earnest devotion of religious ceremony above the food she was cooking for him was enough to drive him mad with love and hunger.

In such a moment he could not restrain himself. He would get up and begin to pace the room in a wordless ecstasy. He would lather his face for shaving, shave one side of it, and then begin to walk up and down the room again, singing, making strange noises in his throat, staring vacantly out of the window at the tree, pulling books from the shelves, reading a line, a page, sometimes reading her a passage from a poem as she cooked, and then forgetting the book, letting it fall upon the cot or on the floor, until the room was covered with them. Then he would sit on the edge of the cot for minutes, staring vacantly ahead, holding one sock in his hand. Then he would spring up again and begin to pace the room, shouting and singing, with a convulsion of energy surging through his body that could find no utterance and that ended only in a wild goat-like cry of joy.

From time to time he would go to the door of the kitchen where she stood above the stove, and for a moment he would draw into his lungs the maddening fragrance of the food. Then he would fling about the room again, until he could control himself no longer. The sight of her tender face, earnestly bent and focused in its work of love, her sure and subtle movements, and her full lovely figure—together with the maddening fragrance of glorious food, evoked an emotion of tenderness and hunger in him which was unutterable.

He could not say what he wished to say, but he could restrain himself no longer. A wild cry would be torn from his throat, and he would leap upon her. He devoured her face with kisses, crushed her figure in his embrace, dragged her, shrieking protests, but yet delighted with his frenzy, across the room, and hurled her down upon the cot.

Or he would grip her tender thigh between his knees, hug her till she cried out for pain; sometimes he was so mad with joy that he gripped his paws around her slender arms, lifted his face crowing with exuberance, and shook her back and forth violently in the single music of a tongueless ecstasy.

II

Meanwhile, the cat crept trembling at its merciless stride along the ridges of the backyard fence. The young leaves turned and rustled in the light winds of April, and the sunlight came and went with all its sudden shifting hues into the pulsing heart of that enchanted green. The hoof and the wheel went by upon the street, as they had done forever, the man-swarm milled and threaded in the million-footed stupefaction of the streets, and the high, immortal sound of time, murmurous and everlasting, brooded forever in the upper air above the fabulous walls and towers of the city.

And, at such a time, as the exultancy of love and hunger surged in upon them, these were the things they said, the words they spoke:

"Yes! He loves me now!" she cried out in a jolly voice. "He loves me when I cook for him!" she said. "I know! I know!" she went on, with a touch of knowing and cynical humor. "He loves me then, all right!"

"Why—you!" he would say convulsively, shaking her deliberately to and fro as if he could speak no more. "Why, my . . . delicate . . . damned . . .

darling," he concluded, still slowly, but with a note of growing jubilation in his voice. "Why . . . my delicate little plum-skinned wench . . . Love you? . . . Why, damn you, my darling, I adore you! . . . I am so mad about you, my sweet, that I shall have you for my dinner," he said with a gloating softness, shaking her gently to and fro, with a tender savagery of hunger. "Why, you fragrant and juicy little hussy . . . let me kiss your rosy little face for you," he said, gripping her between his knees, and brooding prayerfully over her with a kind of exultant difficulty. "I will kiss you ten thousand times, my sweet girl," he now yelled triumphantly as he choked her in his rapture, "because you are the one who cooks for me—oh! you damned . . . delectable . . . little . . . plum-skinned . . . trollop . . . of a cook!" he cried.

Then for a moment he would step back, releasing her, and breathing slowly and heavily. Her delicate flushed face was lifted with the flowerful thirstiness of a child, eager and unquenchable. His eye fed for a moment on her slender succulence with a deliberate and almost material potency of vision, his lower lip bulged outward sensually, his face smoldered sullenly, and briefly and unknowingly he would lick his chops. A heavy surge of blood began to thud and pulse thickly along his veins, beating heavy and slow at his pulse and temples, making his thighs solid with a brutal potency, and impending warmly in his loins with a slow and sultry menace. It beat slowly down into his hands, curving the paws and filling his fingers with a heavy rending power.

Deliberately he would step forward again, gripping her tender thighs between his knees, impending over her like a cloud crested and gathered darkly with its laden storm. Then, tentatively, he would take her arm and pull it gently like a wing.

"Shall it be a wing," he would say, a little hoarsely, "a tender wing done nicely with a little parsley and a butter sauce? Or shall it be the sweet meat of a haunch done to a juicy turn?"

"*Und ganz im Butter gekocht,*" she cried, with a merry face.

"*Ganz im besten Butter gekocht,*" he said. And suddenly he lifted his face, and wildly, with a beast-like cry past reason, crowed: "O yes! O yes indeed!"

"Or shall it be the lean meat of the rib?" he continued in a moment, "or the ripe melons that go ding-dong in April?" he cried, "or shall it be a delicate morsel now of woman's fingers?" he said with a rising jubilation in his heart, "a trifle of delicate knuckles tinged with paprika!" he cried and thrust them in his mouth, "or the juicy lip?" he said, and kissed her, "or belly, or back, or side, or throat—or her damned delicate apple-cheeks!" he yelled, and pressed her red face fiercely in his palms and fell ravenously upon her with a hundred savage kisses.

"Don't bite my face!" she screamed. "You don't know how it hurts! The last time it was all sore and bitten and full of marks!" she said resentfully.

"Why, damn you, my sweet," he cried, "I will leave my mark upon you so all of them will see what I have done. Why, you lovely little trollop, I will bite your red-apple cheeks from hell to breakfast and feed upon your tender lips forever. I will eat you like honey, you sweet little hussy."

Then, they would draw apart once more, and for a moment she would look at him with a somewhat hurt and reproachful look, and then, shaking her head with a slight bitter smile, she said:

"God, but you're a wonder, you are! How have you the heart to call me names like that!"

"Because I love you so!" he yelled exultantly. "That's why. It's love, pure love, nothing on earth but love!" He would look at her a moment longer with a lustful hunger, and then seize her once again in his fierce grip. "Why, you delicate and delectable little wench!" he cried. "I will eat you, devour you, entomb you in me: I will make you a part of me and carry you with me wherever I go."

She cast her head back suddenly, her face glowed fiercely with a heated and almost swollen intensity, and like a person in a trance, she cried out strongly: "Yes! Yes!"

"I will get you inside of me—yes! here and now!—so that you will be mixed and mingled with my blood for ever."

"Yes!" she cried again, staring upward with a kind of focal savagery of feeling. "Yes! Yes!"

"And I will plaster your cherry cheeks with ten thousand kisses," he said fiercely. "By God, I will!" and then he fell upon her once more.

Presently they drew apart again, both flushed and heated now, and breathing hard. In a moment she said in a soft and yet eager voice;

"Do you like my face?"

He tried to speak, but for a moment he could not. He turned away, flinging his arms up in a wild convulsive movement, and suddenly cried out extravagantly in a singing tone:

"I like her face, and I like her pace, and I like her grace!" And then, because he felt such hunger and such madness in him at the moment, he crowed jubilantly again: "O yes! O yes indeed!"

And she, too, now as absurdly beyond reason as he was, would lift her glowing face, and say with a rich and earnest seriousness:

"And he likes my chase, and he likes my place, and he likes my base!"

Then separately, each of them would begin to dance about the room—he leaping and cavorting, flinging his head back in goat-like cries of joy, she more demurely, singing, with hands spread wing-wise, and with the delicate wheelings and pacings of a waltz.

Suddenly he would pause as the purport of her words came clearly to him for the first time. He would come back to her seriously, accusingly, but with laughter welling up in him and an inclination to convulsive lewdness at the corners of his mouth.

"Why, what is this? What did you say, girl? Like your base?" he would say sternly, but with a vulgar emphasis.

She grew serious for a moment, considering, then her face grew beet-red with a sudden wave of choking laughter:

"Yes!" she screamed. "O God! I didn't know how funny it would sound!" And then rich, yolky screams of laughter filled her throat, clouded her eyes with tears, and echoed about the high bare walls of the room.

"Why, this is shocking talk, my lass!" he would say in tones of chiding condemnation. "Why, woman, I am shocked at you." And then, with a sudden return to that separate jubilation in which their words, it seemed, were spoken not so much to each other as to all the elements of the universe, he would lift his head and sing madly out again: "I am astounded and dumbfounded, and confounded at you, woman!"

"He is astonished and admonished and demolished and abolished!" she cried, as she lifted her red face earnestly to heaven.

"You missed that time; it doesn't rhyme!" he cried. "I'll rhyme you any word you like, my girl!" he now said, with a boastful confidence. "I am a poet, you must know it, give me a woid, I'll sing like a boid!" he said.

"Ceiling!" she cried instantly.

"The ceiling has no feeling," he replied at once. "Table?" he would then suggest.

"The table is unstable," she answered.

"Floors?"

"The floors have no doors," she answered triumphantly.

"The floors have cuspidors," he said. "Kitchen?"

"If you want your lunch I've got to pitch in," she said warningly.

"When you get in there, there'll be a bitch in," he shouted with a roar of laughter. "That's what you should have said!"

Again her face would be touched with a reproachful bitterness. She looked at him accusingly for a moment and then said:

"How can you talk to me like that! How can you say such things to anyone who loves you as I do!"

"Oh—I mean that's where I want to see my witch in," he would amend, and putting his arms around her, he would fall to kissing her again.

III

They were filled with folly, love, and jubilation, and they would not have cared how their words might sound to anyone on earth—how foolish, mad, or sensual. They looted their lives out with an insatiate desire, they loved, embraced, and clung and questioned, imagined, answered, believed, denied, giving the full measure of their lives and then beginning all over with a quenchless thirst—but it was like a great fire burning all the time. They lived ten thousand hours together, and each hour was like the full course of a packed and crowded life. And always it was like hunger: it began like hunger, and it went on forever like a hunger that was never satisfied—he felt a literal, physical, and insatiate hunger that could have eaten her alive. When she was with him, he was mad because he could not have her and consume her utterly as he desired, and when she had left him, he would go mad with thinking of her.

She was central, like an inexorable presence, to every action, every feeling, every memory of his life. It was not that he thought directly of her at all times. It was not that he was unable for a moment to free his brain of an all-obsessing image on which the whole energy of his life was focused. No. Her conquest was ten thousand times more formidable than this. For had she dwelt there in the courts of the heart only as some proud empress throned in the temporal images of the brain, she could perhaps have been expelled by some effort of the will, some savage act of violence and dismissal, some oblivion of debauch, or some deliberate scourging of the soul to hate. But she had entered into the porches of the blood, she had soaked through all the tissues of the flesh, she had permeated the convolutions of the brain until now she inhabited his flesh, his blood, his life, like a subtle and powerful spirit that could never again be driven out any more than a man could drive out of him the blood of his mother, secrete unto himself the blood and tissue of his father's life.

Thus, whether he thought of her with deliberate consciousness or not, she was now present, with a damnable and inescapable necessity, in every act and moment of his life. Nothing was his own any more, not even the faintest, farthest memories of his childhood. She inhabited his life relentlessly to its remotest sources, haunting his memory like a witness to every proud and secret thing that had been his own. She was founded in the center of his life now so that she could never for a second be forgotten, and as if she had dwelt there forever. She was mixed and mingled with his flesh, diffused through all the channels of his life, coming and going with every breath he took with respiring hues of brightness, beating and moving in every pulse.

And sometimes she was the subtle, potent bait of life, the fabled lure of proud evil cities, cunningly painted with the hues of innocence and morning, the evil snare that broke the backs of youth, and spread corruption in the hearts of living men, and took all of their visions and their strength in fee.

And sometimes she was like morning, joy, and triumph, the lights of April, and the glorious and wholesome succulence of good food. Thus, as he stood there, he would smell suddenly and remember again the food she was cooking in the kitchen, and a wild and limitless gluttony, which somehow identified her with the food she cooked, would well up in him. He would grip her savagely in a powerful vise of knees and hands, and cry out in a hoarse and passionate tone: "Food! Food! Food!"

Then he would loosen her from the vise-like grip: they would embrace more gently, she would kiss him and say in a tender and eager tone:

"Are you hungry, are you hungry, my dear?"

"Oh, if music be the food of love, play on Macduff, and damned be him that first cries hold, enough!"

"I'll feed you," she said eagerly. "I'll cook for you; I'll get the food for you, my dear."

"You are my food!" he cried, seizing her again. "You are meat, drink, butter, and bread and wine to me!" he said, with a feeling of hunger and madness rising up in him. "You are my cake, my caviar, you are my onion soup!"

"Shall I make you some onion soup?" she then said eagerly. "Is that what you would like?"

Again the glorious smell of the food would come to him, and he would say: "You are my Yankee pot roast, my broiled tenderloin, my delicate and succulent chop!" shaking her gently to and fro, and covering her small glowing face with kisses.

"Shall I make you a Yankee pot roast? Would you like a chop? Shall I broil you a steak?" she said eagerly.

"Why, you—you—you!" he cried, with a movement of convulsive difficulty. "You are my fresh fruit salad, you are my big yellow salad bowl, you are my crisp green leaves of lettuce, my great ripe pears and oranges, my celery, pineapple, cherries, apples, and the rich French dressing that goes with it."

"Shall I make you one?" she said.

"You are my dinner and my cook in one: you are my girl with the subtle soul and the magical hand, you are the one who feeds me, and now, my sweet pet, now, my delicate darling," he cried, seizing her and drawing her to him, "now my jolly and juicy wench, I am going to have my dinner."

"Yes!" the woman cried, lifting her glowing face and staring straight before her, in a tranced and focal cry of complete surrender. "Yes!"

"Are you my girl? Are you my tender, rich, and juicy girl?" he said.

"Yes," she said.

"Are you my delicate damned darling and my dear?"

"Yes," she said, "I am your darling and you dear!"

"Are you my duck?" he crowed with a fierce exultant joy. "Are you my darling and my duck?"

"Yes," she said, "I am your darling and your duck. I am the duck that loves you," she said.

"Is that my arm?"

"Yes," she said.

"Is that my haunch? Is that my velvet thigh? Are those my ribs? Is that my tender satin hide? Is that my neck? Is that my warm round throat, are these my delicate fingers and my apple-cheeks? Is that my red-rose lip, and the sweet liquor of my juicy tongue?"

"Yes!" she said. "Yes, it is all yours!"

"Can I beat you, my duck?"

"Yes," she said.

"Can I eat you, my sweet pet? Can I broil you, roast you, stew you, have you with a little parsley and a golden buttered sauce?"

"Yes," she said, "in any way you like!"

"Can I devour you? Can I feed my hunger on you? Can I entomb you in my flesh forever?"

And for a moment, a black convulsion of madness, shame, and death swept through his brain as he bent with ravening hunger over her, and he cried out the burden of his hatred and despair:

"Can I feed, replenish, and fill with all the fountains of my life all the unsated ocean of your hot desire? Oh, tell me now! Can I wring from you as a reward for ruin and defeat the yolky cries of prayerful pleading, rich satiety? Can I depend upon you now to drive me mad with shame and horror and defeat, to feed the dead men with the life and passion of a living man? Will you stab me to the entrails of my life in the cruel green of Spring, lapse languorously with soft lying words of noble giving to the embraces of your lovers, betray me to my enemies in April, defeat me with the pride of scorn and the ruinous lusts of the old faithless race of man?"

"Oh, you are mad," she cried, "and your mind is black and twisted with its evil."

But instantly the wave of death and horror would pass out of him as quickly as it came, as if he had not heard her voice—and he would say again with swelling joy and certitude:

"Or can I feed my life on your rich flower, get all your life and richness into me, walk about with you inside me, breathe you into my lungs like harvest, absorb you, eat you, melt you, have you in my brain, my heart, my pulse, my blood forever, to confound the enemy and to laugh at death, to love and comfort me, to strengthen me with certitude and wisdom, to make my life prevail, and to make me sound, strong, glorious, and triumphant with your love forever!"

"Yes!" the woman cried out strongly, with the final, fierce, and absolute surrender of her conquest. "Yes! . . . Yes! . . . Yes! . . . Forever!"

And the cat crept trembling at its merciless stride along the ridges of the backyard fence. The young leaves turned and rustled in the light winds of April, and the sunlight came and went with all its sudden shifting hues into the pulsing heart of that enchanted green. The hoof and the wheel went by upon the street as they had done forever, the man-swarm milled and threaded in the million-footed stupefaction of the streets, and the high, immortal sounds of time, murmurous and everlasting, brooded forever in the upper air above the fabulous walls and towers of the city. And the woman looked at it again and put her hand upon her breast and cried, "Forever!" And all as if it was just the same as it had always been, and both of them were certain it was true.

The Child by Tiger

Tiger, tiger, burning bright
In the forests of the night,
What immortal hand or eye
Could frame thy fearful symmetry?

One day after school, twenty-five years ago, several of us were playing with a football in the yard at Randy Shepperton's. Randy was calling signals and handling the ball. Nebraska Crane was kicking it. Augustus Potterham was too clumsy to run or kick or pass, so we put him at center, where all he'd have to do would be to pass the ball back to Randy when he got the signal.

It was late in October, and there was a smell of smoke, of leaves, of burning in the air. Nebraska had just kicked to us. It was a good kick, too—a high, soaring punt that spiraled out above my head, behind me. I ran back and tried to get it, but it was far and away "over the goal line"—that is to say, out in the street. It hit the street and bounded back and forth with that peculiarly erratic bounce a football has.

The ball rolled away from me down toward the corner. I was running out to get it when Dick Prosser, Shepperton's new Negro man, came along, gathered it up neatly in his great black paw and tossed it to me. He turned in then, and came on down the alleyway, greeting us as he did. He called all of us "Mister" except Randy, and Randy was always "Cap'n"—"Cap'n Shepperton." This formal address—"Mr." Crane, "Mr." Potterham, "Mr." Spangler, "Cap'n" Shepperton—pleased us immensely, gave us a feeling of mature importance and authority.

"Cap'n Shepperton" was splendid! It had a delightful military association, particularly when Dick Prosser said it. Dick had served a long enlistment in the United States Army. He had been a member of a regiment of crack Negro troops upon the Texas border, and the stamp of the military man was evident in everything he did. It was a joy, for example, just to watch him split kindling. He did it with a power, a kind of military order, that was astounding. Every stick he cut seemed to be exactly the same length and shape as every other one. He had all of them neatly stacked against the walls of the Shepperton basement with such a regimented faultlessness that it almost seemed a pity to disturb their symmetry for the use for which they were intended.

It was the same with everything else he did. His little whitewashed basement room was as spotless as a barracks room. The bare board floor was always cleanly swept, a plain bare table and a plain straight chair were stationed exactly in the center of the room. On the table there was always just one object: an old Bible almost worn out by constant use, for Dick was a deeply religious man. There was a little cast-iron stove and a little wooden box with a few lumps of coal and a neat stack of kindling in it. And against the wall, to the left, there was an iron cot, always precisely made and covered cleanly with a coarse gray blanket.

The Sheppertons were delighted with him. He had come there looking for work just a month or two before, and modestly presented his qualifications. He had, he said, only recently received his discharge from the Army and was eager to get employment, at no matter what wage. He could cook, he could tend the furnace, he knew how to drive a car—in fact, it seemed to us boys that there was very little that Dick Prosser could not do. He could certainly shoot. He gave a modest demonstration of his prowess one afternoon, with Randy's .22, that left us gasping. He just lifted that little rifle in his powerful black hands as if it were a toy, without seeming to take aim, pointed it toward a strip of tin on which we had crudely marked out some bull's-eye circles, and he simply peppered the center of the bull's eye, putting twelve holes through a space one inch square, so fast that we could not even count the shots.

He knew how to box, too. I think he had been a regimental champion. At any rate, he was as cunning and crafty as a cat. He never boxed with us, of course, but Randy had two sets of gloves, and Dick used to coach us while we sparred. There was something amazingly tender and watchful about him. He taught us many things—how to lead, to hook, to counter and to block—but he was careful to see that we did not hurt each other.

He knew about football, too, and today he paused, a powerful, respectable-looking Negro man of thirty years or more, and watched us for a moment as we played.

Randy took the ball and went up to him. "How do you hold it, Dick?" he said. "Is this right?"

Dick watched him attentively as he gripped the ball, and held it back over his shoulder. The Negro nodded approvingly and said, "That's right, Cap'n Shepperton. You've got it. Only," he said gently, and now took the ball in his own powerful hand, "when you get a little oldah, yo' handses gits biggah and you gits a bettah grip."

His own great hand, in fact, seemed to hold the ball as easily as if it were an apple. And holding it so a moment, he brought it back, aimed over his outstretched left hand as if he were pointing a gun, and rifled it in a beautiful, whizzing spiral thirty yards or more to Gus. He then showed us how to kick, how to get the ball off the toe in such a way that it would rise and spiral cleanly. He knew how to do this, too. He must have got off kicks there, in the yard at the Sheppertons', that traveled fifty yards.

He showed us how to make a fire, how to pile the kindling so that the flames shot up cone-wise, cleanly, without smoke or waste. He showed us how to strike a match with the thumbnail of one hand and keep and hold the flame in the strongest wind. He showed us how to lift a weight, how to tote a burden on our shoulders in the easiest way. There was nothing that he did not know. We were all so proud of him. Mr. Shepperton himself declared that Dick was the best man he'd ever had, the smartest darkey that he'd ever known.

And yet? He went too softly, at too swift a pace. He was there upon you sometimes like a cat. Looking before us, sometimes, seeing nothing but the world before us, suddenly we felt a shadow at our backs and, looking up, would find that Dick was there. And there was something moving in the night. We never saw him come or go. Sometimes we would waken, startled, and feel that we had heard a board creak, the soft clicking of a latch, a shadow passing swiftly. All was still.

"Young white fokes, oh, young white gent'mun,"—his soft voice ending in a moan, a kind of rhythm in his hips—"Oh, young white fokes, Ise tellin' *you*"—that soft low moan again—"you gotta love each othah like a brothah." He was deeply religious and went to church three times a week. He read his Bible every night. It was the only object on his square board table.

Sometimes Dick would come out of his little basement room, and his eyes would be red, as if he had been weeping. We would know, then, that he had been reading his Bible. There would be times when he would almost moan when he talked to us, a kind of hymnal chant that came from some deep and fathomless intoxication of the spirit, and that transported him. For us, it was a troubling and bewildering experience. We tried to laugh it off and make jokes about it. But there was something in it so dark and strange and full of feeling that we could not fathom that our jokes were hollow, and the trouble in our minds and in our hearts remained.

Sometimes on these occasions his speech would be made up of some weird jargon of Biblical phrases, of which he seemed to have hundreds, and which he wove together in this strange pattern of his emotion in a sequence that was meaningless to us, but to which he himself had the coherent clue. "Oh, young white fokes," he would begin, moaning gently, "de dry bones in de valley. I tell you, white fokes, de day is comin' when He's comin' on dis earth again to sit in judgment. He'll put the sheep upon de right hand and de goats upon de left. Oh, white fokes, white fokes, de Armageddon day's a comin', white fokes, an de dry bones in de valley."

Or again, we could hear him singing as he went about his work, in his deep rich voice, so full of warmth and strength, so full of Africa, singing hymns that were not only of his own race but familiar to us all. I don't know where he learned them. Perhaps they were remembered from his Army days. Perhaps he had learned them in the service of former masters. He drove the Sheppertons to church on Sunday morning, and would wait for them throughout the morning service. He would come up to the side door of the church while the service was going on, neatly dressed in his good dark suit, holding his chauffeur's hat respectfully in his hand, and stand there humbly and listen during the course of the entire sermon.

And then, when the hymns were sung and the great rich sound would swell and roll out into the quiet air of Sunday, Dick would stand and listen, and sometimes he would join in quietly in the song. A number of these favorite Presbyterian hymns we heard him singing many times in a low rich voice as he went about his work around the house. He would sing "Who Follows in His Train?" or "Alexander's Glory Song," or "Rock of Ages," or "Onward, Christian Soldiers!"

And yet? Well, nothing happened—there was just "a flying hint from here and there," and the sense of something passing in the night. Turning into the square one day as Dick was driving Mr. Shepperton to town, Lon Everett skidded murderously around the corner, sideswiped Dick, and took the fender off. The Negro was out of the car like a cat and got his master out. Shepperton was unhurt. Lon Everett climbed out and reeled across the street, drunk as a sot at three o'clock. He swung viciously, clumsily, at the Negro, smashing him in the face. Blood trickled from the flat black nostrils and from the thick liver-colored lips. Dick did not move. But suddenly the whites of his eyes were shot with red, his bleeding lips bared for a moment over the white ivory of his teeth. Lon smashed at him again. The Negro took it full in the face again; his hands twitched slightly, but he did not move. They collared the drunken sot and hauled him off and locked him up. Dick stood there for a moment; then he wiped his face and turned to see what damage had been done to the car. No more now, but there were those who saw it who remembered later how the eyes went red.

Another thing: the Sheppertons had a cook named Pansy Harris. She was a comely Negro wench, young, plump, black as the ace of spades, a good-hearted girl with a deep dimple in her cheeks and faultless teeth, bared in a most engaging smile. No one ever saw Dick speak to her. No one ever saw her glance at him, or him at her, and yet that smilingly good-natured wench became as mournful-silent and as silent-sullen as midnight pitch. She went about her work as mournfully as if she were going to a funeral. The gloom deepened all about her. She answered sullenly now when spoken to.

One night toward Christmas she announced that she was leaving. In response to all entreaties, all efforts to find the reason for her sudden and unreasonable decision, she had no answer except a sullen repetition of the assertion that she had to leave. Repeated questionings did finally wring from her a sullen statement that her husband needed her at home. More than this she would not say, and even this excuse was highly suspect, because her husband was a Pullman porter, only home two days a week and well accustomed to do himself such housekeeping tasks as she might do for him.

The Sheppertons were fond of her. They tried to find the reason for her leaving. Was she dissatisfied? "No'm"—an implacable monosyllable, mournful, unrevealing as the night. Had she been offered a better job elsewhere? "No'm"—as untelling as before. If they offered her more wages, would she stay with them? "No'm," again and again, sullen and unyielding until finally the exasperated mistress threw up her hands in a gesture of defeat and said, "All right, then, Pansy. Have it your own way, if that's the way you feel. Only for heaven's sake don't leave us in the lurch until we get another cook."

This, at length, with obvious reluctance, the girl agreed to. Then, putting on her hat and coat and taking her bag of "leavings" she was allowed to take home with her at night, she went out the kitchen door and made her sullen and morose departure.

This was Saturday night, a little after eight o'clock. That afternoon Randy and I had been fooling around the basement and, seeing that Dick's door was slightly ajar, we looked in to see if he was there. The little room was empty, swept and spotless, as it had always been.

But we didn't notice that! We saw it! At the same moment, our breaths caught sharply in a gasp of startled wonderment. Randy was the first to speak. "Look!" he whispered. "Do you see it?"

See it! My eyes were glued upon it. Squarely across the bare board table, blue-dull, deadly in its murderous efficiency, lay a modern repeating rifle. Beside it lay a box containing one hundred rounds of ammunition, and behind it, squarely in the center, face downward on the table, was the familiar cover of Dick's worn old Bible.

Then he was on us like a cat. He was there like a great dark shadow before we knew it. We turned, terrified. He was there above us, his thick lips bared above his gums, his eyes gone small and red as rodents'.

"Dick!" Randy gasped, and moistened his dry lips. "Dick!" he fairly cried now.

It was all over like a flash. Dick's mouth closed. We could see the whites of his eyes again. He smiled and said softly, affably, "Yes, suh, Cap'n Shepperton. Yes, suh! You gent'mun lookin' at my rifle?" he said, and moved into the room.

I gulped and nodded my head and couldn't say a word, and Randy whispered, "Yes." And both of us still stared at him, with an expression of appalled and fascinated interest.

Dick shook his head and chuckled. "Can't do without my rifle, white fokes. No, suh!" he shook his head good-naturedly again. "Ole Dick, he's—he's—he's an ole Ahmy man, you know. If they take his rifle away from him, why, that's just like takin' candy from a little baby. Yes, suh!" he chuckled, and picked the weapon up affectionately. "Ole Dick felt Christmas comin' on—he—he—I reckon he must have felt it in his bones"—he chuckled—"so I been savin' up my money. I just thought I'd hide this heah and keep it as a big supprise fo' the young white fokes untwil Christmas morning.

Then I was goin' to take the young white fokes out and show 'em how to shoot."

We had begun to breathe more easily now, and almost as if we had been under the spell of the Pied Piper of Hamelin, we had followed him, step by step into the room.

"Yes, suh," Dick chuckled, "I was just fixin' to hide this gun away twill Christmas Day, but Cap'n Shepperton—hee!" He chuckled heartily and slapped his thigh. "You can't fool ole Cap'n Shepperton. He just must've smelled this ole gun right out. He comes right in and sees it befo' I has a chance to tu'n around. . . . Now, white fokes"—Dick's voice fell to a tone of low and winning confidence—"now that you's found out, I'll tell you what I'll do. If you'll just keep it a supprise from the other white fokes twill Christmas Day, I'll take all you gent'mun out and let you shoot it. Now, cose," he went on quietly, with a shade of resignation, "if you want to tell on me, you can, but"—here his voice fell again, with just the faintest yet most eloquent shade of sorrowful regret—"ole Dick was lookin' fahwad to this; hopin' to give all the white fokes a supprise Christmas Day."

We promised earnestly that we would keep his secret as if it were our own. We fairly whispered our solemn vow. We tiptoed away out of the little basement room as if we were afraid our very footsteps might betray the partner of our confidence.

This was four o'clock on Saturday afternoon. Already, there was a somber moaning of the wind, gray storm clouds sweeping over. The threat of snow was in the air.

Snow fell that night. It came howling down across the hills. It swept in on us from the Smokies. By seven o'clock the air was blind with sweeping snow, the earth was carpeted, the streets were numb. The storm howled on, around houses warm with crackling fires and shaded light. All life seemed to have withdrawn into thrilling isolation. A horse went by upon the street with muffled hoofs. Storm shook the houses. The world was numb. I went to sleep upon this mystery, lying in the darkness, listening to that exultancy of storm, to that dumb wonder, that enormous and attentive quietness of snow, with something dark and jubilant in my soul I could not utter.

A little after one o'clock that morning I was awakened by the ringing of a bell. It was the fire bell of the city hall, and it was beating an alarm—a hard fast stroke that I had never heard before. Bronze with peril, clangorous through the snow-numbed silence of the air, it had a quality of instancy and menace I had never known before. I leaped up and ran to the window to look for the telltale glow against the sky. But almost before I looked, those deadly strokes beat in upon my brain the message that this was no alarm for fire. It was a savage clangorous alarm to the whole town, a brazen tongue to warn mankind against the menace of some peril, secret, dark, and un-known, greater than fire or flood could ever be.

I got instantly, in the most overwhelming and electric way, the sense that the whole town had come to life. All up and down the street the houses were beginning to light up. Next door, the Shepperton house was ablaze with light from top to bottom. Even as I looked, Mr. Shepperton, wearing an overcoat over his pajamas, ran down the snow-covered steps and padded out across the snow-covered walk toward the street.

People were beginning to run out of doors. I heard excited shouts and questions everywhere. I saw Nebraska Crane come pounding down the middle of the street. I knew that he was coming for me and Randy. As he ran by Sheppertons', he put his fingers to his mouth and whistled piercingly. It was a signal we all knew.

I was all ready by the time he came running down the alley toward our cottage. He hammered on the door; I was already there.

"Come on!" he said, panting with excitement, his black eyes burning with an intensity I'd never seen before. "Come on!" he cried. We were halfway out across the yard by now. "It's that nigger. He's gone crazy and is running wild."

"Wh-wh-what nigger?" I gasped, pounding at his heels. Even before he spoke, I had the answer. Mr. Crane had already come out of his house, buttoning his heavy policeman's overcoat as he came. He had paused to speak for a moment to Mr. Shepperton, and I heard Shepperton say quickly, in a low voice, "Which way did he go?"

Then I heard somebody cry, "It's that nigger of Shepperton's!"

Mr. Shepperton turned and went quickly back across his yard toward the house. His wife and two girls stood huddled in the open doorway, white, trembling, holding themselves together, their arms thrust into the wide sleeves of their kimonos.

The telephone in the Sheppertons' house was ringing like mad, but no one was paying any attention to it. I heard Mrs. Shepperton say quickly, as he ran up the steps, "Is it Dick?" He nodded and passed her brusquely, going toward the phone.

At this moment Nebraska whistled piercingly again upon his fingers, and Randy Shepperton ran past his mother and down the steps. She called sharply to him. He paid no attention to her. When he came up, I saw that his fine thin face was white as a sheet. He looked at me and whispered, "It's Dick!" And in a moment, "They say he's killed four people."

"With—" I couldn't finish.

Randy nodded dumbly, and we both stared there for a minute, aware now of the murderous significance of the secret we had kept, with a sudden sense of guilt and fear, as if somehow the crime lay on our shoulders.

Across the street a window banged up in the parlor of the Suggs's house, and Old Man Suggs appeared in the window, clad only in his nightgown, his brutal old face inflamed with excitement, his shock of silvery white hair awry, his powerful shoulders, and his thick hands gripping his crutches.

"He's coming this way!" he bawled to the world in general. "They say he lit out across the square! He's heading out in this direction!"

Mr. Crane paused to yell back impatiently over his shoulder, "No, he went down South Dean Street! He's heading for Wilton and the river! I've already heard from headquarters!"

Automobiles were beginning to roar and sputter all along the street. Across the street I could hear Mr. Potterham sweating over his. He would whirl the crank a dozen times or more; the engine would catch for a moment, cough and putter, and then die again. Gus ran out-of-doors with a kettle of boiling water and began to pour it feverishly down the radiator spout.

Mr. Shepperton was already dressed. We saw him run down the back steps toward the carriage house. All three of us, Randy, Nebraska, and myself, streaked down the alleyway to help him. We got the old wooden doors open. He went in and cranked the car. It was a new one, and started up at once. Mr. Shepperton backed out into the snowy drive. We all clambered up on the running board. He spoke absently, saying, "You boys stay here. . . . Randy, your mother's calling you," but we tumbled in, and he didn't say a word.

He came backing down the alleyway at top speed. We turned into the street and picked up Mr. Crane at the corner. We lit out for town, going at top speed. Cars were coming out of alleys everywhere. We could hear people shouting questions and replies at one another. I heard one man shout, "He's killed six men!"

I don't think it took us over five minutes to reach the square, but when we got there, it seemed as if the whole town was there ahead of us. Mr. Shepperton pulled up and parked the car in front of the city hall. Mr. Crane leaped out and went pounding away across the square without another word to us.

From every corner, every street that led into the square, people were streaking in. One could see the dark figures of running men across the white carpet of the square. They were all rushing in to one focal point.

The southwest corner of the square where South Dean Street came into it was like a dog fight. Those running figures streaking toward that dense crowd gathered there made me think of nothing else so much as a fight between two boys upon the playgrounds of the school at recess time. The way the crowd was swarming in was just the same.

But then I *heard* a difference. From that crowd came a low and growing mutter, an ugly and insistent growl, of a tone and quality I had never heard before. But I knew instantly what it meant. There was no mistaking the blood note in that foggy growl. And we looked at one another with the same question in the eyes of all.

Only Nebraska's coal-black eyes were shining now with a savage sparkle even they had never had before. "Come on," he said in a low tone, exultantly. "They mean business this time, sure. Let's go." And he darted away toward the dense and sinister darkness of the crowd.

Even as we followed him, we heard coming toward us now, growing, swelling at every instant, one of the most savagely mournful and terrifying sounds that night can know. It was the baying of the hounds as they came up upon the leash from Niggertown. Full-throated, howling deep, the savagery of blood was in it, and the savagery of man's guilty doom was in it, too.

They came up swiftly, fairly baying at our heels as we sped across the snow-white darkness of the square. As we got up to the crowd, we saw that it had gathered at the corner where my uncle's hardware store stood. Cash Eager had not yet arrived, but, facing the crowd which pressed in on them so close and menacing that they were almost flattened out against the glass, three or four men were standing with arms stretched out in a kind of chain, as if trying to protect with the last resistance of their strength and eloquence the sanctity of private property.

Will Hendershot was mayor at that time, and he was standing there, arm to arm with Hugh McNair. I could see Hugh, taller by half a foot than anyone around him, his long gaunt figure, the gaunt passion of his face, even the attitude of his outstretched bony arms, strangely, movingly Lincolnesque, his one good eye blazing in the cold glare of the corner lamp with a kind of cold inspired Scotch passion.

"Wait a minute! You men wait a minute!" he cried. His words cut out above the clamor of the mob like an electric spark. "You'll gain nothing, you'll help nothing, if you do this thing!"

They tried to drown him out with an angry and derisive roar. He shot his big fist up into the air and shouted at them, blazed at them with that cold single eye, until they had to hear. "Listen to me!" he cried. "This is no time for mob law! This is no case for lynch law! This is a time for law and order! Wait till the sheriff swears you in! Wait until Cash Eager comes! Wait—"

He got no further. "Wait, hell!" cried someone. "We've waited long enough! We're going to get that nigger!"

The mob took up the cry. The whole crowd was writhing angrily now, like a tormented snake. Suddenly there was a flurry in the crowd, a scattering. Somebody yelled a warning at Hugh McNair. He ducked quickly, just in time. A brick whizzed past him, smashing the plate glass window into fragments.

And instantly a bloody roar went up. The crowd surged forward, kicked the fragments of jagged glass away. In a moment the whole mob was storming into the dark store. Cash Eager got there just too late. He arrived in time to take out his keys and open the front doors, but as he grimly remarked, it was like closing the barn doors after the horse had been stolen.

The mob was in and helped themselves to every rifle they could find. They smashed open cartridge boxes and filled their pockets with the loose cartridges. Within ten minutes, they had looted the store of every rifle, every cartridge, in the stock. The whole place looked as if a hurricane had hit it. The mob was streaming out into the street, was already gathering round the dogs a hundred feet or so away, who were picking up the scent at that point, the place where Dick had halted last before he had turned and headed south, downhill along South Dean Street toward the river. The hounds were scampering about, tugging at the leash, moaning softly with their noses pointed to the snow, their long ears flattened down. But in that light and in that snow it almost seemed no hounds were needed to follow Dick. Straight as a string, right down the center of the sheeted car tracks, the Negro's footsteps led away until they vanished downhill in the darkness.

But now, although the snow had stopped, the wind was swirling through the street and making drifts and eddies in the snow. The footprints were fading rapidly. Soon they would be gone.

The dogs were given their head. They went straining on softly, sniffing at the snow; behind them the dark masses of the mob closed in and followed. We stood there watching while they went. We saw them go on down the street and vanish. But from below, over the snow-numbed stillness of the air, the vast low mutter of the mob came back to us.

Men were clustered now in groups. Cash Eager stood before his shattered window, ruefully surveying the ruin. Other men were gathered around the big telephone pole at the corner, pointing out two bullet holes that had been drilled cleanly through it. And swiftly, like a flash, running from group to group, like a powder train of fire, the full detail of that bloody chronicle of night was pieced together.

This was what had happened. Somewhere between nine and ten o'clock that night, Dick Prosser had gone to Pansy Harris's shack in Niggertown. Some say he had been drinking when he went there. At any rate, the police had later found the remnants of a gallon jug of raw corn whiskey in the room. What happened, what passed between them, was never known. And, besides, no one was greatly interested. It was a crazy nigger with "another nigger's woman."

Shortly after ten o'clock that night, the woman's husband appeared upon the scene. The fight did not start then. According to the woman, the real trouble did not come until an hour or more after his return.

The men drank together. Each was in an ugly temper. Shortly before midnight, they got into a fight. Harris slashed at Dick with a razor. In a second they were locked together, rolling about and fighting like two madmen on the floor. Pansy Harris went screaming out-of-doors and across the street into a dingy little grocery store.

A riot call was telephoned at once to police headquarters on the public square. The news came in that a crazy nigger had broken loose on Gulley Street in Niggertown, and to send help at once. Pansy Harris ran back across the street toward her little shack.

As she got there, her husband, with blood streaming from his face, staggered out into the street, with his hands held up protectively behind his head in a gesture of instinctive terror. At the same moment, Dick Prosser appeared in the doorway of the shack, deliberately took aim with his rifle, and shot the fleeing Negro squarely through the back of the head. Harris dropped forward on his face into the snow. He was dead before he hit the ground. A huge dark stain of blood-soaked snow widened out around him. Dick Prosser seized the terrified Negress by the arm, hurled her into the shack, bolted the door, pulled down the shades, blew out the lamp, and waited.

A few minutes later, two policemen arrived from town. They were a young constable named Willis, and John Grady, a lieutenant of police. The policemen took one look at the bloody figure in the snow, questioned the frightened keeper of the grocery store, and after consulting briefly, produced their weapons and walked out into the street.

Young Willis stepped softly down onto the snow-covered porch of the shack, flattened himself against the wall between the window and the door, and waited. Grady went around to the side and flashed his light through the window, which, on this side, was shadeless. Grady said in a loud tone: "Come out of there!"

Dick's answer was to shoot him cleanly through the wrist. At the same moment Willis kicked the door in and without waiting, started in with pointed revolver. Dick shot him just above the eyes. The policeman fell forward on his face.

Grady came running out around the house, rushed into the grocery store, pulled the receiver of the old-fashioned telephone off the hook, rang frantically for headquarters and yelled out across the wire that a crazy nigger had killed Sam Willis and a Negro man, and to send help.

At this moment Dick stepped out across the porch into the street, aimed swiftly through the dirty window of the little store, and shot John Grady as he stood there at the phone. Grady fell dead with a bullet that entered just below his left temple and went out on the other side.

Dick, now moving in a long, unhurried stride that covered the ground with catlike speed, turned up the long snow-covered slope of Gulley Street and began his march toward town. He moved right up the center of the street, shooting cleanly from left to right as he went. Halfway up the hill, the second-story window of a two-story Negro tenement flew open. An old Negro man stuck out his ancient head of cotton wool. Dick swiveled and shot casually from his hip. The shot tore the top of the old Negro's head off.

By the time Dick reached the head of Gulley Street, they knew he was coming. He moved steadily along, leaving his big tread cleanly in the middle of the sheeted street, shifting a little as he walked, swinging his gun crosswise before him. This was the Negro Broadway of the town, but where those poolrooms, barbershops, drugstores, and fried-fish places had been loud with dusky life ten minutes before, they were now silent as the ruins of Egypt. The word was flaming through the town that a crazy nigger was on the way. No one showed his head.

Dick moved on steadily, always in the middle of the street, reached the end of Gulley Street, and turned into South Dean—turned right, uphill, in the middle of the car tracks, and started toward the square. As he passed the lunchroom on the left, he took a swift shot through the window toward the counter man. The fellow ducked behind the counter. The bullet crashed into the wall above his head.

Meanwhile, at police headquarters, the sergeant had sent John Chapman out across the square to head Dick off. Mr. Chapman was perhaps the best-liked man on the force. He was a pleasant florid-faced man of forty-five, with curling brown mustaches, congenial and good-humored, devoted to his family, courageous, but perhaps too kindly and too gentle for a good policeman.

John Chapman heard the shots and ran. He came up to the corner by Eager's hardware store just as Dick's last shot went crashing through the lunchroom window. Mr. Chapman took up his post there at the corner behind the telephone post that stood there at that time. Mr. Chapman, from his vantage point behind this post, took out his revolver and shot directly at Dick Prosser as he came up the street.

By this time Dick was not more than thirty yards away. He dropped quietly on one knee and aimed. Mr. Chapman shot again and missed. Dick fired. The high-velocity bullet bored through the post a little to one side. It grazed the shoulder of John Chapman's uniform and knocked a chip out of the monument sixty yards or more behind him in the center of the square.

Mr. Chapman fired again and missed. And Dick, still coolly poised upon his knee, as calm and as steady as if he were engaging in rifle practice, fired again, drilled squarely through the center of the post and shot John Chapman through the heart. Then Dick rose, pivoted like a soldier in his tracks, and started down the street, straight as a string, right out of town.

This was the story as we got it, pieced together like a train of fire among the excited groups of men that clustered there in trampled snow before the shattered glass of Eager's store.

But now, save for these groups of talking men, the town again was silent. Far off in the direction of the river, we could hear the mournful baying of the hounds. There was nothing more to see or do. Cash Eager stooped, picked up some fragments of the shattered glass, and threw them in the window. A policeman was left on guard, and presently all five of us—Mr. Shepperton, Cash Eager, and we three boys—walked back across the square and got into the car and drove home again.

But there was no more sleep, I think, for anyone that night. Black Dick had murdered sleep. Toward daybreak, snow began to fall again. The snow continued through the morning. It was piled deep in gusting drifts by noon. All footprints were obliterated; the town waited, eager, tense, wondering if the man would get away.

They did not capture him that day, but they were on his trail. From time to time throughout the day, news would drift back to us. Dick had turned east along the river and gone out for some miles along the Fairchilds road. There, a mile or two from Fairchilds, he crossed the river at the Rocky Shallows.

Shortly after daybreak, a farmer from the Fairchilds section had seen him cross a field. They picked the trail up there again and followed it across the field and through a wood. He had come out on the other side and got down into the Cane Creek section, and there, for several hours, they lost him. Dick had gone right down into the icy water of the creek and walked upstream a mile or so. They brought the dogs down to the creek, to where he broke the trail, took them over to the other side, and scented up and down.

Toward five o'clock that afternoon they picked the trail up on the other side, a mile or more upstream. From that point on, they began to close in on him. The dogs followed him across the fields, across the Lester road, into a wood. One arm of the posse swept around the wood to head him off. They knew they had him. Dick, freezing, hungry, and unsheltered, was hiding in that wood. They knew he couldn't get away. The posse ringed the wood and waited until morning.

At 7:30 the next morning he made a break for it. He got through the line without being seen, crossed the Lester road, and headed back across the field in the direction of Cane Creek. And there they caught him. They saw him plunging through the snowdrift of a field. A cry went up. The posse started after him.

Part of the posse were on horseback. The men rode in across the field. Dick halted at the edge of the wood, dropped deliberately upon one knee, and for some minutes held them off with rapid fire. At two hundred yards he dropped Doc Lavender, a deputy, with a bullet through the throat.

The posse came in slowly, in an encircling, flankwise movement. Dick got two more of them as they closed in, and then, as deliberately as a trained soldier retreating in good order, still firing as he went, he fell back through the wood. At the other side he turned and ran down through a sloping field that bordered on Cane Creek. At the creek edge, he turned again, knelt once more in the snow, and aimed.

It was Dick's last shot. He didn't miss. The bullet struck Wayne Foraker, a deputy, dead center in the forehead and killed him in his saddle. Then the posse saw the Negro aim again, and nothing happened. Dick snapped the breech open savagely, then hurled the gun away. A cheer went up. The posse came charging forward. Dick turned, stumblingly, and ran the few remaining yards that separated him from the cold and rock-bright waters of the creek.

And here he did a curious thing—a thing that no one ever wholly understood. It was thought that he would make one final break for freedom, that he would wade the creek and try to get away before they got to him. Instead, he sat down calmly on the bank, and as quietly as if he were seated on his cot in an Army barracks, he unlaced his shoes, took them off, placed them together neatly at his side, and then stood up like a soldier, erect, in his bare bleeding feet, and faced the mob.

The men on horseback reached him first. They rode up around him and discharged their guns into him. He fell forward in the snow, riddled with bullets. The men dismounted, turned him over on his back, and all the other men came in and riddled him. They took his lifeless body, put a rope around his neck, and hung him to a tree. Then the mob exhausted all their ammunition on the riddled carcass.

By nine o'clock that morning the news had reached the town. Around eleven o'clock, the mob came back along the river road. A good crowd had gone out to meet it at the Wilton Bottoms. The sheriff rode ahead. Dick's body had been thrown like a sack and tied across the saddle of the horse of one of the deputies he had killed.

It was this way, bullet-riddled, shot to pieces, open to the vengeful and morbid gaze of all, that Dick came back to town. The mob came back right to its starting point in South Dean Street. They halted there before an undertaking parlor, not twenty yards away from where Dick had killed John Chapman. They took that ghastly mutilated thing and hung it in the window of the undertaker's place, for every woman, man, and child in town to see.

And it was so we saw him last. We said we wouldn't look. But in the end we went. And I think it has always been the same with people. They protest. They shudder. And they say they will not go. But in the end they always have their look.

At length we went. We saw it, tried wretchedly to make ourselves believe that once this thing had spoken to us gently, had been partner to our confidence, object of our affection and respect. And we were sick with nausea and fear, for something had come into our lives we could not understand.

We looked and whitened to the lips, and craned our necks and looked away, and brought unwilling, fascinated eyes back to the horror once again, and craned and turned again, and shuffled in the slush uneasily, but could not go. And we looked up at the leaden reek of day, the dreary vapor of the sky, and, bleakly, at these forms and faces all around us—the people come to gape and stare, the poolroom loafers, the town toughs, the mongrel conquerors of earth—and yet, familiar to our lives and to the body of our whole experience, all known to our landscape, all living men.

And something had come into life—into our lives—that we had never known about before. It was a kind of shadow, a poisonous blackness filled with bewildered loathing. The snow would go, we knew; the reeking vapors of the sky would clear away. The leaf, the blade, the bud, the bird, then April would come back again, and all of this would be as it had ever been. The homely light of day would shine again familiarly. And all of this would vanish as an evil dream. And yet not wholly so. For we would still remember the old dark doubt and loathing of our kind, of something hateful and unspeakable in the souls of men. We knew that we should not forget.

Beside us a man was telling the story of his own heroic accomplishments to a little group of fascinated listeners. I turned and looked at him. It was Ben Pounders of the ferret face, the furtive and uneasy eye, Ben Pounders of the mongrel mouth, the wiry muscles of the jaw, Ben Pounders, the collector of usurious lendings to the blacks, the nigger hunter. And now Ben Pounders boasted of another triumph. He was the proud possessor of another scalp.

"I was the first one to git in a shot," he said. "You see that hole there?" He pointed with a dirty finger. "That big hole right above the eye?" They turned and goggled with a drugged and feeding stare.

"That's mine," the hero said, turned briefly to the side and spat tobacco juice into the slush. "That's where I got him. Hell, after that he didn't know what hit him. He was dead before he hit the ground. We all shot him full of holes then. We sure did fill him full of lead. Why, hell yes," he declared, with a decisive movement of his head, "we counted up to two hundred and eighty-seven. We must have put three hundred holes in him."

And Nebraska, fearless, blunt, outspoken, as he always was, turned abruptly, put two fingers to his lips, and spat between them, widely and contemptuously.

"Yeah—*we!*" he grunted. "*We* killed a big one! We—we killed a ba'r, we did! . . . Come on, boys," he said gruffly. "Let's be on our way!"

And, fearless and unshaken, untouched by any terror or any doubt, he moved away. And two white-faced nauseated boys went with him.

A day or two went by before anyone could go into Dick's room again. I went in with Randy and his father. The little room was spotless, bare, and tidy as it had always been. But even the very austerity of that little room now seemed terribly alive with the presence of its black tenant. It was Dick's room. We all knew that. And somehow we all knew that no one else could ever live there again.

Mr. Shepperton went over to the table, picked up Dick's old Bible that still lay there, open and face downward, held it up to the light, and looked at it, at the place that Dick had marked when he last read in it. And in a moment, without speaking to us, he began to read in a quiet voice:

"'The Lord is my shepherd; I shall not want.

"'He maketh me to lie down in green pastures: he leadeth me beside the still waters.

"'He restoreth my soul: he leadeth me in the paths of righteousness for his name's sake.

"'Yea, though I walk through the valley of the shadow of death, I will fear no evil: for thou art with me—'"

Then Mr. Shepperton closed the book and put it down upon the table, the place where Dick had left it. And we went out the door, he locked it, and we went back into that room no more forever.

The years passed, and all of us were given unto time. We went our ways. But often they would turn and come again, these faces and these voices of the past, and burn there in my memory again, upon the muted and immortal geography of time.

And all would come again—the shout of the young voices, the hard thud of the kicked ball, and Dick moving, moving steadily, Dick moving, moving silently, a storm-white world and silence, and something moving, moving in the night. Then I would hear the furious bell, the crowd a-clamor and the baying of the dogs, and feel the shadow coming that would never disappear. Then I would see again the little room that we would see no more, the table and the book. And the pastoral holiness of that old psalm came back to me, and my heart would wonder with perplexity and doubt.

For I had heard another song since then, and one that Dick, I know, had never heard, and one perhaps he might not have understood, but one whose phrases and imagery it seemed to me would suit him better:

> *What the hammer? What the chain?*
> *In what furnace was thy brain?*
> *What the anvil? What dread grasp*
> *Dare its deadly terrors clasp?*
>
> *When the stars threw down their spears*
> *And water'd heaven with their tears*
> *Did He smile His work to see?*
> *Did He who made the lamb make thee?*

"*What* the hammer? *What* the chain?" No one ever knew. It was a mystery and a wonder. There were a dozen stories, a hundred clues and rumors; all came to nothing in the end. Some said that Dick had come from Texas, others that his home had been in Georgia. Some said it was true that he had been enlisted in the Army, but that he had killed a man while there and served a term at Leavenworth. Some said he had served in the Army and had received an honorable discharge, but had later killed a man and had served a term in a state prison in Louisiana. Others said that he had been an Army man, but that he had gone crazy, that he had served a period in an asylum when it was found that he was insane, that he had escaped from this asylum, that he had escaped from prison, that he was a fugitive from justice at the time he came to us.

But all these stories came to nothing. Nothing was ever proved. Men debated and discussed these things a thousand times—who and what he had been, what he had done, where he had come from—and all of it came to nothing. No one knew the answer. But I think that I have found the answer. I think that I know from where he came.

He came from darkness. He came out of the heart of darkness, from the dark heart of the secret and undiscovered South. He came by night, just as he passed by night. He was night's child and partner, a token of the other side of man's dark soul, a symbol of those things that pass by darkness and that still remain, a symbol of man's evil innocence, and the token of his mystery, a projection of his own unfathomed quality, a friend, a brother, and a mortal enemy, an unknown demon, two worlds together—a tiger and a child.

Katamoto

Not more than five hours away from Manhattan, in the capital city of one of the great American States, there is a hill of pleasant green, surmounted by the tremendous edifice of the State Capitol. That innocent-looking hill might provide some future historian of our times with a quite considerable chapter in the history of political manipulation in this country.

The great Capitol Building itself is a monument of spoliation, for of the thirty million dollars it cost, not over half is supposed to have been honestly expended. The remainder found its way, in one fashion or another, into the pockets of the faithful.

And the faithful themselves have not been forgotten by their grateful State. That whole green hill, in fact, is a stately memorial to them. With that touching fidelity to political corruption which in our land keeps the names of its most eminent practitioners green in the hearts of their countrymen, the adoring populace have here memorialized in sculptures of enduring bronze some of the most illustrious scoundrels who ever betrayed a public trust.

There they are, each a little green with age, a little mildewed by the weather, somewhat bespattered on the head with pigeon dung—but noble and enduring to the end. They survey the scene with eyes of far-seeing vacancy as if raptly searching out the possibilities of new corruption in the Civil Service. They start forward from their places with beetling brows, grim mouths, and sheaves of important-looking documents crushed in the hard grip of a bronze hand, as if the sculptor had caught them in the very act of passionately crying, "Never! Never! By Heaven, gentlemen, while the red blood of life flows in the veins of J. Alonzo Guff, let it never be said of him that he betrayed the interests of the working people for less than ten percent!"

I was there again this spring, after an absence of several years, revisiting this pleasant hill and paying my respectful addresses to these honored dead. All of it was much the same as it had always been. The time was dusk, just at the end of one of the first fine days in April: the flowers were bursting from the earth, the grass and trees were coming into life with that feathery delicacy of young green that lasts so short a time and that can never be recaptured, and in the boughs of the fine trees some late birds sang.

Nothing, it seemed, had changed a bit. The immortal dead still kept their sculptured stance, each in his old and proud position, and April had come back again. It was all so calm, so peaceful, somehow so comforting—for in this busy world of swift and brutal change the hill preserved a kind of serene immortality which sweetly said, "All passes—all changes—all is new, save only I, but I remain."

Such, at any rate, was the comforting assurance with which it spoke to me again. And then I saw a change! There had been an addition to that familiar gallery of brazen sculptures. Suddenly I found myself confronted with it, goggling helplessly at it, aghast and shocked and somehow overwhelmed by it, as if I had all at once stumbled upon one of the great pyramids that had *always* been here, but which, in some miraculous way, I had always missed before.

Not that I had actually missed it! For after that first shocked moment of discovery, I saw that the figure was really new and had been put there since my last visit. Neither was there anything in the composition or style of the figure that should have caused me any astonishment. It fitted perfectly in the company of its celebrated brethren. It was punctiliously faithful to all the most cherished traditions of political sculpture. True, the costume was somewhat more modern than the costume of some of its fellows. But aside from this accidental detail of time and fashion, the other elements ran true to form.

There was, for example, the small bronze chair of state behind the figure—such a chair as might befit the dignities of the Roman Senate, with a classically rounded back and the fasces and coat-of-arms of a great State engraven upon it. The figure itself, of course, was standing—and standing in one of the familiar attitudes of statesmanship, one great brazen hoof, complete even to its bronze shoe-laces, heavily advanced before the other, the big jowl-like head lifted in an attitude of grim resolve, and one clenched fist raised in the air above the head, with a fat finger pointing heavenward in a gesture of hoggish majesty.

And yet I was still puzzled. The figure was one of the largest and most costly on the hill, and for a moment I was sorely tried because I could not think of any political crook in recent years who had occupied a position of sufficient magnitude to command a monument of this size.

And then it all came to me in a flash! Of course! This surely could be no other than W. Voorhees Spaugh, who had died and been gathered to his fathers since I was last here and who now, exalted into bronze, was surveying mighty vistas of unexplored pork-barreling with brazen eyes of thoughtful meditation.

I approached and read the legend at the base of his pedestal. Yes, there he was: William Voorhees Spaugh—1856–1928—Semper Fidelis. Here he was, and God had been merciful to His servant until the last. He had been taken away in the full tide of his advancing years before he could ever hear the sinister reverberations of the great crash—or witness the malevolent encroachments of the New Deal. He had gone to his Maker with a peaceful smile on his face and the unshaken conviction that for the faithful there would always be a hog in every trough.

Here he was—fittingly memorialized among his compeers through the generous devotion of a grateful people. Here he was, the man who had created, in one of the greatest of the American States, a political machine which had a record of corrupt efficiency that need not yield its primacy to any other the fathers of the Republic had ever fashioned. Here he was—the man who could carry a million votes around in his vest pocket and "deliver" them to anyone he chose; the man who never needed to ask the count or to find out how and where the result was going because he knew these matters in advance; the man who had been for thirty years the kingmaker of his party, who had named four Presidential candidates from the smoky confines of a hotel room while a thousand sweating delegates milled and stamped and shouted in the convention hall and yet had no more to do with the ultimate decision than a set of rubber stamps. Here he was—the man who is said to have looked over his party's leading candidate at midnight, and while the distinguished aspirant looked back and trembled and made silently his prayers, to have grunted hoarsely, "Hell, let's get another one who's got more chin!"

Well, here he was, all right, where he ought to be. Everything had run magnificently true to form, and W. Voorhees Spaugh had attained in death the brazen eminence that he would have jeeringly refused in life, but that was none the less his due.

And yet—I did not know why, but I was still puzzled, still unsatisfied. It seemed to me that somewhere, somehow—God knows where or how—I had seen this figure before. I don't know what it was, but I think most of all it was the attitude of that brazen fist with the fat finger hoggishly upraised that set off in my memory a powder train of recollection. And all of a sudden, something flared and flashed: an image of a house I lived in and the life I knew, a woman's step upon the stair at noon, the cat that crept along the ridges of the backyard fence, the brief lost moment we had called "forever." I leaned forward in the gathering dusk and peered at the bronze base of the pedestal. And as I read the small and careful letters at one side, traced faintly out in roughened metal, my breath caught sharply and it all came back: K. Katamoto—1929.

In the old house in Eleventh Street where I was living then, Mr. Katamoto occupied the floor below me, and during the course of that year I got to know him very well. I think it might be said that our friendship began in a moment of crisis and continued to a state of security and staunch understanding. Not that Mr. Katamoto ever forgave me when I erred. He was instantly ready to inform me that I had taken a false step again—the word is used advisedly—but he was so infinitely patient, so unflaggingly hopeful of my improvement, so unfailingly good-natured and so courteous, that no one possibly could have been angry or failed to try to mend his ways. I am sure that the thing that saved the situation was Katamoto's gleeful, childlike sense of humor: the man was scarcely more than five feet tall, and small and wiry in his build, and I think my towering height inspired his comic risibilities from the very beginning, because even before I knew him, when we would just pass each other in the hall, he would begin to giggle when he saw me, and then wag a finger at me roguishly, saying, "Tramp-ling! Tramp-ling!"

I thought these words were very mysterious and at first could not fathom their meaning or why the sound of them was sufficient to set him off in a paroxysm of mirth. And yet when he would utter these words and I would look at him in an inquiring sort of way, he would bend double with convulsive laughter, and before I had a chance to say anything, he would stamp at the floor with a tiny foot, shrieking hysterically, "Yis—yis—yis! You are tramp-ling!"—after which he would flee away.

I inferred, however, that these mysterious references to "tramp-ling" had something to do with the size of my feet, for he would always look at them quickly and slyly when he passed me, and then giggle. However, a fuller explanation was presently to be provided me. He came upstairs one afternoon and knocked at my door. When I opened it, he giggled and flashed his teeth and looked somewhat embarrassed. After a moment, with evident hesitancy, he said:

"If you ple-e-e-eze, sir! Will—you—have—some—tea—with—me—yis?" He spoke the words with a kind of deliberate formality, after which he flashed an eager and ingratiating smile at me. I told him I should be glad to, got my coat, and started downstairs with him: he padded swiftly on ahead, his little feet shod in felt slippers that made absolutely no sound.

Half-way down the stairs, as if the sound of my heavy tread had touched his funny bone again, he turned and pointed at my feet, and giggled coyly, "Tramp-ling! You are tramp-ling!" After which he turned and fairly fled away down the stairs, shrieking like a gleeful child. Then he ushered me into his place, introduced me to the slender, agile little Japanese girl, who seemed to stay with him all the time, and brought me back into his studio and served me tea.

It was an amazing place. He had taken the fine old rooms and redecorated them according to the whims of his curious taste. I remember vividly that the big back room had a very crowded, partitioned-off appearance. He had, in fact, for what reasons I never knew, screened off several small compartments with beautiful Japanese screens. In addition, he had constructed a flight of stairs which ran up to a balcony that extended around three sides of the room. And on this balcony I could see a couch, and I judged that he slept there. The room was crowded with little chairs and tables, and there was an opulent-looking couch and cushions. There were a great many small carved objects and a smell of incense.

The center of the room had been left entirely bare save for a big strip of spattered canvas and the plaster model of the enormous hog-like native sons which apparently provided the means of his curious living. He did, I gathered, a thriving business turning out sculptures for expensive speakeasies or immense fifteen-foot statues of native politicians which were to decorate public squares in little towns, or in the State capitals of Arkansas, Nebraska, Iowa, and Wyoming. Where and how he had learned this curious profession I never found out, but he had mastered it somewhere with true Japanese fidelity, and in such a way that his products were apparently in greater demand than those of native sculptors. In spite of his small size and fragile build, the man was a powerful dynamo of energy and could perform the labors of a Titan.

God knows how he did it—where he found the strength. Again and again, in the months that followed, when I came in, I would find the hall below full of sweating, panting movers over whom Katamoto, covered from head to foot with clots of plaster, would hover prayerfully lest they harm his work, twisting his small hands together convulsively, and saying meanwhile with an elaborate, pleading courtesy:

"Now, *if*—*you*—gentlemen! a little! You-u—yis-s—yis-s—yis-s!" with a convulsive grin. "*Oh-h-h!*—yis-s! yis-s!—if you-u—ple-e-eze, sir!—would *down*—a little—yis-s!—yis-s!—yis-s!" he hissed softly with that prayerful grin. And the movers would carry out of the house and stow into their van the enormous piecemeal fragments of some North Dakota Pericles, whose size was such that one would wonder how such a fragile little man could possibly have fashioned such a leviathan as this.

Then the movers would depart, and for a space Mr. Katamoto would loaf and invite his soul. He would come out in the backyard with his girl, the slender, agile little Japanese, and for hours at a time they would play beneath the tree at handball. The pair were usually alone: occasionally, however, they were accompanied by a friend, a young Japanese who would sometimes take part in the game, and who was, I believe, the only visitor they ever had.

Mr. Katamoto would knock the ball up against the projecting brick wall of the house next door and scream with laughter, clapping his small hands together like a child, bending over weakly and pressing his hand against his stomach, staggering about with merriment every time he scored a point.

Choking and screaming with laughter, he would cry out in a high, delirious voice, as rapidly as he could, "Yis, yis, yis!—Yis, yis, yis!—Yis, yis, yis!" He would bend over again, stamping his small feet, and holding his hands weakly over his shaking stomach. Then he would straighten up and catch sight of me looking at him from my window, and this would set him off again, for he would wag his finger at me roguishly, and then fairly scream, "You were tramp-ling! . . . Yis, yis, yis! You were tramp-ling!"— which would finally reduce him to such a paroxysm of mirth that he would stagger across the court and lean against the wall, all caved in, holding his narrow stomach with his slender hands and shrieking faintly.

By this time, however, his humorous allusiveness no longer held any mystery for me. I got the answer that my puzzled mind was seeking, indeed, on this very day when he invited me to tea. I asked him a question about the big plaster model in the center of the room and he took me over and showed it to me, remarking as he pointed to the huge cast of the creature's feet: "He is like you! He is tramp-ling! Yis! He is tramp-ling!"

Then he took me up the stairs onto the balcony, which I dutifully admired. "Yis?—You like?—" He smiled a little doubtfully at me, then, pointing at his couch, he said, "I sleep here!" Then he pointed to the ceiling, which was so painfully low that I had to stoop. "You sleep there?" said Katamoto eagerly. I nodded. Then Katamoto went on again with an ingratiating smile, but with a kind of embarrassed hesitancy that I had noticed before, "I here," said Katamoto pointing, "you there—yis?" He looked at me almost pleadingly, and suddenly I caught the point. "Oh! You mean that I am right above you—" he nodded eagerly, "and sometimes when I stay up late you hear me?"

"Yis! Yis!" he nodded his head vigorously with relief, "sometimes—you will be tramp-ling." He shook his finger at me with coy reproof and giggled. "You are tramp-ling!" said Mr. Katamoto.

"I am awfully sorry," I said. "Of course, I didn't know you slept so near— so near the ceiling. Maybe I can move my cot to the other side of the room where I won't be in your way."

"Oh, no-o—" he cried, genuinely distressed. "If you ple-ee-ze—sir! if you would only not wear shoes at night—if you would—" he pointed at his own small felt-shod feet, "you would like slippers—yis?" and he smiled persuasively at me again.

After that, of course, I wore slippers. Sometimes, however, I would forget, and the next morning Katamoto would be rapping at my door again. He was never angry, he was always beautifully courteous, but he would always call me to account. "You were tramp-ling!" he would cry, "last night, again, you were tramp-ling!" And I would tell him that I was sorry, I would try not to do it again, and he would go away giggling—pausing to turn and wag his finger roguishly at me and to call out "Tramp-ling," after which he would flee downstairs, shrieking with laughter. We were good friends.

Spring came and early summer. One day I came in to find the movers in the house again. This time, obviously, a work of considerable magnitude was in course of transit. Mr. Katamoto, spattered and caked from head to foot with gobs of plaster, was fluttering prayerfully around the husky, coarse-fisted trucking people. As I came in, two of the men backed slowly down the hall, sweating and cursing on each side of an immense head, monstrously jowled and mustached, and set in an expression of hoggish nobility.

A moment later three more men backed slowly from the studio, grunted painfully around the huge and flowing garments of a long frock coat, the vested splendor of a bulging belly. A little later some more men came out, staggering beneath the trousered shank of a mighty leg, the boot of an Atlantean hoof, saying coarsely as they passed, "If the son-of-a-bitch stepped on you with that foot, he wouldn't leave a grease spot, would he, Eddy?"

The last piece of all was an immense fragment of the solon's arm and fist, with one huge fat finger pointed upward in an attitude of solemn objurgation!

I believe that figure was Katamoto's masterpiece; and I knew that the enormous upraised finger was the apple of his eye—the consummation of his life and art. I had never seen him in such a state of agitation as he was that day. He fairly prayed over the sweating men. It was obvious that the coarse indelicacy of their touch made him shudder. The grin was frozen on his face in an expression of congealed terror. He writhed, he wriggled, he wrung his little hands, he crooned to them. And if anything had happened to that fat, pointed finger I believe he would have dropped dead on the spot.

At length, however, they got everything stowed away in their big van without mishap. The last fragment of this huge Ozymandias was packed away, and at length the van with its crew of sweating men drove off, leaving Mr. Katamoto, frail, plaster-spattered, utterly exhausted, at the curb. He came back into the house and smiled wanly at me. "Tramp-ling," he said feebly, and shook his finger, and for the first time there was no mirth or energy in his movements.

He was like some kind of haggard, mud-bespattered doll: I think I had never seen him tired before. I don't think it had ever occurred to me that he could get tired. He had always been so full of inexhaustible life and energy. And now, somehow, I felt an uncontrollable kind of sadness to see the little man so wan, so weary, and so curiously gray. He was silent for a moment, and then he lifted his gray face and said, wearily, yet with a kind of wistful eagerness, "You see statue—yis?"

"Yes, Kato, I saw it."

"And you like?"

"Yes, very much."

"And"—he giggled a little and made a shaping movement with his hands—"you see foot?"

"Yes."

"I s'ink," he said, "he will be *tramp-ling*—yis?" he said, and laughed gleefully.

"He ought to," I said, "with a hoof like that. It's almost as big as mine," I added, as an afterthought.

He seemed delighted with this observation, for he laughed gleefully and said, "Yis! Yis!" nodding his head emphatically. He was silent for another moment, then hesitantly, but with a kind of wistful eagerness that he could not conceal, he said, "And you see finger?"

"Yes, Kato."

"And you like?"—quickly, earnestly.

"Very much."

"Big finger—eh?" he cried gleefully.

"Very big, Kato."

"And *pointing*—yis?" he said ecstatically, grinning from ear to ear, and pointing his own small finger heavenward in the same gesture as the statue used.

"Yes, pointing."

"But not tramp-ling!" he cried gleefully, and giggled. "Finger is not tramp-ling."

"No, Kato."

"Well, z'en," he said, with the appeased air of a child, "I'm glad you like."

I told him that I was going away to Europe soon and that I had stopped for a moment to say good-bye. I did not say any more to him, but I felt the sadness people feel when they are leaving an old house where they have lived and when somehow they know that no matter what may come again, the house, the yard, Katamoto and his girl, and a woman's step upon the stair at noon, the trembling cat that crept upon the ridges of the backyard fence—such things are gone and will not come again. I think he felt a little of this, too: in a moment he smiled wanly, extended his small, bespattered hand in a gesture of farewell, and said, "Good-bye"—a flicker of his childish gaiety flared up in him again—"and do not trample!" said Katamoto, as he shook his finger at me. "You mustn't trample!" Then he was gone.

I did not see him after that. Indeed, for several days, I doubt that I even thought of him. I was busy getting ready to go away, packing up my belongings, storing away the accumulation of several years. And then, one day, as I stood in my empty, now so curiously barren, rooms, among the big packing-cases that waited only the coming of the storage people, I thought of him again. I remembered suddenly that I had not seen him since I had last spoken to him and that I had not even heard the familiar thud of the little ball against the wall outside or the sound of Katamoto's high, shrill laughter. And this sudden discovery, with its sense of loss, so troubled me that I went downstairs immediately and pressed his bell. There was no answer. All was as silent as a tomb; I waited—no one came. Then I went downstairs to the basement and found the caretaker of the old house and spoke to him. He told me that Mr. Katamoto had been ill—no, it was not serious, he thought, but the doctor had advised a brief rest from his furious labors, and had sent him for a few days' care and observation to a nearby hospital.

Then, for several days, I heard no more about him. One day, as I was coming home again, I found a moving van before the house, and saw that Katamoto's door was open and that the moving people had already stripped his quarters almost bare. I went to the door and looked in. In the center of the room, where Katamoto had performed his prodigies of work, I saw the young Japanese, whom I had seen there several times before. He was standing in the middle of the bare floor supervising the conclusion of the moving operations. He looked up quickly, with a toothy grin of frozen courtesy, as I came in. He did not speak until I asked how Mr. Katamoto was and then, with the same toothy, frozen grin upon his face, the same impenetrable courtesy, he told me that Mr. Katamoto was dead.

There was nothing more to say. I suppose some people may find this admission strange—or think it callous or inhuman. But it was not. I can't even say that I felt particularly shocked or surprised at the news. Neither had I expected it. I just accepted it: when I heard it, I had a feeling of strange quietness; but really the strangest thing about the feeling was that it was so quiet, and seemed somehow so natural and familiar. I don't know if I am right or not, but it has always seemed to me this is the way things are when we hear that someone has died: perhaps we did not expect it, perhaps we had no inkling of it, but really we are not often shocked, we are not often surprised.

And I believe the reason for this is that death is one of the two most familiar things in life. We are really not surprised at death: surprise comes later—grief is really *recollective* feeling, isn't it? I just stood there for a moment, knowing, as everyone must know, that there was nothing more to say, and yet feeling somehow as people always feel on these occasions that there is something that they *ought* to say. I looked at him quickly and started to speak, but found myself looking into the dark, untelling eye, the imperturbably courteous face of Asia. And I said nothing more. I just thanked him and went out. And it really has always seemed to me, whenever I thought of it, that there was nothing I could say—was there?

And that was all. Just as the earth possessed again its little man, so did the great honeycomb of life, the labyrinth of our billion destinies, possess these others, and we went our ways. I never saw the young Japanese again. I never saw the slender, agile little girl who had been, in some strange half-childlike way, the mate of Katamoto. They vanished utterly, taking with them every atom of the little man's belongings, leaving the old rooms as bare as if they had never lived in them, leaving a mystery as complete and baffling as the heart of Asia. Who were they? Where did they go? What became of them? It was all lost, faded away as utterly as sunlight passing on a wall on a forgotten day. And all of us were given unto time.

And now I stood ten years later in this green and pleasant park at dusk and felt again the poignant evocation of lost time as I saw the grotesque pathos of that fat, uplifted finger pointing heavenward and knew that it had been the little man's delight and that all of it had happened long ago. I thought again of Katamoto, knowing he was dead, the old house and the step upon the stair, the cat that crept along the ridges of the fence, knowing that all these things were lost in time and never would come back again. And I knew so many other men would pass and see this fat and lifted finger here, and then, like us, would vanish, having known, heard, of none of us—and that others would come after them, like us, so thinking, feeling, pondering on such things as these and on the miracle of time: where now?

The Lost Boy

The light came and went, the booming strokes of three o'clock beat out across the town in thronging bronze, light winds of April blew the fountain out in rainbow sheets, until the plume returned and pulsed, as Robert turned into the Square. He was a child dark-eyed and grave, birthmarked upon his neck—a berry of warm brown—and with a gentle face, perhaps too quiet and listening for his years. The scuffed boy's shoes, the thick-ribbed stockings gartered at the knees, the short knee pants cut straight with three small useless buttons at the side, the sailor blouse, the old cap battered out of shape, perched sideways up on top the raven head—these friendly shabby garments, shaped by Robert, uttered him. He turned and passed along the north side of the Square, and in that moment felt the union of Forever and Now.

Light came and went and came again; the great plume of the fountain pulsed, and the winds of April sheeted it across the Square in rainbow gossamer of spray. The street-cars ground into the Square from every portion of the town's small compass and halted briefly like wound toys in their old quarter-hourly formula of assembled Eight. The courthouse bell boomed out its solemn warning of immediate Three, and everything was just the same as it had always been.

He saw with quiet eyes that haggis of vexed shapes, that hodge-podge of ill-sorted masonries, and he did not feel lost. For "Here," thought Robert, "here's the Square as it has always been—and Papa's shop, the fire department and the city hall, the fountain pulsing with its plume, the drug-store on the corner there, the row of old brick buildings on this side, the people passing and the cars that come and go, the light that comes and changes and that always will come back again, and everything that comes and goes and changes in the Square, and yet will be the same—here," Robert thought, "here is the Square that never changes; here is Robert almost twelve—and here is Time."

For so it seemed to him: small center of his little universe, itself the accidental masonry of twenty years, the chance agglomerate of time and of disrupted strivings, it was for him earth's pivot and the granite core of

359

changelessness, the eternal Place where all things came and passed, the Place that would abide forever and would never change.

The Square walked past him then with steady steps—plume, pulse, and fountain, and the sheeting spray, the open arches of the fire department doors, the wooden stomp of the great hoofs, the casual whiskings of the dry coarse tails. He passed the firetrap of a wiener stand; and the Singer shop, the steel-bright smartness of the new machines, with their swift evocations of the house, the whir, the treadle, and the mounting hum—the vague monotony of women's work. He passed the music-store, the coffined splendor of piano shapes, the deep-toned richness, and the smell of proud dark wood, the stale yet pleasant memory of parlors.

He passed the grocery store then, the gaunt gray horse, the old head leaning to its hitching block; within, the pickle-barrels, the fans, the sultry coffee and the cloven cheese, the musty compost of cool plenty, the delicious All-Smell, and the buttered unction of the grocer with his straw-cuffed sleeves.

He was going past the hardware store now. He always had to stop by places that had shining perfect things in them, and windows full of geometric tools, of hammers, saws, and planing-boards, and strong new rakes and hoes with unworn handles of white perfect wood, stamped hard and vivid with the maker's seal. Ah, how he loved such things as these, strong perfect shapes and pungent smells, the great integrities of use and need, the certitude of this unchanging pattern, set to the grand assurance of the everlasting Square. He turned a corner, and he *was* caught, held. A waft of air, warm, chocolate-laden, filled his nostrils. He tried to pass the white front of the little eight-foot shop; he paused, struggling with conscience; he could not go on. It was the little candy-shop run by old Crocker and his wife. And Robert could not pass.

"Old stingy Crockers!" he thought scornfully. "I'll not go there again. They're so stingy they stop the clocks at night. But—" The maddening fragrance of rich cooking chocolate touched him once again. "I'll just look in the window and see what they've got." He paused a moment, looking with his dark and quiet eyes into the window of the candy shop. His dark eyes rested for a moment on a tray of chocolate drops. Unconsciously he licked his lips. Put one of them upon your tongue and it just melted there like honey. And then the trays full of rich home-made fudge. He looked longingly at the deep body of the chocolate fudge, reflectively at the maple walnut, more critically, yet with longing, at the mints, the nougatines, and all the other tempters.

"Old stingy Crockers!" Robert muttered once again, and turned to go. "I wouldn't go in *there* again."

And yet—he did not go away. "Old stingy Crockers," it was true; still, they did make the best candy in town, the best, in fact, that he had ever tasted.

. . .

He looked through the window back into the little shop and saw Mrs. Crocker there. A customer had made a purchase, and as Robert looked, he saw Mrs. Crocker, with her little wrenny face, lean over and peer primly at the scales. She had a piece of fudge in her clean bony fingers—and now she broke it, primly, in her little bony hands. She dropped a morsel down into the scales. They weighted down alarmingly, and her thin lips tightened. She snatched a piece of fudge out of the scales and broke it carefully once again. This time the scale wavered, went down very slowly, and came back again. Mrs. Crocker carefully put the reclaimed piece of fudge back in the tray, put the remainder in a paper bag, folded it and gave it to the customer, counted the money carefully, and doled it out into the till.

Robert stood there, looking scornfully. "Old stingy Crocker—afraid that she might give a crumb away."

He grunted, and again he turned to go. But now Mr. Crocker came out from the little partitioned place behind, bearing a tray of fresh-made candy in his skinny hands. Old man Crocker rocked along the counter to the front and put it down. He was a cripple. One leg was inches shorter than the other, and on this leg there was an enormous thick-soled boot, with a kind of wooden rocker-like arrangement, six inches high at least, to make up for the deficiency of his game right leg. And on this wooden cradle Mr. Crocker rocked along. He was a little pinched and skinny figure of a man with bony hands and meager features, and when he walked, he really rocked along, with a kind of prim and apprehensive little smile, as if he was afraid he was going to lose something.

"Old stingy Crocker," muttered Robert. "Humph! He wouldn't give you *anything.*"

And yet he did not go away. He hung there curiously, peering through the window, with his dark and gentle face now focused and intent, flattening his nose against the glass. Unconsciously he scratched the thick-ribbed fabric of one stockinged leg with the scuffed toe of his old shoe. The fresh warm odor of the new-made fudge had reached him. It was delicious. It was a little maddening. Half-consciously, he began to fumble in one trouser pocket and pulled out his purse, a shabby worn old black one with a twisted clasp. He opened it and prowled about inside.

What he found was not inspiring: a nickel and two pennies and—he had forgotten them—the stamps. He took the stamps out and unfolded them. There were five twos, eight ones, all that remained of the dollar and sixty cents' worth which Reed, the pharmacist, had given him for running errands a week or two before.

"Old Crocker," Robert thought, looked somberly at the grotesque little form and—"Well—" indefinitely—"He's had all the rest of them. He might as well take these."

So, soothing conscience with this sop of scorn, he went into the shop, and pointing with a slightly grimy finger at the fresh-made tray of chocolate fudge, he said: "I'll take fifteen cents' worth of this, Mr. Crocker."

He paused a moment, fighting with embarrassment; then he lifted his dark face and said quietly: "And please, I'll have to give you stamps again."

Mr. Crocker made no answer. He pressed his lips together. Then he got the candy scoop, slid open the door of the glass case, put fudge into the scoop, and rocking to the scales, began to weigh the candy out. Robert watched him as he peered and squinted, watched him purse his lips together, saw him take a piece of fudge and break it into two parts. And then old Crocker broke two parts in two. He weighed, he squinted, he hovered, until it seemed to Robert that by calling *Mrs.* Crocker stingy he had been guilty of a rank injustice. But finally the scales hung there, quivering apprehensively, upon the very hair-line of nervous balance, as if even the scales were afraid that one more move from old man Crocker and they would be undone.

Mr. Crocker took the candy, dumped it into a paper bag, and rocking back along the counter toward the boy, he said: "Where are the stamps?" Robert gave them to him. Mr. Crocker relinquished his claw-like hold on the bag and set it down upon the counter. Robert took the bag and then remembered. "Mr. Crocker,"—again he felt the old embarrassment that was almost like strong pain,—"I gave you too much," Robert said. "There were eighteen cents in stamps. You—you can just give me three ones back."

Mr. Crocker did not answer for a moment. He was busy unfolding the stamps and flattening them out on top of the glass counter. When he had done so, he peered at them sharply, for a moment, thrusting his scrawny neck forward and running his eye up and down, as a bookkeeper who tots up rows of figures.

Then he said tartly: "I don't like this kind of business. I'm not a post office. The next time you come in here and want anything, you'll have to have the money for it."

Hot anger rose in Robert's throat. His olive face suffused with angry color. His tarry eyes got black and bright. For a moment he was on the verge of saying: "Then why did you take my other stamps? Why do you tell me now, when you have taken all the stamps I had, that you don't want them?"

But he was a quiet, gentle, gravely thoughtful boy, and he had been taught how to respect his elders. So he just stood there looking with his tar-black eyes. Old Man Crocker took the stamps up in his thin, parched fingers, and turning, rocked away down to the till.

He took the twos and laid them in one rounded scallop, then took the ones and folded them and put them in the one next to it. Then he closed the till and started to rock off, down toward the other end. Robert kept looking at him, but Mr. Crocker did not look at Robert. Instead, he began to take some cardboard shapes and fold them into boxes.

In a moment Robert said: "Mr. Crocker, will you give me the three ones, please?"

Mr. Crocker did not answer. But Mrs. Crocker, also folding boxes with her parsley hands, muttered tartly: "Hm! *I'd* give him nothing!"

Mr. Crocker looked at Robert: "What are you waiting for?"

"Will you give me the three ones, please?" Robert said.

"I'll give you nothing," Mr. Crocker said. "Now you get out of here! And don't you come here with any more of those stamps."

"I should like to know where he gets them, that's what *I* should like to know," said Mrs. Crocker.

"You get out of here," said Mr. Crocker. "And don't you come back here with any stamps. . . . Where did you get those stamps?" he said.

"That's just what *I've* been thinking," Mrs. Crocker said.

"You've been coming in here for the last two weeks with stamps," said Mr. Crocker. "I don't like the look of it. Where did you get those stamps?" he said.

"That's what *I've* been thinking all along," said Mrs. Crocker.

Robert had got white underneath his olive skin. His eyes had lost their luster. They looked like dull, stunned balls of tar. "From Mr. Reed," he said. "I got the stamps from Mr. Reed." He burst out desperately: "Mr. Crocker, Mr. Reed will tell you how I got the stamps. I did some work for Mr. Reed; he gave me those stamps two weeks ago."

"Mr. *Reed,*" said Mrs. Crocker acidly. "I call it mighty funny."

"Mr. Crocker," Robert said, "if you'll just let me have the three ones—"

"You get out of here, boy!" cried Mr. Crocker. "Now don't you come in here again! There's something funny about this whole business! If you can't pay as other people do, then I don't want your trade."

"Mr. Crocker," Robert said again, and underneath the olive skin his face was gray, "if you'll just let me have those three—"

"You get out of here," Mr. Crocker cried, and began to rock forward toward the boy. "If you don't get out—"

"*I'd* call a policeman, that's what I'd do," Mrs. Crocker said.

Mr. Crocker came rocking up to Robert, took the boy and pushed him with his bony little hands. Robert felt sick and gray down to the hollow pit of his stomach.

"You've got to give me those three ones," he said.

"You get out of here!" shrilled Mr. Crocker. He seized the screen door, pulled it open, and pushed Robert out. "Don't you come back in here," he said, pausing for a moment, working thinly at the lips. Then he turned and rocked back in the shop again. Robert stood there on the pavement. And light came and went and came again.

The boy stood there for a moment, and a wagon rattled past. There were some people passing by, but Robert did not notice them. He stood there blindly, in the watches of the sun, but something had gone out of the day.

He felt the soul-sickening guilt that all the children, all the good men of the earth, have felt since time began. And even anger had been drowned out, in the swelling tide of guilt. "There is the Square," thought Robert as before. "This is Now. There is my father's shop. And all of it is as it has always been—save I."

And the Square reeled drunkenly around him, light went in blind gray motes before his eyes, the fountain sheeted out to rainbow iridescence and returned to its proud pulsing plume again. But all the brightness had gone out of day.

The scuffed boots of the lost boy moved and stumbled blindly over. The numb feet crossed the pavement—reached the sidewalk, crossed the plotted central Square—the grass plots, the flower-beds, so soon with red and packed geraniums.

"I want to be alone," thought Robert, "where I can not go near him. Oh, God, I hope he never hears, that no one ever tells him—"

The plume blew out; the iridescent sheet of spray blew over him. He passed through, found the other side and crossed the street. "Oh, God, if Papa ever hears," thought Robert, as his numb feet started up the steps into his father's shop.

He found and felt the steps—the thickness of old lumber twenty feet in length. He saw it all: the iron columns on his father's porch, painted with the dull anomalous black-green that all such columns in this land and weather come to; two angels, fly-specked, and the waiting stones. Beyond and all around, in the stonecutter's shop, cold shapes of white and marble, rounded stone, the limestone base, the languid angel with strong marble hands of love.

He went on down the aisle; the white shapes stood around him. He went on back into the workroom. This he knew—the little cast-iron stove in the left-hand corner, the high, dirty window, looking down across the market square, the rude old shelves, upon the shelves the chisels and a layer of stone dust; an emery wheel with pump tread, and two trestles of coarse wood upon which rested gravestones. At one trestle was a man, at work.

The boy looked numbly, saw the name was *Creasman:* the carved analysis of John, the symmetry of S, the fine finality of *Creasman—November, Nineteen-Three.*

The man looked up and then returned to work. He was a man of fifty-three, immensely long and tall and gaunt. He wore good dark clothes, save he had no coat. He worked in shirt-sleeves with his vest on, a strong watch-chain stretching across his vest; wing collar and black tie, Adam's apple, bony forehead, bony nose, light eyes, gray-green, undeep and cold, and somehow lonely-looking, a striped apron going up around his shoulders, and starched cuffs. And in one hand a tremendous rounded wooden mallet like a butcher's bole; and in his other hand, implacable and cold, the chisel.

"How are you, son?"

He did not look up as he spoke. He spoke quietly, absently. He worked upon the chisel and the wooden mallet as delicately as a jeweler might work upon a watch, except that in the man and the wooden mallet there was power, too.

"What is it, son?" he said.

He moved around the table from the head, and started up on *J* again.

"Papa, I never stole the stamps," said Robert.

The man put down the mallet, laid the chisel down. He came around the trestle.

"What?" he said. And Robert winked his tar-black eyes; they brightened; the hot tears shot out. "I never stole the stamps," he said.

"Hey? What is this?" the man said. "What stamps?"

"That Mr. Reed gave to me, when the other boy was sick and I worked there for three days. . . . And old man Crocker," Robert said, "he took all the stamps. And I told him Mr. Reed had given them to me. And now he owes me three ones—and old man Crocker says—he says—I must have taken them."

"The stamps that Reed gave to you—hey?" the stonecutter said. "The stamps you had—" He wet his great thumb briefly on his lips, strode from his workshop out into the storeroom aisle.

The man came back, cleared his throat, and as he passed the old gray board-partition of his office, he cleared his throat and wet his thumb, and said: "I tell you, now—"

Then he turned and strode up toward the front again and cleared his throat and said: "I tell you, now—" And coming back, along the aisle between the rows of marshaled gravestones, he muttered underneath his breath: "By God, now—"

He took Robert by the hand. They went out flying down along the aisle by all the gravestones, the fly-specked angels waiting there, the wooden steps, across the cobbles and the central plot—across the whole·thing, but they did not notice it.

And the fountain pulsed, the plume blew out in sheeted spray and swept across them, and an old gray horse, with a peaceful look about its torn lips, swucked up the cool, the flowing mountain water from the trough as Robert and his father went across the Square.

They went across the Square through the sheeted iridescence of the spray and to the other street and to the candy-shop. The man was dressed in his striped apron still; he was still holding Robert by the hand. He opened the screen door and stepped inside. "Give him the stamps," he said.

Mr. Crocker came rocking forward behind the counter, with a prim and careful look that now was somewhat like a smile. "It was just—" he said.

"Give him the stamps," the man said, and threw some coins down on the counter.

Mr. Crocker rocked away and got the stamps. "I just didn't know—" he said.

The stonecutter took the stamps and gave them to the boy. And Mr. Crocker took the coins.

"It was just that—" Mr. Crocker said, and smiled.

The man in the apron cleared his throat: "You never were a father," the man said. "You never knew the feeling of a child. And that is why you acted as you did. But a judgment is upon you. God has cursed you. He has afflicted you. He has made you lame and childless—and miserable as you are, you will go lame and childless to your grave—and be forgotten!"

And Crocker's wife kept kneading her bony little hands and said imploringly: "Oh, no—oh, don't say that! Please don't say that!"

The stonecutter, the breath still hoarse in him, left the store. Light came again into the day.

"Well, son," he said, and laid his hand on the boy's back. "Now don't you mind."

They walked across the Square, the sheeted spray of iridescent light swept out on them; a horse swizzled at the water-trough.

"Well, son," the gaunt man said again, "now don't you mind."

And he trod his own steps then with his great stride and went back again into his shop.

The lost boy stood upon the Square, close by the porch of his father's shop: light came again into the Square. A car curved in, upon the billboard of the car-end was a poster and some words: "*St. Louis*" and "*Excursion*" and "*The Fair.*"

And light came and went into the Square, and Robert stood there thinking quietly: "Here is the Square that never changes; here is Time."

And light came and went and came again into the Square—but now not quite the same as it had done before. He saw that pattern of familiar shapes, and knew that they were just the same as they had always been. But something had gone out of the day, and something had come in again: out of the vision of those quiet eyes some brightness had been lost; into their vision some deeper color come. He could not say, he did not know through what transforming shadows life had passed within that quarter-hour. He only knew that something had been gained forever—something lost.

As we went down through Indiana—you were too young, child, to remember it, but I always think of all of you, the way you looked that morning, when we went down through Indiana, going to the Fair. All of the apple trees were coming out, and it was April; all of the trees were coming out; it was the beginning of the spring in Indiana, and everything was getting green. Of course we don't have farms at home like those in Indiana. The children had never seen such farms as those, and I reckon, kid-like, had to take it in.

So all of them kept running up and down the aisle—well, no, except for you and *Robert*—*you* were too young; you were just three; I kept you with me. As for Robert: well, I'm going to tell you about that. But the rest of them kept running up and down the aisle and from one window to another. They kept calling out and hollering to each other every time they saw something new. They kept trying to look out on all sides in every way at once, as if they wished they had eyes in the back of their heads. It was the first time any of them had been in Indiana, and I reckon, that, kid-like, it all seemed strange and new.

And so it seemed they couldn't get enough. It seemed they never could be still.

You see, they were excited about going to St. Louis and so curious over everything they saw. They couldn't help it, and they wanted to see everything. But "I'll vow," I said, "if you children don't sit down and rest, you'll be worn to a frazzle before we ever get to see St. Louis and the Fair!"

Except for Robert! He—no sir, not him! Now, boy, I want to tell you— I've raised the lot of you, and if I do say so, there wasn't a numbskull in the lot. But *Robert!* Well, you've all grown up now, all of you have gone away, and none of you are children any more. . . . And of course, I hope that, as the fellow says, you have reached the dignity of man's estate. . . . I suppose you have the judgment of a grown man. . . . But Robert! *Robert* had it, even then!

Oh, even as a child, you know—at a time I was almost afraid to trust the rest of you out of my sight—I could depend on Robert. I could send him anywhere, and I'd always know he'd get back safe, and do exactly what I told him to!

Why, I didn't even have to tell him—you could send that child to market and tell him what you wanted, and he'd come home with *twice* as much as you could get yourself for the same money.

Now you know, I've always been considered a good trader, but *Robert!* Why, it got so finally that your papa said to me: "You'd be better off if you just tell him what you want and leave the rest to him. For," your papa says, "damned if I don't believe he's a better trader than you are. . . . He gets more for the money than anyone I ever saw."

Well, I had to admit it, you know. . . . I had to own up then. . . . Robert, even as a child, was a far better trader than I was. . . . Why, yes, they told it on him all over town, you know. . . . They said all of the market men, all of the farmers, would begin to laugh when they saw him coming. They'd say, "Look out! Here's Robert! Here's one trader you're not going to fool!"

And they were right! . . . *That* child! . . . I'd say: "Robert, suppose you run uptown and see if they've got anything good to *eat* today. Suppose you take this dollar and just see what you can do with it."

Well, sir, that was all that was needed. The minute that you told that child that you depended on his judgment, he'd have gone to the ends of the earth for you—and let me tell you something, he wouldn't *miss*, either!

His eyes would get black as coals—oh, the way that child would look at you, the intelligence and sense in his expression! He'd say, "Yes, *ma'am!*

Now don't you worry, Mamma, you leave it all to me—and I'll do *good!*" said Robert.

And he'd be off like a streak of lightning and oh, Lord! As your father said to me, "I've been living in this town for almost thirty years," he said, "and I thought I knew everything there was to know about it—but that child," your papa says, "he knows places that I never heard of!" Oh, he'd go right down there to that place below your papa's shop where the draymen used to park their wagons—or he'd go down there to those old lots on Concord Street where the farmers used to keep their wagons. And child that he was, he'd go right in among them, *sir—Robert* would!—go right in and barter with them like a grown man!

And he'd come home with things he'd bought that would make your eyes stick out. . . . Here he comes one time with another boy, dragging a great bushel basket full of ripe termaters between them. "Why, Robert," I says, "how on earth are we ever going to use them? Why, they'll go bad on us before we're half-way through them." "Well, Mamma," he says, "I know,"— oh, just as solemn as a judge—"but they were the last the man had," he says, "and he wanted to go home, and so I got them for ten cents," he says. "I thought it was a shame to let 'em go, and I figgered what we couldn't eat— why," says Robert, "you could *put up!*" Well, the way he said it, so earnest and so serious, I had to laugh. "But I'll vow," I said, "if you don't beat all!" . . . But that was *Robert* the way he was in *those* days! As everyone said, boy that he was, he had the sense and judgment of a grown man. . . . Child, child, I've seen you all grow up, and all of you were bright enough, but for all-round intelligence, judgment, and general ability, Robert surpassed the whole crowd. . . . I've never seen his equal, and everyone who knew him as a child will say the same.

So that's what I tell them now, when they ask me about all of you. I have to tell the truth. I always said that you were smart enough—but when they come around and brag to me about you, and I reckon how you have got on and have a kind of name—I don't let on to them, I never say a word. Why, yes! Why, here, you know—oh, 'long about a month ago, this feller comes. He said he came from New Jersey, or somewhere up in that part of the country—and he began to ask me all sorts of questions, what you were like when you were a boy and all such stuff as that.

I just pretended to study it all over; then I said, "Well, yes," real serious-like, you know. "Well, yes—I reckon I ought to know a little something about him: he was my child, just the same as all the others were; I brought him up just the the way I brought up all the others. And," I says—oh, just as solemn as you please, "he wasn't a *bad* sort of a boy. Why," I says, "up to the time that he was twelve years old he was just about the same as any other boy—a good average normal sort of fellow."

"Oh," he says. "But didn't you notice something? Didn't you notice how brilliant he was? He must have been more brilliant than the rest!"

"Well, now," I says, and pretended to study that all over, too. "Now let me see. . . . Yes," I says—I just looked him in the eye, as solemn as you please. "I guess he was a fairly bright sort of a boy. I never had no complaints to make of him on that score. He was bright enough," I says. "The only trouble with him was that he was lazy."

"Lazy!" he says—oh, you should have seen the look upon his face, you know—he jumped like someone had stuck a pin in him. "Lazy!" he says, "Why, you don't mean to tell me—"

"Yes," I says, "I was telling him the same thing myself the last time that I saw him. I told him it was a mighty lucky thing for him that he had the gift of gab. Of course, he went off to college and read a lot of books, and I reckon that's where he got this flow of language they say he has. . . . But as I said to him, 'Now look a-here,' I said, 'if you can earn your living doing a light easy class of work like this you do,' I says, 'you're mighty lucky, because none of the rest of your people had any such luck as that. They had to work hard for a living.'"

Oh, I told him, you know. I made no bones about it. And I tell you what—I wish you could have seen his face. It was a study.

"Well," he says, at last, "you've got to admit this, haven't you—he was the brightest boy you had, now wasn't he?"

I just looked at him a moment. I had to tell the truth. I couldn't fool him any longer. "No," I says. "He was a good bright boy—I have no complaint to make about him on that score; but the brightest boy I had, the one that surpassed all the rest of them in sense, and in understanding, and in judgment—the best boy that I had, the smartest boy I ever saw, was—well, it wasn't him," I said. "It was another one."

He looked at me a moment; then he said: "Which boy was that?"

Well, I just looked at him, and smiled. I shook my head. I wouldn't tell him. "I never brag about my own," I said. "You'll have to find out for yourself."

But—I'll have to tell *you:* the best one of the whole lot was—*Robert!*

. . . And when I think of Robert as he was along about that time, I always see him sitting there, so grave and earnest-like, with his nose pressed to the window, as we went down through Indiana in the morning, to the Fair.

So Robert sat beside this gentleman and looked out the window. I never knew the man—I never asked his name—but I tell you what! He was certainly a fine-looking, well-dressed, good substantial sort of man, and I could see that he had taken a great liking to Robert, and Robert sat there looking out, and then turned to this gentleman, as grave and earnest as a grown-up man, and says: "What kind of crops grow here, sir?" Well, this gentleman threw his head back and just ha-ha-ed. "Well, I'll see if I can tell you," says this gentleman, and then, you know, he talked to him, and Robert took it all in, as solemn as you please, and asked this gentleman every sort of question—what the trees were, what was growing there, how big the farms were—all sorts of questions, which this gentleman would answer, until I said: "I'll vow, Robert! You'll bother the very life out of this gentleman."

The gentleman threw his head back and laughed right out. "Now you leave that boy alone. He's all right," he said. "He doesn't bother me a bit, and if I know the answers to his questions, I will answer him. And if I don't know, why, then, I'll tell him so. But he's *all right*," he said, and put his arm around Robert's shoulders. "You leave him alone. He doesn't bother me a bit."

And I can still remember how he looked, that morning, with his black eyes, his black hair, and with the birthmark on his neck—so grave, so serious, so earnest-like—as he looked out the windows at the apple trees, the farms, the barns, the houses, and the orchards, taking it all in because it was, I reckon, strange and new to him.

It was so long ago, but when I think of it, it all comes back, as if it happened yesterday. And all of you have grown up and gone away, and nothing is the same as it was then. But all of you were there with me that morning, and I guess I should remember how the others looked, but every time I think of it, I still see Robert just the way he was, the way he looked that morning when we went down through Indiana, by the river, to the Fair.

Can you remember how Robert used to look? . . . I mean the birthmark, the black eyes, the olive skin—the birthmark always showed because of those open sailor blouses kids used to wear. . . . But I guess you must have been too young . . . . I was looking at that old photograph the other day—that picture showing all of us before the house in Orchard Street? . . . *You* weren't there. . . . *You* hadn't arrived. . . . You remember how mad you used to get when we used to tell you that you were only a dish-rag hanging out in Heaven, when something happened?

I was looking at that old picture just the other day. There we were. . . . And my God, what is it all about? . . . I mean, when you see the way you were—Mary and Dick and Robert, Bill and all of us—and then—look at us now! Do you ever get to feeling funny? You know what I mean—do you ever get to feeling *queer*?—when you try to figure these things out. . . . You've been to college, and you ought to know the answer. . . . And I wish you'd tell me if you know. . . .

My Lord, when I think sometimes of the way I used to be—the dreams I used to have. . . . Taking singing lessons from Aunt Nell because I felt that some day I was going to have a great career in opera. . . . Can you beat it now? . . . Can you imagine it? . . . *Me!* In grand opera! . . . Now I want to ask you. . . . I'd like to know. . . .

My Lord! When I go uptown and look at all these funny-looking little boys and girls hanging around the drug-store—do you suppose any of them have ambitions the way we did? . . . Do you suppose any of these funny-looking little girls are thinking about a big career in opera? . . . Didn't you ever see that picture of us? It was made before the old house down on

Orchard Street, with Papa standing there in his swallow-tail, and Mamma there beside him—and Robert and Dick and Jim, and Mary, Bill, and me, with our feet up on our bicycles.

Well, there I was, and my poor old skinny legs and long white dress, and two pigtails hanging down my back. And all the funny-looking clothes we wore, with the doo-lolly business on them. . . . But I guess you can't remember. You weren't born.

But—well, we were a right nice-looking set of people, if I do say so. And there was *86* the way it used to be, with the front porch, the grape-vines, and the flower-beds before the house. And Miss Martha standing there by Papa with a watch-charm pinned to her waist. . . . I shouldn't laugh, but Miss Martha. . . . Well, Mamma was a pretty woman then—and Papa in his swallow-tail was a good-looking man. Do you remember how he used to get dressed up on Sunday? And how grand he thought he was? And how wonderful that dinky little shop on the Square looked to us! . . . Can you beat it, now? . . . Why, we thought that Papa was the biggest man in town and—oh, you can't tell me! You can't tell me! He had his faults, but Papa was a wonderful man. You know he was!

And there was Jim and Dick and Robert, Mary, Bill, and me lined up there before the house with one foot on our bicycles. . . . And I got to thinking back about it all. It all came back.

Do you remember anything about St. Louis? You were only three or four years old then, but you must remember something. . . . Do you remember how you used to bawl when I would scrub you? How you'd bawl for Robert? . . . Poor kid, you used to yell for Robert every time I'd get you in the tub. He was a sweet kid, and he was crazy about you: he almost brought you up.

That year Robert was working at the Inside Inn out on the Fair Grounds . . . Do you remember the old Inside Inn? That big old wooden thing inside the Fair? . . . And how I used to take you there to wait for Robert when he got through working? . . . And Billy Pelham at the news-stand, how he used to give you a stick of chewing-gum?

They were all crazy about Robert. . . . Everybody liked him. . . . And how proud Robert was of you! . . . Don't you remember how he used to show you off? . . . How he used to take you around and make you talk to Billy Pelham? . . . And Mr. Curtis at the desk? . . . And how Robert would try to make you talk and get you to say, "Robert"? And you couldn't pronounce the "*r*"—and you'd say "*Wobbut*." Have you forgotten that? . . . You shouldn't forget *that*, because . . . you were a *cute* kid, then . . . Ho-ho-ho-ho-ho. . . . I don't know where it's gone to, but you were a big hit in those days. . . .

And I was thinking of it all the other day: how we used to go and meet Robert there and how he'd take us to the Midway. . . . Do you remember the Midway? The Snake-Eater and the Living Skeleton, the Fat Woman and the Shoot the Chute, the Scenic Railway and the Ferris Wheel? . . . How you bawled the night we took you up on the Ferris Wheel! You yelled your head off. . . . I tried to laugh it off, but I tell you, I was scared myself . . . And how Robert laughed at us and told us there was no danger. . . . My Lord, poor little Robert! He was only twelve years old at the time, but he seemed so grown-up to us. I was two years older, but I thought he knew it all.

It was always that way with him. . . . Looking back now, it sometimes seems that it was Robert who brought us up. He was always looking after us, telling us what to do, bringing us something—some ice-cream or some candy, something he had bought out of the poor little money he'd got at the Inn. . . .

Then I got to thinking of the afternoon we sneaked away from home. . . . Mamma had gone out somewhere. And Robert and I got on the street-car and came downtown. . . . And my Lord, in those days, that was what we called a *trip*. A ride on the street-car was something to write home about in those days. . . . I hear that it's all built up around there now.

So we got on the car and rode the whole way down into the business section of St. Louis. Robert took me into a drug-store and set me up to soda-water. Then we came out and walked around some, down to the Union Station and clear over to the river. . . . And both of us half scared to death at what we'd done and wondering what Mamma would say if she found out.

We stayed there till it was getting dark, and we passed by a lunch-room— an old joint with one-armed chairs and people eating at the counter. . . . We read all the signs to see what they had to eat and how much it cost, and I guess nothing on the menu was more than fifteen cents, but it couldn't have looked grander to us if it had been Delmonico's. . . . So we stood there with our noses pressed against the window, looking in. . . . Two skinny little kids, both of us scared half to death, getting the thrill of a lifetime out of it. . . . You know what I mean? . . . And smelling everything with all our might and thinking how good it all smelled. . . . Then Robert turned to me and whispered, "Come on, Sue. . . . Let's go in. . . . It says fifteen cents for pork and beans. And I've got money," Robert said. "I've got sixty cents."

I was so scared I couldn't speak. . . . I'd never been in a place like that before. . . . But I kept thinking, "Oh, Lord, if Mamma should find out!" . . . Don't you know how it is when you're a kid? It was the thrill of a lifetime. . . . I couldn't resist. So we both went in and ordered pork and beans and a cup of coffee. . . . I suppose we were too frightened at what we'd done really to enjoy anything. We just gobbled it all up in a hurry, and gulped our coffee down. And I don't know whether it was the excitement—

I guess the poor kid was already sick when we came in there and didn't know it. But I turned and looked at him, and he was as white as death. . . . And when I asked him what was the matter, he wouldn't tell me. . . . He was too proud. He said he was all right, but I could see that he was sick as a dog. . . . So he paid the bill. . . . It came to forty cents; I'll never forget *that* as long as I live. . . . And sure enough, we no more than got out the door—he'd hardly time to reach the curb—before it all came up. . . .

And the poor kid was so scared and so ashamed. What scared him so was not that he had got sick but that he had spent all that money, and it had come to nothing. And Mamma would find out. . . . Poor kid, he just stood there looking at me and he whispered, "Oh, Sue, don't tell Mamma. She'll be mad if she finds out." Then we hurried home, and he was still white as a sheet when we got there.

Mamma was waiting for us. . . . She looked at us—you know how Miss Martha looks at you, when she thinks you've been doing something that you shouldn't? . . . Mamma said: "Why, where on earth have you two children been?" I guess she was all set to lay us out. Then she took one look at Robert's face. That was enough for her. She said: "Why, child, what in the world—" She was white as a sheet herself. . . . And all that Robert said was "Mamma, I feel sick."

He was sick as a dog. He fell over on the bed, and we undressed him, and Mamma put her hand upon his forehead and came out in the hall—she was so white you could have made a black mark on her face with chalk—and whispered to me:

"Go and get the doctor quick; he's burning up."

And I went running, my pigtails flying, to get Dr. Packer. I brought him back with me. When he came out of Robert's room, he told Mamma what to do, but I don't know if she even heard him.

Her face was white as a sheet. She looked at me and looked right through me. . . . And oh, my Lord, I'll never forget the way she looked, the way my heart stopped and came up in my throat. . . . I was only a skinny little kid of fourteen. But she looked as if she was dying right before my eyes. . . . And I knew that if anything happened to him, she'd never get over it, if she lived to be a hundred.

Poor old Mamma. You know, he always was her eyeballs—you know that, don't you?—Not the rest of us!—No, sir! I know what I'm talking about. It always has been Robert—she always thought more of him than she did of any of the others and—Poor kid! I can see him lying there white as a sheet and remember how sick he was, and how scared I was! . . . I don't know why—all we'd done had been to sneak away from home and go to a lunch-room—but I felt guilty about the whole thing, as if it was my fault. . . .

It all came back to me the other day when I was looking at that picture, and I thought, my God, we were two kids together, and I was only two years older than Robert was. . . . And now I'm forty-six. . . . Can you imagine that—the way we all grow up and change and go away? . . . And my Lord, Robert seemed so grown-up to me even then. He was only a kid; yet he seemed older than the rest of us.

I was thinking of it just the other day, and I wonder what Robert would say now if he could see that picture. For when you look at it, it all comes back—the boarding house, St. Louis and the Fair. . . . And all of it is just the same as it has always been, as if it happened yesterday. . . . And all of us have grown up and gone away. And nothing has turned out the way we thought it would. . . . And all my hopes and dreams and big ambitions have come to nothing.

It's all so long ago, as if it happened in another world. And then it all comes back, as if it happened yesterday. . . . And sometimes I will lie awake at night and think of all the people who have come and gone, and all the things that happened. And hear the trains down by the river, and the whistles and the bell. . . . And how we went to St. Louis back in 1904.

And then I go out into the street and see the faces of the people that I pass. . . . Don't you see something funny in their eyes, as if they were wondering what had happened to them since they were kids—what it was that they had lost? . . . Now am I crazy, or do they look that way to you?

My God, I'd like to find out what is wrong. . . . What has changed since then. . . . And if we have that same queer funny look in our eyes, too. . . . And if it happens to us all, to everyone. . . . Robert and Jim and Dick and me—all standing there before that house on Orchard Street—and then you see the way we were—and how it all gets lost. . . .

The way it all turns out is nothing like the way we thought that it would be. . . . And how it all gets lost, until it seems that it has never happened— that it is something that we dreamed somewhere. . . . You see what I mean now? . . . That it is something that we hear somewhere, that it happened to someone else. . . . And then it all comes back again.

And there you are, two funny, frightened, skinny little kids with their noses pressed against a dirty window thirty years ago. . . . The way it felt, the way it smelled, even the funny smell in that old pantry of our house. And the steps before the house, the way the rooms looked. Those two little boys in sailor suits who used to ride up and down before the house on their tricycles. . . . And the birthmark on Robert's neck. . . . The Inside Inn. . . . St. Louis and the Fair. . . . It all comes back as if it happened yesterday. And then it goes away and seems farther off and stranger than if it happened in a dream.

"This is King's Highway," a man said. I looked and saw that it was just a street. There were some new buildings, and a big hotel; some restaurants, "bar-grill" places of the modern kind, the livid monotone of neon lights, the ceaseless traffic of the motorcars—all this was new, but it was just a street. And I knew that it had always been a street and nothing more. But somehow—I stood there looking at it, wondering what else I had expected to find.

The man kept looking at me, and I asked him if the Fair had been out this way.

"Sure, the Fair was out beyond here," the man said. "Where the park is now. But this street you're looking for? Don't you remember the name of the street or nothing?"

I said I thought the name was Edgemont Street, but that I was not sure. And I said the house was on the corner of this street and another street. And then the man said, "What street was that?" I said I did not know, but that King's Highway was a block or so away and that an interurban line ran past about a block or so from where we lived.

"What line was this?" the man said, and stared at me.

"The interurban line," I said.

Then he stared at me again and finally, "I don't know no interurban line," he said.

I said it was a line that ran behind some houses and that there were board fences there and grass beside the tracks. But somehow I could not say that it was summer in those days and that you could smell the ties, a kind of wooden tarry smell, and feel a kind of absence in the afternoon, after the car had gone. I could not say that King's Highway had not been a street in those days but a kind of road that wound from magic out of some dim land, and that along the way it had got mixed with Tom the Piper's son, with hot cross buns, with all the light that came and went, and with cloud shadows passing on the mountains, with coming down through Indiana in the morning, and the smell of engine smoke, the Union Station, and most of all with voices lost and far and long ago that said, "King's Highway."

I didn't say those things about King's Highway because I looked about me and I saw what King's Highway was. I left him then and went on till I found the place. And again, again, I turned into the street, finding the place where the two corners meet, the huddled block, the turret, and the steps, and paused a moment, looking back, as if the street was Time.

So I waited for a moment for a word, for a door to open, for the child to come. I waited, but no words were spoken; no one came.

Yet all of it was just as it had always been except the steps were lower and the porch less high, the strip of grass less wide than I had thought. A gray-stone front, St. Louis style, three-storied, with a slant slate roof, the side red brick and windowed, still with the old arched entrance in the center for the doctor's use.

There was a tree in front, a lamp-post, and behind and to the side more trees than I had known there would be. And all the slaty turret gables, all the slaty window gables going into points, the two arched windows, in strong stone, in the front room.

It was all so strong, so solid and so ugly—and so enduring and good, the way I had remembered it, except I did not smell the tar, the hot and caulky dryness of the old cracked ties, the boards of backyard fences and the coarse and sultry grass, and absence in the afternoon when the street-car had gone, and the feel of the hot afternoon, and that everyone was absent at the Fair.

It was a hot day. Darkness had come; the heat hung and sweltered like a sodden blanket in St. Louis. The heat soaked down, and the people sweltered in it; the faces of the people were pale and greasy with the heat. And in their faces was a kind of patient wretchedness, and one felt the kind of desolation that one feels at the end of a hot day in a great city in America—when one's home is far away across the continent, and he thinks of all that distance, all that heat, and feels: "Oh, God, but it's a big country!"

Then he hears the engine and the wheel again, the wailing whistle and the bell, the sound of shifting in the sweltering yard, and walks the street, and walks the street, beneath the clusters of hard lights, and by the people with sagged faces, and is drowned in desolation and no belief.

He feels the way one feels when one comes back, and knows that he should not have come, and when he sees that, after all, King's Highway is—a street; and St. Louis—the enchanted name—a big hot common town upon the river, sweltering in wet dreary heat, and not quite South, and nothing else enough to make it better.

It had not been like this before. I could remember how it got hot in the afternoons, and how I would feel a sense of absence and vague sadness when everyone had gone away. The house would seem so lonely, and sometimes I would sit inside, on the second step of the hall stairs, and listen to the sound of silence and absence in the afternoon. I could smell the oil upon the floor and on the stairs, and see the sliding doors with their brown varnish and the beady chains across the door, and thrust my hand among the beady chains, and gather them together in my arms, and let them clash, and swish with light beady swishings all round me. I could feel darkness, absence, and stained light, within the house, through the stained glass of the window on the stairs, through the small stained glasses by the door, stained light and absence, and vague sadness in the house in a hot mid-afternoon. And all these things themselves would have a kind of life: would seem to wait attentively, to be most living and most still.

Then I would long for evening and return, the slant of light, and feet along the street, the sharp-faced twins in sailor-suits upon their tricycles, the smell of supper and the sound of voices in the house again, and Robert coming from the Fair.

And again, again, I turned into the street, finding the place where two corners meet, turning at last to see if Time was there. I passed the house; some lights were burning in the house; the door was open, and a woman sat upon the porch. And presently I turned and stopped before the house again. I stood looking at it for a moment, and I put my foot upon the step.

Then I said to the woman who was sitting on the porch: "This house—excuse me, but could you tell me, please, who lives here?"

I knew my words were strange and hollow and I had not said what I wished to say. She stared at me a moment, puzzled.

Then she said: "I live here. Who are you looking for?"

I said, "Why, I am looking for—There used to be a house—" I said.

The woman was now staring hard at me.

"I used to live here in this house," I said.

She was silent for a moment; then she said: "When was it that you lived here?"

"In 1904."

Again she was silent, looking at me for a moment. Then presently: "Oh. . . . That was the year of the Fair. You were here then?"

"Yes." I now spoke rapidly, with more confidence: "My mother had the house, and we were here for seven months . . . . And the house belonged to Dr. Packer," I went on. "We rented it from him."

"Yes," the woman said, and nodded now. "This was Dr. Packer's house. He's been dead for many years. But this was the Packer house, all right."

"That entrance on the side," I said, "where the steps go up—that was for Dr. Packer's patients. That was the entrance to his office."

"Oh," the woman said, "I didn't know that. I've often wondered what it was. I didn't know what it was for."

"And this big room here in front," I said, "that was the office. And there were sliding doors, and next to it a kind of alcove for his patients."

"Yes, the alcove is still there, only all of it has been made into one room now—and I never knew just what the alcove was for."

"And there were sliding doors on this side, too, that opened on the hall—and a stairway going up upon this side. And halfway up the stairway, at the landing, a little window of stained glass—and across the sliding doors here in the hall a kind of curtain made of strings of beads."

She nodded, smiling. "Yes, it's just the same—we still have the sliding doors and the stained glass window on the stairs. There's no bead curtain any more," she said, "but I remember when people had them. I know what you mean."

"When we were here," I said, "we used the Doctor's office for a parlor—except later on, the last month or two; and then we used it for a bedroom."

"It is a bedroom now," she said. "I rent rooms—all of the rooms upstairs are rented—but I have two brothers and they sleep in this front room."

And we were silent for a moment; then I said, "My brother stayed there, too."

"In the front room?" the woman said.

I answered: "Yes."

She paused a moment; then she said: "Won't you come in? I don't believe it's changed much. Would you like to see?"

I thanked her and said I would, and I went up the steps. She opened the screen door, and I went in.

And it was just the same—the stairs, the hallway, and the sliding doors, the window of stained glass upon the stairs. All of it was just the same except the stained light of absence in the afternoon, and the child who sat there, waiting on the stairs, and something fading like a dream, something coming like a light, something going, passing, fading like the shadows of a wood. And then it would be gone again, fading like cloud shadows in the hills, coming like the vast, the drowsy rumors of the distant enchanted Fair, and coming, going, coming, being found and lost, possessed and held and never captured, like lost voices in the mountains, long ago, like the dark eyes and the quiet face, the dark lost boy, my brother, who himself like shadows, or like absence in the house, would come, would go, and would return again.

The woman took me into the house and through the hall. I told her of the pantry, and I told her where it was and pointed to the place, but now it was no longer there. And I told her of the back yard, and the old board fence around the yard. But the old board fence was gone. And I told her of the carriage-house, and told her it was painted red. But now there was a small garage. And the back yard was still there, but smaller than I thought, and now there was a tree.

"I did not know there was a tree," I said. "I do not remember any tree."

"Perhaps it wasn't there," she said. "A tree could grow in thirty years." And then we came back through the house and paused a moment at the sliding doors.

"And could I see this room?" I said.

She slid the doors back. They slid open smoothly, with a kind of rolling heaviness, as they used to do. And then I saw the room again. It was the same. There was a window to the side, the two arched windows to the front, the alcove and the sliding doors, the fireplace with the tiles of mottled green, the mantel of dark mission wood, a dresser and a bed, just where the dresser and the bed had been so long ago.

"Is this the room?", the woman said. "It hasn't changed?"

I told her it was the same.

"And your brother slept here where my brothers sleep?"

"This was his room," I said.

And we were silent for a moment. Then I turned to go, and said: "Well, thank you. I appreciate your showing me."

The woman said that she was glad and that it was no trouble. And she said, "And when you see your family, you can tell them that you saw the house," she said. "And my name is Mrs. Bell. You can tell your mother that a Mrs. Bell has got the house. And when you see your brother, you can tell him that you saw the room he slept in, and that you found it just the same."

I told her then that he was dead.

The woman was silent for a moment. Then she looked at me and said: "He died here, didn't he? In this room?"

I told her that he did.

"Well, then," she said, "I knew it. I don't know how. But when you told me he was here, I knew it."

I said nothing. In a moment the woman said: "What did he die of?"

"Typhoid."

She looked shocked and troubled, and began involuntarily:

"My two brothers—"

"That was so long ago," I said. "I don't think you need to worry now."

"Oh, I wasn't thinking about that," she said. . . . "It was just hearing that a little boy—your brother—was—was in this room that my two brothers sleep in now—"

"Well, maybe I shouldn't have told you then. But he was a good boy— and if you'd known him, you wouldn't mind."

She said nothing, and I added quickly: "Besides, he didn't stay here long. This wasn't really his room—but the night he came back with my sister, he was so sick—they didn't move him."

"Oh," the woman said, "I see." And in a moment: "Are you going to tell your mother you were here?"

"I don't think so."

"I—I wonder how she feels about this room."

"I don't know. She never speaks of it."

"Oh. . . . How old was he?'

"He was twelve."

"You must have been pretty young yourself."

"I was four."

"And—you just wanted to see the room, didn't you? Is that why you came back?"

"Yes."

"Well"—indefinitely—"I guess you've seen it now."

"Yes, thank you."

"I guess you don't remember much about him, do you? I shouldn't think you would."

"No, not much."

The years dropped off like fallen leaves: the face came back again—the soft dark oval, the dark eyes, the soft brown berry on the neck, the raven hair, all bending down, approaching—the whole ghost-wise, intent and instant, like faces from a haunted wood.

"Now say it: *Robert!*"

"Wobbut."

"No, not *Wobbut: Robert.* . . . Say it."

"Wobbut."

"Ah-h—you *didn't* say it. . . . You said Wobbut: *Robert!* . . . Now say it."

"Wobbut."

"Look, I'll tell you what I'll do if you say it right. . . . Would you like to go down to King's Highway? Would you like Robert to set you up? All right, then. . . . If you say Robert right, I'll take you to King's Highway and set you up to ice-cream. . . . Now say it right: say *Robert*."

"Wobbut."

"Ah-h you-u! . . . Old tongue-tie, that's what you are. Some day I'm going to . . . . Well, come on, then. I'll set you up, anyway."

It all came back and faded and was lost again. I turned to go, and thanked the woman, and I said: "Good-bye."

"Well, then, good-bye," the woman said, and we shook hands. "I'm glad if I could show you. I'm glad if—" She did not finish, and at length she said: "Well, then, that was a long time ago. You'll find it all changed now, I guess. It's all built up around here now—way out beyond here, out beyond where the Fair grounds used to be. I guess you'll find it changed," she said.

We could find no more to say. We stood there for a moment on the steps, and shook hands once more.

"Well, then, good-bye."

And again, again, I turned into the street, finding the place where corners meet, turning to look again to see where Time had gone. And all of it was just the same, it seemed that it had never changed since then, except all had been found and caught and captured for forever. And so, finding all, I knew all had been lost.

I knew that I would never come again, and that lost magic would not come again, and that the light that came, that passed and went and that returned again, the memory of lost voices in the hills, cloud shadows passing in the mountains, the voices of our kinsmen long ago, the street, the heat, King's Highway, and the piper's son, the vast and drowsy murmur of the distant Fair—oh, strange and bitter miracle of Time—come back again.

But I knew that it could not come back—the cry of absence in the afternoon, the house that waited and the child that dreamed; and through the thicket of man's memory, from the enchanted wood, the dark eye and the quiet face,—poor child, life's stranger and life's exile, lost, like all of us, a cipher in blind mazes, long ago—my parent, friend, and brother, the lost boy, was gone forever and would not return.

Chickamauga

On the seventh day of August 1861, I was nineteen years of age. If I live to the seventh day of August this year, I'll be ninety-five years old. And the way I feel this morning I intend to live. Now I guess you'll have to admit that that's goin' a good ways back.

I was born up at the forks of the Toe River back in 1842; your grandpaw was born at the same place in 1828. His father, Bill Pentland, *your* great-grandfather, was born at Stockade, back in 1805. Bill Pentland's father moved his family up across the Blue Ridge in 1807, when Bill Pentland was jest two years old. They settled at the forks of Toe. The real Indian name fer hit was Estatoe, but the white man shortened hit to Toe, and hit's been known as Toe River ever since.

Hit was Indian country in those days: I've heard the Cherokees helped Bill Pentland's father build the house they lived in where some of us was born. I've heard Bill Pentland's father came from Scotland back before the Revolution and that thar was three brothers. That's all the Pentlands that I ever heared of in this country: if you ever meet a Pentland anywheres you can rest assured he's descended from those three. Bill Pentland married twice, and thar was twenty-three of us in all, nine by his first wife and fourteen by his second. They used to say you couldn't throw a rock in Zebulon County without hittin' either a Pentland or a Patton, and I reckon right out here along the Toe you'll find a good many of us livin' yet.

Well, now, as I was tellin' you, upon the seventh day of August 1861, I was nineteen years of age. At seven-thirty in the mornin' of that day I started out from home and walked the whole way to Clingman. Jim Weaver had come over from Big Hickory, where he lived, the night before and stayed with me. And now he went along with me. He was the best friend that I had. We had growed up alongside of each other: now we was to march alongside of each other fer many a long and weary mile—how many neither of us knowed that mornin' when we started out. Hit was a good twenty mile away from where we lived to Clingman, and I reckon young folks nowadays would consider twenty mile a right smart walk. But fer people in those days hit wasn't anything at all. All of us was good walkers.

381

Your grandpaw could keep goin' without stoppin' all day long: he was a great hunter and they tell hit on him that one time he ran hounds the whole way over into Tennessee and never knowed how far away from home he was until he stopped.

Jim was big and I was little, about the way you see me now, except that I've shrunk up a bit, but I could keep up with him anywheres he went. We made hit into Clingman before twelve o'clock—hit was a hot day, too—and by three o'clock that afternoon we had both joined up with the Twenty-ninth. That was my regiment from then on, right to the end of the War. Anyways, I was an enlisted man that night, the day that I was nineteen years of age, and I didn't see my home again fer four long years. Bob Saunders was our captain; L. C. McIntyre our major; and Leander Briggs the colonel of our regiment. They kept us thar at Clingman fer two weeks. Then they marched us into Altamont and drilled us fer the next two months. Our drillin' ground was right up and down where Parker Street is now: in those days thar was nothin' thar but open fields. That was where we did our drillin' fer the next two months. We camped right out thar in the fields. Hit's all built up now: to look at hit today you'd never know thar'd ever been an open field thar. But that's where hit was, all right.

Late in October we was ready, and they moved us on. The day they marched us out, Martha Patton came in all the way from Zebulon to see Jim Weaver before he went away. He'd known her fer jest two months; he'd met her the very week we joined up, and I was with him when he met her. She came from out along Cane River. Thar was a Camp Revival meetin' goin' on outside of Clingman at the time, and she was visitin' this other gal in Clingman while the Revival lasted; and that was how Jim Weaver met her. We was walkin' along one evenin' towards sunset, and we passed this house where she was stayin' with this other gal. And both of them was settin' on the porch as we went past. The other gal was fair, and she was dark: she had black hair and eyes, and she was plump and sort of little, and she had the pertiest complexion, and the pertiest white skin and teeth you ever seed; and when she smiled, thar was a dimple in her cheeks.

Well, neither of us knowed these gals, and so we couldn't stop to talk to them, but when Jim seed the little 'un he stopped short in his tracks like he was shot, and then he looked at her so hard she had to turn her face. Well, then, we walked on down the road a piece, and then Jim stopped and turned and looked again, and when he did, sure enough, he caught *her* lookin' at him, too; and then her face got red: she looked away again.

Well, that was where she landed him. He didn't say a word, but, Lord! I felt him jerk thar like a trout upon the line—and I knowed right then and thar she had him hooked. We turned and walked on down the road a ways, and then he stopped and looked at me and said: "Did you see that gal back thar?"

"Do you mean the light one or the dark one?"

"You know damn good and well which one I mean," said Jim.

"Yes, I seed her. What about her?" I said.

"Well, nothin'—only I'm a-goin' to marry her," he said.

I knowed then that she had him hooked. And yet I never believed at first that hit would last. Fer Jim had had so many gals—I'd never had a gal in my whole life up to that time, but, Lord! Jim would have him a new gal every other week. We had some fine lookin' fellers in our company, but Jim Weaver was the handsomest feller that you ever seed. He was tall and lean and built jest right, and he carried himself as straight as a rod: he had black hair and coal-black eyes, and when he looked at you, he could burn a hole right through you. And I reckon he'd burned a hole right through the heart of many a gal before he first saw Martha Patton; he could have had his pick of the whole lot—a born lady-killer if ever you seed one—and that was why I never thought that hit'd last.

And maybe hit was a pity that hit did. Fer Jim Weaver until the day that he met Martha Patton had been the most happy-go-lucky feller that you ever seed. He didn't have a care in the whole world—full of fun—ready fer anythin' and into every kind of devilment and foolishment. But from that moment on, he was a different man. And I've always thought that maybe hit was a pity hit had to come jest at that time. If hit could only have waited till the War was over! He'd wanted to go so much—he'd looked at the whole thing as a big lark—but now! Well, she had him, and he had her: the day they marched us out of town, he had her promise, and in his watch he had her picture and a little lock of her black hair, and as they marched us out, and him beside me, we passed her, and she looked at him, and I felt him jerk again and knowed the look she gave him had gone through him like a knife.

From that time on he was a different man; from that time on he was like a man in hell. Hit's funny how hit all turns out—how none of hit is like what we expect. Hit's funny how war and a little black-haired gal will change a man—but that's the story that I'm goin' to tell you now.

The nearest railhead in those days was eighty mile away at Locust Gap. They marched us out of town right up the Fairfield Road along the river up past Crestville, and right across the Blue Ridge thar, and down the mountain. We made Old Stockade the first day's march and camped thar fer the night. It was twenty-four mile of marchin' right across the mountain with the roads the way they was in those days, too. And let me tell you, fer new men with only two months' trainin' that was doin' good.

We made Locust Gap in three days and a half, and I wish you'd seed the welcome they gave us! People were hollerin' and shoutin' the whole way. All the women folk and the childern were lined up along the road, bands a-playin', boys runnin' along beside us, good shoes, new uniforms, the finest lookin' set of fellers that you *ever* seed—Lord! you'd a-thought we was goin' to a picnic from the way hit looked. And I reckon that was the way most of us felt about hit, too. We thought we was goin' off to have a lot of fun. If anyone had knowed what he was in fer or could-a seed the passel o' scarecrows that came limpin' back barefoot and half naked four years later, I reckon he'd a-thought again before he 'listed up.

Lord, when I think of hit! When I try to tell about hit, thar jest ain't words enough to tell what hit was like. And when I think of the way I was when I joined up—and the way I was when I came back four years later!—When I went away I was an ignerant country boy, so tender-hearted that I wouldn't harm a fly. And when I came back when the war was over, I could-a stood by and seed a man murderd right before my eyes with no more feelin' than I'd have fer a stuck hog. I had no more feelin' about human life than I had fer the life of a sparrer. I'd seed a ten-acre field so thick with dead men that you could have walked all over hit without steppin' on the ground a single time.

And that was where I made my big mistake. If I'd only knowed a little more, if I'd only waited jest a little longer after I got home, things would have been all right. That's been the big regret of my whole life. I never had no education. I never had a chance to git one before I went away. And when I came back, I could-a had my schoolin' but I didn't take it. The reason was I never knowed no better: I'd seed so much fightin' and killin' that I didn't care fer nothin'. I jest felt dead and numb like all the brains had been shot out of me. I jest wanted to git me a little patch of land somewheres and settle down and fergit about the world.

That's where I made my big mistake. I didn't wait long enough. I got married too soon, and after that the childern came and hit was root, hawg, or die: I had to grub fer hit. But if I'd only waited jest a little while, hit would have been all right. In less'n a year hit all cleared up. I got my health back, pulled myself together and got my feet back on the ground, and had more mercy and understandin' in me jest on account of all the sufferin' I'd seed than I ever had. And as fer my head, why hit was better than hit ever was:—with all I'd seed and knowed, I could-a got a schoolin' in no time. But you see I wouldn't wait. I didn't think that hit'd ever come back. I was jest sick of livin'. And that's where I played smash!—

But as I say—they marched us down to Locust Gap in less'n four days' time, and then they put us on the cars fer Richmond. We got to Richmond on the mornin' of one day:—up to that very moment we had thought that they were sendin' us to join Lee's army in the North. But the next mornin' we got our orders—and they were sendin' us out West. They had been fightin' in Kentucky: we was in trouble thar; they sent us out to stop the Army of the Cumberland. And that was the last I ever seed of old Virginny. From that time on we fought hit out thar in the West and South. That's where we was, the Twenty-ninth, from then on to the end.

We had no real big fights until the spring of Sixty-two. And hit takes a fight to make a soldier of a man. Before that, there was skirmishin' and raids in Tennessee and in Kentucky. That winter we seed hard marchin' in the cold and wind and rain. We learned to know what hunger was, and what hit was to have to draw your belly in to fit your rations. I reckon by that time we knowed hit wasn't goin' to be a picnic like we thought that hit would be. We was a-learnin' all the time, but we wasn't soldiers yet. Hit takes a good big fight to make a soldier, and we hadn't had one yet. Early in Sixty-two we almost had one: they marched us to the relief of Donelson—but—law! they had taken her before we got thar—and I'm goin' to tell you a good story about that.

U. S. Grant was thar to take her, and we was marchin' to relieve her before Old Butcher could git in. We was seven mile away, and hit was comin' on to sundown; we'd been marchin' hard. We got the order to fall out and rest. And that was when I heard the gun and knowed that Donelson had fallen. Thar was no sound of fightin'. Everything was still as Sunday. We was sittin' thar aside the road, and then I heard a cannon boom. Hit boomed five times, real slow like—Boom!—Boom!—Boom!—Boom!— Boom! And the moment that I heared hit, I had a premonition. I turned to Jim and I said: "Well, thar you are! That's Donelson—and she's surrendered!"

Cap'n Bob Saunders heard me, but he wouldn't believe me and he said: "You're wrong!"

"Well," said Jim, "I hope to God he's right. I wouldn't care if the whole War has fallen through. I'm ready to go home."

"Well, he's wrong," said Cap'n Bob, "and I'll bet money on hit that he is."

Well, I tell you, that jest suited me. That was the way I was in those days— right from the beginnin' of the war to the very end. If there was any fun or devilment goin' on, any card playin' or gamblin', or any other kind of foolishness, I was right in on hit. I'd a-bet a man that red was green or day was night, and if a gal looked at me from a persimmon tree, why, law! I reckon I'd a-clumb the tree to git at her. That's jest the way hit was with me all through the War. I never made a bet or played a game of cards in my life before the War or after hit was over, but while the War was goin' on, I was ready fer anything.

"How much will you bet," I said.

"I'll bet you a hundred dollars even money," said Bob Saunders, and no sooner got the words out of his mouth than the bet was on.

We planked the money down right thar and gave hit to Jim to hold the stakes. Well, sir, we didn't have to wait half an hour before a feller on a horse came ridin' up and told us hit was no use goin' any farther—Fort Donelson had fallen.

"What did I tell you?" I said to Cap'n Saunders, and I put the money in my pocket.

Well, the laugh was on him then—I wish you could a-seed the expression on his face—he looked mighty sheepish, I tell you what he did. But he admitted hit, you know, he had to own up.

"You were right," he said. "You won the bet. But—I'll tell you what I'll do!" He put his hand into his pocket and pulled out a roll of bills—"I've got a hundred dollars left—and with me it's all or nothin'! We'll draw cards fer this last hundred—high card wins!"

Well, I was ready fer him. I pulled out my hundred, and I said, "Git out the deck!"

So they brought the deck out then, and Jim shuffled hit and held hit while we drawed. Bob Saunders drawed first, and he drawed the eight of spades. When I turned my card up, I had one of the queens.

Well, sir, you should have seen the look upon Bob Saunders' face. I tell you what, the fellers whooped and hollered till he looked like he was ready to crawl through a hole in the floor. We all had some fun with him, and then, of course, I gave the money back. I never took a penny in my life I made from gamblin'.

But that's the way hit was with me in those days—I was ready fer hit—fer anything. If any kind of devilment or foolishness came up, I was right in on hit with the ring-leaders.

Fort Donelson was the first big fight that we was in—and as I say, we wasn't really in hit because we couldn't git to her in time. And after Donelson that spring, in April, thar was Shiloh. Well—all that I can tell you is, we was thar on time at Shiloh. Oh, Lord! I reckon that we was! Perhaps we had been country boys before, perhaps some of us still made a joke of hit before—but after Shiloh we wasn't country boys no longer. We didn't make no joke about hit after Shiloh. They wiped the smile off of our faces thar at Shiloh. And after Shiloh we was boys no longer: we was vet'ran men.

From then on hit was fightin' to the end. That's where we learned what hit was like—at Shiloh. From then on we knew what it would be until the end.

Jim got wounded thar at Shiloh. Hit wasn't bad—not bad enough to suit him anyways—fer he wanted to go home fer good. Hit was a flesh wound in the leg, but hit was some time before we could git to him, and he was layin' out thar on the field, and I reckon that he lost some blood. Anyways, I heared he was unconscious when they picked him up; they carried him back and dressed his wound right thar upon the field. They cleaned hit out, I reckon, and they bandaged hit—thar was so many of 'em they couldn't do much more than that. Oh, I tell you what, in those days thar wasn't much that they could do. I've seed the surgeons workin' underneath an open shed with meat-saws, choppin' off the arms and legs and throwin' 'em out thar in a pile like they was sticks of wood, without no chloroform or nothin', and the screamin' and the hollerin' of the men enough to make your head turn gray. And that was as much as anyone could do: hit was live or die and take your chance—and thar was so many of 'em wounded so much worse than Jim that I reckon he was lucky they did anything fer him at all.

I heared them tell about hit later, how he come to, a-layin', stretched out thar on an old dirty blanket on the bare floor, and an army surgeon seed him lookin' at his leg all bandaged up, and I reckon he thought he'd cheer him up and said: "Oh, that ain't nothin'—you'll be up and fightin' Yanks again in two weeks' time."

Well, with that, they said, Jim got to cursin' and a-takin' on somethin' terrible: they said the language he used was enough to make your hair stand on end—they said he screamed and raved and reached down thar and jerked the bandage off and said: "Like hell I will!" They said the blood spouted up thar like a fountain, and they said that army doctor was so mad he throwed Jim down upon his back and sat on him and took that bandage, all bloody as hit was, and he tied hit back around his leg again and he said: "Goddam you, if you pull that bandage off again, I'll let you bleed to death."

And Jim, they said, came ragin' back at him until you could have heard him fer a mile, and said: "Well, by God, I don't care if I do; I'd rather die than stay here any longer."

They say they had hit back and forth thar until Jim got so weak he couldn't talk no more. I know that when I come to see him a day or two later, he was settin' up and I asked him: "Jim, how is your leg? Are you hurt bad?"

And he answered quick as a flash: "Not bad enough. They can take the whole damn leg off as far as I'm concerned, and bury hit here at Shiloh if they'll only let me go back home and not come back again. Me and Martha will git along somehow," he said. "I'd rather be a cripple the rest of my life than have to come back and fight in this damn War."

Well, I knowed he meant hit, too. I looked at him and seed how much he meant hit, and I knowed thar wasn't anything that I could do. When a man begins to talk that way, thar hain't much you can say to him. Well, sure enough, in a week or two, they let him go upon a two months' furlough, and he went limpin' away upon a crutch. He was the happiest man I ever seed. "They gave me two months' leave," he said, "but if they jest let me git back home, old Bragg'll have to send his whole damn army before he gits me out of thar again."

Well, he was gone two months or more, and I never knowed what happened—whether he got ashamed of himself when his wound healed up all right, or whether Martha talked him out of hit. But he was back with us by late July—the grimmest, bitterest-lookin' man you ever seed. He wouldn't talk to me about hit, he wouldn't tell me what happened, but I knowed from that time on he'd never draw his breath in peace until he left the Army and got back home fer good.

Well, that was Shiloh, that was the time we didn't miss, that was where we found out war was no picnic, where we knowed at last what hit would be until the end.

We seed some big fights in the War. And we was in some bloody battles. But the biggest fight we fought was Chickamauga. The bloodiest fight I ever seed was Chickamauga. Thar was big battles in the War, but thar never was a fight before, thar'll never be a fight again, like Chickamauga. I'm goin' to tell you how hit was at Chickamauga.

All through the spring and summer of that year, Old Rosey follered us through Tennessee.

We had him stopped the year before, the time we whupped him at Stone's River at the end of Sixty-two: we tarred him out so bad he had to wait. He waited thar six months at Murfreesboro. But we knowed he was a-comin' all the time. Old Rosey started at the end of June and drove us out of Shelbyville. We fell back on Tullahoma in rains the like of which you never seed. But Rosey kept a-comin' on.

He drove us out of Tullahoma, too. We fell back across the Cumberland: we pulled back behind the mountain, but he follered us.

I reckon thar was fellers that was quicker when a fight was on, and when they'd seed just what hit was they had to do. But when hit came to plannin' and a-figgerin', old Rosey Rosecrans took the cake. Old Rosey was a fox. Fer sheer natural cunnin' I never knowed the beat of him.

While Bragg was watchin' him at Chattanooga to keep him from gittin' across Tennessee, he sent some fellers forty mile upstream. And then he'd march 'em back and forth and round the hill and back in front of us again where we could look at 'em, until you'd a-thought that every Yankee in the world was thar.—But law! All that was jest a dodge! He had fellers a-sawin' and a-hammerin', a-buildin' boats, a-blowin' bugles and a-beatin' drums, makin' all the noise they could—you could hear 'em over yonder gittin' ready—and all the time Old Rosey was fifty mile or more downstream, ten mile *past* Chattanooga, a-fixin' to git over way down thar. That was the kind of feller Rosey was.

We got to Chattanooga early in July and waited fer two months. Old Rosey had to cross the Cumberland, push his men and pull his trains across the ridges and through the gaps before he got to us. July went by, we had no news of him—"Oh Lord!" said Jim, "perhaps he ain't a-comin'!"—I knowed he was a-comin', but I let Jim have his way.

Some of the fellers would git used to hit. A feller'd git into a frame of mind where he wouldn't let hit worry him. He'd let termorrer look out fer hitself. That was the way hit was with me.

With Jim hit was the other way around. Now that he knowed Martha Patton he was a different man. I think he hated the War and army life from the moment that he met her. From that time he was livin' fer only one thing—to go back home and marry that gal. When mail would come and some of us was gittin' letters, he'd be the first in line: and if she wrote him, why he'd walk away like someone in a dream. And if she failed to write, he jest go off somers and set down by himself: he'd be in such a state of misery he didn't want to talk to no one. He got the name with the fellers for bein' queer—unsociable—always a-broodin' and a-frettin' about somethin' and a-wantin' to be left alone. And so, after a time, they let him be: he wasn't popular with most of them—but they never knowed what was wrong, they never knowed that he wasn't really the way they thought he was at all—hit was jest that he was hit so desperate hard, the worst-in-love man that I ever seed. But law! I knowed! I knowed what was the trouble from the start.

Hit's funny how war took a feller. Before the War I was the serious one, and Jim had been the one to play.

I reckon that I'd had to work too hard. We was so poor. Before the War, hit almost seemed I never knowed the time I didn't have to work. And when the War came, why at first I thought hit would be different from the way hit was. I only thought of all the fun and frolic I was goin' to have, and then at last when I knowed what hit was like, why I was used to hit and didn't care.

I always could git used to things. And I reckon maybe that's the reason that I'm here. I wasn't one to worry much, and no matter how rough the goin' got, I always figgered I could hold out if the others could. I let termorrer look out fer hitself. I reckon that you'd have to say that I was an optimist. If things got bad, well, I always figgered that they could be worse, and if they got so bad that they couldn't be no worse, why, then I'd figger that they couldn't last this way ferever, they'd have to git some better some time later on. I reckon you'd have to say that was the Pentland in me: our belief in what we call predestination.

Now, Jim was jest the other way. The War changed him round the other way. And, as I say, hit didn't happen all at once. Jim was the happiest man I ever seed that mornin' that we started out from home. I reckon he thought of the War, as we all did, as a big frolic. We gave hit just about six months: we figgered we'd be back by then, and, of course, that jest suited Jim. I reckon that hit suited all of us. Hit would give us all a chance to wear a uniform and to see the world, to shoot some Yankees and to run 'em north, and then to come back home and lord it over those who hadn't been, and be a hero and court the gals.

That was the way it looked to us when we set out from Zebulon. We never thought about the winter. We never thought about the mud and cold and rain. We never knowed what it would be to have to march on an empty belly, to have to march barefoot with frozen feet and with no coat upon your back, to have to lay down on bare ground and try to sleep with no coverin' above you, and thankful half the time if you could find dry ground to sleep upon and too tard the rest of hit to care. We never knowed or thought about such things as these. We never knowed how hit would be thar in the cedar thickets beside Chickamauga Creek. And if we had a-knowed, if someone had a-told us, why I reckon that none of us would a-cared. We was too young and ignerant to care. And as fer *knowin'*—law! the only trouble about *knowin'* is that you've got to know what knowin's *like* before you can know what knowin' *is*. Thar's no one that can tell you, you've got to know hit fer yourself.

We never knowed about these things the mornin' we started out from home to join. And Jimmy never knowed of Martha Patton.

Well, winter of the first year came, six months had passed, we was with Bragg up in Kentucky, and they pushed us back to Tennessee. And still there was no sign of the war endin'. We fought 'em off at Perryville in October, but they kept a-comin' on, and winter came again. We stopped 'em at Stone's River at the start of Sixty-three. Then spring came, thar was some skirmishin' in May, and then the rains. But Rosey kept a-follerin' us and "Lord!" said Jimmy, "will hit never end?"

He'd been a-prayin' and a-hopin' from the first that soon hit would be over and that he could go back and git that gal. And fer a year or more I'd tried to cheer him up. I told him that hit couldn't last ferever. Now hit was no use to tell him any longer. He wouldn't have believed me if I had.

Because Old Rosey kept a-comin' on: we'd whup him, and we'd stop him fer a while, but then he'd git his wind, he'd be on our trail again, he'd drive us back—"Oh, Lord!" said Jimmy, "will hit never stop?"

That summer he was drivin' us through Tennessee. He drove us out of Shelbyville. We fell back on Tullahoma to the passes of the hills. Then we pulled back across the Cumberland—"Now, we've got him," I told Jim. "He'll have to cross the mountains now to get at us. And when he does, we'll have him—that's all that Bragg's been waitin' fer. We'll whup the day-lights out of him this time," I said, "and after that there'll be nothin' left of him. We'll be home by Christmas, Jim—you wait and see—" And Jim just looked at me and shook his head and said: "Lord, Lord, I don't believe this War'll ever end!"

Hit wasn't that he was afraid—or if he was, hit made a wildcat out of him in the fight. Jim could go fightin'-mad like no one else I ever seed. But I reckon hit was just because he was so desperate. He hated hit so much. He couldn't git used to hit the way the others could. He couldn't take hit as hit came. Hit wasn't so much he was afraid to die. I guess hit was that he was still so full of livin'. . . .

So, like I say, Old Rosey pushed us back across the Cumberland. We was in Chattanooga in July, and fer a few weeks hit was quiet thar. But all the time I knowed that Rosey would keep a-comin' on. We got wind of him again along in August. He pushed his trains across the Cumberland, with the roads so bad, what with the rains, his wagons sunk down to the axle hubs. But he got them over, came down in the valley, then across the ridge, and early in September he was on our heels again.

We cleared out of Chattanooga on the eighth. And our tail end was pullin' out at one end of the town as Rosey come in through the other. We dropped down around the mountain south of town, and Rosey thought he had us on the run again.

But this time he was fooled. We was ready fer him now, a-pickin' our spots and layin' low. Old Rosey follered us. He sent McCook around down towards the south to head us off. He thought he had us in retreat, but when McCook got thar, we wasn't thar at all. We'd come down south of town and taken our positions along Chickamauga Creek. McCook had gone too far. Thomas was follerin' us from the north, and when McCook tried to git back to join Thomas, he couldn't pass us fer we blocked the way. They had to fight us or be cut in two.

We were in position on the Chickamauga on the seventeenth. The Yankees streamed in on the eighteenth, and took their position in the woods a-facin' us. We had our backs to Chickamauga Creek. The Yankees had their line thar in the woods before us on a rise, with Missionary Ridge behind them to the west. . . .

The Battle of Chickamauga was fought in a cedar thicket: that cedar thicket, from what I knowed of hit, was about three miles long and one mile wide. We fought fer two days all up and down that thicket and to and fro across hit. When the fight started, that cedar thicket was so thick and dense you could a-took a butcher knife and drove hit in thar anywheres and hit would a-stuck. And when that fight was over, that cedar thicket had been so torn to pieces by shot and shell you could a-looked in thar anywheres with your naked eye and seed a black snake run a hundred yards away. If you'd a-looked at that cedar thicket the day after that fight was over, you'd a-wondered how a hummin' bird the size of your thumbnail could a-flown through thar without bein' torn to pieces by the fire. And yet more than half of us who went into that thicket came out of hit alive and told the tale. You wouldn't have thought that hit was possible. But I was thar and seed hit, and hit was. . . .

A little after midnight—hit may have been about two o'clock in the mornin'—while we lay there waitin' for the fight we knowed was bound to come next day—Jim woke me up. I woke up like a flash—you got used to hit in those days—and though hit was so dark you could hardly see your hand a foot away, I knowed his face at once. He was white as a ghost, and he had got thin as a rail in that last year's campaign. In the dark his face looked white as paper. He dug his hand into my arm so hard hit hurt. I roused up sharp-like; then I seed him and knowed who it was.

"John!" he said, "John!"—and dug his fingers in my arm so hard he made hit ache—"John! I've seed him! He was here again!"

I tell you what, the way he said hit made my blood run cold. The sight of that white face and those black eyes a-burnin' at me in the dark—the way he said hit and the way hit was—fer I could feel the men around me and hear somethin' movin' in the woods—I heared a trace chain rattle and hit was enough to make your blood run cold. I grabbed a-hold of him—I shook him by the arm—I didn't want the rest of 'em to hear—I told him to hush up.

"John, he was here!" he said.

I never asked him what he meant—I knowed too well to ask. Hit was the third time he'd seed hit in a month—a man upon a horse—I didn't want to hear no more—I told him that hit was a dream and I told him to go back to sleep—

"I tell you, John, hit was no dream!" he said. "Oh, John, I heared hit—

and I heared his horse—and I seed him sittin' there as plain as day—and he never said a word to me—he jest sat thar lookin' down and then he turned and rode away into the woods—John, John, I heared him, and I don't know what hit means!"

Well, whether he seed hit or imagined hit or dreamed hit, I don't know. But the sight of his black eyes a-burnin' holes through me in the dark made me feel almost as if I'd seed hit too. I told him to lay down by me—and still I seed his eyes a-blazin thar. I know he didn't sleep a wink the rest of that whole night—I closed my eyes and tried to make him think that I was sleepin', but hit was no use:—we lay thar wide awake. And both of us was glad when mornin' came.

The fight began upon our right at ten o'clock. We couldn't find out what was happenin'—the woods thar was so close and thick we never knowed fer two days what had happened, and we didn't know fer certain then. We never knowed how many we was fightin' or how many we had lost. I've heard them say that even Old Rosey himself didn't know jest what had happened when he rode back into town the next day, and didn't know that Thomas was standin' like a rock. And if Old Rosey didn't know no more than this about hit, what could a common soldier know? We fought back and forth across that cedar thicket for two days, and thar was times when you would be right up on top of them before you even knowed that they was thar. And that's the way the fightin' went—the bloodiest fightin' that was ever knowed until that cedar thicket was soaked red with blood, and thar was hardly a place left where a sparrer could have perched.

And as I say, we heared them fightin' out upon our right at ten o'clock, and then the fightin' came our way. I heared later that this fightin' started out when the Yanks come down to the Creek and run into a bunch of Forrest's men and drove 'em back. And then they had hit back and forth until they got drove back themselves, and that's the way we had hit all day long. We'd attack and then they'd throw us back, then they'd attack and we'd beat them off. And that was the way hit went from mornin' to night. We piled up thar upon their left: they mowed us down with canister and grape until the very grass was soakin' with our blood, but we kept comin' on. We must have charged a dozen times that day—I was in four of 'em myself. We fought back and forth across that wood until thar wasn't a piece of hit as big as the palm of your hand we hadn't fought on. We busted through their right at two-thirty in the afternoon and got way over by the Widder Glenn's, where Rosey had his quarters, and beat 'em back until we got the whole way cross the Lafayette Road and took possession of hit. And then they drove us out again. And we kept comin' on and both sides was still at hit when darkness fell.

We fought back and forth across that road all day, with first one side and then t'other holdin' hit until the road itself was soaked in blood: they called that road the Bloody Lane, and that was jest the name for hit.

We kept fightin' fer an hour or more after hit had gotten dark, and you could see the rifles flashin' in the woods, but then hit all died down. I tell you what, that night was somethin' to remember and to marvel at as long as you live. The fight had set the woods afire in places, and you could see the smoke and flames and hear the screamin' and the hollerin' of the wounded until hit made your blood run cold. We got as many as we could—but some, we didn't even try to—we jest let 'em lay. Hit was an awful thing to hear—I reckon many a wounded man was jest left thar to die or burn to death because we couldn't git 'em out.

You could see the nurses and the stretcher-bearers movin' through the woods, and each side huntin' fer hits dead; you could see 'em movin' in the smoke an' flames, an' you could see the dead men layin' there as thick as wheat, with their corpse-like faces an' black powder on their lips, an' a little bit of moonlight comin' through the trees, and all of hit more like a nightmare out of hell than anything I ever knowed before.

But we had other work to do. All through the night we could hear the Yanks a-choppin' and a-thrashin' round, and we knowed that they was fellin' trees to block us when we went fer them next mornin'. Fer we knowed the fight was only jest begun. We figgered that we'd had the best of hit, but we knowed no one had won the battle yet. We knowed the second day would beat the first.

Jim knowed hit, too. Poor Jim, he didn't sleep that night—he never seed the man upon the horse that night—he jest sat thar, a-grippin' his knees and starin', and a-sayin', "Lord God, Lord God, when will hit ever end?"

Then mornin' come at last. This time we knowed jest where we was and what hit was we had to do. Bragg knowed at last where Rosey had his line, and Rosey knowed where we was; so we waited thar, both sides, till mornin' came. Hit was a foggy mornin' with mist upon the ground. Around ten o'clock the mist began to rise, we got the order, we went chargin' through the wood again.

We knowed the fight was goin' to be upon the right—upon our right, that is, on Rosey's left. And we knowed that Thomas was in charge of Rosey's left. And we all knowed that hit was easier to crack a flint rock with your teeth than to make Old Thomas budge. But we went after him, and I tell you what, that was a fight! The first day's fight had been like playin' marbles compared to this.

We hit Old Thomas on his left at half past ten, and Breckinridge came sweepin' round and turned Old Thomas' flank and came in at his back, and then we had hit hot and heavy. Old Thomas whupped his men around like he would crack a rawhide whup, and drove Breckinridge back around the flank again, but we was back on top of him before you knowed the first attack was over.

The fight went ragin' down the flank, down to the center of Old Rosey's army and back and forth across the left, and all up and down Old Thomas' line. We'd hit right and left and in the middle, and he'd come back at us and throw us back again. And we went ragin' back and forth thar like two bloody lions, with that cedar thicket so tore up, so bloody and so thick with dead by that time, that hit looked as if all hell had broken loose in thar.

Rosey kept a-whuppin' men around off of his right, to help Old Thomas on the left to stave us off. And then we'd hit Old Thomas left of center, and we'd bang him in the middle, and we'd hit him on the left again, and he'd whup those Yankees back and forth off of the right into his flanks and middle as we went fer him, until we run those Yankees ragged. We had them gallopin' back and forth like kangaroos, and in the end that was the thing that cooked their goose.

The worst fightin' had been on the left, on Thomas' line, but to hold us thar they'd thinned their right out and hadn't closed up on the center of their line. And when Longstreet seed the gap in Wood's position on the right, he took five brigades of us and poured us through. That whupped them. That broke their line and smashed their whole right all to smither-eens. We went after them like a pack of ragin' devils. We killed 'em, and we took 'em by the thousands, and those we didn't kill and take right thar, went streamin' back across the hill as if all hell was at their heels.

That was a rout if ever I heared tell of one! They went streamin' back across the hill—hit was each man fer himself and the devil take the hind-most. They caught Rosey comin' up—he rode into them—he tried to check 'em, face 'em round, and git 'em to come up again—hit was like tryin' to swim the Mississippi upstream on a bone-yard mule! They swept him back with them as if he'd been a wooden chip. They went streamin' into Rossville like the ragtag of creation—the worst whupped Army that you ever seed, and Old Rosey Rosecrans was along with all the rest!

He knowed hit was all up with him, or thought he knowed hit, fer every-body told him the Army of the Cumberland had been blown to smithereens and that hit was a general rout. And Old Rosey turned and rode to Chat-tanooga, and he was a beaten man. I've heard tell that when he rode up to his headquarters thar in Chattanooga, they had to help him from his horse, and that he walked into the house all dazed and fuddled-like, like he never knowed what had happened to him—and that he jest sat thar struck dumb and never spoke.

This was at four o'clock of that same afternoon. And then the news was brought to him that Thomas was still thar upon the field and wouldn't budge. Old Thomas stayed thar like a rock. We'd smashed the right, we'd sent hit flyin' back across the ridge, the whole Yankee right was broken into bits and streamin' back into Rossville for dear life. Then we bent Old Thomas back upon his left: we thought we had him, he'd have to leave the field or else surrender. But Old Thomas turned and fell back along the Ridge and put his back against the wall thar, and he wouldn't budge.

Longstreet pulled us back at three o'clock when we had broken up the right, and sent them streamin' back across the Ridge. We thought that hit was over then; we moved back stumblin' like men walkin' in a dream. And I turned to Jim—I put my arm around him, and I said, "Jim, what did I say, I knowed hit, we've licked 'em and this is the end!" I never even knowed if he heared me, he went stumblin' on beside me with his face as white as paper and his lips black with the powder of the cartridge-bite, mumblin' and mutterin' to himself like someone talkin' in a dream. And we fell back to position, and they told us all to rest. And we leaned thar on our rifles like men who hardly knowed if they had come out of that hell alive or dead.

"Oh, Jim, we've got 'em and this is the end!" He leaned thar swayin' on his rifle, starin' through the wood, he jest leaned and swayed thar, and he never said a word, and those great eyes of his a-burnin' through the wood—

"Jim, don't you hear me?"—and I shook him by the arm. "Hit's over, man! We've licked 'em and the fight is over—can't you understand?"

And then I heard them shoutin' on the right, the word came down the line again, and Jim—poor Jim!—he raised his head and listened, and "Oh God!" he said. "We've got to go again!"

Well, hit was true. The word had come that Thomas had lined up upon the Ridge, and we had to go for him again. After that I never exactly knowed what happened—hit was like fightin' in a bloody dream—like doin' somethin' in a nightmare—only the nightmare was like death and hell. Longstreet threw us up that hill five times, I think, before darkness came. We'd charge up to the very muzzle of their guns, and they'd mow us down like grass, and we'd come stumblin' back—or what was left of us—and form again at the foot of the hill, and then come on again. We'd charge right up the Ridge and drive 'em through the gap and fight 'em with cold steel, and they'd come back again, and we'd brain each other with the butt end of our guns. Then they'd throw us back, and we'd re-form and come on after 'em again.

The last charge happened jest at dark. We came along and stripped the ammunition off the dead—we took hit from the wounded—we had nothin' left ourselves. Then we hit the first line—and we drove 'em back—we hit the second and swept over 'em. We were goin' to take the third and last— they waited till they saw the color of our eyes before they let us have hit. Hit was like a river of red-hot lead had poured down on us: the line melted thar like snow. Jim stumbled and spun round as if somethin' had whupped him like a top. He fell right towards me, with his eyes wide open and the blood a-pourin' from his mouth: I took one look at him and then stepped over him like he was a log. Thar was no more to see or think of now—no more to reach—except that line. We reached hit and they let us have hit— and we stumbled back again.

And yet we knowed that we had won a victory. That's what they told us later—and we knowed hit must be so because when daybreak come the next mornin' the Yankees was all gone. They had all retreated into town, and we was left thar by the Creek at Chickamauga in possession of the field.

I don't know how many men got killed—I don't know which side lost the most. I only know that you could have walked across the dead men without settin' foot upon the ground. I only know that cedar thicket, which had been so dense and thick two days before you could've drove a knife into hit and hit would've stuck, had been so shot to pieces that you could've looked in thar on Monday mornin' with your naked eye and seed a black snake run a hundred yards away.

I don't know how many men we lost or how many of the Yankees we may have killed—the generals on both sides can figger all that out to suit themselves. But I know that when the fight was over you could've looked in thar and wondered how a hummin' bird could've flown through that cedar thicket and come out alive. And yet that happened, yes, and somethin' more than hummin' birds—fer men came out, alive.

And on Monday mornin', when I went back up the Ridge to where Jim lay, thar just beside him on a little torn piece of bough, I heard a redbird sing. I turned him over and got his watch, his pocket knife, and what few papers and belongin's that he had, and some letters that he'd had from Martha Patton. And I put them in my pocket.

And then I got up and looked around. Hit all seemed funny after hit had happened, like somethin' that had happened in a dream. Fer Jim had wanted so desperate hard to live, and hit had never mattered half so much to me, and now I was a-standin' thar with Jim's watch and Martha Patton's letters in my pocket and a-listenin' to that little redbird sing.

And I would go all through the War and go back home and marry Martha later on, and fellers like poor Jim were layin' thar at Chickamauga Creek. . . .

Hit's all so strange now when you think of hit. Hit all turned out so different from the way we thought. And that was long ago, and I'll be ninety-five years old if I am livin' on the seventh day of August, of this present year. Now that's goin' back a long ways, hain't hit? And yet hit all comes back to me as clear as if hit happened yesterday. And then hit all will go away and be as strange as if hit happened in a dream.

But I have been in some big battles, I can tell you: I've seen strange things and been in bloody fights. But the biggest fight that I was ever in—the bloodiest battle anyone ever fought—was Chickamauga in that cedar thicket—at Chickamauga Creek in that great War.

The Company

I

When Joe went home that year, he found that Mr. Merrit also was in town. Almost before the first greetings at the station were over, Jim told him. The two brothers stood there grinning at each other. Jim, with his lean, thin, deeply furrowed face, that somehow always reminded Joe so curiously and poignantly of Lincoln, and that also somehow made him feel a bit ashamed, looked older and more worn than he had the last time Joe had seen him. He always looked a little older and a little more worn; the years, like the slow gray ash of time, wore at his temples and at the corners of his eyes. The two brothers stood there looking at each other, grinning, a little awkward, but delighted. In Jim's naked worn eyes, Joe could see how proud the older brother was of him, and something caught him in the throat.

But Jim just grinned at him, and in a moment said: "I guess we'll have to sleep you out in the garage. Bob Merrit is in town, you, you—or if you like, there's a nice room at Mrs. Parker's right across the street, and she'd be glad to have you."

Joe looked rather uncomfortable at the mention of Mrs. Parker's name. She was a worthy lady, but of a literary turn of mind, and a pillar of the Woman's Club. Kate saw his expression and laughed, poking him in the ribs with her big finger: "Ho, ho, ho, ho, ho! You see what you're in for, don't you? The prodigal son comes home, and we give him his choice of Mrs. Parker or the garage! Now is that life, or not?"

Jim Doaks, as was his wont, took this observation in very slowly. One could see him deliberating on it, and then as it broke slowly on him, it sort of spread all over his seamed face; he bared his teeth in a craggy grin; a kind of rusty and almost unwilling chuckle came from him; he turned his head sideways, and said "Hi—I," an expletive that with him was always indicative of mirth.

"I don't mind a bit," protested Joe. "I think the garage is swell. And then"—they all grinned at each other again with the affection of people who know each other so well that they are long past knowledge—"if I get to

397

helling around at night, I won't feel that I am disturbing you when I come in. . . . And how is Mr. Merrit, anyway?"

"Why, just fine," Jim answered with that air of thoughtful deliberation which accompanied most of his remarks. "He's just fine, I think. And he's been asking about you," said Jim seriously. "He wants to see you."

"And we knew you wouldn't mind," Kate said more seriously. "You know, it's business; he's with the Company, and of course it's good policy to be as nice to them as you can."

But in a moment, because such designing was really alien to her own hospitable and wholehearted spirit, she added: "Mr. Merrit is a nice fellow. I like him. We're glad to have him, anyway."

"Bob's all right," said Jim. "And I know he really wants to see you. Well," he said, "if we're all ready, let's get going. I'm due back at the office now. Merrit's coming in. If you'd like to fool around uptown until one o'clock and see your friends, you could come by then, and I'll run you out. Why don't you do that? Merrit's coming out to dinner, too."

It was agreed to do this, and a few minutes later Joe got out of the car upon the Public Square of the town he had not seen for a year.

The truth of the matter was that Joe not only felt perfectly content at the prospect of sleeping in the garage, but he also felt a pleasant glow at the knowledge that Mr. Robert Merrit was in town, and staying at his brother's house.

Joe had never known exactly just what Mr. Robert Merrit did. In Jim's spacious but rather indefinite phrase, he was referred to as "the Company's man." And Joe did not know what the duties of a "Company's man" were, but Mr. Merrit made them seem mighty pleasant. He turned up ruddy, plump, well-kept, full of jokes, and immensely agreeable, every two or three months, with a pocket that seemed perpetually full, and like the Jovian pitcher of milk of Baucis and Philemon, perpetually replenished, in some miraculous way, with big fat savory cigars, which he was always handing out to people.

Joe understood, of course, that there was some business connection in the mysterious ramifications of "the Company" between his brother and Robert Merrit. But he had never heard them "talk business" together, nor did he know just what the business was. Mr. Merrit would "turn up" every two or three months like a benevolent and ruddy Santa Claus, making his jolly little jokes, passing out his fat cigars, putting his arm around people's shoulders—in general making everyone feel good. In his own words, "I've got to turn up now and then just to see that the boys are behaving themselves, and not taking any wooden nickels." Here he would wink at you in such an infectious way that you had to grin. Then he would give you a fat cigar.

His functions did seem to be ambassadorial. Really, save for an occasional visit to the office, he seemed to spend a good deal of his time in inaugurating an era of good living every time he came to town. He was always taking the salesmen out to dinner and to lunch. He was always "coming out to the house," and when he did come, one knew that Kate would have one of her best meals ready, and that there would be some good drinks. Mr. Merrit usually brought the drinks. Every time he came to town he always seemed to bring along with him a plentiful stock of high-grade beverages. In other words, the man really did carry about with him an aura of good fellowship and good living, and that was why it was so pleasant now to know that Mr. Merrit was in town and "staying out at the house."

Mr. Merrit was not only a nice fellow. He was also with "the Company." And since Jim was also a member of "the Company," that made everything all right. Because "the Company," Joe knew, was somehow a vital, mysterious form in all their lives. Jim had begun to work for it when he was sixteen years old—as a machinist's helper in the shops at Akron. Since then he had steadily worked his way up through all the stages until now, "well-fixed" apparently, he was a district manager—an important member of "the sales organization."

"The Company," "the sales organization"—mysterious titles, both of them. But most comforting.

II

The sales organization—or, to use a word that at this time was coming into common speech, the functional operation—of the Federal Weight, Scale & Computing Co., while imposing in its ramified complexity of amount and number, was in its essence so beautifully simple that to a future age, at least, the system of enfeoffments in the Middle Ages, the relation between the liege lord and his serf, may well seem complex by comparison.

The organization of the sales system was briefly just this, and nothing more: the entire country was divided into districts, and over each district an agent was appointed. This agent, in turn, employed salesmen to cover the various portions of his district. In addition to these salesmen there was also an "office man" whose function, as his name implies, was to look after the office, attend to any business that might come up when the agent and his salesmen were away, take care of any stray sheep who might stray in of their own volition without having been enticed thither by the persuasive herdings of the salesmen and their hypnotic words; and a "repair man" whose business it was to repair damaged or broken-down machines.

Although in the familiar conversation of the agents a fellow agent was said to be the agent for a certain town—Smith, for example, was the "Knoxville man," Jones, the Charleston one, Robinson the one at Richmond, etc., these agencies, signified by the name of a town in which the agent had his office, comprised the district that surrounded them.

In Catawba there were six agencies and six agents. The population of the state was about three million. In other words, each agent had a district of approximately one-half million people. Not that the distribution worked out invariably in this way. There was no set rule for the limitation of an agency; some agencies were larger than others and considerably more profitable, depending upon the amount of business and commercial enterprise that was done in any given district. But the median of one agent to a half-million people was, in probability, a fairly accurate one for the whole country.

Now, as to the higher purposes of this great institution, which the agent almost never referred to by name, as who should not speak of the deity with coarse directness, but almost always with a just perceptible lowering and huskiness of the voice, as "the Company"—these higher purposes were also, when seen in their essential purity, characterized by the same noble directness and simplicity as marked the operations of the entire enterprise. This higher purpose, in the famous utterance of the great man himself, invariably repeated every year as a sort of climax or peroration to his hour-long harangue to his adoring disciples at the national convention, was—sweeping his arm in a gesture of magnificent and grandiloquent command toward the map of the entire United States of America—"There is your market. Go out and sell them."

What could be simpler or more beautiful than this? What could be more eloquently indicative of that quality of noble directness, mighty sweep, and far-seeing imagination, which has been celebrated in the annals of modern literature under the name of "vision"? "There is your market. Go out and sell them."

Who says the age of romance is dead? Who says there are no longer giants on the earth in these days? It is Napoleon speaking to his troops before the pyramids. "Soldiers, forty centuries are looking down on you." It is John Paul Jones: "We have met the enemy and they are ours." It is Dewey, on the bridge deck of the *Oregon:* "You may fire when you are ready, Gridley." It is Grant before the works of Petersburg: "I propose to fight it out on this line if it takes all summer."

"There's your market. Go out and sell them." The words had the same spacious sweep and noble simplicity that have always characterized the utterances of the great leaders of every age and epoch of man's history.

It is true that there had been a time when the aims and aspirations of "the Company" had been more modest ones. There had been a time when the founder of the institution, the father of the present governor, John S. Appleton, had confined his ambitions to these modest words: "I should like to see one of my machines in every store, shop, or business in the United States that needs one, and can afford to pay for one."

The high aims expressed in these splendid words would seem to the inexperienced observer to be far-reaching enough, but as any agent upon the company's roster could now tell you, they were so conventional in their modest pretensions as to be practically mid-Victorian. Or, as the agent himself might put it: "That's old stuff now—we've gone way beyond that. Why, if you wanted to sell a machine to someone who *needs* one, you'd get nowhere. Don't wait until he *needs* one—make him buy one now. Suppose he doesn't need one; all right, we'll make him see the need of one. If he has no need of one, why, we'll create the need." In a more technical phrase, this was known as "creating the market," and this beautiful and poetic invention was the inspired work of one man, the fruit of the vision of none other than the great John S. Appleton, Jr., himself.

In fact, in one impassioned flight of oratory before his assembled parliaments, John S. Appleton, Jr., had become so intoxicated with the grandeur of his own vision that he is said to have paused, gazed dreamily into unknown vistas of magic Canaan, and suddenly to have given utterance in a voice quivering with surcharged emotion to these words: "My friends, the possibilities of the market, now that we have created it, are practically unlimited." Here he was silent for a moment, and those who were present on that historic occasion say that for a moment the great man paled, and then he seemed to stagger as the full impact of his vision smote him with its vistas. His voice is said to have trembled so when he tried to speak that for a moment he could not control himself. It is said that when he uttered those memorable words, which from that moment on were engraved upon the hearts of every agent there, his voice faltered, sank to an almost inaudible whisper, as if he himself could hardly comprehend the magnitude of his own conception.

"My friends," he muttered thickly, and was seen to reel and clutch the rostrum for support, "my friends, seen properly . . . " he whispered and moistened his dry lips, but here, those who were present say, his voice grew stronger and the clarion words blared forth " . . . seen properly, with the market we have created, there is no reason why one of our machines should not be in the possession of every man, woman, and child in the United States of America."

Then came the grand familiar gesture to the great map of these assembled states: "There's your market, boys. Go out and sell them."

Such, then, were the sky-soaring aims and aspirations of the Federal Weight, Scale & Computing Co. in the third decade of the century, and such, reduced to its naked and essential simplicity, was the practical effort, the concrete purpose, of every agent in the company. Gone were the days forever, as they thought, when their operations must be confined and limited merely to those business enterprises who needed, or thought they needed, a weight scale or computing machine. The sky was the limit, and for any agent to have hinted that anything less or lower than the sky was possibly the limit would have been an act of such impious sacrilege as to have merited his instant expulsion from the true church and the living faith—the church and faith of John S. Appleton, Jr., which is called "the Company."

In the pursuit and furtherance and consummation of this grand and elemental aim, the organization of the company worked with the naked drive, the beautiful precision of a locomotive piston. Over the salesmen was the agent, and over the agent was the district supervisor, and over the district supervisor was the district manager, and over the district manager was the general manager, and over the general manager was . . . was . . . God himself, or as the agents more properly referred to him, in voices that fell naturally to the hush of reverence, "the Old Man."

The operation of this beautiful and powerful machine can perhaps best be described to the lay reader by a series of concrete and poetic images. Those readers, for example, with an interest in painting, who are familiar with some of the terrific drawings of old Pieter Brueghel, may recall a certain gigantic product of his genius which bears the title *The Big Fish Eating Up the Little Ones,* and which portrays just that. The great whales and monster leviathans of the vasty deep swallowing the sharks, the sharks swallowing the swordfish, the swordfish swallowing the great bass, the great bass swallowing the lesser mackerel, the lesser mackerel eating up the herrings, the herrings gulping down the minnows, and so on down the whole swarming and fantastic world that throngs the sea-floors of the earth, until you get down to the tadpoles, who, it is to be feared, have nothing smaller than themselves to swallow.

Or, to a reader interested in history, the following illustration may make the operation of the system plain: at the end of a long line that stretches from the pyramids until the very portals of his house, the great Pharaoh, with a thonged whip in his hands, which he vigorously and unmercifully applies to the bare back and shoulders of the man ahead of him, who is great Pharaoh's great chief overseer, and in the hand of Pharaoh's great chief overseer likewise a whip of many tails which the great chief overseer unstintingly applies to the quivering back and shoulders of the wretch before him, who is the great chief overseer's chief lieutenant, and in the lieutenant's hand a whip of many tails which he applies to the suffering hide of his head sergeant, and in the head sergeant's hand a wicked flail with which he belabors the pelt of a whole company of groaning corporals, and in the hand of every groaning corporal, a wicked whip with which they lash and whack the bodies of a whole regiment of grunting slaves, who toil and sweat and bear burdens and pull and haul and build the towering structure of the pyramid.

Or, finally, for those readers with an interest in simple mechanics, the following illustration may suffice. Conceive an enormous flight of stairs with many landings, and at the very top of it, supreme and masterful, a man, who kicks another man in front of him quite solemnly in the seat of the pants; this man turns a somersault and comes erect upon the first and nearest landing and immediately, and with great decision, kicks the man in front of him down two more landings of these enormous stairs, who, on arriving, kicks the next incumbent down three landing flights, and so on to the bottom, where there is no one left to kick.

Now these, in their various ways, and by the tokens of their various imagery, fairly describe the simple but effective operation of the Company. Four times a year, at the beginning of each quarter, John S. Appleton called his general manager before him and kicked him down one flight of stairs, saying, "You're not getting the business. The market is there. You know what you can do about it—or else . . . "

And the general manager repeated the master's words and operations on his chief assistant managers, and they in turn upon the district managers, and they in turn upon the district supervisors, and they in turn upon the district agents, and they in turn upon the lowly salesmen, and they in turn, at long and final last, upon the final recipient of all swift kicks—the general public, the amalgamated Doakses of the earth.

It is true that to the lay observer the operation did not appear so brutally severe as has been described. It is true that the iron hand was cunningly concealed in the velvet glove, but there was no mistaking the fact, as those who had once felt its brutal grip could testify, that the iron hand was there and could be put to ruthless use at any moment. It is true that the constant menace of the iron hand was craftily disguised by words of cheer, by talk of fair rewards and bonuses, but these plums of service could turn bitter in the mouth, the plums themselves were just a threat of stern reprisal to those who were not strong or tall enough to seize them. One was not given his choice of having plums or not having plums. It was no exaggeration to say that one was told he must have plums, that he must get plums, that if he failed to gather plums another picker would be put in his place.

And of all the many wonderful and beautiful inventions which the great brain of John S. Appleton had created and conceived, this noble invention of plum-picking was the simplest and most cunning of the lot. For be it understood that these emoluments of luscious fruit were not wholly free. For every plum the picker took unto himself, two more were added to the plenteous store of Mr. Appleton. And the way this agricultural triumph was achieved was as follows:

Mr. Appleton was the founder of a great social organization known as the Hundred Club. The membership of the Hundred Club was limited exclusively to Mr. Appleton himself and the agents, salesmen, and district managers of his vast organization. The advantages of belonging to the Hundred Club were quickly apparent to everyone. Although it was asserted that membership in the Hundred Club was not compulsory, if one did not belong to it, the time was not far distant when one could not belong to Mr. Appleton. The club, therefore, like all the nobler Appleton inventions, was contrived cunningly of all the familiar ingredients of simplicity and devilish craft, of free will and predestination.

The club had the extraordinary distinction of compelling people to join it while at the same time giving them, through its membership, the proud prestige of social distinction. Not to belong to the Hundred Club, for an agent or a salesman, was equivalent to living on the other side of the railroad tracks. If one did not get in, if one could not reach high enough to make it, he faded quickly from the picture, his fellows spoke of him infrequently. When someone said, "What's Bob Klutz doing now?" the answers would be sparse and definitely vague, and, in course of time, Bob Klutz would be spoken of no more. He would fade out in oblivion. He was "no longer with the Company."

Now, the purpose and the meaning of the Hundred Club was this. Each agent and each salesman in the company, of no matter what position or what rank, had what was called a "quota"—that is to say, a certain fixed amount of business which was established as the normal average of his district and capacity. A man's quota differed according to the size of his territory, its wealth, its business, and his own experience and potentiality. If he was a district agent, his personal quota would be higher than that of a mere salesman in a district. One man's quota would be sixty, another's eighty, another's ninety or one hundred. Each of these men, however, no matter how small or large his quota might be, was eligible for membership in the Hundred Club, provided he could average 100 percent of his quota—hence the name. If he averaged more, if he got 120 percent of his quota, or 150 percent, or 200 percent, there were appropriate honors and rewards, not only of a social but of a financial nature. One could be high up in the Hundred Club or low down in the Hundred Club: it had almost as many degrees of honor and of merit as the great Masonic order. But of one thing, one could be certain: one must belong to the Hundred Club if one wanted to continue to belong to "the Company."

The unit of the quota system was "the point." If a salesman or an agent stated that his personal quota was eighty, it was understood that his quota was eighty points a month, that this was the desired goal, the average, toward which he should strive, which he should not fall below, and which, if possible, he should try to better. If a salesman's quota was eighty points a month, and he averaged eighty points throughout the year, he became automatically a member of the Hundred Club. And if he surpassed this quota, he received distinction, promotion, and reward in the Hundred Club, in proportion to the degree of his increase. The unit of the point itself was fixed at forty dollars. Therefore, if a salesman's quota was eighty points a month and he achieved it, he must sell the products of the Federal Weight, Scale & Computing Co. to the amount of more than three thousand dollars every month, and almost forty thousand dollars in the year.

The rewards were high. A salesman's commission averaged from 15 to 20 percent of his total sales; an agent's, from 20 to 25 percent, in addition to the bonuses he could earn by achieving or surpassing his full quota. Thus, it was entirely possible for an ordinary salesman in an average district to earn from six to eight thousand dollars a year, and for an agent to earn from twelve to fifteen thousand dollars, and even more if his district was an exceptionally good one.

So far, so good. The rewards, it is now apparent, were high, the inducements great. Where does the iron hand come in? It came in in many devious and subtle ways, of which the principal and most direct was this: once a man's quota had been fixed at any given point, the Company did not reduce it. On the contrary, if a salesman's quota was eighty points in any given year and he achieved it, he must be prepared at the beginning of the new year to find that his quota had been increased to ninety points. In other words, the plums were there, but always, year by year, upon a somewhat higher bough. "June Was the Greatest Month in Federal History"—so read the gigantic posters which the Company was constantly sending out to all the district offices—"*Make July a Greater One!* The Market's There, Mr. Agent, the Rest Is Up to You," etc.

In other words, this practice as applied to salesmanship resembled closely the one that has been known in the cotton mills as the stretch-out system. June was the greatest month in Federal history, but July must be a bigger one, and one must never look back on forgotten Junes with satisfaction. One must go on and upward constantly, the race was to the swift. The pace was ever faster and the road more steep.

The result of this on plain humanity may be inferred. It was shocking and revolting. If the spectacle of the average Federal man at work was an alarming one, the spectacle of that same man at play was simply tragic. No more devastating comment could be made on the merits of that vaunted system, which indeed in its essence was the vaunted system at that time of all business, of all America, than the astounding picture of the assembled cohorts of the Hundred Club gathered together in their yearly congress for a "Week of Play." For, be it known, one of the chief rewards of membership in this distinguished body, in addition to the bonuses and social distinctions, was a kind of grandiose yearly outing which lasted for a week and which was conducted "at the Company's expense." These yearly excursions of the fortunate group took various forms, but they were conducted on a lavish scale. The meeting place would be in New York, or in Philadelphia, or in Washington; sometimes the pleasure trip was to Bermuda, sometimes to Havana, sometimes across the continent to California and back again, sometimes to Florida, to the tropic opulence of Miami and Palm Beach; but wherever the voyage led, whatever the scheme might be, it was always grandiose, no expense was spared, everything was done on the grand scale, and the Company—the immortal Company, the paternal, noble, and great-hearted Company—"paid for everything."

If the journey was to be by sea, to Bermuda or to Cuba's shores, the Company chartered a transatlantic liner—one of the smaller but luxurious twenty-thousand tonners of the Cunard, the German Lloyd, or the Holland-American lines. From this time on, the Hundred Club was given a free sweep. The ship was theirs, and all the minions of the ship were theirs, to do their bidding. All the liquor in the world was theirs, if they could drink it. And Bermuda's coral isles, the most unlicensed privilege of gay Havana. For one short week, for one brief gaudy week of riot, everything on earth was theirs that money could buy or that the Company could command. It was theirs for the asking—and the Company paid for all.

It was, as we have said, a tragic spectacle: the spectacle of twelve or fifteen hundred men, for on these pilgrimages, by general consent, women—or their wives at any rate—were disbarred—the spectacle of twelve or fifteen hundred men, Americans, of middle years, in the third decade of this century, exhausted, overwrought, their nerves frayed down and stretched to the breaking point, met from all quarters of the continent "at the Company's expense" upon a greyhound of the sea for one wild week of pleasure. That spectacle had in its essential elements connotations of such general and tragic force in its relation and its reference to the entire scheme of things and the plan of life that had produced it that a thoughtful Martian, had he been vouchsafed but thirty minutes on this earth and could he have spent those thirty minutes on one of the crack liners that bore the Hundred Club to tropic shores, might have formed conclusions about the life on this tormented little cinder where we live that would have made him sorrowful that he had ever come and eager for the moment when his thirty-minute sojourn would be ended.

III

It was a few minutes before one o'clock when Joe entered his brother's office. The outer sales room, with its glittering stock of weights, scales, and computing machines, imposingly arranged on walnut pedestals, was deserted. From the little partitioned space behind, which served Jim as an office, he heard the sound of voices.

He recognized Jim's voice—low, grave, and hesitant, deeply troubled—at once. The other voice he had never heard before.

But as he heard that voice, he began to tremble and grow white about the lips. For that voice was a foul insult to human life, an ugly sneer whipped across the face of decent humanity, and as it came to him that this voice, these words, were being used against his brother, he had a sudden blind feeling of murder in his heart.

And what was, in the midst of this horror, so perplexing and troubling, was that this devil's voice had in it as well a curiously human note, as of someone he had known.

Then it came to him in a flash—it was Merrit speaking. The owner of that voice, incredible as it seemed, was none other than that plump, well-kept, jolly-looking man who had always been so full of cheerful and good-hearted spirits every time he had seen him.

Now, behind that evil little partition of glazed glass and varnished wood, this man's voice had suddenly become fiendish. It was inconceivable, and as Joe listened, he grew sick with horror, as a man does in some awful nightmare when suddenly he envisions someone familiar doing some perverse and abominable act. And what was most dreadful of all was the voice of his brother, humble, low, submissive, modestly entreating. He could hear Merrit's voice cutting across the air like a gob of rasping phlegm, and then Jim's low voice—gentle, hesitant, deeply troubled—coming in from time to time by way of answer.

"Well, what's the matter? Don't you want the job?"

"Why—why, yes, you know I do, Bob," and Jim's voice lifted a little in a troubled and protesting laugh.

"What's the matter that you're not getting the business?"

"Why—why . . . " Again the troubled and protesting little laugh. "I *thought* I was . . . !"

"Well, you're not!" The rasping voice fell harsh upon the air with the brutal nakedness of a knife. "This district ought to deliver thirty percent more business than you're getting from it, and the Company is going to have it, too—or *else!* You deliver or you go right on upon your can! See? The Company doesn't give a damn about you. It's after the business. You've been around a long time, but you don't mean a damn bit more to the Company than anybody else. And you know what's happened to a lot of other guys who got to feeling they were too big for their job, don't you?"

"Why—why, yes, Bob. . . . " Again the troubled and protesting laugh. "But—honestly, I never thought . . . "

"We don't give a damn what you thought!" the brutal voice ripped in. "I've given you fair warning now. You get the business or out you go!"

Merrit came out of the little partition-cage into the cleaner light of the outer room. When he saw Joe, he looked startled for a moment. Then he was instantly transformed. His plump and ruddy face was instantly wreathed in smiles; he cried out in a hearty tone: "Well, well, well! Look who's here! If it's not the old boy himself!"

He shook hands with Joe, and as he did so, turned and winked humorously at Jim, in the manner of older men when they are carrying on a little bantering by-play in the presence of a younger one.

"Jim, I believe he gets better-looking every time I see him. Has he broken any hearts yet?"

Jim tried to smile, gray-faced and haggard.

"I hear you're burning them up in the big town," said Merrit, turning to the younger man. "Great stuff, son, we're proud of you."

And with another friendly pressure of the hand, he turned away with an air of jaunty readiness, picked up his hat, and said cheerfully: "Well, what d'ya say, folks? Didn't I hear somebody say something about one of the madam's famous meals, out at the old homestead? Well, you can't hurt my feelings. I'm ready if you are. Let's go."

And smiling, ruddy, plump, cheerful, a perverted picture of amiable good-will to all the world, he sauntered through the door. And for a moment the two brothers just stood there looking at each other, drawn and haggard, with a bewildered expression in their eyes.

In Jim's decent eyes, also, there was a look of shame. In a moment, with that instinct for loyalty which was one of the roots of his soul, he said: "Bob's a good fellow . . . . You . . . you see, he's got to do these things. . . . He's . . . he's with the Company."

Joe didn't say anything. He couldn't. He had just found out something about life he hadn't known before.

And it was all so strange, so different from what he thought it would be.

A Prologue to America

SCENE: A night of dazzling light above America. As the action begins, the body and bones of the American continent are revealed from East to West. The vision at first is governed by silence and the still white radiance of the blazing moon. The view in this first instant is appalling—it seems lifeless and inhuman, like the design and landscape of a prehistoric world. And yet one knows at once that life is here. The place is burning with terrific instancy, and suddenly one knows that it is alive and swarming with the tremendous energies of forever and of now.

Steeped in this moon-bright stillness of essential time, the vision sweeps the planetary distance of the continent: southward from Maine, around the thumb of Florida, up and around the belly of the Gulf, southward again along the curve of Mexico, and up and out again toward Oregon along the tremendous outward bulge and surge of the Pacific shore.

The vision nears and deepens with the speed of light: the million smaller shapes and contours of the earth appear. And now, for the first time, through the steep silence of the moon, a sound is heard. Vast, low, and murmurous and like a sigh that breathes forever at the ledges of eternity, it is the sea, that feathers constantly upon the shores of time and darkness—and America.

THE SEA (immensely far below, upon twelve thousand miles of coast, with lapse and reluctation of its breath, a vast recessive sigh):

> The sea—
> It is the sea—the sea
> It is the sea—the sea
> It is the sea—the sea
> The sea—the sea—the sea

The vision nears and deepens once again. Faintly, mournfully, infinitely far away, the cry of a great train is heard, as it wails back across America: Whoo-hoo-oo-hoo-oo-hoo-oo. (The cry fades back, away, into the moon-drenched scenery of America: there is faint thunder of wheels pounding at the river's edge. The scene nears and deepens with terrific in-

409

stancy—the train is now heard plainly: it is the great *Pacific Nine* stroking the night with the pistoned velocity of its full speed): chucka-lucka, chucka-lucka, chucka-lucka, chucka-lucka, chucka-lucka. (The scene nears and deepens through the night: *Pacific Nine,* like a lighted thunderbolt, is smashing westward through Nebraska.)

PACIFIC NINE: Ho-Idaho! Ho-Idaho! Ho-Idaho—ho-ho-ho-ho-ho-ho-ho-ho! (Chucka-lucka, chucka-lucka, chucka-lucka, chucka-lucka, chucka-lucka: with fierce bull-bellows, hoarse with pride, she laughs her jolly laughter.)

The scene nears and deepens once again: it is a country road in Illinois, the moon burns brightly on an unpaved road that goes straight as a string between tall walls of corn.

THE CORN BLADES (very softly, rustling stiffly): Ah coarse and cool, ah coarse and cool, America.

(The breeze dies, the corn stands motionless, moon-white the silence of the road again.)

A Listener:

. . . Is it a lion in the mouth sulfurous . . . a cat in the eye humorous, a fox in the paw felonious that prowls the edge of night's great wall forever, and that will not let us sleep?

Who are you that keep vigil in the night? Who are you that from night's consistory the watches of the earth's huge conscience bear? Who are you that from outer dark bring to the cell of this our waiting and most mortal solitude the eye of all your dark enormous listening—child, brother, demon, parent of the night, oh, you Communicant of this America, to us, your tongueless children of the night, on this dark land and waiting, we your children waiting, turn to you, as from the beginning, waiting—dark father of our waiting, speak!

Heart of the night, the spirit of our unsung hope we bring to you! Lord of the night, the freight of all our huge unuttered longing, we bring to you! Tongue of the night, to whom so tongueless we have tongueless spoken, knowledgeless so knowing known, and all unuttered uttered all the unspoke quantity of our impossible desire, the wild unuttered blood of this America and its unuttered prophecy—great hound of darkness ever running in our blood, we bring to you!

Caves the mined darkness to the yellow flood, we turn to you! Still, from the silence heard, the unheard foot, we turn to you! Or waits in silentness, as here to-night, the blazing crater of the moon, on this our large unfinished land—oh, hound, forever running in our blood, we turn to you!

Son of the night, we speak to you.

Eye of the night, we speak to you.

Lord of the night, to whom so often, from the million cells of night, out of the wilderness ourselves, the children of the night, have spoken—oh hound, forever running in the blood of these ourselves, and all our dark Americas, we speak to you.

. . . No answer? Waiting? Forever, as it was from the beginning, waiting? As it was from the beginning, waiting, knowing always you were there? No word, then? Silence again, tonight? No sound, then? But the rustle of the leaves across America.

THE LEAVES: . . . promise . . . promise . . . promise promise.

Where shall we go now? What shall we do?

'Twixt beetling seas, the star-flung crustaceans of the continent and darkness, darkness, and the cool enfolding night, and stars and magic on America—where shall we go now, and what shall we do?

Where shall we go now and what shall we do? Down in the South beside the road, the country Negro, clay-caked, marching, mournful, and the car's brief glare—the sudden spoke and forking of the dusty roads, a sleeping town—street-lights make spangles through the moving leaves, the corner houses are so bright—and then the earth, the pine-land, and the rushing cars again across America—and where shall we go now, and what shall we do?

Here South by radiance of the mill at night, dynamic humming behind light-glazed glass, the weft and shuttle of the spindle room, and then the pines, the clay, the cotton-fields again.

"Do you remember how we used to take an hour to Reynolds-town on Sunday afternoons—and doin' good if we could make it in an hour? Well, it's twenty-seven minutes now, not pushing it. The roads are so much better now—did you see that cat! did you see its eyeballs in the glare? Sure, that's the Willoughby: she's running full-time now: that and the other mills are what makes the town. . . . The houses? Sure, that's the mill-town village—yes, they're all alike. You mustn't think it is so bad; I know these people: they're better off than they ever have been. Wages?—sure, they're low—but you don't get the idea: in most of those little houses that you see there, you'll find three or four members of the family all at work. That's fifty-six bucks a week—more than these people ever dreamed about before. Why, they're in clover now—see there's the mill store—"

A plain brick front, and plate-glass and lights burning late: the provender of poor white people, the sacks of flour piled in the middle, and slabs of fatback racked up crudely like essential stuff, the loaded shelves upon each side with canned familiar articles, tea, coffee, sugar, the proven-der of a meal, a little glass case toward the front with sticks of licorice, tobacco, penny-candies, a tin ice-cooler, brilliant red and modern-looking, provided by the Coca-Cola people, filled with freezing water, floating ice, and soda-pop—a slattern-looking woman with hanked hair, and the slow, distrustful look poor people have when they come in to trade—the mill-store keeper, with grayed hair and ruined teeth—a poor white just a little better off and—thus mistrustful—"these mill-hands are a pretty sorry lot— as tough as they make them, poor white trash"—he is unhappy, too; behind the flour sacks is a jug of corn—

"You see, now: they're in clover. They're better off than they have ever been before: that's the thing these labor agitators from the North can't understand."

Where shall we go now? What shall we do?

The punctual flash across the darkness of the beacon-light; lost in the upper air, the night-plane roaring North from Jacksonville, a small blue light that bores across the night as Brat and Nell sit on the porch and listen: the children are asleep, the bolls are opening—"She's going North tonight"—the vast and thrilling sadness of the katydids are making sound— where shall we go now, and what shall we do?

Two thousand miles away, upon the coast of Maine, a silent road beside the sea, thick-set with spruce, so close, so near, and yet almost you'd never know the sea was there—save where the lighthouse flashes from the darkness of the point, so close beside the sea, you'd hardly know the sea was there: the little houses sleep beneath the moon, in moonlit fields the cows lie bedded on their haunches in the moon, white as a string and wind- ing, the road winds back beneath the moon, so close beside the sea, so sheltered from the sea, so hidden from the sea, you know is there.

Where shall we go now? And what shall we do?

"There's almost nothing quite so good this time of night in New Orleans: they split a crispy, French, and flaky loaf of bread in two and pave the inside with beef or pork or ham, salt, pepper, and some kind of pungent relish—or if the oyster season's on, with six or eight big oysters, fried flaky brown, the way they know how to do it there—I don't know how they do it, but they call the thing a Poor Boy Sandwich, and the price of it is just ten cents, a dime. I guess they got the name from this, because that's the only thing that's poor about it. Why don't you and Pat go down and bring us back about a half-dozen?—we'll sit here in the garden, I'll take beef for mine.—I have remembered nights like these when people plugged a watermelon with champagne—you cut a plug out, and you poured iced champagne in—and you would sit there in the garden, eating watermelon on a night like this: how bright and still it is tonight, the moon makes brightness through magnolia leaves, there is so much of death, of life, of stillness, and of fragrance here around us; on nights like these, the river hooks around you like an elbow, and you always know it is above the town.

What shall we do now, and where shall we go?

Fast-heard, soon-lost, the wheeling noises of the carnival; and sinners wailing in a church in Niggertown. At night, the cars pick tattered tidings from the sides of barns: the ragged remnants of the circus clowns, and mangled notice that Carl Hagenbeck has been to town, Sapolio. Across the width of Indiana the merits of Carter's Little Liver Pills are blazoned in the moon, and from the upper sweep of the Brooklyn Bridge, the blank walls of the tenements advise man that departed ghosts of Cardui were there.

The fields are dreaming through Virginia, there is the silent stature of the moonlit trees, far off and running the faint baying of the hound, moon-white in silence and the ghosts of absence, the houses are so sad, and there is something lost and dead and long ago, something too haunting in Virginia, that horses cannot cure.

OH, WASHINGTON

Where shall we go now? And what shall we do?

It's all the Government—that's Washington—the buildings are all lighted up—the Capitol and the Monument—the White House is just down the street, across the Park. At half-past four you can watch them pouring from the Veterans' Bureau, and you wonder where they all come from. A lot of them are young kids from Carolina, Mississippi, Alabama—from Texas, Massachusetts, Illinois, Ohio, way out West . . . they pass the civil service, and they get their little ninety or a hundred per . . . of course, they think it's wonderful, the kids, I mean. Later on, it's not so good. Of course, you read about the big stuff—the President, the Cabinet, and the Embassies . . . the High Society stuff . . . but the tadpoles never get in on that—you'd know as much about it if you were still living down in Libya Hill . . . you get so you don't care—you wouldn't walk across the street to see the President—it gives the tourists a great thrill, but here, well—it's all old stuff to us, we're used to it . . . taxi-drivers, drifters, people hunting for a job, people with an axe to grind, all the kids from Carolina and Virginia—kids from everywhere, old maids, worn-out people, all the broken-down old people with a little pension—they all come here, and—Go out and take a walk before you go to bed—it's all the Government—but the way the search-lights flash across the air and cross—somehow it makes you feel as if—as if—well, over there upon the other side, that is Virginia—and beyond that, well, you'll like the way the searchlights flash and cross—

Where shall I go now? What shall I do?

Great barns sleep proudly in the swelling earth of Pennsylvania Dutch; at night-time, there are furnace flares across New Jersey: and then dumb ears beneath the river-bed and voices in the tunnel, stopped for Brooklyn; upon the elevated platforms, people waiting for the trains, within the lighted canyons of the city's gulch, the lighted serpent of the train roars by—where shall we go now, and what shall we do?

Upon the tide, the tugs slide moveless in the water, the loaded barge-strings come down after them in silent linkages of light—green, red, and white—in patterned schemes of loneliness, light moves in silence, and the chasmed hackles of Manhattan are blazing in the moon.

OH, MANHATTAN

Where shall we go now? What shall we do?

Here on Manhattan's swarming rock to-night a million feet are moving toward the sky-flung faery and the great Medusa of the night, the star-sown lights incredible are wrought into the robe of night itself, so masoned in the architecture of the night that there is nothing now but lights and darkness, the jewelled pollen of the lights that climb, in linkless chains, sustained and fixed upon the great wall of the night, until we know that there are only the great vertices of dark and light, and that the buildings never were.

Where shall we go now? And what shall we do?

Perhaps to-night, to-night, we shall all find at last what we are waiting for here in America. Or perhaps tonight again we'll prowl the facades of Rat's Alley where the dead men live. Night has a million windows and a million feet are marching somewhere in the night—where shall we go now? And what shall we do?

Perhaps to-night we'll prowl the livid glare of light upon the swarming rock—perhaps we'll go uptown to-night and look up at enormous signs where the electric fishes play. Along toward dusk they change the bulbs: you know, a sign like that has so many million bulbs, it keeps a guy busy changing them. There are so many bulbs; so many bulbs burn out—and Jesus! you should see the size of him, the way he looks up there beside the fish.

But where shall we go now? And what shall we do?

Perhaps we'll sit on porches in the little towns to-night, in leafy streets, behind respiring points of lighted ash, and listen to cars passing and the radios, and certain sounds of music from afar.

Where shall we go now? And what shall we do?

It is so cool to-night: down by the railroad tracks the whores sit with their faces pressed against the grating on the doors, and breathe the sweetness of the air, and switching engines going by: "Gee, Grace, I wish we could get in a swim to-night. . . . If Eddie comes around at closing time, let's see if he won't take us to the lake."

Put dimes and nickels in the old piano, Johnny; we'll play for you again "Love's Old Sweet Song."

.   .   .

Where shall we go now? And what shall we do?

It is so cool to-night, and everywhere there are young lovers, somewhere, and young voices, and the faint and broken music of a dance, and the promise of the leaves across America.

OH, BOSTON

Where shall we go now? And what shall we do?

The cop in Boston, twirling at the stick—"Just one lone bum"—and ruminant—"just one lone bum upon the Common. That was all to-night . . . well, good-night, Joe"—the windows fogged with pungent steam of hamburgers; the blackened fingers of compositors, pressing ink and hunger into spongy bread—"I see these guys in Spain have started in again"—and "Good-night, good-night."

Where shall we go now? And what shall we do?

The Parson strokes his lantern jaws reflectively and smiles with artificial teeth to-night upon his ruined town. The two-million-dollar courthouse is bathed in secret, solid light just like the lighted buildings of Government at Washington. The million-dollar jail and city hall, also the Parson's work, is bathed with baleful reds and purples on its pyramided crest. The Boom is over, and six hundred ruined men are rotting in their graves to-night, and sixty-four have shattered bullet fractures in their skulls—ten thousand more are living as shells live and watch the darkness from their beds to-night in Pleasanton—the town is still and lovely in the darkness, you'd never know to see such lovely buildings that the town is dead.—"We're coming back," the Parson says, and smiles at his police force: they're all young men now, they have such snappy uniforms, neat khaki trousers, crisp brown shirts—you see their guns now, the deadly butt-ends holstered from the waist, a deadly arsenal of cartridge belts around them—they cruise in high-powered cars right down the middle of the streets, just waiting, purring softly their high-powered cars, and waiting in the streets of Pleasanton—there is something in their eyes that young men in the streets of Pleasanton did not use to have.

The cops on the new force are such nice young fellows now—two kids are spitting through their shredded lips to-night, out through the gap-holes where their good teeth have been—they're country kids from Zebulon, and they had a little too much corn to drink—well, they're coming round now, and they're asking fuddled questions of each other, they'll have the whole night through to sober up and think it over in the Parson's million-dollar jail. Out at the country club a dance is on, the saxophones are wailing loud: the Club has good Scotch nowadays, some of the crowd, however, sticks to corn. But, as the Parson says, "It's Progress, and we're coming back"—the Parson will address the federated civic clubs tomorrow upon Progress and Coming Back—and so good-night. Good-night, good-night. Good-night, sweet prince, and flights of angels guide thee to thy rest.

What shall we do now? And where shall we go?

Outside of town, at Lester's Cabins—after the Boom, it folded up, but they're getting a big crowd out there every night these days, they're coming back—the kids with waggish fingers are doing—with a one! a two! a three! a four!—The Big Apple—there's so much nigger-drollness in it, they are so expert now, the girls have lovely legs—and there is something in them that the Parson maybe with his Progress never thought about. And so good-night, good-night. Where shall we go now? And what shall we do?

OH, CHICAGO

Who comes by darkness to the blasted land shall not find darkness in the blasted land; the hills are ruined in the blasted land, but who comes by darkness to the blasted land will find hell's beauty in the blasted land, the forge of Tubal in the blasted land, the flare of Vulcan and the tide of Styx: smoke-flares of torment, fires of burning, hell, beauty, Pittsburgh in the blasted land, the vast smoke-haunted limbo of earth's travail and man's labor in the blasted land. What shall we do now? And where shall we go?

The lake out here tonight is vast and dark and cool: and there is nothing in this world more arrogant and proud and splendid than the shirt-front of Chicago. It has the best shirt-front on earth, and underneath that shirt-front is nothing but the naked flesh. Upon one side the lake: the vast curve of the linked lights, the parkways and the boulevard, the tides of traffic thronging ceaseless into unknown power and mystery—upon the other side, the battlemented shirt-front of America, the cliff-like wall of mighty buildings, sown with a diamond dust of lights, the clubs, the great hotels, the vast apartment-houses. And behind that is—a million miles of brutal jungle that is called Chicago.

It is a place that you're at home in right away: perhaps it is the train-smoke that does the thing to you. You smell the smoke the minute you get off the train, and it does something fierce and wonderful to you: it's better than a shot of gin, it's better than the breath of air off of the prairies which for the most part you can't smell anyway, you just breathe it in and you know that here comes everybody: Wops, Swedes, Jews, Dutchmen, Micks, and all the rest of them, and you can take it, and you are in America, Chicago, U.S.A.

It is so cool along the lake to-night, and you are sitting on the roof beneath the moon, with music playing, a cold drink in your hand, with well-dressed men and women all around you on the lake to-night, you don't smell train-smoke on the lake to-night, but there is something in your heart you cannot say.

Where shall I go now? What shall I do?

She said with silver laughter, and echoes of the Riviera in her voice: "Oh, Jim, how simply priceless that you are the way you are!—I mean, I've been so long away. I'm really such a *foreigner*, if you see what I mean. . . . I mean, I really think my way of thinking and living have become completely European—I mean, you're so Chicago, if you see what I mean. But tell me all the news—I'm simply dying to hear all the news. Of course, Bob Sprague is living in the East!—Anne's living in the South of France, I see her all the time—where's Steve Garrison—and Ed—and Emily—tell me—"

It is so cool and sweet along the lake to-night, there is the lighted panoply of the greatest shirt-front in America, but a wind has risen from the West, across the roofs tonight there sweeps the thick and fat aroma of the slaughtered swine.

"Is Jimmy Oberholt still here?—Did Billy Wade ever marry Sally Ellinger—"

The butchers stand upon raised platforms with their polished knives, one has a very quiet face, and watches carefully. The nigger curses, slipping in the blood, as he plunges booted to the hips among the hogs, he gets the chains around the small protesting hoofs, the hog jerks, squealing in the air, and squealing, swings along the runway to the doom he knows is there. But the butchers are such kindly thoughtful men, they stand there on raised platforms, patiently at ease, the hog comes to them squealing, the butcher shifts the quid of plug tobacco in his cheek, offers, then waits, the hog squeals, it is so swiftly and so softly done, the long knife just slides over, the fat throat divides, the wine-bright hog-blood, redder than you ever dreamed that red could be, outgushes downward to the floor, the hog just jerks a little squealing faintly, so relieved to find it has not been so bad, and another hog is on its way again.

"And what about the Hunt? Is Hugh still Master of the Hounds? You see, I'm simply starved for news. I've been away so long—I know absolutely nothing of what's happened since I left."

But a wind is rising from the West to-night.

OH, ROCKY MOUNTAINS

Where shall we go now? And what shall we do?

The song sweeps westward to the painted rock, to-night there is the silence of the moon on painted rock and there is hackled moonlight on the Rocky Mountains. *The Santa Fe* winds past the painted buttes. Miss Crocker for the fourteenth time is going to the Hopi Dance. She's quite an expert now on Indian customs in the great Southwest—"You see," she says to spellbound tenderfeet, with just the proper touch of Beacon Hill refinement, with a very nice and telling thumb-and-finger gesture of her bony little hand: "The relation between the Indian and the snake is quite remarkable." *The Santa Fe* winds on and leaves the painted buttes, but takes Miss Crocker with *The Santa Fe*.

Where shall we go now? What shall we do?

But moonlight on the painted buttes again, the fiendish silence of the desert world, the mesa's lift, and off the road in an arroyo bed, a shattered Ford, a dead man, two drunk Mexicans—"Meestaire—oh, Meestaire"—so eager, soft-tongued, plaintive, pleading, strange—"Meestaire"—and then the eerie nearness of the wild coyote yelp, and seven miles to go to Santa Fe. What shall we do now? And where shall we go?

OH, HOLLYWOOD

"It's something that you shouldn't miss out here in California— I mean a preem-year is a great experience: Joe's working on the set, he's got seats tonight—it's something you ought not to miss, so come along."

To these dense herdings, thrusting at the breach, here to the glare of light before a facade like a most appallingly splendiferous chop-suey joint—the crowd is here—that maddened thrust of brutal violence, that empty yawn of Kansas gone to Hollywood with maw insatiate to be fed on vacancy, hats knocked askew on reddened faces, sometime-people thrusting, swaying, shoving, out of mind—The uniformed police thrust back, force, maul and snarl—"Get back there! Get back now, or I'll throw you back!" and heaving, sweating, swaying, Kansas, unmanned, ignoble, most inhuman-human, surges to the very ledges of the canopy—the sleek cars arrive, the lights explode, the dazzling sweethearts of the land appear— "That's her!" cries Kansas—is mauled back into line and surges forward with reddened face and all its hairpins gone awry—"That's her!" it roars and surges forward obscenely—and something perfect, empty, glittering, passes by, pauses, responds with a smile of brilliant vacancy—and passes on. "That's her!" screams Kansas—and "Yes, sir. Yes, sir," replies assuring Mike, "The little lady's here herself—and just a moment, folks, just a moment— I'm trying to get her—she's coming this way—ah-h-h—hah-hah-hah, what a crowd! *What* a crowd!—I'm trying to get her attention now!—and yes, sir! I believe I've got her. She's coming toward the microphone now!—And *here* she is, folks! *Here—she—is!!*"

"Hello, everybody! Hello, America! I—I—well, I'm just so happy I don't know what to say! This is the greatest, most beautiful and wonderful moment in my whole life. And well—ah-hah-hah—I guess you know what I mean! I'd just like to give you all a great big hug! And—well, that's about all I can say! Good-night, everybody! And God bless you all! Good-night, America!" And good-night, good-night.

What shall we do now? Where shall we go?

The last street-car going for the night, a sound of absence after it has gone, somewhere a screen door slammed and voices going, and "Good-night." "Good-night, Ollie, good-night, May . . . where's Checkers: did you let him out?" and silence, silence, and "Good-night, good-night," and voices going in Carlisle, "Good-night, good-night"—and voices going in Meridian, "Good-night, good-night . . . and hurry back again!"—and voices going in a thousand little towns—in Macon and Montgomery, in Asheville, Tallahassee, Waco, and Columbia—and "Good-night, good-night"—in Ann Arbor, Wichita, Fort Wayne, Des Moines, Tacoma, Oakland, Monterey—"Good-night."

For everywhere, through the immortal dark, across the land, there has been something moving in the night, and something stirring in the hearts of men, and something crying in their wild unuttered blood, the wild unuttered tongues' huge prophecies. Where shall we go now? And what shall we do? Smoke-blue by morning in the chasmed slant, on-quickening the tempo of the rapid steps, up to the pinnacles of noon; by day and ceaseless, the furious traffics of the thronging streets; forever now, upbuilding through the mounting flood-crest of these days, sky-hung against the crystal of the frail blue weather, the slamming racketing of girdered steel, the stunning riveting of the machines.

And blazing moonlight on the buttes to-night, a screen door slammed, the clicking of a latch and silence in ten thousand little towns, and people lying in the darkness, waiting, wondering, listening as we— "Where shall we go now and what shall we do?"

For there is something marching in the night; so soon the morning, soon the morning—oh, America.

Portrait of a Literary Critic

I

The personality of the celebrated Dr. Turner—or Dr. Hugo Twelvetrees Turner as he was generally known to the reading public—was not an unfamiliar one to Joseph Doaks, the novelist. Dr. Turner's wider reputation had been well known to the public for fifteen years or more. And for ten years he had been the guiding spirit of the splendid journal he had himself established, the *Fortnightly Cycle of Reading, Writing, and the Allied Arts*.

The establishment of the *Fortnightly Cycle* marked, as one critic says, "one of the most important literary events of our time," and life without it, another offered, would have been "simply unthinkable." The *Cycle* came into being at a time when the critical field was more or less divided between the somewhat prosaic conservatism of the *Saturday Review of Literature* and the rather mannered preciosity of the *Dial*. Between the two, Dr. Turner and the *Cycle* struck a happy medium; the position of the *Cycle* might be best classified as a middle-of-the-road one, and Dr. Turner himself might be described as the nation's leading practitioner of middle-of-the-roadism. Here, really, lay his greatest contribution.

It is true that there were certain skeptics who stubbornly disputed Dr. Turner's right to such a title. These critics, instead of being reassured by the broad yet sane liberalism of the Doctor's views, were seriously alarmed by it: they professed to see in Dr. Turner's critical opinions a tendency toward a disturbing—nay dangerous!—radicalism. Such a judgment was simply ridiculous. Dr. Turner's position was neither too far to the right nor too far to the left, but "a little left of center." To such a definition he himself would have instantly agreed; the phrasing would have pleased him.

True, there had been a period in Dr. Turner's rich career when his position had been a much more conservative one than it now was. But to his everlasting credit, let it be said that his views had grown broader as the years went on; the years had brought increase of tolerance, depth of knowledge, width of understanding; ripeness with this valiant soul was all.

There had been a time when Dr. Turner had dismissed the works of some of the more modern writers as being the productions of "a group of dirty

420

little boys." Indeed the first use of this delightfully homely and pungent phrase may be safely accredited to Dr. Turner himself; people on Beacon Hill read it with appreciative chuckles, gentlemen in clubs slapped the *Fortnightly Cycle* on their thighs and cried out "Capital!" It was just the way they had always felt about the fellow themselves, except that they had never found quite the words to put it so; but *this* man now, this What's-His-Name, this Turner—oh, Capital! Capital! It was evident that a fearless, new, and salutary force had come into the Nation's Letters!

A little later on, however, Dr. Turner's dirty little boy had been qualified by the adjectival words "Who scrawls bad words which he hopes may shock his elders upon the walls of privies." This was even better! For a pleasing image was thus conveyed to the readers of Dr. Turner's *Fortnightly Cycle* that brought much unction to their souls. For what could be more comfortable for a devoted reader of the *Fortnightly Cycle* than the reassuring sense that just as he was settling comfortably to attend to one of the most inevitable of the natural functions, he might look up and read with an amused and tolerating eye certain words that various dirty little boys like Anatole France, George Bernard Shaw, Theodore Dreiser, Sherwood Anderson, and D. H. Lawrence had scrawled up there with the intention of shocking him.

If Dr. Turner had made no further contribution, his position would have been secure. But more, much more, was yet to come. For even at this early stage one of the salient qualities of Dr. Turner's talent had revealed itself. He was always able to keep at least two jumps ahead not only of his own critics, but of his own admirers. It was Dr. Turner, for example, who first made the astonishing discovery that Sex was Dull. The news at first stunned the readers of the *Fortnightly Cycle,* who had begun to be seriously alarmed about the whole matter, shocked, appalled, and finally reduced to a state of sputtering indignation by "This, this Sort of Thing, now; Sort of Thing they're writing nowadays; this, this, why, this Filth! This fellow Lawrence, now!"

Dr. Turner put these perturbed spirits to rest. Dr. Turner was neither appalled, shocked, nor incensed by anything he read about sex. He didn't get indignant. He knew a trick worth six of these. Dr. Turner was amused. Or would have been amused, that is, if he had not found the whole business so excessively boring. Even as early as 1924, he was writing the following in comment on a recent book of D. H. Lawrence:

This preoccupation with Sex—really not unlike the preoccupation of a *naughty* little boy with certain four-letter words which he surreptitiously scrawls upon the sides of barns—[*observe how the earlier exuberances of the Doctor are here subtly modified*]—would on the whole be mildly amusing to an adult intelligence who had presumed that these were things that one had lived through and forgotten in one's salad days, if it were not for the fact that the author contrives to make the whole business so appallingly dull. . . .

The readers of the *Fortnightly Cycle* were at first amazed, then simply enchanted by this information. They had been dismayed and sore perplexed—but now! Why, ah-hah-hah, the whole thing was very funny, wasn't it? The extreme seriousness of the fellow about the Kind of Thing they had themselves forgotten since their Sophomore days—would really be quite amusing if he did not contrive to make it so abysmally Dull!

II

But there was more, much more, to come. The whole tormented complex of the twenties was upon good Dr. Turner. People everywhere were bewildered by the kaleidoscopic swiftness with which things changed. It was a trial that might have floored a less valiant spirit than that of Dr. Turner. Hardly a week went by but that a new great poet was discovered. Scarcely an issue of the *Fortnightly Cycle* appeared but that a new novel to equal *War and Peace* was given to the world. And not a month passed but that there was a new and sensational movement in the bewildering flux of fashion: Charles Chaplin was discovered to be not primarily a comedian at all, but the greatest tragic actor of the time (learned adepts of the arts assured the nation that his proper role was Hamlet). The true art-expression of America was the comic-strip (the productions of the Copleys, Whistlers, Sargents, Bellowses, and Lies could never hold a candle to it). The only theater that truly was native and was worth preserving was the burlesque show. The only music that was real was Jazz. There had only been one writer in America (his name was Twain, and he had been defeated just because he was—American; he was so good just because he was—American; but if he had not been American he could have been—so good!). Aside from this the only worthwhile writing in the land was what the advertising writers wrote; this was the true expression of the Yankee clime—all else had failed us, all was dross.

The madness grew from week to week. With every revolution of the clock the Chaos of the Cultures grew. But through it all, the soul of Dr. Turner kept its feet. Turner hewed true and took the Middle Way. To all things in their course, in their true proportion, he was just.

True, he had lapses. In culture's armies, he was not always foremost to the front. But he caught up. He always caught up. If there were errors sometimes in his calculations, he always rectified them before it was too late; if he made mistakes, like the man he was, he gallantly forgot them.

It was inspiring just to watch his growth. In 1923, for instance, he referred to the *Ulysses* of James Joyce as "that encyclopedia of filth which has become the bible of our younger intellectuals"; in 1925, more tolerantly, as "the bible of our younger intellectuals, which differs from the real one in that it manages to be so consistently dull"; in 1929 (behold this man!) as "that amazing *tour de force* which has had more influence on our young writers than any other work of our generation"; and in 1933, when Justice

Woolsey handed down the famous decision that made the sale of *Ulysses* legally permissible throughout these States (in a notable editorial that covered the entire front page of the *Fortnightly Cycle*) as "a magnificent vindication of artistic integrity . . . the most notable triumph over the forces of bigotry and intolerance that has been scored in the Republic of Letters in our time. . . ."

Similarly, when one of the earlier books of William Faulkner appeared, Dr. Turner greeted it with an editorial that was entitled, "The School of Bad Taste." He wrote:

> One wonders what our bright young men will do for material now that the supply of four-letter words and putrescent situations has been so exhausted that further efforts in this direction can only rouse the jaded reader to a state of apathy. Is it too much to hope that our young writers may grow tired of their own monsters and turn their talents to a possible investigation of—dare we hope it?—normal life?

A few years later, however, when Mr. Faulkner's *Sanctuary* appeared, the Doctor had so altered his views that, after likening the author to Poe in "the quality of his brooding imagination . . . his sense of the Macabre . . . his power to evoke stark fear, sheer horror, as no other writer of his time has done," he concluded his article by saying darkly to his readers, "This man may go far."

Thus, although Dr. Turner was occasionally out of step, he always fell in again before the Top Sergeant perceived his fault. Moreover, once he got into the fore, he had a very brave and thrilling way of announcing his position to his readers as if he himself had been in the crow's nest and cried, "Land Ho!" at the very moment when the faint shore of some new and brave America was first visible.

These then were among the Doctor's more daring discoveries; some of the more conservative of his following were made uneasy by such risky venturesomeness, but they should not have been alarmed. For if the Doctor ever stuck his neck out, it was only when he had it safely armor-plated: his bolder sorties out among the new and strange were always well-hedged round by flanking guards of reservations. Upon more familiar ground, however, the Doctor went the whole hog in a way that warmed the soul. His praises of the Joyces, Faulkners, Eliots, and Lawrences were always fenced in by a parenthesis of safe reserve; even the Dreisers and the Lewises had their moderating checks; but when the Millays, Glasgows, Cabells, Nathans, and Morleys were his meat, he spoke out of the fullness of his heart— in vulgar phrase, the Doctor went to town.

And curiously enough, it was just here, when Dr. Turner was on what he himself was fond of classifying as "safe ground," that his judgment was likely to grow giddy and was prone to err. This exuberance caused him some embarrassment; at various stages of his editorial career he had described

Christopher Morley as being the possessor of "the most delightful prose style that the familiar essay has known since the days of his true contemporary and, may I say, *almost* his equal, Charles Lamb. Aside from Lamb there is no other essayist since Montaigne's time to match him." Of Ellen Glasgow: "Not only our greatest living novelist, but one of the greatest novelists that ever lived"; and of that lady's many works, as ". . . in their entirety comprising a picture of a whole society that, for variety and scope, has no parallel in literature except the *Comédie Humaine,* and that, in the perfection of their form and style, achieve a faultless artistry that Balzac's cruder talent never reached"; of the whimsy-whamsy of Robert Nathan as ". . . sheer genius. There is no other word for it; it's sheer elfin genius of a kind that not even Barrie attained and that has no rival in our language unless perchance it be the elfin loveliness of the Titania-Oberon scenes in *A Midsummer Night's Dream*"; of the baroque pilgrimage of Mr. Cabell in his Province of Cockaigne ". . . our greatest ironist. . . . The greatest prose style in the language. . . . Perhaps the only Pure Artist that we have"; and of a young gentleman who wrote a book about a Bridge in South America: "A great writer. . . . Certainly the greatest writer that the Younger Generation has produced. And the book! Ah, what a book! A book to be treasured, cherished, and re-read; a book to put upon your shelves beside *War and Peace, Don Quixote, Moby Dick, Candide* . . . and withal a book, that, without one touch of the dreary and degrading realism that disfigures the work of most of our younger writers, is so essentially, splendidly American . . . as American as Washington, Lincoln, or the Rocky Mountains, since in its story are implicit the two qualities that are most characteristic of our folk: Democracy through Love; Love through Democracy. . . ."

The world being the grim place it sometimes is, it is sorrowful but not surprising to relate that there were a few wicked spirits who took a cruel delight in unearthing these lush phrases years after they had been uttered, and after they had lain decently interred in old copies of the *Fortnightly Cycle* for so long presumably they were as dead as most of the books that had evoked them. Then the worthy Doctor had to pretend he did not know they were there, or else eat them, and of all forms of diet this is the toughest and least palatable.

But on the whole the Doctor came through nobly. The sea at times was stormy and the waves ran very high, but the staunch ship that was Turner weathered through.

Among his followers, it is true, there are some whose tendencies were so conservative that they deplored the catholicity of the Doctor's tastes. And among his enemies, there were some who were cruel enough to suggest that he wanted to be all things to all people, that Turner was not only the proper, but the inevitable, name for him, that the corkscrew shaped his course, and that if he went around the corner he would run into himself on the way back. Doctor Turner's answer to both these groups was simple, dignified, and complete: "In the Republic of Letters," said he, "of which I am a humble citizen, there are, I am glad to say, no factions, groups, or class distinctions. It is a true Democracy, perhaps the only one that now exists. And as long as I am privileged to belong to it, in however modest a capacity, I hope I shall be worthy of it, too, and broad enough to see all sides." The simple dignity of this ringing utterance had answered all of Doctor Turner's critics more effectively than any vituperative tirade could have done. And it was in tribute to these celebrated words that Peter Bilke, the Doctor's editorial colleague who for years, under the nom de plume of Kenelm Digby, had delighted readers of the *Cycle* in his weekly accounts of his whimsical explorations in unknown corners of Manhattan, Brooklyn, and Hoboken—which he had made immortal with the tender appellation of "Old Hobey"—had dubbed the Doctor with a nickname fashioned from his own reply—"Old Broadsides"—a name by which he was now invariably known to his intimates and to those who loved him best.

III

In appearance, Old Broadsides was scarcely prepossessing. He was so much below middle height that at first sight it seemed that one of Singer's Midgets had enjoyed a run of extra growth. He may have been four inches over five feet tall; as for his *sides,* so far from being broad, the whole man, from his shoulders right down to the ground, was astonishingly narrow—he was a mere forked radish of a man, if ever one was ever made. His little breadcrumb of a body, for in appearance he suggested nothing so much as a piece of well-done toast, was surmounted by a head of normal size which appeared too large for the meager figure that supported it. In its other qualities it resembled somewhat the face of the little man one so often sees in political cartoons, and which bears the caption of The Common People. It was such a face as one might see upon the streets a hundred times a day, and never think of later: it may have belonged to a bank clerk, a bookkeeper, an insurance agent, or someone going home to Plainfield on the 5:15.

Doaks himself was one of the good Doctor's more belated discoveries. When the author's first book, *Home to Our Mountains,* had appeared some time before, Dr. Turner had not been favorably impressed. The review in the *Fortnightly Cycle* had been a very gem of bland dismissal: "No doubt the thing is well enough," said Turner, "but after all, old Rabelais is really so much better"—a conclusion which the unhappy author was by no means minded to dispute.

Five years later, upon the publication of Doaks's second book the good Doctor was still undecided just what he was going to do about it or him. Three weeks before the book was released for general sale, in fact, the Doctor had met Doaks's publisher and, after confessing that an advance copy of the new work had been sent to him, had added grimly: "I haven't made up my mind about Doaks yet. But," said he bodingly, "I'll make it up within a week or two." Within the next two weeks, however, Dr. Turner felt the telepathy of moderating influences—"You can always tell," he was wont to say, "when Things are in the Air"—to such a degree that when his critique ultimately appeared, it was much more favorable than Doaks or his publisher had dared to hope. Not that the Doctor was thoroughly persuaded, but he took a more conciliating tone. The book, he averred, "could hardly be called a novel"—he did not trouble to explain what could—it was really "a Spiritual Autobiography," and having arrived at this sounding definition, he discussed the volume freely in spiritual-autobiographical terms, and on the whole was pretty favorable about it, too, having neatly furnished forth a special little nest for Mr. Doaks without in any way impinging on the jealous precincts of more splendid birds on more important boughs.

The way for rapprochement was thus opened gracefully, and when the author met the Doctor some months later, their greetings were of a friendly kind.

"Darling," said Dr. Turner to his wife, "I want you to meet Mr. Doaks. By George! I can't get used to this 'Mister' stuff, I'm going to call you *Joe!*" cried Dr. Turner with an air of bluff heartiness that was simply irresistible. "I know so many people that you know, and I've heard them call you Joe for years, no other name seems possible."

Doaks murmured that he was enchanted thus to be addressed, meanwhile feeling a little helpless and confused under the hypnotic influence of Mrs. Turner, who, still holding him by the hand, was looking steadily into his eyes with a slow, strange smile.

"You," she said at length, very slowly and decidedly. "*You!* You wrote the book," she concluded simply.

He felt definitely vague about this, but managed to mumble that he had. The lady's answer to this was to continue to hold the author by the hand, to regard him steadily with a fixed smile that seemed to harbor some dawning mirth to which no one else was a party.

"You," she said presently again. "I don't know, but somehow you make me laugh. You amuse me. There is something about you that is like—is like—an Elf!"

"Yes," said Dr. Turner quickly, and meeting Doaks's bewildered eye, he went on with an air of hasty explanation in the manner of people steering away from well-known reefs: "My wife was *awfully* interested in that book of yours. *Awfully.* Of course, we *all* were," he went on rapidly. "Matter of fact, I wrote three full columns on it," he went on with just a tinge of nervous constraint, as if he hoped this would make everything all right. "I believe it was the longest review I have done since *An American Tragedy.* I was *awfully* interested in it," said the Doctor, now like Yser, rolling rapidly. "Did you see my review, by any chance?" he asked, and then quickly, before the other had a chance to answer, "I was really *awfully* interested; I called it a kind of spiritual autobiography," he went on. "I mean," he said quickly, as the other opened his mouth as if to speak, "it really made me think of

Wilhelm Meister. Not," the Doctor quickly cried, as Doaks started to open his mouth again, "not that that was all of it—of course there were passages in it that were very much like *War and Peace*—I remember saying to Mrs. Turner at the time, 'You know, there are times when he is very much like Tolstoi.'"

"And like *an—Elf,*" said Mrs. Turner at this point, never for a moment relinquishing her grasp on the author's hand, and continuing to smile steadily at him in a slow, strange way—"So—like—an—Elf," she said, and laughed deliberately.

"And, of course," said Doctor Turner rapidly, "there's the *Moby Dick* influence, too. I know I told my wife at the time that there were passages, magnificent passages," cried Doctor Turner, "that were very much like Herman Melville—"

"And—like—an—Elf!" the wife said.

"And *very* much like *Moby Dick!*" the Doctor said decidedly.

"And *very,*" Doaks, whose mind at last was beginning to work slowly, thought, "oh, *very, very,* like a whale!"

Meanwhile, the critic's lady continued to hold him by the hand, looking steadily at him, smiling a slow smile.

In this way, after so long and perilous a voyage, the storm-tossed mariner, Mr. Doaks, came to port. And if he was not berthed among the mighty liners, at least he now had anchorage in the slips where some of the smaller vessels in the Turnerian heaven were.

The Birthday

Out of the nameless and unfathomed weavings of billion-footed life, out of the dark abyss of time and duty, blind chance had brought these two together on a ship, and their first meeting had been upon the timeless and immortal seas that beat forever at the shores of old earth.

Yet later, it would always seem to him that he had met her for the first time, had come to know and love her first, one day at noon in bright October. That day he was twenty-five years old; she had said that she would meet him for his birthday lunch; they had agreed to meet at noon before the Public Library. He got there early. It was a fine shining day, early in October, and the enormous library, set there at the city's furious heart, with its millions of books, with the beetling architecture that towered around it, and the nameless brutal fury of the manswarm moving around it in the streets, had come to evoke for him a horrible mockery of repose and study in the midst of the blind wildness and savagery of life, to drown his soul with hopelessness, and to fill him with a feeling of weariness and horror.

But now his excitement and happiness over meeting her, together with the glorious life and sparkle of the day, had almost conquered these feelings, and he was conscious of a powerful swelling certitude of hope and joy as he looked at the surging crowds upon the street, the thronging traffic, and the great buildings that soared on every side.

It was the day when for the first time in his life he could say, "Now I am twenty-five years old," and, like a child who thinks that he has grown new muscle, a new stature over night, the magic numerals kept beating in him like a pulse, and he leaned there on the balustrade feeling a sense of exultant power inside him, a sense of triumph for the mastery, the conviction, that the *whole* of this was his.

A young man of twenty-five is the Lord of Life. The very age itself is, for him, the symbol of his mastery. It is the time for him when he is likely to feel that now, at last, he has really grown up to man's estate, that the confusions and uncertainties of his youth are behind him. Like an ignorant fighter, for he has never been beaten, he is exultant in the assurance of his knowledge and his power. It is a wonderful time of life, but it is also a time that is pregnant with a deadly danger. For that great flask of ether which feels within itself the illusions of an invincible and hurtless strength may explode there in so many ways it does not know about—that great engine of life charged with so much power and speed, with a terrific energy of its high velocity so that it thinks that nothing can stop it, that it can roar like a locomotive across the whole continent of life, may be derailed by a pebble, by a grain of dust.

It is a time when a man is so full of himself, of his own strength and pride and arrogant conceit, that there is not much room left at the center of his universe for broad humanity. He is too much the vaunting hero of his cosmic scheme to have a wise heart for the scheme of others: he is arrogant and he does not have a simple heart, and he is intolerant and lacks human understanding, for men learn understanding—courage also!—not from the blows they give to others, but from those they take.

It is the time of life when a man conceives himself as earth's great child. He is life's darling, fortune's pet, the world's enhaloed genius: all he does is right. All must give way to him, nothing must oppose him. Are there traces of rebellion there among the rabble? Ho, varlets, scum—out of the way! Here's royalty! Must we rejoice, then, at the beatings which this fool must take? Not so, because there is so much virtue in the creature also. He is a fool, but there is a touch of angel in him, too. He is so young, so raw, so ignorant, and so grievously mistaken. And he is so right. He would play the proud Lord, brook no insolences, and grind his heel into the world's recumbent neck. And inside the creature is a shaft of light, a jumping nerve, a plate so sensitive that the whole picture of this huge tormented world is printed in the very hues and pigments of the life of man. He can be cruel, and yet hate cruelty with the hate of hell; he can be so unjust, and give his life to fight injustice; he can, in moments of anger, jealousy, or wounded vanity, inflict a grievous hurt upon others who have never done him wrong. And the next moment, thrice wounded, run through and pinioned to the wall upon the spear of his own guilt, remorse and scalding shame, he can endure such agonies that if there really were a later hell there would be no real damnation left in it.

For at the end, the creature's spirit is a noble one. His heart is warm and generous, it is full of faith and noble aspiration. He wants to be the best man in the world, but it is a good world that he wants to be the best man in. He wants to be the greatest man on earth, but in the image of his mind and heart it is not among mean people, but among his compeers of the great, that he wishes to be first. And remember this thing of this creature, too, and let it say a word in his defense: he does not want monopoly, nor is his fire expended upon a pile of dung. He does not want to be the greatest rich man in the world, to beetle up out of the blood sweat of the poor the gold of his accretions. It is not his noble proud ambition to control the slums, to squeeze out in his own huge cider-press the pulp of plundered and betrayed humanity. He does not want to own the greatest bank on earth, to steal the greatest mine, to run the greatest mill, to exploit the labor and to profit on the sweat of ninety thousand lesser men. He has a higher goal than this: at very least he wants to be the greatest fighter in the world, which would take courage and not cunning; and at the very most he wants to be the greatest poet, the greatest writer, the greatest composer, or the greatest leader in the world—and he wants to paint instead of own the greatest painting in the world.

He was the Lord of Life, the master of the earth, he was the city's conqueror, he was the only man alive who ever had been twenty-five years old, the only man who ever loved or ever had a lovely woman come to meet him, and it was morning in October; all of the city and sun, the people passing in the slant of light, all of the wine and gold of singing in the air had been created for his christening, and it was morning in October, and he was twenty-five years old.

And then the golden moments' wine there in the goblet of his life dropped one by one, the minutes passed, and she did not come. Some brightness had gone out of day. He stirred, looked at his watch, searched with a troubled eye among the thronging crowd. The minutes dropped now like cold venom. And now the air was chilled, and all the singing had gone out of day.

Noon came and passed, and yet she did not come. His feeling of jubilant happiness changed to one of dull, sick apprehension. He began to pace up and down the terrace before the library nervously, to curse and mutter, already convinced that she had fooled him, that she had no intention of coming, and he told himself savagely that it did not matter, that he did not care.

He had turned and was walking away furiously toward the street, cursing under his breath, when he heard a clatter of small brisk feet behind him. He heard a woman's voice raised above the others, calling a name, and though he could not distinguish the name, he knew at once that it was his own. His heart gave a bound of the most unspeakable joy and relief, and he turned quickly, and there across the pavement of the court, threading her way through the fast weavings of the crowd, he saw her coming toward him, eager and ruddy as an apple, and clad in rich, russet autumnal brown. Bright harvestings of young October sun fell over her, she trotted toward him briskly as a child, with rapid step and short-paced runs. She was panting for breath: at that moment he began to love her, he loved her with all his heart, but his heart would not utter or confess its love, and he did not know of it.

She was so lovely, so ruddy, and so delicate, she was so fresh and healthy-looking, and she looked like a good child, eager and full of belief in life, radiant with beauty, goodness, and magic. There was an ache of bitter, nameless joy and sorrow in him as he looked at her: the immortal light of time and of the universe fell upon her, and the feet swarmed past upon the pavements of the street, and the old hunger for the wand and the key pierced his entrails—for he believed the magic word might come to unlock his heart and say all that he felt as he saw Esther there at noon in bright October on the day when he was twenty-five years old.

He went striding back toward her, she came hurrying up, they came together in a kind of breathless collision and impulsively seized each other by the hands, and stood there too excited to speak.

"Oh!" she gasped when she could speak. "I ran so! . . . I saw you walking away—my heart jumped so!" And then, more quietly, looking at him, with a shade of reproach, "You were going away," she said.

"I thought—" then paused, groping, not knowing what, in this intoxication of joy and relief, he *had* thought. "I waited for you," he blurted out. "I've been here almost an hour—you said twelve."

"Oh, no, my dear," she answered quietly. "I told you I had an appointment at the costumer's at twelve. I'm a few minutes late, I'm sorry—but I said twelve-thirty."

The emotion of relief and happiness was still so great that he scarcely heard her explanation.

"I thought—I'd given you up," he blurted out. "I thought you weren't coming."

"Oh," she said quietly but reproachfully again, "how could you think that? You must have known I would."

For the first time now they released each other from the hard clasp which, in their excitement, they had held each other fast. They stepped back a little and surveyed each other, she beaming, and he grinning, in spite of himself, with delight.

"Well, young fellow," she cried in a jolly tone. "How does it feel to be twenty-five years old?"

Still grinning, and staring at her foolishly, he stammered: "It—it feels all right. . . . Gosh!" he cried impulsively, "you look swell in brown."

"Do you like it, hah?" she said, eagerly and brightly. She stroked the bosom of her dress with the kind of pride and satisfaction a child might take in its belongings. "It is one of my Indian dresses," she said, "a sari. I'm glad you like it."

Arm in arm, still looking at each other and so absorbed that they were completely oblivious of the crowd, the people passing, and the city all around them, they had begun to walk along, and down the steps that led to the street. On the curb they paused, and for the first time became aware of their surroundings.

"Do you know . . . " she began doubtfully, looking at him. "Where are we going?"

"Oh!" he recollected himself with a start. "Yes! I thought we'd go to a place I know about—an Italian place on the West Side."

She took her purse from under her arm and patted it.

"This is to be a celebration," she said. "I got paid this morning."

"Oh, no you don't! not this time. This is my party."

Meanwhile, he had stopped a taxicab and was holding the door open for her. They got in, he gave the driver the address, and they were driven across town toward the place he had chosen.

It was an Italian speakeasy on West 46th Street, in a row of brownstone houses, of which almost every one harbored an establishment similar to this. Certainly New York at that period must have contained thousands of such places, none of which differed in any essential detail from Joe's.

The setting and design of the establishment was one which a few years under the Prohibition Act had already made monotonously familiar to millions of people in New York. The entrance was through the basement, by means of a grated door which opened underneath the brownstone steps. To reach this door, one went down a step or two from the sidewalk into what had formerly been the basement areaway, pressed a button, and waited. Presently the basement door was opened, a man came out, peered through the grating of the gate, and if he recognized the visitor, admitted him.

Within, too, the appearance of the place was one that had already grown familiar, through thousands of duplications, to city dwellers. The original design of a city house had not been altered very much. There was a narrow hallway which led through the place from front to rear, and at the end of it there was a kitchen; to the left, as one entered, there was a very small room for the hat-check woman. On the right-hand side, in a larger but still very dark and narrow room, there was a small bar. From the bar one entered through a door into a small dining room of about the same dimensions. Across the hall there was a larger dining room, which had been created by knocking out the wall between two rooms. And upstairs, on what had once been the first floor of the house, there were still other dining rooms, and private ones, too, if one desired them. On the floors above were—God knows what!—more rooms and lodgings, and shadowy-looking lodgers who came in and out, went softly up and down the carpeted tread of the old stairs, and, quickly, softly, through the entrance of the upper door. It was a life secret, flitting, and nocturnal, a life rarely suspected and never felt, that never intruded upon the hard, bright gaiety, the drunken voices, and the raucous clatter of the lower depths.

The proprietor of this establishment was a tall, thin, and sallow man with a kind of patient sadness, a gentle melancholy which one somehow liked because he felt and understood in the character of the man a sense of decency and of human friendliness. The man was an Italian, by name Pocallipo, and since he had been christened Giuseppe, the patrons of the place referred to it as "Joe's."

The history of Joe Pocallipo was also, if one could probe that great catacomb of life that hives the obscure swarmings of the city millions, a familiar one. He was one of those simple, gentle, and essentially decent people whom circumstance, occasion, and the collusions of a corrupt period had kicked upstairs, and who did not really like this ruthless betterment.

Before the advent of the Prohibition Act he had been a waiter in a large hotel. His wife had run this same house as a lodging house, her clientele being largely derived from actors, vaudeville performers, and somewhat down-at-the-heels theatrical people of all sorts. As time went on, the woman began to provide some of her guests with an occasional meal when they would ask for it, and Joe, whose skill as a chef was considerable, began himself, on his "off day," to prepare a Sunday dinner, to which paying guests were invited. The idea, begun really as a kind of concession to the lodgers in the house, caught on: the meals were cheap, the food was excellent, people came and came again, returning often with their friends, until Joe's Sunday dinners had achieved a kind of celebrity, and the man and his wife were sorely taxed to accommodate the numbers that now came.

This involved of course the taking on of extra service and the enlargement of the dining space; meanwhile, the Prohibition Act had gone into effect, and now people at these Sunday dinners began to suggest the advisability of serving wine to those who wanted it. To an Italian this request seemed not only simple but completely reasonable; he found, moreover, that although Prohibition was a law, the supply of wine, both new and old, was plentiful to those who could afford to pay for it. Although the price was high, as he soon found from investigation carried on among his friends and colleagues, who had also been led in some such way into the labyrinth of this strange profession, the profit, once the corks were pulled, was great.

The remainder of the road was certain. There was a moment—just a moment—when Joe was faced with a decision, when he saw the perilous way this casual enterprise had led him into, when it was plain to him the kind of decision he had to make; but the dice were loaded, the scales too weighted down upon one side to admit a balanced judgment. Before him lay the choice of two careers. On the one hand, he could continue working as a waiter in a big hotel, which meant the insecurity of employment, subservience, and dependence for his living on a waiter's tips; and this way, as Joe well knew, the end was certain—old age, poverty, and broken feet. Before him on the other hand lay a more perilous and more ruthless way, but one made tempting by its promise of quick wealth. It was a way that would lead him, if not into full membership in the criminal underworld, at least into collusion with it; into a bought-and-paid-for treaty with the criminal police; and to violence, dishonesty, and crime. But it promised to him also wealth and property and eventual independence, and like many another simple man of the corrupted period, it seemed to him there was no choice to make.

He made it, and the results within four years had been more glittering than he had dared hope. His profit had been enormous. Now he was a man of property. He owned this house, and a year before had bought the next one to it. He was even now considering the purchase of a small apartment house uptown. And if not in actual fact a rich man now, he was destined to be a very rich one soon.

And yet—that sad, dark face, that tired eye, the melancholy patience with a tired tone. It was all so different from the way he thought it would turn out—so different from the life that he had thought he would have.

It was, in some ways, so much better; it was, wearily and sadly, so much worse—the dense enmeshment of that tangled scheme, the dark unhappy weavings of the ugly web, the complications of this world of crime, with its constantly growing encroachments, its new and ever uglier demands, the constant mulctings of all its graft, of blackmail, and of infamy, the fear of merciless reprisal, the knowledge that he was now imprisoned in a deadly world from which he could never hope again to escape—a world controlled by criminals, and by the police, each in collusion with the other, and himself so tarred now with the common stick of their iniquity that there was no longer any appeal left to him to any court of justice and authority, if there had been one. And there was none.

So here he stood today, peering out behind the grating of his basement gate, a sad and gentle man with weary eyes, looking out between the bars of his own barricade, to see what new eventuality the ringing of the bell had brought to him, and whether enemy or friend.

For a moment he stood there, looking out through the bars with a look of careful anxiousness; then, when he saw the young man, his face brightened, and he said: "Oh, good-morning, sir. Come in."

He unlocked the door then and held it open for his visitors as they came in, smiling in a gentle, kindly way, as they passed him. He closed the gate behind them and stood aside while they went in. Then he led the way along the narrow little corridor into a dining room. The first one they came to had some people in it, but the smaller one behind was empty. They chose this one, and took a table, Joe pulling back the chairs and standing behind Esther until she was seated, with the air of a kind and gentle dignity that, one felt, was really a part of the decency and the goodness of the man.

"I have not seen you for so long, sir," he said to the young man in his quiet voice; "you've been away?"

"Yes, Joe, I've been away a year," said the young man, secretly warmed and pleased that the man should have remembered him, and a little proud, too, that this mark of recognition should be given in front of Esther.

"We've missed you," Joe said with his quiet smile. "You've been to Europe?"

"Yes," the other said casually, but quite pleased just the same that the proprietor had asked him, for he was of that age when one likes to boast a little of his voyages. "I was there a year," he added, and then realized he had said something of this sort before.

"Where were you?" Joe inquired politely. "You were in Paris, sir, I am sure," he said, and smiled.

"Yes," the other answered carelessly, with just a trace of the nonchalance of the old boulevardier, "I lived there for six months," he said, tossing this off carelessly in a tone of casual ease, "and then I stayed in England for a while."

"You did not go to EEtaly?" inquired Joe, with a smile.

"Yes, I was there this spring," the traveler replied in an easy tone that indicated that this season of the year was always the one he preferred when taking his Italian holiday. He did not think it worth mentioning that he had gone back again in August to sail from Naples: that trip hardly counted, for he had gone straight through by train and had seen nothing of the country.

"Ah, EEtaly is beautiful in spring," Joe said. "You were at Rome?"

"Not long," said the voyager, whose stay in Rome, to tell the truth, had been limited to a stop between trains. "In the spring I remained in the North"—he tossed this off with some abandon, too, as if to say that at this season of the year "the North" is the only portion of the Italian peninsula that a man of cultivated taste could tolerate.

"You know Milano?" said Joe.

"Oh, yes," the other cried, somewhat relieved to have some place mentioned at last that he could honestly say he did know. "I stayed there for some time"—a slight exaggeration of the fact, perhaps, as his sojourn had been limited to seven days. "And Venezia," he went on quickly, getting a lascivious pleasure from his pronunciation of the word.

"Venezia is very beautiful," said Joe.

"Your own home is near Milano, isn't it?"

"No, near Turino, sir," Joe replied.

"And the whole place here," the youth went on, turning eagerly to Esther—"all the waiters, the hat-check girl, the people out in the kitchen, come from the same little town—don't they, Joe?"

"Yes, sir, yes, sir," said Joe, smiling, "all of us." In his quiet and gentle way he turned to Esther and with a movement of the hand explained: "First one man came—and he writes back that he is doing"—he moved his shoulders slightly—"not so bad. Then others came. Now I think we are more here than we are left at home."

"How interesting," murmured Esther, pulling off her gloves and looking round the room. "Look," she said quickly, turning to her companion, "could you get a cocktail—hah? I want to drink to your health."

"Well, of course," said Joe, "you can have anything you like."

"It's my birthday, Joe, and this is my birthday party."

"You shall have everything. What will the lady drink?"—he turned to her.

"Oh, I think—" she meditated a moment; then turning to the youth, said brightly, "a nice Martini—hah?"

"Yes, I'll have that, too. Two of them, Joe."

"Two Martinis. Very good, *very* good," said Joe, with an air of complaisance, "and after that—"

"Well, what have you?"

He told them what he had, and they ordered the dinner—antipasto, minestrone, fish, chicken, salad, cheese, and coffee. It was too much, but they had the spirit of true celebrants: they ordered a quart flask of Chianti to go with it.

"I'm not doing anything else all afternoon," said Esther. "I saved it for you."

Joe disappeared, and they could hear him giving the order in fast Italian. A waiter brought two cocktails on a tray. They clinked glasses, and Esther said, "Well, here's to you, young fellow." She was silent for a moment, looking at him very seriously, then she said: "To your success—the real kind—the kind you want inside of you—the best."

They drank, but her words, her presence here, the feeling of wonderful happiness and pride that the day had brought to him, a sense that somehow this was the true beginning of his life, and that a fortunate and happy life such as he had always visioned now lay immediately before him, gave him an exalted purpose, the intoxication of a determined and irresistible strength that even drink could add nothing to. He leaned forward across the table and seized her hand in both of his: "Oh, I'll do it!" he cried exalted. "I'll do it!"

"You will," she said. "I know you will!" And putting her other hand on top of his, she squeezed it hard, and whispered: "The best! You are the best!"

The wild happiness of that moment, the mounting total of that enchanted day, left now only the overpowering sense of some miraculous consummation that was about to be realized immediately. It seemed to him that he had "the whole thing" within his grasp—what, he did not know, and yet he was sure he had it. The concrete distillation of all this overwhelming certainty, this overwhelming joy—that the great success, the magnificent achievement, the love, the honor, the glory, were already his—lay there palpable, warm and heavy as a ball does, in his hand. And then, feeling this impossible realization so impossibly near that he already had it in his grasp, feeling this certitude so exultantly, the sense of purpose so powerfully, that he was sure he knew exactly what certitude and purpose were—feeling the language he had never uttered so eloquently there at the very hinges of his tongue, the songs that he had never sung, the music he had never heard, the great books, the novels, the poems he had never fashioned—they were all so magnificently, so certainly, his that he could utter them at any moment—now—a moment after—within five minutes—at any moment that he chose to make them his!

That boiling confidence of wild elements proved too much for the fragile tenement of flesh, of bone, of thinking, and of sense that it inhabited, and he began to talk "a blue streak." As if every secret hope, every insatiate desire, every cherished and unspoken aspiration, every unuttered feeling, thought, or conviction that had ever seethed and boiled in the wild ferment of his youth, that had ever rankled, eaten like an acid in the secret places of his spirit, that had ever been withheld, suppressed, pent-up, dammed, concealed through pride, through fear of ridicule, through doubt or disbelief, or because there was no other ear to hear him, no other tongue to answer back, to give them confirmation—this whole tremendous backwater of the spirit burst through its walls and rushed out in an inundating flood.

Words rushed from him in wild phrases, hurled spears, flung and broken staves of thought, of hope, of purpose, and of feeling. If he had had a dozen tongues, yet he could not have had the means to utter them, and still they charged and foamed and thrust there at the portals of his speech, and still not a thousandth part of what he wished to say was shaped or uttered. On the surface of this tremendous superflux he was himself whirled and swept away like a chip, spun round and carried onward, helpless on his own raging flood, and finding all the means at his disposal insufficient, failing him, like a man who pours oil on a raging fire, he ordered one drink after another and gulped them down.

He became very drunk. He became more wild, more incoherent all the time. And yet it seemed to him that he must say it finally, get it out of him, empty himself clean, get it all clear and straight and certain.

When they got out into the street again, darkness had come, and he was still talking. They got into a cab. The thronging streets, the jammed congestion of the traffic, the intolerable glare, the insane kaleidoscope of Broadway burned there in his inflamed and maddened vision, not in a blur, not in a drunken maze, but with a kind of distorted and insane precision, a grotesque projection of what it really was. His baffled and infuriated spirit turned against it—against everyone, everything—against her. For suddenly he realized that she was taking him home to his hotel. The knowledge infuriated him; he felt that she was deserting him, betraying him. He shouted to the driver to stop, she caught hold of his arm and tried to keep him in the car, he wrenched free, shouted at her that she had gone back on him, sold him out, betrayed him—that he wanted to see her no more, that she was no good—and even while she pleaded with him, tried to persuade him to get back in the car with her, he told her to be gone, slammed the door in her face, and lunged away into the crowd.

The whole city now reeled past him—the lights, the crowds, the glittering vertices of night, now bedimmed and sown with a star-flung panoply of their nocturnal faëry—it all burned there in his vision in a pattern of grotesque distortion, it seemed cruel and insane to him. He was filled with a murderous fury; he wanted to batter something into a pulp, to smash things down, to stamp them into splintered ruins. He slugged his way through the streets like a maddened animal, he hurled himself against the crowd, lunged brutally against people and knocked them out of his way, and finally, having stunned himself into a kind of apathy, he reached the end of that blind and blazing passage, he found himself in front of his hotel, exhausted, sick, and with no more hope for a singing in his heart. He found his room, went in, and fell senseless, face downward, on the bed.

The flask of ether had exploded.

A Note on Experts:
Dexter Vespasian Joyner

I have often noticed that it is easier for a man to achieve distinction as an expert here in America than to attain eminence in almost any other branch of the nation's life. One must spend years, for example, at hard labor on small wages to become a first-rate carpenter. The apprenticeship of the master mechanic, the mason, the plasterer, or the stone-cutter is also long, arduous, and impecunious. To become a locomotive engineer, which I should say is almost the highest and the most authoritative of the mechanical positions, a man must undergo an apprenticeship that is only infrequently less than twenty years, and that requires a long and grueling period of preparation as round-house helper, round-house mechanic, and locomotive fireman, before the candidate is deemed worthy of this highest office. Similarly, in the more professional activities, the period of preparation is also long and difficult. A young man must go through ten years of painful study and unpaid service before he is even allowed to begin his practice as a physician. The lawyer must go through a period of training involving six years or more. So, too, the architect, the civil engineer, the piano player, or the opera singer; all these men at all these various trades and labors and professions, from pastry baker to steamship pilot, from locomotive engineer to surgical specialist, must go through the discipline of a long and arduous preparation that requires from five to twenty years of their lives, and that even then leaves them just ready to essay their first modest, independent beginnings in their chosen field. But so far as I know, a man requires no preparation whatever to be an expert. He can be an expert in anything without having to study, without having to serve an apprenticeship, without having had any previous experience in the thing he is expert on—what is most delightful of all, without having to know anything whatever about it. It may be that the more conservative and cautious of my readers—and I confess it is to this type of reader that I have always tried chiefly to address myself, and with whom I find myself personally most in accord—it may be, I say, that this type of reader will find some faint tingeing of extravagance in my assertion, may perhaps too hastily conclude that for the first time in my life I have allowed impulse somewhat to overbalance the more reasoned and deliberate judgment which is characteristic of me. I confess that my apprehensions on this score have always been so great that I have deliberately leaned backward, time and again, in order to avoid the remotest suspicion that anything I have said or written may have been swayed even faintly by that incondite exuberance to which, alas, so many people are susceptible. Accordingly, it is in this same spirit of caution that I now address myself to these same readers, and I repeat, with all the deliberate calculation of which I am capable, that I know no other field in American life in which it is so delightfully easy to attain fame and eminence as the field of experting. And in substantiation of this assertion, all I need do, I think, is to ask the more thoughtful reader to review their own experience and the experience of some of the experts they know—for every American citizen past the age of twenty has known hundreds of experts—and assure themselves that if I err in my assertions, I err from the side of understatement.

Consider for a moment a few of the many activities in which people that we know have won high distinction for their ability as experts—to mention but a few, aesthetics, horse-racing, politics and economics, newspaper comic strips, primitive Negro sculpture and Negro hymns and folk-songs, short-story writing, dramatic composition and the novel, planned economy and world revolution, the art of the cinema in especial relation to Mr. Charles Chaplin considered as Hamlet, Lear, Macbeth, the Trojan Women or the "Tragic Soul of Man," surrealism, post-war expressionism, the Revolution of the Word and the works of Mr. Joyce and Gertrude Stein, what is going on in Germany (by people who have never been there and cannot speak the language), what is going on in Russia (by people who have, or have not, been there for ten days and who cannot speak the language), what is going on in Georgia or in California, among the share-croppers of Arkansas or the coal miners of West Virginia, what is going on on the Pacific coast, in the dust bowls of the West, in the mill towns of New England, in the Negro settlements of the South, in the minds and hearts and lives of the workers, in the whole suffering mind and heart and soul of man—all dished up to you in smoking portions, all smacked down across the counter in neatly done-up packages, all given to you, crammed down your throat, stuffed through your craw, forcibly fed into you, in that spirit of sweet charity, benevolent understanding, divine impartiality, and liberal sweet reasonableness that characterize the more inflamed and choleric utterances of a Jesuit priest. They are all written about, shouted about, dogmatized about, and banged and whacked over the head about by all these wonderful Know-it-alls who, by the simple process of studying nothing, going nowhere, seeing, knowing, understanding no one, nothing, except what they want to see and understand and know, are divinely privileged to lam into you, poor misbegotten ignoramus that you are, who sweat and swelter with the common herd and who know nothing except what you know, that you pay your money but you have no choice except to take it or leave it, what the experts give to you. And if you take it, why, then, you leave it also, for it is a fundamental rule of experting that you take only what your chosen expert has to offer. If you take any of the 957 other varieties of pap which his fellow medicine men are dishing out, why, then, in the spirit of sweet Christian charity, God damn your soul to hell for the moribund and dissolute bourgeois that you are; it's thumbs down now, poison in your soup, and a good swift kick below the belt, a gouge in the eye, a few thousand knife thrusts in the back, and all the other delicate approved stratagems of fair play and sportsmanship, which the saviors of the arts, the politics and economics of the world, the improvement and betterment of one's fellow men, are practiced in.

I have known hundreds of the crew throughout my lifetime. So has everyone. Few of them, I think, are really formidable. Not many of them are even dangerous. Some of them, of course, are downright harmless and amusing. In this class I would put newspaper sporting men.

There used to be a sporting writer on the *New York Sun* whose name was Joe Vila. Poor Joe is dead now. I never got to know him in the flesh. But now that he is gone, I miss him like a friend. Joe was an expert, one of the greatest sporting experts we have ever had. For years I read his columns every day. If I missed it once, I should have felt an aching void. It was essential to me as a cup of coffee. And if ever sports columns—and I have been the devoted reader of thousands of them—ever reached a lower depth of imbecilic foolishness, a higher peak of enthusiastic idiocy, I do not know where they can be found. Statements that seemed to have fallen hot from the lips of Wordsworth's idiot boy were uttered with an inspired authority, an omniscience of conviction that was wonderful; impassioned debates that, in all their elements of logical sequence, reasoned acuity, seemed to have been taken verbatim from the wilder passages between the walrus and the carpenter, were here reproduced with a fidelity that left one gasping, with a rhetorical punch that had one hanging on the ropes. "If Kid Getti," Joe would observe, "displays the same form that he displayed in his fights with Rocky Boozer, Punch-drunk Pipgrass, and One-Eye Maglone, if that wicked sleep-producing right is operating with the same murderous efficiency as it did when it sent Pete Pappadopolos and Irish Dickstein crashing to the mat, he is likely to be returned the winner from his bout with Cyclone McGillicuddy tomorrow evening. On the other hand, if McGillicuddy manages to land often and hard enough with that fast-working left hook that put such gladiators as Jumping Joe Dubinsky and Tornado Tate *hors de combat,* he may be awarded the decision before the fight has gone its scheduled route."

I used to read it and gulp, and then lick my lips for more. There was something so beautifully complete about it. There were no cracks in the armor of Joe Vila's logic. The perfection of his reason was absolute. If some one knocked out some one else, some one would win. If some one else knocked out some one, some one else would win. You couldn't beat that kind of reasoning; Joe Vila had you nailed. All you could do was gulp submissively and stammer, "I—I guess you're right, sir."

Moreover, no matter who won the fight, no matter on which side the decision lay, Joe Vila's confidence was unperturbed, his prognostications in the light of retrospect were infallible. If Kid Getti were the winner, Joe Vila could be depended on next day to emphasize his own triumphant vindication. "As we have been telling the so-called wise boys all along," he would modestly begin, "McGillicuddy was nothing but a set-up for the Brownsville Bomber. Early in the second stanza Getti hung his right on Cyclone's jaw, which put the Boston boy on Queer Street for the remainder of the go." Similarly, if McGillicuddy won the fight, Joe would hold next day an ironic inquest. "We tried to tell the suckers, but they wouldn't listen," he would observe. "Getti was a pushover for the Bean Town Bull. The Kid has nothing but a right-hand punch, and as everybody knows, no boxer with the knowledge of the rudiments will ever get hit with a right."

Joe, by the way, was full of expert knowledge of this sort. He was constantly asserting most impressively that "no one trained in the rudiments of boxing could ever be hit with a right hand"—a statement which I always found surprising, since I had seen a number of bouts myself in which people who *had* been trained in the rudiments of boxing *did* get hit and very forcibly hit with a right hand. I used to ponder this particular assertion very earnestly, and the more I pondered it, the stranger it became. Why, I reflected, if no boxer who is trained in the rudiments of boxing could ever be hit by a right hand—why should any boxer bother to have a right hand? Why, since a right hand was such a very rudimentary possession, and of absolutely no value to a well-trained boxer, why shouldn't he amputate it and save the trouble and expense of having it carried into the ring with him? Why, in fact,—the idea would develop very brilliantly as its manifold possibilities took hold of me—why shouldn't we develop a race of one-armed boxers, each equipped solely and simply with a left hand, trained to the very apex of perfection? Surely, a bout of this sort between two crafty, one-armed strategists of the ring would be a thrilling one. Again, as their knowledge and skill increased, might it not be that each of them would become so cunning and so skillful in the uses of his weapon that he could completely and effectually checkmate the other one in every move. Then—the logic of this development was beautifully apparent—then we could cut off the left hands of all boxers and have bouts thereafter between boxers with *no hands* at all. This would undoubtedly be an improvement over most of the contests one saw, anyway, and besides that, how much greater was the appeal to one's intelligence, how much more fascinating its imaginative possibilities. Boxers would no longer crudely feint and thrust and smash at each other with their physical appendages. No, on the contrary, what we would see would be a kind of boxing match of the wits, a kind of inspired chess play of the roped arena, where one feinted swiftly with the left ventricle of his brain and countered with his right, left-hooked by intuition or uppercutted with a crafty sneak-punch of the subconscious mind. The possibilities of this kind of warfare were apparent. It was really intellectual warfare of the highest and most subtle nature. Its benefits to all mankind would be enormous. I became fascinated with all the brilliant possibilities of my own discovery. I was just on the point of proposing it to my favorite expert in a public letter when poor Joe Vila died. And, as I say, I missed him. In looking back, I think it is just as well now that I did not write the letter. For now it is apparent to me the kind of handless, armless boxing match that I was on the point of putting forth before the world as my own unique discovery had really been familiar to Joe Vila and to all the other experts for many years. It was, in fact, a fundamental tool of their equipment, an essential part of their method, an indispensable property of their paraphernalia. They carried on forever these handless, armless contests of the wit and imagination. They were forever fighting with themselves, forever chasing their own shadows around the ring, forever ducking, weaving, shifting, feinting, bobbing against opponents of their own creation, and finally knocking themselves out with a terrific uppercut, to the accompaniment of tremendous roars of applause delivered by themselves. Joe Vila was himself, in fact, a master of this kind of shadow-boxing. He was forever carrying on sanguinary but completely imaginary contests between imaginary opponents of his own choosing in contests conceived in his own feverish imagination and staged within the roped arena of his own fancy. What, for example, would have been the result if Bob Fitzsimmons, Fitzsimmons of the Nineties, had met Jack Dempsey—the Dempsey of the Twenties—at a time when both were "at their best"? I leave the rest to Joe Vila's superior descriptive power. "The bell clangs. Fitzsimmons shuffles awkwardly out of his corner on his knock-kneed spindly legs, advances cautiously toward his opponent when already, with the tigerish spring of a cat, the Manassa Mauler is upon him. Dempsey shoots his left and misses; close in he smashes savagely with a deadly right that has sent Willard, Carpentier, and Firpo reeling to the canvas. Long Bob does not seem to move. He merely shifts his head. The deadly, dynamite-laden glove whizzes harmlessly past. Dempsey finds himself tied up, unable to use his arms; for the first time a look of dazed surprise comes into the Mauler's eyes"—etc. And so on to the thrilling end, in which Fitzsimmons sometimes won with his terrible solar plexus punch in the fourteenth round, in which Dempsey sometimes got up, dazed and bleeding, from the canvas to hurl himself upon his opponent and fairly beat him to the earth with the last surges of a furious fighter's instinct, but which usually, I am glad to say, ended in a gory but an honorable draw.

For Joe Vila, unlike many other experts, really tried to be impartial. He really tried to referee his own straw battles fairly. He was an expert, but in the end he had a good heart and a sense of justice. He did little harm. He was for the winner. He was against the loser. He was loyal to one while he was the champion, but he didn't betray one when he lost. He always knew just where Joe Vila stood. Of all the types of experts, his was the best. He was a newspaper expert. And newspaper experts are the best. You always know where you stand with newspaper experts, because newspapermen are whores. And you always know where you stand with whores. For that reason, I have always had an uneasy and a stubborn liking for both kinds. You may not like what a whore does to you, but you're really not much surprised about it later, because you always know why she did it. You pay your money and take your choice. You don't always know what you're getting, but at any rate you know the chance you're taking. You may be mistaken but you are not fooled. A whore may rob you, or get you drunk or drug you, or pick your pockets when you are not looking, but she won't say later that she did it because of her great love for you. She may welcome you with open arms and call you sweetheart when your luck is in and you have money in your pockets, and she may throw you out of doors and tell you that you're a dirty bum when your luck is out and there is no money left, but she won't say later that she did it out of love of all mankind, devotion to a sacred principle, the conviction that her obligation to her own ideals, her duty to her fellow men, was greater than her own love. If she stabs you in the back, she stabs you in the back, and that's all there is to it. There are no fancy reasons given for it later unless she's talking to the police. A whore is also a kind of expert in her line and one, it seems to me, of the least harmful kind. And so it is also with her spiritual twin, the newspaperman. I have known a good number of them, and most of them I liked. Those I didn't like were those that tried to lie about it, who had fancy reasons for it later. The newspaper criticos, the tony uppercrust of journaldom, half in, half out and hanging by their fangs upon the fringes of the arts, the gossip-scavengers with the daily columns, the gossip-mongers of the literary life, the musicos, the dramaticos, the criticos, politicos, aestheticos of every sort. You can't put faith in this kind of expert. They are much too fast and fancy for you. They've got a reason ready on their lips for every stab, an argument for every slander, a justification for every cowardly attack. No, give me the good old homely, ink-stained harlot of the city room, the plain old whore of daily print. Give me the fellow who will come to see you for an interview, who will read your mail when you've gone out to get a drink for him, who will look at your telephone bill to see how much you owe, who will try the telephone to see if the service has been cut off, who will poke around in dusty corners, investigate your dirty linen, take advantage of your youth, your excitement, your enthusiasm, your eagerness to make a good impression and have a good piece in the paper and will twist it all around, garble it all, mangle it all, make a fool out of you, betray your honesty and your youth, betray the innocence and belief of man, all for the purpose of "getting a good story" out of it. Give me this kind of whore, I say, because you know just where you stand with him, and in the end you won't be fooled. You know that he is with you when you win; you know he is against you when you lose. You know he will write well of you when you are a public favorite, when the public wishes to hear good news of you. You know that he will write badly of you when you are no longer fortune's child, when that same public which applauded wants to hear the worst. You know that if the worst is not bad enough, the whore of print will make it so. And knowing this, you can remember—and forget. And in the end, somehow, you like the rascal. In the end, you take him as he is, you see what he has to do. You forgive him. You see that he usually does not wish you harm. You see that usually he wishes well. You see that only he does not wish well hard enough. You see that usually he wants what is good in life, but he did not want it hard enough. And you see that usually the whole nature of his fault is here; he sold out along the road. But he sold out not because he was bad but just because he wasn't good enough. But the remnants of that ruined goodness are still in him, and you like him for it. You see it somehow in his sallow face. You see it in his weary eyes. You see it in his shabby, somewhat wilted person, which always carries with it, somehow, something of the weary yet not wholly disagreeable relaxation of the deserted city room after the day's work is over, of the quiet press room, the quiet presses, the smell of ink when the last edition has been run off. You see, finally, that even the fellow's cynicism is just a diverted form of sentiment, his shallow hardness—just a shell. You see that he became a whore not because he wanted to become one, but because he didn't want to become something else quite hard enough. So you know where you are with him. You see finally just where you stand. You learn to understand the newspaper expert, the journalistic whore, which brings me to another, and it seems to me, a worse type of both.

His name was Dexter Vespasian Joyner. He was the greatest expert that I ever knew. As to his eminence in prostitution, I must allow the reader to judge for himself. All I can attempt to do is to give some account of the beginning of his career as an expert—a career which, it seems to me, for astonishing versatility, for flexible adaptability, for swift reflex and for chameleon-like change, for the possession of a large and easy swallow that took everything and that balked at nothing, surpassed any similar career that I have ever known. And I have known many. If I had to give the reason for Dexter Joyner's amazing success as an expert and the eminence which he was destined to attain, I think I should have to attribute it first of all to a kind of astonishing intellectual "nose for news," a sort of uncanny quickness of instinct and reflex, a kind of sensory perspicuity, which felt things coming before most other people even knew that they were on the way, which smelled them in the air before most other people even knew that they had arrived and were knocking at the outposts of the city. He got the jump on every one, and in the end, I think, he suffered the fate other bright young men so often suffer—he got the jump on himself.

Even at college Dexter was always three or four jumps ahead of the rest of us. We were for the most part a benighted crowd, students at a little· country college in the South; and Dexter, at the time when he first burst upon our vision, had already spent a year at Yale. It was my privilege as a Freshman to hear my fellows and, I am afraid, myself, dismissed by this young magnificent as "a crowd of yockels." Yes, Dexter called us Yockels, very properly, no doubt, but, as I remember it, any indignation we may have felt was overwhelmed by hearing the word pronounced that way. The pronunciation fascinated us. All of us who had ever heard or seen the word before had concluded rashly that the proper pronunciation of the word was "yoakels." Furthermore, I think that most of us had heretofore assumed that the expression was not one in general use in the more familiar episodes of American life. We felt, I think, that the word had decided poetical and literary connotations—it was such a word, for instance, as might be used in Shakespeare's time for the description of a clown. It was such a word as the lord of the manor bound from London in Fielding's time might have used for the description of the country fellows in the village. We were country fellows, that was true enough, and most of us were from a village, but I think most of us had previously assumed that a yockel was a country fellow who wore a smock, who gaped and touched his hat when young Lord Sneeringford rode by, and who said, "They do be saying, lads, there's girt doings at his lardship's." Well, maybe Dexter was right about us. I suppose we really looked like yockels to him, and he certainly looked like young Lord Sneeringford to us. But, as I say, if we felt any resentment at the word I think it was all blotted out by the admiration and the wonder which his pronunciation of the word evoked. In fact, after that we became so fascinated with the word that it became a form of familiar address. Someone would knock at our door, and when we would cry, "Who's there?" a voice would answer, "A couple of yockels come to see you." "Come in, you yockels," we would cry. The name became so famous that we even had a Yockels Club, with secret rites, governed by a Head Yockel, a First-Assistant Yockel, a Second-Assistant Yockel, a Lord High Yockel of the British Seal, and a Chief Yockel of the King's Wardrobe. In fact, when Dexter finally left us, and leave us he did—it was asserted he had been yockeled out of college. He departed in his Junior year and went to Harvard, and I think we missed him. We felt that something precious had gone out of life. We continued to call one another yockels for a time, but somehow there didn't seem to be much point in it any more. Even the Yockels Club went out of fashion; deprived of its chief inspiration, cut off from its energizing source, it lost the energies of its first conception, grew anemic, and like many other worthy institutions which have outlived their purpose, it withered finally and died.

I was not privileged to see Dexter for several years after this. And during this time great changes had been wrought. Dexter had been to Oxford for a year or two, and now we companions of an earlier time had become "the peasants." It was, I think, a much more bitter word than "yockel." He uttered it quite venomously, I thought. It had, unquestionably, a sharper bite, a deeper penetration than had "yockel." But personally I regretted the change. I felt that Dexter had grown away from us, that he was too much of the world, that he had become too sophisticated, that he was cutting himself away from his roots. A strangeness had come up between us. I missed the good old homely smack of yockel. There was something so familiar, so plain, so quaint—so—so damned intimate about it. I hated to see it go. It was on the tip of my tongue to tell Dexter so. But by now he had become so grand. He was so much a part of the great world of travel, of fashion, and the arts, that I did not dare even timidly suggest to him that I missed the word, and would he not go back to it. I heard, however, later on, one illuminating story of this Oxford period in his life. My informer was an English youth who had been at Oxford while Dexter was there and was, in fact, a member of his college. According to my English friend, he had been present on the occasion and at the exact moment when Dexter had first appeared upon the Oxford scene. This was at the first dinner of the term in the hall. Dexter appeared, as was his custom, a little late, and when the others of his table were already seated. He bowed and then took the place assigned to him and pursued his meal with quiet dignity until one of the dons who sat at the head of the table broke the silence hospitably and asked him for his name and origins. Dexter gave his name with satisfaction, admitted with a smile that he *was* American, and when pressed for more explicit information as to his native geography, finally confessed with a quiet little shrug and an ironic lifting of the brows, "Oh, I'm sure it's no-where in America that you've ever heard of. My people (all of English stock of course) were from Virginia, but I, alas, grew up among the peasants down in North Carolina." No one, according to my English friend, said anything for a moment, but finally the don, lifting *his* eyebrows with an air of polite astonishment, remarked: "But—how extraordinary—I never knew that there *were* peasants in North Carolina."

After this Dexter was allowed not only to resume but to complete his meal in silence.

Three O'Clock

George Webber lay on the grass one afternoon before his uncle's house. George Webber had good eyes, a sound body, he was twelve years old. He had a wonderful nose, a marvelous sense of smell, nothing fooled him. He lay there in the grass before his uncle's house, thinking: "This is the way things are. Here is the grass, so green and coarse, so sweet and delicate, but with some brown rubble in it. There are the houses all along the street, the concrete blocks of walls, somehow so dreary, ugly, yet familiar, the slate roofs and the shingles, the lawns, the hedges, and the gables, the backyards with their accidental structures of so many little and familiar things as hen houses, barns. All common and familiar as my breath, all accidental as the strings of blind chance, yet all somehow fore-ordered as a destiny: the way they are, because they are the way they are!"

He really knew the way things were. He lay in the grass and pulled some grass blades and looked upon them contentedly and chewed upon them. And he knew the way the grass blades were. He dug bare toes into the grass and thought of it. He knew the way it felt. Among the green grass he saw patches of old brown, and he knew the way that was too. He put out his hand and felt the maple tree. He saw the way it came out of the earth; the grass grew right around it; he felt the bark and got its rough coarse feeling. He pressed hard with his fingers; a little rough piece of the bark came off: he knew the way that was, too. The wind kept howling faintly the way it does in May. All the young leaves of the maple tree were turned back, straining in the wind. He heard the sound it made; it touched him with some sadness; then the wind went and came again.

He turned and saw his uncle's house, its bright red brick, its hard, new, cement columns, everything about it raw and ugly; and beside it, set farther back, the old house his grandfather had built, the clapboard structure, the porch, the gables, the bay windows, the color of the paint. It was all accidental, like a million other things in America. George Webber saw it, and he knew that this was the way things were. He watched the sunlight come and go, across backyards with all their tangle of familiar things; he saw the hills against the eastern side of town, sweet green, a little mottled, so com-

447

mon, homely, and familiar, and, when remembered later, wonderful, the way things are.

There was a certain stitch of afternoon while the boy lay there. Bird chir-rupings and maple leaves, pervading quietness, boards hammered from afar, and a bumbling hum. The day was drowsed with quietness and defunctive turnip greens at three o'clock, and Carlton Leathergood's tall, pock-marked, yellow nigger was coming up the street. The big dog trotted with him, breathing like a locomotive, the big dog Storm, that knocked you down with friendliness. Tongue rolling, heavy as a man, the great head swaying side to side, puffing with joy continually, the dog came on, and with him came the pock-marked nigger, Simpson Simms. Tall, lean, grinning cheer-fully, full of dignity and reverence, the nigger was coming up the street the way he always did at three o'clock. He smiled and raised his hand to George with a courtly greeting. He called him "Mister" Webber as he always did; the greeting was gracious and respectful, and soon forgotten as it is and should be in the good, kind minds of niggers and of idiots, and yet it filled the boy somehow with warmth and joy.

"Good day, dar, Mistah Webbah. How's Mistah Webbah today?"

The big dog swayed and panted like an engine, his great tongue lolling out; he came on with his great head down and with the great black brisket and his shoulders working.

Something happened suddenly, filling that quiet street with instant men-ace, injecting terror in the calm pulse of the boy. Around the corner of the Potterham house across the street came Potterham's bulldog. He saw the mastiff, paused; his forelegs widened stockily, his grim-jowled face seemed to sink right down between the shoulder blades, his lips bared back along his long-fanged tusks, and from his baleful red-shot eyes fierce lightning shone. A low snarl rattled in the folds of his thick throat, the mastiff swung his ponderous head back and growled, the bulldog came on, halted, leaning forward on his widened legs, filled with hell-fire, solid with fight.

And Carlton Leathergood's pock-marked yellow Negro man winked at the boy and shook his head with cheerful confidence, saying:

"He ain't goin' to mix up wid my dawg, Mistah Webbah! . . . No, sah! . . . He knows bettah dan dat! . . . Yes, sah!" cried Leathergood's nigger with unbounded confidence. "He knows too well fo' *dat!*"

The pock-marked nigger was mistaken! Something happened like a flash: there was a sudden snarl, a black thunderbolt shot through the air, the shine of murderous fanged teeth. Before the mastiff knew what had happened to him, the little bull was in and had his fierce teeth buried, sunk, gripped with the lock of death, in the great throat of the larger dog.

What happened after that was hard to follow. For a moment the great dog stood stock still with an eloquence of stunned surprise and bewildered consternation that was more than human; then a savage roar burst out upon the quiet air, filling the street with its gigantic anger. The mastiff swung his great head savagely, the little bull went flying through the air but hung on with embedded teeth; great drops of bright arterial blood went flying everywhere across the pavement, and still the bull held on. The end came like a lightning stroke. The great head flashed once through the air and down: the bull, no longer dog now—just a wad of black—smacked to the pavement with a sickening crunch.

From Potterham's house a screen door slammed, and fourteen-year-old Augustus Potterham, with his wild red hair aflame, came out upon the run. Up the street, paunch-bellied, stiff-legged, and slouchy-uniformed, Mr. Matthews, the policeman, pounded heavily. But Leathergood's nigger was already there, tugging furiously at the leather collar around the mastiff's neck, and uttering imprecations.

But it was all too late. The little dog was dead the moment that he struck the pavement—back broken, most of his bones broken, too; in Mr. Matthews' words, "He never knowed what hit him," and this was true. And the big dog came away quietly enough, now that the thing was done: beneath the Negro's wrenching tug upon his neck, he swung back slowly, panting, throat dripping blood in a slow rain, bedewing the street beneath him with bright red flakes.

Suddenly, like a miracle, the quiet street was full of people. They came from all directions, from everywhere: they pressed around in an excited circle, all trying to talk at once, each with his own story, everyone debating, explaining, giving his own version. In Mr. Potterham's house, the screen door slammed again, and Mr. Potterham came running out at his funny little bandy-legged stride, his little red apple-cheeks aglow with anger, indignation, and excitement, his funny chirping little voice heard plainly over all the softer, deeper, heavier, more Southern tones.

" 'Ere now! Wot did I tell you? I always said his bloody dog would make trouble! 'Ere! *Look* at him now! The great bleedin', blinkin' thing! Big as a helephant 'e is! Wot chance 'ud a dog like mine 'ave against a brute like that! 'E ought to be put out of the way—that's wot! You mark my words—you let that brute run loose, an' there won't be a dog left in town! That's wot!"

And Leathergood's big pock-marked nigger, still clutching to the mastiff's collar as he talks, and pleading with the policeman almost tearfully:

"Fo' de Lawd, Mistah Matthews, my dawg didn't do *nuffin!* No, sah! He don't bothah nobody—*my* dawg don't! He wa'nt even noticin' dat othah dawg—you ask *anybody!*—ask Mistah Webbah heah!"—suddenly appealing to the boy with pleading entreaty—"Ain't dat right, Mistah Webbah? You saw de whole thing yo'se'f, didn't you? You tell Mistah Matthews how it was! Me an' my dawg was comin' up de street, a-tendin' to ouah business, I jus' tu'ned my haid to say good day to Mistah Webbah heah, when heah comes dis othah dawg aroun' de house, jus' a-puffin' an' a-snawtin', and befo' I could say Jack Robinson, he jumps all ovah my dawg an' grabs him by de t'roat—you ask Mistah Webbah if dat ain't de way it happened."

.   .   .

And so it goes, everyone debating, arguing, agreeing, and denying, giving his own version and his own opinion; and Mr. Matthews asking questions and writing things down in a book; and poor Augustus Potterham blubbering like a baby, holding his dead little bulldog in his arms, his homely, freckled face contorted piteously, and dropping scalding tears upon his little dead dog; and the big mastiff panting, dripping blood upon the ground and looking curious, detached from the whole thing, and a little bored; and presently the excitement subsiding, people going away; Mr. Matthews telling the Negro to appear in court; Augustus Potterham going away into the house blubbering, with the little bulldog in his arms; Mr. Potterham behind him, still chirping loudly and excitedly; and the dejected, pock-marked nigger and his tremendous dog going away up the street, the big dog dropping big blood-flakes on the pavement as he goes. And finally, silence as before, the quiet street again, the rustling of young maple leaves in the light wind, the brooding imminence of three o'clock, a few bright blood-flakes on the pavement, and all else the way it had always been, and George Webber, as before, stretched out upon the grass beneath the tree there in his uncle's yard, chin cupped in hands, adrift on time's great dream, and thinking:

"Great God, this is the way things are, I understand this is the way things are: and, Great God! Great God! this being just the way things are, how strange, and plain, and savage, sweet and cruel, lovely, terrible, and mysterious, and how unmistakable and familiar all things are!"

The Winter of Our Discontent

I

You would have loved Daddy. He was so wild and beautiful, everybody adored him. That was the trouble: things came too easy for him; he never had to work for anything.

The year before Daddy died, Richard Brandell made a production of *Richard III,* and he sent my father tickets for the performance, with a very urgent and excited note asking us to come to see him before the show began. At this time my father had not played in the theater for almost a year. His deafness had got so bad he could no longer hear his cues, and Uncle Bob had given him a job as his secretary at Police Headquarters. I used to go there to meet him every Saturday—the policemen were very nice to me and gave me bundles of pencils and great packages of fine stationery.

Mr. Brandell had not seen my father for several months. When we got to the theater, we went backstage for a few moments before the curtain. As my father opened the door and went into the dressing room, Brandell turned and sprang out of his chair like a tiger; he threw both arms around my father and embraced him, crying out in a trembling and excited voice as if he were in some great distress of mind and spirit:—

"Choe! Choe! I am glad to see you have come! It's good to zee you!"

When he was excited, he always spoke like this, with a pronounced accent. Although he insisted he was English by birth, he had been born in Leipzig, his father was a German; his real name was Brandl, which he had changed to Brandell after becoming an actor.

He had the most terrific vitality of any man I have ever seen. He was very handsome, but at the moment his features, which were smooth, powerful, and infinitely flexible, were so swollen and distorted by some convulsion of the soul that he looked like a pig. At his best, he was a man of irresistible charm and warmth; he greeted me in a very kind and affectionate way, and kissed me, but he was overjoyed to see my father. He stood for a moment without speaking, grasping him by the arms and shaking him gently; then he began to speak in a bitter voice of "they" and "them." He thought everyone was against him; he kept saying that Daddy was his only friend on earth, and he kept asking in a scornful and yet eager tone:—

"What are *they* saying, Joe? Have you heard *them* talk?"

"All that I've heard," my father said, "is that it's a magnificent performance, and that there's no one on the stage today who can come anywhere near you—no, that there's no one who can touch you, Dick—and that's the way I feel about it, too."

"Not even His Snakeship? Not even His Snakeship?" Mr. Brandell cried, his face livid and convulsed.

We knew he was speaking of Henry Irving, and we said nothing. For years, ever since the failure of his tour in England, he had been convinced that Irving was responsible for his failure. He had become obsessed with the idea that almost everyone on earth hated him and was trying to get the best of him, and he seized my father's hand, and looking very earnestly in his eyes, he said:—

"No, no! You mustn't lie to me! You mustn't fool me! You are the only man on earth I'd trust!" '

Then he began to tell us all the things his enemies had done to injure him. He said the stagehands were all against him, that they never got the stage set on time, that the time they took between scenes was going to ruin the production. I think he felt his enemies were paying the crew to wreck the show. Daddy told him this was foolish, that no one would do a thing like that, and Mr. Brandell kept saying:—

"Yes, they would! They hate me! They'll never rest until they ruin me! *I* know, I know!" in a very mysterious manner. "I could tell you things. . . . *I* know things. . . . You wouldn't believe it if I told you, Joe." Then, in a bitter voice, he said: "Why is it, then, that I've toured this country from coast to coast, playing in a new town every night, and I've never had any trouble like this before? I've had my scenery arrive two hours before the performance, and they always set it up for me on time! Yes! They'll do that much for you in any one-horse town! Do you mean to tell me they can't do as well here in New York?"

In a moment he said, in a bitter tone: "I've given my life to the theater, I've given the public the best that was in me—and what is my reward? The public hates me, and I am tricked, betrayed, and cheated by the members of my own profession. I started life as a bank clerk in a teller's cage, and sometimes I curse the evil chance that took me away from it. Yes," he said in a passionate voice, "I should have missed the tinsel, the glitter, and the six-day fame—the applause of a crowd that will forget about you tomorrow, and spit upon you two days later—but I should have gained something priceless—"

"What's that?" my father said.

"The love of a noble woman and the happy voices of the little ones."

"Now I can smell the ham," my father said in a cynical tone. "Why, Dick, they couldn't have kept you off the stage with a regiment of infantry. You sound like all the actors that ever lived."

"Yes," said Mr. Brandell with an abrupt laugh, "you're right. I was talking like an actor." He bent forward and stared into the mirror of his dressing table. "An actor! Nothing but an actor! 'Why should a dog, a horse, a rat, have life—and thou no breath at all?'"

"Oh, I wouldn't say that, Dick," my father said. "You've got plenty of breath—I've never known you to run short of it."

"Only an actor!" cried Mr. Brandell, staring into the mirror. "A paltry, posturing, vain, vile, conceited rogue of an actor! An actor—a man who lies and does not know he lies, a fellow who speaks words that better men have written for him, a reader of mash notes from shop girls and the stage-struck wives of grocery clerks, a fellow who could not go into the butcher's to buy his dog a bone without wondering what appearance he was making, a man who cannot even pass the time of day without acting—an actor! Why, by God, Joe," he cried, turning to my father, "when I look into the glass and see my face, I hate the sight of it!"

"Where's that ham?" said Daddy, sniffing about the place.

"An actor!" Mr. Brandell said again. "A man who has imitated so many feelings that he no longer has any of his own! Why, Joe," he said, in a whispering voice, "do you know that when the news came to me that my own mother was dead, I had a moment—yes, I think I really had a moment—of genuine sorrow. Then I ran to look at my face in the mirror, and I cursed because I was not on the stage where I could show it to an audience. An actor! A fellow who has made so many faces he no longer knows his own—a collection of false faces! . . . What would you like, my dear?" he said to me ironically. "Hamlet?"—instantly he looked the part. "Dr. Jekyll and Mr. Hyde?"—here his face went through two marvelous transformations: one moment he was a benevolent-looking gentleman, and the next the deformed and horrible-looking monster. "Richelieu?"—all at once he looked like a crafty and sinister old man. "Beau Brummell?"—he was young, debonair, arrogant, and a fop. "The Duke of Gloucester?"—and in a moment he had transformed himself into the cruel and pitiless villain he was to portray that night.

It was uncanny and fascinating; and there was something horrible in it, too. It was as if he were possessed by a powerful and fluent energy which had all been fed into this wonderful and ruinous gift of mimicry: a gift which may have, as he said, destroyed and devoured his proper self, since one got haunting and fleeting glimpses between these transformations of a man—a sense, an intuition, rather than a memory, of what the man was like and looked like—a sense of a haunted, lost, and lonely spirit which looked out with an insistent, mournful, and speechless immutability through all the hundred changes of his mask.

It seemed to me there was a real despair, a real grief, in Mr. Brandell. I think he had been tormented, like my father, by the eternal enigma of the theater: its almost impossible grandeur and magnificence, its poetry and its magic, which are like nothing else on earth; and the charlatanism and cheapness with which it corrupts its people. Richard Brandell was not only the greatest actor I have ever seen upon the stage; he was also a man of the highest quality. He possessed almost every gift a great actor should possess. And yet his spirit was disfigured as if by an ineradicable taint—a taint which he felt and recognized, as a man might recognize the action of a deadly poison in his blood without being able either to cure or to control it.

He had an astounding repertory of plays which ranged all the way from the great music of *Hamlet* to grotesque and melodramatic trash which he commissioned some hack to write for him, and he would use his great powers in these parts with as much passion and energy as he used in his wonderful portrayals of Iago, Gloucester, or Macbeth. Like most men who are conscious of something false and corrupt in them, he had a kind of Byronic scorn and self-contempt. He was constantly discovering that what he thought had been a deep and honest feeling was only the posturings of his own vanity, a kind of intoxication of self-love, an immense romantic satisfaction at the spectacle of himself having such a feeling; and while his soul twisted about in shame, he would turn and mock and jeer himself and his fellow actors most bitterly.

II

That night was the last time Mr. Brandell ever saw my father. Just before we left, he turned to me, took me by the hand, and said very simply and earnestly: "Esther, earn your living in the sweat of your brow, if you have to; eat your bread in sorrow, if you have to—but promise me you will never attempt to go on the stage."

"I have already made her promise that," my father said.

"Is she as good as she's pretty? Is she smart?" said Mr. Brandell, still holding me by the hand and looking at me.

"She's the smartest girl that ever lived," my father said. "She's so smart she should have been my son."

"And what is she going to do?" said Mr. Brandell, still looking at me.

"She's going to do what I could never do," my father said. He lifted his great hands before him and shook them suddenly in a gesture of baffled desperation. "She's going to take hold of something!" Then he took my hands in his and said: "Not to want the whole earth, and to get nothing! Not to want to do everything, and to do nothing! Not to waste her life dreaming about India when India is around her here and now! Not to go mad thinking of a million lives, wanting the experience of a million people, when everything she has is in the life she's got! Not to be a fool, tortured with hunger and thirst when the whole earth is groaning with its plenty. . . .

My dear child," my father cried, "you are so good, so beautiful, and so gifted, and I love you so much! I want you to be happy and to have a wonderful life." He spoke these words with such simple and urgent feeling that all the strength and power in him seemed to go out through his great hands to me, as if all of the energy of his life had been put into his wish.

"Why, Dick," he said to Mr. Brandell, "this child was born with more wisdom than either of us will ever have. She can go into the park and come back with a dozen kinds of leaves and study them for days. And when she gets through, she will know all about them. She knows their size, their shape and color—she knows every marking on them; she can draw them from memory. Could you draw a leaf, Dick? Do you know the pattern and design of a single leaf? Why, I have looked at forests, I have walked through woods and gone across continents in trains, I have stared the eyes out of my head trying to swallow up the whole earth at a glance—and I hardly know one leaf from another. I could not draw a leaf from memory if my life depended on it. And she can go out on the street and tell you later what clothes the people wore, and what kind of people wore them. Can you remember anyone you passed by on the street today? I walk the streets, I see the crowds, I look at a million faces until my brain goes blind and dizzy with all that I have seen, and later all the faces swim and bob about like corks in water. I can't tell one from the other. I see a million faces, and I can't remember one. But she sees one and remembers a million. That's the thing, Dick. If I were young again, I'd try to live like that: I'd try to see a forest in a leaf, the whole earth in a single face."

"Why, Esther," Mr. Brandell said. "Have you discovered a new country? How does one get to this wonderful place where you live?"

"Well, I tell you, Mr. Brandell," I said. "It's easy. You just walk out in the street and look around and there you are."

"There you are!" Mr. Brandell said. "Why, my dear child, I have been walking out and looking around for fifty years, and the more I walk and look, the less I see that I care to look at. What are these wonderful sights that you have found?"

"Well, Mr. Brandell," I said, "sometimes it's a leaf, and sometimes it's the pocket of a coat, and sometimes it's a button or a coin, and sometimes it's an old hat, or an old shoe on the floor. Sometimes it's a little boy, and sometimes it's a girl looking out a window, and sometimes it's an old woman with a funny hat. Sometimes it's the color of an ice wagon, and sometimes the color of an old brick wall, and sometimes a cat creeping along the backyard fence. Sometimes it's the feet of the men on the rail when you pass a saloon, and the sawdust floors, and the sound of their voices, and that wonderful smell you get of beer and orange peel and angostura bitters. Sometimes it's people passing underneath your window late at night, and sometimes it's the sound of a horse in the street early in the morning, and sometimes it's the ships blowing out in the harbor at night. Sometimes it's the way you feel at night when you wake up in wintertime and you know it's snowing, although you can't see or hear it. Sometimes it's the harbor, sometimes the docks, and sometimes it's the Bridge with people coming across it. Sometimes it's the markets and the way the chickens smell; sometimes it's all the new vegetables and the smell of apples. Sometimes it's the people in a train that passes the one you're in: you see all the people, you are close to them, but you cannot touch them; you say good-bye to them, and it makes you feel sad. Sometimes it's all the kids playing in the street: they don't seem to have anything to do with the grown-ups, they seem to be kids, and yet they seem to be grown up and to live in a world of their own—there is something strange about it. And sometimes it's like that with the horses, too—sometimes you go out and there is nothing but the horses; they fill the streets, you forget about all the people; the horses seem to own the earth; they talk to one another, and they seem to have a life of their own that people have nothing to do with. I know all about this and what is going on inside them, but it's no use telling you and Daddy—you wouldn't know what I was talking about. Well— there's a lot more—do you give up?"

"Good God, yes!" said Mr. Brandell, picking up a towel from his dressing table and waving it at me. "I surrender! O brave new world that has such wonders in it! . . . O, Joe, Joe!" he said to my father. "Will that ever happen to us again? Are we nothing but famished beggars, weary of our lives? Can you still see all those things when you walk the streets? Would it ever come back to us that way again?"

"Not to me," my father said. "I was a Sergeant, but I've been rejuced."

He smiled as he spoke, but his voice was old and tired and weary. I know now he felt that his life had failed. His face had got very yellow from his sickness, and his shoulders stooped, his great hands dangled to his knees; as he stood there between Mr. Brandell and me, he seemed to be half-erect, as if he had just clambered up from all fours. And yet his face was as delicate and wild as it had ever been; it had the strange, soaring look—as if it were in constant flight away from a shackling and degrading weight—that it had always worn, and to this expression of uplifted flight there had now been added the intent listening expression that all deaf people have.

It seemed to me that the sense of loneliness and exile, of a brief and alien rest, as if some winged spirit had temporarily arrested flight upon a foreign earth, was more legible on him now than it had ever been. Suddenly I felt all the strangeness of his life and destiny—his remoteness from all the life I knew. And I felt more than ever before a sense of our nearness and farness; I felt at once closer to him than to anyone on earth, and at the same time farther from him. Already his life had something fabulous and distant in it; he seemed to be a part of some vanished and irrevocable time.

I do not think Mr. Brandell had noticed how tired and ill my father looked. He had been buried in his own world, burning with a furious, half-suppressed excitement, an almost mad vitality which was to have that night its consummation. Before we left him, however, he suddenly glanced sharply and critically at my father, took his hand, and said with great tenderness:—

"What is it, Joe? You look so tired. Is anything wrong?"

My father shook his head. He had become very sensitive about his deafness, and any reference to the affliction that had caused his retirement from the stage or any suggestion of pity from one of his former colleagues because of his present state deeply wounded him. "Of course not," he said. "I never felt better! I used to be Joe the Dog-Faced Actor, now I'm Joe the Dog-Faced Policeman, and I've got a badge to prove it, too." Here he produced his policeman's badge, of which he was really very proud. "If that's not a step up in the world, what is it? Come on, daughter," he said to me. "Let's leave this wicked man to all his plots and murders. If he gets too bad, I'll arrest him!"

We started to go, but for a moment Mr. Brandell stopped us and was silent. The enormous and subdued excitement, the exultant fury, which had been apparent in him all the time, now became much more pronounced. The man was thrumming like a dynamo; his strong hands trembled, and when he spoke, it was as if he had already become the Duke of Gloucester: there was a quality of powerful cunning and exultant prophecy in his tone, something mad, secret, conspiratorial, and knowing.

"Keep your eyes open tonight," he said. "You may see something worth remembering."

We left him and went out into the theater.

III

When we got out into the auditorium the house was almost full, although the people were still going down the aisles to their seats. Because of my father's deafness, Brandell had given us seats in the front row. For a few minutes I watched the people come in and the house fill up, and I felt again the sense of elation and joy I have always felt in the theater before the curtain goes up. I looked at the beautiful women, the men in evening clothes, and all the fat and gaudy ornamentation of the house; I heard the rapid and excited patter of the voices, the stir and rustle of silks, the movement—and I loved it all.

Then in a few minutes the lights darkened. There was a vast, rustling sigh all over the theater, the sound of a great bending forward, and then, for a moment, in that dim light I saw the thing that has always seemed so full of magic and beauty to me: a thousand people who have suddenly become a single living creature, and all the frail white spots of faces blooming like petals there in a velvet darkness, upturned, thirsty, silent, and intent and beautiful.

Then the curtain went up, and on an enormous and lofty stage stood the deformed and solitary figure of a man. For a moment I knew the man was

Brandell; for a moment I could feel nothing but an astounded surprise, a sense of unreality, to think of the miracle of transformation which had been wrought in the space of a few minutes, to know that this cruel and sinister creature was the man with whom we had just been talking. Then the first words of the great opening speech rang out across the house, and instantly all this was forgotten:—the man was no longer Brandell—he was the Duke of Gloucester.

With the opening words, the intelligence was instantly communicated to the audience that it was about to witness such a performance as occurs in the theater only once in a lifetime. And yet, at first, there was no sense of characterization, no feeling of the cruel and subtle figure of Richard—there was only a mighty music which sounded out across the house, a music so grand and overwhelming that it drowned the memory of all the baseness, the ugliness, and the pettiness in the lives of men. In the sound of the words it seemed there was the full measure of man's grandeur, magnificence, and tragic despair, and the words were flung against immense and timeless skies like a challenge and an evidence of man's dignity, and like a message of faith that he need not be ashamed or afraid of anything.

> *Now is the winter of our discontent*
> *Made glorious summer by this sun of York;*
> *And all the clouds that lour'd upon our house*
> *In the deep bosom of the ocean buried. . . .*

Then swiftly and magnificently, with powerful developing strokes of madness, fear, and cruelty, the terrible figure of Richard began to emerge; almost before the conclusion of the opening speech it stood complete. That speech was really a speech of terror, and set clearly the picture of the warped, deformed, agonized Gloucester, for whom there was no beautiful thing in life, a man who had no power to raise himself except by murder. As the play went on, the character of Richard became so real to me, the murders so frightful, the lines filled with such music and such terror, that when the curtain rose on that awful nightmare scene in the tent, I felt I could not stay there if one more drop of blood was shed.

That evening will live in my memory as the most magnificent evening I ever spent in the theater. On that evening Richard Brandell reached the summit of his career. That night was literally the peak. Immediately after the performance Brandell had a nervous collapse: the play was taken off; he never appeared as Richard again. It was months before he made any appearance whatever, and he never again, during the remainder of his life, approached the performance he gave that night.

The Dark Messiah

George had not been in Germany since 1928 and the early months of 1929. At that time he had stayed for a while in a little town in the Black Forest, and he remembered that there had been great excitement because an election was being held. The state of politics was chaotic, with a bewildering number of parties, and the Communists polled a surprisingly large vote. People were disturbed and anxious, and there seemed to be a sense of impending calamity in the air.

This time, things were different. Germany had changed.

Ever since 1933, when the change occurred, George had read, first with amazement, shock, and doubt, then with despair and a leaden sinking of the heart, all the newspaper accounts of what was going on in Germany. He found it hard to believe some of the reports. Of course, there were irresponsible extremists in Germany as elsewhere, and in times of crisis no doubt they got out of hand, but he thought he knew Germany and the German people, and on the whole he was inclined to feel that the true state of affairs had been exaggerated and that things simply could not be as bad as they were pictured.

And now, on the train from Paris, he met some Germans who gave him reassurance. They said there was no longer any confusion or chaos in politics and government, and no longer any fear among the people, because everyone was so happy. This was what George wanted desperately to believe, and he was prepared to be happy, too.

The month of May is wonderful everywhere. It was particularly wonderful in Berlin that year. All along the streets, in the Tiergarten, in all the great gardens, and along the Spree canal, the horse chestnut trees were in full bloom. The crowds sauntered underneath the trees on the Kurfürstendamm, the terraces of the cafés were jammed with people, and always, through the golden sparkle of the days, there was a sound of music in the air. George saw the chains of endlessly lovely lakes around Berlin, and for the first time he knew the wonderful golden bronze upon the tall poles of the kiefern trees. Before, he had visited only the south of Germany, the Rhinelands, and Bavaria; now the north seemed even more enchanting.

It was the season of the great Olympic games, and almost every day

George went to the stadium in Berlin. George observed that the organizing genius of the German people, which has been used so often to such noble purpose, was now more thrillingly displayed than he had even seen it before. The sheer pageantry of the occasion was overwhelming, so much so that he began to feel oppressed by it. One sensed a stupendous concentration of effort, a tremendous drawing together and ordering of the vast collective power of the whole land. And the thing that made it seem ominous was that it so evidently went beyond what the games themselves demanded. The games were overshadowed, and were no longer merely sporting competitions to which other nations had sent their chosen teams. They became, day after day, an orderly and overwhelming demonstration in which the whole of Germany had been schooled and disciplined. It was as if the games had been chosen as a symbol of the new collective might, a means of showing to the world in concrete terms what this new power had come to be.

With no past experience in such affairs, the Germans had constructed a mighty stadium which was the most beautiful and most perfect in its design that had ever been built. And all the accessories of this monstrous plant—the swimming pools, the enormous halls, the lesser stadia—had been laid out and designed with this same cohesion of beauty and use. The organization was superb. Not only were the events themselves, down to the minutest detail of each competition, staged and run off like clockwork, but the crowds—such crowds as no other great city has ever had to cope with, and the like of which would certainly have snarled and maddened the traffic of New York beyond hope of untangling—were handled with a quietness, order, and speed that was astounding.

The daily spectacle was breath-taking in its beauty and magnificence. The stadium was a tournament of color that caught the throat; the massed splendor of the banners made the gaudy decorations of America's great parades, presidential inaugurations, and World's Fairs seem like shoddy carnivals in comparison. And for the duration of the Olympics, Berlin itself was transformed into a kind of annex to the stadium. From one end of the city to the other, from the Lustgarten to the Brandenburger Tor, along the whole broad sweep of Unter den Linden, through the vast avenues of the faery Tiergarten, and out through the western part of Berlin to the very portals of the stadium, the whole town was a thrilling pageantry of royal banners—not merely endless miles of looped-up bunting, but banners fifty feet in height, such as might have graced the tent of some great emperor.

And all through the day, from morning on, Berlin became a mighty Ear, attuned, attentive, focused on the stadium. Everywhere the air was filled with a single voice. The green trees along the Kurfürstendamm began to talk: from loudspeakers concealed in their branches an announcer in the stadium spoke to the whole city—and for George Webber it was a strange experience to hear the familiar terms of track and field translated into the tongue that Goethe used. He would be informed now that the *Vorlauf* was

about to be run—and then the *Zwischenlauf*—and at length the *Endlauf*—
and the winner:

"Owens—Oo Ess Ah!"

Meanwhile, through those tremendous banner-laden ways, the crowds
thronged ceaselessly all day long. The wide promenade of Unter den Linden
was solid with patient, tramping German feet. Fathers, mothers, children,
young folks, old—the whole material of the nation was there, from every
corner of the land. From morn to night they trudged, wide-eyed, full of
wonder, past the marvel of those banner-laden ways. And among them one
saw the bright stabs of color of Olympic jackets and the glint of foreign
faces: the dark features of Frenchmen and Italians, the ivory grimace of the
Japanese, the straw hair and blue eyes of the Swedes, and the big Americans,
natty in straw hats, white flannels, and blue coats crested with the Olympic
seal.

And there were great displays of marching men, sometimes ungunned
but rhythmic, as regiments of brown shirts went swinging through the
streets. By noon each day all the main approaches to the games, the emban-
nered streets and avenues of the route which the Leader would take to the
stadium, miles away, were walled in by the troops. They stood at ease,
young men, laughing and talking with each other—the Leader's bodyguards, the Schutz Staffel units, the Storm Troopers, all ranks and divisions
in their different uniforms—and they stretched in two unbroken lines from
the Wilhelmstrasse up to the arches of the Brandenburger Tor. Then, suddenly, the sharp command, and instantly there would be the solid smack of
ten thousand leather boots as they came together with the sound of war.

It seemed as if everything had been planned for this moment, shaped to
this triumphant purpose. But the people—they had not been planned. Day
after day, behind the unbroken wall of soldiers, they stood and waited in a
dense and patient throng. These were the masses of the nation, the poor
ones of the earth, the humble ones of life, the workers and the wives, the
mothers and the children—and day after day they came and stood and
waited. They were there because they did not have money enough to buy
the little cardboard squares that would have given them places within the
magic ring. From noon till night they waited for just two brief and golden
moments of the day: the moment when the Leader went out to the stadium,
and the moment when he returned.

At last he came—and something like a wind across a field of grass was
shaken through that crowd, and from afar the tide rolled up with him, and
in it was the voice, the hope, the prayer of the land. The Leader came by
slowly in a shining car, a little dark man with a comic-opera mustache, erect
and standing, moveless and unsmiling, with his hand upraised, palm outward, not in Nazi-wise salute, but straight up, in a gesture of blessing such
as the Buddha or Messiahs use.

·   ·   ·

The first weeks passed, and George began to hear some ugly things. From time to time, at parties, dinners, and the like, when George would speak of his enthusiasm for Germany and the German people, various friends that he had made would, if they had had enough to drink, take him aside afterward and, after looking around cautiously, lean toward him with an air of great secrecy and whisper, "But have you heard . . . ? And have you heard . . . ?"

He did not see any of the ugly things they had whispered about. He did not see anyone beaten. He did not see anyone imprisoned, or put to death. He did not see any men in concentration camps. He did not see openly anywhere the physical manifestations of a brutal and compulsive force.

True, there were men in brown uniforms everywhere, and men in black uniforms, and men in uniforms of olive green, and everywhere in the streets there was the solid smack of booted feet, the blare of brass, the tootling of fifes, and the poignant sight of young faces shaded under iron helmets, with folded arms and ramrod backs, precisely seated in great army lorries. But all of this had become so mixed in with the genial temper of the people making holiday, as he had seen and known it so many pleasant times before, that even if it did not now seem good, it did not seem sinister or bad.

Then something happened. It didn't happen suddenly. It just happened as a cloud gathers, as a fog settles, as rain begins to fall.

A man George had met was planning to give a party for him and asked him if he wanted to ask any of his friends. George mentioned one. His host was silent for a moment; he looked embarrassed; then he said that the person George had named had formerly been the editorial head of a publication that had been suppressed, and that one of the people who had been instrumental in its suppression had been invited to the party, so would George mind—?

George named another, an old friend named Franz Heilig whom he had first met in Munich years before, and who now lived in Berlin, and of whom he was very fond. Again the anxious pause, the embarrassment, the halting objections. This person was—was—well, George's host said he knew about this person and knew that he did not go to parties—he would not come if he were invited—so would George mind—?

George next spoke of a lady named Else von Kohler, and the response to this suggestion was of the same kind. How long had he known this woman? Where, and under what circumstances, had he met her? George tried to reassure his host on all these scores. He told the man he need have no fear of any sort about Else. His host was instant, swift, in his apologies: oh, by no means—he was sure the lady was eminently all right—only, nowadays, with a mixed gathering—he had tried to pick a group of people whom George had met and who all knew one another—he had thought it would be much more pleasant that way—strangers at a party were often shy, constrained, and formal—Frau von Kohler would not know anybody there—so would George mind—?

Not long after this baffling experience a friend came to see him. "In a few days," his friend said, "you will receive a phone call from a certain person. He will try to meet you, to talk to you. Have nothing to do with this man."

George laughed. His friend was a sober-minded German, rather on the dull and heavy side, and his face was so absurdly serious as he spoke that George thought he was trying to play some lumbering joke upon him. He wanted to know who this mysterious personage might be who was so anxious to make his acquaintance.

To George's amazement and incredulity, his friend named a high official in the government.

But why, George asked, should this man want to meet him? And why, if he did, should he be afraid of him?

At first his friend would not answer. Finally he muttered circumspectly:

"Listen to me. Stay away from this man. I tell you for your own good." He paused, not knowing how to say it; then: "You have heard of Captain Roehm? You know about him? You know what happened to him?" George nodded. "Well," his friend went on in a troubled voice, "there were others who were not shot in the purge. This man I speak of is one of the bad ones. We have a name for him—it is 'The Prince of Darkness.'"

George did not know what to make of all this. He tried to puzzle it out but could not, so at last he dismissed it from his mind. But within a few days, the official whom his friend had named did telephone, and did ask to meet him. George offered some excuse and avoided seeing the man, but the episode was most spectacular and very unsettling.

Both of these baffling experiences contained elements of comedy and melodrama, but those were the superficial aspects. George began to realize now the tragedy that lay behind such things. There was nothing political in any of it. The roots of it were much more sinister and deep and evil than politics or even racial prejudice could ever be. For the first time in his life he had come upon something full of horror that he had never known before—something that made all the swift violence and passion of America, the gangster compacts, the sudden killings, the harshness and corruption that infested portions of American business and public life, seem innocent beside it. What George began to see was a picture of a great people who had been psychically wounded and were now desperately ill with some dread malady of the soul. Here was an entire nation, he now realized, that was infested with the contagion of an ever-present fear. It was a kind of creeping paralysis which twisted and blighted all human relations. The pressures of a constant and infamous compulsion had silenced this whole people into a sweltering and malignant secrecy until they had become spiritually septic with the distillations of their own self-poisons, for which now there was no medicine or release.

So the weeks, the months, the summer passed, and everywhere about him George saw the evidences of this dissolution, this shipwreck of a great spirit. The poisonous emanations of suppression, persecution, and fear permeated the air like miasmic and pestilential vapors, tainting, sickening, and blighting the lives of everyone he met. It was a plague of the spirit—invisible, but as unmistakable as death. Little by little it sank in on him through all the golden singing of that summer, until at last he felt it, breathed it, lived it, and knew it for the thing it was.

The Hollyhock Sowers

I

There are some men who are unequal to the conditions of modern life, and who have accordingly retreated from the tough realities which they cannot face. They form a separate group or family or race, a little world which has no boundary lines of country or of place. One finds a surprising number of them in America, particularly in the more sequestered purlieus of Boston, Cambridge, and Harvard University. One finds them also in New York's Greenwich Village, and when even that makeshift little Bohemia becomes too harsh for them, they retire into a kind of desiccated country life.

For all such people the country becomes the last refuge. They buy little farms in Connecticut or Vermont, renovate the fine old houses with just a shade too much of whimsy or restrained good taste. Their quaintness is a little too quaint, their simplicity a little too subtle, and on the old farms that they buy no utilitarian seeds are sown and no grain grows. They go in for flowers, and in time they learn to talk very knowingly about the rarer varieties. They love the simple life, of course. They love the good feel of "the earth." They are just a shade too conscious of "the earth," and one hears them say, the women as well as the men, how much they love to work in it.

And work in it they do. In spring they work on their new rock garden, with the assistance of only one other man—some native of the region who hires himself out for wages, and whose homely virtues and more crotchety characteristics they quietly observe and tell amusing stories about to their friends. Their wives work in the earth, too, attired in plain yet not unattractive frocks, and they even learn to clip the hedges, wearing gloves to protect their hands. These dainty and lovely creatures become healthily embrowned; their comely forearms take on a golden glow, their faces become warm with soaked-up sunlight, and sometimes they even have a soft, faint down of gold just barely visible above the cheekbone. They are good to see.

In winter there are also things to do. The snows come down, and the road out to the main highway becomes impassable to cars for three weeks at a time. Not even the truck of the A. & P. can get through. So for three whole weeks on end they have to plod their way out on foot, a good three-

465

quarters of a mile, to lay in provisions. The days are full of other work, as well. People in cities may think that country life is dull in winter, but that is because they simply don't know. The squire becomes a carpenter. He is working on his play, of course, but in between times he makes furniture. It is good to be able to do something with one's hands. He has a workshop fitted up in the old barn. There he has his studio, too, where he can carry on his intellectual labors undisturbed. The children are forbidden to go there. And every morning, after taking the children to school, the father can return to his barn-studio and have the whole morning free to get on with the play.

It is a fine life for the children, by the way. In summer they play and swim and fish and get wholesome lessons in practical democracy by mingling with the hired man's children. In winter they go to an excellent private school two miles away. It is run by two very intelligent people, an expert in planned economy and his wife, an expert in child psychology, who between them are carrying on the most remarkable experiments in education.

Life in the country is really full of absorbing interests which city folk know nothing about. For one thing, there is local politics, in which they become passionately involved. They attend all the town meetings, become hotly partisan over the question of a new floor for the bridge across the creek, take sides against old Abner Jones, the head selectman, and in general back up the younger, more progressive element. Over week-ends they have the most enchanting tales to tell their city friends about these town meetings. They are full of stories, too, about all the natives, and can make the most sophisticated visitor howl with laughter when, after coffee and brandy in the evening, the squire and his wife go through their two-part recital of Seth Freeman's involved squabble and lawsuit with Rob Perkins over a stone fence. One really gets to know his neighbors in the country. It is a whole world in itself. Life here is simple, yet it is good.

II

In their old farmhouse they eat by candlelight at night. The pine paneling in the dining room has been there more than two hundred years. They have not changed it. In fact, the whole front part of the house is just the same as it has always been. All they have added is the new wing for the children. Of course, they had to do a great deal when they bought the place. It had fallen into shocking disrepair. The floors and sills were rotten and had to be replaced. They also built a concrete basement and installed an oil furnace. This was costly, but it was worth the price. The people who had sold them the house were natives of the region who had gone to seed. The farm had been in one family for five generations. It was incredible, though, to see what they had done to the house. The sitting-room floor had been covered with an oilcloth carpet. And in the dining room, right beside this beautiful old Revolutionary china chest, which they had persuaded the people to sell with the house, had been an atrocious phonograph with one of those old-fashioned horns. Can one imagine that?

Of course they had to furnish the house anew from cellar to garret. Their city stuff just wouldn't do at all. It had taken time and hard work, but by going quietly about the countryside and looking into farmer's houses, they have managed to pick up very cheaply the most exquisite pieces, most of them dating back to Revolutionary times, and now the whole place is in harmony at last. They even drink their beer from pewter mugs. Grace discovered these, covered with cobwebs, in the cellar of an old man's house. He was eighty-seven, he said, and the mugs had belonged to his father before him. He'd never had no use for 'em himself, and if she wanted 'em he calc'lated that twenty cents apiece would be all right. Isn't it delicious! And everyone agrees it is.

The seasons change and melt into one another, and they observe the seasons. They would not like to live in places where no seasons were. The adventure of the seasons is always thrilling. There is the day in late summer when someone sees the first duck flying south, and they know by this token that the autumn of the year has come. Then there is the first snowflake that melts as it falls to usher in the winter. But the most exciting of all is the day in early spring when someone discovers that the first snowdrop has opened or that the first starling has come. They keep a diary of the seasons, and they write splendid letters to their city friends:

"I think you would like it now. The whole place is simply frantic with spring. I heard a thrush for the first time today. Overnight, almost, our old apple trees have burst into full bloom. If you wait another week, it will be too late. So do come, won't you? You'll love our orchard and our twisted, funny, dear old apple trees. They've been here, most of them, I suspect, for eighty years. It's not like modern orchards, with their little regiments of trees. We don't get many apples. They are small and sharp and tart, and twisted like the trees themselves, and there are never too many of them, but always just enough. Somehow we love them all the better for it. It's so New England."

So year follows year in healthy and happy order. The first year the rock garden gets laid down and the little bulbs and Alpine plants set out. Hollyhocks are sown all over the place, against the house and beside the fences. By the next year they are blooming in gay profusion. It is marvelous how short a time it takes. That second year he builds the studio in the barn, doing most of the work with his own hands, with only the simple assistance of the hired man. The third year—the children are growing up now, they grow fast in the country—he gets the swimming pool begun. The fourth year it is finished. Meanwhile, he is busy on his play, but it goes slowly because there is so much else that has to be done.

The fifth year—well, one does miss the city sometimes. They would never think of going back there to live. This place is wonderful, except for three months in the winter. So this year they are moving in and taking an apartment for the three bad months. Grace, of course, loves music and misses the opera, while he likes the theater, and it will be good to have again the companionship of certain people whom they know. This is the greatest handicap of country life—the natives make fine neighbors, but one sometimes misses the intellectual stimulus of city life. And so this year he has decided to take the old girl in. They'll see the shows and hear the music and renew their acquaintance with old friends and find out what is going on. They might even run down to Bermuda for three weeks in February. Or to Haiti. That's a place, he's heard, that modern life has hardly touched. They have windmills and go in for voodoo worship. It's all savage and most primitively colorful. It will get them out of the rut to go off somewhere on a trip. Of course they'll be back in the country by the first of April.

Such is the fugitive pattern in one of its most common manifestations. And always with this race of men the fundamental inner structure of illusion and defeat is the same. All of them betray themselves by the same weaknesses. They flee a world they are not strong enough to meet. If they have talent, it is a talent that is not great enough to win for them the fulfillment and success which they pretend to scorn, but for which each of them would sell the pitifully small remnant of his meager soul. If they want to create, they do not want it hard enough to make and shape and finish something in spite of hell and heartbreak. If they want to work, they do not want it genuinely enough to work and keep on working till their eyeballs ache and their brains are dizzy, to work until their loins are dry, their vitals hollow, to work until the whole world reels before them in a gray blur of weariness and depleted energy, to work until their tongues cleave to their mouths and their pulses hammer like dry mallets at their temples, to work until no work is left in them, until there is no rest and no repose, until they cannot sleep, until they can do nothing and can work no more—and then work again.

They are the pallid half-men of the arts, more desolate and damned than if they had been born with no talent at all, more lacking in their lack, possessing half, than if their lack had been complete. And so, half full of purpose, they eventually flee the task they are not equal to—and they potter, tinker, garden, carpenter, and drink.

Nebraska Crane

The train had hurtled like a projectile through its tube beneath the Hudson River to emerge in the dazzling sunlight of a September afternoon, and now it was racing across the flat desolation of the Jersey meadows. George Webber sat by the window and saw the smoldering dumps, the bogs, the blackened factories slide past, and felt that one of the most wonderful things in the world is the experience of being on a train. It is so different from watching a train go by. To anyone outside, a speeding train is a thunderbolt of driving rods, a hot hiss of steam, a blurred flash of coaches, a wall of movement and of noise, a shriek, a wail, and then just emptiness and absence, with a feeling of "there goes everybody!" without knowing who anybody is. And all of a sudden the watcher feels the vastness and loneliness of America, and the nothingness of all those little lives hurled past upon the immensity of the continent. But if one is *inside* the train, everything is different. The train itself is a miracle of man's handiwork, and everything about it is eloquent of human purpose and direction. One feels the brakes go on when the train is coming to a river, and one knows that the old gloved hand of cunning is at the throttle. One's own sense of manhood and of mastery is heightened by being on a train. And all the other people, how real they are! One sees the fat black porter with his ivory teeth and the great swollen gland on the back of his neck, and one warms with friendship for him. One looks at all the pretty girls with a sharpened eye and an awakened pulse. One observes all the other passengers with lively interest, and feels that he has known them forever. In the morning most of them will be gone out of his life; some will drop out silently at night through the dark, drugged snoring of the sleepers; but now all are caught upon the wing and held for a moment in the peculiar intimacy of this pullman car which has become their common home for a night.

At the far end of the car a man stood up and started back down the aisle toward the washroom. He walked with a slight limp and leaned upon a cane, and with his free hand he held onto the backs of the seats to brace himself against the lurching of the train. As he came abreast of George, who sat there gazing out the window, the man stopped abruptly. A strong, good-natured voice, warm, easy, bantering, unafraid, unchanged—exactly as it was when it was fourteen years of age—broke like a flood of living light upon his consciousness.

"Well I'll be dogged! Hi, there, Monkus! Where you goin'?"

At the sound of the old jesting nick-name George looked up quickly. It was Nebraska Crane. The square, freckled, sunburned visage had the same humorous friendliness it had always had, and the tar-black Cherokee eyes looked out with the same straight, deadly fearlessness. The big brown paw came out and they clasped each other firmly. And, instantly, it was like coming home to a strong and friendly place. In another moment they were seated together, talking with the familiarity of people whom no gulf of years and distance could alter or separate.

George had seen Nebraska Crane only once in all the years since he himself had first left Libya Hill and gone away to college. But he had not lost sight of him. Nobody had lost sight of Nebraska Crane. That wiry, fearless little figure of the Cherokee boy who used to come down the hill on Locust Street with the bat slung over his shoulder and the well-oiled fielder's mitt protruding from his hip pocket had been prophetic of a greater destiny, for Nebraska had become a professional baseball player, he had crashed into the big leagues, and his name had been emblazoned in the papers every day.

The newspapers had had a lot to do with his seeing Nebraska that other time. It was in August 1925, just after George had returned to New York from his first trip abroad. That very night, in fact, a little before midnight, as he was seated in a Childs Restaurant with smoking wheatcakes, coffee, and an ink-fresh copy of next morning's *Herald Tribune* before him, the headline jumped out at him: "Crane Slams Another Homer." He read the account of the game eagerly and felt a strong desire to see Nebraska again and to get back in his blood once more the honest tang of America. Acting on a sudden impulse, he decided to call him up. Sure enough, his name was in the book, with an address way up in the Bronx. He gave the number and waited. A man's voice answered the 'phone, but at first he didn't recognize it.

"Hello! . . . Hello! . . . Is Mr. Crane there? . . . Is that you, Bras?"

"Hello." Nebraska's voice was hesitant, slow, a little hostile, touched with the caution and suspicion of mountain people when speaking to a stranger. "Who is that? . . . Who? . . . Is that *you*, Monk?"—suddenly and quickly as he recognized who it was. "Well, I'll be dogged!" he cried. His tone was delighted, astounded, warm with friendly greeting now, and had the somewhat high and faintly howling quality that mountain people's voices often have when they are talking to someone over the telephone: the tone was full, sonorous, countrified, and a little puzzled, as if he were yelling to someone on an adjoining mountain peak on a gusty day in autumn when the wind was thrashing through the trees. "Where'd you come from? How the hell are you, boy?" he yelled before George could answer. "Where you been all this time, anyway?"

"I've been in Europe. I just got back this morning."

"Well, I'll be dogged!"—still astounded, delighted, full of howling friend-liness. "When am I gonna see you? How about comin' to the game tomor-row? I'll fix you up. And say," he went on rapidly, "if you can stick aroun' after the game, I'll take you home to meet the wife and kid. How about it?"

So it was agreed. George went to the game and saw Nebraska knock another home run, but he remembered best what happened afterward. When the player had had his shower and had dressed, the two friends left the ball park, and as they went out, a crowd of young boys who had been waiting at the gate rushed upon them. They were those dark-faced, dark-eyed, dark-haired little urchins who spring up like dragons' teeth from the grim pavements of New York, but in whose tough little faces and raucous voices there still remains, curiously, the innocence and faith of children everywhere.

"It's Bras!" the children cried. "Hi, Bras! Hey, Bras!" In a moment they were pressing round him in a swarming horde, deafening the ears with their shrill cries, begging, shouting, tugging at his sleeves, doing everything they could to attract his attention, holding dirty little scraps of paper toward him, stubs of pencils, battered little notebooks, asking him to sign his au-tograph.

He behaved with the spontaneous warmth and kindliness of his character. He scrawled his name out rapidly on a dozen grimy bits of paper, skillfully working his way along through the yelling, pushing, jumping group, and all the time keeping up a rapid fire of banter, badinage, and good-natured reproof:

"All right—give it here, then! . . . Why don't you fellahs pick on some-body else once in a while? . . . Say, boy!" he said suddenly, turning to look down on one unfortunate child, and pointing an accusing finger at him— "What are you doin' aroun' here again today? I signed my name for you at least a dozen times!"

"No, sir, Misteh Crane!" the urchin earnestly replied. "Honest—not me!"

"Ain't that right?" Nebraska said, appealing to the other children. "Don't this boy keep comin' back here every day?"

They grinned, delighted at the chagrin of their fellow-petitioner. "Dat's right, Misteh Crane! Dis guy's got a whole book wit' nuttin' but yoeh name in it!"

"Ah-h!" the victim cried, and turned upon his betrayers bitterly. "What youse guys tryin' to do—get wise or somep'n? Honest, Misteh Crane!"— he looked up earnestly again at Nebraska—"Don't believe 'em! I jest want yoeh ottygraph! Please, Misteh Crane, it'll only take a minute!"

For a moment more Nebraska stood looking down at the child with an expression of mock sternness; at last he took the outstretched notebook, rapidly scratched his name across a page, and handed it back. And as he did so, he put his big paw on the urchin's head and gave it a clumsy pat; then, gently and playfully, he shoved it from him and walked off down the street.

The apartment where Nebraska lived was like a hundred thousand others in the Bronx. The ugly yellow-brick building had a false front, with meaningless little turrets at the corners of the roof, and a general air of spurious luxury about it. The rooms were rather small and cramped, and were made even more so by the heavy overstuffed Grand Rapids furniture. The walls of the living room, painted a mottled, rusty cream, were bare except for a couple of sentimental prints, while the place of honor over the mantel was reserved for an enlarged and garishly tinted photograph of Nebraska's little son at the age of two, looking straight and solemnly out at all comers from a gilded oval frame.

Myrtle, Nebraska's wife, was small and plump, and pretty in a doll-like way. Her corn-silk hair was frizzled in a halo about her face, and her chubby features were heavily accented by rouge and lipstick. But she was simple and natural in her talk and bearing, and George liked her at once. She welcomed him with a warm and friendly smile and said she had heard a lot about him.

They all sat down. The child, who was three or four years old by this time, and who had been shy, holding on to his mother's dress and peeping out from behind her, now ran across the room to his father and began climbing all over him. Nebraska and Myrtle asked George a lot of questions about himself, what he had been doing, where he had been, and especially what countries he had visited in Europe. They seemed to think of Europe as a place so far away that anyone who had actually been there was touched with an unbelievable aura of strangeness and romance.

"Whereall did you go over there, anyway?" asked Nebraska.

"Oh, everywhere, Bras," George said—"France, England, Holland, Germany, Denmark, Sweden, Italy—all over the place."

"Well, I'll be dogged!"—in frank astonishment. "You sure do git aroun', don't you?"

"Not the way *you* do, Bras. You're traveling most of the time."

"Who—me? Oh, hell, I don't git anywhere—just the same ole places. Chicago, St. Looie, Philly—I seen 'em all so often I could find my way blindfolded!" He waved them aside with a gesture of his hand. Then suddenly he looked at George as if he were seeing him for the first time, and he reached over and slapped him on the knee and exclaimed: "Well, I'll be dogged! How you doin', anyway, Monkus?"

"Oh, can't complain. How about you? But I don't need to ask that. I've been reading all about you in the papers."

"Yes, Monkus," he said. "I been havin' a good year. But, boy!"—he shook his head suddenly and grinned—"Do the ole dogs feel it!"

He was silent a moment, then he went on quietly:

"I've been up here since 1919—that's seven years, and it's a long time in this game. Not many of 'em stay much longer. When you been shaggin' flies as long as that, you may lose count, but you don't need to count—your legs'll tell you."

"But, good Lord, Bras, *you're* all right! Why, the way you got around out there today, you looked like a colt!"

"Yeah," Nebraska said, "maybe I *looked* like a colt, but I felt like a plow horse." He fell silent again, then he tapped his friend gently on the knee with his brown hand and said abruptly: "No, Monkus. When you've been in this business as long as I have, you know it."

"Oh, come on, Bras, quit your kidding!" said George, remembering that the player was only two years older than himself. "You're still a young man. Why, you're only twenty-seven!"

"Sure, sure," Nebraska answered quietly. "But it's like I say. You can't stay in this business much longer than I have. Of course Cobb an' Speaker an' a few like that—they was up here a long time. But eight years is about the average, an' I been here seven years already. So if I can hang on a few years more, I won't have no kick to make . . . . Hell!" he said in a moment, with the old hearty ring in his voice, "I ain't got no kick to make, no-way. If I got my release tomorrow, I'd still feel I done all right. . . . Ain't that so, Buzz?" he cried genially to the child, who had settled down on his knee, at the same time seizing the boy and cradling him comfortably in his strong arm. "Ole Bras has done all right, ain't he?"

"That's the way me an' Bras feel about it," remarked Myrtle, who during this conversation had been rocking back and forth, placidly ruminating on a wad of gum. "Along there last year it looked once or twice as if Bras might git traded. He said to me one day before the game, 'Well, ole lady, if I don't git some hits today, somethin' tells me you an' me is goin' to take a trip.' So I says, 'Trip where?' An' he says, 'I don't know, but they're goin' to sell me down the river if I don't git goin', an' somthin' tells me it's now or never!' So I just looks at him," continued Myrtle placidly, "an' I says, 'Well, what do you want me to do? Do you want me to come today or not?' You know, gener'ly, Bras won't let me come when he ain't hittin'—he says it's bad luck. But he just looks at me a minute, an' I can see him sort of studyin' it over, an' all of a sudden he makes up his mind an' says, 'Yes, come on if you want to; I couldn't have no more bad luck than I've been havin', no-way, an maybe it's come time fer things to change, so you come on.' Well, I went— an' I don't know whether I brought him luck or not, but somethin' did," said Myrtle, rocking in her chair complacently.

"Dogged if she didn't!" Nebraska chuckled. "I got three hits out of four times up that day, an' two of 'em was home runs!"

"Yeah," Myrtle agreed, "an' that Philadelphia fast-ball thrower was throwin' 'em, too."

"He sure was!" said Nebraska.

"I know," went on Myrtle, chewing placidly, "because I heard some of the boys say later that it was like he was throwin' 'em up there from out of the bleachers, with all them men in shirt-sleeves behind him, an' the boys said half the time they couldn't even see the ball. But Bras must of saw it—

or been lucky—because he hit two home runs off of him, an' that pitcher didn't like it, either. The second one Bras got, he went stompin' and tearin' around out there like a wild bull. He sure did look mad," said Myrtle in her customary placid tone.

"Maddest man I ever seen!" Nebraska cried delightedly. "I thought he was goin' to dig a hole plumb through to China. . . . But that's the way it was. She's right about it. That was the day I got goin'. I know one of the boys said to me later, 'Bras,' he says, 'we all thought you was goin' to take a ride, but you sure dug in, didn't you?' That's the way it is in this game. I seen Babe Ruth go fer weeks when he couldn't hit a balloon, an' all of a sudden he lams into it. Seems like he just cain't miss from then on."

All this had happened four years ago. Now the two friends had met again, and were seated side by side in the speeding train, talking and catching up on each other. Nebraska's right ankle was taped and bandaged; a heavy cane rested between his knees. George asked him what had happened.

"I pulled a tendon," Nebraska said, "an' got laid off. So I thought I might as well run down an' see the folks. Myrtle, she couldn't come—the kid's got to git ready fer school."

"How are they?" George asked.

"Oh, fine, fine. All wool an' a yard wide, both of 'em!" He was silent for a moment, then he looked at his friend with a tolerant Cherokee grin and said: "But I'm crackin' up, Monkus. Guess I cain't stan' the gaff much more."

The quiet resignation of the player touched his friend with sadness. It was hard and painful for him to face the fact that this strong and fearless creature, who had stood in his life always for courage and for victory, should now be speaking with such a ready acceptance of defeat.

"But, Bras," he protested, "you've been hitting just as well this season as you ever did! I've read about you in the papers, and the reporters have all said the same thing."

"Oh, I can still hit 'em," Nebraska quietly agreed. "It ain't the hittin' that bothers me. That's the last thing you lose, anyway. Leastways, it's goin' to be that way with me, an' I talked to other fellahs who said it was that way with them." After a pause he went on in a low tone: "If this ole leg heals up in time, I'll go on back and git in the game again an' finish out the season. An' if I'm lucky, maybe they'll keep me on a couple more years, because they know I can still hit. But, hell," he added quietly, "they know I'm through. They already got me all tied up with string."

As Nebraska talked, George saw that the Cherokee in him was the same now as it had been when he was a boy. His cheerful fatalism had always been the source of his great strength and courage. That was why he had never been afraid of anything, not even death. But seeing the look of regret on George's face, Nebraska smiled again and went on lightly:

"That's the way it is, Monk. You're good up there as long as you're good.

After that they sell you down the river. Hell, I ain't kickin'. I been lucky. I had ten years of it already, an' that's more than most. An' I been in three World Series. If I can hold on fer another year or two—if they don't let me go or trade me—I think maybe we'll be in again. Me an' Myrtle has figgered it all out. I had to help her people some, an' I bought a farm fer Mama an' the Ole Man—that's where they always wanted to be. An' I got three hundred acres of my own in Zebulon—all paid fer, too!—an' if I git a good price this year fer my tobacco, I stan' to clear two thousand dollars. So if I can git two years more in the League an' one more good World Series, why—" he turned his square face toward his friend and grinned his brown and freckled grin, just as he used to as a boy—"we'll be all set."

"And—you mean you'll be satisfied?"

"Huh? Satisfied?" Nebraska turned to him with a puzzled look. "How do you mean?"

"I mean after all you've seen and done, Bras—the big cities and the crowds, and all the people shouting—and the newspapers, and the headlines, and the World Series—and—and—the first of March, and St. Petersburg, and meeting all the fellows again, and spring training—"

Nebraska groaned.

"Why, what's the matter?"

"Spring trainin'."

"You mean you don't like it?"

"Like it! Them first three weeks is just plain hell. It ain't bad when you're a kid. You don't put on much weight durin' the winter, an' when you come down in the spring, it only takes a few days to loosen up an' git the kinks out. In two weeks you're loose as ashes. But wait till you been aroun' as long as I have!" He laughed loudly and shook his head. "Boy! The first time you go after a grounder, you can hear your joints creak. After a while you begin to limber up—you work into it an' git the soreness out of your muscles. By the time the season starts, along in April, you feel pretty good. By May you're goin' like a house a-fire, an' you tell yourself you're as good as you ever was. You're still goin' strong along in June. An' then you hit July, an' you git them double-headers in St. Looie! Boy, oh boy!" Again he shook his head and laughed, baring big square teeth. "Monkus," he said quietly, turning to his companion, and now his face was serious, and he had his black Indian look—"you ever been in St. Looie in July?"

"No."

"All right, then," he said very softly and scornfully. "An' you ain't played *ball* there in July. You come up to bat with sweat bustin' from your ears. You step up an' look out to where the pitcher ought to be, an' you see four of him. The crowd in the bleachers is out there roastin' in their shirt-sleeves, an' when the pitcher throws the ball, it just comes from nowheres—it comes right out of all them shirt-sleeves in the bleachers. It's on top of you before you know it. Well, anyway, you dig in an' git a toe-hold, take your cut, an' maybe you connect. You straighten out a fast one. It's good fer two bases if you hustle. In the old days you could've made it standin' up. But now—boy!" He shook his head slowly. "You cain't tell me nothin' about that ball park in St. Looie in July! They got it all growed out in grass in April, but after July first"—he gave a short laugh—"hell! it's paved with concrete! An' when you git to first, them dogs is sayin', 'Boy, let's stay here!' But you gotta keep on goin'—you know the manager is watchin' you—you're gonna ketch hell if you don't take that extra base, it may mean the game. An' the boys up in the press box, they got their eyes glued on you, too—they've begun to say old Crane is playin' on a dime—an' you're thinkin' about next year an' maybe gittin' another Series—an' hope to God you don't git traded to St. Looie. So you take it on the lam, you slide into second like the Twentieth Century comin' into the Chicago yards—an' when you git up an' feel yourself all over to see if any of your parts is missin', you gotta listen to one of the second baseman's wisecracks: 'What's the hurry, Bras? Afraid you'll be late fer the Veterans' Reunion?'"

"I begin to see what you mean, all right," said George.

"See what I mean? Why, say! One day this season I ast one of the boys what month it was, an' when he told me it was just the middle of July, I says to him: 'July, hell! If it ain't September, I'll eat your hat!' 'Go ahead, then,' he says, 'an' eat it, because it ain't September, Bras—it's July.' 'Well,' I says, 'they must be havin' sixty days a month this year—it's the longest damn July I ever felt!' An' lemme tell you, I didn't miss it fer, either—I'll be dogged if I did! When you git old in this business, it may be only July, but you think it's September." He was silent for a moment. "But they'll keep you in there, gener'ly, as long as you can hit. If you can smack that ole apple, they'll send you out there if they've got to use glue to keep you from fallin' apart. So maybe I'll git in another year or two if I'm lucky. So long's I can hit 'em, maybe they'll keep sendin' me out there till all the other players has to grunt every time ole Bras goes after a ground ball!" He laughed. "I ain't that bad yet, but soon's I am, I'm through."

"You won't mind it, then, when you have to quit?"

He didn't answer at once. He sat there looking out the window. Then he laughed a little wearily:

"Boy, this may be a ride on the train to you, but to me—say!—I covered this stretch so often that I can tell you what telephone post we're passin' without even lookin' out the window. Why, hell yes!"—he laughed loudly now, in the old infectious way—"I used to have 'em numbered—now I got 'em *named!*"

"And you think you can get used to spending all your time out on the farm in Zebulon?

"Git used to it?" In Nebraska's voice there was now the same note of scornful protest that it had when he was a boy, and for a moment he turned and looked at his friend with an expression of astonished disgust. "Why, what are you talking about? That's the greatest life in the world!"

"And your father? How is he, Bras?"

The player grinned and shook his head: "Oh, the Ole Man's happy as a possum. He's doin' what he wanted to do all his life."

"And is he well?"

"If he felt any better, he'd have to go to bed. Strong as a bull," said Nebraska proudly. "He could wrastle a bear right now an' bite his nose off! Why, hell yes!" the player went on with an air of conviction—"he could take any two men I know today an' throw them over his shoulder!"

"Bras, do you remember when you and I were kids and your father was on the police force, how he used to wrestle all those professionals that came to town? There were some good ones, too!"

"You're damn right there was!" said the player, nodding his head. "Tom Anderson, who used to be South Atlantic champion, an' that fellah Petersen—do you remember him?"

"Sure. And that big fellow they called the Strangler Turk—"

"Yeah, an' he was good, too! Only he wasn't no Turk—he only called hisself one. The Ole Man told me he was some kind of Polack from the steel mills, an' that's how he got so strong."

"And Bull Dakota—and Texas Jim Ryan—and the Masked Marvel?"

"Yeah—only there was a whole lot of them—guys cruisin' all over the country callin' theirselves the Masked Marvel. The Ole Man wrastled two of 'em. Only the real Masked Marvel never came to town. The Ole Man told me there was a real Masked Marvel, but he was too damn good, I guess, to come to Libya Hill."

"Do you remember the night, Bras, when your father was wrestling one of these Masked Marvels, and we were there in the front row rooting for him, and he got a stranglehold on this fellow with the mask, and the mask came off—and the fellow wasn't the Masked Marvel at all, but only that Greek who used to work all night at the Bijou Cafe for Ladies and Gents down by the depot?"

"Yeah—haw-haw!" Nebraska threw back his head and laughed loudly. "I'd clean fergot that damn Greek, but that's who it was! The whole crowd hollered frame-up an' tried to git their money back—I'll swear, Monk! I'm glad to see you!" He put his big hand on his companion's knee. "It don't seem no time, does it? It all comes back!"

"Yes, Bras—" for a moment George looked out at the flashing landscape with a feeling of sadness and wonder in his heart—"it all comes back."

So This Is Man

In the infinite variety of common, accidental, oft-unheeded things one can see the web of life as it is spun. Whether we wake at morning in the city, or lie at night in darkness in the country towns, or walk the streets of furious noon in all the dusty, homely, and enduring lights of present time, the universe around us is the same. Evil lives forever—so does good. Man alone has knowledge of these two, and he is such a little thing.

For what is man?

First, a child, soft-boned, unable to support itself on its rubbery legs, that howls and laughs by turns, cries for the moon but hushes when it gets its mother's breast; a sleeper, eater, guzzler, howler, laugher, idiot, and a chewer of its toe; a little tender thing all blubbered with its spit, a reacher into fires, a beloved fool.

After that, a boy, hoarse and loud before his companions, but afraid of the dark; will beat the weaker and avoid the stronger; worships strength and savagery, loves tales of war and murder, and violence done to others; joins gangs and hates to be alone; makes heroes out of soldiers, sailors, prize fighters, football players, cowboys, gunmen, and detectives; would rather die than not out-try and out-dare his companions, wants to beat them and always to win, shows his muscle and demands that it be felt, boasts of his victories and will never own defeat.

Then the youth: goes after girls, is foul behind their backs among the drugstore boys, hints at a hundred seductions, but gets pimples on his face; begins to think about his clothes, becomes a fop, greases his hair, smokes cigarettes with a dissipated air, reads novels and writes poetry on the sly. He knows hate, love, and jealousy; he is cowardly and foolish; he cannot endure to be alone; he lives in a crowd, thinks with the crowd, is afraid to be marked off from his fellows by any eccentricity. He joins clubs and is afraid of ridicule; he is bored and unhappy and wretched most of the time. There is a great cavity in him; he is dull.

Then the man: he is busy, he is full of plans and reasons, he has work. He gets children, buys and sells small packets of everlasting earth, intrigues against his rivals, is exultant when he cheats them. He wastes his little three score years and ten in spendthrift and inglorious living; from his cradle to his grave he scarcely sees the sun or moon or stars; he is unconscious of the immortal sea and earth; he talks of the future, and he wastes it as it comes. If he is lucky, he saves money. At the end his fat purse buys him flunkies to carry him where his shanks no longer can; he consumes rich food and golden wine that his wretched stomach has no hunger for; his weary and lifeless eyes look out upon the scenery of strange lands for which in youth his heart was panting. Then the slow death, prolonged by costly doctors, and finally the graduate undertakers, the perfumed carrion, the suave ushers with palms outspread to leftwards, the fast motor hearses, and the earth again.

This is man: a writer of books, a putter-down of words, a painter of pictures, a maker of ten thousand philosophies. He grows passionate over ideas, he hurls mockery and scorn at another's work, he finds the one way, the true way, for himself, and calls all others false—yet in the billion books upon the shelves there is not one that can tell him how to draw a single fleeting breath in peace and comfort. He makes histories of the universe, he directs the destiny of nations, but he does not know his own history, and he cannot direct his own destiny with dignity or wisdom for ten consecutive minutes.

Here, then, is man, this moth of time, this dupe of brevity and numbered hours, this travesty of waste and sterile breath. Yet if the gods could come here to a desolate, deserted earth where only the ruin of man's cities remained, where only a few marks and carvings of his hand were legible upon his broken tablets, where only a wheel lay rusting in the desert sand, a cry would burst out of their hearts, and they would say: "He lived, and he was here!"

Behold his works:

He needed speech to ask for bread—and he had Christ! He needed songs to sing in battle—and he had Homer! He needed words to curse his enemies—and he had Dante, he had Voltaire, he had Swift! He needed cloth to cover up his hairless, puny flesh against the seasons—and he wove the robes of Solomon, he made the garments of great kings, he made the samite for the young knights! He needed walls and a roof to shelter him—and he made Blois! He needed a temple to propitiate his God—and he made Chartres and Fountains Abbey! He was born to creep upon the earth—and he made great wheels, he sent great engines thundering down the rails, he launched great wings into the air, he put great ships upon the angry sea!

Plagues wasted him and cruel wars destroyed his strongest sons, but fire, flood, and famine could not quench him. No, nor the inexorable grave—his sons leaped shouting from his dying loins. The shaggy bison with his thews of thunder died upon the plains; the fabled mammoths of the unrecorded ages are vast scaffoldings of dry, insensate loam; the panthers have learned caution and move carefully among tall grasses to the water hole; and man lives on amid the senseless nihilism of the universe.

For there is one belief, one faith, that is man's glory, his triumph, his immortality—and that is his belief in life. Man loves life, and, loving life, hates death, and because of this he is great, he is glorious, he is beautiful, and his beauty is everlasting. He lives below the senseless stars and writes his meanings in them. He lives in fear, in toil, in agony, and in unending tumult, but if the blood foamed bubbling from his wounded lungs at every breath he drew, he would still love life more dearly than an end of breathing. Dying, his eyes burn beautifully, and the old hunger shines more fiercely in them—he has endured all the hard and purposeless suffering, and still he wants to live.

Thus it is impossible to scorn this creature. For out of his strong belief in life, this puny man made love. At his best, he *is* love. Without him there can be no love, no hunger, no desire.

So this is man—the worst and best of him—this frail and petty thing who lives his day and dies like all the other animals, and is forgotten. And yet, he is immortal, too, for both the good and evil that he does live after him.

The desire for fame is rooted in the hearts of men. It is one of the most powerful of human desires, and perhaps for that very reason, and because it is so deep and secret, it is the desire that men are most unwilling to admit, particularly those who feel most sharply its keen and piercing spur.

The politician, for example, would never have us think that it is love of office, the desire for the notorious elevation of public place, that drives him on. No, the thing that governs him is his pure devotion to the common weal, his selfless and high-minded statesmanship, his burning idealism to turn out the rascal who usurps the office and betrays the public trust which he himself, he assures us, would so gloriously and devotedly maintain.

So, too, the soldier. It is never love of glory that inspires him to his profession. It is never love of battle, love of war, love of all the resounding titles and the proud emoluments of the heroic conqueror. Oh, no. It is devotion to duty that makes him a soldier. He is inspired simply by the endless ardor of his patriotic abnegation. He regrets that he has but one life to give for his country.

So it goes through every walk of life. Even the businessman will not admit a selfish motive in his money-getting. On the contrary, he is the developer of the nation's resources. He is the benevolent employer of thousands of working men who would be lost and on the dole without the organizing genius of his great intelligence. He is the defender of the American ideal of rugged individualism, the shining exemplar to youth of what a poor country boy may achieve in this nation through a devotion to the national virtues of thrift, industry, obedience to duty, and business integrity. He is, he assures us, the backbone of the country, the man who makes the wheels go round, the leading citizen, Public Friend No. 1.

All these people lie, of course. They know they lie, and everyone who hears them also knows they lie. The lie, however, has become a part of the convention of American life. People listen to it patiently, and if they smile at it, the smile is weary, touched with resignation and the indifferent dismissals of fatigue.

Curiously enough, the lie has also invaded the world of creation—the one place where it has no right at all to exist. There was a time when the poet, the painter, the musician, the artist of whatever sort was not ashamed to confess that the desire for fame was one of the driving forces of his life and labor. But what a transformation from that time to this! Nowadays one will travel far and come back fruitless if he hopes to find an artist who will admit that he is devoted to anything except the service of some ideal—political, social, economic, religious, or esthetic—which is outside himself, and to which his own humble fame-forsaking person is reverently and selflessly consigned.

Deluded man! Poor vassal of corrupted time! We have freed ourselves from all degrading vanities, choked off the ravening desire for individual immortality, and now, having risen out of the ashes of our father's earth into the untainted ethers of collective consecration, we are clear at last of all that vexed, corrupted earth—clear of the sweat and blood and sorrow, clear of the grief and joy, clear of the hope and fear and human agony of which our father's flesh and that of every other man alive before us was ever wrought.

And yet: Made of our father's earth, blood of his blood, bone of his bone, flesh of his flesh—born like our father, here to live and strive, here to win through or be defeated—here, like all the other men who went before us, not too nice or dainty for the uses of this earth—here to live, to suffer, and to die—O brothers, like our fathers in their time, we are burning, burning, burning in the night.

The Promise of America

Go, seeker, if you will, throughout the land and you will find us burning in the night.

There where the hackles of the Rocky Mountains blaze in the blank and naked radiance of the moon, go make your resting stool upon the highest peak. Can you not see us now? The continental wall juts sheer and flat, its huge black shadow on the plain, and the plain sweeps out against the East, two thousand miles away. The great snake that you see there is the Mississippi River.

Behold the gem-strung towns and cities of the good, green East, flung like star-dust through the field of night. That spreading constellation to the north is called Chicago, and that giant wink that blazes in the moon is the pendant lake that it is built upon. Beyond, close-set and dense as a clenched fist, are all the jeweled cities of the eastern seaboard. There's Boston, ringed with the bracelet of its shining little towns, and all the lights that sparkle on the rocky indentations of New England. Here, southward and a little to the west, and yet still coasted to the sea, is our intensest ray, the splintered firmament of the towered island of Manhattan. Round about her, sown thick as grain, is the glitter of a hundred towns and cities. The long chain of lights there is the necklace of Long Island and the Jersey shore. Southward and inland, by a foot or two, behold the duller glare of Philadelphia. Southward farther still, the twin constellations—Baltimore and Washington. Westward, but still within the borders of the good, green East, that nighttime glow and smolder of hell-fire is Pittsburgh. Here, St. Louis, hot and humid in the cornfield belly of the land, and bedded on the mid-length coil and fringes of the snake. There at the snake's mouth, southward six hundred miles or so, you see the jeweled crescent of old New Orleans. Here, west and south again, you see the gemmy glitter of the cities on the Texas border.

Turn, now, seeker, on your resting stool atop the Rocky Mountains, and look another thousand miles or so across moon-blazing

482

fiend-worlds of the Painted Desert and beyond Sierra's ridge. That magic congeries of lights there to the west, ringed like a studded belt around the magic setting of its lovely harbor, is the fabled town of San Francisco. Below it, Los Angeles and all the cities of the California shore. A thousand miles to north and west, the sparkling towns of Oregon and Washington.

Observe the whole of it, survey it as you might survey a field. Make it your garden, seeker, or your backyard patch. Be at ease in it. It's your oyster—yours to open if you will. Don't be frightened, it's not so big now, when your footstool is the Rocky Mountains. Reach out and dip a hatful of water from Lake Michigan. Drink it—we've tried it—you'll not find it bad. Take your shoes off and work your toes down in the river oozes of the Mississippi bottom—it's very refreshing on a hot night in the summertime. Help yourself to a bunch of Concord grapes up there in northern New York State—they're getting good now. Or raid that watermelon patch down there in Georgia. Or, if you like, you can try the Rockyfords here at your elbow, in Colorado. Just make yourself at home, refresh yourself, get the feel of things, adjust your sights, and get the scale. It's your pasture now, and it's not so big—only three thousand miles from east to west, only two thousand miles from north to south—but all between, where ten thousand points of light prick out the cities, towns, and villages, there, seeker, you will find us burning in the night.

Here, as you pass through the brutal sprawl, the twenty miles of rails and rickets, of the South Chicago slums—here, in an unpainted shack, is a Negro boy, and, seeker, he is burning in the night. Behind him is a memory of the cotton fields, the flat and mournful pineland barrens of the lost and buried South, and at the fringes of the pine another nigger shack, with mammy and eleven little niggers. Farther still behind, the slave-driver's whip, the slave ship, and, far off, the jungle dirge of Africa. And before him what? A roped-in ring, a blaze of lights, across from him a white champion; the bell, the opening, and all around the vast sea-roaring of the crowd. Then the lightning feint and stroke, the black panther's paw—the hot, rotating presses, and the rivers of sheeted print! O seeker, where is the slave ship now?

Or there, in the clay-baked piedmont of the South, that lean and tan-faced boy who sprawls there in the creaking chair among admiring cronies before the open doorways of the fire department, and tells them how he pitched the team to shut-out victory today. What visions burn, what dreams possess him, seeker of the night? The packed stands of the stadium, the bleachers sweltering with their unshaded hordes, the faultless velvet of the diamond, unlike the clay-baked outfields down in Georgia. The mounting roar of eighty thousand voices and Gehrig coming up to bat, the boy himself upon the pitching mound, the lean face steady as a hound's; then the nod, the signal, and the windup, the rawhide arm that snaps and crackles like a whip, the small white bullet of the blazing ball, its loud report in the oiled pocket of the catcher's mitt, the umpire's thumb jerked upward, the clean strike.

Or there again, in the East-Side Ghetto of Manhattan, two blocks away from the East River, a block away from the gas-house district and its thuggery, there in the swarming tenement, shut in his sweltering cell, breathing the sun-baked air through opened window at the fire escape, celled there away into a little semblance of privacy and solitude from all the brawling and vociferous life and argument of his family and the seething hive around him, the gaunt boy sits and pores upon his book. In shirt-sleeves, bent above his table to meet the hard glare of a naked bulb, he sits with weak eyes squinting painfully through his thick-lens glasses. And for what? For what this agony of concentration? For what this hell of effort? For what this intense withdrawal from the poverty and squalor of dirty brick and rusty fire escapes, from the raucous cries and violence and never-ending noise? For what? Because, brother, he is burning in the night. He sees the class, the lecture room, the shining apparatus of gigantic laboratories, the open field of scholarship and pure research, certain knowledge, and the world distinction of an Einstein name.

So, then, to every man his chance—to every man, regardless of his birth, his shining golden opportunity—to every man the right to live, to work, to be himself, and to become whatever thing his manhood and his vision can combine to make him—this, seeker, is the promise of America.

The Hollow Men

How often have we read the paper in America! How often have we seen it *blocked* against our doors! Little route-boys fold and block it, so to throw it—and so we find it and unfold it, crackling and ink-laden, at our doors. Sometimes we find it tossed there lightly with a flat *plop*: sometimes we find it thrown with a solid, whizzing *whack* against the clapboards (clapboards here, most often, in America): sometimes servants find just freshly folded sheets laid neatly down in doorways, and take them to the table for their masters. No matter how it got there, we always find it.

How we do love the paper in America! How we do love the paper, all!

Why do we love the paper in America? Why do we love the paper, all?

Mad masters, I will tell ye why.

Because the paper is "the news" here in America, and we love the *smell* of news. We love the smell of news that's "fit to print." We also love the smell of news *not* fit to print. We love, besides, the smell of *facts* that news is made of. Therefore we love the paper because the news is so fit-printable—so unprintable—and so fact-printable.

Is the news, then, like America? No it's not.

The news is *not* America, nor is America the *news*—the news is *in* America. It is a kind of light at morning, and at evening, and at midnight in America. It is a kind of growth and record and excrescence of our life. It is not good enough—it does not tell our story—yet it is the news.

Take the following, for instance:

An unidentified man fell or jumped yesterday at noon from the twelfth story of the Admiral Francis Drake Hotel in Brooklyn. The man, who was about thirty-five years old, registered at the hotel about a week ago, according to the police, as C. Green. Police are of the opinion that this was an assumed name. Pending identification, the body is being held at the King's County Morgue.

This, then, is news. Is it the whole story, Admiral Drake? No! Yet we do not supply the whole story—we who have known all the lights and weathers of America.

Well, then, it's news, and it happened in your own hotel, brave Admiral Drake, so, of course, you'll want to know what happened.

"An unidentified man"—well, then, this man was an American. "About thirty-five years old" with "an assumed name"—well, then, call him C. Green, as he called himself ironically in the hotel register. C. Green, the unidentified American, "fell or jumped," then, "yesterday at noon . . . in Brooklyn"—worth six lines of print in today's *Times* —one of seven thousand who died yesterday upon this continent—one of three hundred and fifty who died yesterday in this very city (see dense, close columns of obituaries, page 15: begin with "Aaronson," so through the alphabet to "Zorn"). C. Green came here "a week ago"—

And came from where? From the deep South, or the Mississippi Valley, or the Middle West? From Minneapolis, Bridgeport, Boston, or a little town in Old Catawba? From Scranton, Toledo, St. Louis, or the desert whiteness of Los Angeles? From the pine barrens of the Atlantic coastal plain, or from the Pacific shore?

And so—was *what*, brave Admiral Drake? In what way an American? In what way different from the men *you* knew, old Drake?

When the ships bore home again and Cape St. Vincent blazed in Spaniard's eye—or when old Drake was returning with his men, beating coastwise from strange seas abreast, past the Scilly Isles toward the slant of evening fields, chalk cliffs, the harbor's arms, the town's sweet cluster and the spire—where was Green?

When, in red-oak thickets at the break of day, coon-skinned, the huntsmen of the wilderness lay for bear, heard arrows rattling in the laurel leaves, the bullet's whining plunk, and waited with cocked musket by the tree—where was Green?

Or when, with strong faces turning toward the setting sun, hawk-eyed and Indian-visaged men bore gunstocks on the western trails and sternly heard the fierce war whoops around the Painted Buttes—where, then, was Green?

Was never there with Drake's men in the evening when the sails stood in from the Americas! Was never there beneath the Spaniard's swarthy eye at Vincent's Cape. Was never there in the red-oak thicket in the morning! Was never there to hear the war-cries round the Painted Buttes!

No, no. He was no voyager of unknown seas, no pioneer of western trails. He was life's little man . . . life's nameless cipher, life's manswarm atom, life's American—and now he lies disjected and exploded on a street in Brooklyn!

He was a dweller in mean streets, was Green, a man-mote in the jungle of the city, a resident of grimy steel and stone, a stunned spectator of enormous salmon-colored towers, hued palely in the morning. He was a waker in bleak streets at morning, an alarm-clock watcher, saying, "Jesus, I'll be late!"—a fellow who took short cuts through the corner lot, behind the advertising signs; a fellow used to concrete horrors of hot day and blazing noon; a man accustomed to the tormented hodgepodge of our architecture—used to broken pavements, ash cans, shabby store fronts, dull green paint, the elevated structure, grinding traffic, noise, and streets be-tortured with a thousand bleak and dismal signs. He was accustomed to the gas tanks going out of town, he was an atom of machinery in an endless flow, going, stopping, going to the winking of the lights; he tore down concrete roads on Sundays, past the hot-dog stands and filling stations; he would return at darkness; hunger lured him to the winking splendor of the chop-suey signs; and midnight found him in The Coffee Pot, to prowl above a mug of coffee, tear a coffee-cake in fragments, and wear away the slow gray ash of time and boredom with other men in gray hats and with skins of tallow-gray, at Joe the Greek's.

C. Green could read (which Drake could not), but not too accurately; could write, too (which the Spaniard couldn't), but not too well. C. Green had trouble over certain words, spelled them out above the coffee mug at midnight, with a furrowed brow, slow-shaping lips, and "Jesus!" when news stunned him—for he read the news. Preferred the news "hot," straight from the shoulder—socko!—biff!—straight off the griddle, with lots of mustard, shapely legs, roadside wrecks and mutilated bodies, gangster's molls and gunmen's hideouts, tallow faces of the night that bluntly stare at flashlight lenses—this and talk of "heart-balm," "love-thief," "sex-hijacker"—all of this liked Green.

Yes, Green liked the news—and now, a bit of news himself (six lines of print in the *Times*), has been disjected and exploded on a Brooklyn pavement!

Behold him, Admiral Drake! Observe the scene now! Listen to the people! Here's something strange as the Armadas, the gold-laden cargoes of the bearded Spaniards, the vision of unfound Americas!

What do you see here, Admiral Drake?

Well, first a building—your own hotel—a great block of masonry, grimy-white, fourteen stories tall, stamped in an unvarying pattern with many windows. Sheeted glass below, the store front piled with medicines and toilet articles, perfumes, cosmetics, health contrivances. Within, a soda fountain, Admiral Drake. The men in white with monkey caps, soda jerkers sullen with perpetual overdriven irritation. Beneath the counter, pools of sloppy water, filth, and unwashed dishes. Across the counter, women with fat, rouged lips consuming ice cream sodas and pimento sandwiches.

Outside upon the concrete sidewalk lies the form of our exploded friend, C. Green. A crowd has gathered round—taxi drivers, passers-by, hangers-on about the subway station, people working in the neighborhood, and the police. No one has dared to touch the exploded Green as yet—they stand there in a rapt and fascinated circle, looking at him.

Not much to look at, either, Admiral Drake; not even those who trod your gory decks would call the sight a pretty one. Our friend has landed on his head—"taken a nose dive," as we say—and smashed his brains out at the iron base of the second lamp post from the corner.

So here Green lies, on the concrete sidewalk all disjected. No head is left, the head is gone now, head's exploded; only brains are left. The brains are pink and almost bloodless, Admiral Drake. (There's not much blood here—we shall tell you why.) But brains exploded are somewhat like pale sausage meat, fresh-ground. Brains are stuck hard to the lamp post, too; there is a certain driven emphasis about them, as if they had been shot hydraulically out of a force-hose against the post.

The head, as we have said, is gone completely; a few fragments of the skull are scattered round—but of the face, the features, forehead—nothing! They have all been blown *out*, as by some inner explosion. Nothing is left but the back of the skull, which curiously remains, completely hollowed out and vacant, and curved over, like the rounded handle of a walking stick.

The body, five feet eight or nine of it, of middling weight, is lying—we were going to say "face downward"; had we not better say "stomach downward"?—on the sidewalk. And save for a certain indefinable and curiously "disjected" quality, one could scarcely tell that every bone in it is broken. The hands are still spread out, half-folded and half-clenched, with a still-warm and startling eloquence of recent life. (It happened just four minutes ago!)

Well, where's the blood, then, Drake? You're used to blood; you'd like to know. Well, you've heard of casting bread upon the waters, Drake, and having it return—but never yet, I'll vow, of casting blood upon the streets—and having it run away—and then come back to you! But here it comes now, down the street now toward C. Green, the lamp post, and the crowd!—a young Italian youth, his black eyes blank with horror, tongue mumbling thickly, arm held firmly by the policeman, suit and shirt all drenched with blood, and face be-spattered with it! A stir of sudden interest in the crowd, sharp nudges, low-toned voices whispering:

"Here he is! Th' guy that 'got it'! . . . he was standin' *deh* beside the post! Sure, *that's* the guy!—talkin' to anotheh guy—he got it all! *That's* the reason you didn't see more blood—*this* guy got it!—Sure! The guy just missed him by six inches!—Sure! I'm tellin' you I *saw* it, ain't I! I looked up an' saw him in the air! He'd a hit this guy, but when he saw he was goin' to hit the lamp post, he put out his hands an' tried to keep away! *That's* the reason that he didn't hit this guy! . . . But this guy heard him when he hit, an' turned around—and zowie!—he got it right in his face!"

And another, whispering and nudging, nodding toward the horror-blank, thick-mumbling Italian boy: "Jesus! Look at th' guy, will yuh! . . . He don't know yet what happened to him! . . . Sure! He got it *all*. I tell yuh! An' when it happened—when he got it—he just stahted runnin' . . . He don't know yet what's happened! . . . That's what I'm tellin' yuh—th' guy just stahted runnin' when he got it."

And the Italian youth, thick-mumbling: " . . . Jeez! . . . W'at happened? . . . Jeez! . . . I was standin' talkin' to a guy—I heard it hit . . . Jeez! . . . W'at happened anyway? . . . I got it all oveh me! . . . Jeez! . . . I just stahted runnin' . . . Jeez! I'm sick!"

Voices: "Here, take 'im into the drug store! . . . Wash 'im off! . . . That guy needs a shot of liquor! . . . Sure! Take him into the drug stoeh *deh!* . . . *They'll* fix him up!"

The plump young man who runs the newsstand in the corridor, talking to everyone around him, excitedly and indignantly: ". . . Did I *see* it? Listen! I saw *everything!* I was coming across the street, I looked up, and saw him in the air! . . . *See* it? . . . *Listen!* If someone had taken a big ripe watermelon and dropped it on the street from the fourteenth floor, you'd have some idea what it was like! . . . *See* it! *I'll* tell the world I saw it! I don't want to see anything like *that* again!" Then, excitedly, with a kind of hysterical indignation: "Shows no consideration for other people, that's all *I've* got to say! If a man is going to do a thing like that, why does he pick a place like *this*—one of the busiest corners in Brooklyn? . . . How did *he* know he wouldn't hit someone? Why, if that boy had been standing six inches nearer to the post, he'd have killed him, as sure as you live! . . . And here he does it right in front of all these people who have to look at it! It shows he had no consideration for other people! A man who'd do a thing like that . . . ."

(Alas, poor youth! As if C. Green, now past considering, had considered nice "considerations.")

A taxi driver, impatiently: "That's what I'm tellin' yuh! . . . I watched him for five minutes before he jumped. He crawled out on the window sill an' stood there for *five* minutes, makin' up his mind! . . . Sure, I saw him! Lots of people saw him!" Impatiently, irritably: "Why didn't we *do* somthin' to stop him? A guy who'd do a thing like that is nuts to start with! You don't think he'd listen to anything we had to say, do you? . . . Sure, we *did* yell at him! . . . Jesus! . . . We was almost *afraid* to yell at him—we made motions to him to get back—tried to hold his attention while the cops sneaked round the corner into the hotel . . . . Sure, the cops got there just the second he jumped—I don't know if he jumped when he heard 'em comin' or what happened, but Christ!—he stood there gettin' ready for five minutes while we watched!"

Observe now, Admiral, with what hypnotic concentration the people are examining the grimy white facade of your hotel. Watch their faces and expressions. Their eyes go traveling upward slowly—up—up—up until they finally arrive and come to rest with focal concentration on that single open window twelve floors up. It is no jot different from all the other windows, but now the vision of the crowd is fastened on it with a fatal and united interest. And after staring at it fixedly, the eyes come traveling slowly down again—down—down—down—the faces strained a little, the mouths all slightly puckered as if something set the teeth on edge—and slowly, with fascinated measurement—down—down—down—until the eyes reach side-walk, lamp post, and—the Thing again.

The pavement finally halts all, stops all, answers all. It is the American pavement, Admiral Drake, our universal city sidewalk, a wide, hard, stripe of gray-white cement, blocked accurately with dividing lines. It is the hardest, coldest, cruelest, most impersonal pavement in the world: all of the indifference, the atomic desolation, the exploded nothingness of one hundred million nameless "Greens" is in it.

It came from the same place where all our sidewalks come from—from Standard Concentrated Production Units of America, No. 1. This is where all our streets and lamp posts (like the one on which Green's brains are spattered) come from, where all our white-grimy bricks (like those of which your hotel is constructed) come from, where the red facades of our standard-unit tobacco stores (like the one across the street) come from, where our motor cars come from, where our drug stores and our drug-store window and displays come from, where our soda-fountains (complete with soda jerkers attached) come from, where our cosmetics, toilet articles, and the fat rouged lips of our women come from, where our soda water, slops and syrups, steamed spaghetti, ice cream, and pimento sandwiches come from, where our clothes, our hats (neat, standard stamps of gray, our faces, false stamps of gray, not always neat), our language, conversation, sentiments, feelings, and opinions come from. All these things are made for us by Standard Concentrated Production Units of America, No.1.

So here we are, then, Admiral Drake. You see the street, the sidewalk, the front of your hotel, the constant stream of motor cars, the cops in uniform, the people streaming in and out of the subway, the rusty, pale-hued jungle of the buildings, old and new, high and low. There is no better place to see it, Drake. For this is Brooklyn, which means ten thousand streets and blocks like this one. Brooklyn, Admiral Drake, is the Standard Concentrated Chaos No. 1 of the Whole Universe. That is to say, it has no size, no shape, no heart, no joy, no hope, no aspiration, no center, no eyes, no soul, no purpose, no direction, and no anything—just Standard Concentrated Units everywhere—exploding in all directions for an unknown number of square miles like a completely triumphant Standard Concentrated Blot upon the Face of the Earth. And here, right in the middle, upon a minute portion of this magnificent Standard Concentrated Blot, where all the Standard Concentrated Blotters can stare at him, and with the brains completely out of him—lies Green!

And this is bad—most bad—oh, *very* bad—and should not be allowed! For, as our young news-vendor friend has just indignantly proclaimed, it "shows no consideration for other people"—which means, for other Standard Concentrated Blotters. Green has no right to go falling in this fashion in a public place. He has no business *being* where he is at all. A Standard Concentrated Blotter is not supposed to *be* places, but to *go* places.

You see, dear Admiral, this sidewalk, this Standard Concentrated Mobway, is not a place to walk on, really. It is a place to swarm on, to weave on, to thrust and dodge on, to scurry past on, to crowd by on. One of the earliest precepts in a Concentrated Blotter's life is: "Move on there! Where th' hell d'you think you are, anyway—in a cow pasture?" And, most certainly, it is not a place to lie on, to sprawl out on.

But look at Green! Just *look* at him! No wonder the plump youth is angry with him!

Green has willfully and deliberately violated every Standard Concentrated Principle of Blotterdom. He has not only gone and dashed his brains out, but he has done it in a public place—upon a piece of Standard Concentrated Mobway. He has messed up the sidewalk, messed up another Standard Concentrated Blotter, stopped traffic, taken people from their business, upset the nerves of his fellow Blotters—and now lies there, all *sprawled* out, in a place where he has no right to *be*. And, to make his crime unpardonable, C. Green has—

—Come to Life!

What's that, Admiral? You do not understand it? Small wonder, though it's really very simple:

For just ten minutes since, C. Green was a Concentrated Blotter like the rest of us, a nameless atom, swarming with the rest of us, just another "guy" like a hundred million other "guys." But now, observe him! No longer is he just "another guy"—already he has become a "special guy"—he has become "*The* Guy." C. Green at last has turned into a—*Man!*

The Anatomy of Loneliness

My life, more than that of anyone I know, has been spent in solitude and wandering. Why this is true, or how it happened, I cannot say; yet it is so. From my fifteenth year—save for a single interval—I have lived about as solitary a life as modern man can have. I mean by this that the number of hours, days, months, and years that I have spent alone have been immense and extraordinary. I propose, therefore, to describe the experience of human loneliness exactly as I have known it.

The reason that impels me to do this is not that I think my knowledge of loneliness different in kind from that of other men. Quite the contrary. The whole conviction of my life now rests upon the belief that loneliness, far from being a rare and curious phenomenon, peculiar to myself and to a few other solitary men, is the central and inevitable fact of human existence. When we examine the moments, acts, and statements of all kinds of people—not only the grief and ecstasy of the greatest poets, but also the huge unhappiness of the average soul, as evidenced by the numerous strident words of abuse, hatred, contempt, mistrust, and scorn that forever grate upon our ears as the manswarm passes us in the streets—we find, I think, that they are all suffering from the same thing. The final cause of their complaint is loneliness.

But if my experience of loneliness has not been different in kind from that of other men, I suspect it has been sharper in intensity. This gives me the best authority in the world to write of this, our general complaint, for I believe I know more about it than anyone of my generation. In saying this, I am merely stating a fact as I see it, though I realize that it may sound like arrogance or vanity. But before anyone jumps to that conclusion, let him consider how strange it would be to meet with arrogance in one who has lived alone as much as I. The surest cure for vanity is loneliness. For, more than other men, we who dwell in the heart of solitude are always the victims of self-doubt. Forever and forever in our loneliness, shameful feelings of inferiority will rise up suddenly to overwhelm us in a poisonous flood of horror, disbelief, and desolation, to sicken and corrupt our health and confidence, to spread pollution at the very root of strong, exultant joy. And the eternal paradox of it is that if a man is to know the triumphant labor of creation, he must for long periods resign himself to loneliness, and suffer loneliness to rob him of the health, the confidence, the belief and joy which are essential to creative work.

To live alone as I have lived, a man should have the confidence of God, the tranquil faith of a monastic saint, the stern impregnability of a Gibraltar. Lacking these, there are times when anything, everything, all or nothing, the most trivial incidents, the most casual words, can in an instant strip me of my armor, palsy my hand, constrict my heart with frozen horror, and fill my bowels with the gray substance of shuddering impotence. Sometimes it is nothing but a shadow passing on the sun; sometimes nothing but the torrid milky light of August, or the naked, sprawling ugliness and squalid decencies of streets in Brooklyn fading in the weary vistas of that milky light and evoking the intolerable misery of countless drab and nameless lives. Sometimes it is just the barren horror of raw concrete, or the heat blazing on a million beetles of machinery darting through the torrid streets, or the cindered weariness of parking spaces, or the slamming smash and racket of the El, or the driven manswarm of the earth, thrusting on forever in exacerbated fury, going nowhere in a hurry.

Again, it may be just a phrase, a look, a gesture. It may be the cold, disdainful inclination of the head with which a precious, kept, exquisite princeling of Park Avenue acknowledges an introduction, as if to say: "You are nothing." Or it may be a sneering reference and dismissal by a critic in a high-class weekly magazine. Or a letter from a woman saying I am lost and ruined, my talent vanished, all my efforts false and worthless—since I have forsaken the truth, vision, and reality which are so beautifully her own.

And sometimes it is less than these—nothing I can touch or see or hear or definitely remember. It may be so vague as to be a kind of hideous weather of the soul, subtly compounded of all the hunger, fury, and impossible desire my life has ever known. Or, again, it may be a half-forgotten memory of the cold wintry red of waning Sunday afternoons in Cambridge, and of a pallid, sensitive, esthetic face that held me once in earnest discourse on such a Sunday afternoon in Cambridge, telling me that all my youthful hopes were pitiful delusions and that all my life would come to naught, and the red and waning light of March was reflected on the pallid face with a desolate impotence that instantly quenched all the young ardors of my blood.

Beneath the evocations of these lights and weathers, and the cold disdainful words of precious, sneering, and contemptuous people, all of the joy and singing of the day goes out like an extinguished candle, hope seems lost to me forever, and every truth that I have ever found and known seems false. At such a time a lonely man will feel that all the evidence of his own senses has betrayed him, and that nothing really lives and moves on earth but creatures of the death-in-life—those of the cold, constricted heart and the sterile loins, who exist forever in the red waning light of March and Sunday afternoon.

All this hideous doubt, despair, and dark confusion of the soul a lonely man must know, for he is united to no image save that which he creates himself, he is bolstered by no other knowledge save that which he can gather for himself with the vision of his own eyes and brain. He is sustained and cheered and aided by no party, he is given comfort by no creed, he has no faith in him except his own. And often that faith deserts him, leaving him shaken and filled with impotence. And then it seems to him that his life has come to nothing, that he is ruined, lost, and broken past redemption, and that morning—bright, shining morning, with its promise of new beginnings—will never come upon the earth again as it once did.

He knows that dark time is flowing by him like a river. The huge, dark wall of loneliness is around him now. It encloses and presses in upon him, and he cannot escape. And the cancerous plant of memory is feeding at his entrails, recalling hundreds of forgotten faces and ten thousand vanished days, until all life seems as strange and insubstantial as a dream. Time flows by him like a river, and he waits in his little room like a creature held captive by an evil spell. And he will hear, far off, the murmurous drone of the great earth, and feel that he has been forgotten, that his powers are wasting from him while the river flows, and that all his life has come to nothing. He feels that his strength is gone, his power withered, while he sits there drugged and fettered in the prison of his loneliness.

Then suddenly, one day, for no apparent reason, his faith and his belief in life will come back to him in a tidal flood. It will rise up in him with a jubilant and invincible power, bursting a window in the world's great wall and restoring everything to shapes of deathless brightness. Made miraculously whole and secure in himself, he will plunge once more into the triumphant labor of creation. All his old strength is his again: he knows what he knows, he is what he is, he has found what he has found. And he will say the truth that is in him, speak it though the whole world deny it, affirm it though a million men cry it is false.

At such a moment of triumphant confidence, with this feeling in me, I dare now assert that I have known Loneliness as well as any man, and will now write of him as if he were my very brother, which he is. I will paint him for you with such fidelity to his true figure that no man who reads will ever doubt his visage when Loneliness comes to him hereafter.

II

The most tragic, sublime, and beautiful expression of human loneliness which I have ever read is in the Book of Job; the grandest and most philosophical, Ecclesiastes. Here I must point out a fact which is so much at variance with everything I was told as a child concerning loneliness and the tragic underweft of life that, when I first discovered it, I was astounded and incredulous, doubting the overwhelming weight of evidence that had revealed it to me. But there it was, as solid as a rock, not to be shaken or denied; and as the years passed, the truth of this discovery became part of the structure of my life.

The fact is this: the lonely man, who is also the tragic man, is invariably the man who loves life dearly—which is to say, the joyful man. In these statements there is no paradox whatever. The one condition implies the other, and makes it necessary. The essence of human tragedy is in loneliness, not in conflict, no matter what the arguments of the theater may assert. And just as the great tragic writer (I say, "the tragic writer" as distinguished from "the writer of tragedies," for certain nations, the Roman and French among them, have had no great tragic writers, for Virgil and Racine were none, but great writers of tragedy): just as the great tragic writer—Job, Sophocles, Dante, Milton, Swift, Dostoevski—has always been the lonely man, so he has also been the man who loved life best and had the deepest sense of joy. The real quality and substance of human joy is to be found in the works of these great tragic writers as nowhere else in all the records of man's life upon the earth. In proof of this, I can give here one conclusive illustration:

In my childhood, any mention of the Book of Job evoked instantly in my mind a long train of gloomy, gray, and unbrokenly dismal associations. This has been true, I suspect, with most of us. Such phrases as "Job's comforter," and "the patience of Job," and "the afflictions of Job," have become part of our common idiom and are used to refer to people whose woes seem uncountable and unceasing, who have suffered long and silently, and whose gloom has never been interrupted by a ray of hope or joy. All these associations had united to make for me a picture of the Book of Job that was grim, bleak, and constant in its misery. But any reader of intelligence and experience who has read that great book in his mature years will realize how false such a picture is.

For the Book of Job, far from being dreary, gray, and dismal, is woven entire, more than any single piece of writing I can recall, from the sensuous, flashing, infinitely various, and gloriously palpable material of great poetry; and it wears at the heart of its tremendous chant of everlasting sorrow the exulting song of everlasting joy.

In this there is nothing strange or curious, but only what is inevitable and right. It is the sense of death and loneliness, the knowledge of the brevity of his days, and the huge impending burden of his sorrow, growing always, never lessening, that makes joy glorious, tragic, and unutterably precious to a man like Job. Beauty comes and passes, is lost the moment that we touch it, can no more be stayed or held than one can stay the flowing of a river. Out of this pain of loss, this bitter ecstasy of brief having, this fatal glory of the single moment, the tragic writer will therefore make a song of joy. That, at least, he may keep and treasure always. And his song is full of grief because he knows that joy is fleeting, gone the instant that we have it, and that is why it is so precious, gaining its full glory from the very things that limit and destroy it.

He knows that joy gains its glory out of sorrow, bitter sorrow, and man's loneliness, and that it is haunted always with the certainty of death, dark death, which stops our tongues, our eyes, our living breath, with the twin oblivions of dust and nothingness. Therefore a man like Job will make a chant for sorrow, too, but it will still be a song for joy as well, and one more strange and beautiful than any other that man has ever sung:

> *Hast thou given the horse strength? hast thou clothed his neck with thunder?*
> *Canst thou make him afraid as a grasshopper? the glory of his nostrils is terrible.*
> *He paweth in the valley, and rejoiceth in his strength: he goeth on to meet the armed men.*
> *He mocketh at fear, and is not affrighted; neither turneth he back from the sword.*
> *The quiver rattleth against him, the glittering spear and the shield.*
> *He swalloweth the ground with fierceness and rage; neither believeth he that it is the sound of the trumpet.*
> *He saith among the trumpets, Ha, ha; and he smelleth the battle afar off, the thunder of the captains and the shouting.*

That is joy—joy solemn and triumphant; stern, lonely, everlasting joy, which has in it the full depth and humility of man's wonder, his sense of glory, and his feeling of awe before the mystery of the universe. An exultant cry is torn from our lips as we read the lines about that glorious horse, and the joy we feel is wild and strange, lonely and dark like death, and grander than the delicate and lovely joy that men like Herrick and Theocritus described, great poets though they were.

III

Just as the Book of Job and the sermon of Ecclesiastes are, each in its own way, supreme histories of man's loneliness, so do all the books of the Old Testament, in their entirety, provide the most final and profound literature of human loneliness that the world has known. It is astonishing with what a coherent unity of spirit and belief the life of loneliness is recorded in those many books—how it finds its full expression in the chants, songs, prophecies, and chronicles of so many men, all so various, and each so individual, each revealing some new image of man's secret and most lonely heart, and all combining to produce a single image of his loneliness that is matchless in its grandeur and magnificence.

The total, all-contributory unity of this conception of man's loneliness in the books of the Old Testament becomes even more astonishing when we begin to read the New. For, just as the Old Testament becomes the chronicle of the life of loneliness, the gospels of the New Testament, with the same miraculous and unswerving unity, become the chronicle of the life of love. What Christ is always saying, what he never swerves from saying, what he says a thousand times in a thousand different ways, but always with a central unity of belief, is this: "I am my Father's son, and you are my brothers." And the unity that binds us all together, that makes this earth a family, and all men brothers and the sons of God, is love.

The central purpose of Christ's life, therefore, is to destroy the life of loneliness and to establish here on earth the life of love. It should be obvious to everyone that when Christ says: "Blessed are the poor in spirit: for theirs is the kingdom of heaven," "Blessed are they that mourn: for they shall be comforted," "Blessed are the merciful: for they shall obtain mercy,"—Christ is not here extolling the qualities of humility, sorrow, and mercy as virtues sufficient in themselves, but he promises to men who have these virtues the richest reward that men were ever offered—a reward that promises not only the inheritance of the earth, but the kingdom of heaven, as well.

Such was the final intention of Christ's life, the purpose of his teaching. And its total import was that the life of loneliness could be destroyed forever by the life of love. Or such, at least, has been the meaning which I read into his life. For in these recent years when I have lived alone so much, and known loneliness so well, I have gone back many times and read the story of this man's words and life to see if I could find in them a meaning for myself, a way of life that would be better than the one I had. I read what he said, not in a mood of piety or holiness, not from a sense of sin, a feeling of contrition, or because his promise of a heavenly reward meant much to me. But I tried to read his bare words nakedly and simply, as it seems to me he must have uttered them, and as I have read the words of other men—of Homer, Donne, and Whitman, and the writer of Ecclesiastes—and if the meaning I have put upon his words seems foolish or extravagant, childishly simple or banal, mine alone are no different from what ten million other men have thought; I have only set it down here as I saw it, felt it, found it for myself, and have tried to add, subtract, and alter nothing.

And now I know that though the way and meaning of Christ's life is a far, far better way and meaning than my own, yet I can never make it mine; and I think that this is true of all the other lonely men that I have seen or known about—the nameless, voiceless, faceless atoms of this earth as well as Job and Everyman and Swift. And Christ himself, who preached the life of love, was yet as lonely as any man that ever lived. Yet I could not say that he was mistaken because he preached the life of love and fellowship, and lived and died in loneliness; nor would I dare assert his way was wrong because a billion men have since professed his way and never followed it.

I can only say that I could not make his way my own. For I have found the constant, everlasting weather of man's life to be, not love, but loneliness. Love itself is not the weather of our lives. It is the rare, the precious flower. Sometimes it is the flower that gives us life, that breaches the dark walls of all our loneliness and restores us to the fellowship of life, the family of the earth, the brotherhood of man. But sometimes love is the flower that brings us death; and from it we get pain and darkness; and the mutilations of the soul, the maddening of the brain, may be in it.

How or why or in what way the flower of love will come to us, whether with life or death, triumph or defeat, joy or madness, no man on this earth can say. But I know that at the end, forever at the end for us—the houseless, homeless, doorless, driven wanderers of life, the lonely men—there waits forever the dark visage of our comrade, Loneliness.

But the old refusals drop away, the old avowals stand—and we who were dead have risen, we who were lost are found again, and we who sold the talent, the passion, and belief of youth into the keeping of the fleshless dead, until our hearts were corrupted, our talent wasted, and our hope gone, have won our lives back bloodily, in solitude and darkness; and we know that things for us will be as they have been, and we see again, as we saw once, the image of the shining city. Far flung, and blazing into tiers of jeweled lights, it burns forever in our vision as we walk the Bridge, and strong tides are bound round it, and the great ships call. And we walk the Bridge, always we walk the Bridge alone with you, stern friend, the one to whom we speak, who never failed us. Hear:

"Loneliness forever and the earth again! Dark brother and stern friend, immortal face of darkness and of night, with whom the half part of my life was spent, and with whom I shall abide now till my death forever—what is there for me to fear as long as you are with me? Heroic friend, blood-brother of my life, dark face—have we not gone together down a million ways, have we not coursed together the great and furious avenues of night, have we not crossed the stormy seas alone, and known strange lands, and come again to walk the continent of night and listen to the silence of the earth? Have we not been brave and glorious when we were together, friend? Have we not known triumph, joy, and glory on this earth—and will it not be again with me as it was then, if you come back to me? Come to me, brother, in the watches of the night.

"Come to me in the secret and most silent heart of darkness. Come to me as you always came, bringing to me again the old invincible strength, the deathless hope, the triumphant joy and confidence that will storm the earth again."

The Lion at Morning

It was morning, shining morning, bright motes of morning in the month of May, when James awoke. An old man in a big room in a great house in the East Seventies near Central Park. A little, wiry, bright-eyed man in the great master's chamber of one of those lavish, fatly sumptuous, limestone-and-marble, mansard-roof, bastard-French-château atrocities which rich men were forever building for their wives forty or fifty years ago. But this was 1929, and shining morning in the month of May, when James awoke.

He awoke as he did everything, very cleanly, abruptly, and aggressively, with a kind of grim pugnacity. He would not fool with slumber: once he was done with sleep, he was done with it. He liked comfort and the best of everything, but he hated softness, sloth, and feeble indecision. There was a proper time and place for everything—a time for work; a time for sport, travel, pleasure, and society; a time for a good dinner, brandy, and a good cigar; and last of all, a time for sleep. James knew when the time for everything should be.

For when a thing was finished, it was finished. This applied to sleep as well as to every other useful, pleasant thing in life. He had discharged his debt to sleep and darkness for eight hours, now he was done with it. He paid sleep off as he would sign a check—cleanly, sharply, vigorously, with a final flourish of the pen—"Pay to the order of—Sleep . . . Eight—and no/100 hrs.—James Wyman, Sr." There you are, sir! You are satisfied, I hope? Good! The matter's settled! But, come now! No silly business, if you please, of yawning sleepily, stretching out luxuriously, rolling over on your other side, and mumbling some damned nonsense about "just five minutes more," or some such stuff as that! And none of this business of pulling cobwebs from your brain, getting your eyes unglued, brushing the filaments of sleep away, trying to wake up, come out of it, remember where you are! No! Wake up at once! Come out of it cleanly! Be done with it the moment your eyes are open! Get up and go about your work—day's beginning, night is over, sleep-time's done!

James awoke like this. He was a small and wiry figure of a man, aged seventy-four, with a cold fighter's face. It was not a hard face, in no respect a brutal, savage, or distempered face—no, on the whole it was a rather

499

pleasant face, certainly a very decisive face, and just as certainly a fighting face.

The face was very bright, and had a brisk, sharp, and rather frosty look. The eyes were very blue, frosty looking, and as cold and straight as steel. The hair was white and close-cropped, likewise the mustache. The nose was long and cold and definite, the whole structure of the face slightly concave, the straight, grim mouth touched faintly at the edges with the eternal suggestion of a grin—a grin that was good-humored enough, but also straight, hard, cold, naturally truculent. It was the face of a man who hated fear and despised those who were afraid, which could respect another face that looked right back at it and told it to go to hell, and feel contempt for the face that trembled and the eye that shifted from its own cold steel; a face which could be savage, ruthless, merciless to what it hated and despised, and gravely generous, loyal, and devoted to what it liked; a face which could be intolerant, arrogant, insensitive, and occasionally unjust; but a face which could not be mean.

James lay awake for a moment with his cold blue eyes wide awake and staring at the ceiling. Then he looked at his watch. It lacked only a few minutes of eight o'clock, his invariable time for rising every morning in the city for the past fifty years. In the country, save for Sundays, he rose one hour and fifteen minutes earlier. He fumbled in the bosom of his nightshirt, and scratched himself hairily and reflectively. He had worn a nightshirt all his life, as his father had before him, and as any sensible man would do. He had enough of the discomforts of clothing during the business day. When he went to bed, he wasn't going to put on a damned monkey suit with bright green stripes all over it, rope himself in around the belly like a sack of meal, and incase his legs in trousers. No! The place to wear pants was on the street and in the office. When he went to bed, he wanted all the free space he could get for his legs and belly.

He swung to a sitting position, worked his toes into his bedroom slippers, got up, walked across the room, and stood looking out the window at the street. For a moment he felt giddy: the clear mind reeled a little, the knees felt weak, he shook his head impatiently, and breathed deep; pushed the heavy corded curtains as far back as they could go, opened the window wider. His heart was pumping hard; the thin, grim smile around the firm mouth deepened. Seventy-four! Well, then—what? And for a moment, still holding to the heavy curtain with the veined old hand, he stood looking out into the street. Few people were about and stirring. Across the street, in a big limestone-and-marble mansion similar to his own, a housemaid on her knees was mopping marble steps. A rickety-looking wagon drawn by a shaggy little horse went rattling by. Six doors away a taxi drilled past in the early morning of Fifth Avenue; and, beyond, old James could see the trees and shrubs of Central Park just greening into May. Here in his own street, before the ugly, lavish houses, there were a few trees, all spangled with young green. Bright, shining morning slanted on the house fronts of the street, and from the tender, living green of the young trees the bird song rose.

A fine morning, then, and from nature, May, and sunlight it borrowed a too pleasant coloring, James thought, for such a damned ugly street. It was a typical street of the rich in the East Seventies—a hodgepodge of pretentious architecture. The starkly bleak and solid ugliness of brownstone fronts was interrupted here and there by lavish bastard-French châteaux like his, and in the middle of the block by the pale salmon brick facade, the fashionable flat front, and the green canopy of a new apartment house.

He turned, still smiling grimly. Out in the hall the deep-toned grandfather clock was striking eight through the morning's quietness, and on the last stroke the handle of the great walnut door was turned; his valet entered.

The man said, "Good morning, sir," in a quiet tone. James grunted "Morning" in reply, and without another word walked across the room into the bathroom, and after a moment flushed the toilet noisily, then washed his hands in the old streaked-marble basin, turned the tumbling water on full blast into the big old-fashioned ivory-yellow tub, and while the tub filled, surveyed himself in the mirror, craning his neck, and rubbing his hand reflectively across the wiry gray stubble of his beard. He got his shaving things out of the cabinet and set them in readiness, stropped his old straight razor vigorously, and with an air of satisfaction tested its deadly whetted blade, laid his razor down beside the other shaving things, turned off the water, stripped the nightshirt off over his head, stepped into the tub, and let himself down gingerly and with an easeful grunt into the water.

It took him four minutes to bathe and dry himself, and just six more to lather his face, crane cautiously, and shave the tough gray stubble of his beard as smooth as grained wood. By the time he had finished, cleaned his old, worn razor with tender pride, and put his shaving things away again, it was eight ten.

As he re-entered his bedroom in his dressing gown, the servant had just finished laying out his clothes. From the old walnut dresser or bureau, the man had taken socks, fresh underwear, a clean shirt, cuff-links, and a collar; and from the huge old walnut wardrobe a suit of dark clothes, a black necktie, and a pair of shoes. James would have none of "this new-fangled furniture" in his room. By this he meant that he would have neither the modern styles of recent years, nor the passionately revived colonial. His bedroom was furnished with massive Victorian pieces that had come from his father's bedroom many years before. The high and hideous old dresser, or bureau, had a tall mirror with a carved, towering, cornice-like frame of wood, and a slab of gray-streaked marble, indented and sunk between some little box-like drawers (God knows what these were for, but probably for collar buttons, shirt studs, cuff links, collars, and what he called "thing-ma-jigs"); below were some ponderous walnut drawers with brass knobs, which held his shirts, socks, underwear, and nightshirts. The huge walnut wardrobe was at least ten feet tall; and there was a monstrous walnut table with thick curved legs and a top of the same hideous gray-streaked marble that the bureau had.

James crossed the room to the chair beside the bed, threw off his dressing gown, and grunting a little and holding onto the man with one hand for support, thrust first one wiry shank, and then the other, into a pair of long, half-weight flannel drawers, buttoned a light flannel undershirt across his hairy chest, put on his white starched shirt and buttoned it, got the starched cuffs linked together, and looked around for his trousers, which the man was holding for him, when he changed his mind suddenly, and said:

"Wait a minute! Where's that gray suit—the one I got last year? I think I'll wear it today."

The valet's eyes were startled, his quiet voice touched just traceably with surprise.

"The *gray*, sir?"

"I said gray, didn't I?" said James grimly, and looked at him with a naked challenge of the cold blue eyes.

"Very well, sir," the man said quietly; but for a moment their eyes met, and although the face of each was grave, and that of James a trifle grim and truculent, there was also a sharp enkindled twinkle in the eyes of each, a kind of "tickled" quality that would not speak because there was no need to speak.

Gravely, imperturbably, the man went to the doors of the great walnut wardrobe, opened them, and took out a neat, double-breasted suit of light gray—a decidedly gay and skittish suit for James, whose apparel was habitually dark and sober. Still imperturbable, the man came back, laid out the coat, held out the trousers to his master, and gravely held the trouser ends as James grunted and thrust gingerly into them. The servant did not speak again until James had hitched his braces over his square shoulder and was buttoning up the neat buttons of the vest.

"And the necktie, sir?" the man inquired. "You will not be wearing the dark one now, I suppose."

"No," said James, hesitated for a moment, then looked the man pugnaciously in the eye and said: "Give me a light one—something that goes with this suit of clothes, something gay."

"Yes, sir," the man answered calmly; and again their eyes met, their faces grave and stern, but in their eyes again the sly, enkindled twinkle of their recognition.

It was not until James was carefully knotting under his wing collar a distinctly fashionable cravat of light spring gray, slashed smartly with black stripes, that the man found occasion to say smoothly:

"It's a fine morning, isn't it, sir?"

"It is! Yes, sir!" said James firmly and grimly, and looked at his servant truculently again; but again there was the enkindled sparkle in their eyes, and the man was smiling quietly behind his master's back as James marched sprucely from his chamber.

Outside the master's door the hall was dark and heavy, cushioned to the tread, still with silence, sleep, and morning, filled with walnut light and the slow ticking of the clock.

James glanced toward the door of his wife's chamber. The huge walnut door was also eloquent with silence, deep, inviolable repose. He smiled grimly and went down lavish marble stairs. They swept down with magnificence: the ghostly feet of memory and old event thronged on them—the rustle of silk and satin and the gleam of naked shoulders, proud tiaras, bustles, dog collars of hard diamonds, ropes of pearls.

He smiled grimly to himself and with displeasure. Damned old barn! From the great reception hall at the bottom he looked in at the lush magnificence of the huge salon: at the red carpet, velvet to the tread; at the fat red plush chairs with gold backs and gilded arms; at the straight, flimsy, ugly, brutally uncomfortable little chairs of gold, with faded coverings of silk; at the huge mirrors with gilt frames, also a little faded; at the French clock, a mass of fat gilt cupids, gewgaws, "thing-ma-jigs"; at the damned ugly tables, cabinets, glass cases, all loaded down with more thing-ma-jigs, gewgaws, china figures, vases, fat gilt cupids. Junk!

Well, this was what they wanted forty years ago—what they thought they wanted, anyway—what the women wanted—what she wanted. He had let her have it! He had always hated it. He had said often and grimly that the only comfortable room in the whole damned place was his bathroom; the only easy chair was the stool. They had tried to change that a year ago; he wouldn't let them!

As for the rest of it, it was no home. It was a kind of rigid mausoleum for what people used to call "Society." It had been built for that purpose forty years ago, when people went in for that kind of thing, and when everyone was trying to outdo his neighbor in ugliness, vulgarity, lavish pretentiousness—in strident costliness, blind waste, and arrogant expense.

As such, no doubt, it had served its purpose well! It had cost him a quarter of a million dollars, but he doubted if he'd get a hundred thousand if he put it on the block tomorrow. You couldn't even keep the damned barn warm! And now? And for the future? Well, *she* would outlive him. The Parrotts always lived longer than the Wymans. What would happen? He didn't have to die and go to heaven to find out the answer to that one! She'd try to swing it for a while, then she'd find out! It'd be her money then, she'd run the show, and she'd find out! She'd give a reception or two, attempt a party in the old grand manner, try to revive dog-collardom—and find out dog-collardom was dead forever!

She'd get a few old hags, their skinny necks and bony arms encrusted with their jewelry; a few doddering old fools creaking at the joints and lisping through their artificial teeth—all trying to revive the ghostly pomps of Mrs. Astor! She'd get a few furiously bored young people, there at grandma's imperative command, wondering when in God's name the ghastly business would be over, when they could decently escape from the Morgue and flee to glittering spots of music, dancing, noise, and alcohol—and she'd find out!

Grimly, he fancied he could already hear her anguished screech when bills came in and she discovered what it cost, discovered further that it was her money she was spending now, and that money didn't grow on trees—or if it did, it was her own tree now, the *Parrott* tree.

That made a difference, didn't it? For the Parrotts, he reflected grimly, were known for their tender solicitude where their own tree was concerned—whether it was a family tree or a money tree. Her father—damned old fool!—had spent the last twenty years of his life writing a single book. And what a book! *The Beginnings of the New England Tradition: A History of the Parrott Family.* Great God, had anyone ever heard such conceited bilge as that since time began! And he, James Wyman, Sr.—had had trouble to persuade one of his publishing acquaintances to print the damned thing; and then he had to endure the jibes, the digs, the witticisms of all his friends at the club—or else listen to the Parrott screech. Of the two evils he had taken, he thought, the lesser one. Swift ridicule, he had concluded, was better than slow torture; a silly book is soon forgotten, but a woman's tongue cannot be stilled.

Well, *she'd* find out, he thought, and grimly paused upon the marble flags of the reception hall, and grimly stared into the faded splendors of the great salon. He thought he foresaw the anguished progress of events already: the screech of pained astonishment when she saw the bills—the bills for coal alone—those ten-ton truck loads, barge loads, train loads of black coal required just to keep the grave-damp chill of this damned tomb reduced to a degree of semi-frigidness from October until May. And the caretakers, the nightwatchmen, the housekeepers, and so on, required to keep it guarded, watched and mended, dusted off—from May until October—when the family was away! As if anyone was going to walk off with the damned thing! Oh, if someone only would!—if a parliament of public-spirited second-story men, yeggmen, dynamiters, roof-and-cellar men, elegant silk-hatted Raffleses, and plain common-garden burglars in secret session assembled would only, in their large benevolence of soul, agree to enter, search, seize, and take away everything they could lay their hands on while the family was out of town: if they would only turn up before the barn at night in five-ton trucks, armored motor cars, swift sedans: if they would only come with any vehicle they had—wheelbarrows, furniture vans, or covered wagons—and walk out with every bit of junk in sight—all the damned plush chairs, and gilt French clocks; all of the vases, statuettes, and figurines; all of the painted china, crimson carpets, agonizing chairs, and hideous tables; all of the gewgaws and thing-ma-jigs, the imposing sets of unread books and the bad portraits of the ancestors, including the atrocious one of Parrott, Sr., author of *The Beginnings of the New England Tradition*—the old fool!—and while they were about it, also overpower, gag, chloroform, and spirit away into oblivion all of the caretakers, housekeepers, nightwatchmen, and—

"Breakfast is served, sir."

At the soft, the whispered, the oh-most-elegant, refined and sugared tones, James started. As if shocked with an electric current, he turned and stared grimly into the unctuous, oily visage of his butler, Mr. Warren.

—And yes! above all, and by all means, if some kindhearted gang of kidnapers would only remove out of his hearing, sight, and memory forever the pompous person and the odious presence of Old Sugarlips—

"Coming," James said curtly.

"Very good, sir," Sugarlips replied with maddening unctuousness. Then the butler turned solemnly and departed down the hall—departed with the pompous waddle of his big, fat buttocks, his bulging and obscenely sensual calves; departed like the disgusting fat old woman that he was, with his oily face and his fat lips set in an expression of simpering propriety—

—Oh, if only Sugarlips would depart for good! If only noblehearted kidnapers would do their merciful work! If only he—James Wyman, Sr.,—could somehow free himself from Sugarlips, somehow detach this fat Old Woman of the Sea from his life, so that he could enjoy a moment's peace and privacy in his own house without being told that something was "Very good, sir," enjoy a moment's rest and relaxation without Sugarlips "Begging your pardon, sir," sit down at his own table to feed himself in his own way without feeling Sugarlips' damned moist breath upon his neck, eat as he chose and what he chose and help himself the way he chose without having every movement censured by the interrogation of that fishy eye, the infuriating assurance of "Allow me, sir."

If only he—James Wyman, Sr., free, white, and . . . seventy-four!—a free American citizen, by God!—could come and go the way he chose to come and go, sit where he wanted, eat as he wished to eat, do as he pleased and as a free man had a right to do—without having all the acts, engagements, and arrangements of his personal and most private life subjected to the constant supervision of a fool! He was tired; he was ill, he knew; he was getting sour and crotchety—yes, he knew all this—but, Great God! Great God!—he was an old man, and he wanted to be left alone! He'd seen and known it all, now—he'd tried all the arguments, found all the answers, done all the things he should have done—that the world of his time, his wife, his family, and society, had expected of him—even *this*—and Great God! why had he done them? Was it worth it? He stared in again among the splendors of the great salon, and for a moment his cold blue eyes were clouded by the shade of baffled doubt. He had wanted a home to live in, hadn't he?—a place of warmth, of light, a dwelling place of love and deep security—he had all the means of getting it, hadn't he?—wealth, courage, character, and intelligence—and he had come to this? Somewhere, somehow, he had missed out in life, something had been put over on him. But where? And how? How and where had he failed?

He had been one of the conspicuous men of his time and generation—conspicuous not alone for his material achievements, but conspicuous for character, honesty, integrity, and fair-dealing in the world of money-getting, pirate-hearted, and red-handed Yankeedom. Of all the men of that time and generation, he was among the first. There were great names in America today—names great for wealth, power, for ruthlessness, for their stupendous aggrandizements. And he knew the way most of those names were tainted with dishonor, those names of men who had so ruthlessly exploited life, destroyed their fellows, betrayed mankind and their own country. Those names, he knew, would be a stench in the nostrils of future generations, a shame and a disgrace to the unfortunate children and grandchildren who would have to acknowledge them; and from this shameful taint he knew that his own name was triumphantly secure. And yet something had gone wrong. Where? How?

He was no whiner; he was a brave man and a fighter; and he knew that wherever lay the fault, the fault, dear Brutus, lay not in his stars, but in himself! But (James stared grimly in among the faded splendors of the great salon) his life had come to *this!* And why? Why? Why?

Had all gone ill, then? By no means! There had been high effort, great accomplishment. There had been true friendship; rooted deep affection: the confident regard of kings and Presidents, statesmen, men of letters, great industrialists, other leading bankers and financiers like himself.

He had yielded to no man to his own dishonor; he had yielded to many with fair dealing, generous concession, unresentful pardon. He had fought hardest when the odds were all against him, but he had eased pressure when he was on top; he had not withheld the stroke in battle, but he had not exulted over a fallen foe.

No, the slate was clean, the mirror was unclouded—yet, he had come to this. An old man, living with an old wife, in an old graveyard of a house—alone.

Old James looked in upon the faded gilt of morning with a baffled eye. Where had it gone to, then—all the passion and the fire of youth, and the proud singing; all of the faith, the clean belief of fifty years ago? Where had it gone to, then—the strength, the faith, the wisdom, the sound health and substance of his lost America? Had it only been a dream, then? No, it was no dream—"for he lay broad awaking"—or, if dream, then such a dream as men have lived a million years to dream—to hope for—to achieve. But where now?

Gone—all gone—gone like phantasmal images of smoke, the shining bright reality of that deathless dream submerged in ruin. In the great world all around him now he saw black chaos exploding into unpurposeful and blatant power: confusion swarming through the earth, the howling jargons of a million tongues, each one dissimilar, none speaking to another; brute corruption crowned with glory, privilege enthroned. Where once there had been the patient hard confusion of honest doubt, the worried perturbation of strong faith, was now the vile smirk of a passive acceptance, the cheap sneer of the weakling lip, the feeble gibe of the ignoble vanquished, gibing their own treason and their lack of faith, the fattied heart no longer sound enough for battle, the clouded and beclamored mind no longer clear enough for truth, the bleared eye murked with rotten mockeries. The thin venom of the tongues just sneered and said, "Well, what are you going to do about it?"—and so were lost, all joined together in the corrupt defenses of their shame and cowardice—all kneeling basely at the feet of their own traitors, all bent in obscene reverence before their own monsters, all yielding, all submissive to the gods of money getting and of mockery, all bent forward to kiss the dyer's bloody hand subdued to its own dye. So was his lost America rotted out. Gone, now, the faith of youth, the morning and the passion: the gold, the singing, and the dream—all vanished like phantasmal smoke, and come to this!

And *from* this, too! For had he not sold out somewhere along the line? But where? Where? The *hour,* the *moment,* and the actual point of *crisis*—where?

Had not he who was James Wyman fifty years ago—young and brave and an American who had the faith, and felt the strength and heard the singing, who had seen the plains, the rivers, and the mountains, the quiet blueness in a farmhand's eyes, and had heard the voices in the darkness talking, known how the land went, and the shapes of things, and known, too, that the dream was something more than dream, the great hope something more than hope—had not he, James Wyman, who had seen and heard and felt and known all these things, as all men in this land have known them—had he not sold out somewhere down the line? taken what the others had to give?—believed what others had to say?—accepted what they had to offer? And what was that? Dog-collardom, vulgarity, and empty show, the hypocrisies and shrill pretenses of a clown-like aristocracy, the swinish gluttonies of last year's hog all varnished over with this year's coat of arms, the no-questions-asked philosophy of money-sewerdom, proud noses lifted with refined disdain at uncouth table manners, but not too nice or dainty to appraise with charity the full, rich droppings of a scoundrel's bank account.

Yes, he had so accepted, he had been so persuaded, he had so believed; or, so believing that he so believed, and so sold out somewhere, being young along the line—and so had come to this: an old man, living with an old wife, in an old graveyard of a house—alone.

And, looking grimly in upon the faded gilt of morning in the great salon, James reflected that not even morning entered here. No, nothing young and sweet and fresh and alive and shining could exist here. Even light, the crystal shining light of spring, of morning, and of May, was staled and deadened here. It forced its way in dustily, it thrust in through the reluctant folds of the plush curtains, it came in in mote-filled beams of dusty light, it was old and dead before it got here—like the plush, the gilt, the carpets, the chairs and tables, the gewgaws, bric-a-brac, and thing-ma-jigs—as musty, stale, and full of death as all the things it fell upon.

No, it was not like Morning, really, by the time it had forced its painful entrance in that room. Rather, James reflected grimly, it was like the Morning After—it was—it was—well, it was like After the Ball Is Over.

The whole house, he thought, is like After the Ball Is Over. It had always been like that. "After the Ball," he thought, would be an excellent name for the damned thing: that had always been the effect it had produced on him. It had never been a home, never a place to come back to at night, and find rest and peace and warmth and homeliness and comfort. No, it had always been the cold mausoleum of departed guests; a great, frigid, splendid, and completely lifeless temple to the memory of the glittering and fashionable parties which should have been given here last night, but which probably had not occurred.

Thus, the great house was haunted constantly by the haughty ghosts of stuffed-shirtdom and dog-collardom; but by the presences of living warmth, familiar usage, genial homeliness—never! The great marble steps with their magnificent sweep, the marble entrance hall, the great salon, always seemed to be congealing mournfully, fading again into a melancholy staleness, mustiness, and frigid loneliness after the rustling silks and satins, the blazing chandeliers, the refined and cultivated voices, the silvery laughter and the champagne bubbles, the dog collars, ropes of pearls, bare backs, stiff shirts, and glowing shoulders of last night's splendid gathering had departed.

All that was needed to complete the illusion was a corps of caterer's men—twenty or thirty swarthy little fellows in monkey suits marching in to clear up the litter of the party—the empty champagne glasses, salad dishes, the cigar butts; the ashes on the carpet, and the filaments of colored paper hanging from the chandeliers—tattered remnants of the ball.

James sighed a little, then turned brusquely and marched down the hall into the great dining room.

The dining room, too, was splendid and magnificent—cold, cold, cold—like eating in a tomb. The room was on the west side of the house: the morning sun had not yet entered here. The great table was a somber polished slab, the large buffet, resplendent as a coffin, set with massive plate.

At one end of the enormous table, a great high-backed chair, of carved and somber darkness, a big plate, a great heavy knife and fork and spoon, the slender elegance of a silver coffeepot, a fragile purity of cups and saucers, another plate domed richly with an enormous silver warming-cover, a glass of orange juice, and stiff, heavy, spotless napery.

James seated himself down there, a lonely little figure at the end of the enormous table—and surveyed the feast. First he looked at the glass of orange juice, raised it to his lips, shuddered, and set it down. Then, gingerly, he lifted the great silver warming-lid and peered beneath the cover: three thin brown slices of dry toast lay chastely on a big white plate. James let the silver cover fall with a large clatter. Sugarlips appeared. James poured black fluid from the coffeepot into his cup and tasted it: a slight convulsion twisted his firm mouth; he said:

"What is this stuff?"

"Coffee, sir," said Sugarlips.

"Coffee?" said James coldly.

"A new coffee, sir," breathed Sugarlips, "that has no caffeine in it."

James made no answer, but his cold blue eyes were bright and hard, and nodding toward the covered dish, he spoke coldly, tonelessly, as before:

"And this?"

"Your toast, sir," breathed Sugarlips moistly.

"*My* toast?" James inquired, in the same cold and unpersuaded tone.

"Yes, sir," breathed Sugarlips. "*Your* toast—dry toast, sir."

"Oh, no," said James grimly, "you're wrong there. It's not *my* toast—dry toast has never been *my* toast! . . . What's this?" he said with brutal suddenness, jerking his head toward the glass of orange juice.

"Your fruit juice, sir," breathed Sugarlips.

"Oh, no," said James, more cold and grim than ever. "It's not *my* fruit juice. You're wrong again! You never saw me drink it yet." For a moment he surveyed the butler with blue blazing eyes. Cold fury choked him. "Look here," he rasped suddenly, "what the hell's the meaning of all this? Where's my breakfast? You told me it was ready!"

"Begging your pardon, sir—" Sugarlips began, dilating his full lips moistly.

"'Begging my pardon,' hell!" cried James, and threw his napkin to the floor. "I don't want my pardon begged—I want my breakfast! Where is it?"

"Yes, sir," Sugarlips began, and moistened his full lips nervously, "but the doctor, sir—the diet he prescribed, sir! . . . It was the mistress's orders that you get it, sir."

"Whose breakfast is this, anyway?" said James, "mine or your mistress's?"

"Why, *yours,* sir," Sugarlips hastily agreed.

"Who's *eating* it," James went on brusquely. "Your mistress or me?"

"Why, you are, sir," said Sugarlips. "Of course, sir!"

"Then bring it to me!" shouted James. "At once! When I need anyone's help to tell me what I have to eat, I'll let you know!"

"Yes, sir," Sugarlips breathed, all of a twitter now. "Then you desire—"

"You know what I desire," James yelled. "I desire my breakfast! At once! Now! Right away! . . . The same breakfast that I always have! The breakfast that I've had for forty years! The breakfast that my father had before me! The breakfast that a working man has *got* to have—as it was in the beginning, is now, and ever shall be! Amen!" James shouted. "Namely, a dish of oatmeal, four slices of buttered toast, a plate of ham and eggs, and a pot of coffee—strong black *coffee—real* coffee!" James shouted. "Do you understand?"

"Y-y-yes, sir," stammered Sugarlips. "P-p-perfectly, sir."

"Then go and get it! . . . Have you got any real coffee in the house?" he demanded sharply.

"Of course, sir."

"Then bring it!" James cried, and struck the table. "At once! Now! . . . And hurry up with it! I'll be late to work as it is!" He picked up the folded pages of the *Times* beside his plate and opened it with a vicious rattle— "And take this slop away!" he barked, as an afterthought, indicating the rejected breakfast with a curt nod. "Do what you like with it—throw it down the sink—but take it away!" And he went back savagely to the crisp pages of the *Times* again.

The coffee came in, Sugarlips poured it, and James was just on the point of drinking it when something happened. He bent forward sharply, ready with the cup of real, right coffee almost to his lips, grunted suddenly with surprise, put the cup down sharply, and leaned forward with the paper tightly gripped in his two hands, reading intently. What he read—what caught and held his startled interest—ran as follows:

"ACTRESS SUES SUNDAY SCHOOL SUPERINTENDENT CLAIMING HEART BALM

"Notice of suit was filed yesterday before Mr. Justice McGonigle in an action for breach of promise brought by Mrs. Margaret Hall Davis, 37, against W. Wainwright Parsons, 58. Mr. Parsons is well known as the author of many books on religious subjects, and for the past fifteen years he has been Superintendent of the Church School at the fashionable Episcopal Church of St. Balthazar, whose vestrymen include such leading citizens of New York as Mr. James Wyman, Sr., the banker, and . . . "

Old James swore softly to himself at this linking of his own name with such a scandal. He skimmed swiftly through the list of his fellow vestrymen and read on avidly:

.   .   .

"Mr. Parsons could not be found last night at the University Club, where he lives. Officials at the club said he had occupied his rooms there until three days ago, when he departed, leaving no address. Members of the club, when questioned, expressed surprise when informed of Mrs. Davis's suit. Mr. Parsons, they said, was a bachelor of quiet habits, and no one had ever heard of his alleged connection with the actress.

"Mrs. Davis, interviewed at her Riverside Drive apartment, answered questions willingly. She is a comely blonde of mature charms, and was formerly, she said, a member of the Ziegfeld Follies, and later a performer on the musical-comedy stage. She said that she met the elderly Mr. Parsons two years ago, during a week-end at Atlantic City. Their friendship, she asserted, developed rapidly. Mr. Parsons proposed marriage to her, she claims, a year ago, but requested a postponement until New Year's Day, pleading business and financial difficulties and the illness of a member of his family as reasons for the delay. To this the pretty divorcee agreed, she says, and as a result of his ardent persuasions consented to a temporary alliance prior to their marriage. Since the first of last October, she asserted, they have occupied the Riverside Drive apartment jointly, and were known to the landlord and the other tenants of the building as 'Mr. and Mrs. Parsons.'

"As the time of their marriage approached, the woman alleges, Mr. Parsons pleaded further complications on his personal affairs, and asked for another postponement until Easter. To this she also agreed, still confident of the sincerity of his intentions. Early in March, however, he left the apartment, telling her he had been called to Boston on business, but would return in a few days. Since that time, she says, she has not seen him, and all efforts to communicate with him have been fruitless. The woman further asserts that, in reply to repeated letters from her, Mr. Parsons finally wrote her three weeks ago, stating it would now be impossible for him to fulfill his promise of marriage, and suggesting that 'for the good of all concerned, we call the whole thing off.'

"This, Mrs. Davis asserted, she is unwilling to do.

"'I loved Willy,' she declared, with tears in her eyes. 'God is my witness that I loved him with the deepest, purest love a woman ever had to give a man. And Willy loved me, loves me still. I know he does. I am *sure* of it! If you could only see the letters that he wrote me—I have dozens of them here'—she indicated a thick packet of letters on the table, tied with a pink ribbon—'the most passionate and romantic letters any lover ever wrote,' she declared. 'Willy was a wonderful lover—so gentle, so tender, so poetic— and always such a perfect gentleman! I cannot give him up!' she passionately declared. 'I *will* not! I love him still in spite of everything that has happened. I am willing to forgive all, forget all—if only he will come back to me.'

"The actress is suing for damages of one hundred thousand dollars. The firm of Hoggenheimer, Blaustein, Glutz, and Levy, of 111 Broadway, are her legal representatives.

"Mr. Parsons is well known for his books in the religious field. According to *Who's Who,* he was born in Lima, Ohio, April 19, 1871, the son of the Reverend Samuel Abner Parsons, and the late Martha Elizabeth Bushmiller Parsons. Educated at DePauw University, and later at the Union Theological Seminary, he was himself ordained to the ministry in 1897, and during the next ten years filled successive pulpits in Fort Wayne, Indiana, Pottstown, Pennsylvania, and Elizabeth, New Jersey. In 1907, he retired from the ministry to devote his entire time to literary activity. Always a prolific writer, and gifted with a facile pen, his success in this field was rapid. He is the author of more than a score of books on devotional subjects, several of which have run through repeated editions, and one of which, a travel book, 'Afoot in the Holy Land,' enjoyed a tremendous sale, not only in this country but abroad. Some of his other works, according to *Who's Who,* are as follows:

"'Following After the Master' (1907); 'Almost Thou Persuadest Me' (1908); 'Job's Comforters' (1909); 'Who Follows in His Train' (1910); 'For They Shall See God' (1912); 'Jordan and the Marne' (1915); 'Armageddon and Verdun' (1917); 'Christianity and the Fuller Life' (1921); 'The Way of Temptation' (1927); 'The Song of Solomon' (1927); 'Behold, He Cometh' (1928)."

James saw the item just as he had been bending forward to sip his coffee. The name of W. Wainwright Parsons leaped out at him and hit him in the eye. Down went the cup of coffee with a bang. James read on. It was not reading so much as a kind of lightning-like absorption. He tore through the column, ripping splintered fragments from the thing—all he needed!—until he had it clear and blazing in his mind. Then for a moment, after he had finished, he sat completely motionless, with a look of utter stupefaction on his face. Finally he raised the outspread paper in both hands, banged it down emphatically on the table, leaned back in his great chair, stared straight and far and viewlessly across the enormous polished vista of the table, and said slowly and with emphasis:

"I'll-be-damned!"

Just then Sugarlips came in with the oatmeal, smoking hot, and slid it unctuously before him. James dashed thick cream all over it, spread sugar with a copious spoon, and dug in savagely. At the third mouthful he paused again, picked up the paper in one old hand and stared at it, flung it down with an impatient growl, took another mouthful of hot oatmeal, couldn't keep away from the accursed paper—took it finally and propped it up against the coffeepot with the accusing article staring blank and square in his cold eye, and then re-read it slowly, carefully, precisely, word for word and comma for comma, and between mouthfuls of hot oatmeal let out a running commentary of low-muttered growls:

" 'I loved Willy—' "

"Why, the damned—"

" 'Willy was a wonderful lover—so gentle, so tender, so poetic—' "

"Why—that damned mealy-mouthed, butter-lipped, two-faced—!"

" 'Mr. Parsons is well known as the author of many books on religious subjects—' "

James dug savagely into the oatmeal and swallowed. " 'Religious subjects'! Bah!"

" 'Superintendent . . . Church School . . . fashionable Episcopal Church of St. Balthazar . . . whose vestrymen include . . . Mr. James Wyman, Sr.' "

James groaned, picked up the offending paper, folded it, and banged it down with the story out of sight. The ham and eggs had come, and he ate savagely, in a preoccupied silence, broken by an occasional angry growl. When he got up to go, he had composed himself, but his bright blue eyes were as hard and cold as glacial ice, and the suggestion of a faint grim grin about the edges of his mouth was sharper, finer, more deadly than it had ever been before.

He looked at the paper, growled impatiently, started for the door, paused, turned round, looked back, came back growling, picked up the paper, thrust it angrily into his pocket, and marched down the enormous hall. He paused at the entrance, took a derby hat, and placed it firmly, a trifle jauntily, and at an angle on his well-shaped head, stepped down and opened the enormous front door, went out and down the street at a brisk pace, turned left, and so into Fifth Avenue.

To one side, the Park and the young greening trees; in the roadway, the traffic beginning to thicken and drill past; everywhere, people thronging and hurrying; directly ahead, the frontal blaze and cliff of the terrific city, and morning, shining morning, on the tall towers—while an old man with cold blazing eyes went sprucely swinging through the canyoned slant, muttering to himself:

—" 'Following After the Master'—*Bah!*"

—" 'Almost Thou Persuadest Me'—*Bah!*"

—" 'The Way of Temptation' "—

Suddenly he whipped the folded newspaper out of his pocket, turned it over, and peered intently at the story again. The faint grim grin around the edges of his mouth relaxed a little.

—" 'The Song of Solomon' "—

The grin spread over his face, suffusing it with color, and his old eyes twinkled as, still peering intently, he re-read the last line of the story.

—" 'Behold, He Cometh' "—

With a jaunty motion he slapped the folded paper against his thigh, and chuckling to himself with a full return of his good humor, he muttered:

"By God! I didn't know he had it in him!"

The Plumed Knight

Theodore Joyner was old William Joyner's youngest son. As so often happens with the younger children of a self-made man, he got more education than the others. "And," said his older brother Zachariah whenever the fact was mentioned, "just *look* at him!" For mingled with the Joyner reverence for learning, there was an equally hearty contempt among them for those who could not use it for some practical end.

Like his two more able brothers, Theodore had been destined for the law. He followed them to Pine Rock College and had his year of legal training. Then he "took the bar," and failed ingloriously; tried and failed again; and—

"Hell!" old William said disgustedly—"hit looked like he wa'nt fit fer nothin' else, so I jest sent him back to school!"

The result was that Theodore returned to Pine Rock for three years more, and finally succeeded in taking his diploma and bachelor's degree.

Schoolmastering was the trade he turned to now, and, Libya Hill having grown and there being some demand for higher learning, he set up for a "Professor." He "scratched about" among the people he knew—which was everyone, of course—and got twenty or thirty pupils at the start. The tuition was fifteen dollars for the term, which was five months; and he taught them in a frame church.

After a while "'Fessor Joyner's School" grew to such enlargement that Theodore had to move to bigger quarters. His father let him have the hill he owned across the river two miles west of town, and here Theodore built a frame house to live in and another wooden building to serve as a dormitory and classroom. The eminence on which the new school stood had always been known as Hogwart Heights. Theodore did not like the inelegant sound of that, so he rechristened it Joyner Heights, and the school, as befitted its new grandeur, was now named the Joyner Heights Academy. The people in the town, however, went on calling the hill Hogwart as they had always done, and to Theodore's intense chagrin they even dubbed the academy Hogwart, too.

In spite of this handicap the school prospered in its modest way. It was by no means a flourishing institution, but as people said, it was a good thing for Theodore. He could not have earned his living at anything else, and the

514

school at least gave him a livelihood. The years passed uneventfully, and Theodore seemed settled forever.

Then, three years before the outbreak of the Civil War, a startling change occurred. By that time the fever of the approaching conflict was already sweeping through the South, and that fact gave Theodore his great opportunity. He seized it eagerly, and overnight transformed his school into the Joyner Heights *Military* Academy. By this simple expedient he jumped his enrollment from sixty to eighty, and—more important—transmogrified himself from a rustic pedagogue into a military man.

So much is true, so cannot be denied—although Zachariah, in his ribald way, was forever belittling Theodore and his accomplishments. On Zachariah's side it must be admitted that Theodore loved a uniform a good deal better than he wore one; and that he, as Master, with the help of a single instructor who completed the school's faculty, undertook the work of military training, drill, and discipline with an easy confidence which, if not sublime, was rather staggering. But Zachariah *was* unjust.

"I have heard," Zachariah would say in later years, warming up to his subject and assuming the ponderously solemn air that always filled his circle of cronies with delighted anticipation of what was to come—"I have heard that fools rush in where angels fear to tread, but in the case of my brother Theodore, it would be more accurate to say that he *leaps* in where God Almighty crawls! . . . I have seen a good many remarkable examples of military chaos," he continued, "but I have never seen anything so remarkable as the spectacle of Theodore, assisted by a knock-kneed fellow with the itch, tripping over his sword and falling on his belly every time he tried to instruct twenty-seven pimply boys in the intricacies of squads right."

That was unfair. Not *all*, assuredly, were pimply, and there were more than twenty-seven.

"Theodore," Zack went on with the extravagance that characterized these lapses into humorous loquacity—"Theodore was so short that every time he —— he blew dust in his eyes; and the knock-kneed fellow with the itch was so tall that he had to lay down to let the moon go by. And somehow they got their uniforms mixed up, so that Theodore had the one that was meant for the knock-kneed fellow, and the knock-kneed fellow had on Theodore's. The trousers Theodore was wearing were so baggy they looked as if a nest of kangaroos had spent the last six months in them, and the knock-kneed fellow's pants were stretched so tight that he looked like a couple of long sausages. In addition to all this, Theodore had a head shaped like a balloon—and about the size of one. The knock-kneed fellow had a peanut for a head. And whoever had mixed up their uniforms had also got their hats exchanged. So every time Theodore reared back and bawled out a command, that small hat he was wearing would pop right off his head into the air, as if it had been shot from a gun. And when the knock-kneed fellow would repeat the order, the big hat he had on would fall down over his ears and eyes as if someone had thrown a bushel basket over his head, and he would come clawing his way out of it with a bewildered expression on his face, as if to say, 'Where the hell am I, anyway?' . . . They had a devil of a time getting those twenty-seven boys straightened up as straight as they could get—which is to say, about as straight as a row of crooked radishes. Then, when they were all lined up at attention, ready to go, the knock-kneed fellow would be taken with the itch. He'd shudder up and down, all over, as if someone had dropped a cold worm down his back; he'd twitch and wiggle, and suddenly he'd begin to scratch himself in the behind."

The truth of the matter is that the "pimply boys" drilled so hard and earnestly that the grass was beaten bare on the peaceful summit of Hogwart Heights. Uniforms and muskets of a haphazard sort had been provided for them, and all that could be accomplished by the pious reading of the drill manual and a dry history of Napoleonic strategy was done for them by Theodore and his knock-kneed brother in arms. And when war was declared in April 1861, the entire enrollment of the academy marched away to battle with Theodore at their head.

The trouble between Zachariah and Theodore afterward was that the war proved to be the great event in Theodore's life, and he never got over it. His existence had been empty and pointless enough before the war, and afterward, knowing there was nothing to live for that could possibly match the glories he had seen, he developed rather quickly into the professional warrior, the garrulous hero forever talking of past exploits. This is what annoyed Zachariah more and more as time went on, and he never let a chance go by to puncture Theodore's illusions of grandeur and to take him down a peg or two.

Theodore should have had a group photograph taken of himself. He should have been blocked out by Rubens, painted in his elemental colors by fourteen of Rubens' young men, had his whiskers done by Van Dyck, his light and shade by Rembrandt, his uniform by Velasquez; then if the whole thing had been gone over by Daumier, and touched up here and there with the satiric pencil of George Belcher, perhaps in the end you might have got a portrait that would reveal, in the colors of life itself, the august personage of Colonel Theodore Joyner, C.S.A.

Theodore rapidly became almost the stock type of the "Southern Colonel—plumed knight" kind of man. By 1870, he had developed a complete vocabulary and mythology of the war—"The Battle of the Clouds," Zachariah termed it. Nothing could be called by its right name. Theodore would never dream of using a plain or common word if he could find a fancy one. The Southern side of the war was always spoken of in a solemn whisper, mixed of phlegm and reverent hoarseness, as "Our Cause." The Confederate flag became "Our Holy Oriflamme—dyed in the royal purple of the heroes' blood." To listen to Theodore tell about the war, one would have thought it had been conducted by several hundred thousand knighted Galahads upon one side, engaged in a struggle to the death against several hundred million black-hearted rascals, the purpose of said war being the protection "of all that we hold most sacred—the purity of Southern womanhood."

The more completely Theodore emerged as the romantic embodiment of Southern Colonelcy, the more he also came to look the part. He had the great mane of warrior hair, getting grayer and more distinguished looking as the years went by; he had the bushy eyebrows, the grizzled mustache, and all the rest of it. In speech and tone and manner he was leonine. He moved his head exactly like an old lion, and growled like one, whenever he uttered such proud sentiments as these:

"Little did I dream, sir," he would begin—"little did I *dream,* when I marched out at the head of the Joyner Military Academy—of which the entire enrollment, sir—the *entire* enrollment had volunteered to a man—all boys in years, yet each breast beating with a hero's heart—one hundred and thirty-seven fine young men, sir—the flower of the South—all under nineteen years of age—think of it, sir!" he growled impressively—"one hundred and thirty-seven under nineteen!—"

"Now wait a minute, Theodore," Zachariah would interpose with a deceptive mildness. "I'm not questioning your veracity, but if my memory is not playing tricks, your facts and figures are a little off."

"What do you mean, sir?" growled Theodore, and peered at him suspiciously. "In what way?"

"Well," said Zachariah calmly, "I don't remember that the enrollment of the academy had risen to any such substantial proportions as you mention by the time the war broke out. One hundred and thirty-seven under nineteen?" he repeated. "Wouldn't you come closer to the truth if you said there were nineteen under one hundred and thirty-seven?"

"Sir—sir—" said Theodore, breathing heavily and leaning forward in his chair. "Why, you—Sir!" he spluttered, and then glared fiercely at his brother and could say no more.

To the credit of Theodore's lads, and to the honor of the times and Colonel Joyner's own veracity, let it be admitted here and now that whether there were nineteen or fifty or a hundred and thirty-seven of them, they did march out "to a man," and many of them did not return. For four years and more the grass grew thick and deep on Hogwart Heights: the school was closed, the doors were barred, the windows shuttered.

When the war was over and Theodore came home again, the hill, with its little cluster of buildings, was a desolate sight. The place just hung there stogged in weeds. A few stray cows jangled their melancholy bells and wrenched the coarse, cool grass beneath the oak trees, before the bolted doors. And so the old place stood and stayed for three years more, settling a little deeper into the forgetfulness of dilapidation.

The South was stunned and prostrate now, and Theodore himself was more stunned and prostrate than most of the men who came back from the war. The one bit of purpose he had found in life was swallowed up in the great defeat, and he had no other that could take its place. He did not know what to do with himself. Halfheartedly, he "took the bar" again, and for the third time failed. Then in 1869 he pulled himself together, and using money that his brothers loaned him, he repaired the school and opened it anew.

It was a gesture of futility, really—and a symptom of something that was happening all over the South in that bleak decade of poverty and reconstruction. The South lacked money for all the vital things, yet somehow, like other war-struck and war-ravaged communities before it, the South found funds to lay out in tin-soldierism. Pygmy West Points sprang up everywhere, with their attendant claptrap of "Send us the boy, and we'll return you the man." It was a pitiable spectacle to see a great region and a valiant people bedaubing itself with such gim-crack frills and tin-horn fopperies after it had been exhausted and laid waste by the very demon it was making obeisance to. It was as if a group of exhausted farmers, singed whiskers and lackluster eyes, had come staggering back from some tremendous conflagration that had burned their homes and barns and crops right to the ground, and then had bedecked themselves in outlandish garments and started banging on the village gong and crying out: "At last, brothers, we're all members of the fire department!"

Theodore took a new lease on life with the reopening of the Joyner Military Academy. When he first decided to restore the place, he thought he could resume his career at the point where the war had broken in upon it, and things would go on as if the war had never been. Then, as his plans took shape and he got more and more into the spirit of the enterprise, his attitude and feelings underwent a subtle change. As the great day for the reopening approached, he knew that it would not be just a resuming of his interrupted career. It would be much better than that. For the war was a heroic fact that could not be denied, and it now seemed to Theodore in some strange and transcendental way the South had been gloriously triumphant even in defeat, and that he himself had played a decisive part in bringing about this transcendental victory.

Theodore was no more consciously aware of the psychic processes by which he had arrived at this conclusion than were thousands of others all over the South who, at this same time, were coming to the same conclusion themselves. But once the attitude had crystallized and become accepted, it became the point of departure for a whole new rationale of life. Out of it grew a vast mythology of the war—a mythology so universally believed that to doubt its truth was worse than treason. In a curious way, the war became no longer a thing finished and done with, a thing to be put aside and forgotten as belonging to the buried past, but a dead fact recharged with a new vitality, and one to be cherished more dearly than life itself. The mythology to which this gave rise acquired in time the force of an almost supernatural sanction. It became a kind of folk-religion. And under its soothing, other-worldly spell, the South began to turn its face away from the hard and ugly realities of everyday living that confronted it on every hand, and escape into the soft dream of vanished glories—imagined glories—glories that had never been.

The first concrete manifestation of all this in Theodore was an inspiration that came to him as he lay in bed the night before the great day when the Joyner Military Academy was to reopen its doors. As he lay there, neither quite awake nor yet asleep, letting his mind shuttle back and forth between remembered exploits on the field of battle and the exciting event scheduled for the morrow, the two objects of his interest became fused: he felt that they were really one, and he saw the military school as belonging to the war, a part of it, a continuation and extension of it into the present, and on down through the long, dim vista of the future. Out of this there flowed instantly into his consciousness a sequence of ringing phrases that brought him as wide awake as the clanging of a bell, and he saw at once that he had invented a perfect slogan for his school. The next day he announced it at the formal convocation.

It is true that Theodore's slogan occasioned a good deal of mirth at his expense when it was repeated all over town with Zachariah's running commentary upon it. The father of one of the students was one of Zack's most intimate friends; this man had attended the convocation, and he told Zack all about it afterward.

"Theodore," this friend reported, "gave the boys a rousing new motto to live up to—earned, he said, by their predecessors on the glorious field of battle. Theodore made such a moving speech about it that he had all the mothers in tears. You never heard such a blubbering in your life. The chorus of snifflings and chokings and blowing of noses almost drowned Theodore out. It was most impressive."

"I don't doubt it," said Zack. "Theodore always did have an impressive manner. If he only had the gray matter that ought to go with it, he'd be a wonder. But what did he say? What was the motto?"

"*First at Manassas—*"

"First to eat, he means!" said Zachariah.

"*—fightingest at Antietam Creek—*"

"Yes, fightingest to see who could get back first across the creek!"

"*—and by far the farthest in the Wilderness.*"

"By God, he's right!" shouted Zachariah. "Too far, in fact, to be of any use to anyone! They thrashed around all night long, bawling like a herd of cattle and taking potshots at one another in the belief that they had come upon a company of Grant's infantry. They had to be gathered together and withdrawn from the line in order to prevent their total self-destruction. My brother Theodore," Zachariah went on with obvious relish, "is the only officer of my acquaintance who performed the remarkable feat of getting completely lost in an open field and ordering an attack upon his own position. . . . His wounds, of course, are honorable, as he himself will tell you on the slightest provocation—but he was shot in the behind. So far as I know, he is the only officer in the history of the Confederacy who possesses the distinction of having been shot in the seat of the pants by one of his own sharpshooters, while stealthily and craftily reconnoitering his own breastworks in search of any enemy who was at that time nine miles away and marching in the opposite direction!"

From this time on, the best description of Theodore is to say that he "grew" with his academy. The institution thrived in the nostalgic atmosphere that had made its resurrection possible in the first place, and Theodore himself became the personal embodiment of the post-war tradition, a kind of romantic vindication of rebellion, a whole regiment of plumed knights in his own person. And there can be no doubt whatever that he grew to believe it all himself.

According to the contemporary accounts, he had been anything but a prepossessing figure when he went off to war, and if any part of Zachariah's extravagant stories can be believed, anything but a master strategist of arms on the actual field of battle. But with the passage of the years he grew into his role, until at last, in his old age, he looked a perfect specimen of the grizzled warrior.

Long before that, people had stopped laughing at him. No one but Zachariah now dared to question publicly any of Theodore's pronouncements, and Zachariah's irreverence was tolerated only because he was considered to be a privileged person, above the common *mores*. Theodore was now held in universal respect. Thus the youngest of "the Joyner boys"—the one from whom the least had been expected—finally came into his own as a kind of sacred symbol.

In Libya Hill during those later years it was to be a familiar spectacle every Monday—the day when the "cadets" enjoyed their holiday in town— to see old Colonel Joyner being conveyed through the streets in an old victoria driven by an aged Negro in white gloves and a silk hat. The Colonel was always dressed in his old uniform of Confederate gray; he wore his battered old Confederate service hat, and, winter or summer, he was never seen without an old gray cape about his shoulders. He did not loll back among the faded leather cushions of the victoria: he sat bolt upright—and when he got too old to sit bolt upright under his own power, he used a cane to help him. He would ride through the streets, always sitting soldierly erect, gripping the head of his supporting cane with palsied hands, brown with the blotches of old age, and glowering out to left and right beneath bushy eyebrows of coarse white with kindling glances of his fierce old eyes, at the same time clenching his jaw firmly and working sternly at his lips beneath his close-cropped grizzled mustache. This may have been just the effect of his false teeth, but it suggested to awed little boys that he was uttering war-like epithets. That is what every inch of him seemed to imply, but actually he was only growling out such commands as "Go on, you scoundrel! Go on!" to his aged charioteer, or muttering with fierce scorn as he saw the slovenly posture of his own cadets lounging in drugstore doors.

"Not a whole man among 'em! Look at 'em now! A race of weaklings, hollow-chested and hump-backed—not made of the same stuff their fathers were—not like the crowd we were the day we all marched out to a man— the bravest of the brave, the flower of our youth and our young manhood! One hundred and thirty-seven under nineteen! Hrumph! Hrumph!—Get along, you scoundrel! Get along!"

The Newspaper

Time: A hot night in June 1916.

Scene: The city room of a small-town newspaper

The room has three or four flat-topped desks, typewriters, green-shaded lights hanging from the ceiling by long cords, some filing cabinets. Upon the wall, a large map of the United States. Upon the desks, newspaper clippings, sheets of yellow flimsy, paste pots, pencils, etc. Over all, a warm smell of ink, a not unpleasant air of use and weariness.

To the right, a door opening to a small room which houses the A.P. man, his typewriter, and his instruments. To the left, a glass partition and a door into the compositor's room. This door stands open, and the compositors may be seen at work before the linotype machines, which make a quiet slotting sound. The A.P. man's door is also open, and he can be seen within, typing rapidly, to the accompaniment of the clattering telegraph instrument on the table beside him.

In the outer room, Theodore Willis, a reporter, sits at his desk, banging away at a typewriter. He is about twenty-eight years old, consumptive, very dark of feature, with oval-shaped brown eyes, jet black hair, thin hands, and a face full of dark intelligence, quickness, humor, sensitivity. At another desk, his back toward Willis, sits another reporter—young, red-headed, red-necked, stocky—also typing. All of the men wear green eye-shades. Theodore Willis is smoking a cigarette, which hangs from the corner of his mouth and which he inhales from time to time, narrowing his eyes to keep the smoke out.

THE A.P. WIRE (*clattering rapidly*): . . . Wash June 18 Walter Johnson was invincible today held Athletics to four scattered hits Senators winning three to nothing batteries Washington Johnson and Ainsmith Philadelphia Bender Plank and Schalk.

(The telegraph instrument stops suddenly. The A.P man gets up, pulls a sheet from the machine, comes out in the city room, and tosses it on Theodore Willis's desk.)

THE A.P. MAN: Well, the big Swede was burning 'em in today.

WILLIS (*typing, without looking up*): Washington win?

THE A.P. MAN: Three-nothing.

WILLIS: How many did he fan?

522

A.P. MAN: Fourteen. (*He lights a cigarette and inhales.*) Christ! If he had a decent team behind him, he'd never lose a game.

(*Far off across the town, the screeching noise of Pretty Polly is heard, coming from the roof of the Appalachicola Hotel. She is a local character who for years has earned her living by singing in public places, and nobody ever calls her anything but Pretty Polly.*)

PRETTY POLLY (*singing away in the distance, and plainly audible to the last syllable*): . . . threels—mee-uh—and stuh-heels—mee-uh—and luh-hulls—mee-uh—to r-r-r-rest . . .

(*Benjamin Gant passes through the city room on way to compositors' room. Pauses a moment with lean fingers arched upon his hips, head cocked slightly in direction of the sound.*)

PRETTY POLLY (*as before, but fading away now*): . . . threels—mee-uh—and stuh-heels—mee-uh—and luh-hulls—mee-uh—to r-r-r-rest.

BEN GANT (*jerking his head up scornfully and speaking to some unknown auditor*): Oh for God's sake! Listen to that, won't you? (*He goes into the compositors' room.*)

A.P. MAN: Christ, what a voice!

WILLIS: Voice! That's not a voice! It's a distress signal! They ought to take her out to sea and anchor her off Sandy Hook as a warning to incoming liners.

(*Harry Tugman, the chief pressman, enters at this moment with a bundle tied in a newspaper under his arm. He is a powerful man, brutally built, with the neck, shoulders, and battered features of a prize fighter. His strong, pitted face is colorless, and pocked heavily with ink marks.*)

TUGMAN (*yelling as he enters*): Wow! Wouldn't that old battle-ax be something in a fog! She's hot tonight! Boy, she's goin' good! (*These remarks are addressed to no one in particular, but now he pauses beside the little group of reporters and speaks to them with abusive good nature.*) Hello, you lousy reporters. Is that lousy rag of yours ready to be run off yet?

WILLIS (*quietly, and without looking up*): Hello, you gin-swizzling sot. Yes, the lousy rag is ready to be run off, and so are you if the Old Man ever gets a whiff of that breath of yours. You'd better beat it downstairs now and get your press to rolling before he comes in and takes you for a brewery.

TUGMAN (*with riotous good nature*): Whew! That's it, Ted—give 'em hell! (*Boisterously*) Boys, I've been in a crap game, and I took 'em for a hundred and fifty bucks.

WILLIS: Which means you're a dollar and a quarter to the good, I suppose. (*Quietly, viciously*) A hundred and fifty bucks—why, God damn your drunken soul, you never saw that much money at one time in your whole life.

A.P. MAN: How much of it you got left, Tug?

TUGMAN: Not a lousy cent. They took me to the cleaners afterwards. Tell you how it was, boys. We was down at Chakales Pig. When I picked up the loot, I looked around and counted up the house and decided it was safe to buy a round of drinks, seein' as there was only five guys there. (*His manner grows more riotously extravagant as with coarse but eloquent improvisation he builds up the farce.*) Well, I goes up to the bar, thinkin' I'm safe, and says, "Step right up, gentlemen. This one's on me." And do you know what happens? (*He pauses a moment for dramatic effect.*) Well, boys, I ain't hardly got the words out of my mouth when there is a terrific crash of splintered glass and eighteen booze hounds bust in from the sidewalk, six more spring through the back windows, and the trap doors of the cellar come flyin' open and thirty-seven more swarm up like rats out of the lower depths. By that time the place is jammed. Then I hear the sirens goin' in the street, and before I know it, the village fire department comes plungin' in, followed by two-thirds of the local constabulary. I tries to crawl out between the legs of One-Eye McGloon and Silk McCarthy, but they have me cornered before I gets as far as the nearest spittoon. Well, to make a long story short, they rolled me for every nickel I had. Somebody got my socks and B.V. D.'s, and when I finally crawled to safety, Chakales had my shirt and told me he was holdin' it as security until I came through with the six bits I still owed him for the drinks.

(*Ben Gant returns from the compositors' room, and as he passes, Tugman slaps him violently on his bony back.*)

TUGMAN (*yelling boisterously*): How's that, Ben? Is that gettin' 'em told, or not?

BEN (*arching his hands upon his hips, sniffing scornfully, and jerking his head toward his unknown auditor*): Oh, for God's sake! Listen to this, won't you?

TUGMAN (*still boisterously*): Did I ever tell you boys about the time I came back from Scandinavia, where I'd been managin' Jack Johnson on a barn-stormin' tour?

WILLIS (*starting up suddenly, laughing, and seizing a paper weight*): Get out of here, you son-of-a-bitch. Scandinavia! You've never been north of Lynchburg. The last time you told that story it was South America.

TUGMAN (*laughing heartily*): That was another time. (*Loudly, immensely pleased with himself*): Whew! God-*damn!* Give 'em hell, boys!

WILLIS: On your way, bum. It's time to roll.

TUGMAN (*going out in high spirits, singing loudly a bawdy parody of Pretty Polly's song*): . . . sla-hays—mee-uh—and la-hays—mee-uh—and luh-hulls—mee-uh—to r-r-r-rest.

WILLIS (*now standing at his desk and reading a sheet of yellow flimsy with an air of growing stupefaction*): Well, I'll be—in the name of God, who wrote this, anyway? (*Reads*) "By this time the police had arrived and thrown a cordon around the blazing tenement in an effort to keep the milling throngs at a safe distance." (*With an air of frank amazement*) Well, I'll be God-damned! (*Suddenly, irritably, in a rasping voice*) Who wrote this crap? "Blazing tenement"—"milling throngs"—now ain't that nice? (*Reading again, slowly, deliberately*) "By—this—time—the—police—had—arrived—and—thrown—a—cordon—" . . . a—*cordon*—

RED (*the young reporter, whose neck and face during this recital has become redder than ever*): We always said "cordon" on the *Atlanta Constitution.*

WILLIS (*looking at him with an air of stunned disbelief*): Did you write this? Is this your story?

RED (*sulkily*): Who the hell do you think wrote it, the Angel Gabriel?

WILLIS (*with an air of frank defeat*): Well, I'll be damned! If that's not the damnedest description of a fire in Niggertown, I'll kiss a duck. (*With wicked insistence*) "Blazing tenement." What blazing tenement are you talking about—a two-roomed nigger shack in Valley Street? For Christ's sake, you'd think the whole East Side of New York was afire. And "milling throngs." Well, I'm a monkey's uncle if that ain't perfectly God-damned delightful! What do you mean by milling throngs—forty-two niggers and a couple of one-eyed mules? And "cordon." (*A trifle more emphatically*): "Cordon!" (*He holds the paper at arm's length and surveys it daintily, with a show of mincing reflection.*)

RED (*sulkily*): We always said "cordon" on the *Constitution.*

WILLIS: *Constitution,* my ass! If old man Matthews, John Ledbetter, and Captain Crane constitute a cordon, then I'm a whole God-damned regiment of United States Marines!

RED (*angrily*): All right, then. If you don't like the way the story's written, why the hell don't you write it yourself?

WILLIS: Why the hell should I? That's your job, not mine. Christ Almighty, man! I've got enough to do on my own hook without having to rewrite your whole damned story every time I send you out to cover a lousy little fire in Niggertown.

RED: That story would have gone on the *Constitution.* (*Sarcastically*) But apparently it's not good enough for a one-horse paper in a hick town. (*He pulls off his eye-shade and tosses it down upon the desk; puts on his vest and coat and begins to button himself up viciously.*) To hell with it, anyway! To hell with this whole damn outfit! I'm through with it! The trouble with you guys is that you're a bunch of illiterate half-wits who don't know anything about style and don't appreciate a piece of writing when you see one!

WILLIS: Style, hell! What I'd appreciate from you is a simple declarative sentence in the English language. If you've got to get all that fancy palaver out of your system, write it in your memory book. But for God's sake, don't expect to get it published in a newspaper.

RED (*savagely, tugging at his vest*): I'll get it published all right, and it won't be in your lousy paper, either!

WILLIS (*ironically, sitting down and adjusting his eye-shade*): No? Where are you going to get it published—in the *Woman's Home Companion?*

RED (*contemptuously*): You guys give me a pain. Wait till my book comes out. Wait till you read what the critics have to say about it.

WILLIS (*beginning to work on the unhappy story with a blue pencil*): Go on, go on. The suspense is awful. What are we going to do when we read it? Turn green with envy, I suppose?

RED (*wagging his head*): All right, all right. Have it your own way. Only you'll be laughing out the other corner of your mouth some day. You wait and see.

WILLIS (*working rapidly with the blue pencil and still speaking ironically, but in a more kindly tone than before*): Don't make us wait too long, Red. I've got only one lung left, you know. (*He coughs suddenly into a wadded handkerchief, stares intently for an instant at the small stain of spreading red, then thrusts the crumpled handkerchief back into his pocket.*)

RED (*flushing uncomfortably, suddenly moved*): Oh, well—(*eagerly*) Jesus, Ted, I've got a whale of an idea! If I can come through with this one, it'll knock 'em loose!

WILLIS (*a trifle absently, still working busily on the story*): What is it this time, Red—something hot? The love affairs of a police reporter, or something like that?

RED: Nah, nah. Nothing like that! It's a historical novel. It's about Lincoln.

WILLIS: Lincoln! You mean Abe?

RED (*nodding vigorously*): Sure! It's a romance—an adventure story. I've been working on the idea for years, and boy, it's a lulu if I can put it over! (*Looks around craftily toward the door to see if he is being overheard, lowers his voice carefully, with an insinuating tone*) Listen, Ted—

WILLIS (*absently*): Well?

RED (*in a tone of cunning secrecy*): If I let you in on the idea (*he peers around apprehensively again*), you won't tell anyone, will you?

WILLIS: You know me, Red. Did you ever hear of a newspaper reporter giving away a secret? All right, kid, spill it.

RED (*lowering his voice still more, to a confidential whisper*): The big idea is this. Lincoln—you know Lincoln—

WILLIS: Sure. You mean the guy that got shot.

RED: Sure. (*Then, cunningly, secretively*) Well, Ted, all the history books—all the big authorities and the wise guys—*they* tell you he was born in Kentucky—

WILLIS: And you mean to tell me he wasn't?

RED (*scornfully*): You're God-damn right he wasn't! Nah! (*Coming closer and whispering earnestly*) Why, Ted, that guy was no more born in Kentucky than you or I were. (*Nodding vigorously*) Sure. I'm telling you. I've got the dope—I know. (*Whispering impressively*) Why, Ted, that guy grew up right out here in Yancey County, not more than fifty miles from town.

WILLIS (*in a tone of mock astonishment*): Go on! You're kidding me!

RED (*very earnestly*): No I'm not. It's the truth, Ted! I know what I'm talking about. I've got the dope now—I've been working on the thing for years. (*He looks around cautiously again, then whispers*) And say, Ted, you know what else I've got? I've got a little dress that Lincoln wore when he was a baby. And say (*his voice sinking now to an awed whisper*), do you know what I found?

WILLIS (*working absently*): What was it, Red?

RED (*whispering*): They say, you know, that Lincoln's parents were poor—but that little baby dress is made of the finest lace! And Ted, it's all embroidered, too. It's got initials on it! (*His voice sinks to an almost inaudible whisper*) Ted, it's embroidered with the letter N. (*He pauses significantly to let this sink in, then repeats in a meaningful tone*) N, Ted. . . . N. . . . Do you get it?

WILLIS: Do I get what? N what?

RED (*impatiently*): N nothing. Just N, Ted. (*He pauses anxiously for this to sink in, but gets no response.*)

WILLIS (*after waiting a moment*): Well? What about it?

RED (*disappointedly, whispering*): Why, don't you see, Ted? Lincoln's name begins with an L, and this little dress I got is embroidered with the letter N. (*Again he waits for a satisfactory response and gets none.*) N, Ted. . . . N. . . . Don't you see?

WILLIS (*looking up a trifle impatiently and slapping his blue pencil down on the desk*): What are you driving at, Red? Spill it, for Christ's sake!

RED: Why, Ted, Lincoln's name begins with an L, and this little dress I got is embroidered with the letter—

WILLIS (*nodding wearily*): The letter N. Sure, I get you, Red. (*Picks up the pencil and resumes work again*) Well, maybe the laundry got the tags mixed.

RED (*in a disgusted tone*): Nah, Ted. (*Slowly, significantly*) N . . . N . . . (*Slyly*) Can't you think of anyone, Ted, whose name begins with N?

WILLIS (*Casually*): Napoleon Bonaparte.

RED (*patiently*): Nah-ah, Ted—that's not it—(*he looks around craftily again before he speaks, then whispers cunningly*) You're coming close, kid—you're getting hot.

WILLIS (*throwing down his pencil, pushing up his eye-shade, and settling back in his chair with an air of weary resignation*): Look here, what the hell are you trying to give me? Are you trying to hint that Lincoln was related to Napoleon?

RED (*glancing around, then in a cunning whisper*): No, Ted—not Napoleon. (*He looks craftily around again, then whispers*)—Marshal Ney. (*A look of triumphant satisfaction expands across his countenance, he nods his head in satisfied affirmal*) Sure! I'm telling you! Marshal Ney.

WILLIS (*staring at him with frank amazement*): Well, what the hell—you mean to tell me that Abraham Lincoln was Marshal Ney's son?

RED (*after glancing around craftily again, in a cunning whisper*): No, Ted—not his son—(*he glances around again before he lets it out*)—his grandson.

WILLIS (*appalled, staring helplessly*): Well, I'll be—

RED (*nodding vigorously*): Sure, sure, I'm telling you! (*He looks around again before he speaks*) You see, Ted, Marshal Ney didn't die in France. (*He peers craftily again before he whispers*) No one knows where he died. Except (*He peers slyly around again*) except me. I know. You see, it was like this— After the Battle of Waterloo, Marshal Ney escaped. He was never heard of again. No one knows what became of him. (*He looks around cautiously before he whispers*) But I found out. I got the dope. I've been working on the thing for years—I got it nailed down now. Marshal Ney escaped to this country, after the Battle of Waterloo, in a sailing ship.

WILLIS: In a sailing ship—(*in a tone of astounded disbelief*) Go on! You know a big man like that never would have taken a common sailing ship, Red. He'd at least have come over on a freighter. (*His sarcasm is wasted on his earnest communicant.*)

RED (*whispering earnestly*): Nah-ah, Ted. It was a sailing ship. I've got all the dope—the name of the ship, the captain, everything. And Marshal Ney escaped under an assumed name—he called himself Nye.

WILLIS (*astounded*): Go on, I don't believe you! Why hell, Red, you're thinking of Bill Nye—that's who it was. You got the two mixed up.

RED (*earnestly*): Nah-ah, Ted. I've got all the dope: it was Marshal Ney, all right. He landed at Baltimore and then came South. He settled near Salisbury—and he lived to be an old, old man. (*He looks around again cautiously before he whispers*) Why, hell, Ted! He died only about five years ago! He was way over a hundred when he died (*looking around again before he whispers*): And there's people down there, around Salisbury, who knew him! Do you get that, Ted? They knew him, they talked to him. And they say it was Marshal Ney all right. I got all the dope. And it was his son (*he looks around again before he reveals his last astonishing item of historical fact*), it was his son who came up here to Yancey County—and his son, his son, Ted— (*He looks around most cunningly now, in fact for a moment he seems about to investigate the doors, the spittoons, and the space beneath the tables*)—his son was Lincoln's father.

WILLIS (*lying sprawled in his chair as though he had collapsed, and with his thin hand upon the desk, his mouth slightly ajar, staring at his companion with paralyzed astonishment, and speaking very slowly*): Well—I'll—be—God — damned!

RED (*taking the words as tribute, beaming triumphantly*): Ain't it a lulu, boy? Ain't it a wham? Won't it knock 'em for a goal?

WILLIS (*waving his hand groggily before his face*): You win, kid. Pick up the marbles. You've got me licked.

RED (*exuberantly*): Boy, I've got the hit of the century here—the greatest story since *The Count of Monte Cristo!*

WILLIS (*feebly*): Don't stop at *Monte Cristo,* kid. You can go the whole way back to the Holy Bible as far as I'm concerned.

RED (*delighted, yet a trifle anxiously*): You won't say anything about it, Ted? You won't let it out?

WILLIS (*exhausted*): Not for the world and a cage of pet monkeys. (*He holds out a thin, limp hand.*) Put it there.

(*Red, his face crimson with happiness, seizes Theodore Willis's thin hand and wrings it heartily. And then, with a jubilant "Good night," he goes out. For a moment Willis sits quietly, in an exhausted attitude, then he opens his mouth and lets out a long sigh.*)

WILLIS: Whew-w!

THE A.P MAN (*coming to his door and peering out*): What is it?

WILLIS (*slowly shaking his head*): That wins the gold-enameled mustache cup. That guy!

A.P. MAN: What is it now—a new idea for a book he's going to write?

WILLIS: Yep—and he's got the whole idea nailed down, trussed up, and hog-tied. It's going to paralyze the public, upset history, and make the faculty at Harvard look like a set of boobs.

A.P. MAN: What is it? What's the idea?

WILLIS (*shaking his head solemnly*): That, sir, I can nevermore divulge. He has my promise, my word of honor. And the word of a Willis is as good as his bond—in fact, a damn sight better. Wild horses could not drag his secret from me. But I'll tell you this, my friend. If you should suddenly read absolute historic proof that Shakespeare had come over on the *Mayflower* and was the father of George Washington, you'd get some faint notion of what this book is going to do to us. (*He coughs suddenly, rackingly, spits carefully into his wadded handkerchief, looks intently at the small red stain, then, with an expression of weariness and disgust, thrusts the wadded rag back in his pocket.*) Christ! Maybe someday I'll write a book myself—about all the poor hams I've known in this game who were going to write a book—and never did. What a life!

(*The A.P. man shrugs and goes back into his little room. The telephone rings. With an expression of weariness Theodore Willis takes the receiver from the hook.*)

WILLIS: Hello. . . . Yes, this is the *Courier*. . . . (*in an agreeable tone that is belied by the expression of extreme boredom on his face*) Yes, Mrs. Purtle. Yes, of course. . . . Oh, yes, there's still time. . . . No, she's not here, but I'll see that it gets in. . . . Certainly, Mrs. Purtle. Oh, absolutely. . . . (*He rolls his dark eyes aloft with an expression of anguished entreaty to his Maker.*) Yes, indeed, I promise you. It will be in the morning edition. . . . Yes, I can well imagine how important it is. (*He indicates his understanding of its importance by scratching himself languidly on the hind quarter.*) . . . Oh, absolutely without fail. You can depend on it. . . . Yes, Mrs. Purtle. . . . (*He sprawls forward on one elbow, takes the moist fag end of a cigarette from his mouth and puts it in a tray, picks up a pencil, and wearily begins to take notes.*) Mr. and Mrs. S. Frederick Purtle. . . . No, I won't forget the S. . . . Yes, I know we had it Fred last time. We had a new man on the job. . . . No, we'll get it right this time. Mr. and Mrs. S. Frederick Purtle . . . dinner and bridge . . . tomorrow night at eight . . . at their residence, "Oaknook," 169 Woodbine Drive . . . in honor of—Now just a moment, Mrs. Purtle. I want to be sure to get this straight. (*Then, very slowly, with an expression of fine concern*) In honor of their house guest . . . Mrs. J. Skidmore Pratt, of Paterson, New Jersey, . . . the former Miss Annie Lou Bass of this city. (*Writing casually as he continues*) Those invited include Mr. and Mrs. Leroy Dingley . . . Mr. and Mrs. E. Seth Hooten . . . Mr. and Mrs. Claude Belcher . . . Mr. Nemo McMurdie . . . all of this city . . . and Miss May Belle Buckmaster of Florence, South Carolina. . . . Now, just a moment, Mrs. Purtle, to see if I've got it all straight. (*He reads it over to her. The lady is apparently satisfied, for at length he says*) Oh, absolutely. No, I won't forget. . . . Not at all, Mrs. Purtle. (*He laughs falsely.*) Delighted, of course. . . . Good-bye.

(*He hangs up the receiver, lights a cigarette, inserts a fresh sheet in the typewriter, and begins to type it out. The A.P. man comes out chuckling with a piece of paper in his hand.*)

A.P. MAN: Here's a hot one. Fellow out in Kansas has made himself a pair of wings and sent word around to all the neighbors that tomorrow's to be the last day of the world and he's going to take off for the Promised Land at four o'clock. Everyone's invited to be present. And what's more, all of them are coming.

WILLIS (*typing*): Not a bad idea at that. (*Pulls the paper from the machine viciously and looks at it*) Christ! If I could only be sure tomorrow was going to be the last day of the world, what a paper I'd get out! That's my idea of heaven—to have, just for once in my life, that chance to tell these bastards what they are.

A.P. MAN (*grinning*): Boy, you could sure go to town on that, couldn't you? Only, you couldn't get it in the ordinary edition. You'd need an extra-extra-extra feature edition with fourteen supplements.

WILLIS (*clutching the sheet he has just typed and shaking it viciously*): Listen to this, will you. (*Reads*) "Mr. and Mrs. Fred Purtle" (*he coughs in an affected tone*)—I beg your pardon, "Mr. and Mrs. S. Frederick Purtle"—and be sure to get in the Frederick and don't leave out the S . . . "Mr. and Mrs. Leroy Dingley . . . Mr. and Mrs. E. Seth Hooten"—and don't leave out the E . . . "in honor of Mrs. J. Skidmore Pratt"—now there's a good one! (*Throws down the paper savagely*) Why, God-damn, it's enough to make your butt want buttermilk. That bunch of mountaineers—half of 'em never owned an extra pair of pants until they were twenty-one. As for Fred Purtle, he was brought up out in Yancey County on hawg and hominy. His father used to go over him with a curry comb and horse clippers every Christmas, whether he needed it or not. Why, hell yes. They had to throw him down to hold him while they put shoes on him. And now, for Christ's sake, it's Mr. S. Frederick Purtle—and don't leave out the S. My God! What a world! And what a job I could do on all the bastards in this town if I only had the chance! To be able, just for once, to tell the truth, to spill the beans, to print the facts about every crooked son-of-a-bitch of them. To tell where they came from, who they were, how they stole their money, who they cheated, who they robbed, whose wives they slept with, who they murdered and betrayed, how they got here, who they really are. My God, it would be like taking a trip down the sewer in a glass-bottomed boat! But it would be wonderful—if tomorrow were the last day of the world. Only it's not (*he coughs suddenly, chokingly, and spits carefully into his handkerchief and stares intently for a moment at the small blot of spreading blood*)—not for most of us.

(*In the little office the telegraph instrument begins to clatter, and the A.P. man goes back, types rapidly for a moment, and returns with another paper in his hand.*)

A.P. MAN: Here's something, Ted. It might be a story for you. Did you know this guy?

WILLIS (*taking the paper and reading it*): "In an official communiqué the French Air Ministry today confirmed the report that Flight Lieutenant Clifford McKinley Brownlow of the Lafayette Escadrille was killed in action Tuesday morning over the lines near Soissons. Lieutenant Brownlow, who in point of service was one of the oldest pilots in the Escadrille, had previously brought down fourteen German planes and had been decorated with the Croix de Guerre. He was twenty-four years old, and a native of Altamont, Old Catawba."

(*When he has finished reading, Theodore Willis is silent for a moment and stares straight ahead of him. Then*):

WILLIS (*speaking very slowly, as if to himself*): Did I know him? . . . Clifford Brownlow . . . Mrs. Brownlow's darling boy . . . the one we used to call "Miss Susie" . . . and chase home from school every day, calling (*changing his voice to a parody of throaty refinement*): "Oh, Clifford! Are you the-ah?" . . . His mother used to call him like that, and we all took it up. Poor little devil! He must have had a wretched life. Clifford seemed a perfect name for him—for his ice cream pants, his effeminate way of walking and of talking, and all the rest of him. And now? Lieutenant Clifford Brownlow . . . Lafayette Escadrille . . . killed in action. . . . Somehow, that seems perfect, too. And not funny, either. There'll be speeches now, and ceremonies for "Miss Susie." There'll be a statue, too, a park named after him, a Clifford Brownlow school, a Brownlow auditorium. And why? What makes a hero, anyway? . . . Was it because we used to call him "Miss Susie" and run him home, calling after him: "Oh, Clifford! Are you the-ah?" Was it because we tormented the poor little bastard until we almost drove him mad? Was it because his mother wouldn't let him play with us, wouldn't let him mingle with the rough, rude boys? Is that the way a hero's made? . . . Poor kid, he used to have a game he had invented that he played all by himself. It was a sort of one-man football game. She wouldn't let him play with us, so he had a dummy rigged up in the yard, something he had made himself, stuffed with straw and hung on a pulley and a wire. He had a football uniform, too, shoes with cleats, a jersey, shoulder-pads, a brand-new football—everything that all the rest of us didn't have—she always bought him the best of everything. And we used to go by in the afternoon and see him playing at his one-man game, running with his brand-new ball, tackling his home-made dummy, sprinting for a touchdown through an imaginary broken field. And we—may God have mercy on our souls—we used to stand by the fence and jeer at him! . . . Well, he's a hero now—about the only hero we have. And there'll be ceremonies, honors, letters to his mother from the President of the French Republic. He's a hero, and he's dead. And we? (*He coughs suddenly, chokingly, spits into his wadded handkerchief, and stares intently at the spreading blot.*) Well, Joe, (*huskily*) tomorrow may be the last day of the world. Is there any other war news?

A.P. MAN: Just the usual run. The French claim they've broken through and gained another hundred yards upon a half-mile front. The Germans say they killed six hundred Frenchmen.

WILLIS (*looking at his watch*): Twelve-two. Two minutes after five o'clock in France . . . and some bastard's getting his right at this moment. . . . Another day. . . . For how many will it be the last day of the world? God, if I only knew that it would be for me! (*Coughs, goes through the ritual with the handkerchief, then rises, takes off his eye-shade, throws it on the desk, and stretches slowly with an air of great weariness and disgust.*) Ah-h Christ!

(*The scene fades out. Far off, in the darkness, is heard the baying of a hound.*)

No Cure for It

"Son! son! Where are you, boy?"

He heard her call again, and listened plainly to her now, and knew she would break in upon his life, his spell of time, and wondered what it was she wanted of him. He could hear her moving in the front of the house.

Suddenly he heard her open the front door and call out sharply: "Oh, Doctor McGuire! . . . Will you stop in here a minute? . . . There's something I want to ask you."

He heard the iron gate slam, and the doctor's slow, burly tread, the gruff rumble of his voice, as he came up the steps. Then he heard them talking in low voices at the front hall door. He could not distinguish their words until, after a minute or two, she raised her voice somewhat and he heard her say reflectively, "Why-y, no-o!"—and knew that she was pursing her lips in a startled, yet thoughtful manner, as she said it. Then she went on in her curiously fragmentary, desperate, and all-inclusive fashion: "I don't think so. At least, he's always seemed all right. Never complained of anything. . . . It's only the last year or so. . . . I got to thinkin' about it—it worried me, you know. . . . He seems strong and healthy enough. . . . But the way he's growin'! I was speakin' to his father about it the other day—an' he agreed with me, you know. Says, 'Yes, you'd better ask McGuire the next time you see him.'"

"Where is he?" McGuire said gruffly. "I'll take a look at him."

"Why, yes!" she said quickly. "That's the very thing! . . . Son! . . . Where are you, boy?"

Then they came back along the hall, and into the sitting room. The gangling boy was still stretched out on the smooth, worn leather of his father's couch, listening to the time-strange tocking of the clock, and regarding his bare brown legs and sun-browned toes with a look of dreamy satisfaction as they entered.

"Why, boy!" his mother cried in a vexed tone. "What on earth do you mean? I've been callin' for you everywhere!"

He scrambled up sheepishly, unable to deny that he had heard her, yet knowing, somehow, that he had not willfully disobeyed her.

533

Doctor McGuire came over, looking like a large, tousled bear, smelling a little like his horse and buggy, and with a strong stench of cigar and corn whisky on his breath. He sat his burly figure down heavily on Gant's couch, took hold of the boy's arm in one large, meaty hand, and for a moment peered at him comically through his bleared, kindly, dark-yellow eyes.

"How old are you?" he grunted.

Eugene told him he was seven, going on eight, and McGuire grunted indecipherably again.

He opened the boy's shirt and skinned it up his back, and then felt carefully up and down his spinal column with thick, probing fingers. He wriggled the boy's neck back and forth a few times, held the skinny arm out and inspected it solemnly, and then peered with grave, owlish humor at the boy's enormous hands and feet. After that he commanded the boy to stoop over without bending his knees and touch the floor.

Eugene did so; and when the doctor asked him if he could bend no farther, the boy put his hands down flat upon the floor, and remained bent over, holding them that way, until the doctor told him to stand up and let his arms hang naturally. When he stood up and let his arms fall, his hands hung level with his knees, and for a moment McGuire peered at him very carefully. Then he turned and squinted comically at Eliza with his look of owlish gravity, and said nothing. She stood there, her hands clasped in their loose, powerful gesture at her apron strings, and when he looked at her, she shook her puckered face rapidly in a movement of strong concern and apprehension.

"Hm! Hm! Hm! Hm! Hm!" she said. "I don't like it! It don't seem natural to me!"

McGuire made no comment and did not answer her. After staring owlishly at her a moment longer, he turned to the boy again and told him to lie down upon the couch. Eugene did so. McGuire then told him to raise his legs and bend them back as far as they would go, and kept grunting, "Farther! Farther!" until the boy was bent double. Then McGuire grunted sarcastically:

"Go on! Is that the best you can do? I know a boy who can wrap his legs all the way around his neck."

When he said this, the boy stuck his right leg around his neck without any trouble at all, and remained in that posture for some time, happily wriggling his toes under his left ear. McGuire looked at him solemnly, and at last turned and squinted at his mother, saying nothing.

"Whew-w!" she shrieked with a puckered face of disapproval. "Get out of here! I don't like to look at anything like that! . . . Hm! Hm! Hm! Hm! Hm!" she muttered, shaking her head rapidly with an expression of strong concern, as the boy unwound his legs and straightened out again.

Eugene stood up. For a moment McGuire held him by the arm and squinted comically at him through his bleared eyes, without saying a word. Then his burly, bearlike shoulders began to heave slowly, a low hoarse chuckle rose in his throat, and he said, poking the boy in the ribs with one fat thumb:

"Why, you little monkey!"

"Hah! What say? What is it?" cried his mother in a sharp, startled tone.

The doctor's huge shoulders heaved mountainously again, the hoarse sound rumbled in his throat, and shaking his head slowly, he said:

"I've seen them when they were knock-kneed, bow-legged, cross-eyed, pigeon-toed, and rickety—but that's the damnedest thing I ever saw! I never saw the beat of it!" he said—and the boy grinned back at him proudly.

"Hah! What say? What's wrong with him?" Eliza said sharply.

The burly shoulders heaved again:

"Nothing," McGuire said. "Nothing at all! He's all right! He's just a little monkey!"—and the rumbling noises came from his inner depths again.

He was silent for a moment, during which he squinted at Eliza as she stood pursing her lips at him, then he went on:

"I've seen them when they shot up like weeds, and I've seen them when you couldn't make them grow at all," he said, "but I never saw one before who grew like a weed in one place while he was standing still in another! . . . Look at those arms and legs!" he cried. "And good God! Will you look at his hands and feet! Did you ever in your life see such hands and feet on a child his age?"

"Why, it's awful!" his mother agreed, nodding. "I know it is! We can't find anything in the stores to fit him now! What's it goin' to be like when he gets older? It's an awful thing!" she cried.

"Oh, he'll be all right," McGuire said, as he heaved slowly. "He'll get all of his parts together some day and grow out of it! . . . But God knows what he'll grow into!" he said, rumbling inside again and shaking his head as he peered at the boy. "A mountain or an elephant—I don't know which!" He paused, then added: "But at the present time he's just a little monkey. . . . That's what you are—a monkey!" and the tremendous shoulders heaved again.

Just then the iron gate slammed, and the boy heard his father lunge across the walk, take the front porch steps in bounds of three, and come striding around the porch into the sitting room. He was muttering madly to himself, but stopped short as he came upon the little group, and with a startled look in his uneasy cold-gray eyes, he cried out—"Hey?" although no one had spoken to him.

Then, wetting his great thumb briefly on his lips, and slamming down the package he was carrying, he howled:

"Woman, this is your work! Unnatural female that you are, you have given birth to a monster who will not rest until he has ruined us all, eaten us out of house and home, and sent me to the poorhouse to perish in a pauper's grave! Nor man nor beast hath fallen so far! . . . Well, what's your opinion, hey?" he barked abruptly at McGuire, half bending toward him in a frenzied manner.

"He's all right," McGuire said, heaving slowly. "He's just a monkey."

For a moment Gant looked at his son with his restless, cold-gray eyes.

"Merciful God," he said. "If he had hair on him, they couldn't tell him from a monkey now!" Then, wetting his great thumb, he grinned thinly and turned away. He strode rapidly about the room, his head thrown back, his eyes swinging in an arc about the ceiling; then he paused, grinned again, and came over to the boy. "Well, son," he said kindly, putting his great hand gently upon the boy's head, "I'm glad to know that it's all right. I guess it was the same with me. Now don't you worry. You'll grow up to be a big man some day."

They all stood looking at the boy—his mother with pursed, tremulous, bantering, proudly smiling lips, his father with a faint, thin grin, and McGuire with his owlish, bleared, half-drunken kindly stare. The boy looked back at them, grinning proudly, worried about nothing. He thought his father was the grandest, finest person in the world, and as the three of them looked at him he could hear, in the hush of brooding noon, the time-strange tocking of his father's clock.

On Leprechauns

An Armenian friend of ours, a Mr. Vladimir Adzigian of South Brooklyn, has mentioned among the defects of our literary style a certain coldness and economy of manner, which, while it makes for precision and temperance, is likely to err too much on the side of understatement. This critic feels— and rightly, too, we think—that our work would profit if it had a little more exuberance, a more impulsive warmth, even a little exaggeration here and there. "For," says he, "exaggeration is in itself a form of enthusiasm, and enthusiasm, in my opinion, is the quality that your work, together with almost all American writing, lacks." This cultivated gentleman then goes on to say that here in America we have never overcome the repressive influences of our Puritan ancestry, and he thinks we will never completely realize ourselves until we do.

While admitting the truth of our friend's observations and conceding regretfully that our own style does suffer from a kind of puritanic sparseness, an almost frigid restraint, we think we might interpose a few mild, although apologetic, reservations to the general tenor of his remarks. In the first place, if our style does suffer from a puritanic frigidity, it is because we, in our own person, suffer from the same defect. And however much we may regret it, however much we may want to burst through the barriers of our reserve to a warm and free communication with the universe, it is probably better to reflect the color of our soul—even though that color be cold and hard—than to assume a false, unwarranted spontaneity that we do not have. Moreover, even if we could overcome the constrained reserve of our nature and break through to a more impulsive spontaneity, we should hesitate to attempt it, because we have so many friends and readers whose own sense of propriety and personal modesty would be affronted if we did.

Chief among these people are our Irish friends, whom we number by the hundreds. Our admiration and affection for the Irish is, we believe, well known. In addition to the traditional affection for the race in which every American boy is brought up, and which is as natural to him as a sore toe, we have had the privilege time and again in our written works of expressing—as soberly and temperately as any man could, it seemed to us, and certainly far too soberly and temperately to suit the tastes of Mr. Adzigian—

what seemed to us to be the shining and distinguishing qualities of the race, its great and lasting contributions to our nation's life.

We have found frequent occasion to pay tribute to their sterling honesty, the devotion of their public service, their brilliant skill in politics and government, which have given them a record of unselfish and incorruptible administration that is, we believe, unequaled by any other people in the world. Where else in the world may a people be found who will so cheerfully and uncomplainingly take over the onerous and thankless burden of running the government, and whose devotion to the principles of law and order, sobriety, reasonable conciliation, and selfless and unseeking consecration to the common weal are as high, loyal, and untarnished in their idealism as are those of the Irish? Where else, among all the peoples who make up the vast polyglot of American life, will another people be found whose patriotism is not only one hundred per cent American, but maintains a constant average of one hundred and thirty-seven per cent?

We have considered it not only a duty but an agreeable privilege to refer to these well-known facts on several occasions, and if we finally desisted, it was largely because of the quiet protests of our Irish friends themselves.

For, said they, the only reward they ever desired or hoped for was the knowledge of public duty modestly done and honorably completed. Virtue was its own exceeding great reward. There were, it is true, among other peoples, certain odious demagogues who were always making public speeches in their own behalf, and slapping themselves proudly on their own breasts; there were even those contemptible characters who regarded politics as a means of feathering their own nests out of the common funds. As for themselves, however, all they asked was the joyful privilege of serving their state or their city as well as they could, giving to their country the last full measure of their devotion. That was reward enough, and the knowledge that one had given his *all* for his country should be sufficient for any man. Certainly, the thought of public acknowledgment for such a noble and idealistic service was odious, and would we please not affront their deepest and most sacred feelings by speaking of it further?

Since the matter was presented to us in this way by many of our Irish friends, we consented reluctantly to refrain from further public display of our enthusiasm rather than incur the reproaches of a people who, as is well known, are among the shyest and most modest races in the world. In matters of literary judgment, however, we trust we may be allowed a more full and free expression of our emotions, since every race, no matter how innately modest, how consecrated to a public trust, may be justly proud of its artistic achievements, and justly boastful of all its men of genius.

We take it as a matter of general consent that Ireland has always swarmed with geniuses. Old Erin has been for centuries running over with them—has, in fact, so many of this glorious type that it has been necessary to establish a kind of emigration service for the exportation of Irish geniuses to other nations which, though bigger, are lamentably deficient in their genius supply.

The leading customer for the importation of Irish geniuses has been our own fair land. In fact, we do not believe it any extravagant exaggeration to say that where genius is concerned, the Irish brand tops the list with us. Here in America we'd rather have one good, bona fide, Irish genius than a half-dozen Polish, Swedish, Czechoslovakian, or Hungarian specimens, no matter what their reputations.

It is true that visiting Englishmen are still in considerable demand, and ply a thriving trade before the Culture Clubs and Female Forums of the Corn Belt. Almost any ninth-rate scribbler from Great Britain can still come over here and insult the country with the choicest and most indecipherable sneers in his whole Oxford vocabulary, and command prices from his adoring audiences that no American could dream of asking. Yes, there is still a good market for the English genius, but among the *haut ton,* so to say, the true sophisticates of culture, the Irish bards and story tellers come first. A bad English writer may still put in a profitable six or eight months and eat and drink his way across the pampas from Portland, Maine, to Tacoma, Washington, at the expense of this great, benevolent, and culture-loving people. But to do so requires considerable traveling, and the English genius cannot always pick his spots; he must occasionally prepare himself for the uncomfortable exigencies of one-night stands, bad accommodations, and poor food.

An Irish genius is faced with none of these embarrassing possibilities. He can pick his spots and do as he damn pleases. He can remain in New York in the perfumed salons of the art-loving plutocracy, and can always have the very best of everything at no cost to himself, provided he exercises only a very small degree of caution and has sense enough to know upon which side his cake is caviared. An Englishman may have to stand an occasional round of drinks, or stay with the second-best family in Hamtramck, Michigan, but a visiting Irishman—never! A visiting Englishman may have to have at least the vestige of a reputation—to have received the endorsement of Hugh Walpole, or to have in his pocket a letter of introduction from J. B. Priestley—but a visiting Irishman needs nothing. It is naturally preferable if someone has heard of him before, but it is by no means essential. The main thing is that he be a visiting Irish writer, and, of course, all visiting Irish writers are geniuses, and not only geniuses, but the most Extra-Special, A-Number-1, Eighteen-Carat Geniuses in existence.

After that, no introduction is necessary, He can just call himself Sean Mulligan or Seamus O'Toole or some other whimsical appellative of this nature, and everything will be all right. He needs only to get off the boat and announce to the reporters that he is the author of an untranslated and untranslatable epic, written in pure Gaelic (he disdains, of course, to use the English speech, unless it be to cash a check; otherwise he abhors the race that has cruelly, bloodily, and damnedly oppressed Old Erin for a thousand years, etc., etc., etc.), and from that time on, his path is smooth, his bed is roses.

If, in addition, he will only come down the gangplank muttering through his whiskers something about "a green leprechaun which they do be sayin' an old man in the west was afther seein' on the hill behint his house, year afther year, bedad," or some other elfin talk of this nature, by which the bearded adults of his race strive to convince themselves and other people that they are really just a lot of little boys, the whole thing will be lapped up greedily, will travel the rounds of the salons, and be hailed as a perfect masterpiece of whimsy, just too Irish, quaint, and delightful for words. Many a visiting Irish bard has established a reputation, achieved celebrity, and eaten and drunk his way into the Great American Heart on no better grounds than this.

It may be perfectly true, of course, that while all this is going on—while the Irish genius is muttering through his whiskers about the fairies and the leprechauns, and is being coddled in the silken laps of the adoring plutocracy as a reward for his whimsical caprice—some poor, benighted bastard of a native son, some gaunt-eyed yokel from Nebraska, Texas, Tennessee, or Minnesota, may be eating his heart out in a Greenwich Village garret, opening canned beans at midnight, and wreaking out his vision of his life here in America with all the passion, fury, terror, suffering, poverty, cruelty, and neglect which a young man in this abundant land can know. It may be true, we say, that while the visiting Seans and Seamuses are chirping on Park Avenue about their leprechauns to an adoring audience of silken wenches, some wild-eyed native youth may be pounding at the wall of his garret with bloody knuckles, wondering where, when, and how in God's name, in a swarming city of eight million, he can find a woman, or even slake his hunger for a moment with the bought and bitter briefness of a whore.

Yet, while the lovely legs cross slowly, and slide the silken thighs, while the fragrant bellies heave in unction to the elfin blandishments of Sean, a boy may be burning in the night, burning in the lone, stern watches of darkness, and giving a tongue to silence that will shape new language long after silken thighs and Sean and Seamus are no more.

But have no perturbations, gentle reader. When the boy has won through from the agony of silence to an uttered fame, when his toiling and imperiled soul has beat its way to shore, when by his own unaided effort he stands safe on land, you may depend on it that he will be at once encumbered with the help he no longer needs. Lovely legs and silken thighs and fragrant bellies will then heave amorously for him, as they do now for Sean, and every little whore of wealth and fashion will contend for the honors of the bed that poverty had bachelored and that fame has filled. The youth, once left to rot and starve, will now be fawned upon and honeyed over by the very apes of fashion who previously ignored him, and who now seek to make him their ape. And the treachery of their adoration will be more odious than the treachery of their neglect, for it stands written in Fame's lexicon that he who lets himself be whored by fashion will be whored by time.

Perhaps the reader may detect in these grave lines a color of some bitterness. Perhaps he may be shocked to realize that there is some slight neglect among the people of this present age, in this enlightened and art-loving nation, toward the young native artist. It is conceivable that the reader may espy here, in this true picture of our native customs, some tincture of injustice, some snobbery of fashion, some conceit of taste. But there are high authorities on these matters who will quickly inform the reader that if he thinks any of these things he is seriously mistaken.

It is necessary to look at what George Webber learned in college to call "The Deeper and More Significant Aspects of the Situation." Seen in this light, things which may have seemed a little difficult and puzzling become beautifully clear. Elsewhere I have told the story of George Webber's life in considerable detail, and in that chronicle I have shown that the usual reception of our young native artist during the years of his apprenticeship is a good, swift kick in the teeth, followed by a good, swift kick in the seat of the pants that will send him flying out of doors onto the pavement. The reason why this happens to the poor, young, native son, while Sean and Seamus eat and drink and wench it to their heart's content, is not because anyone means to be cruel or indifferent, but because great men and lovely women of the Cultured Classes have found out long since that the best thing that could possibly happen to a poor young man of native stock and talent is to get a few good kicks in the face. They know that he can come to his full maturity only through adversity, so they kick him out of doors just to help him along.

In this way he is prevented from getting soft. People who live in luxury, on assured incomes, have very stern and Spartan notions about getting soft. To be sure, everyone is willing to sympathize with a young man's early struggles after he has had them, but, obviously, there can be no sympathy unless he *has* had them.

Any enlightened millionaire can explain "The Deeper and More Significant Aspects of the Situation." It is really part of what we call "The American Dream." It belongs to our ideal of rugged individualism. The more often one gets kicked in the teeth, the more rugged he becomes. It is our method of doing things, and such a simple and direct expression of our life that we have even invented a name for it. We speak of it proudly as "The American Way."

The Return of the Prodigal

1. The Thing Imagined

Eugene Gant was a writer, and in the great world he had attained some little fame with his books. After a while, indeed, he became quite a famous person. His work was known, and everywhere he went he found that his name had preceded him. Everywhere, that is, except where he would most have wished it—at home.

The reason for this anomaly was not far to seek. His first novel had been based in large measure upon a knowledge of people derived from his boyhood in a little town. When the book came out, the townspeople read it and thought they recognized themselves in the portraits he had drawn, and almost to a man the town rose up against him. He received threatening letters. He was warned never to show his face again in the precincts from which his very life had sprung.

He had not expected anything like this, and the shock of it had a profound effect upon him. He took it hard. And for seven years thereafter he did not go home again. He became an exile and a wanderer.

And through all these seven years when he did not go back, his thoughts went back forever. At night as he walked the streets of distant cities or tossed sleepless in his bed in foreign lands, he would think of home, recalling every feature of the little town's familiar visage, and wondering what reception he would get at home if he should decide at last to visit it again.

He thought of this so often with the intensity of nostalgic longing that in the end his feelings built up in his mind an image which seemed to him more true than anything that he had ever actually experienced. After that it became an image that never varied. It came back to haunt him a thousand times—this image of what it would be like if he did go home again:

One blustery night toward the end of October a man was walking swiftly down a street in the little town of Altamont in the hill district of Old Catawba. The hour was late, and a small, cold rain was falling, swept by occasional gusts of wind. Save for this solitary pedestrian, the street was bare of life.

542

The street itself was one of those shabby and nondescript streets whereon the passage of swift change and departed grandeur is strikingly apparent. Even at this dreary season and hour it was possible to see that the street had known a time of greater prosperity than it now enjoyed and that it had once been a pleasant place in which to live. The houses were for the most part frame structures in the style of that ugly, confused, and rather pretentious architecture which flourished forty or fifty years ago, and, so late at night, they were darkened and deserted looking. Many of them were set back in yards spacious enough to give an illusion of moderate opulence and security, and they stood beneath ancient trees, through the bare branches of which the wind howled mournfully. But even in the darkness one could see on what hard times the houses and the street had fallen. The gaunt and many-gabled structures, beaten and swept by the cold rain, seemed to sag and to be warped by age and disrepair, and to confer there dismally like a congress of old crones in the bleak nakedness of night and storm that surrounded them. In the dreary concealments of the dark, one knew by certain instinct that the old houses had fallen upon grievous times and had been unpainted for many years, and even if one's intuition had not conveyed this, the strangely mixed and broken character of the street would have afforded telling evidence of the fate which had befallen it. Here and there the old design of pleasant lawns had been brutally deformed by the intrusion of small, cheap, raw, and ugly structures of brick and cement blocks. These represented a variety of enterprises: one or two were grocery stores, one was a garage, some were small shops which dealt in automobile accessories, and one, the most pretentious of the lot, was a salesroom for a motor car agency. In the harsh light of a corner lamp, broken by the stiff shadows of bare, tangled boughs, the powerful and perfect shapes of the new automobiles glittered splendidly, but in this splendor there was, curiously, a kind of terrible, cold, and desolate bleakness which was even more cruel, lonely, and forbidding than all the other dismal bleakness of the dark old street.

The man, who was the only evidence of life the street provided at this hour, seemed to take only a casual and indifferent interest in his surroundings. He was carrying a small suitcase, and from his appearance he might have been taken for a stranger, but his manner—the certain purpose in his stride, and the swift, rather detached glances he took from time to time at objects along the way—indicated that the scene was by no means an unfamiliar one but had at some period in his life been well known to him.

Arrived at length before an old house set midway down the street, he paused, set down his suitcase on the pavement, and for the first time showed signs of doubt and indecision. For some moments he stood looking with nervous and distracted intentness at the dark house as if trying to read upon its blank and gloomy visage some portent of the life within, or to decipher in one of its gaunt and ugly lineaments some answer to the question in his mind. For some time he stood this way, but at length, with an impatient movement, he picked up his suitcase, mounted the brief flight of concrete steps that went up to the yard, advanced swiftly along the walk and up the steps onto the porch, set down his suitcase at the door, and after a final instant of disturbed hesitancy shook his head, impatiently and almost angrily, and rang the bell.

The bell sent through the old dark hall within, lit dimly at the farther end by one small light, a sharp and vital thring of sound that drew from the man a shocked and involuntary movement, almost of protest and surprise. For a moment his jaw muscles knotted grimly; then, thrusting his hands doggedly into the pockets of his raincoat, he lowered his head and waited.

—They flee us who beforetime did us seek, with desolate pauses sounding between our chambers, in old chapters of the night that sag and creak and pass and stir and come again. They flee us who beforetime did us seek. And now, in an old house of life, forever in the dark mid-pause and watches of the night, we sit alone and wait.

What things are these, what shells and curios of outworn custom, what relics here of old, forgotten time? Festoons of gathered string and twines of thread, and boxes filled with many buttons, and bundles of old letters covered with scrawled and faded writings of the dead, and on a warped old cupboard, shelved with broken and mended crockery, an old wooden clock where Time his fatal, unperturbed measure keeps, while through the night the rats of time and silence gnaw the timbers of the old house of life.

A woman sits here among such things as these, a woman old in years, and binded to the past, remembering while storm shakes the house and all the festoons of hung string sway gently and the glasses rattle, the way the dust rose on a certain day, and the way the sun was shining, and the sound of many voices that are dead, and how sometimes in these mid-watches of the night a word will come, and how she hears a step that comes and goes forever, and old doors that sag and creak, and something passing in the old house of life and time in which she sits alone.

The naked, sudden shock of the bell broke with explosive force against her reverie. The old woman started as if someone had spoken suddenly across her shoulder. Her swollen, misshapen feet were drawn quickly from the edge of the open oven door where she had been holding them for warmth, and glancing around and upward sharply with the sudden attentiveness of a startled bird, she cried out instinctively, although no one was there: "Hah? What say?"

Then, peering through her glasses at the wooden clock, she got up slowly, stood for a moment holding her broad, work-roughened hands clasped loosely at the waist, and after a few seconds' troubled indecision went out into the hall and toward the closed front door, peering uncertainly and with a puzzled, troubled look upon her face as she approached. Arrived at the door, she paused again, and still holding her hands in their loose clasp across her waist, she waited a moment in uncertain and troubled meditation. Then, grasping the heavy brass knob of the door, she opened it cautiously a few inches, and prying out into the dark with curious, startled face, she repeated to the man she saw standing there the same words she had spoken to herself in solitude a minute or two before: "Hah? What say?"—and immediately, with a note of sharp suspicion in her voice: "What do you want?"

He made no answer for a moment, but had there been light enough for her to observe the look upon his face, she might have seen him start and change expression, and be about to speak, and check himself with an almost convulsive movement of control. Finally he said quietly:

"A room."

"What's that?" she said, peering at him suspiciously and almost accusingly. "A room, you say?" Then sharply, after a brief pause: "Who sent you?"

The man hesitated, then said: "Someone I met in town. A man in the lunchroom. I told him I had to put up somewhere overnight, and he gave me your address." She answered him as before, repeating his words in the same suspicious manner, yet her tone also had in it now a certain quality of swift reflection, as if she were not so much questioning him as considering his words. "A man—lunchroom—say he told you?" she said quickly. And then instantly, as if for the first time recognizing and accepting the purpose of this nocturnal visit, she added: "Oh, yes! MacDonald! He often sends me people. . . . Well, come in," she said, and opened the door and stood aside for him to enter. "You say you want a room?" she went on now more tolerantly. "How long do you intend to stay?"

"Just overnight," he said. "I've got to go on in the morning."

Something in his tone awoke a quick and troubled recollection in her. In the dim light of the hall she peered sharply and rather painfully at him with a troubled expression on her face, and speaking with the same abrupt and almost challenging inquiry that had characterized her former speech but now with an added tinge of doubt, she said: "Say you're a stranger here?"—although he had said nothing of the sort. "I guess you're here on business, then?"

"Well—not exactly," he answered hesitantly. "I guess you could almost call me a stranger, though. I've been away from here so long. But I came from this part of the country."

"Well, I was thinkin'," she began in a doubtful but somewhat more assured tone, "there was somethin' about your voice. I don't know what it was, but—" she smiled a tremulous yet somewhat friendly smile—"it seemed like I must have heard it somewhere. I knew you must have come from somewheres around here. I knew you couldn't be a Northern man—you don't have that way of talkin'. . . . Well, then, come in," she said conciliatingly, as if satisfied with the result of her investigation, "if it's only a room for the night you want, I guess I can fix you up. You'll have to take things as you find them," she said bluntly. "I used to be in the roomin'-house business, but I'm not young enough or strong enough to take the interest in it I once did. This house is gettin' old and run-down. It's got too big for me. I can't look after it like I used to. But I try to keep everything clean, and if you're satisfied with the way things are, why—" she folded her hands across her waist in a loose, reflective gesture and considered judicially for a moment—"why," she said, "I reckon you can have the room for fifty cents."

"It's little enough," she thought, "but still it looks as if that's about all he's able to pay, an' things have got to such a state nowadays it's either take what you can get an' get somethin', or take nothin' at all an' lose everything. Yes, he's a pretty seedy-lookin' customer, all right," she went on thinking. "A fly-by-night sort of feller if I ever saw one. But then I reckon MacDonald had a chance to size him up, an' if MacDonald sent him, I guess it's all right. An', anyway, that's the only kind that comes here nowadays. The better class all have their automobiles an' want to get out in the mountains. An' besides, no one wants to come to an old, cold, run-down sort of place like this if they can afford to go to a hotel. So I'd better let him in, I guess, an' take what little he can pay. It's better than nothin' at all."

During the course of this reflection she was peering through her glasses at him sharply and intently, and with a somewhat puzzled and troubled expression on her face. The figure that her old, worn, and enfeebled eyes made out in the dim, bleak light of the hall was certainly far from prepossessing. It was that of an uncommonly tall man, heavily built, and shabbily dressed in garments which were badly in need of pressing, and which, as she phrased it to herself, "looked as if he'd come the whole way across the country in a day coach." His face was covered with the heavy black furze of a week-old beard, and although the features were neither large nor coarse, they had, somewhere in life, suffered a severe battering. The nose, which was short, tilted, and pugnacious-looking, had been broken across the ridge and was badly set, and there was a scar which ran slant-wise across the base of the nose. This disfigurement gave the man's face a somewhat savage appearance, an impression which was reinforced by the look in his eyes. His eyes, which were brown, had a curiously harsh and dark and hurt look in them, as though the man had been deeply wounded by life and was trying to hide the fact with a show of fierce and naked truculence as challenging as an angry word.

Nevertheless, it was the cold anger in his eyes that somehow finally reassured the old woman. As he returned her prying stare with his direct and angry look, she felt vaguely comforted, and reflected: "Well, he's a rough-lookin' customer, sure enough, but then he looks honest—nothin' hang-dog about him—an' I reckon it's all right."

And, aloud, she repeated: "Well, then, come on. If you're satisfied with things the way they are, I guess I can let you have this room here."

Then turning, she led the way into a room which opened from the hall to the right and switched on the dingy light. It was a large front room, gaunt in proportions like the house, high-ceilinged, cheerless, bare and clean and cold, with white-washed walls. There was a black old fireplace, fresh-painted and unused, which gave a bleak enhancement to the cold white bareness of the room. A clean but threadbare carpet covered the worn planking of the floor. In one corner there was a cheap dresser with an oval mirror, in another a small washstand with a bowl and pitcher and a rack of towels, and in the ugly bay window which fronted the street side of the house there was a nondescript small table covered with a white cloth. Opposite the door stood a clean but uninviting white iron bed.

The old woman stood for a moment with her hands clasped loosely at her waist as she surveyed the room with a reflective stare.

"Well," she remarked at last with an air of tranquil and indifferent concession, "I reckon you'll find it pretty cold in here, but then there's no one in the house but one roomer an' myself, an' I can't afford to keep fires burnin' in a house like this when there's nothin' comin' in. But you'll find things clean enough," she added quietly, "an' there's lots of good, warm covers on the bed. You'll sleep warm enough, an' if you're gettin' up to make an early start tomorrow, I don't guess you'll want to sit up late, anyway."

"No, ma'am," he answered, in a tone that was at once harsh and hurt. "I'll get along all right. And I'll pay you now," he said, "in case I don't see you in the morning when I leave."

He fished into his pockets for a coin and gave it to her. She accepted it with the calm indifference of old, patient, unperturbed people, and then remained standing there in a reflective pause while she gave the room a final meditative look before leaving him.

"Well, then," she said, "I guess you've got all you need. You'll find clean towels on the washstand rack, and the bathroom's upstairs at the end of the first hallway to the left."

"Thank you, ma'am," he answered in the same tone as before. "I'll try not to disturb anyone."

"There's no one to disturb," she said quietly. "I sleep at the back of the house away from everything, an' as for Mr. Gilmer—he's the only steady roomer I've got left—he's been here for years, an' he's so quiet I hardly know when he's in the house. Besides, he sleeps so sound he won't even know you're here. He's still out, but he ought to be comin' in any minute now. So you needn't worry about disturbin' us. An' no one will disturb you, either," she said, looking straight at him suddenly and smiling the pale tremulous smile of an old woman with false teeth. "For there's one thing sure—this is as quiet a house as you could find. So if you hear anyone comin' in, you needn't worry; it's only Mr. Gilmer goin' to his room."

"Thank you," the man said coldly. "Everything's all right. And now," he added, turning away as if anxious to terminate a more protracted conversation, "I'm going to turn in. It's past your bedtime, too, and I won't keep you up, ma'am, any longer."

"Yes," she said hastily, turning to go, yet still regarding him with a puzzled, indecisive look. "Well, then, if there's anythin' else you need—"

"No, ma'am," he said. "I'll be all right. Good night to you."

"Good night," she answered, and after one more parting glance around the cold walls of the room, she went out quietly and closed the door behind her.

For a moment after she was gone, the man stood motionless and made no sound. Then he looked about him slowly, rubbing his hand reflectively across the rough furze-stubble of his beard. His traveling gaze at length rested on his reflected image in the dresser mirror, and for a brief instant he regarded himself intently, with a kind of stupid and surprised wonder. And suddenly his features were contorted by a grimace as anguished and instinctive as a cornered animal's.

Almost instantly, however, it was gone. He ran his hands through his disheveled hair and shook his head angrily as though throwing off a hurt. Then quickly and impatiently he took off his coat, flung it down across a chair, sat down upon the bed, bent and swiftly untied his muddy shoes and removed them, and then sat there numbly in a stupor for some minutes, staring before him blindly at the wall. The cold, white bareness of the room stole over him and seemed to hold his spirit in a spell.

At length he stirred. For a moment his lips moved suddenly. Slowly he looked around the bare white walls with an expression of dawning recognition and disbelief. Then shaking his head and shrugging his thick shoulders with an involuntary and convulsive shudder, he got up abruptly, switched off the light, and without removing the rest of his clothes, lay down upon the bed and drew a quilt across his body.

And then, while storm beat against the house and cold silence filled it, he lay there, flat and rigid on his back, staring up with fixed eyes into blackness. But at last the drug of cold, dark silence possessed him, his eyes closed, and he slept.

In the old house of time and silence there is something that creaks forever in the night, something that moves and creaks forever, and that never can be still.

The man woke instantly, and instantly it was as if he had never slept at all. Instantly it was as if he had never been absent from the house, had never been away from home.

Strong, unreasoning terror gripped him, numb horror clove his breath, the cold, still silence laid its hand upon his heart. For in his brain it seemed a long-forgotten voice had just re-echoed, in his heart a word, and in his ear it seemed a footfall, soft and instant, had just passed.

"Is anybody there?" he said.

Storm beat about the house, and darkness filled it. There was nothing but cold silence and the million drumming hoof-beats of small rain.

"But I heard it!" his mind repeated. "I heard a voice now lost, belonging to a name now seldom spoken. I heard a step that passed here—that of a phantom stranger and a friend—and with it was a voice that spoke to me, saying the one word, 'Brother!'

"Is it the storm," he said to himself, "that has a million voices? Is it the rain? Is it the darkness that fills an old house of life and gives a tongue to silence, a voice to something that moves and creaks forever in the night? Or is it the terror of cold silence that makes of my returning no return, and of me an alien in this house, where my very mother has forgotten me? Oh, is it the cold and living silence of strong terror moving in the house at night that stabs into the living heart of man the phantom daggers of old time and memory? Is there a tongue to silence and the dark?"

Light and instant as the rain a footfall passed above him. "Who's there?" he said.

Storm beat upon the house, and silence filled it. Strong darkness prowled there, and the bare boughs creaked, and something viewless as the dark had come into the house, and suddenly he heard it again and knew that it was there.

Above his head, in Ben's old room—the room of his brother, Ben, now dead these many years, and, like himself, forgotten, too—he heard a light, odd step, nimble as a bird's, as soft as ashes, and as quick as rain.

And with the step he heard once more the old familiar voice, saying softly:

"Brother! Brother! . . . What did you come home for? . . . You know now that you can't go home again!"

2. The Real Thing

Eugene Gant had been seven years from home, and many times in those long years of absence he had debated with himself, saying: "I will go home again. I shall lay bare my purposes about the book, say my piece, speak so that no man living in the world can doubt me. Oh, I shall tell them till the thing is crystal clear when I go home again."

Concerning the town's bitter and ancient quarrel with him, he knew that there was much to say that could be said. He also knew that there was much to say that could never be spoken. But time passes, and puts halters on debate. And one day, when his seven years were up, he packed his bag and started out for home.

Each man of us has his own America, his own stretch, from which, here outward, the patterns are familiar as his mother's face and the prospect is all his. Eugene's began at Gettysburg, his father's earth; then southward through Hagerstown, and down the Valley of Virginia.

First, the great barns, the wide sweep and noble roll of Pennsylvania fields, the neat-kept houses. Lower down, still wide fields, still neat-kept houses, white fences and painted barns, a grace and sweetness that still lingers in the Valley of Virginia. But now, for the first time, the hodden drab of nigger gray also appears—gray barns, gray sheds, gray shacks, and lean-tos sturdy to the weather that had given them this patina to make up for the lack of paint. Now, too, the gashed and familiar red of common clay. To Eugene Gant returning home it was all most beautiful, seen so with the eyes of absence.

The rains of spring were heavy through Virginia, the land was sodden, and everywhere was spotted with wet pools of light. It was almost the time of apple blossoms, and faintly there was the smell of rain and apple blossoms on the air.

Through the Valley of Virginia he went down very slowly. And slowly the rains lifted, and one day, in sun and light, the blue veil round the shouldering ramparts of the great Blue Ridge appeared.

Quickly, now, the hills drew in out of wide valleydom, and signs of old kept spaciousness vanished into the blue immediate. Here was another life, another language of its own—the life and language of creek, hill, and hollow, of gulch and notch and ridge and knob, and of cabins nestling in their little patches of bottom land.

And suddenly Eugene was back in space and color and in time, the weather of his youth was round him, he was home again.

Following some deep, unreasoning urge that sought to delay the moment and put off the final impact of his return, he took a circuitous course that carried him southward from Virginia into Tennessee, then south again, beyond the high wall of the mountains, to Knoxville. From there the road to Altamont is long and roundabout. Almost at once it starts to mount the ramparts of the Great Smokies. It winds in and out, and goes by rocky waters boiling at the bottom of steep knolls, then climbs, climbs, winds and climbs. May is late and cold among the upper timber. Torn filaments of mist wash slowly round the shoulders of the hills. Here the chestnut blight is evident: ruined, in the blasted sweeps, the great sentries of the heights appear.

Very steep now, the road went up across the final crest of mountains. The ruined hulks of the enormous chestnut trees stood bleakly on the slopes. High up on the eroded hillsides, denuded of their growth, were the raw scars of mica pits. Beyond, stretching into limitless vistas, were the blue and rugged undulations of a lost and forgotten world. And suddenly a roadside sign—Eugene was back in Old Catawba, and the road started down again, to Zebulon.

Zebulon—the lost world. Zebulon—the syllables that shaped the very clay of his mother's ancestral earth.

And all at once he heard his mother's voice echo across the years: "Son! Son! . . . Where are you, boy? I'll vow—where has he gone?" And with it came faint echoes of the bell that came and went like cloud shadows passing on a hill, and like the lost voices of his kinsmen in the mountains long ago. With it returned old memories of his mother's endless stories about her people, stories of Marches long ago, of bleak dust and rutted clay, of things that happened at sunset in the mountains when the westering red was pale, ragged, cold, and desolate, and winter was howling in the oak.

And with the echoes of his mother's voice, that had seemed to fill all the days of his childhood with its unending monotone, there returned to him an immediate sense of everything that he had ever known: the front porch of the old house in Altamont where he had lived, the coarse and cool sound of Black's cow munching grass in the alleyway, along the edges of the back-yard fence, the mid-morning sound of sawn ice out in the hot street of summer, the turbaned slatterns of good housewives awaiting noon, the smell of turnip greens, and upon the corner up above, the screeching halt of the street car, and the sound of absence after it had gone, then the liquid smack of leather on the pavement as the men came home at noon for dinner, and the slam of screen doors and the quiet greetings; and, inside the house, the cool, stale smell of the old parlor, and the coffined, rich piano smell, the tinkling glasspoints of the chandelier, the stereopticon of Gettysburg, the wax fruit on the mantel underneath its glass hood, and he himself reclining on his father's couch, buried in a book, his imagine soaring with Hans Grimm, and with thoughts of witches, a fair princess, fairies, elves, and gnomes, and of a magic castle on a rock.

Then a memory of one particular day, and his mother's voice again:

"Child! Child! . . . I'll vow—where is that boy? . . . Son! Son! Where are you? . . . Oh, here! Boy, here's your Uncle Bacchus. He comes from Zebulon, where he was born a hundred years ago—an' Uncle Bacchus, he was my father's brother."

And then the voice of Uncle Bacchus, drawling, quiet as the sifting of the winter ash, impregnant with all time and memory, and in its suggestive overtones of the voices of lost kinsmen long ago: "I knowed the minute I seed him, 'Liza—fer he looks like you." The voice was benevolent, all-sure, triumphant, unforgettable—as hateful as the sound of good and unctuous voices that speak softly while men drown. It was the very death-watch of a voice, the voice of one who waits and watches, all-triumphant, while others die, and then keeps vigil by the dead in a cabin in the hills, and drawls the death-watch out to the accompaniment of crackling pine-knots on the hearth and the slow crumbling of the ash.

"Your Uncle Bacchus, child, from Zebulon—"

So memory returned with Eugene Gant's return. And this was Zebulon. Now down the stretch of road he went his own way home. The tallest hills in all the eastern part of North America soared on every side. The way wound steeply down by blighted chestnut trees and brawling waters into the mountain fastness of old Zebulon.

And the voice of Uncle Bacchus came back again:

"Yore grandpaw, son, was my own brother. He was born, like all of us, out on the South Toe out in Zebulon. He married yore grandmaw thar and settled down and raised a family. His paw before him—my paw, too—he come in thar long years before. I've heerd him tell it was wild country then. Thar was Cherokees when yore great-grandpaw first come in thar. Yes, sir. And he hunted, fished, and laid traps fer bear. He growed or trapped everything he et. He was a great hunter, and one time they say he run the hounds the whole way over into Tennessee."

Then his mother's voice again:

"That is the way it was, all right. I've heard father tell about it a thousand times. . . . You must go out there some day, son. It's many years since I was there, but dozens of my people are still livin' out in Zebulon. There's Uncle John, an' Thad an' Sid, an' Bern, Luke, an' James—they're all there with the families they have raised. . . . Well, now, I'll tell you what—Uncle Bacchus is right about it. It was a wild place back in those days. Why, father used to tell us how much wild life there was even in his time. But look here—why, wasn't I readin' about it just the other day?—an article, you know—says the wild life has all gone now."

The county seat of Zebulon is a little town. Eugene decided to stay overnight and see if he could hunt out any of his mother's people. There was no hotel, but he found a boarding house. And the moment he began to make inquiries about the Pentlands, his mother's family, he seemed to run into people everywhere who said they were relatives of his. Most of them he had never seen before, or even heard of, but as soon as he identified himself, they all appeared to know who he was, and the first show of mountain aloofness with which they had greeted him when they thought him a stranger quickly melted into friendly interest when they placed him as "Eliza Pentland's boy." One man in particular proved most obliging.

"Why, hell," he said, "we've all heard of you from your cousin Thad. He lives a mile from town. And your Uncle Johnny and Bern and Sid—the whole crowd of them out upon the Toe. They'll want to see you. I can drive you out tomorrow. My name is Joe Pentland, and we're fifth cousins. Everybody's kinfolks here. There are only fifteen thousand people in Zebulon County, and we're all related somehow . . . . So you're goin' home again? Well, it's all blown over now. The people who were mad about the book have forgotten it. They'll be glad to see you. . . . Well, you won't find this much of a town after the cities you have seen. Six hundred people, a main street, a few stores and a bank, a church or two—that's all there is . . . Yes, you can get cigarettes in the drug store. It's still open—this is Saturday night. You'd better wear your coat. We're thirty-seven hundred feet up here—we've got a thousand feet on Altamont—you'll find it cooler than it is down there. . . . I'll go with you."

The night had the chill cool of mountain May, and as the two men walked along, a nerve, half ecstasy, was set atremble in Eugene's blood. The country street was fronted by a few brick stores, their monotony broken only by the harsh rawness of the Baptist Church. A light was burning inside the church, and the single squat and ugly window that faced the street depicted Christ giving mercy in the bleak colors of raw glass. The drug store was on the corner at the crossroads. Next door was a lunchroom. Three or four ancient and very muddy Fords were parked slanting at the curb before the drug store. A few feet away, outside the lunchroom, there was a huddled group of men in overalls, attentive, watching, like men looking at a game of cards. From the center of the group came a few low words—drawling, mountain-quiet, somehow ominous. Eugene's companion spoke casually to one of the men:

"What is it, Bob?"

The answer came evasive, easy, mountain-quiet again:

"Oh, I don't know. A little argument, I guess."

"Who was that?" asked Eugene as they entered the drug store.

"That was Bob Creasman. Said there was some argument going on. Ted Reed's there—he's my cousin—and he's drunk again. It happens every Saturday night. A bunch of 'em was at the quarry this afternoon, and they've been drinkin' corn. I guess they're arguin' a bit. . . . What's yours? A Coca-Cola? . . . Make it two cokes and a couple of packs of Chesterfields."

Five minutes later, as the two men emerged from the drug store, there was a just-perceptible stir in the attentive group of men outside.

"Wait a minute," said Joe Pentland. "Let's see what's goin' on."

There was the same quietness as before, but the waiting men were now drawn back against the lunchroom window, and in front of them two others stood and faced each other. One of them was in overalls, and he was saying:

"Now, Ted. . . . "

The other was more urbanely clothed in dark trousers and a white shirt without a collar. His hat was pushed to the back of his head, and he just stood there staring heavily, his sullen face, sleepy eyed, thrust forward, silent, waiting.

"Now, Ted," the one in overalls repeated. "I'm warnin' ye. . . . You're goin' too fer now. . . . Now leave me be."

Drowsy-eyed, swart-visaged, and unspeaking, a little sagging at the jowls, a little petulant like a plump child, darkly and coarsely handsome, with his head thrust forward, the other listens sullenly, while the men, attentive, feeding, wait.

"You leave me be now, Ted. . . . I'm not lookin' fer no trouble, so you leave me be."

Still sullen and unspeaking, the swart visage waits.

"Ted, no, I'm tellin' ye. . . . When ye cut me up six years ago, yore family and yore kinfolks begged you out of hit. . . . Now you leave me be. . . . I'm not lookin' fer no trouble with ye, Ted, but you're goin' too fer now. . . . You leave me be."

"It's Ted Reed and Emmet Rogers," Joe whispers hoarsely in Eugene's ear, "and they've started in again. They had a fight six years ago. Ted cut Emmet up, and now they always get this way on Saturday night. Ted, he gets to drinkin' and acts big—but pshaw! he wouldn't hurt a fly. He ain't got the kind of guts it takes to be *real* mean. Besides, Will Saggs is here—the one there in the white shirt—he's the cop. Will's scared—you can see that. Not scared of Ted, though. See that big man standin' back of Will—that's Lewis Blake, Ted's cousin. That's who Will's afraid of. Lewis is the kind that won't take nothin' off of nobody, and if it wasn't for him, Will Saggs would break this up. . . . *Wait* a minute! Somethin's happenin'!"

A quick flurry, and—

"Now, goddam you, Ted, you leave me be!" The two men are apart now, Ted circling the other, and slowly his hand goes back upon his hip.

"Look out!"—shouted from the crowd. "He's got his gun!"

There is the dull wink of blue metal at Ted Reed's hip, the overalled line fades back, and every waiting man now jumps for cover. The two principals are left alone.

"Go on and shoot, goddam you! I'm not afraid of you!"

To Eugene, who has dodged back into the recess entrance of the drug store, someone calls out sharply: "Better git behind a car there at the curb, man! You ain't got no protection in that doorway!"

Moving with the urgency of instant fear, Eugene dives across the expanse of open pavement just as the explosion of the first shot blasts the air. The bullet whistles right past his nose as he ducks behind a car. Cautiously he peers around the side to see Emmet moving slowly with a strange grin on his face, circling slowly to the shot, mocking his antagonist with the gun, his big hands spread palms outward in a gesture of invitation.

"Go on, goddam you, shoot! You bastard, I'm not scared of you!"

The second shot blows out a tire on the car Eugene has retreated to. He crouches lower—another shot—the sharp hiss of escaping air from another tire, and Emmet's whine, derisive, scornful:

"Why, go on and shoot, goddam you!"

A fourth shot—

"Go on! Go on! Goddam you, I'm not—"

A fifth—and silence.

Then Ted Reed comes walking slowly past the row of cars. Men step out from behind them and say quietly:

"What's wrong, Ted?"

Sullenly, the gun held straight downward at his thigh: "Oh, he tried to git smart with me."

Other voices now, calling to each other:

"Where'd he git 'im?"

"Right under the eye. He never knowed what hit 'im."

"You'd better go on, Ted. They'll be lookin' fer you now."

Still sullen: "The bastard wasn't goin' to git smart with me. . . . Who's this?"—stopping to look Eugene up and down.

Joe Pentland, quickly: "Must be a cousin of yours, Ted. Leastways, he's a cousin of mine. You know—the feller that wrote that book."

With a slow and sullen grin Ted shifts the gun and offers his hand. The hand of murder is thick flesh, strong, a little sticky, cool and moist.

"Why, sure, I know about you. I know your folks. But, by God, you'd better never put *this* in a book! Because if you do—"

Other voices, coaxingly: "You better go along now, Ted, before the sheriff gits here. . . . Go on, you fool, go on."

"—because if you do—" with a shake of the head and a throaty laugh— "you and me's goin' to git together!"

The voices breaking in again: "You're in fer it this time, Ted. You carried it too fer this time."

"Hell, you couldn't git a jury here in Zebulon to convict a Reed!"

"Go on, now. They'll be lookin' fer ye."

"They don't make jails that can hold a Reed!"

"Go on. Go on."

And he was gone, alone, and with his gun still in his hand—gone right down the middle of the quiet street, still sullen-jowled and sleepy-eyed— leaving a circle of blue-denimed men, and a thing there on the pavement which, two minutes before, had been one of their native kind.

Eugene saw it all, and turned away with a leaden sickness in his heart. And once again he heard the echoes of his mother's voice, saying:

"The wild life has all gone now."

At last Eugene was home again in Altamont, and at first it was good to be home again. How many times in those seven years had he dreamed and thought of going home and wondered what it would be like! Now he was back, and saw, felt, knew it as it really was—and nothing was the way he had imagined it. Indeed, there was very little that was even as he remembered it.

Of course, there were some things that had not changed, some things that were still the same. He heard again all the small familiar sounds of his boyhood: the sounds of night, of voices raised in final greetings, saying "Good night" as screen doors slammed—"Good night," far off, and the receding thunder-drone of a racing motor—"Good night," and the last street car going—"Good night," and the rustle of the maple leaves around the street light on the corner. And he heard in the still-night distance the barking of a dog, the shifting of the engines in the yards, the heavy thunder of the wheels along the river's edge, the clanking rumble of the long freights, and far off, wind-broken, mournful, the faint tolling of the bell. He saw again the first blue light of morning break against the rim of eastern hills, and heard the first cock's crow just as he had heard it a thousand times in childhood.

Niggertown was also still the same, with the branch-mire running in the nigger depths, yellow, rank with nigger sewage. And the smells were just the same—the sour reek from the iron laundry pots mixed in with the branch-mire smell and the acrid tang of woodsmoke from the nigger shacks. So, too, no doubt, were the smells the same inside of nigger-shackdom— the smells of pork, urine, nigger funk, and darkness. He remembered all this with the acid etchings of a thousand wintry mornings, when, twenty- five years ago, with the canvas strap around his neck and the galling weight of the bag forever pulling at him, he had gone down to Niggertown upon his paper route and had heard, a hundred times repeated every morning, the level smack of ink-fresh news against the shanty doors and the drowsy moan of funky wenches in the sleeping jungle depths.

These things were still the same. They would never change. But for the rest, well—

"Hello, there, Gene! I see you've put on weight! How are you, boy?"

"Oh, fine. Glad to see you. You haven't changed much."

"Have you seen Jim yet?"

"No. He came by the house last night, but I wasn't there."

"Well, Jim Orton's been looking for you—he and Ed Sladen, Hershel Brye, Holmes Benson, Brady Chalmers, Erwin Hines. . . . Why, say! Here's Jim now, and all the rest of them."

A chorus of voices, laughing and calling out greetings as they all piled out of the car that had pulled up at the curb:

"Here he is! . . . All right, we've got him now! . . . So you decided to come home again? . . . What was it you said about me in the book—that I concealed the essential vulgarity of my nature behind a hearty laugh?"

"Now look here, Jim—I—I—"

"I—I—hell!"

"I didn't mean—"

"The hell you didn't!"

"Let me explain—"

"Explain nothing! Why, hell, man, what is there to explain? You didn't even get started in that book. If you were going to write *that* kind of book, why didn't you let me know? I could have told you dirt on some of the people in this town that you never even heard about. . . . Look at his face! . . . We've got him now! . . . Hell, son, don't look so backed. It's all forgot- ten now. A lot of them around here were pretty hot about it for a while. Two or three of them were out to get you—or said they were."

Laughter, then a sly voice:

"Have you seen Dan Fagan yet?"

"No, I haven't. Why?"

"Oh, nothing. I just wondered. Only—"

"Hell, he won't do nothing! No one will. The only ones who are mad today are those you left out!"

More laughter.

"Hell, it's true! The rest of 'em are proud of it! . . . We're all proud of you, son. We're glad that you came home. You've been away too long. Stay with us now."

"Why, hello, son! Glad to see you back! . . . You'll find many changes. The town has improved a lot since you were here. I guess the new Courthouse and the County Hall were put up since you left. Cost four million dollars. Have you seen the tunnel they bored under the mountain for the new road-way out of town? Cost two million more. And the High School and the Junior College, and the new streets and all the improvements? . . . And look at the Square here. I think it's pretty now the way they've laid it out, with flower beds and benches for the people. That's the thing this town needs most—some parks, some new amusements. If we hope to bring tourists here and make this a tourist town, we've got to give them some amuse-ments. I've always said that. But you get a bunch of messheads in at City Hall and they can't see it. . . . Fact is, tourists don't stay here any more. They used to come and stay a month. You ought to know—you wrote about them sitting on the porches of the boarding houses. They'd come and sit and rock upon the porches, and they'd stay a month, people from all over—Memphis, Jacksonville, Atlanta, New Orleans. But we don't get them any more. They've all got cars now, and there are good roads every-where, so they just stay overnight and then hit it for the mountains. You can't blame them—we've got no amusements. . . . Why, I can remember when this was a sporting center. The big swells all came here, the million-aires and racing men. And we had seventeen saloons—Malone's, and Creaseman's, and Tim O'Connell's, and Blake's, and Carlton Leather-good's—your father used to go in there, he was a friend of Leathergood's. Do you remember Leathergood's tall, pock-marked, yellow nigger and his spotted dog? All gone now—dead, forgotten. . . . Here's where your fa-ther's shop used to stand. Do you remember the angel on the porch, the draymen sitting on the wooden steps, your father standing in the door, and the old calaboose across the street? It's pretty now, the way they've got all the grass and flower beds where the old calaboose used to be, but some-how the whole Square looks funny, empty at one end. And it's strange to see this sixteen-story building where your father's old marble shop once stood. But, say what you will, they've certainly improved things a lot . . . . Well, good-bye. The whole town wants to see you. I won't keep you. Come to see me sometime. My office is on the eleventh floor—right over where your father's workbench used to be. I'll show you a view you never dreamed of when your father's shop was here."

The return of the prodigal, and the whole town broken into greetings while the on-coming, never-ceasing younger generation just gaped, curiously a-stare:

"He's back. . . . Have you seen him yet? . . . Which one is he?"

"Don't you see him there, talking to all those people? . . . There—over *there*—before the shoe-shine shop."

A girl's voice, disappointed: "Oh-h! Is that him? . . . Why, he's *old!*"

"Oh, Eugene's not so *very* old. He's thirty-six. He only seems old to you, honey. . . . Why I remember him when he was a snotty-nosed little kid, running around the street selling *Saturday Evening Posts,* and delivering a route in Niggertown for the *Courier.*"

"But—why, he's fat around the waist. . . . And look! He just took his hat off. Why, he's getting bald on top! . . . Oh-h, I never thought—"

"What did you think? He's thirty-six years old, and he never was very much to look at, anyway. He's just Eugene Gant, a snot-nosed kid who used to carry a paper route in Niggertown, and whose mother ran a boarding house, and whose father had a tombstone shop upon the Square. . . . And now just look at him! The snot-nosed kid who went away and wrote a book or two—and look there, will you!—look at all those people crowding round him! They called him every name they could think of, and now they're crawling over one another just to shake his hand."

And across the street:

"Hello, Gene!"

"Oh, hello—ah—hello—ah—"

"Come on, now: hello-ah what?"

"Why, hello—ah—"

"Boy, I'll beat your head in if you don't call me by my name. Look at me. Now, what is it? Hello-ah *what?*"

"Why, ah—ah—"

"Come on, now! . . . Well, tell me this: who was it that called you 'Jocko' in that book?"

"Why—ah—ah—Sid! Sidney Purtle!"

"By God, you better *had!*"

"Why, Sid, how are you? Hell, I knew you the minute you spoke to me!"

"The hell you did!"

"Only I couldn't quite . . . Oh, hello, Carl. Hello, Vic. Hello, Harry, Doc, Ike—"

He felt someone plucking at his sleeve and turned:

"Yes, ma'am?"

The lady spoke through artificial teeth, close-lipped, prim, and very hurriedly:

"Eugene I know you don't remember me I'm Long Wilson's mother who used to be in school with you at Plum Street School Miss Lizzy Moody was your teacher and—"

"Oh, yes, Mrs. Wilson. How is Long?"

"He's very well thank you I won't keep you now I see you're busy with your friends I know everyone wants to see you you must be rushed to death but sometime when you aren't busy I'd like to talk to you my daughter-in-law is very talented she paints sculptures and writes plays she's dying to meet you she's written a book and she says the experience of her life is so much like yours that she's sure you'd both have a lot in common if you could only get together to talk about it—"

"Oh, I'd love to. I'd love to, Mrs. Wilson."

"She's sure if she could talk to you you'd be able to give her some suggestions about her book and help her find a publisher I know you're bothered with so many people that you've hardly any time to call your own but if you could only talk to her—"

"Oh, I'd be glad to."

"She's a very in-ter-est-ing person and if you'd only let us see you sometime I know—"

"Oh, I will. I will. Thank you so much, Mrs. Wilson. I will. I will. I will."

And at home:

"Mama, have there been any calls?"

"Why, child, the telephone's been goin' all day long. I've never known the like of it. Sue Black called up an' says for you to ring her back—an' Roy Hitchebrand, an' Howard Bartlett, an'—oh yes, that's so—a lady from out along Big Homing. Says she's written a book an' she's comin' in to see you. Says she wants you to read it an' criticize it for her an' tell her how to make it good so it will sell. . . . An' yes—that's so now—Fred Patton called up for the Rotary Club an' wants to know if you will speak to them at lunch next Tuesday. I think you ought to do that, son. They're good, substantial men, all of them, with a high standin' in the community. That's the kind of people you ought to be in with if you're goin' to keep on writin' books. . . . An'—oh yes!—someone called up from the Veterans' Hospital—a girl named Lake, or Lape, or somethin' like that—says she used to be in the same class with you at Plum Street School, an' she's in charge of the Recreation Center for the veterans—says a lot of 'em have read your books an' want to see you an' won't you be the guest of honor on Saturday night. I wish you'd do that, child. I reckon the poor fellers, most of 'em, are far from home, an' many of 'em will never go back again to where they came from—it might cheer 'em up. . . . An' yes, that's so!—Sam Colton called up for the alumni committee of the university, an' they want you to speak to 'em at the big alumni rally next week at the Country Club. You ought to go, child. They're your old friends an' classmates, an' they want to see you. An' yes!—what about it, now!—why, you're to speak on the same program with 'Our Dick'—Senator Richard L. Williams of the United States Senate, if you please! As Sam said, you and him are the two most famous alumni of the university that the town has yet produced. Hm-m! . . . Then there was Jimmy Stevenson, he called up and wanted you to come to a steak dinner to be given by the Business Men's Convention out at Sharpe's Cabin on the Beetree Creek, nine miles from Gudgerton. I'd certainly go if I were you. I've never seen the place, but they say Ed Sharpe certainly has a beautiful cabin, the best one around here—an' as the feller says, right in the heart of Nature's Wonderland, in the center of these glorious hills. I know the section well, for that's where father an' mother went to live ninety years ago, just after they were married—they moved there from Zebulon—didn't stay, of course—I reckon the pull of Zebulon an' all their kinfolks there was too much for 'em—but you couldn't pick a prettier spot if you hunted all over for it, right out in the heart of nature, with old Craggy Tavern in the background. That's the place I'd go, boy, if I was a writer an' wanted to get inspiration. Get close to nature, as the feller says, an' you'll get close to God. . . . An' yes—two young fellers called up from over in Tennessee—said they're the Blakely boys. You've heard of the famous Blakely Canners. Why, I hear that they own almost every farm in three counties there, an' they've got factories everywhere, through Tennessee, an' way down South, an' all out through the Middle West—why, they're worth millions. Says—oh, just a boy, you know—but says, real slylike, 'Is this Miss Delia?'—givin' me the name you gave me in the book. Well, I just played along with him—'Well, now,' I says, 'I don't know about that. My name's Eliza. Now I've heard that I've been called Delia, but you mustn't believe all that you read,' I says. 'For all you know, I may be human just like everybody else. Now,' I says, 'I looked real good and hard at myself this mornin' in the mirror, an' if there are any horns stickin' out of my head, why I must've missed 'em, I didn't see any. Of course, I'm growin' old, an' maybe my eyesight's failin' me,' I says, 'but you're young an' ought to have good eyes, so why don't you come an' have a look an' tell me what you think.' Well, sir, he laughed right out across the phone as big as you please, and says, 'Well, you're right! I think you're wonderful! An' I'm tryin' to be a writer—even if my father does put up tomatoes—an' I think your son's one of the best writers we have.' Well, I didn't let on, of course. Father always taught us that it was vulgar an' unrefined to brag about your own, so I just said, 'Well, now, I don't know about that. But you come on an' look at him. Up to the time he was twelve years old,' I says, 'he was a good normal sort of boy like everybody else. Now what happened to him after that,' I says—you see, I thought I'd have a little fun with him—'what happened after that I don't know—I'm not responsible. But you come an' take a look at him. Maybe you'll get surprised. Maybe you'll find he doesn't have horns, either.' Well, he laughed right out an' said, 'You're all right! An' I'm goin' to take you up on that. My brother an' I are drivin' over tomorrow afternoon—an' we're goin' to bring him back with us,' he says. 'If he wants a cabin like I hear he does, I've got one here that I can give him, so we're goin' to bring him back,' he says. Well, you can't do that, of course, child, but be nice to them. He spoke like a very well-brought-up sort of boy—an' the Blakelys are the sort of people that you ought to know. . . . An' after that a lot of girls called up an' said they heard you needed someone to type for you—said they'd like to do it, an' knew how to type good. One of 'em said she'd be willin' to do it for nothin'—says she wants to be a writer, an' knew she'd learn so much from you an' what an inspiration it would be. Hm! Pshaw!—I cut her off mighty quick, I can tell you! Sounded funny to me—wantin' to work for nothin', an' all that gushy talk about inspiration. I knew what she was after, all right. You watch out, son—don't let any of these silly women rope you in. . . . Yes, that's so. Cash Hopkins was here askin' about you. Of course he's just a plain, workin' sort of man. He used to do jobs for your father, but your father liked him, an' he's always been our friend, interested in all of you. . . . Mr. Higginson was here, too. He's an Episcopal minister that came to town several years ago for his health—an' what about it!—he's been your friend right from the start. When all the preachers were denouncin' you, an' sayin' you'd disgraced us all, an' everyone was down on you an' said if you ever came back here they'd kill you—he defended you, sir! He stood right up for you! He read everything you wrote, an' he said, 'That boy should have been a preacher. He's got more of the true gospel in his books than all of us preachers put together!' Oh, he came right out for you, you know. 'It's we who have failed,' he said, 'not him!' Child, I hope you'll be nice to Mr. Higginson. He's been your friend from the first, an' as the sayin' goes, he's a scholar an' a Christian gentleman. . . . An' law, what about it! I'm sorry you were not here to see it. I'll vow, I had to turn my head away to keep from laughin'. Why Ernest Pegram, if you please, in his big car—all rared back there in a brand-new Cadillac as fat as a pig, an' with a big cigar stickin' out of his mouth. Why, of course; he's *rich* now! He's well-fixed—every last one of the Pegrams is! You see, when Will Pegram died two years ago up there in the North somewhere, he was a wealthy man, a big official in some large corporation. You see, he was the only one of the Pegrams who got away. But, poor Will! I can remember just as well the day he left here more than forty years ago—this corporation had given him a job down in the eastern part of the State, an', as the sayin' goes, he didn't have an extra shirt to put on his back. An' here he dies two years ago an' leaves close to a million dollars. So they're well-fixed! Of course, Will had no childern, an' his brothers an' sisters got it all. He left Ernest a flat hundred thousand—that's what it was, all right, because I read it in the papers, an' Ernest told me so himself. The others came in for their share, too. Here the rest of us are broke, the whole town ruined, everyone has lost everything they had—as the Bible says, 'How have the mighty fallen!'—but the Pegrams don't have to worry from now on. So Ernest drives up an' stops before the house this afternoon in his big, new car, smokin' his fine cigar. 'Why Ernest,' I says, 'I don't think I ever saw you lookin' better. Are you still workin' at your plumbin' trade?' I says. Of course I knew he wasn't—I just wanted to hear what he would say. 'No, Eliza,' he says—oh, the biggest thing you ever saw, puffin' away at his cigar. 'No,' he says. 'I've reached the age,' he says, 'when I figured it was about time to retire.' Pshaw! *Retire!* I had to turn my head away to keep from laughin'. Who ever heard of a plumber retirin'? What did *he* ever have to retire *on*—that's what I'd like to know—if it hadn't been for Will? But—oh, yes, see here, now—says:

'You tell Gene,' he says, 'that I haven't got anything to do. My time is free,' he says, 'an' if there's any place he wants to go, any place where I can take him, why, my car is here,' he says, 'an' it's at his disposal.' You know how good-hearted he's always been. I reckon he was thinkin' of the days when he used to live next to us on Woodson Street, an' how he watched all you childern grow up. The Pegrams have always been our friends an' taken a great interest in your career. I wish, son, that you'd go to see them all while you're here. They'll be glad to see you. But when I saw Ernest there in his big car, puffin' away on his cigar, an' lookin' fat enough, as the sayin' goes, to pop right out of his britches, an' tellin' me he had retired—well, I just had to turn my head away an' laugh. . . . Well, in all my life I've never seen the beat of it! There's been a steady string of them here all day long, an' the telephone has rung constantly. I'll vow—it seems to me that everyone in town has either been here or called up today. . . . An', oh yes! There are two of 'em out in the sun parlor now—old Cap'n Fitzgerald and a Miss Morgan, a trained nurse. I don't know what they want. They've been waitin' for an hour, so I wish you'd just step out an' say hello to 'em. . . . An' yes! There's three more in the front parlor—a lady who says she's from Charleston an' had read your books an' was just passin' through town an' heard you were here an' wanted to shake hands with you, an' that young Tipton that you used to know, an'—oh yes! that's so!—the reporter from the paper, he's there, too. I guess he wants to write you up, so you'd better go right in. . . . I'll vow! There goes that phone again! Just a minute, son—I'll answer it."

Old Man Rivers

1

When Old Man Rivers woke up in the morning, among the first objects that his eyes beheld were two large and very splendid photographs that faced each other on the top of his tall chiffonier dresser, and that were divided by the heavy, silver-mounted brush and comb that lay between them. It was a good arrangement: each of the two splendid photographs commanded its own half of the dresser like a bull in its own pasture, and the rich dull solidity of the comb and brush seemed to give each just the kind of "frame," the kind of proud division, to which it was entitled. In a way, the two splendid photographs seemed to regard each other with the bellicose defiance of a snorting bull: if anyone of this present generation can remember the Bull Durham advertisements of twenty years ago, he may get the idea—three rails of fence, the pasture, the proud bull dominant with the great neck raised, the eyes flashing fire, and the proud rage of his magnificent possession simply *smoking* from his nostrils, and saying plainer than any words could do: "Here I am and here I mean to stay! This side of the fence is mine! Keep out of here!"

Old Man Rivers more *sensed* than *saw* these things when he opened his old eyes. He didn't see things clearly any more. Things didn't come to him in the morning the way they used to come. He didn't wake up easily, he didn't wake up at once, "all over," as he used to do; rather, his old, tired, faded, somewhat rheumy eyes opened slowly, gluily, and for a moment surveyed the phenomena of the material universe around him with an expression that was tired, old, sad, vague, and unremembering.

Presently he roused himself and got up; he got up slowly, with a heavy sigh, and bent to find his slippers with a painful grunt; he was a heavy old figure of a man—a man who had been a big man, big-boned, big-handed, big-shouldered, and big-muscled, and whose bigness had now shrunk and dwindled to a baggy, sagging heaviness; round baggy shoulders, thin legs, sagging paunch—a big man grown old. It took him a long time to bathe, a long time to look at the sad old face reflected in the mirror, the face with the high cheek-bones, the slanting sockets of the eyes, the long wispy mustache, and the scraggly wispy beard, which, with the sensually full red lips and old tired, yellowed, weary eyes, gave Mr. Rivers a certain distinction of appearance—an appearance not unlike that of a Chinese mandarin.

It took him a long time to shave, too—to do all the delicate work required about the edges of that long, straggling mustache, and that wispy mandarin-like beard to which he owed a good part of the distinction of his personal appearance. He shaved with a straight razor, of course; as he often said, he wouldn't use "one of these confounded safety razor contraptions" if they gave him the *whole* factory. But, really, he had become afraid of his old straight razor, which had once been such a friend to him; his old hands shook with palsy now, he had cut himself badly on more than one occasion, shaving had become a slow and perilous affair.

But he felt better after shaving and four fingers of sound rye:—none of your bromo seltzers, aspirins, or soda-tablets, or any of your other quack remedies for *him;* after a night of old-fashioned cocktails and champagne there was nothing like a good stiff drink of *whiskey* the next morning to set a fellow up.

Warmed by the liquor, and with a sparkle in his eye for the first time, Mr. Rivers finished dressing without great difficulty. He grunted his way into his heavy woolen drawers and undershirt, fumbled with shaky fingers to put cuff links and collar buttons in a clean shirt, grunted as he bent over to pull his socks on, got into his trousers without much effort, but had a hard time with his shoes—confound it, it came hard to have to bend and tie the laces, but he wasn't going to let any fellow tie his shoes for *him!* By George, as long as he could move a muscle, he'd have none of that.

The worst was over now; fully attired, save for his coat and vest and collar, he stood before the chiffonier, buttoned the wing collar, and with trembling fingers fumbled carefully with the knot of his cravat. Then he combed his sparse hair with the heavy silver comb, brushed it with the heavy silver brush, and—looked with satisfaction at the two splendid photographs.

The one on the left was really bull-like; the square face was packed with a savage concentration of energy and power, the mustache curved around two rows of horse teeth bared with tigerish joy, behind the spectacles the eyes looked out upon the world with fighter's glance. Everything about the photograph spoke the brutal eloquence of energy and power, its joyful satisfaction in itself, its delight with life, adventure, friendship, love or hate, its instant readiness for anything. Everything about the picture said: "Here I am, boys! I feel bully!"—and this bully-feeling, brutal, savage, joyful, ready-for-fight-or-fun picture was autographed: "To dear old Ned with heartiest and most affectionate regards from Theodore!"

The other face, no less the fighter's face, was colder, leaner, more controlled. A long, lean face a little horse-like in its bony structure, horse-like, too, in its big teeth, touched coldly, stiffly round the powerful thin mouth with the sparse smile of the school-teacher; the whole long face borne outward by the powerful long jaw, relentless, arrogant, and undershot,—face of school-teacher marking papers, Presbyterian face, to flesh-pots hostile, to wine, women, belly-warmth, exuberance, and life's fluidity, unskilled, opposed, and all unknowledgable, but face of cold high passion, too, fire-glacial face, and face of will unbreakable, no common, cheap, contriving, all-agreeing, all conceding, compromising, and all-promising face of the ignoble politician, but face of purpose, faith, and fortitude—face of arrogance, perhaps, but face, too, of a captain of the earth, a man inviolable, a high man—and signed: "To Edward Rivers—with sincerest good wishes and—may I say—affectionate regards—Cordially yours—Woodrow Wilson."

Old Man Rivers' tired old eyes and haggard face really had the warm glow of life and interest in them now. As he struggled into his vest and coat, he looked at the two photographs, wagged his head with satisfaction, and chuckled:—

Good old Ted! Dear old Tommy! I tell you what, those—those fellows were—were *just bully!* He just wished everyone in the world could have known *both* of them the way he had known them! Why, the minute Ted walked in a room and flung down his hat, the place was his. The minute he met you, shook hands with you—why—he made you his friend forever! By George, there was something about that fellow—just the way he had of coming in a room, or flinging his hat down, or jumping up to shake your hand, and saying, "Delighted"—there—there was just something about everything that fellow *did* that warmed you up all over!

And Tommy? As Mr. Rivers' old tired eyes surveyed the long prim face of Tommy, his expression, if anything, became a little softer, a little more suffused with mellowness than when he had surveyed the vigorous countenance of Ted. . . . Tommy! There was a great fellow! He just wished everyone had known Tommy as *he* had known him!—Why, confound these fellows, anyway (a kind of indignant and impatient mutter rattled in the old man's throat)—writing and saying all this stuff about Tommy's being cold, unfriendly, not able to warm up to people.—By George, *he'd* like to tell 'em what *he* knew! He'd known Tommy almost fifty years, from the time they were at Princeton right up to Tommy's death, and there never was a man on earth who had a warmer "human side" than Tommy had! By George, no! Ask anyone who knew him, ask any of Tommy's friends whether he was cold and unable to warm up—*they'd* tell you pretty quick how cold he was! Confound these fellows, he'd just like to tell them about some of the great times *he'd* had with Tommy—some of the things they'd done in college— yes! And even later—he'd just like to tell them about that time when Tommy had all the fellows in the class come and visit him—that was in 1917, right when he was in the middle of all that trouble, but you'd never have known it from the way he acted, invited the whole class to come and stay two days and all the fellows who could come *came*, too—and that *was* a celebration! The last night they were there, after Tommy had gone to bed, the fellows took Jimmy Mason, who was the baby of the class and also the smallest one among them, and dressed him up in a nightgown and a night-cap and put him in a baby-carriage and wheeled him down the hall to Tommy's room and walked right in, by George, and woke Tommy up and said, "Tommy, here's a child we can't stop crying! What are we going to do with him!" And Tommy got right out of bed, entered right into the spirit of the thing, and says, 'I think we ought to let Ned Rivers take care of him; he's the only bachelor among us, and if anyone is going to be kept awake by that child's crying, *he's* the one who ought to pay the *penalty,* what do *you* fellows think?" Well, by George, they all agreed with him—and Tommy took the baby-carriage and wheeled it away and led the whole procession down the hall, by George, into my room—and some of the fellows found a cradle that had been there ever since Ted's day—or McKinley's—or some-one—and put Jim Mason into it—and made him stay there, by George!—why, confound these fellows, when they begin to say things about how cold and reserved Tommy was, they just don't know what they're talking about. I'd like to tell them!

Mr. Rivers surveyed the two photographs a moment longer with a warm color of affection and tenderness in his tired old face, the glow of pride and loyalty in his weary eyes.

It was something to be able to say that you'd been the friend of two such fellows as that. It did not occur to Mr. Rivers, it had probably never oc-curred to him, that it was not only "something to be able to say," but in the nature of a miracle to be able to accomplish it—something like sitting on Vesuvius and cooling one's heels at the North Pole at the same time. It was part of Mr. Rivers' charm that he had never seen anything at all extraordi-nary in his accomplishment. It is true that there had been times when his friendship for these two celebrated men had been attended by certain mo-ments of embarrassment. There had been the time, for instance, when Theodore had come into his office, tossed his hat across the room, flung himself into a chair, and opened conversation with: "Well, Ned, what's the news? Have you seen or heard anything lately of that lily-livered, weasel-worded milk-sop down in Washington? Look here, how the devil can you put up with such a fellow?"

And there had been the time when Tommy had broken a pause in the conversation, to inquire acidly: "Are your relations still as cordial as ever with the Buzz-Saw of Sagamore? I'm surprised to see there are no scars of battle yet."

Well, now, by George—yes, those fellows did say things about each other now and then, but that was just a way they both had of blowing off steam. I don't think either of them really meant a word of it! By George, I just wish those two fellows could have known each other—and—and—and I just believe they'd have gotten along together *fine!*

2

It may seem from these interior reflections that Mr. Rivers was not lacking in certain extraordinary gifts. Possessing no talent of any kind—except the genuine and attractive talent for friendships that has been indicated—Mr. Edward Rivers had risen to a very considerable position in the nation's life. He was now occasionally referred to in the press as "the Dean of American Letters." Every year upon his birthday, representatives of the New York *Times* and the New York *Herald Tribune* called upon Mr. Rivers, interviewed him, and printed his views on a great variety of subjects at a very considerable and respectful length. When questioned by the representative of the New York *Times* for his opinions on the Modern American Girl, the venerable Dean of American Letters had remarked that by George, he just thought she was fine—he thought she was perfectly splendid! And when the young man from the *Herald Tribune* asked the Dean for his opinion on the state of the nation's letters, and his opinion of the Younger Writers, the Dean said Well, now, he thought the whole thing looked most promising. He liked to see vitality, originality, and a fresh point of view—and he thought these Young Fellows had it, by George he did. What—the *Times* man would now inquire—did the Dean think about the modern freedom of expression—the tendency to "tell all" in modern writing—to put it bluntly, the use of "four letter words" by some of the young writers, even in the pages of some of the higher class magazines? For example, *Rodney's Magazine,* of which the Dean had been for many years the editor, had only a year or two before serialized the latest novel of the young writer, John Bulsavage. What did the Dean think of the use of certain words in that book—the use of words (and of blank spaces!) which had never before appeared on the chaste pages of *Rodney's Magazine?* Was it not true that there had been a great many letters of indignant protest from old subscribers? Had there not been a number of canceled subscriptions? Had the Dean himself approved the inclusion of these debatable scenes and phrases which had caused so much and such excited comment at the time? Was the Dean himself disposed to say that he favored the startling freedom in the use of material and of utterance which characterized the work of some of the leading Young Writers? As a distinguished editor, an arbiter of the nation's taste, as a discoverer and supporter of the best that had been said for the past fifty years, as a friend of Theodore Roosevelt and Woodrow Wilson, as a crony of the late Henry van Dyke and William Lyon Phelps, as the esteemed and honored colleague of such distinguished people as Agnes Repplier, Ellen Glasgow, Robert Underwood Johnson, Edith Wharton, Nicholas Murray Butler, John Galsworthy, Henry Seidel Canby, Percy S. Hutchinson, Walter Pritchard Eaton, Henry Peckinpaugh Saltonstall, Corinne Roosevelt Robinson, and Elizabeth Pipgras Wiggins, Isabel Miranda Patterson, and Irene McGoody Titsworth, Constance Lindsay Skinner and Winona Roberta

Snoddy, Edna Lou Walton and Ella Mae Maird, Sylvia Chatfield Bates and Ishbel Lorine McLush, Ben Ray Redman and Edmund Clarence Stedman, Henry Goddar Leach and Warner Perkins Beach, Charles Forbes Goddard and T. Lothrop Stoddard, Constance D'Arcy Mackay and Edna St. Vincent Millay, Hamilton Fish and Lillian Gish—in fact the whole brilliant and distinguished group of authors, editors, and critics who had always stood for the most liberal—nay, the most *advanced!*—developments in modern literature, but whose judgment was also tempered by a sane balance, a sane adherence to standards of good taste, craftsmanship, and form, and to an unwavering belief in the fundamental wholesomeness, purity, and good sense of American life, which the writing of some of these younger writers was prone to forget—what, considering his intimate association with all these distinguished people, did he, Edward Rivers, the Dean of American Letters, think of the work of these Younger Writers?

Well, now—Mr. Rivers squirmed a little at questions such as these. He foresaw complications, disagreements, arguments, and Mr. Rivers did not like complications, disagreements, arguments. He believed in Tact. Well, now—the Dean of American Letters saw stormy weather: he must trim his canvas and sail close. If he came out with whole-hearted and enthusiastic endorsement of the Young Writers, all of their methods, words, and works, he knew that he must be prepared for a vigorous chorus of protest from certain worthwhile people of his distinguished and extensive acquaintance:—letters from venerable dowagers at whose dinner parties he was a frequent guest (Mr. Rivers was a constant diner-out; he had spent a large part of his life dining out; he dined out every night; his difficulty was not to get invitations, but tactfully to chose between invitations, so that he might not only retain the affection—and future invitations—of those he refused, but could also assure himself of the best dinner, the best liquor, the finest champagne, and the most distinguished and worthwhile gathering among those he accepted)—letters then from venerable old dowagers, from venerable old Vanderbilts, Astors, Morgans, Rhinelanders, Goelets, and Schermerhorns (Mr. Rivers knew *all* the venerable old Vanderbilts, Astors, Morgans, Rhinelanders, and Schermerhorns), letters from distinguished old ladies who wrote or had written essays for *Rodney's*, letters from all the distinguished old widows of all the ambassadors, governors, senators, financiers, college presidents, and presidents of the nation he had known, letters from all the lady writers with three names—the Irene McGoody Titsworths, the Winona Roberta Snoddys, the Elizabeth Pipgras Wigginses, and so on—each letter written in the writer's own inimitable and distinguished vein, of course, but all showing a certain unity of purpose and opinion—viz:—*Could* the Dean of American Letters have been quoted correctly? *Could* they believe their eyes? Could it be possible that the statements attributed to Mr. Rivers in this morning's edition of the *Times* accurately represented the considered judgment of that distinguished editor? Could it be true that the celebrated critic who had for fifty years been not only the wise and temperate appraiser, but the arbiter of what was highest, noblest, purest in the world of letters, who had been, for so long and such an honorable career of service, guardian of the torch, the defender of the "eternal values"—could such a man as *this* have so forgotten all his standards, have so forsaken all that he had ever stood for, as to uphold, praise, and give the support of his authority to iniquitous filth that posed as "literature" (God save the mark), to defend the use of language one might expect to find among the low dives of the Bowery, but never within the pages of *Rodney's Magazine,* and to praise the relentless "realism" (realism, if you please), the "talent" (talent, the Lord help us), the depraved, imbecilic, brutal, vulgar, and ill-written maunderings of people whose obscenity might conceivably be of interest to the specialist in abnormal psychology, the professional criminologist, the pathologist interested in various states of manic-depressivism, but of serious interest to one of the most distinguished critics living—good heavens! *What* had happened to him, anyway?

3

Well, now, it was a hard question to decide. It certainly was! A fellow never knew just what to say: if he praised the works, the words, the talents of these Younger Writers, he would let himself in for all this kind of thing from people he knew, some of them his best friends. And if he *dispraised* the works, the words, the talents of these Younger Writers, then he might expect another flood of letters from the children and the grandchildren of the very people he had sought to please. And these letters from the irreverent young would ask him bluntly who the hell he thought he was, and suggest that he go immediately and reserve accommodations for himself at the Old Woman's Home. They would tell him further that the serialization of Mr. Bulsavage's work was the only useful act that *Rodney's Magazine* had performed in twenty years, that the magazine was moribund, a museum piece, and under Mr. Rivers' direction had become a repository for essays on bee-culture written by the aged widows of former ambassadors to Peru. They would finally suggest that Mr. Rivers close his trap and continue to print the works of Mr. Bulsavage and a few other young people, who were doing the only work worth doing nowadays, or else deposit the decayed remains of *Rodney's* in the nearest garbage can, and go jump in the river.

By George, what was a fellow going to do? If you pleased one crowd, you'd make the other mad. There had been a time when young people had let their elders tell them what to read and what to think, but that was gone. Nowadays you never knew which way to turn. Well, the only way, the Dean decided, was the Middle Way. That was the way he'd always taken; it had always been the right way for him. So when the *Times* man asked him what he thought about the Younger Writers, and whether he approved, Mr. Rivers squirmed a little, looked uncomfortable, then took the Middle Way.

Well, now, that was a hard question to answer—by George it was. He didn't approve of everything they did—not by a jugful. He might be old-fashioned, and all that, but he still believed there were certain Standards—Standards of—of—style, and form, and craftsmanship, and—and—good taste, by George he did! If these things should perish, then the world would be the loser, but he didn't believe for a moment that they would. In the long run, the eternal values would win out. He didn't believe for a moment that the whole picture of American life, the whole truth of it, its fundamental wholesomeness, and sweetness, and—and sanity, was being dealt with by these young writers. He thought that they were too prone to deal with abnormal states pf psychology, to present distorted pictures, to go in too much for—for scenes of violence and cruelty—and—and—abnormal and distorted points of view. The War was probably responsible for this condition, the Dean thought. But just as the pendulum had swung too far in one direction, it would probably swing back in the other. As for the Younger Writers, although he didn't approve of everything they did, he thought their vitality, their freshness, the originality of their point of view, was just splendid! He thought the future of American writing showed great promise. We were undoubtedly going through one of the most interesting and hopeful periods of literary production we had known in a long time. Some of the Younger Writers were people of undoubted talent, and when they had grown a little older, and acquired a more mature point of view, by George, he expected great things from them (headlines for tomorrow: "Dean Sees Golden Future For Young Writers," or "Dean Raps Smut But Praises Promise").

And so it went the whole way down the line. Old Man Rivers' opinion on the moving pictures, the radio, the automobile, the machine age, politics, Mr. Roosevelt, the New Deal—in short, on anything that might come within the range of general interest or a reporter's inquiry—held firmly to this course of "Middle Way"-ism. If he disapproved, his disapproval was such as to cause no general offense. If he approved, his approval was such as the world in general could agree to. There were few things so bad that they might not be worse, almost everything showed promise of betterment. The seeds of hope were in misfortune, the promise of perfection in error.

4

Old Man Rivers, in fact, like that Celebrated Stream which was so much like his own name and which "must know somep'n, but don't say nuthin'," just kept rollin', he kept on rollin' along. The process had been profitable: with no more literary talent than would fit comfortably in the bottom of a thimble, with no more critical ability than the village school-marm possesses, and with no opinions about anything more startling than those usually held by the average filing clerk, he had risen to a position in the nation's life where his literary talent was taken for granted, his critical ability was esteemed as a very rare and penetrating faculty, and his opinions were largely sought after, and printed with pious completeness in the pages of the New York *Times*.

Mr. Rivers had, in short, "arrived"; he had arrived solidly, and with both feet; he had arrived substantially and materially through the possession of no other faculties than a genuine capacity for warm and loyal friendship, a tremendous capacity for saying nothing with the air of saying a great deal, a remarkable talent for being all things to all people, and for pleasing everybody, quite a distinguished, mandarin-like, and somewhat goaty (the ladies preferred to call it faun-like) personal appearance, and a very imposing and exceptional—stuffed shirt.

And yet the old man felt sad and lonely nowadays when he woke up in the morning. Why? Mr. Rivers had never been a man who looked too directly at unpleasant facts; the instinctive tendency of his amiable and agreeing nature was to avoid unpleasant facts: to skip over them, or to get around them if he could. Yet there had been times in recent years when he had felt, sadly and obscurely, that something had gone grievously wrong in his own life. There had been times when doubt and sorrow had penetrated the thick hide of his own genial self-satisfaction—when he had wondered if the imposing front was anything but just a—front.

He was old, he was tired, he was sad, he was lonely. He had never married, his life for forty years had been the life of the assiduous diner-out, the "prominent club-man." Now he wondered if the game was worth it. He had always told himself—and other people, too—that he would know when to quit when the time came. He had celebrated the virtues of the pastoral life, and affirmed his own devotion to the country, time and again, in word and print. Moreover, he had used his money, and a small inheritance, thriftily; no one would ever have to look after Old Man Rivers, he was well-fixed. Part of his funds for many years had been invested in a large and very splendid farm in Pennsylvania. Beautifully stocked with sheep and blooded cattle and good horses, it had been the place to which he was going to retire "in his old age." He had celebrated his country home in conversation and in writing; he had even written a little book about it, called *My Sabine Farm*.

Well, what detained him now? His old age was here, the quitting time had come. The quitting time, Old Man Rivers occasionally and sorrowfully suspected, had come several years before, when he had been deposed as editor of *Rodney's Magazine*. There had been more than a grain of truth in the derisory jibes of young people that *Rodney's Magazine* had become a museum piece, the repository for essays on bee-culture written by the aged widows of ex-ambassadors. The Magazine, itself a languishing reminder of a by-gone and more leisurely age, had lapsed finally into such musty decrepitude that surgical measures had become necessary if it was going to be saved from utter extinction: Mr. Rivers had been removed as editor, and a young man appointed in his place.

Mr. Rivers had always told himself that he would be prepared for such an event. He had told himself that he would never let it happen. He had told himself that "when the time came" he would know the time had come, that he would cheerfully "step out" and give "some of the young fellows a chance." No, he'd be prepared for it, he'd know himself before the others did, the Sabine Farm in Pennsylvania was waiting to receive him.

Comforting fable! Fond delusion! The "time" had come and Old Man Rivers had not known it. He had not stepped out, not known when to quit. Instead, he had been tapped upon the shoulder and told that he had worn out his welcome, it was time to go.

5

When the time came, Old Man Rivers couldn't face it. In a painful scene at a director's meeting—before old James, Pounders, Fox, and Prince, and Dick—the old man had broken down and wept. He had been told that he could be retired upon half pay, that his security would be protected in every way. It was no use. He did not need the money, he was well-off, and they knew it, but he lied, he begged; he said he had dependents, onerous responsibilities, heavy and expensive burdens—that he couldn't live upon the pension, that he needed the money.

It was a wretched business for everyone. They had put it off for years; they had finally compelled his resignation only when no other course was possible if the Magazine was to survive. The upshot of it was, they let him stay on at full pay, called him an "Advisory Editor," gave him a little office where he would be out of people's way, where he could piddle around with worthless manuscripts that never got published, receive old cronies, widows of ambassadors, and venerable dowagers of his acquaintance.

It was a hard blow to his pride, a bitter come-down, but it was better than nothing. Mr. Rivers was not such a fool that he didn't realize that a good part of his social popularity came from his position as editor of one of the most distinguished and eminent magazines in America. In recent years, as the fortunes and influence of the Magazine had declined, Mr. Rivers had noticed a corresponding decline in his own social prominence. He was no longer in such demand as he had been twenty years before. And now? Well, it was going to be tough sledding from now on. "Advisory Editor"? That didn't go down so well. It was all very fine to joke about it, to say in his genial, high, foggy tone that he had decided it was time "for some of us old fogies to step aside and give some of the young fellows a chance. So I decided to resign. But they prevailed on me to stay on as—Advisory Editor." It wasn't completely convincing, and he knew it, but—it was better than nothing, he could not give up.

Yes, Mr. Rivers had worn out his welcome. And the Sabine Farm? Those final years of a long life spent far from the city's whirling noise, in the wise and pastoral meditations of retirement—oh, where now? Faced with the actuality, he couldn't meet it. To give up all the city's life, his clubs, his bars, his dinner parties and his after-dinner speeches, his dowagers, his rich and fashionable acquaintances, for the bucolic tedium of a Pennsylvania farm— he couldn't do it.

And yet, even the pleasures of *this* life had staled on him. A large part of his life had been spent in clubs. He was forever telling someone, with a trace of pride: "I live at the University Club—lived there for twenty years— wouldn't *think* of living anywhere else. Most comfortable life in the world; you don't have to fool with apartments, leases, servants, electricity, cook- ing—it's all done *for* you:—you've got everything you need right there— good food, a good library, and, of course"—here he would wink slyly—"a good bar! I tell you what, *that's* mighty important. You just come up with me sometime—I'll get Tom to fix you one of his famous Old Fashioneds:— Oh, he knows how to fix 'em, too—you just come up and try a few—you know," here Mr. Rivers would wink slyly again—"they *give* 'em to me; I don't have to pay for a thing; all I have to do is sign for it—"

Well, even this business of living in clubs and dining out at night had begun to pall on him. He was bored with it, bored with the club faces, bored with the club food, bored with his room. But when he tried to give the whole thing up, he couldn't. He'd been around too long.

There had been a time when "any old room" had been good enough for Mr. Rivers. "I'm on the go all the time, anyway," he used to say. "All I need is a bed to sleep in and a place to hang my hat." Well, he had that, certainly, and it was no longer good enough. He had never felt the lack before, but now he wanted—he wanted—by George, he didn't know just what, but he wanted "a room of his own." This morning the old man felt lonely, bored, as he looked around his room. He wanted to get out of it! And yet it was a pleasant enough room: large enough, sunny enough, quiet enough—it looked right out on Fifty-fourth Street at the tall and imposing residences of Mr. John D. Rockefeller and his son. It was well furnished, and yet, Mr. Rivers reflected, probably every other room in the club was furnished in the identical fashion of his own room. And if he moved out today, someone else would move in tomorrow morning without ever knowing he had been there; there was nothing about the place to show that it was his own. The thought somehow made Mr. Rivers uncomfortable, he shivered a little as he looked about the room, he picked up his hat, and got out.

6

Once in the corridor, outside his door, his whole demeanor changed. Mr. Rivers was now about to go before the world again; it was up to him, he felt, to put on a good show. His manner became more jaunty, jovial, half- jesting; he walked down the corridor toward the elevator at a springy step, he pressed the elevator button, and as he waited, composed his face into its customary morning expression of jesting raillery.

The elevator came up, the doors opened, Mr. Rivers stepped briskly in, and the bald-headed Irishman who had taken Mr. Rivers up and down for twenty years greeted him with a grin that was really more than casual, a grin that showed a genuine affection and warmth of feeling for his passenger.

"Good-mornin', Mr. Rivers," the man said. "It's a nice fine day, isn't it?"

"Yes, Tim," said Mr. Rivers, "It's going to be a beautiful day. By George, it's a pity that a couple of young fellows like you and me have got to be cooped up on a day like this. Let the *old* fellows go to work; you and I ought to take the day off—go on a picnic somewhere—take our girl for a ride—by George, we ought!"

"Shure, an' ye're right, Mr. Rivers," Tim agreed. "This is no day for two young bucks like you an' me to work. There ought to be a law against it."

"Well, now, that's right," said Mr. Rivers, and wagged his head vigorously. They had reached the bottom and the elevator door had opened— "They ought to make old fellows like Jim here do all the work," he said, indicating a smiling youth in bell-hop's uniform who was coming along the corridor. "Isn't that right, Jim?"

"You're right, Mr. Rivers," the boy agreed with a friendly smile, and passed by.

Mr. Rivers' next move was to cross the lobby of the tremendous building and inquire for mail at the cashier's office.

"Have you got any more bills—or duns—or advertising matter—or any of those love-letters that the girls keep writing me?"—his florid face was decidedly goat-like now, he leered knowingly at the mail clerk, and winked, speaking in a high, foggy, somewhat wheezy voice that was the perfect vehicle for his brand of humor.

"Yes, sir, Mr. Rivers," the mail clerk smiled—"It looks as if the girls had written you quite a stack of them this morning. Here you are, sir."

"Well, now, that's good," wheezed Mr. Rivers, shuffling through his mail. "We young fellows have to make hay while the sun shines, don't we? Tempus fidgets, as the fellow says, and if we don't make the most of our opportunities when we have them, it may be too late before we know it."

The clerk smilingly agreed, and Mr. Rivers, still opening and running through his mail, crossed the lobby to the newsstand.

"Say, young fellow," he wheezed, "I wonder if you have a copy of a rare old publication known as the New York *Times?*"

"Yes, sir, Mr. Rivers," grinned the news clerk. "I've been saving one for you. Here you are, sir."

"Now," said Mr. Rivers warningly, as he picked up the paper and fumbled for a coin—"I don't want it unless it's a genuine First Edition. You know, we collectors have got to be very careful about that sort of thing. Our professional reputation is at stake. If it got around that I'd gone and bought a second, a third, or a fourth edition of the *Times,* thinking that I had a *first*—why, I'd be ruined. So if you think there's any doubt about it, I want you to say so, and we'll call it off."

The news-dealer smiling assured Mr. Rivers that he thought his professional reputation would be safe, and Mr. Rivers, shaking his head vigorously, wheezed, "Well now, that's good"—and walked away.

7

On his way to the huge club breakfast room, his high foggy voice could be heard all over the place, either uttering greetings or responding to them. He knew everyone, and everyone knew him; his remarks to everyone were couched in the same tone of pseudo-serious jocosity. In response to an inquiry concerning the state of his health, he was heard to remark that if he felt any better it would hurt him. In response to someone's comment about feeling "under the weather," Mr. Rivers was heard to say that there was nothing like a good stiff shot of rye to help a fellow get "on top of the weather."

Over breakfast (grapefruit, soft-boiled eggs, dry toast, and strong black coffee) he had time for a more thorough inspection of his mail. It was an average crop. A bill for dues from one of his clubs—Mr. Rivers belonged to eight and was always receiving bills for dues, and always scolding, as he did now, that he was going to "give up" most of them. "It's all foolishness," he muttered angrily, as he read the bill and crumpled it away into his pocket—"I don't go to most of 'em twice a year, and every time I turn around, it seems I get a bill for something." A letter from a colleague inviting Mr. Rivers to join a *new* club—to be called the Editors and Authors—which was just being organized, which would meet on the first Tuesday of every month for dinner, and for "general discussion," and in which Mr. Rivers could enjoy the privileges of Charter Membership for only twenty-five dollars a year ("We're all eager to have you, Ned: everyone feels that we can't really call ourselves the Editors and Authors Club unless *you're* a member—do say you'll join—"). Mr. Rivers swore vigorously under his breath—Damn it all, just when a fellow was trying to get *out* of some of the clubs he did belong to, here comes someone trying to get him *into* another one—No, sir! He was through! No more clubs for him! Nevertheless, his weary old eyes had a rather *appeased* look in them as he read the flattering words of the invitation; he read it a second time, and put it away in his inside coat-pocket. He'd think it over, but damned if he was going to join any more of 'em!

There was a note from the venerable Mrs. Cornelius van Allen Hacker reminding him that she was expecting his attendance Saturday night at the Costume Ball to be given at the Waldorf by the Friends of Finnish Freedom: Costume Period, Louis Quinze. This reminded Mr. Rivers that he had not yet been to the costumer's to attend to the agony of getting rigged up in his monkey-suit, knee-breeches and drawer ruffles for his stringy shanks, flowered waistcoat, and a powdered wig. A letter from the Friends of Finland Society informing Mr. Rivers that they were sure he would be delighted to subscribe to the valuable work the Society was doing when they told him what it was (more muttered profanity from the recipient: Damn it, he didn't *want* to know what they were doing, they were doing what everyone else was doing—trying to do *him!*). A note from the widow of the late manufacturer of roofing materials and member of the United States Senate, Mrs. W. Spenser Drake, inviting him to a dinner given for the Irish playwright, Seamus O'Burke, Saturday at eight. (Confound it! How the hell *could* he when he was going to this Friends of Finland thing; did she expect him to come rigged up in his monkey-suit?) An advertisement by a syndicate of hair-restoring quacks, beginning companionably as follows: "Dear Friend: Your name has been given to us as one of that great and constantly growing group of American business men who are threatened with approaching baldness"—(*Threatened!* Threatened, hell! Threatened as the Red Coats threaten Philadelphia, as Washington is being threatened by Jubal Early's raiders—threatened forty years too late, when threats are useless!)—"Your condition, while serious, is by no means hopeless. So many men when they reach your age"—(when they reach *my* age! Who the hell do they think they're talking to: A God-damn school-boy!) "are prone to think" (—prone to think! Bah!) "—that baldness is incurable. We assure you that this is not the case, if you will act promptly! Act NOW! Even six months' delay at this stage *may be fatal!* The Roberts System offers to you an easy, agreeable, and scientific way of recovering your lost hair"—(Offers! Offers, nothing! Offers you an easy, agreeable, and scientific method of being swindled, fleeced, and robbed by a crowd of quacks and thieves and cut-throats who ought to be in jail! *Offers!—Bah!*)

Muttering angrily, Old Man Rivers crumpled up the offending letter into a wadded ball and threw it on the floor. It was all the same nowadays! There was some sort of trick to everything! Everywhere you turned, someone was out to do you!—Even—even Society—dining out—going to parties—had turned into a kind of—a kind of *Racket!* There wasn't even any real friendship any more; everyone was trying to see what he could get out of you! Even when you got invited out, you had to subscribe to something, give money to some damn fool organization, serve on committees, dance attendance on some visiting Irish popinjay, fill in at the last moment to make a *fourteenth* at dinner, be introduced as "Mr. Edward Rivers, the *former* editor of *Rodney's Magazine.*" By George, he was getting good and sick of it! For—two cents, he'd chuck the whole business, and go down and live on his farm in Pennsylvania! Most sensible life on earth, anyway! And the people down there in the country were *real* people—they had none of your fancy city ways, but they weren't all out to do you! You knew where you stood with them—by George you did!

8

The old man picked up the *Times* with an impatient rattle. There was very little in those crisp soberly packed columns to console him. Strikes—strikes—strikes; picketing and riots; hunger lines; and sixteen million out of work! Confound it, what were we coming to, anyway? Banks closing everywhere, banks being closed forever, banks being partially reopened, thousands of depositors losing all their savings, the President and his counselors pleading with the people for calmness, steadiness, faith, and prophets of doom direly predicting even worse times to come—total collapse—revolution perhaps—communism; armies, armaments, and marching men, threats of war everywhere; the whole world a snarl of passion, hate, and error—confusion everywhere, bewilderment, a new time, a new age, with nothing fixed or certain—nothing he could understand; the Stock Market in a state of bankruptcy—(Mr. Rivers surveyed the shattered columns of the stock reports, and groaned: another three point drop in a stock he had bought at 87, and which was now 12 and a fraction)—nothing but trouble, ruin, and damnation everywhere—

"Oh, Ned! Ned!"—At the sound of the sly voice at his shoulder, Mr. Rivers looked up sharply, startled and bewildered:—

"Hey? . . . What? . . . Oh, hello, Joe. I didn't see you."

Joe Paget bent a little lower over Old Man Rivers' shoulder, and before he spoke looked slyly round with eyes blood-shot, injected from the liquefactions of the night before:—

"Ned," he whispered and nudged the old man with a slyly prodding thumb—"Did you see it? Did you read it?"

"Hey?" said Mr. Rivers, still bewildered. "What's that, Joe? Read what?"

Joe Paget looked slyly round again before he answered. This was a sensual old man's face, high colored, with a thin, corrupted mouth, a face touched always by a sly and obscene humor, the whispering and impotent lecheries of an old worn-out rake.

"Did you read the story about Parsons?" Joe Paget asked in a low tone.

"Who? What?—*Parsons*? No—What about him?" Mr. Rivers said, in a startled tone.

Joe Paget glanced furtively around again; his red face suffused to purple, his red eyes blurred, low laughter struggled in his throat, his shoulders heaved:—

"He's being sued for breach of promise," said Joe Paget, "by an actress: she claims they've been sharing the same apartment since October—has all the letters to prove it. She's suing for a hundred thousand."

"No!" wheezed Mr. Rivers, frankly stupefied. "You don't mean it!" After a moment, however, he wagged his head with energetic decision, and said: "Well, now, we mustn't be too hasty! We mustn't make up our minds too fast! I'm going to wait until I hear what Parsons has to say before making up mine. That kind of woman will try anything. The woods are full of 'em nowadays:—they're just out to fleece anyone they can—they won't stop at blackmail, slander, lies, or anything! By George, if I were a judge, I'd be inclined to treat 'em pretty rough!—For all we know, the woman may be some kind of—of—adventuress, who met Parsons somewhere and—and— why, the whole thing may be nothing but a frame-up! That's what I think it *is!*"

"Well," said Joe Paget in a low voice, looking slyly around again before he spoke—"maybe. I don't know—only the papers say she's got a great stack of letters and—" the lecherous old rake glanced carefully around again, lowered his voice to a confiding whisper, and slyly nudged Old Man Rivers as he spoke—"You know, he's not been round the club much for the past six months—none of the fellows have seen much of him and—" Joe Paget again glanced slyly round, and dropped his voice—"during the past week he hasn't been here at all—"

"No!" said Mr. Rivers, astounded.

"Yes," Joe Paget whispered, and glanced round again, "—and for the last three days he hasn't even showed up at the office. No one knows where he is. So, you see—"

His voice trailed off, he glanced craftily around again, but the suggestion of lecherousness and smothered glee in his lewd old face and thin corrupted mouth was now unmistakable.

"Well, now—" began Old Man Rivers uncertainly, and cleared his throat—"We mustn't be too—"

"I know," Joe Paget said in a low tone and looked around, "—but still, Ned—"

Mr. Rivers fingered his goaty whiskers reflectively, and in a moment looked around slyly at Joe Paget. And Joe Paget looked slyly back at Old Man Rivers. For a moment their sly glances met and crossed and spoke— the old lecher and the aged goat—they looked quickly away again, then back, with sly communication at each other. A sly grin was now faintly printed round the mouth of Old Man Rivers, something low and guttural rattled in Joe Paget's throat, his florid face suffused to purple, he looked around him carefully, and then bent lower, shaking with repressed but obscene mirth:—

"But, Christ," he chortled, "I have to laugh when I think of the look on J. T.'s face when he sees it!" He looked slyly around again, then with suffusing face: "And Parsons! What do you suppose he feels like!—coming into the office every day to finish up that work he's been doing on the Acts of the Apostles—" Joe Paget gasped.

"—And tearing off a little now and then Between the Acts—" wheezed Mr. Rivers.

"You'd better say, Between the Actress, hadn't you?" Joe Paget choked, and nudged his copesmate with lewd fingers.

"God!" wheezed Mr. Rivers, in a high choked gasp and put his napkin to his streaming eyes. "—But that's a good one, 'y God it is!"

"Writing those little Sunday school books of his about Faith, Hope, and Charity—"

"And finding out, by God, there's damned little charity," gasped Mr. Rivers.

"He's got one," Joe Paget choked, "called 'All Is Not Gold That Glitters' "—

"Whew!" wheezed Mr. Rivers, wiping at his streaming eyes, and "Whee!" moaned Joseph Paget softly, and looked around him with injected and lewd-crafty eyes.

So did those two old men, the lecher and the goat, wheeze and chortle with lewd ruminations in the shining morning of young May. Old bald gray heads of other dotards turned toward them be-puzzled, frowned. Behind the cover of respectful fingers waiters smiled.

9

Promptly at nine-twenty, as had been his custom on every working day for twenty years, Mr. Rivers departed briskly from the club, turned round the corner into Fifth Avenue, and directed his morning footsteps toward the office of James Rodney & Co.

As usual, he had some genial wheeze of greeting for everyone: the doorman and the call-boys; club members; the policeman directing traffic at the corner, the elevator men at Rodney's, the office boy on the fifth floor, where he got out and where he had his office, Miss Dorgan, the stenographer, Fox, Pounders, old James, Tom T. Toms—anyone who came within range of his amiable and wheezing observation. All went well—or almost all—this morning along that well-known and often traveled route; the old man received and bestowed greetings everywhere—in the course of twenty years his eccentrically distinguished person had become familiar to a great many people, even in the thronging traffic of the city's life. At an intersection, however, something occurred to break the genial tenor of this morning's journey: just as the old man had started to cross over to the other side of the street, where Rodney's was situated, a taxi, swiftly driven, shot around to turn the corner, and almost clipped him. Mr. Rivers halted with a startled yell, the taxi halted with wheels sharply cut, and screaming brakes. For a moment, the genial appearance of the old man's temper was swallowed utterly in the swelling distemper of an old man's rage—blind, swift, sudden, and malevolent: one clenched and knotted old fist shot out, he shook it menacingly in the taxi-driver's face, and yelled out in a voice that could be heard a block:—

"You God-damn scoundrel, you! I'll have you put in jail, that's what I'll do."

To which the taxi-driver, young, hard, swarthy, and unmoved, made answer: "O.K., Toots. Whatever you say!"

Mr. Rivers then went his way muttering; before he reached the other side, however, he turned again and yelled a final denunciation: "You're a menace to public safety, that's what you are! They've got no business giving fellows like you a license!"

He was still muttering angrily about it when he entered the elevator at Rodney's; he responded curtly to the greeting of the elevator man, got out at the fifth floor, and entered his office without speaking to anyone.

By ten o'clock, however, he had forgotten it. The usual assortment of morning letters absorbed his attention—the useless letters from useless old people who knew him, or who knew useless old people who knew him. Some were letters of introduction from useless old people introducing other useless old people who had a useless old manuscript they wanted to get published. Others were just letters from useless old people sending along the useless old manuscripts which they themselves had written.

The business of reading these letters, of answering them, of examining all the useless old manuscripts, gave Old Man Rivers a glow of pleasure. It was somehow very satisfying to be so eagerly sought and solicited by so many well-placed and important people; to have his opinion eagerly solicited by the widow of a defunct ambassador for the manuscript "Memoirs of an Ambassador's Wife"—By George, that ought to get published! People were getting tired of all this stuff about gangsters and prize-fighters and bull-fighters and street-fighters and booze-fighters—they were getting tired of all this sex and profanity and vulgarity and filth—they'd like to read about Nice People for a change. Well, here it was, then, the very thing, all about the court life and the diplomatic life of Vienna in the days before the War, all kinds of interesting anecdotes about famous people—Franz Josef, the Empress, their children, the great statesmen, the foreign ambassadors— and written by a woman who knows what she's talking about, related to the Stuyvesant family, and more at home in Europe than she is in America, by George! . . . Why wouldn't people want to read a book like that?—written by a real lady, and with nothing in it that's likely to offend the feelings of other people of good taste and breeding.

Or, here now:—here was something that looked promising. This manuscript that came in just this morning, highly recommended too by Mrs. William Poindexter van Loan:—says the author is her brother-in-law, been all over the world, has been a sportsman, yachtsman, big-game hunter, had a racing stable, was a member of the diplomatic service, and is the eldest son of the late Henry C. Gipp, the oil man. "Adventures of an Amateur Explorer" by Henry C. Gipp, Jr.,—by George, it sounded as if there might be something in the thing; it looked Promising, and he was going to look into it right away.

Mr. Rivers' method of "looking into" something which he considered Promising was simple and direct. He had followed it for twenty years or more while he was Editor of *Rodney's Magazine,* and he was faithful to it yet. First of all, when he received a manuscript which sounded Promising, which came to him with the warmest recommendations of people of undoubted standing and the highest Social Position, Mr. Rivers immediately looked up the author of the manuscript in the *Social Register.* If the author of the manuscript was in the *Social Register,* Mr. Rivers was very considerably impressed. Nay, it would be more accurate to say that Mr. Rivers was now weighed down by a feeling of grave and solemn responsibility; the light of serious and concerned reflection would deepen in his eyes; it was evident that a matter of some moment had presented itself, and that all his most mature and serious powers of critical appraisal would be called into use, if he was to arrive at a fair judgment.

10

The second step of Mr. Rivers' critical technique was marked by the same clarity of purpose, the same cold and surgical directness. Having looked up the author of the Promising manuscript in the *Social Register* and found, just as he had suspected all the time, that he was *there,*—Mr. Rivers then turned his eagle-eyed pursuit to an investigation of the bulkier but no less enlightening pages of *Who's Who.* And if he found him here, name, birth, age, parentage, denomination, university, degrees, honors, offices, publications, clubs, all padded out to very imposing proportions (Mr. Rivers always *measured* when he used *Who's Who*), then, by George, that just about clinched the matter as far as he was concerned: his vote was *for* it.

Well, then—"Adventures of an Amateur Explorer," by Henry C. Gipp, Jr.—Mr. Rivers thumbed rapidly with a practiced thumb, through the chaste pages of the *Social Register:*—Yes, sir! just as he thought,—of course, anyone who was the brother-in-law of Mrs. William Poindexter van Loan would be in—together with his wife—his first *three* wives, that is (M. 1st [1905] Ellen Aster de Kaye [see also Mrs. Charles Lamson Turner, Mrs. H. Tracy Spencer]; m. 2nd [1913] Margaret Ferris Stokes [see also Mrs. F. Mortimer Payne, Mrs. H. Tracy Spencer (1st), the Princess Pinchabelli]; and 3rd [1922] Mabel Dodson Sprague [see also Princess Pinchabelli (2nd)])—together with all his children by all three marriages—no wait a minute; his third wife's children by her second marriage, his first wife's children by her third marriage; his second wife's children by her—well, anyway, here it was, a little confusing, perhaps, but all there, a whole page of them!—

—*And*—almost with trembling haste, with darkling apprehension, Mr. Rivers now approached and rapidly thumbed through the bulky pages of *Who's Who*—Now, let him see: Gibbs—Gibson—Gifford—Gilchrist—Gilroy—Gimble—Gipp!—Ah, *there* he was—and, by George, a good stick, too (Mr. Rivers measured with an expert finger)—three good inches at the least! . . . Yes, sir!—let's see now . . . son of the late Henry C. Gipp and Ethel Pratt. . . . St. Paul's and Harvard—hm! . . . Knickerbocker, Union, Racquet, New York Yacht, and Essex County Hunt (better and better). . . . And, yes, and author, too: "Adventures of an Amateur Angler" (1908); "Adventures of an Amateur Mountaineer" (1911); "Adventures of an Amateur Yachtsman" (1913); "Further Adventures of an Amateur Yachtsman" (1924); "Adventures of an Amateur Geologist" (1927).

By George! This looked like something! Breathing heavily, Mr. Rivers got up, picked up the manuscript with trembling fingers, and started down the long aisle that led from his own office at the back of the building to the office of Fox, in the front.

"Now, Edwards," Mr. Rivers began without preliminary in his high foggy voice as he entered Foxhall Edwards' office, "it looks to me we've got something here worth looking into—fellow comes to me with the highest recommendations, brother-in-law of Mrs. William Poindexter van Loan, son of the late Henry Gipp, the big oil man—and all that—looked him up in the *Social Register* myself," wheezed Mr. Rivers—"and yes!—been all over the world, she says—big-game hunter, yachtsman, mountain climber, used to row on the crew at Harvard—"

Fox, who had been standing at the window, hat jammed down over his ears and hands hanging to his coat lapels as he looked down with sea-pale, lonely, and abstracted eyes at the swirling tides of life and traffic in Fifth Avenue, five floors below, now turned slowly, stared at Old Man Rivers with a bewildered expression, and finally, in a low, deaf, puzzled tone, said slowly:—

"Wha-a-t?" Seeing the manuscript in Old Man Rivers' hand, Fox turned slowly, in a tone of quiet resignation: "Oh-h!"—then turned back sadly to his lonely, sea-pale contemplation of the street again.

"Yes," wheezed Mr. Rivers foggily, in a tone indicative of considerable excitement—"says he's been everywhere, all over the world, done everything, says he's really a very remarkable kind of fellow—"

"Wha-a-t?" says Fox, turning slowly, in a slow, deaf, bewildered tone again—"Who-o-o?"

"Why—this—this—this Gipp fellow, Mrs. van Loan, I mean—no! Her brother-in-law—the one who wrote this thing here," Mr. Rivers wheezed excitedly (Confound that fellow, Mr. Rivers thought impatiently, you never know how to talk to him. You tell him all about something—something important like this—and his mind's a thousand miles away from you all the time. He just looks out the window and doesn't hear a word you say)— "but I've gone into the whole matter carefully," wheezed Mr. Rivers, "—and the way it looks to me, Edwards, we've got something here that we ought to consider very carefully. I've looked up his whole record—he's written a half-dozen books—Adventures, you know, in one thing and another and," Mr. Rivers wheezed triumphantly, "—*he's got that much in Who's Who!*"—as he uttered these words, Mr. Rivers made a descriptive gesture with the thumb and forefinger of his right hand, to indicate that "that much" meant at least three or four inches.

For a moment Fox looked at him with an expression of blank astonishment. Still hanging to his coat lapels, he bent, craned his neck, and peered at Mr. Rivers' thumb and forefinger with a look of utter stupefaction.

"I say," screamed Mr. Rivers, at the foggy apex of his voice—"*he's—got— that—much—in—Who's Who!*" (God damn it, he thought, what's wrong with the fellow, anyway? Can't he understand a word you say to him?)

"Oh-h," said Fox slowly. Slowly, and with an effort, his soul swam upward from its sea-sunken depths. "All right, I'll look at it," he said.

"Well, now," Mr. Rivers wheezed, a little mollified, and shaking his head with vigorous emphasis—"that's what I think, now! I think we've got something here we ought to look into."

11

With these words Mr. Rivers departed, going down the aisle, past Fred Busch busy with his telephone, past the two partitioned libraries, past the little reception vestibule where the office boy, a stenographer, and several hopeful-hoping authors were waiting to see Fox, Dick, Fred Busch, George Hauser, or someone else about their manuscripts, and so back into his own little dark, partitioned cubby-hole of an office. As he went, Old Man Rivers wagged his whiskers vigorously and muttered to himself. By George, now, he hoped they'd wake up around this place, and take advantage of their opportunities! They'd turned down everything else he'd ever brought them, but he hoped they'd wake up and do something this time, before they lost this fellow, too. That fellow Edwards, now, might be all right in *a literary sort of a way*, but he didn't seem to have any enterprise—to—to—to show any practical judgment. Here he'd brought him people time and again— well-known people with long write-ups in *Who's Who*—and he'd just let them slip right through his fingers. What was the good of calling yourself an editor, anyway, if you were just going to look out the window all day long and let someone else snap up all the good people you could have had yourself. Sometimes it looked as if some of these young fellows nowadays were fifty years behind the times. It almost looked as if it took the old warhorse to show 'em!

Old Man Rivers had got back to his office by this time. He went in, sat down at his desk, tilted back in his swivel chair for a moment, and with his veinous old hands resting on the armrests, stared reflectively for a moment at his desk. He felt tired, exhausted by his effort, by the excitement of his latest discovery, by his efforts to persuade and impress Edwards. Also he felt a little lonely. He looked at his watch. It was only eleven-thirty in the morning—still too early to go to lunch—and he had finished all he had to do. He had answered all the letters that he had to answer: the neatly typed replies lay in a clean sheaf before him. All he had to do was sign them, and Miss Dorgan would do the rest. So what to do?—How to kill the time?— How to look busy between now and lunch? And after lunch? He could spend three hours comfortably at lunch—from twelve to three with some of his cronies at the University Club: a good meal, good drinks, brandy, and a good cigar. But, then, the rest of the afternoon, from three to five, stretched out before him. He ought to come back to his office if only for the sake of keeping up appearances, but what was there to do? To sit there in that office staring at the fresh green blotter on his tidy desk—the prospect left him desolate.

He straightened with a jerk, dropped pen in ink-well, and began to sign the letters. When he had finished, he wheezed out: "Oh, Miss Dorgan."

"Yes, Mr. Rivers?"—she came at once, a pleasant red-cheeked, friendly-looking girl, who had her typist's desk outside his office.

"Now these letters here," he wheezed and waved toward them—"they're all signed and ready to be mailed. So you can take them when you're ready."

"Yes, Mr. Rivers. And will that be all?"

"Well, now," he wheezed, "was that all the mail there was?"

"Yes, that was all, Mr. Rivers."

"Well, then," he said, "I guess that's all then for the present. . . . There's no one waiting out there to see me?" he demanded, with a flare of hope.

"No, Mr. Rivers. There's been no one today."

"Well, then," he mumbled, "I guess that's all for the present. . . . Oh, I don't suppose there was any more mail?"—hopefully.

"I don't *think* so, Mr. Rivers. If you'll just wait a moment, I'll see if anything came in the second delivery."

"Well, now," the old man mumbled, "maybe you'd better do that."

She left him, and in a moment returned with a single letter. Mr. Rivers snatched it almost greedily.

"This just came, Mr. Rivers." She hesitated a little. "Do you think it's anything that needs to be tended to right away? It—it looks as if it might be an advertising folder."

"Well, now, I don't know," said Mr. Rivers, and shook his head dubiously. "You can't tell about these things—you never know what's in 'em. For all I know, it might be something important, something I ought to attend to right away—"

Meanwhile, he was examining the envelope with palsied hands: suddenly the inscription *Who's Who In America* caught his weary eyes, and fixed them with the sudden spark of interest.

"By George, yes," Mr. Rivers wheezed, and began to run a trembling

finger under the flap—"Just as I thought—this looks as if it might be something I ought to attend to right away."

"Then you'll call me if you need me?" said Miss Dorgan.

Mr. Rivers wagged his goatish head with solemn affirmation:—

"You go right on out there and sit down," he kindly wheezed—"If it's
something we've got to do, why—" solemnly he wagged his goatish head
again—"I'll let you know."

12

Left alone, Mr. Rivers opened the letter and observed the contents. A brief
note informed him that a proof of his biography, as recorded in the last
edition of *Who's Who,* was enclosed, and requested him to make any necessary changes or additions, and return the proof for the forthcoming edition
as soon as possible.

This *was* something! It just went to show that a fellow never could be
too careful—something important that ought to be attended to right away
might turn up at any moment! Well, he'd just look into this right now, and
see what needed to be done.

Mr. Rivers adjusted his spectacles and began to read the proof of his
biography—two-thirds of a column of fine dense type. As he went on, the
last trace of weariness, boredom, and dejection vanished. The old man's eyes
began to sparkle, his cheeks flushed with a glow of ruddy color, he had
begun to read with an air of editorial alertness, but this shortly vanished,
was supplanted almost instantly by a look of growing fascination, the rapt
absorption of the artist enchanted by the contemplation of his own creation.

By George, this *was* something now! When a fellow was feeling blue or
depressed, all he had to do was take a look at *this!* There he *was,* in black
and white, the sum of him, the dense chronicle of his accomplishment! And
if he did say so himself, it was pretty good! Pretty good for the son of a
country doctor! Why (Old Man Rivers thumbed rapidly through the pages
of *Who's Who* before him on the desk—)—there weren't over a half-dozen
fellows in the whole book who had as much as he had (Barr—Barrett—
Burroughs—Butler)—Nick Butler, now, *he* had more, of course, all of those
learned societies and honors he had received abroad, and things he belonged to in France and England, they ran the score up, but there weren't
many like that. And having satisfied himself that this was true, Mr. Rivers
returned to a contemplation of his *own* score, which ran as follows:

Rivers, Edward Schroeder; Publicist and Editor. B. Hamburg Falls, Pa., May
2, 1857, s. of the late Dr. Joseph C. and Augusta (Schroeder) R. Ed. at public
schools and at the Lawrenceville Academy, A.B. Princeton University, 1879:

Student at Heidelberg and the University of Berlin, 1879–1880. Associated with the publishing house of James Rodney & Co. since 1881. Unmarried. Presbyt'n. Associate Editor Rodney's Magazine 1886–1902; Editor-in-Chief Rodney's Magazine, 1902–1930; Advisory Editor James Rodney & Co. since 1930.

Member following societies, organizations, honorary fellowships and institutions: Sons of the American Revolution; Sons and Daughters of the Tribe of Pocahontas; National Affiliation of Colonial Families (Regional Sec. 1919–1924); Children of William Penn; and President Hamburg Falls Historical Ass'n. (since 1894).

Also, Friends of The Pilgrim Fathers; International Union of the Society of Hands Across the Sea; English Speaking Union; National Association of Descendants of Early Huguenots; National Association of the Friends of Lafayette; The Steuben Society; National Preparedness Guild; American League Against War and Fascism; Society of the Friends of the American Constitution; also Friends of the Russian People; Friends of Poland; Friends of Norway; Spanish-American Fellowship for the Promotion of Friendly Relations Between the Republics of the North and South American Continents; American Liberty League; and Society for the Prevention of Cruelty to Animals.

Also, Member International Writers Guild For the Promotion of An International Point of View Among the Writers of All Nations (Founder, and Honorary President since 1913); the International Society for the Dissemination of Good Manners and Standards of Culture; the League for Social Democracy; the League of National Magazine Editors (Affiliated with the International League of Magazine Editors); the League for the Promotion of Friendlier Relations Between Publishers and Authors; the League for the Control of a Wise and Wholesome Censorship; the National League for the Protection of National Ideals, Morals, and Standards of Purity; and the P.E.N. Club.

Also, author of the following books of verse, fiction, essays, travel, biography, autobiography, and criticism: A Yankee Pilgrim on the Rhine (1881); Eternal Values (1884); Literature and Morals (1885); Leadership and Letters (1888); Literature and the Good Life (1891); Rondels for Rita (1894); Maypoles for Margaret (1896); When Prue and I Were Young, Maggie (1897); A Sheaf of Sonnets (1898); A Bouquet of Ballads (1899); Lyrics for Louise (1900); Jed Stone's Conversion (1902); The Ordeal of Abner Ames (1904); Enid's Enigma (1905); Their Golden Wedding (1907); Mrs. Coke's Confession (1909); An Editor's Edifications (1910); Confessions of an Incomplete Angler (1911); My Sabine Farm (1913); Kinsmen Once and Brothers Yet (1914); France and Freedom (1915); Shall England Perish? (1916); The Hun and Hatred (1918); Friendship's Folly (1920); Ted and Tom: A Memoir (1922); and A Greybeard's Garland (1926).

Clubs: The Ivy, University, Princeton, Century, Players, Lotos, Coffee House, Dutch Treat, Collectors, Scriveners, Rod and Gun, Cuff and Link, Hound and Horn, and the Hamburg Falls (Pa.) Country.

Address: The University Club, New York City.

By *George,* now! This *was* something! Mr. Rivers leaned back in his swivel chair, and rocked gently back and forth for a moment, staring at the column of dense print before him with an air of profound and contemplative satisfaction. The weary, sad, dejected old man of a few minutes ago had been transformed. Gone was his dejection, vanished his boredom, flown away on wings of hope the last vestiges of self-doubt, loneliness, and depression. When a fellow was feeling low—when he had doubts—when he wondered if the whole thing had been worth all the trouble, let him look at *that!* And let the others look at it, too. There he was, there was the whole story down in black and white, if they wanted to know who *he* was, what *he* had done, just let them look at that.

For a moment longer he rocked back and forth reflectively. Then, clearing his throat, and raising his head, he wheezed out in a high and foggy tone:—

"Miss Dorgan."

"Yes, Mr. Rivers." Smiling, the girl appeared at once.

"Now," Mr. Rivers wheezed, clearing his throat again. "Hem!" he wheezed, and rocked back and forth reflectively a moment. "Well, now—" he fumbled at the inside pocket of his coat with shaking fingers, took out the letter he had put there that morning, and again inspected it. "Well, now, Miss Dorgan," Mr. Rivers said, "—down there where it says 'Clubs'—do you see where I mean?"

"Yes, Mr. Rivers."

"Well, put in down there, member of the Editors and Authors Club—put down 'Charter Member'."

"Yes, Mr. Rivers. But are you a member yet?"

"Well, now," said Mr. Rivers, a trifle testily, "—*no!* Not exactly! But I'm *going* to be—" In response to the faintly amused question in the girl's eyes, the old man wagged his head defensively, and said: "—Well, now, I know I said I wasn't going to join any more—and I'm *not*—only this is something I've *got* to do! They said they wouldn't feel right calling it an Editors and Authors Club unless they had me in there.—But that's the last one: I'm through after this. But you put that in there where it says 'Clubs'."

"Yes, Mr. Rivers, Member of the Editors and Authors Club."

"—Hem! Yes. . . . *Charter* member: don't forget to put that in."

"Yes, Mr. Rivers. Will that be all?"

"—Hem! Yes, I think so! . . . Now, you'd better get that right off as soon as you can, Miss Dorgan," he wheezed admonishingly. "They say the time is short, and for all we know, we may hold up the whole edition if we're late."

"Yes, Mr. Rivers. I'll mail it right away."

When she had gone, the old man rocked back and forth a moment longer. There was a little smile of pleased reflection around his mouth. It was funny what a thing like that could do. It made him feel good, set him right up! He'd been down in the dumps just half an hour ago, with no interest in anything—and now!—Mr. Rivers looked at his watch and jumped up briskly. It was twelve o'clock. He'd go to the Club, get Tom to fix him an Old Fashioned, and order a whacking good lunch. He felt in the mood for it, by George he did!

The old man picked up his hat and left the office. A moment later he was in the street, walking briskly along among the thronging crowds, in the direction of the Club.

Justice Is Blind

There used to be—perhaps there still exists—a purveyor of *belles lettres* in the older, gentler vein who wrote a weekly essay in one of the nation's genteeler literary publications, under the whimsical *nom de plume* of Old Sir Kenelm. Old Sir Kenelm, who had quite a devoted literary following that esteemed him as a perfect master of delightful letters, was a leisurely essayist of the Lambsian school. He was always prowling around in out-of-the-way corners and turning up with something quaint and unexpected that made his readers gasp and say, "Why, I've passed that place a thousand times and I never *dreamed* of anything like that!"

In the rush, the glare, the fury of modern life many curious things, alas, get overlooked by most of us; but leave it to Old Sir Kenelm, he would always smell them out. He had a nose for it. He was a kind of enthusiastic rubber-up of tarnished brasses, and assiduous ferreter-out of grimy corner-stones. The elevated might roar above him, and the subway underneath him, and a hurricane of machinery all about him, while ten thousand strident tones passed and swarmed and dinned in his ears—above all this raucous tumult Old Sir Kenelm rose serene: if there was a battered inscription anywhere about, caked over with some fifty years of city dirt, he would be sure to find it, and no amount of paint or scaly rust could deceive his falcon eye for Revolutionary brick.

The result of it was, Old Sir Kenelm wandered all around through the highways and byways of Manhattan, Brooklyn, and the Bronx discovering Dickens everywhere; moreover, as he assured his readers constantly, anyone with half an eye could do the same. Whimsical characters in the vein of Pickwick simply abounded in the most unexpected places—in filling stations, automats, and the corner stores of the United Cigar Company. More than this, seen properly, the automat was just as delightful and quaint a place as an old inn, and a corner cigar store as delightfully musty and redolent of good cheer as a tavern in Cheapside. Old Sir Kenelm was at his best when describing the customs and whimsical waterfront life of Hoboken, which he immortalized in a delightful little essay as "Old Hobie"; but he really reached the heights when he applied his talents to the noontime rush hour at the soda counter of the corner pharmacy. His description

589

of the quaint shopgirls who foregathered at the counter, the swift repartee and the Elizabethan jesting of the soda jerkers, together with his mouth-watering descriptions of such Lucullan delicacies as steamed spaghetti and sandwiches of pimento cheese, were enough to make the ghosts of the late William Hazlitt and Charles Lamb roll over in their shrouds and weep for joy.

It is therefore a great pity that Old Sir Kenelm never got a chance to apply his elfin talent to a description of the celebrated partnership that bore the name of Paget and Page. Here, assuredly if ever, was grist for his mill, or in somewhat more modern phrase, here was a subject right down his alley. Since this yearning subject has somehow escaped the Master's hand, we are left to supply the lack as best we can by the exercise of our own modest talents.

The offices of the celebrated firm of Paget and Page were on the thirty-seventh floor of one of the loftier skyscrapers, a building that differed in no considerable respect from a hundred others: unpromising enough, it would seem, for purposes of Dickensian exploration and discovery. But one who has been brought up in the hardy disciplines of Old Sir Kenelm's school is not easily dismayed. If one can find Charles Lamb at soda fountains, why should one not find Charles Dickens on the thirty-seventh floor?

One's introduction to this celebrated firm was swift, and from an eighteenth century point of view perhaps a bit unpromising. One entered the great marble corridor of the building from Manhattan's swarming streets, advanced through marble halls and passed the newspaper and tobacco stand, and halted before a double row of shining elevators. As one entered and to the charioteer spoke the magic syllables, "Paget and Page," the doors slid to and one was imprisoned in a cage of shining splendor; a lever was pulled back, there was a rushing sound, punctuated now and then by small clicking noises—the whole thing was done quite hermetically, and with no sense of movement save for a slight numbness in the ears, very much, no doubt, as a trip to the moon in a projectile would be—until at length, with the same magic instancy, the cage halted, the doors slid open, and one stepped out upon the polished marble of the thirty-seventh floor feeling dazed, bewildered, and very much alone, and wondering how one got there. One turned right along the corridor, and then left, past rows of glazed-glass offices, formidable names, and the clattering cachinnations of a regiment of typewriters, and almost before one knew it, there squarely to the front, at the very dead end of the hall, one stood before another glazed-glass door in all respects identical with the others except for these words:

PAGET AND PAGE
Counselors at Law

This was all—these simple functions of the alphabet in orderly arrange-ment—but to anyone who has ever broached that portal, what memories they convey!

Within, the immediate signs of things to come were also unremarkable. There was an outer office, some filing cases, a safe, a desk, a small telephone switchboard, and two reasonably young ladies seated busily at typewriters. Opening from this general vestibule were the other offices of the suite. First one passed a rather small office with a flat desk, behind which sat a quiet and timid-looking little gentleman of some sixty years, with a white mus-tache, and a habit of peering shyly and quickly at each new visitor over the edges of the papers with which he was usually involved, and a general facial resemblance to the little man who has become well known in the drawings of a newspaper cartoonist as Caspar Milquetoast. This was the senior clerk, a sort of good man Friday to this celebrated firm. Beyond his cubicle a corridor led to the private offices of the senior members of the firm.

As one went down this corridor in the direction of Mr. Page—for it is with him that we shall be principally concerned—one passed the office of Mr. Paget. Lucius Page Paget, as he had been christened, could generally be seen sitting at his desk as one went by. He, too, was an elderly gentleman with silvery hair, a fine white mustache, and gentle patrician features. Be-yond was the office of Mr. Page.

Leonidas Paget Page was a few years younger than his partner, and in appearance considerably more robust. As he was sometimes fond of saying, for Mr. Page enjoyed his little joke as well as any man, he was "the kid member of the firm." He was a man of average height and of somewhat stocky build. He was bald, save for a surrounding fringe of iron-gray hair, he wore a short-cropped mustache, and his features, which were round and solid and fresh-colored, still had something of the chunky plumpness of a boy. At any rate, one got a very clear impression of what Mr. Page must have looked like as a child. His solid, healthy-looking face, and a kind of animal drive and quickness in his stocky figure, suggested that he was a man who liked sports and out-of-doors.

This was true. Upon the walls were several remarkable photographs por-traying Mr. Page in pursuit of his favorite hobby, which was ballooning. One saw him, for example, in a splendid exhibit marked "Milwaukee, 1908," helmeted and begoggled, peering somewhat roguishly over the edges of the wicker basket of an enormous balloon which was apparently just about to take off. There were other pictures showing Mr. Page in sim-ilar attitudes, marked "St. Louis," or "Chicago," or "New Orleans." There was even one showing him in the proud possession of an enormous silver cup: this was marked "Snodgrass Trophy, 1916."

Elsewhere on the walls, framed and hung, were various other evidences of Mr. Page's profession and his tastes. There was his diploma from the Harvard Law School, his license to practice, and most interesting of all, in a small frame, a rather faded and ancient-looking photograph of a lawyer's shingle upon which, in almost indecipherable letters, was the inscription: "Paget and Page." Below, Mr. Page's own small, fine handwriting informed one that this was evidence of the original partnership, which had been formed in 1838.

Since then, fortunately, there had always been a Paget to carry on partnership with Page, and always a Page so to combine in legal union with Paget. The great tradition had continued in a line of unbroken succession from the time of the original Paget and the original Page, who had been great-grandfathers of the present ones. Now, for the first time in almost one hundred years, that hereditary succession was in danger of extinction; for the present Mr. Page was a bachelor, and there were no others of his name and kin who could carry on. But come!—that prospect is a gloomy one and not to be thought of any longer here.

There exist in modern life, as Spangler was to find out, certain types of identities or people who, except for contemoporary manifestations of dress, of domicile, or of furniture, seem to have stepped into the present straight out of the life of a vanished period. This archaism is particularly noticeable among the considerable group of people who follow the curious profession known as the practice of the law. Indeed, as Spangler was now to discover, the archaism is true of that curious profession itself. Justice, he had heard, is blind. Of this he was unable to judge, because in all his varied doings with legal gentlemen he never once had the opportunity of meeting the Lady. If she was related to the law, as he observed it in majestic operation, the relationship was so distant that no one, certainly no lawyer, ever spoke of it.

In his first professional encounter with a member of this learned craft, Spangler was naive enough to mention the Lady right away. He had just finished explaining to Mr. Leonidas Paget Page the reason for his visit, and in the heat of outraged innocence and embattled indignation he had concluded:

"But good Lord! They can't do a thing like this! There's no Justice in it!"

"Ah, now," replied Mr. Page. "Now you're talking about Justice!"

Spangler, after a somewhat startled pause, admitted that he was.

"Ah, now! Justice—" said Mr. Page, nodding his head reflectively as if somewhere he had heard the word before—"Justice. Hm, now, yes. But my dear boy, that's quite another matter. This problem of yours," said Mr. Page, "is not a matter that involves Justice. It is a matter of the Law." And, having delivered himself of these portentous words, his voice sinking to a note of unctuous piety as he pronounced the holy name of Law, Mr. Page settled back in his chair with a relaxed movement, as if to say: 'There you have it in a nutshell. I hope this makes it clear to you.'

Unhappily it didn't. Spangler, still persisting in his error, struck his hand sharply against the great mass of letters and documents he had brought with him and deposited on Mr. Page's desk—the whole accumulation of the damning evidence that left no doubt whatever about the character and conduct of his antagonist—and burst out excitedly:

"But good God, Mr. Page, the whole thing's here! As soon as I found out what was going on, I simply had to write her as I did, the letter I told you about, the one that brought all this to a head."

"And quite properly," said Mr. Page with an approving nod. "Quite properly. It was the only thing to do. I hope you kept a copy of the letter," he added thriftily.

"Yes," said Spangler. "But see here. Do you understand this thing? The woman's *suing* me! Suing *me!*" the victim went on in an outraged and exasperated tone of voice, as of one who could find no words to express the full enormity of the situation.

"But of course she's suing you," said Mr. Page. "That's just the point. That's why you're here. That's why you've come to see me, isn't it?"

"Yes, sir. But good God, she can't do this!" the client cried in a baffled and exasperated tone. "She's in the wrong and she knows it! The whole thing's here, don't you see that, Mr. Page?" Again Spangler struck the mass of papers with an impatient hand. "It's here, I tell you, and she can't deny it. She can't sue me!"

"But she is," said Mr. Page tranquilly.

"Yes—but dammit!—" in an outraged yell of indignation —"this woman *can't* sue me. I've done nothing to be sued about."

"Ah, now!" Mr. Page, who had been listening intently but with a kind of imperturbable, unrevealing detachment which said plainly, "I hear you but I grant you nothing," now straightened with a jerk and with an air of recognition, and said: "Ah, now I follow you. I get your point. I see what you're driving at. You can't be sued, you say, because you've done nothing to be sued about. My dear boy!" For the first time Mr. Page allowed himself a smile, a smile tinged with a shade of good humor and forgiving tolerance, as one who is able to understand and overlook the fond delusions of youth and immaturity. "My dear boy," Mr. Page repeated, "that has nothing in the world to do with it. Oh, absolutely nothing!" His manner had changed instantly as he spoke these words: he shook his round and solid face quickly, grimly, with a kind of bulldog tenacity that characterized his utterance when he stated an established fact, one that allowed no further discussion or debate. "Absolutely nothing!" cried Mr. Page, and shook his bulldog jaw again. "You say you can't be sued unless you've done something to be sued about. My dear sir!"—here Mr. Page turned in his chair and looked grimly at his client with a kind of bulldog earnestness, pronouncing his words now deliberately and gravely, with the emphasis of a slowly wagging finger, as if he wanted to rivet every syllable and atom of his meaning into his client's brain and memory—"My dear sir," said Mr. Page grimly, "you are laboring under a grave misapprehension if you think you have to do something to be sued about. Do not delude yourself. That has nothing on earth to do with it! Oh, absolutely nothing!" Again he shook his bulldog jaws. "From this time on," as he spoke, his words became more slow and positive, and he hammered each word home with the emphasis of his authoritative finger—"from this time on, sir, I want you to bear this fact in mind and never to forget it for a moment, because it may save you much useless astonishment and chagrin as you go on through life. *Anybody*, Mr. Spangler," Mr. Page's voice rose strong and solid, "*anybody*—can sue—*anybody*—about *anything!*" He paused a full moment after he had uttered these words, in order to let their full significance sink in; then he said: "Now have you got that straight? Can you remember it?"

The younger man stared at the attorney with a look of dazed and baffled stupefaction. Presently he moistened his dry lips, and as if he still hoped he had not heard correctly, said: "You—you mean—even if I have not done anything?"

"That has nothing on earth to do with it," said Mr. Page as before. "Absolutely nothing."

"But suppose—suppose, then, that you do not even know the person who is suing you—that you never even heard of such a person—do you mean to tell me—?"

"Absolutely!" cried Mr. Page before his visitor could finish. "It doesn't matter in the slightest whether you've heard of the person or not! That has nothing to do with it!"

"Good Lord, then," the client cried, as the enormous possibilities of legal action were revealed to him, "if what you say is true, then anybody at all—" he exclaimed as the concept burst upon him in its full power, "why you could be sued, then, by a one-eyed boy in Bethlehem, Pennsylvania, even if you'd never seen him!"

"Oh, absolutely!" Mr. Page responded instantly. "He could claim," Mr. Page paused a moment and became almost mystically reflective as the juicy possibilities suggested themselves to his legally fertile mind, "he could claim, for example, that—that, er, one of your books—hm, now, yes!"— briefly and absently he licked his lips with an air of relish, as if he himself were now becoming professionally interested in the case—"he could claim that one of your books was printed in such small type that—that—that the sight of the other eye had been *permanently* impaired!" cried Mr. Page triumphantly. He settled back in his swivel chair and rocked back and forth a moment with a look of such satisfaction that it almost seemed as if he were contemplating the possibility of taking a hand in the case himself. "Yes! By all means!" cried Mr. Page, nodding his head in vigorous affirmation. "He might make a very good case against you on those grounds. While I haven't considered carefully all the merits of such a case, I can see how it might have its points. Hm, now, yes." He cleared his throat reflectively. "It might be very interesting to see what one could do with a case like that."

For a moment the younger man could not speak. He just sat there looking at the lawyer with an air of baffled incredulity. "But—but—" he managed presently to say—"why, there's no Justice in the thing!" he burst out indignantly, in his excitement making use of the discredited word again.

"Ah, Justice," said Mr. Page, nodding. "Yes, I see now what you mean. That's quite another matter. But we're not talking of Justice. We're talking of the Law—which brings us to this case of yours." And, reaching out a pudgy hand, he pulled the mass of papers toward him and began to read them.

Such was our pilgrim's introduction to that strange, fantastic world of twist and weave, that labyrinthine cave at the end of which waits the Minotaur, the Law.

No More Rivers

George awoke at seven-thirty, and for a moment lay flat on his back, and listened to the beating of his heart. With the fingers of one hand, he felt his pulse, and counted: "One-two-three-four"—the great pump beat regularly enough, until "five-six-seven"—blank terror filled him—it had jumped a beat! Great God, it had fluttered for a moment like a wing—now it missed again!—fluttered—beat again—George pressed hot fingers on his wrist and listened. He was sick with fear! His pulse now beat like a sledgehammer in his throat, it pounded thickly, like the muffled beating of a bell in his ear-drums. Gradually, it subsided: his pulse beat regularly again, until the con-vulsion of his fear had passed. His pleasant face resumed its normal quietness.

I have heard, thought George, that it may miss *two* strokes, and yet the man will live. I have even heard it said that it may miss *three* strokes and *still* the man can live. But I have heard it said that if it misses *four*—the man is dead, the heart will never beat again.

Oh, God, he thought, as the agony of horror filled his soul again—to be composed of so much bitter agony, such lust of living and such fear of dying, that all the oceans of the world could never hold the huge unfath-omed sum of it, and all of it dependent for its life upon the beating of a tired pump!

One-two-three-four! It's just a little pump, yet it can never stop—if it should stop for half a minute, we are gone. Great God, do people *know?* Do they never stop to think about the terror of the heart?—that small, frail pulse of pumping blood that is the only thing that stands between them— all they have and strive for and accomplish—and blank nothingness? Do they never lie alone in this great city as I have lain alone here many thousand times—and listen to the beating of their hearts?

Do they not know that really there is nothing in the world but—*heart?* That this whole enormous city is nothing but heart?—that the lives of all men living are nothing more than the beating of a heart?

Have they never lain here in darkness thinking of these things? Have they never lain here at night in all their little rooms—their wretched rabbit-warrens of brick, their dizzy battlements of stone, tier above tier and floor

596

upon floor? In these seven million little cells of men, are seven million little pumps, all beating in the seven million cells of night, all joining seven million heartbeats to the heart of sleep, all uniting to the single beating of the city's heart?

Have they never *counted*? Have they never *listened*? Have they never heard them in the night, as I have heard them all so many times, giving their pulse to sleep and silence and the flowing of the river, ticking like tiny clocks the promise of their pulses to—death?

He lay still on his couch and listened to the steady rumble of the traffic on First Avenue, just half a block away—the heavy rattling of the huge trucks rumbling down to get their morning load; and the smooth, thrumming, projectile-like precision of the motor cars. He had seen it all a thousand times—huge rusty trucks, the gaudy taxis flashing past; huge limousines, or motors of a common make, or speedy roadsters driven by assured young men, driving to their offices from their country homes.

And oh, the certitude, the alert and daring *will* of all these people:—all flashing past with this same overwhelming confidence that faced the swarming complexity of the city's life—but did *they* know? Did *they* know that this invincible will of purpose—that the whole of this gigantic energy—was dependent on the frail, uncertain beating of a heart?

And all these other ones—those unnumbered motes of life who now were being hurled into this tortured rock through tunnels roaring with the blind energy of the subway trains, who were roaring in across the bridges, rushing in by train, sliding in packed in a dense wall across the blunted snouts of ferries—who were pouring out of seven million sleeping cells in all the dense compacted warrens of the city life, to be rushed to seven million other *waking* cells of work—did *they* know? They were being hurled in from every spot upon the compass—the crack trains of the nation were crashing up from Georgia, flashing down out of New England, the crack trains thirty coaches long that had smashed their way all night across the continent— from Chicago, St. Louis, from Montreal, Atlanta, New Orleans, and Texas. These great projectiles of velocity that had bridged America with the pistoned stroke, the hot and furious breath of their terrific drive, were now pounding at the river's edge upon the very lintels of the city. They were filled with people getting up—at sixty miles an hour—filled with people getting dressed—at sixty miles an hour—filled with people getting shaved— at sixty miles an hour—walking down carpeted narrow aisles between the green baize curtains of the Pullman berths—at sixty miles an hour—and sitting down to eat substantial breakfasts in splendid windowed dining cars, while the great train smashes at the edges of that noble wink, the enchanted serpent of the Hudson River. The hot breath of the tremendous locomotive fairly pants against the lintels of the terrific city—all at sixty miles an hour— and all for *what*? for *what*?—Great God, that all these people, dressed and shaved and breakfasted, and hurled halfway across the continent by night— might add, each in his own way, their little sum to the gigantic total of that universal agony! Didn't they ever ask themselves *why* they should get up in the morning at all, *why* they should dress, and gulp down coffee, and then rush out into the streets with a look of grim determination in their eye, to push and be pushed, dodge and scuttle across, be hurled through tunnels and come swarming, clawing their way out of them—for what? for *what?*— So that they could get from one ridiculous little cell where they slept, to another ridiculous little cell where they worked, and go about doing ridiculous things all day long—writing ridiculous letters, making or receiving ridiculous telephone calls, "getting in touch" (which was itself ridiculous, how? why? should you try to "get in touch" with anyone)—with other ridiculous people, looking up ridiculous things in a filing cabinet, or filing them away. Good Lord, couldn't they see that all of it was a spectacle to make the men on Mars—if men on Mars existed—split their sides with laughter. Couldn't they see that everything began with and returned to the only thing for which they should care at all—the frail uncertain beating of a—*heart!*

For him, at any rate, that had become the only thing for which he cared— to keep his own heart beating, to avoid in every way he could the brutal shocks of life and business, of speed, confusion, noise, and violence, of love, of grief, of happiness and heartbreak! Great God! Would people never *learn?* Would they never understand that the frail and naked heart could not be used as a football, kicked about by all the brutal and indifferent feet of life? Oh, if he could only tell them how slight a thing it took to plunge the anguish of a cureless hurt into the heart's deep core—how slight a thing— a tread upon the stairs, the intonation of a voice, the opening of a door— could fill the heart with joy and anguish—if he could only tell them how slight a thing it took to make hearts break!

Therefore, no more, no more! For him, at any rate, his care henceforth would be to keep his heart in one small cell, and so to spare his heart and hearts of other people. No more to dare adventure, or to risk defeat with this frail heart! No more to endure the agony of grief, the cureless pain of loss, the insane devotion, and the wound remediless of love! No more friendship; no more love and no more hatred, no more conflict, no more desire, no more happiness, no more men and no more women.

No more streets! He heard again the heavy thunder of the traffic on First Avenue; again he saw that violence of speed and hot machinery—but no more streets!

George turned his head, and for a moment looked about the room with tired eyes. In the cool sweet light of early morning his beautiful little apartment was spotless as a pin. He did not have much furniture: a table or two, a few good chairs, designed in the clean planes and angles of the modern fashion. There was a fireplace with a small clock upon the mantel and over it a long panoramic photograph of a noble river, with grand special vistas of high buttes and grandly wooded shores.

The piece that dominated the room was George's grand piano, a shining shape of grace and power; his face softened, and he smiled a little as he looked at it. Then he reached out of bed and got his glasses, adjusted them, and began to read the memorandum that lay beside him on the table.

The schedule of the day's activity lay neatly mapped out before him in the pages of the little leather book. Mr. Robert Carpenter was due at ten o'clock; Mr. Milton Weisenborn at eleven; Mr. John Michael at noon. He began again at two o'clock when he received Mr. Tony Bertilotti; Mr. Peter Jorgensen at three; and Mr. Joseph Silverstein, perhaps the most talented of all his students, at four.

This was his program for the day. He was a teacher to young pianists who had shown distinguished promise and who were studying with a view to appearances on the concert stage. That had also been his own life formerly—before he had found out about his heart. He had known some of the most eminent people; he had studied under some of the ablest teachers—they had warned him about all sorts of things, but none of them had ever spoken of the heart.

If someone, in all those years of study and of preparation, had only told him a few very simple, fundamental things. If someone had only told him that before playing he would always feel not ready. If they'd only told him that he'd always feel—no matter how many times he practiced—that if he only had one more day he'd be sure he'd be ready to play the piece. If someone, out of all his teachers, in all the weary years of grinding and incessant practice, had only told him of some way in which he could feel *sure* of what he knew, of some way in which he could control his nerves—so that his subconscious mind would take him through!

But no one ever told him—and George glanced swiftly, briefly, at his wrist watch and then again at the little leather notebook of his day's schedule, before he closed it—and he had come to this!

If only someone had told him what to do when he got out there upon the stage to play, when he saw out in the huge dark pool of the great house that disembodied host of faces blooming there in the darkness, white, innumerable, like petals on a bough, when space, time, everything is gone. If someone had only told him what to do when he first sat down at the piano, how to conquer the nervousness that made him feel as if he'd lost control of the muscles of his hands. It's true he had talked about this to many other people, to concert pianists far better known than himself, and all of them were full of bland encouragements. They would all assure him that he would "find" himself when he struck the first chords. They would assure him that as time went on he would get calmer and surer, and that after the first applause he would feel much better, that encores were always the *best* because a musician is surer of himself by then and not nervous and in "a more exalted frame of mind."

Yes, they had told him this, but it had not worked out according to their telling. His pulse had always beaten like a trip hammer, and his heart had kept time until it seemed the heart strings would be torn right out of him, until it seemed that nothing was worth this agony, no effort, no applause was worth the terror and the peril of this ordeal—until there was nothing left for him in all his consciousness, except that ghastly choking beating of the heart. And so—no more!—no more!—let others dare the ordeal if they liked, let others tempt the perilous, stricken beating of the frail small heart—but as for him—well, he had come to this. And this was better.

George looked at his wrist watch. It was eight-fifteen. He got up, put on his slippers and a dressing gown, took off his gold-rimmed spectacles, and polished them carefully, and put them on again. Without his glasses, his face had the slightly tired, patient look that is common among people with weak eyes. With his glasses on, the expression of his face was somewhat changed: it was a pleasant, most attractive face, well-modeled, firm, distinguished by a look of quiet strength and natural gentleness, all subdued somehow to the suggestive hue of a tranquil but deep-rooted melancholy. It would have been hard for a stranger to believe that this man could be the slave of an obsession, could hold in him such ocean depths of terror, such dread of everything that might disturb the frail small beating of the heart.

George walked over to the windows, pulled up the shutters of one Venetian blind, and for a moment stood looking quietly out upon the river. Everything was touched with morning, and the river was flashing with all the ecstasy and movement of its thousand currents.

A cool breath of morning, sea-fresh, and tide-laden, curiously half-rotten, flowed over his calm features: that living river and its smell, he understood, was like all life. The river was a flowing sewer surging back and forth to the recession of the tides, and bearing in its tainted flood the excremental dumpings of six million men. And yet the river was a tide of flashing life, marked delicately in a hundred places with the silvery veinings of a hundred currents, and pungent with the vital, aqueous, full salt-laden freshness of the sea.

The tide was coming in upon the full; George stood there, watching quietly, and saw it come. It was a steady, flowing, crawling and impulsive surge—a welling flood that would come on forever and knew no limit to the invasion of its power. The river was not quiet; the tide was ruffled by the breath of morning into a million scallop shells of winking light—rose, golden, silver, sapphire, pink—the whole polychrome of morning was reflected in the stream, and within the channel of the river's life, the tide came on.

Morning, shining morning, filled the river, and transformed the town. Across the river, the tormented visage of Long Island City had also been transformed; that grim forest of smokestacks, chimneys, enormous stamped-out factory moulds, million-windowed warehouses, gas tanks and refineries, derricks, tugboats, cranes and docks, was magically translated by the wizardry of every hue that morning knows.

As he looked, a tug set neatly in between two barges, each loaded with twin rows of box-cars, backed out into the stream and quartered slowly, steadily, with its enormous freight, then started head-on up the stream. Thick water foamed against the blunt snouts of the barges, as the little tug between them neatly forged ahead with its great cargo, with a sense of limitless power, and with astonishing speed. The young cool light of morning fell flat and cleanly on the rusty sides of the old freight cars on the barges: everything began to blaze with thrilling color. The excitement, the beauty, the feelings of wonder and recognition which all the associations of the scene evoked, were intoxicating. It was not just the composition of the scene itself; the thing that made the heart beat faster, and the throat get tight, and something stab as swift and instant as a knife—was not so much the beauty and the wonder of the thing as the beauty and wonder which the thing evoked. The little tug was not just a little tug that plied about the waters of Manhattan. No, the little tug was sliding lights at night—red, yellow, green, as hard and perfect as cut gems, as poignant, small, and lonely as the hearts of men. The little tug was like the lights of darkness in America, which stretch across the continent like strung beads, which are so brave, so small, so lonely in that huge vacancy of the attentive and eternal dark. The tug was like dark waters of the night, the poignant lights that slide there in the viewless dark, down past the huge cliff of the silent and terrific city, the eyes of the unnumbered windows, the huge heart of the city, and the small beating hearts of sleep.

The little tug was like the evocation of those things; it was like the great piers blazing in the night at twelve o'clock, the dense packed crowds, the rattling winches, and the lighted ship. It was like the huge turmoil of departure, the shattering blasts of the great ship, the great hawsers straining, taut as thrumming wires, as twelve small bull-dog tugs heave back and get their teeth in, haul her out and straighten her into the stream, until the liner's terrific side turns flat and level to Manhattan. Her lights blaze up from her sheer side, nine rows of light across one thousand feet of length, the proud sweep of all her storied promenades, the great white curve of all her superstructure, breasted like a swan, the racing slant and spurt of the great funnels, the whole thing sliding past the city now. At twelve-fifteen the funnels show along the piers at the end of Eleventh Street, the people in the old red-brick houses down in Greenwich Village see the lights slide past. At twelve-fifteen the *Berengaria* moans, the tugs cut loose, the lighted cliff of the great liner slides past the lighted cliff of the great city, seeks the Narrows, finds the sea. And the tug was like the evocation of these things.

The enormous barges spoke, as did the tugs, of the huge traffic of the harbor, of docks and piers and loadings, of the raw use and labor of America. But more than anything else the barges belonged to the sunset; they belonged to the vast hush of evening, the old-gold of the setting sun that burns the fiery furnace of its last radiance in one pane of glass high up in the great splinter of a sky-scraper, or on one pane of glass there in a warehouse of Long Island City. The barges, then, belong to all the men who lean upon the sills of evening in America, and regard with quiet eyes, and know that night is coming, labor done. The barges belong to all the quiet waters of the evening, to the vast and empty hush of piers, to quiet waters that come in with quiet glut, to slap against old crusted pilings of the wharves, to slap against the sides of rusty barges tethered there, to rock them gently, and to bump their rusty sides together, stiffly to rock the high poles of the derrick-booms. The old barges belonged to all these things, to sunset and the end of work, and to the long last fading slants of light here in America that will fall, like sorrow and an unknown joy, upon the old red brick of houses, so to lie there briefly like the ghost of light and so to wane, to die there, knowing night has come.

As for the freight cars, they were companion to these things, and they belonged to all the rest of it, as well. Even their crude raw color—the color of dried ox-blood, grimed and darkened to the variation of their age— seemed to have been derived from some essential pigment of America, somehow to express the whole weather of her life. George looked at them and saw their faded lettering: he could not read it, but he knew that if he could, he would find the names of most of the great lines of the nation— the Pennsylvania, the New York Central, the Erie, Lackawanna, and New Haven, the Baltimore and Ohio, the Southern, the North Western, and the Santa Fe.

He knew that those irons wheels had pounded back and forth along al- most every mile of rail whose giant web covered the country. He knew that those harsh ox-blood frames of wood and steel had been exposed to every degree and every violence of weather the continent knows. He knew that they had broiled in train yards out in Kansas, all through the sweltering afternoons of mid-July, when the temperature stood at 107°. He knew that they had been beaten upon with torrential rain, frozen over in a six-inch sheath of ice and snow; he knew that in the night-time they had toiled their way, behind the thundering bellows of a "double-header," up through the sinuous grades of the Appalachians, or pounded their way by day, straight as a string across the plains of western Kansas. They had crossed the Mis- sissippi and the Rio Grande; they had known the lonely pine lands of the South, as well as the towering forests of the great Northwest; they had known the cornlands, crossed the plains, gone round or through the Rocky Mountains; they had crossed the blasted fiend-world of Nevada, and they had sought and found the great Pacific shore. He had thundered past un- ending strings of them, lined up across the midlands of the country, and he had seen them for a fleeting instant from the windows of a speeding train, curved back upon a spur of rusty track in lonely pine lands of the South, at red and waning sunset in the month of March, open and deserted, yet in- definably thrilling, filled somehow with all the wildness, loneliness, the mes- sage of enormous distance, that is America.

George turned away from the window with a faint sigh—not so much the sigh of a man who is physically tired, but of one whose weariness has sunk deep into all the secret places of his life. That flashing tide that never ceased was no more for him to be experienced or endured. The living energy of all its veined and weaving currents, the constant traffics of its multiform and never-ending life—with all their evocations of the violence of living—was no more to be endured. Hereafter, one small cell surrounded by his careful walls was all that he desired. There would be no more rivers in the life of George.

As he turned away from the window, the look of melancholy in his quiet face was more marked than it had ever been, but in a moment he stirred himself and set about his preparations for the day.

He went about each task with a sense of order that never varied in its tempo by a jot. The love of order was the very core of him. His apartment almost seemed to clean itself; the quiet and orderly way in which he went about the work of keeping it so gave no sense of effort, no sense of care or worry. It was as if everything he did was as natural to him as his breath, and was a kind of pleasure.

First, he went into his gleaming white-tiled bathroom, opened the cabinet, took out his tooth brush and tooth powder, brushed his teeth, put everything back just as he had found it, and washed out the bowl. Then he took a shower—first a warm one, then a tepid one, and then a cold one— but not too cold. He had serious misgivings concerning the sudden shock of icy water upon the frail small beating of the—heart. Then he dried himself vigorously with a bath-towel, put on his dressing gown and shaved himself, then cleaned and dried his razor carefully, washed out the brush, washed out the basin, and put everything back into the gleaming cabinet, spotless and shining, exactly as he had found them. Then he combed his hair; his hair was abundant, close cropped, dark blond in color, and George parted it into two neat, shining wings exactly in the center.

Then George came out of the bathroom, crossed the big room, opened up the chest of drawers, and took out fresh and neatly folded garments, socks, underwear, a shirt. He put them on, then opened the closet door, selected a suit of clothes from the row of well-cut, faultlessly-kept suits that hung there, and put it on. He selected a pair of shoes from the substantial assortment in the closet, selected with great care a tie marked with a fine gray stripe, adjusted arm-bands of ruffled blue to keep his sleeves up, and now was ready for his breakfast.

George entered his gleaming kitchenette, and with unhurried method, set about the preparation of his morning meal. First, he filled a glistening little pot with water, set it down upon the stove, and got the burner going. Then he filled the container of his drip-machine with Sanka coffee, and screwed it into place. Then he opened the door of his gleaming electric ice box, took out two good-sized Florida oranges, cut them evenly in two, and squeezed their juice into a glass. The water on the stove was boiling now. George poured the water carefully into the round top of the drip-machine, and poured the remainder of the boiling water into the sink. Then while his Sanka coffee dripped, George put three slices of fresh bread into the electric toaster on the breakfast table, set out a knife and fork, a cup and saucer, a square of butter and a napkin, set his glass of orange juice beside the plate, and in faultless taste, impeccable spotlessness, prepared to have a breakfast—with himself.

George drank the orange juice, consumed the buttered toast, and slowly swallowed down a cup of Sanka coffee.

Then he cleared the table, washed the dishes and put each article back into its gleaming cabinet, washed out the sink, wiped off the table, then went out into his bed–living room. George opened the door of a closet in his little entrance hall, took out a mop, an oil mop, a broom, a dustpan and a dusting cloth, and brought them back with him. First he swept the floor of his little kitchenette and dining alcove. Then he swept the three small rugs, and went over the wax-polished floor carefully with the oil mop. Then he took the water-mop, and carefully swabbed the glittering tiling of the bathroom floor. Then he took the soft dust cloth, and very tenderly and lovingly, went over every square inch of the magnificent grand piano. Then he took all the sheets and covers from his couch, put the sheets on tidily, spread the thin gray blanket over them and tucked it in, covered the whole couch with the blue coverlet, took certain plump and tidy-looking cushions from the closet, and arranged them tastefully. Then he stood for a moment in the center of his spotless little universe, with a quiet look of satisfaction upon his face, like the Lord of some small but immaculate creation, who looks upon his work and finds it good.

In the midst of these pleasing contemplations, the telephone rang. George jumped as if he had been shot.

The sharp electric *thring* of the telephone bell had cut across the calm weather of his spirit like a lightning flash. The telephone rang again—again—again—insistent and emphatic, naked as a live wire. George felt his knees give under him, he cast distracted looks about the room, he looked at the telephone as if it were a venomous reptile. Good God, was there no escape, no means by which a man could make himself secure against all the brutal shocks of this huge world? He had burnt all bridges, closed all avenues, built his walls more cunningly than those of Troy, and still the remorseless and inevitable tides of life came in.

But why—for what reason—should his 'phone ring now? No one ever called him in the morning. Swiftly his mind ran over the list of all the people that he knew who were privileged to call. There were only eleven people in the world to whom, after years of cautious acquaintanceship, he had revealed his number.

Even with these people he had never felt entirely free. Moreover, he had never allowed the whole chosen eleven to know one another: he kept them carefully parceled in three groups. One group—a group of four—were people who shared his interest in music; he went to concerts with them, to the symphony, occasionally to opera. A second group, a group of three, were Bridge Players, and George was an excellent hand at bridge. The third group, also of four people, were Theater Goers. George enjoyed the theater, and for eight months of the year went once a week. Thus even in his well-ordered social life, George still displayed his salutary caution: none of the Concert Attenders knew any of the Bridge Players, and none of the Bridge Players had ever met any of the Theater Goers, just as none of the Theater Goers had ever heard of the existence of the Concert Attenders. But these eleven people were the only ones to whom he had confided the number of his telephone. And none of them, he knew, would dream of calling him at this hour of the morning, unless something of a catastrophic nature had occurred.

Then—George stared desperately at that crackling instrument of dread—who could it be, then?—*Who?*

He was more composed now, steeled with resolution, and when at last he took the instrument from the hook, his voice was cadenced to its customary tone of quiet, deep, and pleasant courtesy.

"Hello—Hello!"

"Oh, hello darling. Is it *really* you? I was about to give up hope."

Her voice was husky, full of depth, the cadences of unuttered tenderness, conveying perfectly a sense of quiet irony and affection—the full image of its owner's loveliness. But George, just at the moment, was in no fit mood to estimate its beauty; the voice had gone through him in a searing flash of memory—he was white around the lips, and leaning forward, gripping the instrument with a hand gone bloodless to the fingertips, he stammered hoarsely:

"Hello, hello—Who is it?—Is it—"

"Guess who, darling?" The quiet irony in the husky tone had deepened just a trifle.

"Margaret!" he gasped. "Is that *you!*"

"That's who. You seem a little overcome, my dear." The husky tone was dulcet now.

"Why—why—yes—no—that is," George stammered with an uncertain laugh—"*Yes!* I was a little surprised. I wonder how . . ." He stopped abruptly, fumbled, trying to get out of it.

"How *what?* How I got your number?"

"Why—why—yes! That is—I gave instructions to the company not to let anyone—" he reddened with embarrassment, then blurted out "—of course, I wanted *you* to have it—I—I—I've been intending all along to write and tell you the new number—"

"You have?" the husky voice was faintly accented with cynical amusement. "Only it's just escaped your mind during the past two or three years, hasn't it?"

"Well—you see—" he fumbled.

"I know, darling. It's all right. You're a very secret little boy nowadays, aren't you?" Another pause, a brief one, but for George a very long one. "Well, since you're so curious to know, I'll tell you how I got the number. Stew Taylor gave it to me."

"But he—" George began, puzzled.

"Yes, I know he didn't." The low voice was shaded now with sadness. "You've covered your tracks pretty well these last three years. Stew happened to meet one of your bridge-playing friends, and he let him have it."

"But he *couldn't!*" George said incredulously. "I—I mean he *wouldn't*— that is—"

"Well, he did, my love. It's too bad, but there's no telling what a few drinks will do, is there?"

"Well, whoever it was," George began angrily, "I'd like to find out—because when I gave those numbers out, I told people not to—well, anyway," he broke off, "it's nice to hear from you again, Margaret. We've got to try—"

"Try what? To get together sometime? Yes, I know," the irony of the voice was very quiet now—"I've been trying for the last three years."

"Well, then," he said quickly, "that's what we'll have to do—I'll call you up sometime when—"

"When I'm not looking? Or when I'm dead?"

"Now, Margaret," said George, laughing and speaking in his familiar quiet voice, "you know you're not being fair when you say that. I've been meaning to call you for a long time. Just at present—" he coughed a little, and looked quickly at his watch—"well, anyway, when things slacken up a little—"

"When things slacken up a little? You sound frightfully busy. What's the matter?—have you taken up crocheting?"

"Well, you see—"

"I don't want to take up your valuable time, you know. Have you finished with your daily housekeeping yet?"

"Well—*yes!*" he confessed.

"Had your breakfast?"

"Yes. Oh, yes."

"Washed the dishes?"

"Yes."

"Tidied up the kitchen, and put everything away in his little cubbyhole?"—the husky voice suspiciously dulcet now.

"Yes—but look here—"

"Tidied up the bathroom, swept the floors, dusted the furniture—"

"Look here, Margaret. What are you trying to—"

"Made up his little bed, and spread the cute little cover on it, and plumped the cozy little pillows out—"

"Well, what's the matter with that?" he protested.

"*Matter?*"—innocently—"Why, darling, I didn't say anything was the matter. I think it's *wonderful!*"

"Well, I don't see it's anything for you to make fun of," he said sulkily.

"Make *fun* of—" innocently aggrieved—"But who's making *fun*? I think you're *won*-derful! You can do *everything*! You can keep house, make up beds, wash dishes, sweep floors, keep everything tidy as a pin," piously the voice enumerated these virtues.

"Well, if you're going to be funny about—"

"And play the piano, and play bridge—" the voice continued dulcetly— "Oh, *yes*!"—eagerly excitedly—"And he can *cook*, too! He's a *good* cook, isn't he?" After a moment, slowly, laughingly, the husky tone now carrying its full charge of sarcasm, she concluded: "My, my! I wonder if they know what they're missing?"

"What *who's* missing?" George said suspiciously.

"What the girls are missing—" then sweetly, tenderly, the *coup-de-grâce:* "You'd make a great little mother to some woman's children, Georgy. Don't you know you would?"

"It seems to me—" said George—"Look," he continued quietly, "I'm going to hang up."

"Oh, wait," she said; the woman's husky voice was suddenly subdued to earnest tenderness—"Don't go away. I mean, what I wanted to say was, why couldn't we"—the voice had changed to jesting irony again—"Get on your running shoes, darling—what are you going to be doing tonight?"

He was silent, stunned; and then he floundered:

"Why—why—I—I've—I'm going to the theater with some people that I know."

"I see. . . . And tomorrow night, darling?"—the voice was dulcet now: knowing the tone, he reddened, squirmed, remembered the look in her eye.

"Why—tomorrow," George said slowly, "I—I've promised some friends to play bridge."

"Ah-hah"—just barely audible—"And the day *after* tomorrow, my sweet?"

"Why—now let's see," George mumbled, fumbling desperately for time—"I've promised some people I know to go to a piano recital."

"And Friday?"

"Why—Friday," George began desperately—"I—I've—"

"I know," the husky voice broke in sweetly—"Friday is fish day, isn't it, and you've promised some Catholic friends of yours to go to a clambake, haven't you?—"

"Now, Margaret," George began, with a troubled laugh—"You know—"

"Of course I know, my pet—on Saturday you're going out to the country for the weekend, to visit some 'people you know'—aren't you? And by the way, who are all these 'people you know' anyway? Most of the people you used to know never see you any more."

"Well—you see—"

"Look here," she said quietly—"What's happened to you, anyway? What's wrong with you?—What are you afraid of, anyway? . . . There wasn't one of us five years ago who wouldn't have bet his last nickel upon you—upon everything we thought you were going to do in the world—"

"Oh, wait a minute—" he put in quietly—"I wasn't a genius—and I never pretended to be one."

"No, I know you weren't—But you did have something that is not given to one person in a thousand—the power to feel and know music and to play it in such a way that you could give to other people some of your own feeling. That was a gift that came straight to you from God—and what have you done with it?"

"Now, Margaret," his own voice was hot and angry now—"if that's what you're going to—"

"I'll tell you what you've done with it!"—Her voice cut harshly in across the wire—"You've thrown it away because you got scared, because you were afraid to use it, and what have you got left? Well, you've got your bridge-playing friends, and your little apartment, and your little music students, haven't you?"

"If you're going to sneer at the way I earn my living—"

"Oh, I couldn't sneer at it sufficiently," she said. "I couldn't begin to sneer at it the way it deserves to be sneered at!"

"If you mean to say," he began in a choking voice, "that you think the way I earn my living is not honorable—"

"Oh, honorable, my eye!" she said wearily. "So is ditch-digging! Look here, George Hauser—there are a thousand things that you could do that would be honorable—making kiddy cars or peddling toy balloons. But what you ought to do is the work that you were put here for!"

"Apparently you think, then" he began stiffly, "that teaching young men and women that show signs of musical talent—"

"Oh, talent, my eye!" she said coarsely again. "You know perfectly well that it doesn't matter in the slightest what happens to most of them—whether they learn to play the mouth harp or the accordion—"

"There," he said frigidly, "I cannot agree with you. I assure you that I have some young people of talent who—"

"Well, what if you have?" she said brutally. "Let them get along with their talent as best they may!—Let someone else show them what to do! It's about time you started worrying about *your* talent! Oh, George, George, what in the name of God has happened to you? You used to be so different! Don't you know that everyone adored you—they do still? Have you forgotten the good times we used to have together?—Stew Taylor, Kate, myself, the Crosbys, Buzz Wilton, Doris, you?—What's come over you?—Have you forgotten the time you said, 'Let's go to Brooklyn'—and we went, not knowing where—the times we used to ride back and forth across the Staten Island Ferry—the time you asked the policeman where Red Hook was—and he tried to keep us from going—the times we went to Shorty Gallini's on Sixth Avenue—all of the times we stayed up talking all night long—what's happened to you, George? Have you forgotten all of them?"

"You know," he said slowly—"there was something I found out—"

"Oh, yes, I know," she said quietly, with the shadow of a weary irony, "there was your—heart. You were always bothered by it, weren't you? The college doctor in Ann Arbor told you to take care of it, didn't he?"

"Margaret," George said gravely, "if you knew what you—"

"Oh, darling, but I know. The doctor told you that you ought to watch your heart—and so you watched it. You told me all about your heart—do you remember?—How frail the heart was—how easy it was for the heart to stop beating."

"Those," said George, "are very serious—"

"Do you know something, George—" she now said slowly.

"What?"

"Well, I'll tell you"—very slowly—"Some day you're going to *die* of—*heart*—failure—"

"Oh, *Margaret!*" he gasped.

"You're *going* to die of heart–*failure*," she repeated slowly—"Some day your heart is going to *fail*—it's just going to quit—lie down—stop—"

"Margaret!"

"—Like mine, and like Stew Taylor's, Kate's, Buzz Wilton's—all the rest of us—"

"Yes, but—"

"Listen: what's it all about?—this business of your heart? We know about your heart, and really, George, your heart was not so bad. I used to listen to it in the night-time when I slept with you—"

"Margaret!"

"Oh, but I did—and really, George, your heart was just a—*heart*."

"Margaret, if you're going to—"

"Oh, but I did—I happen to remember—and really, George, your heart was not so bad, until little what's-her-name—the little washed-out blonde with the hank of hair—came along, and took you for a ride."

"Now, Margaret, you look here—"

"—The little ex-chorine who got money from you for her boy friend—ran away with him and came back broke—broke down, confessed, worked on your sympathies—"

"Now, you look here—"

"—And got more money from you for her boy friend—"

"I'm not going to—"

"—Oh, you're not going to what? You had fine friends, a fine career, and everyone adored you and believed in you—you had me, and I'm a nice woman—and you gave everything, all of us, the gate for a little washed-out ex-chorine who gave *you* the gate—"

"Listen, if you think—"

"—And walked all over that poor heart of yours, didn't she?"

"You can—"

"I can what? I can go to hell, you mean? Well, why not? You've sold us out—your friends, yourself, your work—but you've discovered that you have a—heart. So we can go to hell, can't we?"

When George spoke, his voice was quiet, deep, sincere, and sad. "If you feel that way," he said, "I don't see why you bother to call me up."

There was a moment's pause, then the husky voice suddenly charged through with passion:

"Because, you God-damned fool, I happen to adore you!"

The receiver banged up in his face.

When George got up, his face was white, and his hands were shaking. He walked over to the mantel of his room without knowing where he was going or what he was doing. He leaned upon the mantel. Above him was the picture of a river. It was George's river; the upper reaches of the Mississippi in the State of Minnesota. It was a silvery stream that channeled around islands—there were dense woodings of great trees upon the shore; there were long wooded buttes, high promontories, also with the lovely forestings of the great trees dense. In his quiet face, he knew there was the look that one often finds among people who come from this part of the country. It was neither sad nor resigned, but unconsciously it had sadness, resignation in it: what it *really* had, he knew, was a gigantic acceptance, a sense of quiet and enormous *background*, a sense of great scenes gone home to the heart, the hush of the enormous evenings and the gigantic distances, of something immense, and waiting, set there in the silence of repose. He knew this was the way he looked. And his river also looked like this. He had swum in it when young, looked at it a thousand times, known every part of the immense landscapes of its shores. It was his, his country, his America—and his river. But now he was finished with that, too.

That, he knew, had been *his* river. And for him, at least, it had been a good deal more than a river, a good deal more than an aspect of familiar geography. It was, in a way, the image of his whole life; his life had been haunted by that river; it had wound through the landscape of his youth like a haunted thread. In so many ways past knowing and past telling, he knew that this great stream—was his. It was so calm, so homely, so mysterious— like so much else that we have known here, itself a part of the "large unconscious scenery" of this country, so familiar and so strange, so friendly and so indefinably sad—as if, in the utter plainness of our best-known things, there is something undefined and troubling, that plain speech can never know—something at which men can only guess, which comes to pass across a quiet spirit like a troubling light, and to vanish before it can be outlined or defined—Oh, hard and strange enigma of the lonely land! *This* had been his. He, too, had known it, but now—no more!

In a few minutes, when he had grown quieter, he went over and sat down at his piano and began to play grave and tranquil music; he played the Chopin C Minor Prelude; he smote the keys with strong white fingers, and the music came.

The bell rang. George stopped midway among the calm resounding chords. He went to the door and opened it. Ledig, the superintendent of the building, was standing there.

"Good morning, Ledig," George greeted the man in his deep and pleasant tone. "Come in."

Ledig was a man of George's age—in the late thirties—with the common, square, and friendly-brutal face of the Germanic stock, and eyes of china-blue.

"Good morning, Mr. Hauser," Ledig said, and grinned, "I just t'ought I'd speak to you about de apartment—"

"Oh, yes," said George quietly, and waited.

Ledig looked around the room, his round eyes surveyed the scene approvingly; George was his favorite tenant. "You got it goot here," Ledig said. "You keep it nice."

A quick communication passed between them—one of pleasure and swift understanding; George said nothing.

"—about de apartment—you haf deceit-ed?" Ledig asked.

"Yes, Ledig," George said, as before, "I want the other one."

"It is on de udder seit, dough, Mr. Hauser," Ledig said, then added doubtfully, "But you like besser, de udder seit?"

"Yes, Ledig, I think I'll like it better on the other side," said George.

"But," said Ledig very earnestly, "de udder seit, Mr. Hauser, it gifs no more riffers."

"No, that is true," said George in his low and quiet tone.

"But," Ledig's blue eyes were full of puzzled trouble, "you like it besser dat vay, den—mit no more riffers?"

"Yes," said George, "I like it better that way, Ledig."

"But," the china eyes were fuller still of puzzled wonder and regret. "No more *riffers*, Mr. Hauser."

When Ledig had gone, George stood there leaning on the mantel. For a moment he regarded the picture of his river with quiet eyes. Then he walked to the window and looked out. Upon that shining tide of life, a boat was passing. George lowered the Venetian blinds. And suddenly the room was dark with morning.

Now there were no more rivers.

The Spanish Letter

Dear friend, whom I have never seen, you write me in troubled times, and ask a question that is being asked today throughout the world. You ask a question about Spain. Well, I have never been to Spain, and yet my answer to your question will be long. I have so often thought of Spain, dear friend. I have so often gone there in my spirit's voyaging. And because this Spain of which you speak is so close at hand to my discovery, my answer to your question will be long.

A poet said some eighty years ago that when he died the name of Italy would be found engraved upon his heart. Perhaps today it is the same with Spain. Perhaps each man alive today has his own Spain engraved upon his heart. At any rate, it has been so with me.

So first of all, my answer to you will be this: my Spain is here, this world around me here and now. And I shall tell you first about this Spain. For I am thirty-seven years of age, and if I live in Spain, I can no longer live in a Spanish castle.

The Spain of which you speak, while far away from all our voyaging, is yet close to ken. And because of this I want to make an answer to the question that you ask in such a clear and unmistaken way that there will never be a doubt in anyone who reads it how I feel, or what it is that I am saying here.

What I am going to say is going to be personal, and it is going to be personal because any opinion I may utter here has come not through what I have read, nor from anything that has been suggested to me by someone else, nor from the intellectual influence of my associates and friends. It has come, as has every deep conviction of my life, from what I have seen, felt, thought, lived, experienced, and found out for myself. It seems to me this is the way every man alive has got to find out things, and therefore, if what one man has found out in this way has any use or value to you, or seems important to you in any way, here it is:

I came from a state in the Middle South, and from, I think, the most conservative element of American life. All of my people, although for the most part people of modest or even humble circumstances, were people who had lived in this country and known its life for two hundred years or more, and so far as I know, until the last generation, there was not one of them who had ever lived in a city. My father was a stone-cutter, his father was a farm laborer, my mother's family were mountain people: all of them were politically, socially, religiously, and in every other way, a part of the most traditional element of this country's life; and my own childhood, boyhood, and early training was passed under these influences and under these circumstances.

When I began to write, I began, as so many young men do, as a lyrical writer. My first book was a book about the life of a small town, and of the people there. I suppose the book followed a pretty familiar pattern, and that the central conflict was between a young fellow with sensitive feelings, and perhaps some talent, and the social forces around him—that is, the life of the small town, and the collisions of his own personality with it.

The solution, or resolution, of this conflict was also a familiar one: the hero solved it by escaping, by leaving the community and the environment with which he had been in conflict. Like many other young men of my age at the time I wrote that book, which appeared in 1929, my mind, while seething with feelings, thoughts, images, and swift and penetrating perceptions, was nevertheless a confused and troubled one. I was in conflict with the whole baffling complex of life, of society, and of the world around me. I was trying to shape a purpose, to find a way, and to know my own position. But, like many other people of that time, although I was not defeated, I was lost.

I suppose if anyone had questioned me to find out what I thought or what I believed, and above all, why I wanted to write books, I should have said that I wrote books because some day I hoped I would write a great one, that I would rather do this than anything in the world, that it seemed to me art was the highest thing in life, and that the life of the artist was the best and highest life a man could have. I might even have said in those days that art is enough, that beauty is enough, in William Morris' words that "Love is enough though the whole world be waning." And I think I should certainly have disagreed positively with anyone who suggested that the artist's life and work were in any way connected with the political and economic movements of his time.

Now that I no longer feel this way, I would not apologize for having felt so, nor sneer at the work I did, or at the work of other young men at that time who felt and thought as I did. It seems to me natural and almost inevitable that a young man should begin life as a lyrical writer, that his first picture of life, as reflected in his first work, should be a very personal one, and that he should see life and the world largely in terms of its own impingements on his own personality, in terms of his personal conflicts or agreements with the structure of things as they are. As for the way we felt, or thought we felt, about art and love and beauty in those days, and how they were not only sufficient to all things, but that all things else were alien and remote to them, that, too, perhaps, is a natural and inevitable way for young men to feel. And it certainly was a product of the training, the culture, and the aesthetic ideas of that time.

But I have found out something else, for myself at least, in the past few years. And it is this: you can't go home again—back to your childhood, back to the father you have lost, back to the solacements of time and memory—yes, even back to art and beauty and to love. For me, at any rate, it is now manifest that they are not enough. And I do not think that this be treason, but if it be, then—

I began to find out about it six or seven years ago when I was living and working on a book in Brooklyn, and I have been finding out about it ever since. I do not know when it first began, perhaps such things as these have no actual moment of beginning, but I do know that one day I got a letter from a person who was speaking about love and art and beauty. It was a good letter, but after I had read it, I looked out the window, and across the street I saw a man. He was digging with his hand into a garbage can for food: I have a good memory for places and for time, and this was half-way through December 1932. And I know that since then I have never felt the same way about love or art or beauty or thought they were enough.

This thing has all come slowly, because although thinking, feeling, perceiving, even working and writing, have always come to me with a rush, upon a kind of furious and tremendous tide, the resolution of things is very slow, because, as I have said, nothing is any good to me, nor I think to any man, until we find it out for ourselves. And I know that you can't go home again.

For four years, then, I lived and worked in Brooklyn. I worked like a locomotive. I certainly did not get around much in literary circles. But I do not think I missed much of what was going on around me in Brooklyn—which really is the world, or has the whole world in it—among my people down in North Carolina, in my native town, or in the country as a whole. And I think the reason I did not miss much was that I was so hard at work. People have told me that such work shuts one away from life. But that is not true. Such work is life, and enhances the whole sense and understanding of life immeasurably. So it was with me, at any rate.

Early in 1935 I finished a big job of work and went abroad for the first time in four years. I went to Germany, because of all the countries I have ever seen, outside of my own, that, I think, is the country I have liked the best, in which I have felt most at home, with whose people I have felt the most natural, instant, and instinctive sympathy and understanding. It is also the country whose magic and mystery have haunted me the most. I had thought about it many times: after the labor, the fury, and the exhaustion of those four Brooklyn years, it meant peace to me, and release, and happiness, and the old magic again.

I had not been there since the fall of 1930. Then I had stayed in a little town in the Black Forest, and there was great excitement among the people, for a great national election was being held. The state of politics was chaotic, there was a bewildering number of political parties—more than forty million votes, as I recall, were cast in the great *Wahl*. That year the Communists alone got four million votes, or more.

This time, the thing was different. Germany had changed. Some people told me there was no such confusion or chaos in the politics or government now, because everyone was so happy. And I should have been. For I think no man ever went to a foreign land under more propitious conditions than did I early in May 1935.

It is said that Byron awoke one morning at the age of twenty-four to find himself famous. I had to wait ten years longer; I was thirty-four when I reached Berlin, but it was magic just the same. I suppose I was not really very famous. But it was just as good, because for the first and last time in my life I felt as if I were. A letter had reached me from America telling me that my second book had been successful there, and my first book had been translated and published in Germany a year or two before. The German critics had said tremendous things about it; my name was known. When I got to Berlin, people were waiting for me.

It was the month of May: along the streets, in the Tiergarten, in the great gardens, and along the Spree Canal, the horse chestnut trees were in full bloom. The great crowds sauntered underneath the trees on the Kurfürsten-damm, the terraces of the cafés were crowded with people, and always, through the golden sparkle of the days, there was a sound of music in the air, the liquid smack of leather boots upon the streets as men in uniform came by with goose precision. There are so many chains of endless lovely lakes around Berlin, and for the first time I knew the wonderful golden bronze upon the tall poles of the kiefern trees: I had known only the South, the Rhinelands and Bavaria before. And now Brooklyn, and four years of work, the man who prowled into the garbage can, and the memory of grim weather, were far away.

It was a glorious period for a week. I suppose in some way I connected the image of my own success, this happy release after years of toil and desperation, with May, the kiefern trees, the great crowds thronging the Kur-fürstendamm, all of the golden singing of the air—somehow with a feeling that for everyone grim weather was behind and that happy days were here again.

I had heard some ugly things, but I did not see them now. I did not see anyone beaten, I did not see anyone imprisoned, or put to death, I did not see any of the men in concentration camps, I did not see openly anywhere the physical manifestations of a brutal and compulsive force. True, there were men in brown shirts everywhere, there were men in leather boots and black uniforms, in uniforms of olive green around one everywhere, there was about one everywhere in the great streets the solid smack of booted feet, the blare of brass, the tootling fifes, the memory of young faces shaded under iron helmets, with folded arms and ramrod backs, precisely seated in great army lorries.

But all of this was so mixed in with May, and the horse chestnut trees, the great cafés in the Kurfürstendamm, and the genial temper of the people making holiday, as I had seen and known it on so many pleasant times before, that even if it did not now seem good, it did not seem sinister or bad.

Then something happened. It didn't happen suddenly. It just happened as a cloud gathers, as fog settles, as rain begins to fall.

Someone I had met was giving me a party and asked if I should like to ask any of the people I had met to come to it. I mentioned one. My party host was silent for a moment; he looked embarrassed: then he told me the person I had mentioned had formerly been the editorial head of a publication that had been suppressed, and that one of the people who had been instrumental in its suppression had been invited to the party, so would I mind—?

I named another, and again the anxious pause, the embarrassment, the painful silence. This person was—was—well, he knew this person and he knew he did not go to parties, he would not come were he invited, so would I mind—? I named another, a woman I had met, whom I had liked. Again, the anxious pause, the painful silence. How long had I known this woman? Where, under what circumstances, had I met her?

I tried to reassure my host on all these scores. I told him he need have no fear of any sort about this woman. He was instant, swift, in his apologies— oh, by no means: he was sure the lady was eminently all right—only, now-adays—with a mixed gathering—he had tried to pick a group of people I had met and liked, who all knew one another—he had thought that it would be much more pleasant that way—strangers at a party were often shy at first, constrained, and formal with each other—so would I mind—?

A friend came to see me: "In a few days," he said, "you will receive a phone call from a certain person. He will try to meet you, to talk to you. Have nothing to do with this man. His name is —— ." When I asked him why this man should try to meet me, and why, if he did, I should be afraid of him, he would not answer, he just muttered: "This is a bad man. We have a name for him: it is 'the Prince of Darkness.'" In a few days the man that he had named did call up, and did want to meet me. I wish that I could say that all of this was as laughable and as melodramatic as it may sound. But the tragedy is, it was not.

Not that it was political. I am not trying to suggest that it was. The roots of it were much more sinister and deep and evil, and in their whole and tragic implication more far-reaching than politics or even racial prejudice could ever be. For the first time in my life I came upon something that I had never known before—something that made all the swift violence and passion of America, the gangster compacts, the swift killing, all the confu-sion, harshness, and corruption that infect portions of our own life seem innocent in comparison. And this was the picture of a great people who were spiritually sick, psychically wounded: who had been poisoned by the contagion of an ever-present fear, the pressure of a constant and infamous compulsion, who had been silenced into a sweltering and malignant secrecy, until spiritually they were literally drowning in their own secretions, dying from the distillations of their own self poison, for which now there was no medicine or release.

Can anyone be so base as to exult at this great tragedy—a tragedy in which the whole world shares today—or to feel hatred for the great and mighty people who have been the victims of it? Culturally, it seems to me, from the eighteenth century on, the German was the first citizen of Europe. In Goethe there was made sublimely articulate the expression of a world spirit which knew no boundary line of race, or color, or religion, which rejoiced in the inheritance of all mankind, and which wanted no domination and no conquest of that inheritance, save the knowledge of his own contribution and participation in it.

From the eighteenth century, in an unbroken line, down to the present one, that spirit in art, in literature, in music, and in philosophy, has continued, until there is not a man or woman in the world today who is not, in one way or another, the richer for it. When I first went to Germany, in 1926, the evidence of that spirit was manifest everywhere, even in the most simple and unmistakable ways. One could not, for example, pass the crowded window of a bookshop in any town in Germany without observing instantly the overwhelming evidence of the intellectual and cultural enthusiasm of the German people. Now that the indignation of the world is roused, it is too easy to sneer at these things as evidences of Teutonic ponderosity, Prussian pedagogics, another evidence of the unimaginative heaviness of their temperament. But the plain blunt truth of the matter is that it was a magnificent and noble thing, and without drawing an invidious comparison, a careful examination of the contents of a German bookshop or of a bookseller's window, in 1926, would have revealed a breadth of vision, an interest in the cultural production of the whole world that would have made the contents of a French bookshop, with its lingual and geographic constriction, seem paltry by comparison.

The best writers of every country in Europe were as well known in Germany as in their own land. The names of such American writers as Theodore Dreiser, Sinclair Lewis, Upton Sinclair, Jack London, were not only well known, but their books were sold and read everywhere throughout the country; and the work of our younger writers was eagerly published, welcomed, read, and judged as was the work of writers everywhere throughout the world.

Even in 1935 when, after an absence of almost five years, I saw the country again, and for the first time under the regime of Adolph Hitler, the evidences of this noble enthusiasm, now submerged and mutilated, were apparent in the most touching way. It has been said by some people that there are no more good books published in Germany, because good books can no longer be published or read. This is not true, as so many things one reads about Germany today are not true. And about Germany today we must be very true. And the reason that we must be very true is that the thing we are against is false: we cannot turn the other cheek to wrong, but also we cannot be wrong about wrong. We cannot meet wrong with wrong: we must be right about it. And we cannot meet lies and falsehood with lies and falsehood, although there are people who argue that we must. So it is not true to say that good books can no longer be published in Germany. And because it is not true, the tragedy of Germany, and the survival of the great German spirit, even in the devious and distorted ways in which it does now manifest itself, is more movingly evident than it would be if it were true. Good books are still published where the substance and material of good books does not in any way controvert or either openly or by implication criticize the present regime. It would be simply foolish and stupid to assert that any good book must so controvert or criticize the present regime, just because it is a good book.

For all these reasons, the eagerness, the curiosity, and the enthusiasm of Germans for the books which they are still allowed to read has been, if anything, movingly intensified. Their eagerness to find out what is going on in the world, what is being written and published outside of Germany, the generous enthusiasm for such American writing as they are allowed to read, is as overwhelming as it is pathetic. One might liken the survival of the German spirit, under these conditions, to that of a man dying of thirst in a dry land, gulping greedily at a flask of water; or to a man who is drowning, clutching desperately at the floating spar of his own wrecked ship.

Everywhere about me, as time went on during that spring and summer of 1935, I saw the evidences of this dissolution, this shipwreck of a great spirit, this miasmic poison that sank like a pestilential fog through the very air, tainting, sickening, blighting with its corrosive touch, through fear, pressure, suppression, insane distrust, and spiritual disease, the lives of everyone I met. It was, and was everywhere, as invisible as a plague, and as unmistakable as death; it sank in on me through all the golden singing of that May, until at last I felt it, breathed it, lived it, and knew it for the thing it was.

I returned to Germany again for the last time perhaps that I shall ever be allowed to visit or to see that magic land again, in 1936.

This time, the welcome that I got was even greater than it had been the year before. My second book had just been published; it had received a great reception: now everywhere I went there were people who knew my work. But something had gone out of life for me.

It was the season of the great Olympic Games, and every day I went to the Stadium in Berlin. And, just as that year of absence had marked the evidence of a cruel and progressive dissolution in the lives of all the people I had known, so it had also marked the overwhelming evidence of an increased concentration, a stupendous organization, a tremendous drawing together and ordering, in the vast collective power of the whole land. And as if these Games had been chosen as a symbol of this new collected might, the means of showing to the world in concrete terms what this new power had come to be, it seemed that every energy and strength in the whole country had been collected and disciplined to this end. It is probable that no more tremendous demonstration has been known in modern times: the Games were no longer Games, no longer a series of competitive exercises to which the nations of the world had sent their chosen teams. The Games were an orderly and overwhelming demonstration in which the whole nation had been schooled, and in which the whole nation took a part.

No one who ever witnessed that tremendous demonstration will ever forget it. In the sheer pageantry of the occasion, the Games themselves were overshadowed. But the great organizing strength and genius of the German people, which has been used so often to such noble purpose, had never been more thrillingly displayed than it was now. There had never been in the whole history of the Games, such complete and perfect preparation, and such calm and ordered discipline.

With no past experience in such affairs, the German people had constructed a mighty stadium which was not only the most beautiful, but the most perfect in its design and purpose that any nation has designed in modern times.

And all the attendant and accessory elements of this great plant—the swimming pools, the great halls, and the lesser stadia—had all been laid out and designed with the same cohesion of beauty and of use.

The organization was superb. Day after day enormous crowds, such as no other city in modern times has had to cope with, and such as would certainly have congested and maddened the traffics of New York, and all its transportational facilities, were handled with a quietness, an order, and a speed that was astounding.

The daily spectacle was overwhelming in its beauty and magnificence. From one end of Berlin to another, from the Lustgarten to the Brandenburger Tor, along the whole broad sweep of Unter den Linden, through the vast alleys and avenues of the faery green Tiergarten, out through the great West of Berlin to the very portals of the Stadium, the town was a thrilling pageantry of royal banners—not merely endless yards of looped-up bunting, but banners fifty feet in height, such as might have graced the battle tent of some great emperor. It was a thrilling tournament of color that caught the throat, and that in its massed splendor, and grand dignity, made all the gaudy decorations of our own Worlds' Fairs, inaugurations, great parades, look like a scheme of shoddy carnivals in comparison.

And all through the day, from morning on, Berlin became a mighty Ear, attuned, attentive, focused, on the Stadium. From one end of the city to the other, the air became a single voice. The green trees along the Kurfürstendamm began to talk: out of the viewless air, concealed and buried in ten thousand trees, a voice spoke to four million people from the Stadium— and for the first time in his life, a Yankee ear had the strange adventure of hearing the familiar terms of track and field translated in the tongue that Goethe used. He would be informed now that the *Vorlauf* would be run— and now the *Zwischenlauf*—at length the *Endlauf*—and the winner: Owens—Oo—Ess—Ah.

Meanwhile, through those tremendous banner-laden ways, the crowds thronged ceaseless all day long. From end to end the great wide promenade of Unter den Linden was solid with a countless horde of patient, tramping German feet. Fathers, mothers, children, young folk, old, the whole material of the nation was there from every corner of the land, trudged wide-eyed, full of wonder, past the marvel of those ceaseless banner-laden ways from morn to night.

And in between one saw the glint of foreign faces: the dark features of the Frenchman or Italian, the ivory grimace of the Jap, the straw hair and blue eyes of the Swede, the bright stabs of color of Olympic jackets, the big Americans, natty in straw hats, blue coats crested with the Olympic seal, and white flannels: and other teams from other nations, with gay and jaunty colors of their own.

And there were great displays of marching men, sometimes ungunned but rhythmic, great regiments of brown shirts swinging through the streets; again, at ease, young men and laughing, talking with each other, long lines of Hitler's bodyguards, black-uniformed and leather-booted, the Schutz-Staffel men, stretching in unbroken lines from the Leader's residence in the Wilhelmstrasse up to the arches of the Brandenburger Tor; then suddenly the sharp command, and instantly, unforgettably, the liquid smack of ten thousand leather boots as they came together, with the sound of war.

By noon, all of the huge approaches to the Games, that enchanted lane-way that the Leader would himself take from the Wilhelmstrasse to the great Stadium, miles away, were walled in by troops, behind which patient, dense, incredible, the masses of the nation waited day by day.

And if the inside of the Stadium was a miracle of color, structure, planned design, the outside, that enormous mass of people waiting, waiting, was a memory one could not forget. All had been planned and shaped to this triumphant purpose, maybe; but the people—they had not been planned. They just stood there and waited day by day—the poor ones of the earth, the humble ones of life, the workers and the wives, the mothers and the children of the land. They were there because they had not money enough to buy the magic little cardboard square that would have given them a place within the magic ring. They were there for just one purpose—to wait from morn to night for just two brief and golden moments of the day: the moment when the Leader came, the moment when he went.

And at last he came: and something like a wind across a field of grass was shaken through that crowd, and from afar the tide rolled up with him, in which was born the hope, the voice, the prayer of the land. And Hitler came by slowly in a shining car, erect and standing, moveless and unsmiling, with his hand upraised, palm outward, not in Nazi-wise salute, but straight up, with such blessing and such gesture that the Buddha or Messiahs use.

Title Index